EVERYMAN'S LIBRARY

EVERYMAN,
I WILL GO WITH THEE,
AND BE THY GUIDE,
IN THY MOST NEED
TO GO BY THY SIDE

DASHIELL HAMMETT

The Maltese Falcon
The Thin Man
Red Harvest

with an Introduction by Robert Polito

EVERYMAN'S LIBRARY

263

This book is one of 250 volumes in Everyman's Library
which have been distributed to 4500 state schools
throughout the United Kingdom.
The project has been supported by a grant of £4 million
from the Millennium Commission.

First included in Everyman's Library, 2000
The Maltese Falcon first published in Great Britain 1931 by Cassell &
Co Ltd. Copyright Cassell & Co Ltd.
The Thin Man first published in Great Britain 1932 by Cassell & Co
Ltd. Copyright Cassell & Co Ltd.
Red Harvest first published in Great Britain 1950 by Cassell & Co
Ltd. Copyright Cassell & Co Ltd.
This edition is published by permission of the
Orion Publishing Group
Typography by Peter B. Willberg

ISBN 1-85715-263-8

A CIP catalogue record for this book is available from the
British Library

Published by Everyman Publishers plc,
Gloucester Mansions, 140A Shaftesbury Avenue,
London WC2H 8HD

Distributed by Random House (UK) Ltd.,
20 Vauxhall Bridge Road, London SW1V 2SA

DASHIELL HAMMETT

CONTENTS

INTRODUCTION

'Alice B. Toklas did hers and now anybody will do theirs,' Gertrude Stein announced in *Everybody's Autobiography*. 'That is the way any autobiography has to be written which reminds me of Dashiell Hammett.'

When Stein's American lecture tour approached Los Angeles in April 1935, she was asked whom she might wish to meet there. Socialite Lillian Ehrman proposed a welcoming dinner party – 'she said she would get Charlie Chaplin and the Emersons and some others not more than twelve in all would that do'. Alice took the call. 'Later on in the day I never get up early I get up as late as possible I like not to get up in the morning and no one ever wakes me anyway I was told about it and was pleased,' Stein remembered, 'then suddenly the next day I said but I did want to meet Dashiell Hammett.'

Stein esteemed Hammett as a crucial American novelist. She invoked his writing as a counterpart to her own experiments in the assiduous stripping away of nineteenth-century psychology, character, even plot from twentieth-century fiction. The following year she would observe in 'What Are Masterpieces': 'It is curious but the detective story which is you might say the only really modern novel form that has come into existence gets rid of human nature by having the man dead to begin with the hero is dead to begin with and so you have so to speak got rid of the event before the book begins.'

As Stein recalled their conversation at Mrs Ehrman's Beverly Hills home, 'Beverly Hills,' she asserted, 'which is the same as Hollywood':

I said to Hammett there is something that is puzzling. In the nineteenth century the men when they were writing did invent all kinds and a great number of men. The women on the other hand never could invent women they always made the women be themselves seen splendidly or sadly or heroically or beautifully or despairingly or gently, and they never could make any other kind of woman. From Charlotte Bronte to George Eliot and many years

xi

later this was true. Now in the twentieth century it is the men who
do it. The men all write about themselves, they are always themselves
as strong or weak or mysterious or passionate or drunk or controlled
but always themselves as the women used to do in the nineteenth
century. Now you yourself always do it now why is it. He said it's
simple. In the nineteenth century men were confident, the women
were not but in the twentieth century the men have no confidence
and so they have to make themselves as you say more beautiful more
intriguing more everything and they cannot make any other man
because they have to hold on to themselves not having any confidence.
Now I he went on have even thought of doing a father and a son to
see if in that way I could make another one. That's interesting I said.

As Hammett encountered Stein he was scaling the pitch
of his own literary celebrity. His talents for compression,
action and tough talk were conspicuous from his earliest
articles and stories for *The Smart Set* and *Black Mask* in 1922.
But since 1929 he had published five novels with the prestigious
house of Alfred A. Knopf – his four most original and daring,
Red Harvest (1929), *The Dain Curse* (1929), *The Maltese Falcon*
(1930) and *The Glass Key* (1931), appearing during a headlong
twenty-six months to accelerating sales and intensifying critical
appreciation. The previous year *The Thin Man* (1934) sold
some 30,000 copies (20,000 within the first three weeks),
and MGM purchased the screen rights for $21,000 prior to
publication; Paramount also filmed *The Glass Key* (directed by
Frank Tuttle, starring George Raft and Edward Arnold). The
first film version of *The Maltese Falcon* (directed by Roy Del
Ruth, with Ricardo Cortez and Bebe Daniels) had already
been released by Warner Brothers in 1931; a second, titled
Satan Met a Lady (directed by William Dieterle, with Warren
William and Bette Davis), would soon follow in 1936. By
1935 Dashiell Hammett was an iconic figure – the dustjacket
photograph on *The Thin Man* draped the handsome author
flamboyantly in tweeds and expressive shadows, mustache and
walking cane – the ex-Pinkerton detective, the first writer to
slip from the pulp underground (*Black Mask, Saucy Stories, Action
Stories*) into cosmopolitan American culture, edgily receding
into his creations. Hammett's legend eventually spurred at
least two biographical films: his early San Francisco years in

Wim Wenders' stylishly oracular *Hammett* (1983); and his relationship with Lillian Hellman in Kathy Bates' depressed, gossipy *Dash and Lilly* (1999).

Hammett would never complete the 'father and son' story he intimated to Stein, nor any of the other novels he sketched for friends at parties when asked about his work. He lived another twenty-six years, but except for a few political public letters his writing life was over.

*

In his 1944 essay 'The Simple Art of Murder' Raymond Chandler famously celebrated Dashiell Hammett as the writer who 'took murder out of the Venetian vase and dropped it into the alley ... Hammett wrote at first (and almost to the end) for people with a sharp, aggressive attitude to life. They were not afraid of the seamy side of things; they lived there. Violence did not dismay them; it was right down their street. Hammett gave murder back to the kind of people that commit it for reasons, not just to provide a corpse; and with the means at hand, not hand-wrought dueling pistols, curare, and tropical fish. He put these people down on paper as they were, and he made them talk and think in the language they customarily used for such purposes ... He was spare, frugal, hard-boiled, but he did over and over again what only the best writers can ever do at all. He wrote scenes that seemed never to have been written before.'

Chandler perhaps less famously cautioned during the same essay, 'I doubt that Hammett had any deliberate artistic aims whatever; he was trying to make a living by writing something he had firsthand information about.' The tenor of 'deliberate artistic aims' here perhaps is purposefully hazy – after such elaborate accolades Chandler might only have been conserving some strategic space for his own writing (born nearly six years earlier than Hammett, Chandler did not publish his first *Black Mask* story until 1933). For although Hammett could derisively reject his accomplishments as 'blackmasking', no American *noir* novelist until Jim Thompson in the 1950s or James Ellroy in the 1990s would advance bolder artistic ambitions for his crime writing. And no early crime writer – including Chandler – was more self-aware and fluent about his art.

When Hammett submitted his revisions of *Red Harvest* to Blanche Knopf, he signaled his aspirations in a letter dated March 20, 1928:

> I'm one of the few – if there are any more – people moderately literate who take the detective story seriously. I don't mean that I necessarily take my own or anybody else's seriously – but the detective story as a form. Some day somebody's going to make 'literature' of it (Ford's GOOD SOLDIER wouldn't have needed much altering to be a detective story), and I'm selfish enough to have my hopes, however slight the evident justification may be. I have a long speech I usually make on the subject, all about the ground not having been scratched yet, and so on, but I won't bore you with it now.

Earlier in the letter Hammett outlined a stylistic experiment he projected for an upcoming novel – most likely *The Maltese Falcon*:

> Then I want to try adapting the stream-of-consciousness method, conveniently modified, to a detective story, carrying the reader along with the detective, showing him everything as it is found, giving him the detective's conclusions as they are reached, letting the solution break on them together. I don't know whether I made that very clear, but it's something altogether different from the method employed in [*Red Harvest*], for instance, where, though the reader goes along with the detective, he seldom sees deeper into the detective's mind than dialogue and action let him. If I can manage it, I want to do this one without any regard for magazines' thou-shalts and thou-shalt-nots. I hope to get it finished by late summer, in time to do another – a plot I've been waiting to get at for two years – before 1928 is dead.

'Literature, as I see it,' Hammett remarked in 1924, 'is good to the extent that it is art, and bad to the extent that it isn't, and I know of no other standard by which it may be judged.' He resisted the frustrating and muzzling segregation of crime fiction. When Knopf objected to the sex scenes in *The Maltese Falcon*, Hammett wrote to editor Harry Block: 'I should like to leave them as they are, especially since you say they "would be all right perhaps in an ordinary novel". It seems to me that the only thing that can be said against their use in a detective novel is that nobody has tried it yet. I'd like to try it.'

INTRODUCTION

Hammett steadily expounded on intricacies and contradictions of style in interviews and magazine profiles, and also in book reviews. During the late 1920s he covered detective fiction for the *Saturday Review of Literature* and studies of advertising, selling and merchandising for *Western Advertising*. Provocative angles abound. Hammett along with Ernest Hemingway insinuated the American vernacular into American literature; and he argued at a 1939 Writers' Congress that 'The contemporary novelist's job is to take pieces of life and arrange them on paper, and the more direct their passage from street to paper the more lifelike they should turn out.' Yet for *Western Advertising* in 1926 Hammett shrewdly registered the vacancies and evasions of slang, and reinstated the craft inside any literary arrangements of everyday life:

The language of the man in the street is seldom either clear or simple. If you think I exaggerate, have your stenographer eavesdrop a bit with notebook and pencil. You will find this common language, divorced from gesture and facial expression, not only excessively complicated and repetitious, but almost purposeless in its lack of coherence . . .

The favorite words of the plain man are those which enable him to talk without thinking . . .

You may read tons of books and magazines without finding, even in fiction dialogue, any attempt faithfully to reproduce common speech. There are writers who do try it, but they seldom see print. Even such a specialist in the vernacular as Ring Lardner gets his effects of naturalness by skillfully editing, distorting, simplifying, coloring the national tongue, and not by reporting it verbatim.

Simplicity and clarity are not to be got from the man in the street. They are the most elusive and difficult of literary accomplishments, and a high degree of skill is necessary to any writer who would win them. They are the most important qualities in securing the maximum desired effect on the reader. To secure that maximum desired effect is literature's chief goal . . .

Despite the righteous, inflated tone, Hammett's sophistication probably remained matchless among crime writers. Even his own sharpest explanation for why he quit fiction – whatever credence one assigns it – reflects the pains of conscious artistry. 'I stopped writing because I found I was repeating myself,' Hammett told an interviewer in 1957. 'It's the beginning of the end when you discover you have style.'

DASHIELL HAMMETT

*

Samuel Dashiell Hammett was born on May 27, 1884 on the tobacco farm of his grandfather Samuel Hammett in St Mary's County, in southern Maryland. He was the second of three children of Richard Thomas Hammett and Annie Bond Dashiell. His earliest Hammett ancestor emigrated to America from England in 1630. Also early settlers, the Dashiells – the name was pronounced with an accent on the second syllable, 'Da-sheel' – were Huguenots, but Annie converted to Catholicism upon marrying Richard. Hammett was baptized a Catholic at St Nicholas Church.

A failed farmer and politician, Richard moved the family to Philadelphia in 1900, and then to Baltimore in 1901, when his son was seven. He found employment variously as a streetcar conductor, a salesman, the foreman of a lock factory, a seafood peddler and a clerk. Dashiell Hammett grew up in a rented row house off Franklin Square, in a hard-working, middle-income neighborhood. The toilets were out back, their street was not paved, and Annie accepted boarders.

Hammett entered the Baltimore Polytechnic Institute in 1908, but dropped out after less than a year of high school. He was fourteen, with dark red hair, lean and already tall. Newsboy, messenger for the B & O Railroad, brokerage clerk – Hammett apparently was fired from nearly every job he took, usually for lateness. He read far into the night, anything from mysteries to *The Critique of Pure Reason*. He patronized the dice and whore bars around the railroad yards; he quarreled drunkenly with his father over his new socialist friends from the Baltimore waterfront; he caught gonorrhea; and he continued to reside at home past the age of twenty-one.

In 1915 Hammett signed on as a Pinkerton detective, a newspaper want-ad casually summoning him to the work that would shape his life, his fiction, his celebrity. 'I found I could sell stories easily when it became known I was a Pinkerton man,' he later concluded. 'People thought my stuff was authentic.' The logo of the Pinkerton National Detective Agency featured a lone vigilant eye, its motto the laconic warning 'We never sleep.' The Pinkerton mission of perpetual surveillance cast a menacing specter by the time Hammett caught up with it. Once esteemed as wily protectors of presidents and tireless sentinels against sensational crimes, Pinkerton operatives were now infamous as strike breakers and union busters. They safeguarded scabs from pickets, factories and mines from organizers, and business property from labor.

Hammett trained at Pinkerton's Baltimore office in the Continental Building. James Wright was the assistant manager, a short, fat, gruff operative who seven years later would re-emerge as the Continental Op in Hammett's *Black Mask* stories. Any precise docket of Hammett's Pinkerton activities slides into rumor and psychodrama along the slippery slope of his own or Lillian Hellman's retellings and amplifications. Pinkerton's defended the mining corporations around Butte, Montana, when IWW labor leader Frank Little was lynched in 1917. Hammett told Hellman that he had been offered $5,000 by the Anaconda Copper Mining Company to assassinate Little. 'Through the years he was to repeat that bribe offer so many times that I came to believe, knowing him now, that it was a kind of key to his life,' Hellman wrote in *Scoundrel Time*. 'He had given a man the right to think that he would murder, and the fact that Frank Little was lynched with three other men in what was known as the Everett Massacre must have been, for Hammett, an abiding horror. I think I can date Hammett's belief that he was living in a corrupt society from Little's murder.'

The 'horror' – and Hammett's shame – would drift through Poisonville in *Red Harvest* like corrosive fumes. Yet the ex-Pinkerton rarely resisted any occasion to spike his detective pedigree. In the March 1923 *Smart Set* he published twenty-nine numbered extracts 'From the Memoirs of a Private Detective'. Among them:

2

A man whom I was shadowing went into the country for a walk one Sunday afternoon and lost his bearings completely. I had to direct him back to the city.

5

Three times I have been mistaken for a Prohibition agent, but never had trouble clearing myself.

6

Taking a prisoner from a ranch near Gilt Edge, Mont., to Lewistown one night, my machine broke down and we had to sit there until daylight. The prisoner, who stoutly affirmed his innocence, was clothed only in overalls and shirt. After shivering all night on the front seat his morale was low, and I had no difficulty in getting a complete confession from him while walking to the nearest ranch early the following morning.

8

I was once falsely accused of perjury and had to perjure myself to escape arrest.

11

I know a man who will forge the impressions of any set of fingers in the world for $50.

13

I know a detective who once attempted to disguise himself thoroughly. The first policeman he met took him into custody.

17

The slang in use among criminals is for the most part a conscious, artificial growth, designed more to confuse outsiders than for any other purpose, but sometimes it is singularly expressive; for instance, *two-time loser* – one who has been convicted twice; and the older *gone to read and write* – found it advisable to go away for a while.

18

Pocket-picking is the easiest to master of all the criminal trades. Anyone who is not crippled can become an adept in a day.

21

The chief of police of a Southern city once gave me a description of a man, complete even to a mole on his neck, but neglected to mention that he had only one arm.

25

Going from the larger cities out into the remote rural communities one finds a steadily decreasing percentage of crimes that have to do with money and a proportionate increase in the frequency of sex as a criminal motive.

28

I know a man who once stole a Ferris-wheel.

29

That the law-breaker is invariably sooner or later apprehended is probably the least challenged of extant myths. And yet the files of every detective bureau bulge with records of unsolved mysteries and uncaught criminals.

After three years as a Pinkerton, Hammett enlisted in the Army, taking basic training at Camp Mead, Maryland, and in the summer of 1918 he was assigned to the Motor Ambulance Company. He subsequently explained his disinclination to drive a car as a reaction to an accident when he overturned an ambulance of wounded soldiers returning to the States for hospitalization. Hammett lasted in the Army only about eleven months. During the 1918–1919 epidemic he contracted Spanish influenza, followed by bronchial pneumonia. The assault on his lungs released a latent tuberculosis – Hammett's mother Annie was tubercular and coughed chronically throughout his adolescence. Discharged with a small disability pension, he entered the Cushman Hospital in Tacoma, Washington, where he met and made love to a nurse named Josephine 'Jose' Dolan. Recurrent lung problems, relapses and hemorrhages would dog Hammett for much of the 1920s.

He returned to the Pinkerton Agency, operating from the Spokane, Washington office, and then in San Francisco. Hammett recounted his involvement in the Fatty Arbuckle rape case, the Arnstein bond theft case, the Gloomy Gus Schaefer arrest, and the *Sonoma* freighter gold coin theft. In 1921 Jose Dolan wrote him from her family home in Montana – she was pregnant. Hammett sent for Jose, and on July 7 he married her at St Mary's Cathedral. A daughter, Mary Jane, was born on October 15. There would be another daughter, Josephine Rebecca (born May 24, 1926).

When a debilitating bronchial infection forced Hammett to stop working as a detective, he enrolled in stenography and writing classes at Munson's Business College on a vocational training subsidy from the Veterans' Bureau. He started to write advertising, freelance for the first few years; he occasionally bartered ads in exchange for a suit or shoes. By 1926 Hammett was the advertising manager for the Albert S. Samuels Company, the oldest jeweler in San Francisco. (Hammett dedicated *The Dain Curse* to Al Samuels, after lifting his characters' names from Samuels' employees.)

At the same time that he was studying and writing advertising, Hammett started to publish brief pieces in H. L. Mencken and George Jean Nathan's monthly, *The Smart Set* – anecdotes, articles, his first short fiction. In December 1922, he contributed 'The Road Home' to *Black Mask*, the toniest of the pulps and the magazine Mencken and Nathan founded to subsidize *The Smart Set*. He introduced the Continental Op to *Black Mask* in October of the following year, with the story 'Arson Plus'. Hammett eventually published twenty-eight short stories in the voice of the nameless Op.

In 1927 Jose moved with the children to San Anselmo, while Hammett remained in San Francisco. *Black Mask* editor Joseph T. Shaw urged him to write an Op book. The November issue carried the first installment of the novel Hammett was calling 'Poisonville'.

*

Red Harvest (as 'Poisonville' issued from Knopf in February 1929) opens on a political nightmare then tilts into a headlong fever dream. The Op is summoned by newspaper reformer Donald Willsson to Personville, a Northwestern mining town modeled on the corrupt Butte or Anaconda of Hammett's Pinkerton stint. 'An ugly city of forty thousand people, set in an ugly notch between two ugly mountains all dirtied up by mining', Personville – or Poisonville, as the locals drawl it – once was the possession, 'soul, skin and guts', of Willsson's father, Elihu, President of the Personville Mining Corporation and the First National Bank, and owner of the two city newspapers. But after coal prices dropped in 1921 the elder Willsson tore up the miners' contracts; when they struck, the 'czar of Poisonville' crushed the Wobblies with triggermen and goons. 'Old Elihu didn't know his Italian history,' an IWW organizer explains to the Op. 'He won the strike, but he lost his hold on the city and the state. To beat the miners he had to let his hired thugs run wild. When the fight was over he couldn't get rid of them. He had given his city to them and he wasn't strong enough to take it away from them. Personville looked good to them and they took it over. They had won his strike for him and they took the city for their spoils. He couldn't openly break with them. They had too much on him. He was responsible for all they had done during the strike.'

Op, of course, is short for Operative – the Op is a Continental Detective Agency operative, San Francisco branch. But as a 'fat, middle-aged, hard-boiled, pig-headed guy', Op might as well mean the opposite of Hammett: the Op weighs 190 pounds to Hammett's 160, and is roughly 5ft 6in to the writer's 6ft 1in. When Donald Willsson is murdered the night of the Op's arrival, Elihu hires the Op to find the killer, thereby slotting him into his son's crusader's role. The Op will substitute for the progressive editor, yet he lacks his idealism – and his innocence: to reform Poisonville, the Op recognizes, is also to return Personville to Elihu Willsson.

The cops in *Red Harvest* are shabby, mercenary and crooked, but the Op is hardly distinguishable from any of the hoodlums who control Poisonville. He carries multiple IDs (including, cynically, the card of a Wobbly seaman), repeatedly lifts booze from crime scenes, grabs an alibi for himself from a mobster, and even transports a valise of pipe bombs to a shoot-out. He introduces his incentive for cleaning up Poisonville to Elihu Willsson as 'fun':

'Your fat chief of police tried to assassinate me last night. I don't like that. I'm just mean enough to want to ruin him for it. Now I'm going to have my fun. I've got ten thousand dollars of your money to play with. I'm going to use it to open up Poisonville from Adam's apple to ankles. I'll see that you get my reports as regularly as possible. I hope you enjoy them.'

And later, speaking to gambling boss Max 'Whisper' Thaler, the Op tips his intentions brusquely toward revenge:

'No, I don't like the way Poisonville has treated me. I've got my chance now, and I'm going to even up. I take it you're back in the club again, all brothers together, let bygones be bygones. You want to be left alone. If I had been, maybe now I'd be riding back to San Francisco. But I wasn't.'

The Op forgoes familiar fictional detective's tactics for abrupt, explosive flourishes that simultaneously baffle and goad. As a backup Continental operative protests midway, 'this job is plain as astronomy to me. I understand everything about it except what you have done and why, and what you are trying to do and how.' When Dinah Brand, the enigmatic prostitute at the emotional – and criminal – still point of *Red Harvest*, complains, 'you've got the vaguest way of doing things I ever heard of,' the Op replies: 'Plans are all right sometimes ... And sometimes just stirring things up is all right ...' His oblique strategies involve the almost random blasts of what he styles 'dynamite', loaded bits of misinformation and rumor that scramble the hostile factions of Poisonville. 'I've got to have a wedge,' he says. 'If we can smash things up enough – break the combination – they'll have their knives in each other's backs, doing our work for us.'

Something of the chaos the Op triggers can be discovered in this short scene with gangster Reno Starkey:

... [Reno] rubbed his chin and said: 'Well, that settles the Whisper end.'

I said: 'No.'

'What do you mean, no?'

'If his mob don't know where he is,' I suggested, 'let's tell them. They blasted him out of the can when [police chief] Noonan copped him. Think they'd try it again if the news got around that [acting police chief] McGraw had picked him up on the quiet?'

'Keep talking,' Reno said.

'If his friends try to crack the hoosegow again, thinking he's in it, that'll give the department, including Pete's specials, something to do. While they're doing it, you could try your luck in Whiskeytown.'

'Maybe,' he said slowly, 'maybe we'll try just that thing.'

'It ought to work,' I encouraged him, standing up. 'I'll see you –'

'Stick around. This is as good sport as any while there's a reader out for you. And we'll need a good guy like you on the party.'

I didn't like that so much. I knew enough not to say so. I sat down again.

Reno got busy arranging the rumor. The telephone was worked over-time. The kitchen door was worked as hard, letting men in and out. More came in than went out. The house filled with men, smoke, tension.

Op's mastery of criminal slang is a significant undertow of his rampant disorder. Back when he wrote advertising, Hammett speculated that 'The favorite words of the plain man are those which enable him to talk without thinking.' The Op alternately cuts through and exploits the tough chatter that shades Poisonville like dust from the mines. Prior to meeting Dinah Brand, for instance, he hears four descriptions of her. When the Op (and the reader) finally see her, Dinah enters the novel – her hair messy, lipstick crooked, runs in her stockings – as a suddenly complicated woman shedding so many hard-boiled stereotypes. 'This was the Dinah Brand who took her pick of Poisonville's men, according to what I had been told.'

Yet as he pits cops against gangsters, gangsters against gangsters, cops against cops, his distance finally can't protect the Op. 'It's this damned town,' he claims. 'Poisonville is right. It's poisoned me.' His bitter pun sounds knee-jerk, evasive – another hard-bitten cliché – but the Op can't let go of the notion:

'Look. I sat at Willsson's table tonight and played them like you'd play trout, and got just as much fun out of it. I looked at Noonan and knew he hadn't a chance in a thousand of living another day because of what I had done to him, and I laughed, and felt warm and happy inside. That's not me. I've got hard skin all over what's left of my soul, and after twenty years of messing around with crime I can look at any sort of murder without seeing anything in it but my bread and butter, the day's work. But this getting a rear out of planning deaths is not natural to me. It's what this place has done to me.'

In the novel's most famous phrase, the Op senses he is 'blood-simple'. *Red Harvest* teases out the shifting insinuations: murderous – crazy – dumb. When the Op flees Personville all the gangs and crooked cops might be dead, but the city reverts to the ultimate source of the corruption, Elihu Willsson. For the Op the only release is to draft his official report for the Old Man of the Continental Detective Agency – a vain escape into hollow professionalism, since this is a report he has already told us 'is no place for the dirty details anyway'.

Some seventy-plus years after publication, after decades of imitation, the odd, surreal fringes of *Red Harvest* still startle: the Jacobean ghoulishness of the twenty-four murders; the Op's laudanum dreams; and this phantasmagoric snapshot of the Op:

'I don't mean to be the only one that's hurt. I twist the pick out of her hand and stick it in her. You gallop out, coked to the edges, charging at the whole world with both eyes shut. She tumbles into you. You go down, roll around till your hand hits the butt of the pick. Holding on to that, you go to sleep, peaceful as she is.'

*

Dashiell Hammett continued the Op for *The Dain Curse*, also published in 1929. By the time Knopf issued *Red Harvest*, he was already at work on a third novel, *The Maltese Falcon*. In October Hammett moved to New York City with novelist and actress Nell Martin – he would dedicate *The Glass Key* to her. *The Maltese Falcon* appeared in February 1930.

The Maltese Falcon introduced a new detective – Sam Spade – whose physical aspects (shades of his conversation with Stein) now approximated Hammett's. The novel also originated a fresh narrative direction. The Op related his own stories and investigations, lodging his idiosyncrasies, omissions and intuitions at the core of *Red Harvest* and *The Dain Curse*. For *The Maltese Falcon* Hammett shifted to a neutral, but chilling third-person narration that consistently monitors Spade from the outside – often insouciantly as a 'blond satan' or a smiling 'wolfish' cur – but never ventures anywhere Spade does not go or witnesses anything Spade doesn't see.

This cold-eyed yet restricted angle prolongs the suspense; when Spade learns of Archer's murder we hear only his end of the phone call – 'Hello ... Yes, speaking ... Dead? ... Yes ... Fifteen minutes. Thanks.' The name of the deceased stays concealed with the detective until he enters the crime scene and views his partner's corpse. Never disclosing what Spade is feeling and thinking, Hammett positions indeterminacy as an implicit moral stance. By screening the reader from his gumshoe's inner life, he pulls us into Spade's ambiguous world. As Spade consoles Brigid O'Shaughnessy, 'It's not always easy to know what to do.'

The implacable music of *The Maltese Falcon* is the point, counterpoint of the double-cross. Surrounded by liars, Spade discharges the coiling whorl-within-whorls of Kenneth Fearing's poem 'Dear Beatrice Fairfax':

> But just the same, baby, and never forget,
> It takes a neat, smart, fast, good, sweet doublecross

INTRODUCTION

> To doublecross the gentleman who doublecrossed the
>   gentleman who doublecrossed
> Your doublecrossing, doublecrossing, doublecross friend.

A 'tough one to figure out', he plays his corners tight – as a
friendly hotel dick challenges Spade: 'You don't cash many
checks for strangers, do you, Sammy?' The detective appears
susceptible to all dubious turns. As *The Maltese Falcon* opens
his mistress is Archer's wife, Iva, who wonders if he killed her
husband. He tells Brigid O'Shaughnessy that he didn't trust
her story when he accepted her case, but he 'believed your
two hundred dollars'. Spade commands a retainer from Brigid,
then demands another from Cairo. After going to bed with
Brigid, he steals away to search her room. His secretary dubs
him 'too slick for your own good', and the depraved Gutman
imagines him a brother: 'By Gad, sir, you are a character!'

Spade's dodges and bravado refine the chaotic lunges of the
Op. 'My way of learning,' he discloses to Brigid, 'is to heave
a wild and unpredictable monkey wrench into the machinery.'
But more often he bluffs – Brigid, Cairo, Gutman; even when
he's probably telling the truth, Spade radiates self-interest:

> Spade's eyes had lost their warmth. His face was dull and lumpy.
> 'I know what I'm talking about,' he said in a low, consciously patient,
> tone. 'This is my city and my game. I could manage to land on my
> feet – sure – this time, but the next time I tried to put over a fast
> one they'd stop me so fast I'd swallow my teeth. Hell with that. You
> birds'll be in New York or Constantinople or someplace else. I'm in
> business here.'

The worldly cynicism (Brigid and Spade 'maybe' love each
other, Spade says), the coruscating images of compulsive
materialism (Spade no less than the iconic Falcon), the strings of
point-blank maxims (Spade's elegant 'I don't mind a reasonable
amount of trouble'): Sam Spade was Dashiell Hammett's most
appealing and enduring creation, even before Bogart indelibly
limned him for the 1941 film. For as Hammett reflected in his
introduction to the 1934 Modern Library edition of *The Maltese
Falcon*:

> Spade had no original. He is a dream man in the sense that he is
> what most of the private detectives I worked with would like to have

been and what quite a few of them in their cockier moments thought they approached. For your private detective does not – or did not ten years ago when he was my colleague – want to be an erudite solver of riddles in the Sherlock Holmes manner; he wants to be a hard and shifty fellow, able to take care of himself in any situation, able to get the best of anybody he comes in contact with, whether criminal, innocent by-stander, or client.

Yet the novel resists retrospective romanticism. Remember Gutman's daughter Rhea, drugged and full of pin holes. Or Captain Jacobi, nearly seven feet tall and spurting blood, delivering the Falcon. Or the still wondrous Flitcraft story – the parable of a man elaborately going nowhere that impresses Spade 'like somebody had taken the lid off life and let him look at the works,' because this is also his story. The sad final lines of *The Maltese Falcon* drop him back where he started, shooing another woman into his office. As Hammett wrote, Spade 'shivered'.

*

Hammett followed *The Maltese Falcon* with *The Glass Key* early in 1931. By then he was residing in Hollywood at a succession of modish hotels. His friends included the writers Ben Hecht, S. J. Perelman and Dorothy Parker. Hammett wrote *City Streets* – his only original screenplay – for Paramount, and the film, starring Gary Cooper and Sylvia Sidney, was released in April to approving reviews, particularly for the clever, arch dialogue he would revisit in his next novel.

The previous November Hammett had met Lillian Kober, née Hellman, a script reader for MGM and the wife of playwright Arthur Kober, at a Bing Crosby opening at the Roosevelt Hotel. He told her that he was coming off a five-day drunk. She was twenty-five, he thirty-six. The relationship would persist, through infidelities and estrangements, for the rest of his life.

Knopf published *The Thin Man* in January 1934, with a dedication to Lillian. Hellman later wrote in *An Unfinished Woman*: 'So it was a happy day when I was given half the manuscript to read and was told I was Nora. It was nice to be Nora, married to Nick Charles, maybe one of the few

INTRODUCTION

marriages in modern literature where the man and woman like each other and have a fine time together. But I was soon put back in my place – Hammett said I was also the silly girl in the book and the villainess. I don't know now if he was joking...'

For his last novel, the soon to be former detective writer focused on an ex-detective turned sophisticated lush. Hammett restored the first-person mode of *Red Harvest* and *The Dain Curse*, but recast his hard-boiled recitation as a rueful string of one-liners and drollery. Nick and Nora Charles are on holiday in New York City during Christmas 1932. Nick retired six years earlier, when Nora's father passed away and 'left her a lumber mill and a narrow-gauge railroad and some other things and I quit the Agency to look after them'. When members of their old circle soon turn up dead (secretary Julia Wolf) or missing (inventor and chief suspect Clyde Miller Wynant), Nick reluctantly, almost inadvertently wobbles into action. In perhaps the neatest gag here, he manifests no urgent interest in the crimes – and never is he actually hired by anyone; Nick relapses into detection essentially to defend himself against whoever is trying to snooker him into the case.

The Thin Man is a sly, deceptive sexual farce. Through nearly ever scene Hammett layered many pleasures, notably the frisky Nick-and-Nora dialogue that echoes *The Front Page* even as he anticipates the Preston Sturges films of the early 1940s. 'Tell me something, Nick,' Nora asks. 'Tell me the truth: when you were wrestling with Mimi, didn't you have an erection?' (Knopf alluded to this notorious line in their advertising campaign.) Hammett modulated the complicated backstory into self-revealing banter – as Nora poses anxious questions and Nick deflects with wisecracks. In a subtle, mediated reprise of the assault on cliché and cant from *Red Harvest*, he also relished juxtaposing Nick's observations to the glib, distorted articles in the daily papers.

Yet this Depression screwball comedy of an alcoholic Manhattan aristocracy arranges many dark intrusions. The long, almost 2,000-word quotation from Maurice Duke's *Celebrated Criminal Cases in America* about Alfred G. Packer, a Salt Lake City prospector convicted of cannibalism during the late nineteenth century, is an egregious interruption of the plot. Hammett commentators tend to cite Lillian Hellman's opinion that the Packer story merely resulted from the pressure to fill pages. But Duke's book was also a favorite of Sam Spade, and *The Thin Man* is shot through with moments when the careless teasing, kidding and ridicule yield to sudden rifts of anger and madness. These largely involve the Wynant family – if not precisely cannibals, 'the first of a new race of monsters', as Nora styles them. Daughter Dorothy drunkenly divulges her sexual fears of her step-father. Son Gilbert retrogresses into his gaga crime obsessions, his theories about lying and odors, and his 'funny question' about incest. Mother Mimi beats Dorothy, and slips into animal rages – 'She made a claw of her right hand and struck at my face with her pointed nails.' As Nick concludes, 'They're all sex-crazy, I think, and it backs up into their heads.'

The Thin Man sustains an elegiac fable of identity. So many characters assume two, sometimes three lives: Julia Wolf, Chris Jorgensen, Herbert Macauley, Art Nunheim, even Nick Charles, haunted by his detective past. Others, like Clyde Wynant – and perhaps also Nick – end up thin men. 'What was that joke,' a police officer asks, 'about a guy being so thin he had to stand in the same place twice to throw a shadow?'

*

Nick Charles exits *The Thin Man* dazed, weary, a little lost. When Nora wonders what will happen to Mimi, Dorothy and Gilbert Wynant, he responds: 'Nothing new. They'll go on being Mimi and Dorothy and Gilbert just as you and I will go on being us and the Quinns will go on being the Quinns. Murder doesn't round out anybody's life except the murdered's and sometimes the murderer's.'

Dashiell Hammett's life after 1934 is immaterial to his fiction. Although mainsprings of the popular Hammett legend originate from the late '30s, '40s and '50s – the intricate relationship with Hellman; his leadership of the League of American Writers and the Screen Writers Guild; his Marxism and imprisonment for contempt of court in 1951 – there would be no creative work other than an abandoned novel fragment, *Tulip*.

Those around Hammett offered explanations for his silence – alcohol, celebrity, affluence, Hellman, the conviction he would die young. Beyond the prison house of a 'style' and the fears of 'repeating myself', Hammett himself recalled that 'The thing that ruined me was the writing of the last third of *The Glass Key* in one sitting of 30 hours.' The autobiographical *Tulip* glosses the paralysis of ambition – 'You'd never get it all in one book' – and concludes: 'If you are tired you ought to rest, I think, and not try to fool yourself and your customers with colored baubles.' Hammett's table talk with Gertrude Stein suggests also that he felt restless and cornered inside his character, 'Dashiell Hammett'.

*

But for Stein, touring the States back in 1935, Dashiell Hammett was America. In her lecture, 'The Gradual Making of *The Making of Americans*', Stein wrote 'that a space of time is a natural thing for an American to always have inside them as something in which they are continuously moving', and this was 'an American thing', she continued, as American as detective stories:

> Think of anything, of cowboys, of movies, of detective stories, of anybody who goes anywhere or stays at home and is an American and you will realize that it is strictly American to conceive a space that is filled with moving, a space of time that is filled always filled with moving and my first effort to express this thing which is an American thing began in writing *The Making of Americans*.

Dorothy Parker put the same *American thing* about Dashiell Hammett more concisely. 'All I can say is that anyone who doesn't read him misses much of modern America. And hot that sounds!'

Robert Polito

ROBERT POLITO is the author of *Savage Art: A Biography of Jim Thompson*, which won the National Book Critics Circle Award in biography. He directs the graduate writing program at the New School in New York City.

S E L E C T   B I B L I O G R A P H Y

For biographical information about Dashiell Hammett and for quotations from his letters, articles and interviews, the following books were invaluable:

JOHNSON, DIANE, *Dashiell Hammett: A Life* (New York: Random House, 1983).
LAYMAN, RICHARD, *Shadow Man: The Life of Dashiell Hammett* (New York: Harcourt Brace Jovanovich, 1981).
MELLEN, JOAN, *Hellman and Hammett* (New York: HarperCollins, 1996).
STEIN, GERTRUDE, *Everybody's Autobiography* (New York: Random House, 1937).
VAN VECHTEN, CARL, ed., *Selected Writings of Gertrude Stein* (New York: Vintage Books, 1972).

Books by Dashiell Hammett
Red Harvest (New York: Alfred A. Knopf, 1929).
The Dain Curse (New York: Alfred A. Knopf, 1929).
The Maltese Falcon (New York: Alfred A. Knopf, 1930).
The Glass Key (New York: Alfred A. Knopf, 1931).
The Thin Man (New York: Alfred A. Knopf, 1934).
The Big Knockover: Selected Short Stories and Short Novels
(New York: Random House, 1966).
The Continental Op (New York: Random House, 1974).
Woman in the Dark (New York: Alfred A. Knopf, 1988).
Nightmare Town: Stories, edited by Kirby McCauley, Martin H. Greenberg, and Ed Gorman (New York: Alfred A. Knopf, 1999).
Selected Letters of Dashiell Hammett, edited by Richard Layman, with Julie M. Rivett, Foreword by Josephine Hammett Marshall (Washington, D.C.: Counterpoint Press, February 2001).

CHRONOLOGY

DATE	AUTHOR'S LIFE	LITERARY CONTEXT
1894	Samuel Dashiell Hammett born 27 May in St Mary's County, Maryland to Richard Thomas Hammett and Annie Bond Dashiell.	Conan Doyle: *The Memoirs of Sherlock Holmes*. Conan Doyle visits US for lecture tour. Twain: *Pudd'nhead Wilson*.
1896		Fitzgerald born. Chekhov: *The Seagull*. Hardy: *Jude the Obscure*.
1898		
1899		Hemingway born. Hornung: *Raffles: The Amateur Cracksman*. Chopin: *The Awakening*. James: *The Awkward Age*. Nabokov born.
1900		Freud: *The Interpretation of Dreams*. Conrad: *Lord Jim*. Dreiser: *Sister Carrie*.
1901	Family moves to Baltimore.	Mann: *Buddenbrooks*. Kipling: *Kim*.
1902		Conan Doyle: *The Hound of the Baskervilles*. Steinbeck born.
1904		Chekhov dies. James: *The Golden Bowl*.
1905		Conan Doyle: *The Return of Sherlock Holmes*. Wharton: *The House of Mirth*.
1906		Beckett born.
1907		Conrad: *The Secret Agent*. Auden born.
1908	Attends Baltimore Polytechnic Institute. Leaves after less than a year to work at various jobs.	
1909		Stein: *Three Lives*.
1912		Dreiser: *The Financier*.

The US becomes the leading manufacturing nation in the world. Beginning of Freudian psychoanalysis. Nicholas II becomes Tsar.

William McKinley elected US president. Klondike Gold Rush.

Invention of the cash register. Rockefeller 'retires' worth c. $200 million. Spanish-American War.
Outbreak of Boer War. Alfred Hitchcock born.

US population 76 million. US railroad network just under 200,000 miles. First International Socialist Congress in Paris. Planck's quantum theory.

President McKinley assassinated. Succeeded by Theodore Roosevelt, ushering in a progressive era in American politics. Marconi transmits messages across the Atlantic. Death of Queen Victoria; accession of Edward VII.

War breaks out between Japan and Russia.

Einstein's theory of relativity. General strikes, mutiny and incipient revolution in Russia.

San Francisco earthquake.
Cubist exhibition in Paris.

First Ford Model T car.
Woodrow Wilson elected US president. Sinking of *Titanic*. Charlie Chaplin's first film.

DATE	AUTHOR'S LIFE	LITERARY CONTEXT
1913		Frost: *A Boy's Will.* Lawrence: *Sons and Lovers.* Gorky: *Childhood.*
1914		Burroughs: *Tarzan of the Apes.* Joyce: *Dubliners.*
1915	Detective for Pinkerton's National Detective Service.	Ford: *The Good Soldier.* Kafka: *Metamorphosis.* Lawrence: *The Rainbow.*
1917		Conan Doyle: *His Last Bow.* Eliot: 'The Love Song of J. Alfred Prufrock'.
1918	Enlists in army.	
1919	Discharged from army with disability pension following bouts of flu, pneumonia and tuberculosis. Returns to work at Pinkerton's.	*Black Mask*, pulp magazine, set up. Anderson: *Winesburg, Ohio.* Woolf: *Night and Day.*
1920	Works as Pinkerton's operative in Spokane, Washington, Idaho and Montana. Is hospitalised, where he meets nurse Josephine ('Jose') Dolan.	Christie: *The Mysterious Affair at Styles* (first novel). Mansfield: *Bliss.* Fitzgerald: *This Side of Paradise.* Pound: *Hugh Selwyn Mauberly.* Lewis: *Main Street.*
1921	Marries Jose Dolan on 7 July in San Francisco. Daughter Mary Jane born 15 October.	Dos Passos: *Three Soldiers.* Lawrence: *Women in Love.* Pirandello: *Six Characters in Search of an Author.*
1922	First short stories published in *Smart Set* and *Black Mask*.	Carroll John Daly creates the first hard-boiled detective in 'The False Burton Combs'. Eliot: *The Wasteland.* Joyce: *Ulysses.* Mansfield: *The Garden Party.*
1923	Introduces the Continental Op in *Black Mask* short story 'Arson Plus'.	
1925	'The Scorched Face' (novelette) published in *Black Mask*.	Dreiser: *An American Tragedy.* Fitzgerald: *The Great Gatsby.* Loos: *Gentlemen Prefer Blondes.* Stein: *The Making of Americans.* Kafka: *The Trial.* Woolf: *Mrs Dalloway.* Dos Passos: *Manhattan Transfer.*

CHRONOLOGY

HISTORICAL EVENTS

Completion of new, even grander Grand Central Station building. Post-Impressionist exhibition in New York.

Outbreak of World War I. President Wilson proclaims US neutrality. Panama Canal opens.

US joins war in Europe. Russian October Revolution.

World War I ends 11 November.
The Eighteenth Amendment, prohibiting the manufacture and sale of intoxicating liquors, is ratified. Versailles Peace Conference, with Wilson's Fourteen Points. The 'Red Scare' in the US: American steelworkers start year-long strike. Nineteenth Amendment (Female Suffrage) passed by the House.
Warren G. Harding elected US president. Slump in US. League of Nations formed. Russian Civil War ends. The 'jazz age'.

Quota laws restrict immigration to the US. Radio broadcasting.

Mussolini gains power in Italy. Revival of the Ku Klux Klan. Talking pictures developed.

Calvin Coolidge elected president after Harding's death. Moscow becomes capital of USSR; Stalin becomes General Secretary of Communist Party.

Al Capone a powerful force in Chicago. The 'Monkey Trial' in Dayton, Tennessee finds for *Genesis* and signals the withdrawal of Southern culture into other-worldliness.

HAMMETT

DATE	AUTHOR'S LIFE	LITERARY CONTEXT
1926	Advertising manager for jeweller Albert Samuels. Daughter Josephine Rebecca born 24 May.	Fitzgerald: *All the Sad Young Men.* Faulkner: *Soldier's Pay.* Hemingway: *The Sun Also Rises.* Christie: *The Murder of Roger Ackroyd.*
1927	First part of *Red Harvest* (originally called 'Poisonville') published in *Black Mask.*	Woolf: *To the Lighthouse.* Cather: *Death Comes for the Archbishop.* Wilder: *The Bridge of San Luis Rey.* Proust: *Remembrance of Things Past.* Conan Doyle: *The Case Book of Sherlock Holmes.*
1928		Lawrence: *Lady Chatterley's Lover.* Bulgakov: *The Master and Margarita* (to 1940). O'Neill: *Strange Interlude.* Waugh: *Decline and Fall.*
1929	*Red Harvest* and *The Dain Curse* published by Knopf. Moves to New York. First part of *The Maltese Falcon* and 'Fly Paper' (a novelette) published in *Black Mask.*	Hemingway: *A Farewell to Arms.* Faulkner: *The Sound and the Fury.* Wolfe: *Look Homeward, Angel.* Remarque: *All Quiet on the Western Front.*
1930	*The Maltese Falcon* published by Knopf. *Roadhouse Nights,* a movie based on *Red Harvest,* released by Paramount. Moves to Hollywood; meets Lillian Hellman.	Lawrence dies. Faulkner: *As I Lay Dying.* Crane: *The Bridge.* Freud: *Civilization and its Discontents.*
1931	*The Glass Key* published. Moves back to New York. First film version of *The Maltese Falcon,* starring Ricardo Cortez and Bebe Daniels, released by Warner Brothers. Hammett co-writes screenplay.	
1932		Crane dies. Huxley: *Brave New World.* Caldwell: *Tobacco Road.* Erle Stanley Gardner: *The Case of the Velvet Claws* (first Perry Mason novel).

CHRONOLOGY

Television invented by John Logie Baird. First liquid fuel rocket. General strike in UK.

Lindbergh's solo Atlantic flight. Financial crisis in Germany. Trotsky expelled from Communist Party in USSR.

First full-length film, first television broadcast; 26 million cars and 13 million radios in use in US. Herbert Hoover elected US president. First 'Mickey Mouse' cartoon. Gershwin: *An American in Paris*. Amelia Earhart becomes the first woman to fly the Atlantic solo.

Wall Street Crash, 24 October; mass unemployment. US establishes Federal Loans. Beginning of world depression. Al Capone arrested. Museum of Modern Art in New York founded. Land speed record set at 231 mph.

Unemployment rises to 13 million. US tariff raised. France begins Maginot Line. Gandhi begins civil disobedience campaign in India. Empire State Building opened.

Al Capone found guilty of tax evasion and sent to prison (the first time a charge was made to stick). Britain abandons Gold Standard. Invention of the electric razor.

Lindbergh's son kidnapped. Franklin Roosevelt, Democrat, elected US president. Inaugurates New Deal. Stock prices in the US fall to 20% of their 1929 value.

DATE	AUTHOR'S LIFE	LITERARY CONTEXT
1933	Novella 'Woman in the Dark' published in *Liberty*. *Condensed version of The Thin Man* published in *Redbook*.	Book burnings in Nazi Germany. Nathanael West: *Miss Lonelyhearts*.
1934	*The Thin Man* published. Film version starring William Powell and Myrna Loy released by MGM (five other *Thin Man* movies would follow between 1934 and 1947).	Cain: *The Postman Always Rings Twice* (banned in Boston). Fitzgerald: *Tender is the Night*. First Soviet Writers' Congress held in Moscow. Waugh: *A Handful of Dust*. Miller: *Tropic of Cancer*. Christie: *Murder on the Orient Express*.
1935	Meets Gertrude Stein.	Cain: *Double Indemnity*. Wolfe: *Of Time and the River*. Lewis: *It Can't Happen Here*.
1936	Secretly joins Communist Party. *Satan Met a Lady*, a second film version of *The Maltese Falcon*, is released by Warner Brothers. *After the Thin Man* released by MGM.	Mitchell: *Gone with the Wind*. Eliot: *Collected Poems*. Dos Passos: *The Big Money*. Faulkner: *Absalom, Absalom!* Lorca killed by Fascist militia in Spain.
1937		Hemingway: *To Have and Have Not*. Steinbeck: *Of Mice and Men*. Stevens: *The Man with the Blue Guitar*. Woolf: *The Years*. Dos Passos: *U.S.A.*
1938		Cummings: *Collected Poems*. Sartre: *Nausea*. Beckett: *Murphy*. Waugh: *Scoop*.
1939		Chandler: *The Big Sleep*. Joyce: *Finnegans Wake*. Steinbeck: *The Grapes of Wrath*.
1940		Hemingway: *For Whom the Bell Tolls*. Chandler: *Farewell, My Lovely*. Fitzgerald dies. Greene: *The Power and the Glory*.

CHRONOLOGY

HISTORICAL EVENTS

The Twenty-First Amendment, repealing prohibition, ratified. Hitler appointed Chancellor of Germany. USSR recognised by US. By this year 11,000 of the 25,000 banks in the US have failed.

Depth of the Great Depression. Stalin institutes purges of the Communist Party in Russia. Al Capone sent to Alcatraz.

Transcontinental air service begins in US. Mussolini invades Abyssinia. Gershwin: *Porgy and Bess*.

Roosevelt re-elected by a landslide. Spanish Civil War begins. Abdication of King Edward VIII who wishes to marry the American divorcee Wallace Simpson. Hitler and Mussolini form Rome-Berlin axis.

Japan invades China. First jet engine and nylon stockings. In the US approximately 75 million visit movies every week. Moscow show trials of Communist Party opponents of Stalin. Strike against Republic Steel in Chicago: four strikers killed, forty-four injured.

Germany annexes Austria; Munich crisis. Pogroms against Jews in Germany. Hitchcock: *The Lady Vanishes*.

World War II begins. First commercial transatlantic flights. Vivien Leigh and Clark Gable star in *Gone with the Wind*.

The Battle of Britain. Penicillin developed. Fall of Paris. Assassination of Trotsky in Mexico. Churchill prime minister in UK. Extraction of plutonium from uranium.

HAMMETT

DATE	AUTHOR'S LIFE	LITERARY CONTEXT
1941	Elected president of League of American Writers. John Huston's film version of *The Maltese Falcon*, starring Humphrey Bogart and Mary Astor, released by Warner Brothers.	Fitzgerald: *The Last Tycoon* (posthumous). Brecht: *Mother Courage*. Woolf and Joyce die.
1942	Hammett rejoins army as a private.	Chandler: *The High Window*. Paul: *A Narrow Street*. Camus: *The Stranger*.
1943	Sent to Fort Randall, Alaska. Co-writes screenplay *Watch on the Rhine* with Lillian Hellman.	Chandler: *The Lady in the Lake*.
1944		Williams: *The Glass Menagerie*. Eliot: *Four Quartets*.
1945	Honourably discharged as a master sergeant. Returns to New York.	Orwell: *Animal Farm*. Waugh: *Brideshead Revisited*. Thurber: *The Thurber Carnival*. Borges: *Fictions*. Dreiser dies.
1946	Elected president of Communist-sponsored Civil Rights Congress of New York. Begins teaching courses in mystery writing at Jefferson School of Social Science.	Chandler wins Mystery Writers of America's Edgar Allan Poe Award (also in 1954). Goodis: *Dark Passage*.
1947		*The Diary of Anne Frank*. Williams: *A Streetcar Named Desire*.
1948		Eliot wins Nobel Prize. Mailer: *The Naked and the Dead*.
1949		Chandler: *The Little Sister*. Faulkner wins Nobel Prize. Orwell: *1984*. Greene: *The Third Man*. Miller: *Death of a Salesman*.
1950		Chandler: 'The Simple Art of Murder', 'Goldfish'. Eliot: *The Cocktail Party*.
1951	Questioned before US District Court about Civil Rights Congress bail fund. Found guilty of contempt of court and sentenced to six months in prison, where his health deteriorates.	Jones: *From Here to Eternity*. Salinger: *The Catcher in the Rye*. Frost: *Complete Poems*.

xl

CHRONOLOGY

HISTORICAL EVENTS

Japanese attack on Pearl Harbor. US enters war 11 December. Hitler invades Russia. US introduces 'lease-lend' system of aid to Britain. Orson Welles: *Citizen Kane*. Irving Berlin: *White Christmas*. Beginnings of 'bebop'.

Rommel defeated at El Alamein. Build-up of American air force in Free China. World's first nuclear reactor constructed at Chicago University.

Russians defeat Germans at Stalingrad. Allied armies victorious in North Africa. Allied invasion of Italy.

Allied landings in Normandy; German retreat; liberation of Paris. Roosevelt elected for fourth term in US. *Double Indemnity* released (screenplay part written by Raymond Chandler).
Churchill gives 'Iron Curtain' speech. Cold War begins. Unconditional surrender of Germany. Suicide of Hitler. World War II ends after bombing of Hiroshima and Nagasaki. Foundation of United Nations. Truman president of US; Attlee prime minister in UK.

Film of *The Big Sleep* with Humphrey Bogart and Lauren Bacall.

Al Capone dies. Film of *Dark Passage* starring Bogart and Bacall. India proclaimed independent.

Jewish state of Israel comes into existence. Month-long coal miners' strike in America. Hitchcock: *Rope*.
Chinese revolution. Northern Atlantic Treaty signed at Washington. Russian Blockade lifted. Orson Welles stars in *The Third Man*.

Senator Joseph McCarthy accuses State Department of being riddled with Communists, and begins the worst of the American blacklist period. Korean War begins.
President Truman dismisses General MacArthur as commander of the UN forces in Korea. Rogers and Hammerstein: *South Pacific*. Hitchcock: *Strangers on a Train* (screenplay part written by Chandler). Churchill elected prime minister in UK.

DATE	AUTHOR'S LIFE	LITERARY CONTEXT
1952	Moves to Katonah, New York. Begins work on a novel; fragment is later published as *Tulip* in *The Big Knockover*, a collection of his stories published in 1966.	Beckett: *Waiting for Godot.* Ellison: *The Invisible Man.* O'Connor: *Wise Blood.* Steinbeck: *East of Eden.*
1953	Subpoenaed by Senator Joseph McCarthy to testify before his Senate subcommittee.	Chandler: *The Long Goodbye.* Faulkner: *Requiem for a Nun.* Williams: *Camino Real.*
1954		Hemingway wins Nobel Prize. Amis: *Lucky Jim.*
1955	Suffers heart attack at Lillian Hellman's house on Martha's Vineyard.	Nabokov: *Lolita.* Williams: *Cat on a Hot Tin Roof.* Miller: *A View from the Bridge.*
1956		Osborne: *Look Back in Anger.* Brecht dies. Goodis: *Shoot the Piano Player.*
1957		Kerouac: *On the Road.*
1958		Pasternak's *Dr Zhivago* published throughout world (except USSR). Capote: *Breakfast at Tiffany's.*
1959		Burroughs: *The Naked Lunch.* Grass: *The Tin Drum.*
1960		Updike: *Rabbit, Run.* O'Connor: *The Violent Bear It Away.*
1961	Dies of lung cancer on 10 January 1961 in New York City. Buried at Arlington National Cemetery.	Hemingway dies. Heller: *Catch 22.* Williams: *Night of the Iguana.*

CHRONOLOGY

HISTORICAL EVENTS

Eisenhower elected US president. Gary Cooper stars in *High Noon*. China accuses US of waging germ warfare in Korea. Batista overthrows Cuban government. Accession of Elizabeth II. First contraceptive pill.

Experiments in colour television in the US. Stalin dies.

Communist Party outlawed in US. Marlon Brando stars in *On the Waterfront*. Hitchcock: *Dial M for Murder* and *Rear Window*. Vietnamese Communists defeat French at Dien Bien Phu.

Soviets invade Hungary. Suez Crisis. Eisenhower re-elected as US president. Transatlantic telephone service linking Britain and the US.

Civil Rights Act in US; race riots in southern US.
Alaska becomes 49th state of US. Bernstein: *West Side Story*. Hitchcock: *Vertigo*. Beginning of space exploration.

Batista flees Cuba; Castro seizes power.

John F. Kennedy elected US president. Brezhnev becomes president of USSR. John Wayne stars in *The Alamo*.

Berlin Wall constructed. Yuri Gagarin becomes first man in space.

THE MALTESE FALCON

To Jose

1 SPADE & ARCHER

SAMUEL SPADE'S JAW was long and bony, his chin a jutting v under the more flexible v of his mouth. His nostrils curved back to make another, smaller, v. His yellow-gray eyes were horizontal. The v *motif* was picked up again by thickish brows rising outward from twin creases above a hooked nose, and his pale brown hair grew down – from high flat temples – in a point on his forehead. He looked rather pleasantly like a blond satan.

He said to Effie Perine: "Yes, sweetheart?"

She was a lanky sunburned girl whose tan dress of thin woolen stuff clung to her with an effect of dampness. Her eyes were brown and playful in a shiny boyish face. She finished shutting the door behind her, leaned against it, and said: "There's a girl wants to see you. Her name's Wonderly."

"A customer?"

"I guess so. You'll want to see her anyway: she's a knock-out."

"Shoo her in, darling," said Spade. "Shoo her in."

Effie Perine opened the door again, following it back into the outer office, standing with a hand on the knob while saying: "Will you come in, Miss Wonderly?"

A voice said, "Thank you," so softly that only the purest articulation made the words intelligible, and a young woman came through the doorway. She advanced slowly, with tentative steps, looking at Spade with cobalt-blue eyes that were both shy and probing.

She was tall and pliantly slender, without angularity anywhere. Her body was erect and high-breasted, her legs long, her hands and feet narrow. She wore two shades of blue that had been selected because of her eyes. The hair curling from under her blue hat was darkly red, her full lips more brightly red. White teeth glistened in the crescent her timid smile made.

Spade rose bowing and indicating with a thick-fingered hand the oaken armchair beside his desk. He was quite six feet tall. The steep rounded slope of his shoulders made his body seem almost conical – no broader than it was thick – and kept his freshly pressed gray coat from fitting very well.

Miss Wonderly murmured, "Thank you," softly as before and sat down on the edge of the chair's wooden seat.

Spade sank into his swivel-chair, made a quarter-turn to face her, smiled politely. He smiled without separating his lips. All the v's in his face grew longer.

The tappity-tap-tap and the thin bell and muffled whir of Effie Perine's typewriting came through the closed door. Somewhere in a neighboring office a power-driven machine vibrated dully. On Spade's desk a limp cigarette smoldered in a brass tray filled with the remains of limp cigarettes. Ragged gray flakes of cigarette-ash dotted the yellow top of the desk and the green blotter and the papers that were there. A buff-curtained window, eight or ten inches open, let in from the court a current of air faintly scented with ammonia. The ashes on the desk twitched and crawled in the current.

Miss Wonderly watched the gray flakes twitch and crawl. Her eyes were uneasy. She sat on the very edge of the chair. Her feet were flat on the floor, as if she were about to rise. Her hands in dark gloves clasped a flat dark handbag in her lap.

Spade rocked back in his chair and asked: "Now what can I do for you, Miss Wonderly?"

She caught her breath and looked at him. She swallowed and said hurriedly: "Could you – ? I thought – I – that is – " Then she tortured her lower lip with glistening teeth and said nothing. Only her dark eyes spoke now, pleading.

Spade smiled and nodded as if he understood her, but pleasantly, as if nothing serious were involved. He said: "Suppose you tell me about it, from the beginning, and then we'll know what needs doing. Better begin as far back as you can."

"That was in New York."

"Yes."

"I don't know where she met him. I mean I don't know where in New York. She's five years younger than I – only seventeen – and we didn't have the same friends. I don't suppose we've ever been as close as sisters should be. Mama and Papa are in Europe. It would kill them. I've got to get her back before they come home."

"Yes," he said.

"They're coming home the first of the month."

Spade's eyes brightened. "Then we've two weeks," he said.

"I didn't know what she had done until her letter came. I was frantic." Her lips trembled. Her hands mashed the dark handbag in her lap. "I was too afraid she had done something like this to go to the police, and the fear that something had happened to her kept urging me to go. There wasn't anyone I could go to for advice. I didn't know what to do. What could I do?"

"Nothing, of course," Spade said, "but then her letter came?"

"Yes, and I sent her a telegram asking her to come home. I sent it to General Delivery here. That was the only address she gave me. I waited a whole week, but no answer came, not another word from her. And Mama and Papa's return was drawing nearer and nearer. So I came to San Francisco to get her. I wrote her I was coming. I shouldn't have done that, should I?"

"Maybe not. It's not always easy to know what to do. You haven't found her?"

"No, I haven't. I wrote her that I would go to the St. Mark, and I begged her to come and let me talk to her even if

7

she didn't intend to go home with me. But she didn't come. I waited three days, and she didn't come, didn't even send me a message of any sort."

Spade nodded his blond satan's head, frowned sympathetically, and tightened his lips together.

"It was horrible," Miss Wonderly said, trying to smile. "I couldn't sit there like that – waiting – not knowing what had happened to her, what might be happening to her." She stopped trying to smile. She shuddered. "The only address I had was General Delivery. I wrote her another letter, and yesterday afternoon I went to the Post Office. I stayed there until after dark, but I didn't see her. I went there again this morning, and still didn't see Corinne, but I saw Floyd Thursby."

Spade nodded again. His frown went away. In its place came a look of sharp attentiveness.

"He wouldn't tell me where Corinne was," she went on, hopelessly. "He wouldn't tell me anything, except that she was well and happy. But how can I believe that? That is what he would tell me anyhow, isn't it?"

"Sure," Spade agreed. "But it might be true."

"I hope it is. I do hope it is," she exclaimed. "But I can't go back home like this, without having seen her, without even having talked to her on the phone. He wouldn't take me to her. He said she didn't want to see me. I can't believe that. He promised to tell her he had seen me, and to bring her to see me – if she would come – this evening at the hotel. He said he knew she wouldn't. He promised to come himself if she wouldn't. He – "

She broke off with a startled hand to her mouth as the door opened.

The man who had opened the door came in a step, said, "Oh, excuse me!" hastily took his brown hat from his head, and backed out.

"It's all right, Miles," Spade told him. "Come in. Miss Wonderly, this is Mr. Archer, my partner."

Miles Archer came into the office again, shutting the door behind him, ducking his head and smiling at Miss Wonderly, making a vaguely polite gesture with the hat in his hand. He was of medium height, solidly built, wide in the shoulders, thick in the neck, with a jovial heavy-jawed red face and some gray in his close-trimmed hair. He was apparently as many years past forty as Spade was past thirty.

Spade said: "Miss Wonderly's sister ran away from New York with a fellow named Floyd Thursby. They're here. Miss Wonderly has seen Thursby and has a date with him tonight. Maybe he'll bring the sister with him. The chances are he won't. Miss Wonderly wants us to find the sister and get her away from him and back home." He looked at Miss Wonderly. "Right?"

"Yes," she said indistinctly. The embarrassment that had gradually been driven away by Spade's ingratiating smiles and nods and assurances was pinkening her face again. She looked at the bag in her lap and picked nervously at it with a gloved finger.

Spade winked at his partner.

Miles Archer came forward to stand at a corner of the desk. While the girl looked at her bag he looked at her. His little brown eyes ran their bold appraising gaze from her lowered face to her feet and up to her face again. Then he looked at Spade and made a silent whistling mouth of appreciation.

Spade lifted two fingers from the arm of his chair in a brief warning gesture and said:

"We shouldn't have any trouble with it. It's simply a matter of having a man at the hotel this evening to shadow him away when he leaves, and shadow him until he leads us to your sister. If she comes with him, and you persuade her to return with you, so much the better. Otherwise – if she doesn't want

9

to leave him after we've found her – well, we'll find a way of managing that."

Archer said: "Yeh." His voice was heavy, coarse.

Miss Wonderly looked up at Spade, quickly, puckering her forehead between her eyebrows.

"Oh, but you must be careful!" Her voice shook a little, and her lips shaped the words with nervous jerkiness. "I'm deathly afraid of him, of what he might do. She's so young and his bringing her here from New York is such a serious – Mightn't he – mightn't he do – something to her?"

Spade smiled and patted the arms of his chair.

"Just leave that to us," he said. "We'll know how to handle him."

"But mightn't he?" she insisted.

"There's always a chance." Spade nodded judicially. "But you can trust us to take care of that."

"I do trust you," she said earnestly, "but I want you to know that he's a dangerous man. I honestly don't think he'd stop at anything. I don't believe he'd hesitate to – to kill Corinne if he thought it would save him. Mightn't he do that?"

"You didn't threaten him, did you?"

"I told him that all I wanted was to get her home before Mama and Papa came so they'd never know what she had done. I promised him I'd never say a word to them about it if he helped me, but if he didn't Papa would certainly see that he was punished. I – I don't suppose he believed me, altogether."

"Can he cover up by marrying her?" Archer asked.

The girl blushed and replied in a confused voice: "He has a wife and three children in England. Corinne wrote me that, to explain why she had gone off with him."

"They usually do," Spade said, "though not always in England." He learned forward to reach for pencil and pad of paper. "What does he look like?"

"Oh, he's thirty-five years old, perhaps, and as tall as you, and either naturally dark or quite sunburned. His hair is dark too, and he has thick eyebrows. He talks in a rather loud, blustery way and has a nervous, irritable manner. He gives the impression of being – of violence."

Spade, scribbling on the pad, asked without looking up: "What color eyes?"

"They're blue-gray and watery, though not in a weak way. And – oh, yes – he has a marked cleft in his chin."

"Thin, medium, or heavy build?"

"Quite athletic. He's broad-shouldered and carries himself erect, has what could be called a decidedly military carriage. He was wearing a light gray suit and a gray hat when I saw him this morning."

"What does he do for a living?" Spade asked as he laid down his pencil.

"I don't know," she said. "I haven't the slightest idea."

"What time is he coming to see you?"

"After eight o'clock."

"All right, Miss Wonderly, we'll have a man there. It'll help if – "

"Mr. Spade, could either you or Mr. Archer?" She made an appealing gesture with both hands. "Could either of you look after it personally? I don't mean that the man you'd send wouldn't be capable, but – oh! – I'm so afraid of what might happen to Corinne. I'm afraid of him. Could you? I'd be – I'd expect to be charged more, of course." She opened her handbag with nervous fingers and put two hundred-dollar bills on Spade's desk. "Would that be enough?"

"Yeh," Archer said, "and I'll look after it myself."

Miss Wonderly stood up, impulsively holding a hand out to him.

"Thank you! Thank you!" she exclaimed, and then gave Spade her hand, repeating: "Thank you!"

"Not at all," Spade said over it. "Glad to. It'll help some if you either meet Thursby downstairs or let yourself be seen in the lobby with him at some time."

"I will," she promised, and thanked the partners again.

"And don't look for me," Archer cautioned her. "I'll see you all right."

Spade went to the corridor-door with Miss Wonderly. When he returned to his desk Archer nodded at the hundred-dollar bills there, growled complacently, "They're right enough," picked one up, folded it, and tucked it into a vest-pocket. "And they had brothers in her bag."

Spade pocketed the other bill before he sat down. Then he said: "Well, don't dynamite her too much. What do you think of her?"

"Sweet! And you telling me not to dynamite her." Archer guffawed suddenly without merriment. "Maybe you saw her first, Sam, but I spoke first." He put his hands in his trousers-pockets and teetered on his heels.

"You'll play hell with her, you will." Spade grinned wolf-ishly, showing the edges of teeth far back in his jaw. "You've got brains, yes you have." He began to make a cigarette.

2 DEATH IN THE FOG

A TELEPHONE-BELL rang in darkness. When it had rung three times bed-springs creaked, fingers fumbled on wood, something small and hard thudded on a carpeted floor, the springs creaked again, and a man's voice said:

"Hello.... Yes, speaking.... Dead? ... Yes.... Fifteen minutes. Thanks."

A switch clicked and a white bowl hung on three gilded chains from the ceiling's center filled the room with light. Spade, bare-footed in green and white checked pajamas, sat on the side of his bed. He scowled at the telephone on the table while his hands took from beside it a packet of brown papers and a sack of Bull Durham tobacco.

Cold steamy air blew in through two open windows, bringing with it half a dozen times a minute the Alcatraz foghorn's dull moaning. A tinny alarm-clock, insecurely mounted on a corner of Duke's *Celebrated Criminal Cases of America* – face down on the table – held its hands at five minutes past two.

Spade's thick fingers made a cigarette with deliberate care, sifting a measured quantity of tan flakes down into curved paper, spreading the flakes so that they lay equal at the ends with a slight depression in the middle, thumbs rolling the paper's inner edge down and up under the outer edge as forefingers pressed it over, thumbs and fingers sliding to the paper cylinder's ends to hold it even while tongue licked the flap, left forefinger and thumb smoothed the damp seam, right forefinger and thumb twisting their end and lifting the other to Spade's mouth.

13

He picked up the pigskin and nickel lighter that had fallen to the floor, manipulated it, and with the cigarette burning in a corner of his mouth stood up. He took off his pajamas. The smooth thickness of his arms, legs, and body, the sag of his big rounded shoulders, made his body like a bear's. It was like a shaved bear's: his chest was hairless. His skin was childishly soft and pink.

He scratched the back of his neck and began to dress. He put on a thin white union-suit, gray socks, black garters, and dark brown shoes. When he had fastened his shoes he picked up the telephone, called Graystone 4500, and ordered a taxicab. He put on a green-striped white shirt, a soft white collar, a green necktie, the gray suit he had worn that day, a loose tweed overcoat, and a dark gray hat. The street-door-bell rang as he stuffed tobacco, keys, and money into his pockets.

Where Bush Street roofed Stockton before slipping downhill to Chinatown, Spade paid his fare and left the taxicab. San Francisco's night-fog, thin, clammy, and penetrant, blurred the street. A few yards from where Spade had dismissed the taxicab a small group of men stood looking up an alley. Two women stood with a man on the other side of Bush Street, looking at the alley. There were faces at windows.

Spade crossed the sidewalk between iron-railed hatchways that opened above bare ugly stairs, went to the parapet, and, resting his hands on the damp coping, looked down into Stockton Street.

An automobile popped out of the tunnel beneath him with a roaring swish, as if it had been blown out, and ran away. Not far from the tunnel's mouth a man was hunkered on his heels before a billboard that held advertisements of a moving picture and a gasoline across the front of a gap between two store-buildings. The hunkered man's head was bent almost to the sidewalk so he could look under the billboard. A hand flat on the paving, a hand clenched on the billboard's green frame, held him in this grotesque position. Two other men stood awkwardly together at one end of the billboard, peeping through the few inches of space between it and the building at that end. The building at the other end had a blank gray sidewall that looked down on the lot behind the billboard. Lights flickered on the sidewall, and the shadows of men moving among lights.

Spade turned from the parapet and walked up Bush Street to the alley where men were grouped. A uniformed policeman chewing gum under an enameled sign that said *Burritt St.* in white against dark blue put out an arm and asked:

"What do you want here?"

"I'm Sam Spade. Tom Polhaus phoned me."

"Sure you are." The policeman's arm went down. "I didn't know you at first. Well, they're back there." He jerked a thumb over his shoulder. "Bad business."

"Bad enough," Spade agreed, and went up the alley.

Half-way up it, not far from the entrance, a dark ambulance stood. Behind the ambulance, to the left, the alley was bounded by a waist-high fence, horizontal strips of rough boarding. From the fence dark ground fell away steeply to the billboard on Stockton Street below.

A ten-foot length of the fence's top rail had been torn from a post at one end and hung dangling from the other. Fifteen feet down the slope a flat boulder stuck out. In the notch between boulder and slope Miles Archer lay on his back. Two men stood over him. One of them held the beam of an electric torch on the dead man. Other men with lights moved up and down the slope.

One of them hailed Spade, "Hello, Sam," and clambered up to the alley, his shadow running up the slope before him. He was a barrel-bellied tall man with shrewd small eyes, a thick mouth, and carelessly shaven dark jowls. His shoes, knees, hands, and chin were daubed with brown loam.

"I figured you'd want to see it before we took him away," he said as he stepped over the broken fence.

"Thanks, Tom," Spade said. "What happened?" He put an elbow on a fence-post and looked down at the men below, nodding to those who nodded to him.

Tom Polhaus poked his own left breast with a dirty finger. "Got him right through the pump – with this." He took a fat revolver from his coat-pocket and held it out to Spade. Mud inlaid the depressions in the revolver's surface. "A Webley. English, ain't it?"

Spade took his elbow from the fence-post and leaned down to look at the weapon, but he did not touch it.

"Yes," he said, "Webley-Fosbery automatic revolver. That's it. Thirty-eight, eight shot. They don't make them any more. How many gone out of it?"

"One pill." Tom poked his breast again. "He must've been dead when he cracked the fence." He raised the muddy revolver. "Ever seen this before?"

Spade nodded. "I've seen Webley-Fosberys," he said without interest, and then spoke rapidly: "He was shot up here, huh? Standing where you are, with his back to the fence. The man that shot him stands here." He went around in front of Tom and raised a hand breast-high with leveled forefinger. "Lets him have it and Miles goes back, taking the top off the fence and going on through and down till the rock catches him. That it?"

"That's it," Tom replied slowly, working his brows together. "The blast burnt his coat."

"Who found him?"

"The man on the beat, Shilling. He was coming down Bush, and just as he got here a machine turning threw head-lights up here, and he saw the top off the fence. So he came up to look at it, and found him."

"What about the machine that was turning around?"

"Not a damned thing about it, Sam. Shilling didn't pay any attention to it, not knowing anything was wrong then. He says nobody didn't come out of here while he was coming down from Powell or he'd've seen them. The only other way out would be under the billboard on Stockton. Nobody went that way. The fog's got the ground soggy, and the only marks are where Miles slid down and where this here gun rolled."

"Didn't anybody hear the shot?"

"For the love of God, Sam, we only just got here. Somebody must've heard it, when we find them." He turned and put a leg over the fence. "Coming down for a look at him before he's moved?"

Spade said: "No."

Tom halted astride the fence and looked back at Spade with surprised small eyes.

Spade said: "You've seen him. You'd see everything I could."

Tom, still looking at Spade, nodded doubtfully and withdrew his leg over the fence.

"His gun was tucked away on his hip," he said. "It hadn't been fired. His overcoat was buttoned. There's a hundred and sixty-some bucks in his clothes. Was he working, Sam?"

Spade, after a moment's hesitation, nodded.

Tom asked: "Well?"

"He was supposed to be tailing a fellow named Floyd Thursby," Spade said, and described Thursby as Miss Wonderly had described him.

"What for?"

Spade put his hands into his overcoat-pockets and blinked sleepy eyes at Tom.

Tom repeated impatiently: "What for?"

"He was an Englishman, maybe. I don't know what his game was, exactly. We were trying to find out where he lived." Spade grinned faintly and took a hand from his pocket to pat Tom's shoulder. "Don't crowd me." He put the hand in his pocket again. "I'm going out to break the news to Miles's wife." He turned away.

Tom, scowling, opened his mouth, closed it without having said anything, cleared his throat, put the scowl off his face, and spoke with a husky sort of gentleness:

"It's tough, him getting it like that. Miles had his faults same as the rest of us, but I guess he must've had some good points too."

"I guess so," Spade agreed in a tone that was utterly meaningless, and went out of the alley.

In an all-night drug-store on the corner of Bush and Taylor Streets, Spade used a telephone.

"Precious," he said into it a little while after he had given a number, "Miles has been shot. . . . Yes, he's dead . . . . Now don't get excited . . . . Yes . . . . You'll have to break it to Iva . . . . No, I'm damned if I will. You've got to do it . . . . That's a good girl . . . . And keep her away from the office . . . . Tell her I'll see her – uh – some time . . . . Yes, but don't tie me up to anything . . . . That's the stuff. You're an angel. 'Bye."

Spade's tinny alarm-clock said three-forty when he turned on the light in the suspended bowl again. He dropped his hat and overcoat on the bed and went into his kitchen, returning to the bedroom with a wine-glass and a tall bottle of Bacardi. He poured a drink and drank it standing. He put bottle and glass on the table, sat on the side of the bed facing them, and rolled a cigarette. He had drunk his third glass of Bacardi and was lighting his fifth cigarette when the street-door-bell rang. The hands of the alarm-clock registered four-thirty.

Spade sighed, rose from the bed, and went to the telephone-box beside his bathroom-door. He pressed the button that released the street-door-lock. He muttered, "Damn her," and stood scowling at the black telephone-box, breathing irregularly while a dull flush grew in his cheeks.

The grating and rattling of the elevator-door opening and closing came from the corridor. Spade sighed again and moved towards the corridor-door. Soft heavy footsteps sounded on the carpeted floor outside, the footsteps of two men. Spade's face brightened. His eyes were no longer harassed. He opened the door quickly.

"Hello, Tom," he said to the barrel-bellied tall detective with whom he had talked in Burritt Street, and, "Hello, Lieutenant," to the man beside Tom. "Come in."

They nodded together, neither saying anything, and came in. Spade shut the door and ushered them into his bedroom. Tom sat on an end of the sofa by the windows. The Lieutenant sat on a chair beside the table.

The Lieutenant was a compactly built man with a round head under short-cut grizzled hair and a square face behind a short-cut grizzled mustache. A five-dollar gold-piece was pinned to his necktie and there was a small elaborate diamond-set secret-society-emblem on his lapel.

Spade brought two wine-glasses in from the kitchen, filled them and his own with Bacardi, gave one to each of his visitors, and sat down with his on the side of the bed. His face was placid and uncurious. He raised his glass, and said, "Success to crime," and drank it down.

Tom emptied his glass, set it on the floor beside his feet, and wiped his mouth with a muddy forefinger. He stared at the foot of the bed as if trying to remember something of which it vaguely reminded him.

The Lieutenant looked at his glass for a dozen seconds, took a very small sip of its contents, and put the glass on the table at his elbow. He examined the room with hard deliberate eyes, and then looked at Tom.

Tom moved uncomfortably on the sofa and, not looking up, asked: "Did you break the news to Miles's wife, Sam?"

Spade said: "Uh-huh."

"How'd she take it?"

Spade shook his head. "I don't know anything about women."

Tom said softly: "The hell you don't."

The Lieutenant put his hands on his knees and leaned forward. His greenish eyes were fixed on Spade in a peculiarly rigid stare, as if their focus were a matter of mechanics, to be changed only by pulling a lever or pressing a button.

"What kind of gun do you carry?" he asked.

"None. I don't like them much. Of course there are some in the office."

"I'd like to see one of them," the Lieutenant said. "You don't happen to have one here?"

"No."

"You sure of that?"

"Look around." Spade smiled and waved his empty glass a little. "Turn the dump upside-down if you want. I won't squawk – if you've got a search-warrant."

Tom protested: "Oh, hell, Sam!"

Spade set his glass on the table and stood up facing the Lieutenant.

"What do you want, Dundy?" he asked in a voice hard and cold as his eyes.

Lieutenant Dundy's eyes had moved to maintain their focus on Spade's. Only his eyes had moved.

Tom shifted his weight on the sofa again, blew a deep breath out through his nose, and growled plaintively: "We're not wanting to make any trouble, Sam."

Spade, ignoring Tom, said to Dundy: "Well, what do you want? Talk turkey. Who in hell do you think you are, coming in here trying to rope me?"

"All right," Dundy said in his chest, "sit down and listen."

"I'll sit or stand as I damned please," said Spade, not moving.

"For Christ's sake be reasonable," Tom begged. "What's the use of us having a row? If you want to know why we didn't talk turkey it's because when I asked you who this Thursby was you as good as told me it was none of my business. You can't treat us that way, Sam. It ain't right and it won't get you anywheres. We got our work to do."

Lieutenant Dundy jumped up, stood close to Spade, and thrust his square face up at the taller man's.

"I've warned you your foot was going to slip one of these days," he said.

Spade made a depreciative mouth, raising his eyebrows. "Everybody's foot slips sometime," he replied with derisive mildness.

"And this is yours."

Spade smiled and shook his head. "No, I'll do nicely, thank you." He stopped smiling. His upper lip, on the left side, twitched over his eyetooth. His eyes became narrow and sultry. His voice came out deep as the Lieutenant's. "I don't like this. What are you sucking around for? Tell me, or get out and let me go to bed."

"Who's Thursby?" Dundy demanded.

"I told Tom what I knew about him."

"You told Tom damned little."

"I knew damned little."

"Why were you tailing him?"

"I wasn't. Miles was – for the swell reason that we had a client who was paying good United States money to have him tailed."

"Who's the client?"

Placidity came back to Spade's face and voice. He said reprovingly: "You know I can't tell you that until I've talked it over with the client."

"You'll tell it to me or you'll tell it in court," Dundy said hotly. "This is murder and don't you forget it."

"Maybe. And here's something for you to not forget, sweetheart. I'll tell it or not as I damned please. It's a long while since I burst out crying because policemen didn't like me."

Tom left the sofa and sat on the foot of the bed. His carelessly shaven mud-smeared face was tired and lined.

"Be reasonable, Sam," he pleaded. "Give us a chance. How can we turn up anything on Miles's killing if you won't give us what you've got?"

"You needn't get a headache over that," Spade told him. "I'll bury my dead."

Lieutenant Dundy sat down and put his hands on his knees again. His eyes were warm green discs.

"I thought you would," he said. He smiled with grim content. "That's just exactly why we came to see you. Isn't it, Tom?"

Tom groaned, but said nothing articulate.

Spade watched Dundy warily.

"That's just exactly what I said to Tom," the Lieutenant went on. "I said: 'Tom, I've got a hunch that Sam Spade's a man to keep the family-troubles in the family.' That's just what I said to him."

The wariness went out of Spade's eyes. He made his eyes dull with boredom. He turned his face around to Tom and asked with great carelessness: "What's itching your boy-friend now?"

Dundy jumped up and tapped Spade's chest with the ends of two bent fingers.

"Just this," he said, taking pains to make each word distinct, emphasizing them with his tapping finger-ends: "Thursby was shot down in front of his hotel just thirty-five minutes after you left Burritt Street."

Spade spoke, taking equal pains with his words: "Keep your God-damned paws off me."

Dundy withdrew the tapping fingers, but there was no change in his voice: "Tom says you were in too much of a hurry to even stop for a look at your partner."

Tom growled apologetically: "Well, damn it, Sam, you did run off like that."

"And you didn't go to Archer's house to tell his wife," the Lieutenant said. "We called up and that girl in your office was there, and she said you sent her."

Spade nodded. His face was stupid in its calmness.

Lieutenant Dundy raised his two bent fingers towards Spade's chest, quickly lowered them, and said: "I give you ten minutes to get to a phone and do your talking to the girl. I give you ten minutes to get to Thursby's joint – Geary near Leavenworth – you could do it easy in that time, or fifteen at the most. And that gives you ten or fifteen minutes of waiting before he showed up."

"I knew where he lived?" Spade asked. "And I knew he hadn't gone straight home from killing Miles?"

"You knew what you knew," Dundy replied stubbornly. "What time did you get home?"

"Twenty minutes to four. I walked around thinking things over."

The Lieutenant wagged his round head up and down. "We knew you weren't home at three-thirty. We tried to get you on the phone. Where'd you do your walking?"

"Out Bush Street a way and back."

"Did you see anybody that – ?"

"No, no witnesses," Spade said and laughed pleasantly. "Sit down, Dundy. You haven't finished your drink. Get your glass, Tom."

Tom said: "No, thanks, Sam."

Dundy sat down, but paid no attention to his glass of rum.

Spade filled his own glass, drank, set the empty glass on the table, and returned to his bedside-seat.

"I know where I stand now," he said, looking with friendly eyes from one of the police-detectives to the other. "I'm sorry I got up on my hind legs, but you birds coming in and trying to put the work on me made me nervous. Having Miles knocked off bothered me, and then you birds cracking foxy. That's all right now, though, now that I know what you're up to."

Tom said: "Forget it."

The Lieutenant said nothing.

Spade asked: "Thursby die?"

While the Lieutenant hesitated Tom said: "Yes."

Then the Lieutenant said angrily: "And you might just as well know it – if you don't – that he died before he could tell anybody anything."

Spade was rolling a cigarette. He asked, not looking up: "What do you mean by that? You think I did know it?"

"I meant what I said," Dundy replied bluntly.

Spade looked up at him and smiled, holding the finished cigarette in one hand, his lighter in the other.

"You're not ready to pinch me yet, are you, Dundy?" he asked.

Dundy looked with hard green eyes at Spade and did not answer him.

"Then," said Spade, "there's no particular reason why I should give a damn what you think, is there, Dundy?"

Tom said: "Aw, be reasonable, Sam."

Spade put the cigarette in his mouth, set fire to it, and laughed smoke out.

"I'll be reasonable, Tom," he promised. "How did I kill this Thursby? I've forgotten."

Tom grunted disgust. Lieutenant Dundy said: "He was shot four times in the back, with a forty-four or forty-five, from across the street, when he started to go in the hotel. Nobody saw it, but that's the way it figures."

"And he was wearing a Luger in a shoulder-holster," Tom added. "It hadn't been fired."

"What do the hotel-people know about him?" Spade asked.

"Nothing except that he'd been there a week."

"Alone?"

24

"Alone."

"What did you find on him? or in his room?"

Dundy drew his lips in and asked: "What'd you think we'd find?"

Spade made a careless circle with his limp cigarette. "Something to tell you who he was, what his story was. Did you?"

"We thought you could tell us that."

Spade looked at the Lieutenant with yellow-gray eyes that held an almost exaggerated amount of candor. "I've never seen Thursby, dead or alive."

Lieutenant Dundy stood up looking dissatisfied. Tom rose yawning and stretching.

"We've asked what we came to ask," Dundy said, frowning over eyes hard as green pebbles. He held his mustached upper lip tight to his teeth, letting his lower lip push the words out. "We've told you more than you've told us. That's fair enough. You know me, Spade. If you did or you didn't you'll get a square deal out of me, and most of the breaks. I don't know that I'd blame you a hell of a lot – but that wouldn't keep me from nailing you."

"Fair enough," Spade replied evenly. "But I'd feel better about it if you'd drink your drink."

Lieutenant Dundy turned to the table, picked up his glass, and slowly emptied it. Then he said, "Good night," and held out his hand. They shook hands ceremoniously. Tom and Spade shook hands ceremoniously. Spade let them out. Then he undressed, turned off the lights, and went to bed.

3   THREE WOMEN

WHEN SPADE REACHED his office at ten o'clock the following morning Effie Perine was at her desk opening the
morning's mail. Her boyish face was pale under its sunburn.
She put down the handful of envelopes and the brass paper-
knife she held and said: "She's in there." Her voice was low
and warning.

"I asked you to keep her away," Spade complained. He too
kept his voice low.

Effie Perine's brown eyes opened wide and her voice was
irritable as his: "Yes, but you didn't tell me how." Her eyelids
went together a little and her shoulders drooped. "Don't be
cranky, Sam," she said wearily. "I had her all night."

Spade stood beside the girl, put a hand on her head,
and smoothed her hair away from its parting. "Sorry, angel,
I haven't —" He broke off as the inner door opened. "Hello,
Iva," he said to the woman who had opened it.

"Oh, Sam!" she said.

She was a blonde woman of a few more years than
thirty. Her facial prettiness was perhaps five years past its
best moment. Her body for all its sturdiness was finely
modeled and exquisite. She wore black clothes from hat to
shoes. They had as mourning an impromptu air. Having
spoken, she stepped back from the door and stood waiting
for Spade.

He took his hand from Effie Perine's head and entered the
inner office, shutting the door. Iva came quickly to him,
raising her sad face for his kiss. Her arms were around him
before his held her. When they had kissed he made a little

26

movement as if to release her, but she pressed her face to his chest and began sobbing.

He stroked her round back, saying: "Poor darling." His voice was tender. His eyes, squinting at the desk that had been his partner's, across the room from his own, were angry. He drew his lips back over his teeth in an impatient grimace and turned his chin aside to avoid contact with the crown of her hat. "Did you send for Miles's brother?" he asked.

"Yes, he came over this morning." The words were blurred by her sobbing and his coat against her mouth.

He grimaced again and bent his head for a surreptitious look at the watch on his wrist. His left arm was around her, the hand on her left shoulder. His cuff was pulled back far enough to leave the watch uncovered. It showed ten-ten.

The woman stirred in his arms and raised her face again. Her blue eyes were wet, round, and white-ringed. Her mouth was moist.

"Oh, Sam," she moaned, "did you kill him?"

Spade stared at her with bulging eyes. His bony jaw fell down. He took his arms from her and stepped back out of her arms. He scowled at her and cleared his throat.

She held her arms up as he had left them. Anguish clouded her eyes, partly closed them under eyebrows pulled up at the inner ends. Her soft damp red lips trembled.

Spade laughed a harsh syllable, "Ha!" and went to the buff-curtained window. He stood there with his back to her looking through the curtain into the court until she started towards him. Then he turned quickly and went to his desk. He sat down, put his elbows on the desk, his chin between his fists, and looked at her. His yellowish eyes glittered between narrowed lids.

"Who," he asked coldly, "put that bright idea in your head?"

"I thought –" She lifted a hand to her mouth and fresh tears came to her eyes. She came to stand beside the desk, moving with easy sure-footed grace in black slippers whose smallness and heel-height were extreme. "Be kind to me, Sam," she said humbly.

He laughed at her, his eyes still glittering. "You killed my husband, Sam, be kind to me." He clapped his palms together and said: "Jesus Christ."

She began to cry audibly, holding a white handkerchief to her face.

He got up and stood close behind her. He put his arms around her. He kissed her neck between ear and coat-collar. He said: "Now, Iva, don't." His face was expressionless. When she had stopped crying he put his mouth to her ear and murmured: "You shouldn't have come here today, precious. It wasn't wise. You can't stay. You ought to be home."

She turned around in his arms to face him and asked: "You'll come tonight?"

He shook his head gently. "Not tonight."

"Soon?"

"Yes."

"How soon?"

"As soon as I can."

He kissed her mouth, led her to the door, opened it, said, "Good-bye, Iva," bowed her out, shut the door, and returned to his desk.

He took tobacco and cigarette-papers from his vest-pockets, but did not roll a cigarette. He sat holding the papers in one hand, the tobacco in the other, and looked with brooding eyes at his dead partner's desk.

Effie Perine opened the door and came in. Her brown eyes were uneasy. Her voice was careless. She asked: "Well?"

Spade said nothing. His brooding gaze did not move from his partner's desk.

The girl frowned and came around to his side. "Well," she asked in a louder voice, "how did you and the widow make out?"

"She thinks I shot Miles," he said. Only his lips moved.

"So you could marry her?"

Spade made no reply to that.

The girl took his hat from his head and put it on the desk. Then she leaned over and took the tobacco-sack and the papers from his inert fingers.

"The police think I shot Thursby," he said.

"Who is he?" she asked, separating a cigarette-paper from the packet, sifting tobacco into it.

"Who do you think I shot?" he asked.

When she ignored that question he said: "Thursby's the guy Miles was supposed to be tailing for the Wonderly girl."

Her thin fingers finished shaping the cigarette. She licked it, smoothed it, twisted its ends, and placed it between Spade's lips. He said, "Thanks, honey," put an arm around her slim waist, and rested his cheek wearily against her hip, shutting his eyes.

"Are you going to marry Iva?" she asked, looking down at his pale brown hair.

"Don't be silly," he muttered. The unlighted cigarette bobbed up and down with the movement of his lips.

"She doesn't think it's silly. Why should she – the way you've played around with her?"

He sighed and said: "I wish to Christ I'd never seen her."

"Maybe you do now." A trace of spitefulness came into the girl's voice. "But there was a time."

"I never know what to do or say to women except that way," he grumbled, "and then I didn't like Miles."

"That's a lie, Sam," the girl said. "You know I think she's a louse, but I'd be a louse too if it would give me a body like hers."

Spade rubbed his face impatiently against her hip, but said nothing.

Effie Perine bit her lip, wrinkled her forehead, and, bending over for a better view of his face, asked: "Do you suppose she could have killed him?"

Spade sat up straight and took his arm from her waist. He smiled at her. His smile held nothing but amusement. He took out his lighter, snapped on the flame, and applied it to the end of his cigarette. "You're an angel," he said tenderly through smoke, "a nice rattle-brained angel."

She smiled a bit wryly. "Oh, am I? Suppose I told you that your Iva hadn't been home many minutes when I arrived to break the news at three o'clock this morning?"

"Are you telling me?" he asked. His eyes had become alert though his mouth continued to smile.

"She kept me waiting at the door while she undressed or finished undressing. I saw her clothes where she had dumped them on a chair. Her hat and coat were underneath. Her singlette, on top, was still warm. She said she had been asleep, but she hadn't. She had wrinkled up the bed, but the wrinkles weren't mashed down."

Spade took the girl's hand and patted it. "You're a detective, darling, but" – he shook his head – "she didn't kill him."

Effie Perine snatched her hand away. "That louse wants to marry you, Sam," she said bitterly.

He made an impatient gesture with his head and one hand.

She frowned at him and demanded: "Did you see her last night?"

"No."

"Honestly?"

"Honestly. Don't act like Dundy, sweetheart. It ill becomes you."

"Has Dundy been after you?"

"Uh-huh. He and Tom Polhaus dropped in for a drink at four o'clock."

"Do they really think you shot this what's-his-name?"

"Thursby." He dropped what was left of his cigarette into the brass tray and began to roll another.

"Do they?" she insisted.

"God knows." His eyes were on the cigarette he was making. "They did have some such notion. I don't know how far I talked them out of it."

"Look at me, Sam."

He looked at her and laughed so that for the moment merriment mingled with the anxiety in her face.

"You worry me," she said, seriousness returning to her face as she talked. "You always think you know what you're doing, but you're too slick for your own good, and some day you're going to find it out."

He sighed mockingly and rubbed his cheek against her arm. "That's what Dundy says, but you keep Iva away from me, sweet, and I'll manage to survive the rest of my troubles." He stood up and put on his hat. "Have the *Spade & Archer* taken off the door and *Samuel Spade* put on. I'll be back in an hour, or phone you."

Spade went through the St. Mark's long purplish lobby to the desk and asked a red-haired dandy whether Miss Wonderly was in. The red-haired dandy turned away, and then back shaking his head. "She checked out this morning, Mr. Spade."

"Thanks."

Spade walked past the desk to an alcove off the lobby where a plump young-middle-aged man in dark clothes sat at a flat-topped mahogany desk. On the edge of the desk facing the lobby was a triangular prism of mahogany and brass inscribed *Mr. Freed.*

The plump man got up and came around the desk holding out his hand.

"I was awfully sorry to hear about Archer, Spade," he said in the tone of one trained to sympathize readily without intrusiveness. "I've just seen it in the *Call.* He was in here last night, you know."

"Thanks, Freed. Were you talking to him?"

"No. He was sitting in the lobby when I came in early in the evening. I didn't stop. I thought he was probably working and I know you fellows like to be left alone when you're busy. Did that have anything to do with his –?"

"I don't think so, but we don't know yet. Anyway, we won't mix the house up in it if it can be helped."

"Thanks."

"That's all right. Can you give me some dope on an ex-guest, and then forget that I asked for it?"

"Surely."

"A Miss Wonderly checked out this morning. I'd like to know the details."

"Come along," Freed said, "and we'll see what we can learn."

Spade stood still, shaking his head. "I don't want to show in it."

Freed nodded and went out of the alcove. In the lobby he halted suddenly and came back to Spade.

"Harriman was the house-detective on duty last night," he said. "He's sure to have seen Archer. Shall I caution him not to mention it?"

Spade looked at Freed from the corners of his eyes. "Better not. That won't make any difference as long as there's no connection shown with this Wonderly. Harriman's all right, but he likes to talk, and I'd as lief not have him think there's anything to be kept quiet."

Freed nodded again and went away. Fifteen minutes later he returned.

"She arrived last Tuesday, registering from New York. She hadn't a trunk, only some bags. There were no phone-calls charged to her room, and she doesn't seem to have received much, if any, mail. The only one anybody remembers having seen her with was a tall dark man of thirty-six or so. She went out at half-past nine this morning, came back an hour later, paid her bill, and had her bags carried out to a car. The boy

32

who carried them says it was a Nash touring car, probably a hired one. She left a forwarding address – the Ambassador, Los Angeles."

Spade said, "Thanks a lot, Freed," and left the St. Mark.

When Spade returned to his office Effie Perine stopped typing a letter to tell him: "Your friend Dundy was in. He wanted to look at your guns."

"And?"

"I told him to come back when you were here."

"Good girl. If he comes back again let him look at them."

"And Miss Wonderly called up."

"It's about time. What did she say?"

"She wants to see you." The girl picked up a slip of paper from her desk and read the memorandum penciled on it: "She's at the Coronet, on California Street, apartment one thousand and one. You're to ask for Miss Leblanc."

Spade said, "Give me," and held out his hand. When she had given him the memorandum he took out his lighter, snapped on the flame, set it to the slip of paper, held the paper until all but one corner was curling black ash, dropped it on the linoleum floor, and mashed it under his shoe-sole.

The girl watched him with disapproving eyes.

He grinned at her, said, "That's just the way it is, dear," and went out again.

4 THE BLACK BIRD

MISS WONDERLY, IN a belted green crêpe silk dress, opened the door of apartment 1001 at the Coronet. Her face was flushed. Her dark red hair, parted on the left side, swept back in loose waves over her right temple, was somewhat tousled.

Spade took off his hat and said: "Good morning."

His smile brought a fainter smile to her face. Her eyes, of blue that was almost violet, did not lose their troubled look. She lowered her head and said in a hushed, timid voice: "Come in, Mr. Spade."

She led him past open kitchen-, bathroom-, and bedroom-doors into a cream and red living-room, apologizing for its confusion: "Everything is upside-down. I haven't even finished unpacking."

She laid his hat on a table and sat down on a walnut settee. He sat on a brocaded oval-backed chair facing her.

She looked at her fingers, working them together, and said: "Mr. Spade, I've a terrible, terrible confession to make."

Spade smiled a polite smile, which she did not lift her eyes to see, and said nothing.

"That – that story I told you yesterday was all – a story," she stammered, and looked up at him now with miserable frightened eyes.

"Oh, that," Spade said lightly. "We didn't exactly believe your story."

"Then – ?" Perplexity was added to the misery and fright in her eyes.

"We believed your two hundred dollars."

"You mean – ?" She seemed to not know what he meant.

34

"I mean that you paid us more than if you'd been telling the truth," he explained blandly, "and enough more to make it all right."

Her eyes suddenly lighted up. She lifted herself a few inches from the settee, settled down again, smoothed her skirt, leaned forward, and spoke eagerly: "And even now you'd be willing to – ?"

Spade stopped her with a palm-up motion of one hand. The upper part of his face frowned. The lower part smiled. "That depends," he said. "The hell of it is, Miss – Is your name Wonderly or Leblanc?"

She blushed and murmured: "It's really O'Shaughnessy – Brigid O'Shaughnessy."

"The hell of it is, Miss O'Shaughnessy, that a couple of murders" – she winced – "coming together like this get everybody stirred up, make the police think they can go the limit, make everybody hard to handle and expensive. It's not – "

He stopped talking because she had stopped listening and was waiting for him to finish.

"Mr. Spade, tell me the truth." Her voice quivered on the verge of hysteria. Her face had become haggard around desperate eyes. "Am I to blame for – for last night?"

Spade shook his head. "Not unless there are things I don't know about," he said. "You warned us that Thursby was dangerous. Of course you lied to us about your sister and all, but that doesn't count: we didn't believe you." He shrugged his sloping shoulders. "I wouldn't say it was your fault."

She said, "Thank you," very softly, and then moved her head from side to side. "But I'll always blame myself." She put a hand to her throat. "Mr. Archer was so – so alive yesterday afternoon, so solid and hearty and – "

"Stop it," Spade commanded. "He knew what he was doing. They're the chances we take."

"Was – was he married?"

"Yes, with ten thousand insurance, no children, and a wife who didn't like him."

"Oh, please don't!" she whispered.

Spade shrugged again. "That's the way it was." He glanced at his watch and moved from his chair to the settee beside her. "There's no time for worrying about that now." His voice was pleasant but firm. "Out there a flock of policemen and assistant district attorneys and reporters are running around with their noses to the ground. What do you want to do?"

"I want you to save me from – from it all," she replied in a thin tremulous voice. She put a timid hand on his sleeve. "Mr. Spade, do they know about me?"

"Not yet. I wanted to see you first."

"What – what would they think if they knew about the way I came to you – with those lies?"

"It would make them suspicious. That's why I've been stalling them till I could see you. I thought maybe we wouldn't have to let them know all of it. We ought to be able to fake a story that will rock them to sleep, if necessary."

"You don't think I had anything to do with the – the murders – do you?"

Spade grinned at her and said: "I forgot to ask you that. Did you?"

"No."

"That's good. Now what are we going to tell the police?"

She squirmed on her end of the settee and her eyes wavered between heavy lashes, as if trying and failing to free their gaze from his. She seemed smaller, and very young and oppressed.

"Must they know about me at all?" she asked. "I think I'd rather die than that, Mr. Spade. I can't explain now, but can't you somehow manage so that you can shield me from them, so I won't have to answer their questions? I don't think I could stand being questioned now. I think I would rather die. Can't you, Mr. Spade?"

36

"Maybe," he said, "but I'll have to know what it's all about."

She went down on her knees at his knees. She held her face up to him. Her face was wan, taut, and fearful over tight-clasped hands.

"I haven't lived a good life," she cried. "I've been bad – worse than you could know – but I'm not all bad. Look at me, Mr. Spade. You know I'm not all bad, don't you? You can see that, can't you? Then can't you trust me a little? Oh, I'm so alone and afraid, and I've got nobody to help me if you won't help me. I know I've no right to ask you to trust me if I won't trust you. I do trust you, but I can't tell you. I can't tell you now. Later I will, when I can. I'm afraid, Mr. Spade. I'm afraid of trusting you. I don't mean that. I do trust you, but – I trusted Floyd and – I've nobody else, nobody else, Mr. Spade. You can help me. You've said you can help me. If I hadn't believed you could save me I would have run away today instead of sending for you. If I thought anybody else could save me would I be down on my knees like this? I know this isn't fair of me. But be generous, Mr. Spade, don't ask me to be fair. You're strong, you're resourceful, you're brave. You can spare me some of that strength and resourcefulness and courage, surely. Help me, Mr. Spade. Help me because I need help so badly, and because if you don't where will I find anyone who can, no matter how willing? Help me. I've no right to ask you to help me blindly, but I do ask you. Be generous, Mr. Spade. You can help me. Help me."

Spade, who had held his breath through much of this speech, now emptied his lungs with a long sighing exhalation between pursed lips and said: "You won't need much of any-body's help. You're good. You're very good. It's chiefly your eyes, I think, and that throb you get into your voice when you say things like 'Be generous, Mr. Spade.'"

She jumped up on her feet. Her face crimsoned painfully, but she held her head erect and she looked Spade straight in the eyes.

"I deserve that," she said. "I deserve it, but – oh! – I did want your help so much. I do want it, and need it, so much. And the lie was in the way I said it, and not at all in what I said." She turned away, no longer holding herself erect. "It is my own fault that you can't believe me now."

Spade's face reddened and he looked down at the floor, muttering: "Now you are dangerous."

Brigid O'Shaughnessy went to the table and picked up his hat. She came back and stood in front of him holding the hat, not offering it to him, but holding it for him to take if he wished. Her face was white and thin.

Spade looked at his hat and asked: "What happened last night?"

"Floyd came to the hotel at nine o'clock, and we went out for a walk. I suggested that so Mr. Archer could see him. We stopped at a restaurant in Geary Street, I think it was, for supper and to dance, and came back to the hotel at about half-past twelve. Floyd left me at the door and I stood inside and watched Mr. Archer follow him down the street, on the other side."

"Down? You mean towards Market Street?"

"Yes."

"Do you know what they'd be doing in the neighborhood of Bush and Stockton, where Archer was shot?"

"Isn't that near where Floyd lived?"

"No. It would be nearly a dozen blocks out of his way if he was going from your hotel to his. Well, what did you do after they had gone?"

"I went to bed. And this morning when I went out for breakfast I saw the headlines in the papers and read about – you know. Then I went up to Union Square, where I had seen automobiles for hire, and got one and went to the hotel for my luggage. After I found my room had been searched yesterday I knew I would have to move, and I had found this place yesterday afternoon. So I came up here and then telephoned your office."

"Your room at the St. Mark was searched?" he asked.

"Yes, while I was at your office." She bit her lip. "I didn't mean to tell you that."

"That means I'm not supposed to question you about it?"

She nodded shyly.

He frowned.

She moved his hat a little in her hands.

He laughed impatiently and said: "Stop waving the hat in my face. Haven't I offered to do what I can?"

She smiled contritely, returned the hat to the table, and sat beside him on the settee again.

He said: "I've got nothing against trusting you blindly except that I won't be able to do you much good if I haven't some idea of what it's all about. For instance, I've got to have some sort of a line on your Floyd Thursby."

"I met him in the Orient." She spoke slowly, looking down at a pointed finger tracing eights on the settee between them. "We came here from Hongkong last week. He was — he had promised to help me. He took advantage of my helplessness and dependence on him to betray me."

"Betray you how?"

She shook her head and said nothing.

Spade, frowning with impatience, asked: "Why did you want him shadowed?"

"I wanted to learn how far he had gone. He wouldn't even let me know where he was staying. I wanted to find out what he was doing, whom he was meeting, things like that."

"Did he kill Archer?"

She looked up at him, surprised. "Yes, certainly," she said.

"He had a Luger in a shoulder-holster. Archer wasn't shot with a Luger."

"He had a revolver in his overcoat-pocket," she said.

"You saw it?"

"Oh, I've seen it often. I know he always carries one there. I didn't see it last night, but I know he never wears an overcoat without it."

"Why all the guns?"

"He lived by them. There was a story in Hongkong that he had come out there, to the Orient, as a bodyguard to a gambler who had had to leave the States, and that the gambler had since disappeared. They said Floyd knew about his disappearing. I don't know. I do know that he always went heavily armed and that he never went to sleep without covering the floor around his bed with crumpled newspaper so nobody could come silently into his room."

"You picked a nice sort of playmate."

"Only that sort could have helped me," she said simply, "if he had been loyal."

"Yes, if." Spade pinched his lower lip between finger and thumb and looked gloomily at her. The vertical creases over his nose deepened, drawing his brows together. "How bad a hole are you actually in?"

"As bad," she said, "as could be."

"Physical danger?"

"I'm not heroic. I don't think there's anything worse than death."

"Then it's that?"

"It's that as surely as we're sitting here" – she shivered – "unless you help me."

He took his fingers away from his mouth and ran them through his hair. "I'm not Christ," he said irritably. "I can't work miracles out of thin air." He looked at his watch. "The day's going and you're giving me nothing to work with. Who killed Thursby?"

She put a crumpled handkerchief to her mouth and said, "I don't know," through it.

"Your enemies or his?"

"I don't know. His, I hope, but I'm afraid – I don't know."

"How was he supposed to be helping you? Why did you bring him here from Hongkong?"

She looked at him with frightened eyes and shook her head in silence. Her face was haggard and pitifully stubborn.

Spade stood up, thrust his hands into the pockets of his jacket, and scowled down at her. "This is hopeless," he said savagely. "I can't do anything for you. I don't know what you want done. I don't even know if you know what you want."

She hung her head and wept.

He made a growling animal noise in his throat and went to the table for his hat.

"You won't," she begged in a small choked voice, not looking up, "go to the police?"

"Go to them!" he exclaimed, his voice loud with rage. "They've been running me ragged since four o'clock this morning. I've made myself God knows how much trouble standing them off. For what? For some crazy notion that I could help you. I can't. I won't try." He put his hat on his head and pulled it down tight. "Go to them? All I've got to do is stand still and they'll be swarming all over me. Well, I'll tell them what I know and you'll have to take your chances."

She rose from the settee and held herself straight in front of him though her knees were trembling, and she held her white panic-stricken face up high though she couldn't hold the twitching muscles of mouth and chin still. She said: "You've been patient. You've tried to help me. It is hopeless, and useless, I suppose." She stretched out her right hand. "I thank you for what you have done. I – I'll have to take my chances."

Spade made the growling animal noise in his throat again and sat down on the settee. "How much money have you got?" he asked.

The question startled her. Then she pinched her lower lip between her teeth and answered reluctantly: "I've about five hundred dollars left."

DASHIELL HAMMETT

"Give it to me."

She hesitated, looking timidly at him. He made angry gestures with mouth, eyebrows, hands, and shoulders. She went into her bedroom, returning almost immediately with a sheaf of paper money in one hand.

He took the money from her, counted it, and said: "There's only four hundred here."

"I had to keep some to live on," she explained meekly, putting a hand to her breast.

"Can't you get any more?"

"No."

"You must have something you can raise money on," he insisted.

"I've some rings, a little jewelry."

"You'll have to hock them," he said, and held out his hand. "The Remedial's the best place – Mission and Fifth."

She looked pleadingly at him. His yellow-gray eyes were hard and implacable. Slowly she put her hand inside the neck of her dress, brought out a slender roll of bills, and put them in his waiting hand.

He smoothed the bills out and counted them – four twenties, four tens, and a five. He returned two of the tens and the five to her. The others he put in his pocket. Then he stood up and said: "I'm going out and see what I can do for you. I'll be back as soon as I can with the best news I can manage. I'll ring four times – long, short, long, short – so you'll know it's me. You needn't go to the door with me. I can let myself out."

He left her standing in the center of the floor looking after him with dazed blue eyes.

Spade went into a reception-room whose door bore the legend *Wise, Merican & Wise*. The red-haired girl at the switchboard said: "Oh, hello, Mr. Spade."

"Hello, darling," he replied. "Is Sid in?"

He stood beside her with a hand on her plump shoulder while she manipulated a plug and spoke into the mouthpiece: "Mr. Spade to see you, Mr. Wise." She looked up at Spade. "Go right in."

He squeezed her shoulder by way of acknowledgment, crossed the reception-room to a dully lighted inner corridor, and passed down the corridor to a frosted glass door at its far end. He opened the frosted glass door and went into an office where a small olive-skinned man with a tired oval face under thin dark hair dotted with dandruff sat behind an immense desk on which bales of paper were heaped.

The small man flourished a cold cigar-stub at Spade and said: "Pull a chair around. So Miles got the big one last night?" Neither his tired face nor his rather shrill voice held any emotion.

"Uh-huh, that's what I came in about." Spade frowned and cleared his throat. "I think I'm going to have to tell a coroner to go to hell, Sid. Can I hide behind the sanctity of my clients' secrets and identities and what-not, all the same priest or lawyer?"

Sid Wise lifted his shoulders and lowered the ends of his mouth. "Why not? An inquest is not a court-trial. You can try, anyway. You've gotten away with more than that before this."

"I know, but Dundy's getting snotty, and maybe it is a little bit thick this time. Get your hat, Sid, and we'll go see the right people. I want to be safe."

Sid Wise looked at the papers massed on his desk and groaned, but he got up from his chair and went to the closet by the window. "You're a son of a gun, Sammy," he said as he took his hat from its hook.

Spade returned to his office at ten minutes past five that evening. Effie Perine was sitting at his desk reading *Time*. Spade sat on the desk and asked: "Anything stirring?"

"Not here. You look like you'd swallowed the canary."

43

He grinned contentedly. "I think we've got a future. I always had an idea that if Miles would go off and die somewhere we'd stand a better chance of thriving. Will you take care of sending flowers for me?"

"I did."

"You're an invaluable angel. How's your woman's intuition today?"

"Why?"

"What do you think of Wonderly?"

"I'm for her," the girl replied without hesitation.

"She's got too many names," Spade mused, "Wonderly, Leblanc, and she says the right one's O'Shaughnessy."

"I don't care if she's got all the names in the phone-book. That girl is all right, and you know it."

"I wonder." Spade blinked sleepily at Effie Perine. He chuckled. "Anyway she's given up seven hundred smacks in two days, and that's all right."

Effie Perine sat up straight and said: "Sam, if that girl's in trouble and you let her down, or take advantage of it to bleed her, I'll never forgive you, never have any respect for you, as long as I live."

Spade smiled unnaturally. Then he frowned. The frown was unnatural. He opened his mouth to speak, but the sound of someone's entrance through the corridor-door stopped him.

Effie Perine rose and went into the outer office. Spade took off his hat and sat in his chair. The girl returned with an engraved card – *Mr. Joel Cairo.*

"This guy is queer," she said.

"In with him, then, darling," said Spade.

Mr. Joel Cairo was a small-boned dark man of medium height. His hair was black and smooth and very glossy. His features were Levantine. A square-cut ruby, its sides paralleled by four baguette diamonds, gleamed against the deep green of his cravat. His black coat, cut tight to narrow shoulders, flared a little over slightly plump hips. His trousers fitted his round legs more snugly than was the current fashion. The uppers of his patent-leather shoes were hidden by fawn spats. He held a black derby hat in a chamois-gloved hand and came towards Spade with short, mincing, bobbing steps. The fragrance of *chypre* came with him.

Spade inclined his head at his visitor and then at a chair, saying: "Sit down, Mr. Cairo."

Cairo bowed elaborately over his hat, said, "I thank you," in a high-pitched thin voice and sat down. He sat down primly, crossing his ankles, placing his hat on his knees, and began to draw off his yellow gloves.

Spade rocked back in his chair and asked: "Now what can I do for you, Mr. Cairo?" The amiable negligence of his tone, his motion in the chair, were precisely as they had been when he had addressed the same question to Brigid O'Shaughnessy on the previous day.

Cairo turned his hat over, dropping his gloves into it, and placed it bottom-up on the corner of the desk nearest him. Diamonds twinkled on the second and fourth fingers of his left hand, a ruby that matched the one in his tie even to the surrounding diamonds on the third finger of his right hand. His hands were soft and well cared for. Though they were not large their flaccid bluntness made them seem clumsy. He rubbed his palms together and said over the whispering sound they made: "May a stranger offer condolences for your partner's unfortunate death?"

"Thanks."

"May I ask, Mr. Spade, if there was, as the newspapers inferred, a certain – ah – relationship between that unfortunate happening and the death a little later of the man Thursby?"

Spade said nothing in a blank-faced definite way.

Cairo rose and bowed. "I beg your pardon." He sat down and placed his hands side by side, palms down, on the corner of the desk. "More than idle curiosity made me ask

45

that, Mr. Spade. I am trying to recover an – ah – ornament that has been – shall we say? – mislaid. I thought, and hoped, you could assist me."

Spade nodded with eyebrows lifted to indicate attentiveness.

"The ornament is a statuette," Cairo went on, selecting and mouthing his words carefully, "the black figure of a bird."

Spade nodded again, with courteous interest.

"I am prepared to pay, on behalf of the figure's rightful owner, the sum of five thousand dollars for its recovery." Cairo raised one hand from the desk-corner and touched a spot in the air with the broad-nailed tip of an ugly forefinger. "I am prepared to promise that – what is the phrase? – no questions will be asked." He put his hand on the desk again beside the other and smiled blandly over them at the private detective.

"Five thousand is a lot of money," Spade commented, looking thoughtfully at Cairo. "It – "

Fingers drummed lightly on the door.

When Spade had called, "Come in," the door opened far enough to admit Effie Perine's head and shoulders. She had put on a small dark felt hat and a dark coat with a gray fur collar.

"Is there anything else?" she asked.

"No. Good night. Lock the door when you go, will you?"

Spade turned in his chair to face Cairo again, saying: "It's an interesting figure."

The sound of the corridor-door's closing behind Effie Perine came to them.

Cairo smiled and took a short compact flat black pistol out of an inner pocket. "You will please," he said, "clasp your hands together at the back of your neck."

5   THE LEVANTINE

SPADE DID NOT look at the pistol. He raised his arms and, leaning back in his chair, intertwined the fingers of his two hands behind his head. His eyes, holding no particular expression, remained focused on Cairo's dark face.

Cairo coughed a little apologetic cough and smiled nervously with lips that had lost some of their redness. His dark eyes were humid and bashful and very earnest. "I intend to search your offices, Mr. Spade. I warn you that if you attempt to prevent me I shall certainly shoot you."

"Go ahead." Spade's voice was as empty of expression as his face.

"You will please stand," the man with the pistol instructed him at whose thick chest the pistol was aimed. "I shall have to make sure that you are not armed."

Spade stood up pushing his chair back with his calves as he straightened his legs.

Cairo went around behind him. He transferred the pistol from his right hand to his left. He lifted Spade's coat-tail and looked under it. Holding the pistol close to Spade's back, he put his right hand around Spade's side and patted his chest. The Levantine face was then no more than six inches below and behind Spade's right elbow.

Spade's elbow dropped as Spade spun to the right. Cairo's face jerked back not far enough: Spade's right heel on the patent-leathered toes anchored the smaller man in the elbow's path. The elbow struck him beneath the cheek-bone, staggering him so that he must have fallen had he not been held by Spade's foot on his foot. Spade's elbow went on past the

47

astonished dark face and straightened when Spade's hand struck down at the pistol. Cairo let the pistol go the instant that Spade's fingers touched it. The pistol was small in Spade's hand.

Spade took his foot off Cairo's to complete his about-face. With his left hand Spade gathered together the smaller man's coat-lapels – the ruby-set green tie bunching out over his knuckles – while his right hand stowed the captured weapon away in a coat-pocket. Spade's yellow-gray eyes were somber. His face was wooden, with a trace of sullenness around the mouth.

Cairo's face was twisted by pain and chagrin. There were tears in his dark eyes. His skin was the complexion of polished lead except where the elbow had reddened his cheek.

Spade by means of his grip on the Levantine's lapels turned him slowly and pushed him back until he was standing close in front of the chair he had lately occupied. A puzzled look replaced the look of pain in the lead-colored face. Then Spade smiled. His smile was gentle, even dreamy. His right shoulder raised a few inches. His bent right arm was driven up by the shoulder's lift. Fist, wrist, forearm, crooked elbow, and upper arm seemed all one rigid piece, with only the limber shoulder giving them motion. The fist struck Cairo's face, covering for a moment one side of his chin, a corner of his mouth, and most of his cheek between cheek-bone and jaw-bone.

Cairo shut his eyes and was unconscious.

Spade lowered the limp body into the chair, where it lay with sprawled arms and legs, the head lolling back against the chair's back, the mouth open.

Spade emptied the unconscious man's pockets one by one, working methodically, moving the lax body when necessary, making a pile of the pockets' contents on the desk. When the last pocket had been turned out he returned to his own chair, rolled and lighted a cigarette, and began to examine his spoils. He examined them with grave unhurried thoroughness.

There was a large wallet of dark soft leather. The wallet contained three hundred and sixty-five dollars in United States bills of several sizes; three five-pound notes; a much-visaed Greek passport bearing Cairo's name and portrait; five folded sheets of pinkish onion-skin paper covered with what seemed to be Arabic writing; a raggedly clipped newspaper-account of the finding of Archer's and Thursby's bodies; a post-card photograph of a dusky woman with bold cruel eyes and a tender drooping mouth; a large silk handkerchief, yellow with age and somewhat cracked along its folds; a thin sheaf of Mr. Joel Cairo's engraved cards; and a ticket for an orchestra seat at the Geary Theatre that evening.

Besides the wallet and its contents there were three gaily colored silk handkerchiefs fragrant of *chypre*; a platinum Longines watch on a platinum and red gold chain, attached at the other end to a small pear-shaped pendant of some white metal; a handful of United States, British, French, and Chinese coins; a ring holding half a dozen keys; a silver and onyx fountain-pen; a metal comb in a leatherette case; a nail-file in a leatherette case; a small street-guide to San Francisco; a Southern Pacific baggage-check; a half-filled package of violet pastilles; a Shanghai insurance-broker's business-card; and four sheets of Hotel Belvedere writing paper, on one of which was written in small precise letters Samuel Spade's name and the addresses of his office and his apartment.

Having examined these articles carefully – he even opened the back of the watch-case to see that nothing was hidden inside – Spade leaned over and took the unconscious man's wrist between finger and thumb, feeling his pulse. Then he dropped the wrist, settled back in his chair, and rolled and lighted another cigarette. His face while he smoked was, except for occasional slight and aimless movements of his lower lip, so still and reflective that it seemed stupid; but when Cairo presently moaned and fluttered his eyelids Spade's face became bland, and he put the beginning of a friendly smile into his eyes and mouth.

Joel Cairo awakened slowly. His eyes opened first, but a full minute passed before they fixed their gaze on any definite part of the ceiling. Then he shut his mouth and swallowed, exhaling heavily through his nose afterward. He drew in one foot and turned a hand over on his thigh. Then he raised his head from the chair-back, looked around the office in confusion, saw Spade, and sat up. He opened his mouth to speak, started, clapped a hand to his face where Spade's fist had struck and where there was now a florid bruise.

Cairo said through his teeth, painfully: "I could have shot you, Mr. Spade."

"You could have tried," Spade conceded.

"I did not try."

"I know."

"Then why did you strike me after I was disarmed?"

"Sorry," Spade said, and grinned wolfishly, showing his jaw-teeth, "but imagine my embarrassment when I found that five-thousand-dollar offer was just hooey."

"You are mistaken, Mr. Spade. That was, and is, a genuine offer."

"What the hell?" Spade's surprise was genuine.

"I am prepared to pay five thousand dollars for the figure's return." Cairo took his hand away from his bruised face and sat up prim and business-like again. "You have it?"

"No."

"If it is not here" – Cairo was very politely skeptical – "why should you have risked serious injury to prevent my searching for it?"

"I should sit around and let people come in and stick me up?" Spade flicked a finger at Cairo's possessions on the desk. "You've got my apartment-address. Been up there yet?"

"Yes, Mr. Spade. I am ready to pay five thousand dollars for the figure's return, but surely it is natural enough that I should try first to spare the owner that expense if possible."

"Who is he?"

Cairo shook his head and smiled. "You will have to forgive my not answering that question."

"Will I?" Spade leaned forward smiling with tight lips. "I've got you by the neck, Cairo. You've walked in and tied yourself up, plenty strong enough to suit the police, with last night's killings. Well, now you'll have to play with me or else."

Cairo's smile was demure and not in any way alarmed. "I made somewhat extensive inquiries about you before taking any action," he said, "and was assured that you were far too reasonable to allow other considerations to interfere with profitable business relations."

Spade shrugged. "Where are they?" he asked.

"I have offered you five thousand dollars for – "

Spade thumped Cairo's wallet with the backs of his fingers and said: "There's nothing like five thousand dollars here. You're betting your eyes. You could come in and say you'd pay me a million for a purple elephant, but what in hell would that mean?"

"I see, I see," Cairo said thoughtfully, screwing up his eyes. "You wish some assurance of my sincerity." He brushed his red lower lip with a fingertip. "A retainer, would that serve?"

"It might."

Cairo put his hand out towards his wallet, hesitated, withdrew the hand, and said: "You will take, say, a hundred dollars?"

Spade picked up the wallet and took out a hundred dollars. Then he frowned, said, "Better make it two hundred," and did.

Cairo said nothing.

"Your first guess was that I had the bird," Spade said in a crisp voice when he had put the two hundred dollars into his pocket and had dropped the wallet on the desk again. "There's nothing in that. What's your second?"

"That you know where it is, or, if not exactly that, that you know it is where you can get it."

Spade neither denied nor affirmed that: he seemed hardly to have heard it. He asked: "What sort of proof can you give me that your man is the owner?"

"Very little, unfortunately. There is this, though: nobody else can give you any authentic evidence of ownership at all. And if you know as much about the affair as I suppose – or I should not be here – you know that the means by which it was taken from him shows that his right to it was more valid than anyone else's – certainly more valid than Thursby's."

"What about his daughter?" Spade asked.

Excitement opened Cairo's eyes and mouth, turned his face red, made his voice shrill. "*He* is not the owner!"

Spade said, "Oh," mildly and ambiguously.

"Is he here, in San Francisco, now?" Cairo asked in a less shrill, but still excited, voice.

Spade blinked his eyes sleepily and suggested: "It might be better all around if we put our cards on the table."

Cairo recovered composure with a little jerk. "I do not think it would be better." His voice was suave now. "If you know more than I, I shall profit by your knowledge, and so will you to the extent of five thousand dollars. If you do not then I have made a mistake in coming to you, and to do as you suggest would be simply to make that mistake worse."

Spade nodded indifferently and waved his hand at the articles on the desk, saying: "There's your stuff"; and then, when Cairo was returning them to his pockets: "It's understood that you're to pay my expenses while I'm getting this black bird for you, and five thousand dollars when it's done?"

"Yes, Mr. Spade; that is, five thousand dollars less whatever moneys have been advanced to you – five thousand in all."

"Right. And it's a legitimate proposition." Spade's face was solemn except for wrinkles at the corners of his eyes. "You're not hiring me to do any murders or burglaries for you, but simply to get it back if possible in an honest and lawful way."

"If possible," Cairo agreed. His face also was solemn except for the eyes. "And in any event with discretion." He rose and picked up his hat. "I am at the Hotel Belvedere when you wish to communicate with me – room six-thirty-five. I confidently expect the greatest mutual benefit from our association, Mr. Spade." He hesitated. "May I have my pistol?"

"Sure. I'd forgotten it."

Spade took the pistol out of his coat-pocket and handed it to Cairo.

Cairo pointed the pistol at Spade's chest.

"You will please keep your hands on the top of the desk," Cairo said earnestly. "I intend to search your offices."

Spade said: "I'll be damned." Then he laughed in his throat and said: "All right. Go ahead. I won't stop you."

FOR HALF AN hour after Joel Cairo had gone Spade sat alone, still and frowning, at his desk. Then he said aloud in the tone of one dismissing a problem, "Well, they're paying for it," and took a bottle of Manhattan cocktail and a paper drinking-cup from a desk-drawer. He filled the cup two-thirds full, drank, returned the bottle to the drawer, tossed the cup into the wastebasket, put on his hat and overcoat, turned off the lights, and went down to the night-lit street.

An undersized youth of twenty or twenty-one in neat gray cap and overcoat was standing idly on the corner below Spade's building.

Spade walked up Sutter Street to Kearny, where he entered a cigar-store to buy two sacks of Bull Durham. When he came out the youth was one of four people waiting for a street-car on the opposite corner.

Spade ate dinner at Herbert's Grill in Powell Street. When he left the Grill, at a quarter to eight, the youth was looking into a nearby haberdasher's window.

Spade went to the Hotel Belvedere, asking at the desk for Mr. Cairo. He was told that Cairo was not in. The youth sat in a chair in a far corner of the lobby.

Spade went to the Geary Theatre, failed to see Cairo in the lobby, and posted himself on the curb in front, facing the theatre. The youth loitered with other loiterers before Marquard's restaurant below.

At ten minutes past eight Joel Cairo appeared, walking up Geary Street with his little mincing bobbing steps. Apparently he did not see Spade until the private detective touched his shoulder. He seemed moderately surprised for a moment, and then said: "Oh, yes, of course you saw the ticket."

"Uh-huh. I've got something I want to show you." Spade drew Cairo back towards the curb a little away from the other waiting theatre-goers. "The kid in the cap down by Marquard's."

Cairo murmured, "I'll see," and looked at his watch. He looked up Geary Street. He looked at a theatre-sign in front of him on which George Arliss was shown costumed as Shylock, and then his dark eyes crawled sidewise in their sockets until they were looking at the kid in the cap, at his cool pale face with curling lashes hiding lowered eyes.

"Who is he?" Spade asked.

Cairo smiled up at Spade. "I do not know him."

"He's been tailing me around town."

Cairo wet his lower lip with his tongue and asked: "Do you think it was wise, then, to let him see us together?"

"How do I know?" Spade replied. "Anyway, it's done."

Cairo removed his hat and smoothed his hair with a gloved hand. He replaced his hat carefully on his head and said with every appearance of candor: "I give you my word I do not know him, Mr. Spade. I give you my word I have nothing to do with him. I have asked nobody's assistance except yours, on my word of honor."

"Then he's one of the others?"

"That may be."

"I just wanted to know, because if he gets to be a nuisance I may have to hurt him."

"Do as you think best. He is not a friend of mine."

"That's good. There goes the curtain. Good night," Spade said, and crossed the street to board a westbound street-car.

The youth in the cap boarded the same car.

Spade left the car at Hyde Street and went up to his apartment. His rooms were not greatly upset, but showed unmistakable signs of having been searched. When Spade had washed and had put on a fresh shirt and collar he went out again, walked up to Sutter Street, and boarded a westbound car. The youth boarded it also.

Within half a dozen blocks of the Coronet Spade left the car and went into the vestibule of a tall brown apartment-building. He pressed three bell-buttons together. The street-door-lock buzzed. He entered, passed the elevator and stairs, went down a long yellow-walled corridor to the rear of the building, found a back door fastened by a Yale lock, and let himself out into a narrow court. The court led to a dark back street, up which Spade walked for two blocks. Then he crossed over to California Street and went to the Coronet. It was not quite half-past nine o'clock.

The eagerness with which Brigid O'Shaughnessy welcomed Spade suggested that she had been not entirely certain of his coming. She had put on a satin gown of the blue shade called Artoise that season, with chalcedony shoulder-straps, and her stockings and slippers were Artoise.

The red and cream sitting-room had been brought to order and livened with flowers in squat pottery vases of black and silver. Three small rough-barked logs burned in the fireplace. Spade watched them burn while she put away his hat and coat.

"Do you bring me good news?" she asked when she came into the room again. Anxiety looked through her smile, and she held her breath.

"We won't have to make anything public that hasn't already been made public."

"The police won't have to know about me?"

"No."

She sighed happily and sat on the walnut settee. Her face relaxed and her body relaxed. She smiled up at him with admiring eyes. "However did you manage it?" she asked more in wonder than in curiosity.

"Most things in San Francisco can be bought, or taken."

"And you won't get into trouble? Do sit down." She made room for him on the settee.

"I don't mind a reasonable amount of trouble," he said with not too much complacence.

He stood beside the fireplace and looked at her with eyes that studied, weighed, judged her without pretense that they were not studying, weighing, judging her. She flushed slightly under the frankness of his scrutiny, but she seemed more sure of herself than before, though a becoming shyness had not left her eyes. He stood there until it seemed plain that he meant to ignore her invitation to sit beside her, and then crossed to the settee.

"You aren't," he asked as he sat down, "exactly the sort of person you pretend to be, are you?"

"I'm not sure I know what you mean," she said in her hushed voice, looking at him with puzzled eyes.

"Schoolgirl manner," he explained, "stammering and blushing and all that."

She blushed and replied hurriedly, not looking at him: "I told you this afternoon that I've been bad – worse than you could know."

"That's what I mean," he said. "You told me that this afternoon in the same words, same tone. It's a speech you've practiced."

After a moment in which she seemed confused almost to the point of tears she laughed and said: "Very well, then, Mr. Spade, I'm not at all the sort of person I pretend to be. I'm eighty years old, incredibly wicked, and an iron-molder by trade. But if it's a pose it's one I've grown into, so you won't expect me to drop it entirely, will you?"

"Oh, it's all right," he assured her. "Only it wouldn't be all right if you were actually that innocent. We'd never get any-where."

"I won't be innocent," she promised with a hand on her heart.

"I saw Joel Cairo tonight," he said in the manner of one making polite conversation.

Gaiety went out of her face. Her eyes, focused on his profile, became frightened, then cautious. He had stretched his legs out and was looking at his crossed feet. His face did not indicate that he was thinking about anything.

There was a long pause before she asked uneasily:

"You – you know him?"

"I saw him tonight." Spade did not look up and he maintained his light conversational tone. "He was going to see George Arliss."

"You mean you talked to him?"

"Only for a minute or two, till the curtain-bell rang."

She got up from the settee and went to the fireplace to poke the fire. She changed slightly the position of an ornament on the mantelpiece, crossed the room to get a box of cigarettes from a table in a corner, straightened a curtain, and returned to her seat. Her face now was smooth and unworried.

Spade grinned sidewise at her and said: "You're good. You're very good."

Her face did not change. She asked quietly: "What did he say?"

"About what?"

She hesitated. "About me."

"Nothing." Spade turned to hold his lighter under the end of her cigarette. His eyes were shiny in a wooden satan's face.

"Well, what did he say?" she asked with half-playful petulance.

"He offered me five thousand dollars for the black bird."

She started, her teeth tore the end of her cigarette, and her eyes, after a swift alarmed glance at Spade, turned away from him.

"You're not going to go around poking at the fire and straightening up the room again, are you?" he asked lazily.

She laughed a clear merry laugh, dropped the mangled cigarette into a tray, and looked at him with clear merry eyes. "I won't," she promised. "And what did you say?"

"Five thousand dollars is a lot of money."

She smiled, but when, instead of smiling, he looked gravely at her, her smile became faint, confused, and presently vanished. In its place came a hurt, bewildered look. "Surely you're not really considering it," she said.

"Why not? Five thousand dollars is a lot of money."

"But, Mr. Spade, you promised to help me." Her hands were on his arm. "I trusted you. You can't –" She broke off, took her hands from his sleeve and worked them together.

Spade smiled gently into her troubled eyes. "Don't let's try to figure out how much you've trusted me," he said. "I promised to help you – sure – but you didn't say anything about any black birds."

"But you must've known or – or you wouldn't have mentioned it to me. You do know now. You won't – you can't – treat me like that." Her eyes were cobalt-blue prayers.

"Five thousand dollars is," he said for the third time, "a lot of money."

She lifted her shoulders and hands and let them fall in a gesture that accepted defeat. "It is," she agreed in a small dull voice. "It is far more than I could ever offer you, if I must bid for your loyalty."

Spade laughed. His laughter was brief and somewhat bitter. "That is good," he said, "coming from you. What have you given me besides money? Have you given me any of your confidence? any of the truth? any help in helping you? Haven't you tried to buy my loyalty with money and nothing else? Well, if I'm peddling it, why shouldn't I let it go to the highest bidder?"

"I've given you all the money I have." Tears glistened in her white-ringed eyes. Her voice was hoarse, vibrant. "I've thrown myself on your mercy, told you that without your help

59

I'm utterly lost. What else is there?" She suddenly moved close to him on the settee and cried angrily: "Can I buy you with my body?"

Their faces were a few inches apart. Spade took her face between his hands and he kissed her mouth roughly and contemptuously. Then he sat back and said: "I'll think it over." His face was hard and furious.

She sat still holding her numbed face where his hands had left it.

He stood up and said: "Christ! there's no sense to this." He took two steps towards the fireplace and stopped, glowering at the burning logs, grinding his teeth together.

She did not move.

He turned to face her. The two vertical lines above his nose were deep clefts between red wales. "I don't give a damn about your honesty," he told her, trying to make himself speak calmly. "I don't care what kind of tricks you're up to, what your secrets are, but I've got to have something to show that you know what you're doing."

"I do know. Please believe that I do, and that it's all for the best, and –"

"Show me," he ordered. "I'm willing to help you. I've done what I could so far. If necessary I'll go ahead blindfolded, but I can't do it without more confidence in you than I've got now. You've got to convince me that you know what it's all about, that you're not simply fiddling around by guess and by God, hoping it'll come out all right somehow in the end."

"Can't you trust me just a little longer?"

"How much is a little? And what are you waiting for?"

She bit her lip and looked down. "I must talk to Joel Cairo," she said almost inaudibly.

"You can see him tonight," Spade said, looking at his watch. "His show will be out soon. We can get him on the phone at his hotel."

She raised her eyes, alarmed. "But he can't come here. I can't let him know where I am. I'm afraid."

"My place," Spade suggested.

She hesitated, working her lips together, then asked: "Do you think he'd go there?"

Spade nodded.

"All right," she exclaimed, jumping up, her eyes large and bright. "Shall we go now?"

She went into the next room. Spade went to the table in the corner and silently pulled the drawer out. The drawer held two packs of playing-cards, a pad of score-cards for bridge, a brass screw, a piece of red string, and a gold pencil. He had shut the drawer and was lighting a cigarette when she returned wearing a small dark hat and a grey kidskin coat, carrying his hat and coat.

Their taxicab drew up behind a dark sedan that stood directly in front of Spade's street-door. Iva Archer was alone in the sedan, sitting at the wheel. Spade lifted his hat to her and went indoors with Brigid O'Shaughnessy. In the lobby he halted beside one of the benches and asked: "Do you mind waiting here a moment? I won't be long."

"That's perfectly all right," Brigid O'Shaughnessy said, sitting down. "You needn't hurry."

Spade went out to the sedan. When he had opened the sedan's door Iva spoke quickly: "I've got to talk to you, Sam. Can't I come in?" Her face was pale and nervous.

"Not now."

Iva clicked her teeth together and asked sharply: "Who is she?"

"I've only a minute, Iva," Spade said patiently. "What is it?"

"Who is she?" she repeated, nodding at the street-door.

He looked away from her, down the street. In front of a garage on the next corner an undersized youth of twenty or twenty-one in neat gray cap and overcoat loafed with his back

61

against a wall. Spade frowned and returned his gaze to Iva's insistent face. "What is the matter?" he asked. "Has anything happened? You oughtn't to be here at this time of night."

"I'm beginning to believe that," she complained. "You told me I oughtn't to come to the office, and now I oughtn't to come here. Do you mean I oughtn't to chase after you? If that's what you mean why don't you say it right out?"

"Now, Iva, you've got no right to take that attitude."

"I know I haven't. I haven't any rights at all, it seems, where you're concerned. I thought I did. I thought your pretending to love me gave me –"

Spade said wearily: "This is no time to be arguing about that, precious. What was it you wanted to see me about?"

"I can't talk to you here, Sam. Can't I come in?"

"Not now."

"Why can't I?"

Spade said nothing.

She made a thin line of her mouth, squirmed around straight behind the wheel, and started the sedan's engine, staring angrily ahead.

When the sedan began to move Spade said, "Good night, Iva," shut the door, and stood at the curb with his hat in his hand until it had been driven away. Then he went indoors again.

Brigid O'Shaughnessy rose smiling cheerfully from the bench and they went up to his apartment.

7   G IN THE AIR

IN HIS BEDROOM that was a living-room now the wall-bed was up, Spade took Brigid O'Shaughnessy's hat and coat, made her comfortable in a padded rocking chair, and telephoned the Hotel Belvedere. Cairo had not returned from the theatre. Spade left his telephone-number with the request that Cairo call him as soon as he came in.

Spade sat down in the armchair beside the table and without any preliminary, without an introductory remark of any sort, began to tell the girl about a thing that had happened some years before in the Northwest. He talked in a steady matter-of-fact voice that was devoid of emphasis or pauses, though now and then he repeated a sentence slightly rearranged, as if it were important that each detail be related exactly as it had happened.

At the beginning Brigid O'Shaughnessy listened with only partial attentiveness, obviously more surprised by his telling the story than interested in it, her curiosity more engaged with his purpose in telling the story than with the story he told; but presently, as the story went on, it caught her more and more fully and she became still and receptive.

A man named Flitcraft had left his real-estate-office, in Tacoma, to go to luncheon one day and had never returned. He did not keep an engagement to play golf after four that afternoon, though he had taken the initiative in making the engagement less than half an hour before he went out to luncheon. His wife and children never saw him again. His wife and he were supposed to be on the best of terms. He had two children, boys, one five and the other three. He owned his house in a Tacoma suburb, a new Packard, and the rest of the appurtenances of successful American living.

Flitcraft had inherited seventy thousand dollars from his father, and, with his success in real estate, was worth something in the neighborhood of two hundred thousand dollars at the time he vanished. His affairs were in order, though there were enough loose ends to indicate that he had not been setting them in order preparatory to vanishing. A deal that would have brought him an attractive profit, for instance, was to have been concluded the day after the one on which he disappeared. There was nothing to suggest that he had more than fifty or sixty dollars in his immediate possession at the time of his going. His habits for months past could be accounted for too thoroughly to justify any suspicion of secret vices, or even of another woman in his life, though either was barely possible.

"He went like that," Spade said, "like a fist when you open your hand."

When he had reached this point in his story the telephone-bell rang.

"Hello," Spade said into the instrument. "Mr. Cairo? ... This is Spade. Can you come up to my place – Post Street – now? ... Yes, I think it is." He looked at the girl, pursed his lips, and then said rapidly: "Miss O'Shaughnessy is here and wants to see you."

Brigid O'Shaughnessy frowned and stirred in her chair, but did not say anything.

Spade put the telephone down and told her: "He'll be up in a few minutes. Well, that was in 1922. In 1927 I was with one of the big detective agencies in Seattle. Mrs. Flitcraft came in and told us somebody had seen a man in Spokane who looked a lot like her husband. I went over there. It was Flitcraft, all right. He had been living in Spokane for a couple of years as Charles – that was his first name – Pierce. He had an automobile-business that was netting him twenty or twenty-five thousand a year, a wife, a baby son, owned his home in a Spokane suburb, and usually got away to play golf after four in the afternoon during the season."

Spade had not been told very definitely what to do when he found Flitcraft. They talked in Spade's room at the Davenport. Flitcraft had no feeling of guilt. He had left his first family well provided for, and what he had done seemed to him perfectly reasonable. The only thing that bothered him was a doubt that he could make that reasonableness clear to Spade. He had never told anybody his story before, and thus had not had to attempt to make its reasonableness explicit. He tried now.

"I got it all right," Spade told Brigid O'Shaughnessy, "but Mrs. Flitcraft never did. She thought it was silly. Maybe it was. Anyway, it came out all right. She didn't want any scandal, and, after the trick he had played on her – the way she looked at it – she didn't want him. So they were divorced on the quiet and everything was swell all around.

"Here's what had happened to him. Going to lunch he passed an office-building that was being put up – just the skeleton. A beam or something fell eight or ten stories down and smacked the sidewalk alongside him. It brushed pretty close to him, but didn't touch him, though a piece of the sidewalk was chipped off and flew up and hit his cheek. It only took a piece of skin off, but he still had the scar when I saw him. He rubbed it with his finger – well, affectionately – when he told me about it. He was scared stiff of course, he said, but he was more shocked than really frightened. He felt like somebody had taken the lid off life and let him look at the works."

Flitcraft had been a good citizen and a good husband and father, not by any outer compulsion, but simply because he was a man who was most comfortable in step with his sur-roundings. He had been raised that way. The people he knew were like that. The life he knew was a clean orderly sane responsible affair. Now a falling beam had shown him that life was fundamentally none of these things. He, the good citizen-husband-father, could be wiped out between office and restaurant by the accident of a falling beam. He knew then that men died at haphazard like that, and lived only while blind chance spared them.

It was not, primarily, the injustice of it that disturbed him: he accepted that after the first shock. What disturbed him was the discovery that in sensibly ordering his affairs he had got out of step, and not into step, with life. He said he knew before he had gone twenty feet from the fallen beam that he would never know peace again until he had adjusted himself to this new glimpse of life. By the time he had eaten his luncheon he had found his means of adjustment. Life could be ended for him at random by a falling beam: he would change his life at random by simply going away. He loved his family, he said, as much as he supposed was usual, but he knew he was leaving them adequately provided for, and his love for them was not of the sort that would make absence painful.

"He went to Seattle that afternoon," Spade said, "and from there by boat to San Francisco. For a couple of years he wandered around and then drifted back to the Northwest, and settled in Spokane and got married. His second wife didn't look like the first, but they were more alike than they were different. You know, the kind of women that play fair games of golf and bridge and like new salad-recipes. He wasn't sorry for what he had done. It seemed reasonable enough to him. I don't think he even knew he had settled back naturally into the same groove he had jumped out of in Tacoma. But that's the part of it I always liked. He adjusted himself to beams falling, and then no more of them fell, and he adjusted himself to them not falling."

"How perfectly fascinating," Brigid O'Shaughnessy said. She left her chair and stood in front of him, close. Her eyes were wide and deep. "I don't have to tell you how utterly at a disadvantage you'll have me, with him here, if you choose."

Spade smiled slightly without separating his lips. "No, you don't have to tell me," he agreed.

"And you know I'd never have played myself in this position if I hadn't trusted you completely." Her thumb and forefinger twisted a black button on his blue coat.

Spade said, "That again!" with mock resignation.

"But you know it's so," she insisted.

"No, I don't know it." He patted the hand that was twisting the button. "My asking for reasons why I should trust you brought us here. Don't let's confuse things. You don't have to trust me, anyhow, as long as you can persuade me to trust you."

She studied his face. Her nostrils quivered.

Spade laughed. He patted her hand again and said: "Don't worry about that now. He'll be here in a moment. Get your business with him over, and then we'll see how we'll stand."

"And you'll let me go about it − with him − in my own way?"

"Sure."

She turned her hand under his so that her fingers pressed his. She said softly: "You're a God-send."

Spade said: "Don't overdo it."

She looked reproachfully at him, though smiling, and returned to the padded rocker.

Joel Cairo was excited. His dark eyes seemed all irises and his high-pitched thin-voiced words were tumbling out before Spade had the door half-open.

"That boy is out there watching the house, Mr. Spade, that boy you showed me, or to whom you showed me, in front of the theatre. What am I to understand from that, Mr. Spade? I came here in good faith, with no thought of tricks or traps."

"You were asked in good faith." Spade frowned thought-fully. "But I ought to've guessed he might show up. He saw you come in?"

"Naturally. I could have gone on, but that seemed useless, since you had already let him see us together."

Brigid O'Shaughnessy came into the passageway behind Spade and asked anxiously: "What boy? What is it?"

Cairo removed his black hat from his head, bowed stiffly, and said in a prim voice: "If you do not know, ask Mr. Spade. I know nothing about it except through him."

"A kid who's been trying to tail me around town all evening," Spade said carelessly over his shoulder, not turning to face the girl. "Come on in, Cairo. There's no use standing here talking for all the neighbors."

Brigid O'Shaughnessy grasped Spade's arm above the elbow and demanded: "Did he follow you to my apartment?"

"No. I shook him before that. Then I suppose he came back here to try to pick me up again."

Cairo, holding his black hat to his belly with both hands, had come into the passageway. Spade shut the corridor-door behind him and they went into the living-room. There Cairo bowed stiffly over his hat once more and said: "I am delighted to see you again, Miss O'Shaughnessy."

"I was sure you would be, Joe," she replied, giving him her hand.

He made a formal bow over her hand and released it quickly.

She sat in the padded rocker she had occupied before. Cairo sat in the armchair by the table. Spade, when he had hung Cairo's hat and coat in the closet, sat on an end of the sofa in front of the windows and began to roll a cigarette.

Brigid O'Shaughnessy said to Cairo: "Sam told me about your offer for the falcon. How soon can you have the money ready?"

Cairo's eyebrows twitched. He smiled. "It is ready." He continued to smile at the girl for a little while after he had spoken, and then looked at Spade.

Spade was lighting his cigarette. His face was tranquil.

"In cash?" the girl asked.

"Oh, yes," Cairo replied.

She frowned, put her tongue between her lips, withdrew it, and asked: "You are ready to give us five thousand dollars, now, if we give you the falcon?"

Cairo held up a wriggling hand. "Excuse me," he said. "I expressed myself badly. I did not mean to say that I have the money in my pockets, but that I am prepared to get it on a very few minutes' notice at any time during banking hours."

"Oh!" She looked at Spade.

Spade blew cigarette-smoke down the front of his vest and said: "That's probably right. He had only a few hundred in his pockets when I frisked him this afternoon."

When her eyes opened round and wide he grinned.

The Levantine bent forward in his chair. He failed to keep eagerness from showing in his eyes and voice. "I can be quite prepared to give you the money at, say, half-past ten in the morning. Eh?"

Brigid O'Shaughnessy smiled at him and said: "But I haven't got the falcon."

Cairo's face was darkened by a flush of annoyance. He put an ugly hand on either arm of his chair, holding his small-boned body erect and stiff between them. His dark eyes were angry. He did not say anything.

The girl made a mock-placatory face at him. "I'll have it in a week at the most, though," she said.

"Where is it?" Cairo used politeness of mien to express skepticism.

"Where Floyd hid it."

"Floyd? Thursby?"

She nodded.

"And you know where that is?" he asked.

"I think I do."

"Then why must we wait a week?"

"Perhaps not a whole week. Whom are you buying it for, Joe?"

Cairo raised his eyebrows. "I told Mr. Spade. For its owner."

Surprise illuminated the girl's face. "So you went back to him?"

"Naturally I did."

She laughed softly in her throat and said: "I should have liked to have seen that."

Cairo shrugged. "That was the logical development." He rubbed the back of one hand with the palm of the other. His upper lids came down to shade his eyes. "Why, if I in turn may ask a question, are you willing to sell to me?"

"I'm afraid," she said simply, "after what happened to Floyd. That's why I haven't it now. I'm afraid to touch it except to turn it over to somebody else right away."

Spade, propped on an elbow on the sofa, looked at and listened to them impartially. In the comfortable slackness of his body, in the easy stillness of his features, there was no indication of either curiosity or impatience.

"Exactly what," Cairo asked in a low voice, "happened to Floyd?"

The tip of Brigid O'Shaughnessy's right forefinger traced a swift G in the air.

Cairo said, "I see," but there was something doubting in his smile. "Is he here?"

"I don't know." She spoke impatiently. "What difference does it make?"

The doubt in Cairo's smile deepened. "It might make a world of difference," he said, and rearranged his hands in his lap so that, intentionally or not, a blunt forefinger pointed at Spade.

The girl glanced at the pointing finger and made an impatient motion with her head. "Or me," she said, "or you."

"Exactly, and shall we add more certainly the boy outside?"

"Yes," she agreed and laughed. "Yes, unless he's the one you had in Constantinople."

Sudden blood mottled Cairo's face. In a shrill enraged voice he cried: "The one you couldn't make?"

Brigid O'Shaughnessy jumped up from her chair. Her lower lip was between her teeth. Her eyes were dark and wide in a tense white face. She took two quick steps towards Cairo. He started to rise. Her right hand went out and cracked sharply against his cheek, leaving the imprint of fingers there.

Cairo grunted and slapped her cheek, staggering her side-wise, bringing from her mouth a brief muffled scream.

Spade, wooden of face, was up from the sofa and close to them by then. He caught Cairo by the throat and shook him. Cairo gurgled and put a hand inside his coat. Spade grasped the Levantine's wrist, wrenched it away from the coat, forced it straight out to the side, and twisted it until the clumsy flaccid fingers opened to let the black pistol fall down on the rug.

Brigid O'Shaughnessy quickly picked up the pistol.

Cairo, speaking with difficulty because of the fingers on his throat, said: "This is the second time you've put your hands on me." His eyes, though the throttling pressure on his throat made them bulge, were cold and menacing.

"Yes," Spade growled. "And when you're slapped you'll take it and like it." He released Cairo's wrist and with a thick open hand struck the side of his face three times, savagely.

Cairo tried to spit in Spade's face, but the dryness of the Levantine's mouth made it only an angry gesture. Spade slapped the mouth, cutting the lower lip.

The door-bell rang.

Cairo's eyes jerked into focus on the passageway that led to the corridor-door. His eyes had become unangry and wary. The girl had gasped and turned to face the passageway. Her face was frightened. Spade stared gloomily for a moment at the blood trickling from Cairo's lip, and then stepped back, taking his hand from the Levantine's throat.

71

"Who is it?" the girl whispered, coming close to Spade; and Cairo's eyes jerked back to ask the same question.

Spade gave his answer irritably: "I don't know."

The bell rang again, more insistently.

"Well, keep quiet," Spade said, and went out of the room, shutting the door behind him.

Spade turned on the light in the passageway and opened the door to the corridor. Lieutenant Dundy and Tom Polhaus were there.

"Hello, Sam," Tom said. "We thought maybe you wouldn't've gone to bed yet."

Dundy nodded, but said nothing.

Spade said good-naturedly: "Hello. You guys pick swell hours to do your visiting in. What is it this time?"

Dundy spoke then, quietly: "We want to talk to you, Spade."

"Well?" Spade stood in the doorway, blocking it. "Go ahead and talk."

Tom Polhaus advanced saying: "We don't have to do it standing here, do we?"

Spade stood in the doorway and said: "You can't come in." His tone was very slightly apologetic.

Tom's thick-featured face, even in height with Spade's, took on an expression of friendly scorn, though there was a bright gleam in his small shrewd eyes. "What the hell, Sam?" he protested and put a big hand playfully on Spade's chest.

Spade leaned against the pushing hand, grinned wolfishly, and asked: "Going to strong-arm me, Tom?"

Tom grumbled, "Aw, for God's sake," and took his hand away.

Dundy clicked his teeth together and said through them: "Let us in."

Spade's lip twitched over his eyetooth. He said: "You're not coming in. What do you want to do about it? Try to get in? Or do your talking here? Or go to hell?"

Tom groaned.

Dundy, still speaking through his teeth, said: "It'd pay you to play along with us a little, Spade. You've got away with this and you've got away with that, but you can't keep it up forever."

"Stop me when you can," Spade replied arrogantly.

"That's what I'll do." Dundy put his hands behind him and thrust his hard face up towards the private detective's. "There's talk going around that you and Archer's wife were cheating on him."

Spade laughed. "That sounds like something you thought up yourself."

"Then there's not anything to it?"

"Not anything."

"The talk is," Dundy said, "that she tried to get a divorce out of him so's she could put in with you, but he wouldn't give it to her. Anything to that?"

"No."

"There's even talk," Dundy went on stolidly, "that that's why he was put on the spot."

Spade seemed mildly amused. "Don't be a hog," he said. "You oughtn't try to pin more than one murder at a time on me. Your first idea that I knocked Thursby off because he'd killed Miles falls apart if you blame me for killing Miles too."

"You haven't heard me say you killed anybody," Dundy replied. "You're the one that keeps bringing that up. But suppose I did. You could have blipped them both. There's a way of figuring it."

"Uh-huh. I could've butchered Miles to get his wife, and then Thursby so I could hang Miles's killing on him. That's a hell of a swell system, or will be when I can give somebody else the bump and hang Thursby's on them. How long am I supposed to keep that up? Are you going to put your hand on my shoulder for all the killings in San Francisco from now on?"

Tom said: "Aw, cut the comedy, Sam. You know damned well we don't like this any more than you do, but we got our work to do."

"I hope you've got something to do besides pop in here early every morning with a lot of damned fool questions."

"And get damned lying answers," Dundy added deliberately.

"Take it easy," Spade cautioned him.

Dundy looked him up and down and then looked him straight in the eyes. "If you say there was nothing between you and Archer's wife," he said, "you're a liar, and I'm telling you so."

A startled look came into Tom's small eyes.

Spade moistened his lips with the tip of his tongue and asked: "Is that the hot tip that brought you here at this ungodly time of night?"

"That's one of them."

"And the others?"

Dundy pulled down the corners of his mouth. "Let us in." He nodded significantly at the doorway in which Spade stood.

Spade frowned and shook his head.

Dundy's mouth-corners lifted in a smile of grim satisfaction. "There must've been something to it," he told Tom.

Tom shifted his feet and, not looking at either man, mumbled: "God knows."

"What's this?" Spade asked. "Charades?"

"All right, Spade, we're going." Dundy buttoned his overcoat. "We'll be in to see you now and then. Maybe you're right in bucking us. Think it over."

"Uh-huh," Spade said, grinning. "Glad to see you any time, Lieutenant, and whenever I'm not busy I'll let you in."

A voice in Spade's living-room screamed: "Help! Help! Police! Help!" The voice, high and thin and shrill, was Joel Cairo's.

Lieutenant Dundy stopped turning away from the door, confronted Spade again, and said decisively: "I guess we're going in."

The sounds of a brief struggle, of a blow, of a subdued cry, came to them.

Spade's face twisted into a smile that held little joy. He said, "I guess you are," and stood out of the way.

When the police-detectives had entered he shut the corridor-door and followed them back to the living-room.

BRIGID O'SHAUGHNESSY WAS huddled in the armchair by the table. Her forearms were up over her cheeks, her knees drawn up until they hid the lower part of her face. Her eyes were white-circled and terrified.

Joel Cairo stood in front of her, bending over her, holding in one hand the pistol Spade had twisted out of his hand. His other hand was clapped to his forehead. Blood ran through the fingers of that hand and down under them to his eyes. A smaller trickle from his cut lip made three wavy lines across his chin.

Cairo did not heed the detectives. He was glaring at the girl huddled in front of him. His lips were working spasmodically, but no coherent sound came from between them.

Dundy, the first of the three into the living-room, moved swiftly to Cairo's side, put a hand on his own hip under his overcoat, a hand on the Levantine's wrist, and growled: "What are you up to here?"

Cairo took the red-smeared hand from his head and flourished it close to the Lieutenant's face. Uncovered by the hand, his forehead showed a three-inch ragged tear. "This is what she has done," he cried. "Look at it."

The girl put her feet down on the floor and looked warily from Dundy, holding Cairo's wrist, to Tom Polhaus, standing a little behind them, to Spade, leaning against the door-frame. Spade's face was placid. When his gaze met hers his yellow-gray eyes glinted for an instant with malicious humor and then became expressionless again.

76

"Did you do that?" Dundy asked the girl, nodding at Cairo's cut head.

She looked at Spade again. He did not in any way respond to the appeal in her eyes. He leaned against the door-frame and observed the occupants of the room with the polite detached air of a disinterested spectator.

The girl turned her eyes up to Dundy's. Her eyes were wide and dark and earnest. "I had to," she said in a low throbbing voice. "I was all alone in here with him when he attacked me. I couldn't – I tried to keep him off. I – I couldn't make myself shoot him."

"Oh, you liar!" Cairo cried, trying unsuccessfully to pull the arm that held his pistol out of Dundy's grip. "Oh, you dirty filthy liar!" He twisted himself around to face Dundy. "She's lying awfully. I came here in good faith and was attacked by both of them, and when you came he went out to talk to you, leaving her here with this pistol, and then she said they were going to kill me after you left, and I called for help, so you wouldn't leave me here to be murdered, and then she struck me with the pistol."

"Here, give me this thing," Dundy said, and took the pistol from Cairo's hand. "Now let's get this straight. What'd you come here for?"

"He sent for me." Cairo twisted his head around to stare defiantly at Spade. "He called me up on the phone and asked me to come here."

Spade blinked sleepily at the Levantine and said nothing.

Dundy asked: "What'd he want you for?"

Cairo withheld his reply until he had mopped his bloody forehead and chin with a lavender-barred silk handkerchief. By then some of the indignation in his manner had been replaced by caution. "He said he wanted – they wanted – to see me. I didn't know what about."

Tom Polhaus lowered his head, sniffed the odor of *chypre* that the mopping handkerchief had released in the air, and turned his head to scowl interrogatively at Spade. Spade winked at him and went on rolling a cigarette.

Dundy asked: "Well, what happened then?"

"Then they attacked me. She struck me first, and then he choked me and took the pistol out of my pocket. I don't know what they would have done next if you hadn't arrived at that moment. I dare say they would have murdered me then and there. When he went out to answer the bell he left her here with the pistol to watch over me."

Brigid O'Shaughnessy jumped out of the armchair crying, "Why don't you make him tell the truth?" and slapped Cairo on the cheek.

Cairo yelled inarticulately.

Dundy pushed the girl back into the chair with the hand that was not holding the Levantine's arm and growled: "None of that now."

Spade, lighting his cigarette, grinned softly through smoke and told Tom: "She's impulsive."

"Yeah," Tom agreed.

Dundy scowled down at the girl and asked: "What do you want us to think the truth is?"

"Not what he said," she replied. "Not anything he said." She turned to Spade. "Is it?"

"How do I know?" Spade responded. "I was out in the kitchen mixing an omelette when it all happened, wasn't I?"

She wrinkled her forehead, studying him with eyes that perplexity clouded.

Tom grunted in disgust.

Dundy, still scowling at the girl, ignored Spade's speech and asked her: "If he's not telling the truth, how come he did the squawking for help, and not you?"

"Oh, he was frightened to death when I struck him," she replied, looking contemptuously at the Levantine.

Cairo's face flushed where it was not blood-smeared. He exclaimed: "Pfoo! Another lie!"

She kicked his leg, the high heel of her blue slipper striking him just below the knee. Dundy pulled him away from her while big Tom came to stand close to her, rumbling: "Behave, sister. That's no way to act."

"Then make him tell the truth," she said defiantly.

"We'll do that all right," he promised. "Just don't get rough."

Dundy, looking at Spade with green eyes hard and bright and satisfied, addressed his subordinate: "Well, Tom, I don't guess we'll go wrong pulling the lot of them in."

Tom nodded gloomily.

Spade left the door and advanced to the center of the room, dropping his cigarette into a tray on the table as he passed it. His smile and manner were amiably composed. "Don't be in a hurry," he said. "Everything can be explained."

"I bet you," Dundy agreed, sneering.

Spade bowed to the girl. "Miss O'Shaughnessy," he said, "may I present Lieutenant Dundy and Detective-sergeant Polhaus." He bowed to Dundy. "Miss O'Shaughnessy is an operative in my employ."

Joel Cairo said indignantly: "That isn't so. She – "

Spade interrupted him in a quite loud, but still genial, voice: "I hired her just recently, yesterday. This is Mr. Joel Cairo, a friend – an acquaintance, at any rate – of Thursby's. He came to me this afternoon and tried to hire me to find something Thursby was supposed to have on him when he was bumped off. It looked funny, the way he put it to me, so I wouldn't touch it. Then he pulled a gun – well, never mind that unless it comes to a point of laying charges against each other. Anyway, after talking it over with Miss O'Shaughnessy, I thought maybe I could get something out of him about Miles's and Thursby's killings, so I asked him to come up here. Maybe we put the questions to him a little rough, but he wasn't hurt any, not enough to have to cry for help. I'd already had to take his gun away from him again."

As Spade talked anxiety came into Cairo's reddened face. His eyes moved jerkily up and down, shifting their focus uneasily between the floor and Spade's bland face.

Dundy confronted Cairo and bruskly demanded: "Well, what've you got to say to that?"

Cairo had nothing to say for nearly a minute while he stared at the Lieutenant's chest. When he lifted his eyes they were shy and wary. "I don't know what I should say," he murmured. His embarrassment seemed genuine.

"Try telling the facts," Dundy suggested.

"The facts?" Cairo's eyes fidgeted, though their gaze did not actually leave the Lieutenant's. "What assurance have I that the facts will be believed?"

"Quit stalling. All you've got to do is swear to a complaint that they took a poke at you and the warrant-clerk will believe you enough to issue a warrant that'll let us throw them in the can."

Spade spoke in an amused tone: "Go ahead, Cairo. Make him happy. Tell him you'll do it, and then we'll swear to one against you, and he'll have the lot of us."

Cairo cleared his throat and looked nervously around the room, not into the eyes of anyone there.

Dundy blew breath through his nose in a puff that was not quite a snort and said: "Get your hats."

Cairo's eyes, holding worry and a question, met Spade's mocking gaze. Spade winked at him and sat on the arm of the padded rocker. "Well, boys and girls," he said, grinning at the Levantine and at the girl with nothing but delight in his voice and grin, "we put it over nicely."

Dundy's hard square face darkened the least of shades. He repeated peremptorily: "Get your hats."

Spade turned his grin on the Lieutenant, squirmed into a more comfortable position on the chair-arm, and asked lazily: "Don't you know when you're being kidded?"

Tom Polhaus's face became red and shiny.

Dundy's face, still darkening, was immobile except for lips moving stiffly to say: "No, but we'll let that wait till we get down to the Hall."

Spade rose and put his hands in his trousers-pockets. He stood erect so he might look that much farther down at the Lieutenant. His grin was a taunt and self-certainty spoke in every line of his posture.

"I dare you to take us in, Dundy," he said. "We'll laugh at you in every newspaper in San Francisco. You don't think any of us is going to swear to any complaints against the others, do you? Wake up. You've been kidded. When the bell rang I said to Miss O'Shaughnessy and Cairo: 'It's those damned bulls again. They're getting to be nuisances. Let's play a joke on them. When you hear them going one of you scream, and then we'll see how far we can string them along before they tumble.' And – "

Brigid O'Shaughnessy bent forward in her chair and began to laugh hysterically.

Cairo started and smiled. There was no vitality in his smile, but he held it fixed on his face.

Tom, glowering, grumbled: "Cut it out, Sam."

Spade chuckled and said: "But that's the way it was. We – "

"And the cuts on his head and mouth?" Dundy asked scornfully. "Where'd they come from?"

"Ask him," Spade suggested. "Maybe he cut himself shaving."

Cairo spoke quickly, before he could be questioned, and the muscles of his face quivered at the strain of holding his smile in place while he spoke. "I fell. We intended to be struggling for the pistol when you came in, but I fell. I tripped on the end of the rug and fell while we were pretending to struggle."

Dundy said: "Horse feathers."

Spade said: "That's all right, Dundy, believe it or not. The point is that that's our story and we'll stick to it. The news-papers will print it whether they believe it or not, and it'll be just as funny one way as the other, or more so. What are you going to do about it? It's no crime to kid a copper, is it? You haven't got anything on anybody here. Everything we told you was part of the joke. What are you going to do about it?"

Dundy put his back to Spade and gripped Cairo by the shoulders. "You can't get away with that," he snarled, shaking the Levantine. "You belched for help and you've got to take it."

"No, sir," Cairo sputtered. "It was a joke. He said you were friends of his and would understand."

Spade laughed.

Dundy pulled Cairo roughly around, holding him now by one wrist and the nape of his neck. "I'll take you along for packing the gun, anyway," he said. "And I'll take the rest of you along to see who laughs at the joke."

Cairo's alarmed eyes jerked sidewise to focus on Spade's face.

Spade said: "Don't be a sap, Dundy. The gun was part of the plant. It's one of mine." He laughed. "Too bad it's only a thirty-two, or maybe you could find it was the one Thursby and Miles were shot with."

Dundy released Cairo, spun on his heel, and his right fist clicked on Spade's chin.

Brigid O'Shaughnessy uttered a short cry.

Spade's smile flickered out at the instant of the impact, but returned immediately with a dreamy quality added. He steadied himself with a short backward step and his thick sloping shoulders writhed under his coat. Before his fist could come up Tom Polhaus had pushed himself between the two men, facing Spade, encumbering Spade's arms with the closeness of his barrel-like belly and his own arms.

"No, no, for Christ's sake!" Tom begged.

After a long moment of motionlessness Spade's muscles relaxed. "Then get him out of here quick," he said. His smile had gone away again, leaving his face sullen and somewhat pale.

Tom, staying close to Spade, keeping his arms on Spade's arms, turned his head to look over his shoulder at Lieutenant Dundy. Tom's small eyes were reproachful.

Dundy's fists were clenched in front of his body and his feet were planted firm and a little apart on the floor, but the truculence in his face was modified by thin rims of white showing between green irises and upper eyelids.

"Get their names and addresses," he ordered.

Tom looked at Cairo, who said quickly: "Joel Cairo, Hotel Belvedere."

Spade spoke before Tom could question the girl. "You can always get in touch with Miss O'Shaughnessy through me."

Tom looked at Dundy. Dundy growled: "Get her address."

Spade said: "Her address is in care of my office."

Dundy took a step forward, halting in front of the girl. "Where do you live?" he asked.

Spade addressed Tom: "Get him out of here. I've had enough of this."

Tom looked at Spade's eyes – hard and glittering – and mumbled: "Take it easy, Sam." He buttoned his coat and turned to Dundy, asking, in a voice that aped casualness, "Well, is that all?" and taking a step towards the door.

Dundy's scowl failed to conceal indecision.

Cairo moved suddenly towards the door, saying: "I'm going too, if Mr. Spade will be kind enough to give me my hat and coat."

Spade asked: "What's the hurry?"

Dundy said angrily: "It was all in fun, but just the same you're afraid to be left here with them."

"Not at all," the Levantine replied, fidgeting, looking at neither of them, "but it's quite late and – and I'm going. I'll go out with you if you don't mind."

Dundy put his lips together firmly and said nothing. A light was glinting in his green eyes.

83

Spade went to the closet in the passageway and fetched Cairo's hat and coat. Spade's face was blank. His voice held the same blankness when he stepped back from helping the Levantine into his coat and said to Tom: "Tell him to leave the gun."

Dundy took Cairo's pistol from his overcoat-pocket and put it on the table. He went out first, with Cairo at his heels. Tom halted in front of Spade, muttering, "I hope to God you know what you're doing," got no response, sighed, and followed the others out. Spade went after them as far as the bend in the passageway, where he stood until Tom had closed the corridor-door.

9 BRIGID

SPADE RETURNED TO the living-room and sat on an end of the sofa, elbows on knees, cheeks in hands, looking at the floor and not at Brigid O'Shaughnessy smiling weakly at him from the armchair. His eyes were sultry. The creases between brows over his nose were deep. His nostrils moved in and out with his breathing.

Brigid O'Shaughnessy, when it became apparent that he was not going to look up at her, stopped smiling and regarded him with growing uneasiness.

Red rage came suddenly into his face and he began to talk in a harsh guttural voice. Holding his maddened face in his hands, glaring at the floor, he cursed Dundy for five minutes without break, cursed him obscenely, blasphemously, repetitiously, in a harsh guttural voice.

Then he took his face out of his hands, looked at the girl, grinned sheepishly, and said: "Childish, huh? I know, but, by God, I do hate being hit without hitting back." He touched his chin with careful fingers. "Not that it was so much of a sock at that." He laughed and lounged back on the sofa, crossing his legs. "A cheap enough price to pay for winning." His brows came together in a fleeting scowl. "Though I'll remember it."

The girl, smiling again, left her chair and sat on the sofa beside him. "You're absolutely the wildest person I've ever known," she said. "Do you always carry on so high-handed?"

"I let him hit me, didn't I?"

"Oh, yes, but a police official."

"It wasn't that," Spade explained. "It was that in losing his head and slugging me he overplayed his hand. If I'd mixed it

85

with him then he couldn't've backed down. He'd've had to go through with it, and we'd've had to tell that goofy story at headquarters." He stared thoughtfully at the girl, and asked: "What did you do to Cairo?"

"Nothing." Her face became flushed. "I tried to frighten him into keeping still until they had gone and he either got too frightened or stubborn and yelled."

"And then you smacked him with the gun?"

"I had to. He attacked me."

"You don't know what you're doing." Spade's smile did not hide his annoyance. "It's just what I told you: you're fumbling along by guess and by God."

"I'm sorry," she said, face and voice soft with contrition, "Sam."

"Sure you are." He took tobacco and papers from his pockets and began to make a cigarette. "Now you've had your talk with Cairo. Now you can talk to me."

She put a fingertip to her mouth, staring across the room at nothing with widened eyes, and then, with narrower eyes, glanced quickly at Spade. He was engrossed in the making of his cigarette. "Oh, yes," she began, "of course – " She took the finger away from her mouth and smoothed her blue dress over her knees. She frowned at her knees.

Spade licked his cigarette, sealed it, and asked, "Well?" while he felt for his lighter.

"But I didn't," she said, pausing between words as if she were selecting them with great care, "have time to finish talking to him." She stopped frowning at her knees and looked at Spade with clear candid eyes. "We were interrupted almost before we had begun."

Spade lighted his cigarette and laughed his mouth empty of smoke. "Want me to phone him and ask him to come back?"

She shook her head, not smiling. Her eyes moved back and forth between her lids as she shook her head, maintaining their focus on Spade's eyes. Her eyes were inquisitive.

Spade put an arm across her back, cupping his hand over the smooth bare white shoulder farthest from him. She leaned back into the bend of his arm. He said: "Well, I'm listening."

She twisted her head around to smile up at him with playful insolence, asking: "Do you need your arm there for that?"

"No." He removed his hand from her shoulder and let his arm drop down behind her.

"You're altogether unpredictable," she murmured.

He nodded and said amiably: "I'm still listening."

"Look at the time!" she exclaimed, wriggling a finger at the alarm-clock perched atop the book saying two-fifty with its clumsily shaped hands.

"Uh-huh, it's been a busy evening."

"I must go." She rose from the sofa. "This is terrible."

Spade did not rise. He shook his head and said: "Not until you've told me about it."

"But look at the time," she protested, "and it would take hours to tell you."

"It'll have to take them then."

"Am I a prisoner?" she asked gaily.

"Besides, there's the kid outside. Maybe he hasn't gone home to sleep yet."

Her gaiety vanished. "Do you think he's still there?"

"It's likely."

She shivered. "Could you find out?"

"I could go down and see."

"Oh, that's – will you?"

Spade studied her anxious face for a moment and then got up from the sofa saying: "Sure." He got a hat and overcoat from the closet. "I'll be gone about ten minutes."

"Do be careful," she begged as she followed him to the corridor-door.

He said, "I will," and went out.

* * *

Post Street was empty when Spade issued into it. He walked east a block, crossed the street, walked west two blocks on the other side, recrossed it, and returned to his building without having seen anyone except two mechanics working on a car in a garage.

When he opened his apartment-door Brigid O'Shaughnessy was standing at the bend in the passageway, holding Cairo's pistol straight down at her side.

"He's still there," Spade said.

She bit the inside of her lip and turned slowly, going back into the living-room. Spade followed her in, put his hat and overcoat on a chair, said, "So we'll have time to talk," and went into the kitchen.

He had put the coffee-pot on the stove when she came to the door, and was slicing a slender loaf of French bread. She stood in the doorway and watched him with preoccupied eyes. The fingers of her left hand idly caressed the body and barrel of the pistol her right hand still held.

"The table-cloth's in there," he said, pointing the bread-knife at a cupboard that was one breakfast-nook partition.

She set the table while he spread liverwurst on, or put cold corned beef between, the small ovals of bread he had sliced. Then he poured the coffee, added brandy to it from a squat bottle, and they sat at the table. They sat side by side on one of the benches. She put the pistol down on the end of the bench nearer her.

"You can start now, between bites," he said.

She made a face at him, complained, "You're the most insistent person," and bit a sandwich.

"Yes, and wild and unpredictable. What's this bird, this falcon, that everybody's all steamed up about?"

She chewed the beef and bread in her mouth, swallowed it, looked attentively at the small crescent its removal had made in the sandwich's rim, and asked: "Suppose I wouldn't tell you? Suppose I wouldn't tell you anything at all about it? What would you do?"

"You mean about the bird?"

"I mean about the whole thing."

"I wouldn't be too surprised," he told her, grinning so that the edges of his jaw-teeth were visible, "to know what to do next."

"And that would be?" She transferred her attention from the sandwich to his face. "That's what I wanted to know: what would you do next?"

He shook his head.

Mockery rippled in a smile on her face. "Something wild and unpredictable?"

"Maybe. But I don't see what you've got to gain by covering up now. It's coming out bit by bit anyhow. There's a lot of it I don't know, but there's some of it I do, and some more that I can guess at, and, give me another day like this, I'll soon be knowing things about it that you don't know."

"I suppose you do now," she said, looking at her sandwich again, her face serious. "But – oh! – I'm so tired of it, and I do so hate having to talk about it. Wouldn't it – wouldn't it be just as well to wait and let you learn about it as you say you will?"

Spade laughed. "I don't know. You'll have to figure that out for yourself. My way of learning is to heave a wild and unpredictable monkey-wrench into the machinery. It's all right with me, if you're sure none of the flying pieces will hurt you."

She moved her bare shoulders uneasily, but said nothing. For several minutes they ate in silence, he phlegmatically, she thoughtfully. Then she said in a hushed voice: "I'm afraid of you, and that's the truth."

He said: "That's not the truth."

"It is," she insisted in the same low voice. "I know two men

I'm afraid of and I've seen both of them tonight."

"I can understand your being afraid of Cairo," Spade said. "He's out of your reach."

"And you aren't?"

"Not that way," he said and grinned.

She blushed. She picked up a slice of bread encrusted with grey liverwurst. She put it down on her plate. She wrinkled her white forehead and she said: "It's a black figure, as you know, smooth and shiny, of a bird, a hawk or falcon, about that high." She held her hands a foot apart.

"What makes it important?"

She sipped coffee and brandy before she shook her head. "I don't know," she said. "They'd never tell me. They promised me five hundred pounds if I helped them get it. Then Floyd said afterward, after we'd left Joe, that he'd give me seven hundred and fifty."

"So it must be worth more than seventy-five hundred dollars?"

"Oh, much more than that," she said. "They didn't pretend that they were sharing equally with me. They were simply hiring me to help them."

"To help them how?"

She lifted her cup to her lips again. Spade, not moving the domineering stare of his yellow-gray eyes from her face, began to make a cigarette. Behind them the percolator bubbled on the stove.

"To help them get it from the man who had it," she said slowly when she had lowered her cup, "a Russian named Kemidov."

"How?"

"Oh, but that's not important," she objected, "and wouldn't help you" – she smiled impudently – "and is certainly none of your business."

"This was in Constantinople?"

She hesitated, nodded, and said: "Marmora."

He waved his cigarette at her, saying: "Go ahead, what happened then?"

"But that's all. I've told you. They promised me five hundred pounds to help them and I did and then we found that Joe Cairo meant to desert us, taking the falcon with him and leaving us nothing. So we did exactly that to him, first. But then I wasn't any better off than I had been before, because Floyd hadn't any intention at all of paying me the seven hundred and fifty pounds he had promised me. I had learned that by the time we got here. He said we would go to New York, where he would sell it and give me my share, but I could see he wasn't telling me the truth." Indignation had darkened her eyes to violet. "And that's why I came to you to get you to help me learn where the falcon was."

"And suppose you'd got it? What then?"

"Then I'd have been in a position to talk terms with Mr. Floyd Thursby."

Spade squinted at her and suggested: "But you wouldn't have known where to take it to get more money than he'd give you, the larger sum that you knew he expected to sell it for?"

"I did not know," she said.

Spade scowled at the ashes he had dumped on his plate. "What makes it worth all that money?" he demanded. "You must have some idea, at least be able to guess."

"I haven't the slightest idea."

He directed the scowl at her. "What's it made of?"

"Porcelain or black stone. I don't know. I've never touched it. I've only seen it once, for a few minutes. Floyd showed it to me when we'd first got hold of it."

Spade mashed the end of his cigarette in his plate and made one draught of the coffee and brandy in his cup. His scowl had gone away. He wiped his lips with his napkin, dropped it crumpled on the table, and spoke casually: "You *are* a liar."

She got up and stood at the end of the table, looking down at him with dark abashed eyes in a pinkening face. "I am a liar," she said. "I have always been a liar."

"Don't brag about it. It's childish." His voice was good-humored. He came out from between table and bench. "Was there any truth at all in that yarn?"

She hung her head. Dampness glistened on her dark lashes. "Some," she whispered.

"How much?"

"Not – not very much."

Spade put a hand under her chin and lifted her head. He laughed into her wet eyes and said: "We've got all night before us. I'll put some more brandy in some more coffee and we'll try again."

Her eyelids drooped. "Oh, I'm so tired," she said tremulously, "so tired of it all, of myself, of lying and thinking up lies, and of not knowing what is a lie and what is the truth. I wish I –"

She put her hands up to Spade's cheeks, put her open mouth hard against his mouth, her body flat against his body.

Spade's arms went around her, holding her to him, muscles bulging his blue sleeves, a hand cradling her head, its fingers half lost among red hair, a hand moving groping fingers over her slim back. His eyes burned yellowly.

10 THE BELVEDERE DIVAN

BEGINNING DAY HAD reduced night to a thin smokiness when Spade sat up. At his side Brigid O'Shaughnessy's soft breathing had the regularity of utter sleep. Spade was quiet leaving bed and bedroom and shutting the bedroom-door. He dressed in the bathroom. Then he examined the sleeping girl's clothes, took a flat brass key from the pocket of her coat, and went out.

He went to the Coronet, letting himself into the building and into her apartment with the key. To the eye there was nothing furtive about his going in: he entered boldly and directly. To the ear his going in was almost unnoticeable: he made as little sound as might be.

In the girl's apartment he switched on all the lights. He searched the place from wall to wall. His eyes and thick fingers moved without apparent haste, and without ever lingering or fumbling or going back, from one inch of their fields to the next, probing, scrutinizing, testing with expert certainty. Every drawer, cupboard, cubbyhole, box, bag, trunk – locked or unlocked – was opened and its contents subjected to examination by eyes and fingers. Every piece of clothing was tested by hands that felt for telltale bulges and ears that listened for the crinkle of paper between pressing fingers. He stripped the bed of bedclothes. He looked under rugs and at the under side of each piece of furniture. He pulled down blinds to see that nothing had been rolled up in them for concealment. He leaned through windows to see that nothing hung below them on the outside. He poked with a fork into powder and cream-jars on the dressing-table. He held atomizers and bottles up against the light. He examined dishes and pans and food and

93

food-containers. He emptied the garbage-can on spread sheets of newspaper. He opened the top of the flush-box in the bathroom, drained the box, and peered down into it. He examined and tested the metal screens over the drains of bathtub, wash-bowl, sink, and laundry-tub.

He did not find the black bird. He found nothing that seemed to have any connection with a black bird. The only piece of writing he found was a week-old receipt for the month's apartment-rent Brigid O'Shaughnessy had paid. The only thing he found that interested him enough to delay his search while he looked at it was a double-handful of rather fine jewelry in a polychrome box in a locked dressing-table-drawer.

When he had finished he made and drank a cup of coffee. Then he unlocked the kitchen-window, scarred the edge of its lock a little with his pocket-knife, opened the window – over a fire-escape – got his hat and overcoat from the settee in the living-room, and left the apartment as he had come.

On his way home he stopped at a store that was being opened by a puffy-eyed shivering plump grocer and bought oranges, eggs, rolls, butter, and cream.

Spade went quietly into his apartment, but before he had shut the corridor-door behind him Brigid O'Shaughnessy cried: "Who is that?"

"Young Spade bearing breakfast."

"Oh, you frightened me!"

The bedroom-door he had shut was open. The girl sat on the side of the bed, trembling, with her right hand out of sight under a pillow.

Spade put his packages on the kitchen-table and went into the bedroom. He sat on the bed beside the girl, kissed her smooth shoulder, and said: "I wanted to see if that kid was still on the job, and to get stuff for breakfast."

"Is he?"

"No."

94

She sighed and leaned against him. "I awakened and you weren't here and then I heard someone coming in. I was terrified."

Spade combed her red hair back from her face with his fingers and said: "I'm sorry, angel. I thought you'd sleep through it. Did you have that gun under your pillow all night?"

"No. You know I didn't. I jumped up and got it when I was frightened."

He cooked breakfast – and slipped the flat brass key into her coat-pocket again – while she bathed and dressed.

She came out of the bathroom whistling *En Cuba*. "Shall I make the bed?" she asked.

"That'd be swell. The eggs need a couple of minutes more."

Their breakfast was on the table when she returned to the kitchen. They sat where they had sat the night before and ate heartily.

"Now about the bird?" Spade suggested presently as they ate.

She put her fork down and looked at him. She drew her eyebrows together and made her mouth small and tight. "You can't ask me to talk about that this morning of all mornings," she protested. "I don't want to and I won't."

"It's a stubborn damned hussy," he said sadly and put a piece of roll into his mouth.

The youth who had shadowed Spade was not in sight when Spade and Brigid O'Shaughnessy crossed the sidewalk to the waiting taxicab. The taxicab was not followed. Neither the youth nor another loiterer was visible in the vicinity of the Coronet when the taxicab arrived there.

Brigid O'Shaughnessy would not let Spade go in with her. "It's bad enough to be coming home in evening dress at this hour without bringing company. I hope I don't meet any-body."

"Dinner tonight?"

"Yes."

They kissed. She went into the Coronet. He told the chauffeur: "Hotel Belvedere."

When he reached the Belvedere he saw the youth who had shadowed him sitting in the lobby on a divan from which the elevators could be seen. Apparently the youth was reading a newspaper.

At the desk Spade learned that Cairo was not in. He frowned and pinched his lower lip. Points of yellow light began to dance in his eyes. "Thanks," he said softly to the clerk and turned away.

Sauntering, he crossed the lobby to the divan from which the elevators could be seen and sat down beside – not more than a foot from – the young man who was apparently reading a newspaper.

The young man did not look up from his newspaper. Seen at this scant distance, he seemed certainly less than twenty years old. His features were small, in keeping with his stature, and regular. His skin was very fair. The whiteness of his cheeks was as little blurred by any considerable growth of beard as by the glow of blood. His clothing was neither new nor of more than ordinary quality, but it, and his manner of wearing it, was marked by a hard masculine neatness.

Spade asked casually, "Where is he?" while shaking tobacco down into a brown paper curved to catch it.

The boy lowered his paper and looked around, moving with a purposeful sort of slowness, as of a more natural swiftness restrained. He looked with small hazel eyes under somewhat long curling lashes at Spade's chest. He said, in a voice as colorless and composed and cold as his young face: "What?"

"Where is he?" Spade was busy with his cigarette.

"Who?"

"The fairy."

96

The hazel eyes' gaze went up Spade's chest to the knot of his maroon tie and rested there. "What do you think you're doing, Jack?" the boy demanded. "Kidding me?"

"I'll tell you when I am." Spade licked his cigarette and smiled amiably at the boy. "New York, aren't you?"

The boy stared at Spade's tie and did not speak. Spade nodded as if the boy had said yes and asked: "Baumes rush?"

The boy stared at Spade's tie for a moment longer, then raised his newspaper and returned his attention to it. "Shove off," he said from the side of his mouth.

Spade lighted his cigarette, leaned back comfortably on the divan, and spoke with good-natured carelessness: "You'll have to talk to me before you're through, sonny – some of you will – and you can tell G. I said so."

The boy put his paper down quickly and faced Spade, staring at his necktie with bleak hazel eyes. The boy's small hands were spread flat over his belly. "Keep asking for it and you're going to get it," he said, "plenty." His voice was low and flat and menacing. "I told you to shove off. Shove off."

Spade waited until a bespectacled pudgy man and a thin-legged blonde girl had passed out of hearing. Then he chuckled and said: "That would go over big back on Seventh Avenue. But you're not in Romeville now. You're in my burg." He inhaled cigarette-smoke and blew it out in a long pale cloud. "Well, where is he?"

The boy spoke two words, the first a short guttural verb, the second "you."

"People lose teeth talking like that." Spade's voice was still amiable though his face had become wooden. "If you want to hang around you'll be polite."

The boy repeated his two words.

Spade dropped his cigarette into a tall stone jar beside the divan and with a lifted hand caught the attention of a man who had been standing at an end of the cigar-stand for several minutes. The man nodded and came towards them. He was a middle-aged man of medium height, round and sallow of face, compactly built, tidily dressed in dark clothes.

"Hello, Sam," he said as he came up.

"Hello, Luke."

They shook hands and Luke said: "Say, that's too bad about Miles."

"Uh-huh, a bad break." Spade jerked his head to indicate the boy on the divan beside him. "What do you let these cheap gunmen hang out in your lobby for, with their tools bulging their clothes?"

"Yes?" Luke examined the boy with crafty brown eyes set in a suddenly hard face. "What do you want here?" he asked.

The boy stood up. Spade stood up. The boy looked at the two men, at their neckties, from one to the other. Luke's necktie was black. The boy looked like a schoolboy standing in front of them.

Luke said: "Well, if you don't want anything, beat it, and don't come back."

The boy said, "I won't forget you guys," and went out.

They watched him go out. Spade took off his hat and wiped his damp forehead with a handkerchief.

The hotel-detective asked: "What is it?"

"Damned if I know," Spade replied. "I just happened to spot him. Know anything about Joel Cairo – six-thirty-five?"

"Oh, that one!" The hotel-detective leered.

"How long's he been here?"

"Four days. This is the fifth."

"What about him?"

"Search me, Sam. I got nothing against him but his looks."

"Find out if he came in last night?"

"Try to," the hotel-detective promised and went away. Spade sat on the divan until he returned. "No," Luke reported, "he didn't sleep in his room. What is it?"

"Nothing."

"Come clean. You know I'll keep my clam shut, but if there's anything wrong we ought to know about it so's we can collect our bill."

"Nothing like that," Spade assured him. "As a matter of fact, I'm doing a little work for him. I'd tell you if he was wrong."

"You'd better. Want me to kind of keep an eye on him?"

"Thanks, Luke. It wouldn't hurt. You can't know too much about the men you're working for these days."

It was twenty-one minutes past eleven by the clock over the elevator-doors when Joel Cairo came in from the street. His forehead was bandaged. His clothes had the limp unfreshness of too many hours' consecutive wear. His face was pasty, with sagging mouth and eyelids.

Spade met him in front of the desk. "Good morning," Spade said easily.

Cairo drew his tired body up straight and the drooping lines of his face tightened. "Good morning," he responded without enthusiasm.

There was a pause.

Spade said: "Let's go some place where we can talk."

Cairo raised his chin. "Please excuse me," he said. "Our conversations in private have not been such that I am anxious to continue them. Pardon my speaking bluntly, but it is the truth."

"You mean last night?" Spade made an impatient gesture with head and hands. "What in hell else could I do? I thought you'd see that. If you pick a fight with her, or let her pick one with you, I've got to throw in with her. I don't know where that damned bird is. You don't. She does. How in hell are we going to get it if I don't play along with her?"

Cairo hesitated, said dubiously: "You have always, I must say, a smooth explanation ready."

Spade scowled. "What do you want me to do? Learn to stutter? Well, we can talk over here." He led the way to the divan. When they were seated he asked: "Dundy take you down to the Hall?"

"Yes."

"How long did they work on you?"

"Until a very little while ago, and very much against my will." Pain and indignation were mixed in Cairo's face and voice. "I shall certainly take the matter up with the Consulate General of Greece and with an attorney."

"Go ahead, and see what it gets you. What did you let the police shake out of you?"

There was prim satisfaction in Cairo's smile. "Not a single thing. I adhered to the course you indicated earlier in your rooms." His smile went away. "Though I certainly wished you had devised a more reasonable story. I felt decidedly ridiculous repeating it."

Spade grinned mockingly. "Sure," he said, "but its goofiness is what makes it good. You sure you didn't give them anything?"

"You may rely upon it, Mr. Spade, I did not."

Spade drummed with his fingers on the leather seat between them. "You'll be hearing from Dundy again. Stay dummied-up on him and you'll be all right. Don't worry about the story's goofiness. A sensible one would've had us all in the cooler." He rose to his feet. "You'll want sleep if you've been standing up under a police-storm all night. See you later."

Effie Perine was saying, "No, not yet," into the telephone when Spade entered his outer office. She looked around at him and her lips shaped a silent word: "Iva." He shook his head. "Yes, I'll have him call you as soon as he comes in," she said aloud and replaced the receiver on its prong. "That's the third time she's called up this morning," she told Spade.

He made an impatient growling noise.

The girl moved her brown eyes to indicate the inner office. "Your Miss O'Shaughnessy's in there. She's been waiting since a few minutes after nine."

Spade nodded as if he had expected that and asked: "What else?"

"Sergeant Polhaus called up. He didn't leave any message."

"Get him for me."

"And G. called up."

Spade's eyes brightened. He asked: "Who?"

"G. That's what he said." Her air of personal indifference to the subject was flawless. "When I told him you weren't in he said: 'When he comes in, will you please tell him that G., who got his message, phoned and will phone again?'"

Spade worked his lips together as if tasting something he liked. "Thanks, darling," he said. "See if you can get Tom Polhaus." He opened the inner door and went into his private office, pulling the door to behind him.

Brigid O'Shaughnessy, dressed as on her first visit to the office, rose from a chair beside his desk and came quickly towards him. "Somebody has been in my apartment," she explained. "It is all upside-down, every which way."

He seemed moderately surprised. "Anything taken?"

"I don't think so. I don't know. I was afraid to stay. I changed as fast as I could and came down here. Oh, you must've let that boy follow you there!"

Spade shook his head. "No, angel." He took an early copy of an afternoon paper from his pocket, opened it, and showed her a quarter-column headed SCREAM ROUTS BURGLAR.

A young woman named Carolin Beale, who lived alone in a Sutter Street apartment, had been awakened at four that morning by the sound of somebody moving in her bedroom. She had screamed. The mover had run away. Two other women who lived alone in the same building had discovered, later in the morning, signs of the burglar's having visited their apartments. Nothing had been taken from any of the three.

"That's where I shook him," Spade explained. "I went into that building and ducked out the back door. That's why all three were women who lived alone. He tried the apartments that had women's names in the vestibule-register, hunting for you under an alias."

"But he was watching your place when we were there," she objected.

Spade shrugged. "There's no reason to think he's working alone. Or maybe he went to Sutter Street after he had begun to think you were going to stay all night in my place. There are a lot of maybes, but I didn't lead him to the Coronet."

She was not satisfied. "But he found it, or somebody did."

"Sure." He frowned at her feet. "I wonder if it could have been Cairo. He wasn't at his hotel all night, didn't get in till a few minutes ago. He told me he had been standing up under a police-grilling all night. I wonder." He turned, opened the door, and asked Effie Perine: "Got Tom yet?"

"He's not in. I'll try again in a few minutes."

"Thanks." Spade shut the door and faced Brigid O'Shaughnessy.

She looked at him with cloudy eyes. "You went to see Joe this morning?" she asked.

"Yes."

She hesitated. "Why?"

"Why?" He smiled down at her. "Because, my own true love, I've got to keep in some sort of touch with all the loose ends of this dizzy affair if I'm ever going to make heads or tails of it." He put an arm around her shoulders and led her over to his swivel-chair. He kissed the tip of her nose lightly and set her down in the chair. He sat on the desk in front of her. He said: "Now we've got to find a new home for you, haven't we?"

She nodded with emphasis. "I won't go back there."

He patted the desk beside his thighs and made a thoughtful face. "I think I've got it," he said presently. "Wait a minute." He went into the outer office, shutting the door.

Effie Perine reached for the telephone, saying: "I'll try again."

"Afterwards. Does your woman's intuition still tell you that she's a madonna or something?"

She looked sharply up at him. "I still believe that no matter what kind of trouble she's gotten into she's all right, if that's what you mean."

"That's what I mean," he said. "Are you strong enough for her to give her a lift?"

"How?"

"Could you put her up for a few days?"

"You mean at home?"

"Yes. Her joint's been broken into. That's the second burglary she's had this week. It'd be better for her if she wasn't alone. It would help a lot if you could take her in."

Effie Perine learned forward, asking earnestly: "Is she really in danger, Sam?"

"I think she is."

She scratched her lip with a fingernail. "That would scare Ma into a green hemorrhage. I'll have to tell her she's a surprise-witness or something that you're keeping under cover till the last minute."

"You're a darling," Spade said. "Better take her out there now. I'll get her key from her and bring whatever she needs over from her apartment. Let's see. You oughtn't to be seen leaving here together. You go home now. Take a taxi, but make sure you aren't followed. You probably won't be, but make sure. I'll send her out in another in a little while, making sure she isn't followed."

11   THE FAT MAN

THE TELEPHONE-BELL was ringing when Spade returned to his office after sending Brigid O'Shaughnessy off to Effie Perine's house. He went to the telephone.

"Hello ... Yes, this is Spade.... Yes, I got it. I've been waiting to hear from you.... Who?... Mr. Gutman? Oh, yes, sure!... Now – the sooner the better.... Twelve C.... Right. Say fifteen minutes.... Right."

Spade sat on the corner of his desk beside the telephone and rolled a cigarette. His mouth was a hard complacent v. His eyes, watching his fingers make the cigarette, smoldered over lower lids drawn up straight.

The door opened and Iva Archer came in.

Spade said, "Hello, honey," in a voice as lightly amiable as his face had suddenly become.

"Oh, Sam, forgive me! forgive me!" she cried in a choked voice. She stood just inside the door, wadding a black-bordered handkerchief in her small gloved hands, peering into his face with frightened red and swollen eyes.

He did not get up from his seat on the desk-corner. He said: "Sure. That's all right. Forget it."

"But, Sam," she wailed, "I sent those policemen there. I was mad, crazy with jealousy, and I phoned them that if they'd go there they'd learn something about Miles's murder."

"What made you think that?"

"Oh, I didn't! But I was mad, Sam, and I wanted to hurt you."

"It made things damned awkward." He put his arm around her and drew her nearer. "But it's all right now, only don't get any more crazy notions like that."

"I won't," she promised, "ever. But you weren't nice to me last night. You were cold and distant and wanted to get rid of me, when I had come down there and waited so long to warn you, and you – "

"Warn me about what?"

"About Phil. He's found out about – about you being in love with me, and Miles had told him about my wanting a divorce, though of course *he* never knew what for, and now Phil thinks we – you killed his brother because he wouldn't give me the divorce so we could get married. He told me he believed that, and yesterday he went and told the police."

"That's nice," Spade said softly. "And you came to warn me, and because I was busy you got up on your ear and helped this damned Phil Archer stir things up."

"I'm sorry," she whimpered, "I know you won't forgive me. I – I'm sorry, sorry, sorry."

"You ought to be," he agreed, "on your own account as well as mine. Has Dundy been to see you since Phil did his talking? Or anybody from the bureau?"

"No." Alarm opened her eyes and mouth.

"They will," he said, "and it'd be just as well to not let them find you here. Did you tell them who you were when you phoned?"

"Oh, no! I simply told them that if they'd go to your apartment right away they'd learn something about the murder and hung up."

"Where'd you phone from?"

"The drug-store up above your place. Oh, Sam, dearest, I–"

He patted her shoulder and said pleasantly: "It was a dumb trick, all right, but it's done now. You'd better run along home and think up things to tell the police. You'll be hearing from them. Maybe it'd be best to say 'no' right across the board." He frowned at something distant. "Or maybe you'd better see Sid Wise first." He removed his arm from around her, took a card out of his pocket, scribbled three lines on its back, and gave it to her. "You can tell Sid everything." He frowned. "Or almost everything. Where were you the night Miles was shot?"

"Home," she replied without hesitating.

He shook his head, grinning at her.

"I was," she insisted.

"No," he said, "but if that's your story it's all right with me. Go see Sid. It's up on the next corner, the pinkish building, room eight-twenty-seven."

Her blue eyes tried to probe his yellow-gray ones. "What makes you think I wasn't home?" she asked slowly.

"Nothing except that I know you weren't."

"But I was, I was." Her lips twisted and anger darkened her eyes. "Effie Perine told you that," she said indignantly. "I saw her looking at my clothes and snooping around. You know she doesn't like me, Sam. Why do you believe things she tells you when you know she'd do anything to make trouble for me?"

"Jesus, you women," Spade said mildly. He looked at the watch on his wrist. "You'll have to trot along, precious. I'm late for an appointment now. You do what you want, but if I were you I'd tell Sid the truth or nothing. I mean leave out the parts you don't want to tell him, but don't make up anything to take its place."

"I'm not lying to you, Sam," she protested.

"Like hell you're not," he said and stood up.

She strained on tiptoe to hold her face nearer his. "You don't believe me?" she whispered.

"I don't believe you."

"And you won't forgive me for – for what I did?"

"Sure I do." He bent his head and kissed her mouth. "That's all right. Now run along."

She put her arms around him. "Won't you go with me to see Mr. Wise?"

"I can't, and I'd only be in the way." He patted her arms, took them from around his body, and kissed her left wrist between glove and sleeve. He put his hands on her shoulders, turned her to face the door, and released her with a little push. "Beat it," he ordered.

The mahogany door of suite 12-C at the Alexandria Hotel was opened by the boy Spade had talked to in the Belvedere lobby. Spade said, "Hello," good-naturedly. The boy did not say anything. He stood aside holding the door open.

Spade went in. A fat man came to meet him.

The fat man was flabbily fat with bulbous pink cheeks and lips and chins and neck, with a great soft egg of a belly that was all his torso, and pendant cones for arms and legs. As he advanced to meet Spade all his bulbs rose and shook and fell separately with each step, in the manner of clustered soap-bubbles not yet released from the pipe through which they had been blown. His eyes, made small by fat puffs around them, were dark and sleek. Dark ringlets thinly covered his broad scalp. He wore a black cutaway coat, black vest, black satin Ascot tie holding a pinkish pearl, striped grey worsted trousers, and patent-leather shoes.

His voice was a throaty purr. "Ah, Mr. Spade," he said with enthusiasm and held out a hand like a fat pink star.

Spade took the hand and smiled and said: "How do you do, Mr. Gutman?"

Holding Spade's hand, the fat man turned beside him, put his other hand to Spade's elbow, and guided him across a green rug to a green plush chair beside a table that held a siphon, some glasses, and a bottle of Johnnie Walker whiskey on a tray, a box of cigars – Coronas del Ritz – two newspapers, and a small and plain yellow soapstone box.

Spade sat in the green chair. The fat man began to fill two glasses from bottle and siphon. The boy had disappeared. Doors set in three of the room's walls were shut. The fourth wall, behind Spade, was pierced by two windows looking out over Geary Street.

"We begin well, sir," the fat man purred, turning with a proffered glass in his hand. "I distrust a man that says when. If he's got to be careful not to drink too much it's because he's not to be trusted when he does."

Spade took the glass and, smiling, made the beginning of a bow over it.

The fat man raised his glass and held it against a window's light. He nodded approvingly at the bubbles running up in it. He said: "Well, sir, here's to plain speaking and clear under-standing."

They drank and lowered their glasses.

The fat man looked shrewdly at Spade and asked: "You're a close-mouthed man?"

Spade shook his head. "I like to talk."

"Better and better!" the fat man exclaimed. "I distrust a close-mouthed man. He generally picks the wrong time to talk and says the wrong things. Talking's something you can't do judiciously unless you keep in practice." He beamed over his glass. "We'll get along, sir, that we will." He set his glass on the table and held the box of Coronas del Ritz out to Spade. "A cigar, sir."

Spade took a cigar, trimmed the end of it, and lighted it. Meanwhile the fat man pulled another green plush chair around to face Spade's within convenient distance and placed a smoking-stand within reach of both chairs. Then he took his glass from the table, took a cigar from the box, and lowered himself into his chair. His bulbs stopped jouncing and settled into flabby rest. He sighed comfortably and said: "Now, sir, we'll talk if you like. And I'll tell you right out that I'm a man who likes talking to a man that likes to talk."

"Swell. Will we talk about the black bird?"

The fat man laughed and his bulbs rode up and down on his laughter. "Will we?" he asked and, "We will," he replied. His pink face was shiny with delight. "You're the man for me, sir, a man cut along my own lines. No beating about the bush, but right to the point. 'Will we talk about the black bird?' We will. I like that, sir. I like that way of doing business. Let us talk about the black bird by all means, but first, sir, answer me a question, please, though maybe it's an unnecessary one, so we'll understand each other from the beginning. You're here as Miss O'Shaughnessy's representative?"

Spade blew smoke above the fat man's head in a long slanting plume. He frowned thoughtfully at the ash-tipped end of his cigar. He replied deliberately: "I can't say yes or no. There's nothing certain about it either way, yet." He looked up at the fat man and stopped frowning. "It depends."

"It depends on – ?"

Spade shook his head. "If I knew what it depends on I could say yes or no."

The fat man took a mouthful from his glass, swallowed it, and suggested: "Maybe it depends on Joel Cairo?"

Spade's prompt "Maybe" was noncommittal. He drank.

The fat man leaned forward until his belly stopped him. His smile was ingratiating and so was his purring voice. "You could say, then, that the question is which one of them you'll represent?"

"You could put it that way."

"It will be one or the other?"

"I didn't say that."

The fat man's eyes glistened. His voice sank to a throaty whisper asking: "Who else is there?"

Spade pointed his cigar at his own chest. "There's me," he said.

The fat man sank back in his chair and let his body go flaccid. He blew his breath out in a long contented gust. "That's wonderful, sir," he purred. "That's wonderful. I do like a man that tells you right out he's looking out for himself. Don't we all? I don't trust a man that says he's not. And the man that's telling the truth when he says he's not I distrust most of all, because he's an ass and an ass that's going contrary to the laws of nature."

Spade exhaled smoke. His face was politely attentive. He said: "Uh-huh. Now let's talk about the black bird."

The fat man smiled benevolently. "Let's," he said. He squinted so that fat puffs crowding together left nothing of his eyes but a dark gleam visible. "Mr. Spade, have you any conception of how much money can be made out of that black bird?"

"No."

The fat man leaned forward again and put a bloated pink hand on the arm of Spade's chair. "Well, sir, if I told you – by Gad, if I told you half! – you'd call me a liar."

Spade smiled. "No," he said, "not even if I thought it. But if you won't take the risk just tell me what it is and I'll figure out the profits."

The fat man laughed. "You couldn't do it, sir. Nobody could do it that hadn't had a world of experience with things of that sort, and" – he paused impressively – "there aren't any other things of that sort." His bulbs jostled one another as he laughed again. He stopped laughing, abruptly. His fleshy lips hung open as laughter had left them. He stared at Spade with an intentness that suggested myopia. He asked: "You mean you don't know what it is?" Amazement took the throatiness out of his voice.

Spade made a careless gesture with his cigar. "Oh, hell," he said lightly, "I know what it's supposed to look like. I know the value in life you people put on it. I don't know what it is."

"She didn't tell you?"

"Miss O'Shaughnessy?"

"Yes. A lovely girl, sir."

"Uh-huh. No."

The fat man's eyes were dark gleams in ambush behind pink puffs of flesh. He said indistinctly, "She must know," and then, "And Cairo didn't either?"

"Cairo is cagey. He's willing to buy it, but he won't risk telling me anything I don't know already."

The fat man moistened his lips with his tongue. "How much is he willing to buy it for?" he asked.

"Ten thousand dollars."

The fat man laughed scornfully. "Ten thousand, and dollars, mind you, not even pounds. That's the Greek for you. Humph! And what did you say to that?"

"I said if I turned it over to him I'd expect the ten thousand."

"Ah, yes, *if!* Nicely put, sir." The fat man's forehead squirmed in a flesh-blurred frown. "They must know," he said only partly aloud, then: "Do they? Do they know what the bird is, sir? What was your impression?"

"I can't help you there," Spade confessed. "There's not much to go by. Cairo didn't say he did and he didn't say he didn't. She said she didn't, but I took it for granted that she was lying."

"That was not an injudicious thing to do," the fat man said, but his mind was obviously not on his words. He scratched his head. He frowned until his forehead was marked by raw red creases. He fidgeted in his chair as much as his size and the size of the chair permitted fidgeting. He shut his eyes, opened them suddenly – wide – and said to Spade: "Maybe they don't." His bulbous pink face slowly lost its worried frown and then, more quickly, took on an expression of ineffable happiness. "If they don't," he cried, and again: "If they don't I'm the only one in the whole wide sweet world who does!"

Spade drew his lips back in a tight smile. "I'm glad I came to the right place," he said.

The fat man smiled too, but somewhat vaguely. Happiness had gone out of his face, though he continued to smile, and caution had come into his eyes. His face was a watchful-eyed smiling mask held up between his thoughts and Spade. His eyes, avoiding Spade's, shifted to the glass at Spade's elbow.

His face brightened. "By Gad, sir," he said, "your glass is empty." He got up and went to the table and clattered glasses and siphon and bottle mixing two drinks.

Spade was immobile in his chair until the fat man, with a flourish and a bow and a jocular "Ah, sir, this kind of medicine will never hurt you!" had handed him his refilled glass. Then Spade rose and stood close to the fat man, looking down at him, and Spade's eyes were hard and bright. He raised his glass. His voice was deliberate, challenging: "Here's to plain speaking and clear understanding."

The fat man chuckled and they drank. The fat man sat down. He held his glass against his belly with both hands and smiled up at Spade. He said: "Well, sir, it's surprising, but it well may be a fact that neither of them does know exactly what that bird is, and that nobody in all this whole wide sweet world knows what it is, saving and excepting only your humble servant, Casper Gutman, Esquire."

"Swell." Spade stood with legs apart, one hand in his trousers-pocket, the other holding his glass. "When you've told me there'll only be two of us who know."

"Mathematically correct, sir" – the fat man's eyes twinkled – "but" – his smile spread – "I don't know for certain that I'm going to tell you."

"Don't be a damned fool," Spade said patiently. "You know what it is. I know where it is. That's why we're here."

"Well, sir, where is it?"

Spade ignored the question.

The fat man bunched his lips, raised his eyebrows, and cocked his head a little to the left. "You see," he said blandly, "I must tell you what I know, but you will not tell me what you know. That is hardly equitable, sir. No, no, I do not think we can do business along those lines."

Spade's face became pale and hard. He spoke rapidly in a low furious voice: "Think again and think fast. I told that punk of yours that you'd have to talk to me before you got through.

I'll tell you now that you'll do your talking today or you are through. What are you wasting my time for? You and your lousy secret! Christ! I know exactly what that stuff is that they keep in the subtreasury vaults, but what good does that do me? I can get along without you. God damn you! Maybe you could have got along without me if you'd kept clear of me. You can't now. Not in San Francisco. You'll come in or you'll get out – and you'll do it today."

He turned and with angry heedlessness tossed his glass at the table. The glass struck the wood, burst apart, and splashed its contents and glittering fragments over table and floor. Spade, deaf and blind to the crash, wheeled to confront the fat man again.

The fat man paid no more attention to the glass's fate than Spade did: lips pursed, eyebrows raised, head cocked a little to the left, he had maintained his pink-faced blandness throughout Spade's angry speech, and he maintained it now.

Spade, still furious, said: "And another thing, I don't want – "

The door to Spade's left opened. The boy who had admitted Spade came in. He shut the door, stood in front of it with his hands flat against his flanks, and looked at Spade. The boy's eyes were wide open and dark with wide pupils. Their gaze ran over Spade's body from shoulders to knees, and up again to settle on the handkerchief whose maroon border peeped from the breast-pocket of Spade's brown coat.

"Another thing," Spade repeated, glaring at the boy: "Keep that gunsel away from me while you're making up your mind. I'll kill him. I don't like him. He makes me nervous. I'll kill him the first time he gets in my way. I won't give him an even break. I won't give him a chance. I'll kill him."

The boy's lips twitched in a shadowy smile. He neither raised his eyes nor spoke.

The fat man said tolerantly: "Well, sir, I must say you have a most violent temper."

"Temper?" Spade laughed crazily. He crossed to the chair on which he had dropped his hat, picked up the hat, and set it on his head. He held out a long arm that ended in a thick forefinger pointing at the fat man's belly. His angry voice filled the room. "Think it over and think like hell. You've got till five-thirty to do it in. Then you're either in or out, for keeps." He let his arm drop, scowled at the bland fat man for a moment, scowled at the boy, and went to the door through which he had entered. When he opened the door he turned and said harshly: "Five-thirty – then the curtain."

The boy, staring at Spade's chest, repeated the two words he had twice spoken in the Belvedere lobby. His voice was not loud. It was bitter.

Spade went out and slammed the door.

SPADE RODE DOWN from Gutman's floor in an elevator. His lips were dry and rough in a face otherwise pale and damp. When he took out his handkerchief to wipe his face he saw his hand trembling. He grinned at it and said, "Whew!" so loudly that the elevator-operator turned his head over his shoulder and asked: "Sir?"

Spade walked down Geary Street to the Palace Hotel, where he ate luncheon. His face had lost its pallor, his lips their dryness, and his hand its trembling by the time he had sat down. He ate hungrily without haste, and then went to Sid Wise's office.

When Spade entered, Wise was biting a fingernail and staring at the window. He took his hand from his mouth, screwed his chair around to face Spade, and said: "'Lo. Push a chair up."

Spade moved a chair to the side of the big paper-laden desk and sat down. "Mrs. Archer come in?" he asked.

"Yes." The faintest of lights flickered in Wise's eyes. "Going to marry the lady, Sammy?"

Spade sighed irritably through his nose. "Christ, now you start that!" he grumbled.

A brief tired smile lifted the corners of the lawyer's mouth. "If you don't," he said, "you're going to have a job on your hands."

Spade looked up from the cigarette he was making and spoke sourly: "You mean you are? Well, that's what you're for. What did she tell you?"

"About you?"

"About anything I ought to know."

Wise ran fingers through his hair, sprinkling dandruff down on his shoulders. "She told me she had tried to get a divorce from Miles so she could – "

"I know all that," Spade interrupted him. "You can skip it. Get to the part I don't know."

"How do I know how much she – ?"

"Quit stalling, Sid." Spade held the flame of his lighter to the end of his cigarette. "What did she tell you that she wanted kept from me?"

Wise looked reprovingly at Spade. "Now, Sammy," he began, "that's not – "

Spade looked heavenward at the ceiling and groaned: "Dear God, he's my own lawyer that's got rich off me and I have to get down on my knees and beg him to tell me things!" He lowered at Wise. "What in hell do you think I sent her to you for?"

Wise made a weary grimace. "Just one more client like you," he complained, "and I'd be in a sanitarium – or San Quentin."

"You'd be with most of your clients. Did she tell you where she was the night he was killed?"

"Yes."

"Where?"

"Following him."

Spade sat up straight and blinked. He exclaimed incredulously: "Jesus, these women!" Then he laughed, relaxed, and asked: "Well, what did she see?"

Wise shook his head. "Nothing much. When he came home for dinner that evening he told her he had a date with a girl at the St. Mark, ragging her, telling her that was her chance to get the divorce she wanted. She thought at first he was just trying to get under her skin. He knew – "

"I know the family history," Spade said. "Skip it. Tell me what she did."

"I will if you'll give me a chance. After he had gone out she began to think that maybe he might have had that date. You know Miles. It would have been like him to – "

"You can skip Miles's character too."

"I oughtn't to tell you a damned thing," the lawyer said. "So she got their car from the garage and drove to the St. Mark, sitting in the car across the street. She saw him come out of the hotel and she saw that he was shadowing a man and a girl – she says she saw the same girl with you last night – who had come out just ahead of him. She knew then that he was working, had been kidding her. I suppose she was disappointed, and mad – she sounded that way when she told me about it. She followed Miles long enough to make sure he was shadowing the pair, and then she went up to your apartment. You weren't home."

"What time was that?" Spade asked.

"When she got to your place? Between half-past nine and ten the first time."

"The first time?"

"Yes. She drove around for half an hour or so and then tried again. That would make it, say, ten-thirty. You were still out, so she drove back downtown and went to a movie to kill time until after midnight, when she thought she'd be more likely to find you in."

Spade frowned. "She went to a movie at ten-thirty?"

"So she says – the one on Powell Street that stays open till one in the morning. She didn't want to go home, she said, because she didn't want to be there when Miles came. That always made him mad, it seems, especially if it was around midnight. She stayed in the movie till it closed." Wise's words came out slower now and there was a sardonic glint in his eye. "She says she had decided by then not to go back to your place again. She says she didn't know whether you'd like having her drop in that late. So she went to Tait's – the one on Ellis Street – had something to eat and then went home –

alone." Wise rocked back in his chair and waited for Spade to speak.

Spade's face was expressionless. He asked: "You believe her?"

"Don't you?" Wise replied.

"How do I know? How do I know it isn't something you fixed up between you to tell me?"

Wise smiled. "You don't cash many checks for strangers, do you, Sammy?"

"Not basketfuls. Well, what then? Miles wasn't home. It was at least two o'clock by then – must've been – and he was dead."

"Miles wasn't home," Wise said. "That seems to have made her mad again – his not being home first to be made mad by her not being home. So she took the car out of the garage again and went back to your place."

"And I wasn't home. I was down looking at Miles's corpse. Jesus, what a swell lot of merry-go-round riding. Then what?"

"She went home, and her husband still wasn't there, and while she was undressing your messenger came with the news of his death."

Spade didn't speak until he had with great care rolled and lighted another cigarette. Then he said: "I think that's an all right spread. It seems to click with most of the known facts. It ought to hold."

Wise's fingers, running through his hair again, combed more dandruff down on his shoulders. He studied Spade's face with curious eyes and asked: "But you don't believe it?"

Spade plucked his cigarette from between his lips. "I don't believe it or disbelieve it, Sid. I don't know a damned thing about it."

A wry smile twisted the lawyer's mouth. He moved his shoulders wearily and said: "That's right – I'm selling you out. Why don't you get an honest lawyer – one you can trust?"

"That fellow's dead." Spade stood up. He sneered at Wise. "Getting touchy, huh? I haven't got enough to think about: now I've got to remember to be polite to you. What did I do? Forget to genuflect when I came in?"

Sid Wise smiled sheepishly. "You're a son of a gun, Sammy," he said.

Effie Perine was standing in the center of Spade's outer office when he entered. She looked at him with worried brown eyes and asked: "What happened?"

Spade's face grew stiff. "What happened where?" he demanded.

"Why didn't she come?"

Spade took two long steps and caught Effie Perine by the shoulders. "She didn't get there?" he bawled into her frightened face.

She shook her head violently from side to side. "I waited and waited and she didn't come, and I couldn't get you on the phone, so I came down."

Spade jerked his hands away from her shoulders, thrust them far down in his trousers-pockets, said, "Another merry-go-round," in a loud enraged voice, and strode into his private office. He came out again. "Phone your mother," he commanded. "See if she's come yet."

He walked up and down the office while the girl used the telephone. "No," she said when she had finished. "Did – did you send her out in a taxi?"

His grunt probably meant yes.

"Are you sure she – Somebody must have followed her!"

Spade stopped pacing the floor. He put his hands on his hips and glared at the girl. He addressed her in a loud savage voice: "Nobody followed her. Do you think I'm a God-damned schoolboy? I made sure of it before I put her in the cab, I rode a dozen blocks with her to be more sure, and I checked her another half-dozen blocks after I got out."

"Well, but —"

"But she didn't get there. You've told me that. I believe it. Do you think I think she did get there?"

Effie Perine sniffed. "You certainly act like a God-damned schoolboy," she said.

Spade made a harsh noise in his throat and went to the corridor-door. "I'm going out and find her if I have to dig up sewers," he said. "Stay here till I'm back or you hear from me. For Christ's sake let's do something right."

He went out, walked half the distance to the elevators, and retraced his steps. Effie Perine was sitting at her desk when he opened the door. He said: "You ought to know better than to pay any attention to me when I talk like that."

"If you think I pay any attention to you you're crazy," she replied, "only" – she crossed her arms and felt her shoulders, and her mouth twitched uncertainly – "I won't be able to wear an evening gown for two weeks, you big brute."

He grinned humbly, said, "I'm no damned good, darling," made an exaggerated bow, and went out again.

Two yellow taxicabs were at the corner-stand to which Spade went. Their chauffeurs were standing together talking. Spade asked: "Where's the red-faced blond driver that was here at noon?"

"Got a load," one of the chauffeurs said.

"Will he be back here?"

"I guess so."

The other chauffeur ducked his head to the east. "Here he comes now."

Spade walked down to the corner and stood by the curb until the red-faced blond chauffeur had parked his cab and got out. Then Spade went up to him and said: "I got into your cab with a lady at noontime. We went out Stockton Street and up Sacramento to Jones, where I got out."

"Sure," the red-faced man said. "I remember that."

"I told you to take her to a Ninth-Avenue-number. You didn't take her there. Where did you take her?"

The chauffeur rubbed his cheek with a grimy hand and looked doubtfully at Spade. "I don't know about this."

"It's all right," Spade assured him, giving him one of his cards. "If you want to play safe, though, we can ride up to your office and get your superintendent's OK."

"I guess it's all right. I took her to the Ferry Building."

"By herself?"

"Yeah. Sure."

"Didn't take her anywhere else first?"

"No. It was like this: after we dropped you I went on out Sacramento, and when we got to Polk she rapped on the glass and said she wanted to get a newspaper, so I stopped at the corner and whistled for a kid, and she got her paper."

"Which paper?"

"The *Call*. Then I went on out Sacramento some more, and just after we'd crossed Van Ness she knocked on the glass again and said take her to the Ferry Building."

"Was she excited or anything?"

"Not so's I noticed."

"And when you got to the Ferry Building?"

"She paid me off, and that was all."

"Anybody waiting for her there?"

"I didn't see them if they was."

"Which way did she go?"

"At the Ferry? I don't know. Maybe upstairs, or towards the stairs."

"Take the newspaper with her?"

"Yeah, she had it tucked under her arm when she paid me."

"With the pink sheet outside, or one of the white?"

"Hell, Cap, I don't remember that."

Spade thanked the chauffeur, said, "Get yourself a smoke," and gave him a silver dollar.

* * *

Spade bought a copy of the *Call* and carried it into an office-building-vestibule to examine it out of the wind.

His eyes ran swiftly over the front-page-headlines and over those on the second and third pages. They paused for a moment under SUSPECT ARRESTED AS COUNTERFEITER on the fourth page, and again on page five under BAY YOUTH SEEKS DEATH WITH BULLET. Pages six and seven held nothing to interest him. On eight 3 BOYS ARRESTED AS S.F. BURGLARS AFTER SHOOTING held his attention for a moment, and after that nothing until he reached the thirty-fifth page, which held news of the weather, shipping, produce, finance, divorce, births, marriages, and deaths. He read the list of the dead, passed over pages thirty-six and thirty-seven – financial news – found nothing to stop his eyes on the thirty-eighth and last page, sighed, folded the newspaper, put it in his coat-pocket, and rolled a cigarette.

For five minutes he stood there in the office-building-vestibule smoking and staring sulkily at nothing. Then he walked up to Stockton Street, hailed a taxicab, and had himself driven to the Coronet.

He let himself into the building and into Brigid O'Shaughnessy's apartment with the key she had given him. The blue gown she had worn the previous night was hanging across the foot of her bed. Her blue stockings and slippers were on the bedroom floor. The polychrome box that had held jewelry in her dressing-table-drawer now stood empty on the dressing-table-top. Spade frowned at it, ran his tongue across his lips, strolled through the rooms, looking around but not touching anything, then left the Coronet and went downtown again.

In the doorway of Spade's office-building he came face to face with the boy he had left at Gutman's. The boy put himself in Spade's path, blocking the entrance, and said: "Come on. He wants to see you."

The boy's hands were in his overcoat-pockets. His pockets bulged more than his hands need have made them bulge.

Spade grinned and said mockingly: "I didn't expect you till five-twenty-five. I hope I haven't kept you waiting."

The boy raised his eyes to Spade's mouth and spoke in the strained voice of one in physical pain: "Keep on riding me and you're going to be picking iron out of your navel."

Spade chuckled. "The cheaper the crook, the gaudier the patter," he said cheerfully. "Well, let's go."

They walked up Sutter Street side by side. The boy kept his hands in his overcoat-pockets. They walked a little more than a block in silence. Then Spade asked pleasantly: "How long have you been off the goose-berry lay, son?"

The boy did not show that he had heard the question.

"Did you ever –?" Spade began, and stopped. A soft light began to glow in his yellowish eyes. He did not address the boy again.

They went into the Alexandria, rode up to the twelfth floor, and walked down the corridor towards Gutman's suite. Nobody else was in the corridor.

Spade lagged a little, so that, when they were within fifteen feet of Gutman's door, he was perhaps a foot and a half behind the boy. He leaned sidewise suddenly and grasped the boy from behind by both arms, just beneath the boy's elbows. He forced the boy's arms forward so that the boy's hands, in his overcoat-pockets, lifted the overcoat up before him. The boy struggled and squirmed, but he was impotent in the big man's grip. The boy kicked back, but his feet went between Spade's spread legs.

Spade lifted the boy straight up from the floor and brought him down hard on his feet again. The impact made little noise on the thick carpet. At the moment of impact Spade's hands slid down and got a fresh grip on the boy's wrists. The boy, teeth set hard together, did not stop straining against the man's big hands, but he could not tear himself loose, could not keep the man's hands from crawling down over his own hands. The boy's teeth ground together audibly, making a noise that mingled with the noise of Spade's breathing as Spade crushed the boy's hands.

They were tense and motionless for a long moment. Then the boy's arms became limp. Spade released the boy and stepped back. In each of Spade's hands, when they came out of the boy's overcoat-pockets, there was a heavy automatic pistol.

The boy turned and faced Spade. The boy's face was a ghastly white blank. He kept his hands in his overcoat-pockets. He looked at Spade's chest and did not say anything.

Spade put the pistols in his own pockets and grinned derisively. "Come on," he said. "This will put you in solid with your boss."

They went to Gutman's door and Spade knocked.

13 THE EMPEROR'S GIFT

GUTMAN OPENED THE door. A glad smile lighted his fat face. He held out a hand and said: "Ah, come in, sir! Thank you for coming. Come in."

Spade shook the hand and entered. The boy went in behind him. The fat man shut the door. Spade took the boy's pistols from his pockets and held them out to Gutman. "Here. You shouldn't let him run around with these. He'll get himself hurt."

The fat man laughed merrily and took the pistols. "Well, well," he said, "what's this?" He looked from Spade to the boy.

Spade said: "A crippled newsie took them away from him, but I made him give them back."

The white-faced boy took the pistols out of Gutman's hands and pocketed them. The boy did not speak.

Gutman laughed again. "By Gad, sir," he told Spade, "you're a chap worth knowing, an amazing character. Come in. Sit down. Give me your hat."

The boy left the room by the door to the right of the entrance.

The fat man installed Spade in a green plush chair by the table, pressed a cigar upon him, held a light to it, mixed whiskey and carbonated water, put one glass in Spade's hand, and, holding the other, sat down facing Spade.

"Now, sir," he said, "I hope you'll let me apologize for – "

"Never mind that," Spade said. "Let's talk about the black bird."

The fat man cocked his head to the left and regarded Spade with fond eyes. "All right, sir," he agreed. "Let's." He took a sip from the glass in his hand. "This is going to be the most astounding thing you've ever heard of, sir, and I say that knowing that a man of your caliber in your profession must have known some astounding things in his time."

Spade nodded politely.

The fat man screwed up his eyes and asked: "What do you know, sir, about the Order of the Hospital of St. John of Jerusalem, later called the Knights of Rhodes and other things?"

Spade waved his cigar. "Not much – only what I remember from history in school – Crusaders or something."

"Very good. Now you don't remember that Suleiman the Magnificent chased them out of Rhodes in 1523?"

"No."

"Well, sir, he did, and they settled in Crete. And they stayed there for seven years until 1530 when they persuaded the Emperor Charles V to give them" – Gutman held up three puffy fingers and counted them – "Malta, Gozo, and Tripoli."

"Yes?"

"Yes, sir, but with these conditions: they were to pay the Emperor each year the tribute of one" – he held up a finger – "falcon in the acknowledgment that Malta was still under Spain, and if they ever left the island it was to revert to Spain. Understand? He was giving it to them, but not unless they used it, and they couldn't give or sell it to anybody else."

"Yes."

The fat man looked over his shoulders at the three closed doors, hunched his chair a few inches nearer Spade's, and reduced his voice to a husky whisper: "Have you any conception of the extreme, the immeasurable, wealth of the Order at that time?"

"If I remember," Spade said, "they were pretty well fixed."

Gutman smiled indulgently. "Pretty well, sir, is putting it mildly." His whisper became lower and more purring. "They were rolling in wealth, sir. You've no idea. None of us has any idea. For years they had preyed on the Saracens, had taken nobody knows what spoils of gems, precious metals, silks, ivories – the cream of the cream of the East. That is history, sir. We all know that the Holy Wars to them, as to the Templars, were largely a matter of loot.

"Well, now, the Emperor Charles has given them Malta, and all the rent he asks is one insignificant bird per annum, just as a matter of form. What could be more natural than for these immeasurably wealthy Knights to look around for some way of expressing their gratitude? Well, sir, that's exactly what they did, and they hit on the happy thought of sending Charles for the first year's tribute, not an insignificant live bird, but a glorious golden falcon encrusted from head to foot with the finest jewels in their coffers. And – remember, sir – they had fine ones, the finest out of Asia." Gutman stopped whispering. His sleek dark eyes examined Spade's face, which was placid. The fat man asked: "Well, sir, what do you think of that?"

"I don't know."

The fat man smiled complacently. "These are facts, historical facts, not schoolbook history, not Mr. Wells's history, but history nevertheless." He leaned forward. "The archives of the Order from the twelfth century on are still at Malta. They are not intact, but what is there holds no less than three" – he held up three fingers – "references that can't be to anything else but this jeweled falcon. In J. Delaville Le Roulx's *Les Archives de l'Ordre de Saint-Jean* there is a reference to it – oblique to be sure, but a reference still. And the unpublished – because unfinished at the time of his death – supplement to Paoli's *Dell' origine ed instituto del sacro militar ordine* has a clear and unmistakable statement of the facts I am telling you."

"All right," Spade said.

"All right, sir. Grand Master Villiers de l'Isle d'Adam had this foot-high jeweled bird made by Turkish slaves in the castle of St. Angelo and sent it to Charles, who was in Spain. He sent it in a galley commanded by a French knight named Cormier or Corvere, a member of the Order." His voice dropped to a whisper again. "It never reached Spain." He smiled with compressed lips and asked: "You know of Barbarossa, Red-beard, Khair-ed-Din? No? A famous admiral of buccaneers sailing out of Algiers then. Well, sir, he took the Knights' galley and he took the bird. The bird went to Algiers. That's a fact. That's a fact that the French historian Pierre Dan put in one of his letters from Algiers. He wrote that the bird had been there for more than a hundred years, until it was carried away by Sir Francis Verney, the English adventurer who was with the Algerian buccaneers for a while. Maybe it wasn't, but Pierre Dan believed it was, and that's good enough for me.

"There's nothing said about the bird in Lady Frances Ver-ney's *Memoirs of the Verney Family during the Seventeenth Century*, to be sure. I looked. And it's pretty certain that Sir Francis didn't have the bird when he died in a Messina hospital in 1615. He was stony broke. But, sir, there's no denying that the bird *did* go to Sicily. It was there and it came into the posses-sion there of Victor Amadeus II some time after he became king in 1713, and it was one of his gifts to his wife when he married in Chambéry after abdicating. That is a fact, sir. Carutti, the author of *Storia del Regno di Vittorio Amadeo II*, himself vouched for it.

"Maybe they – Amadeo and his wife – took it along with them to Turin when he tried to revoke his abdication. Be that as it may, it turned up next in the possession of a Spaniard who had been with the army that took Naples in 1734 – the father of Don José Monino y Redondo, Count of Floridablanca, who was Charles III's chief minister. There's nothing to show that it didn't stay in that family until at least the end of the Carlist War in '40. Then it appeared in Paris at just about the time that Paris was full of Carlists who had had to get out of Spain. One of them must have brought it with him, but, whoever he was, it's likely he knew nothing about its real value. It had been – no doubt as a precaution during the Carlist trouble in Spain – painted or enameled over to look like nothing more than a fairly interesting black statuette. And in that disguise, sir, it was, you might say, kicked around Paris for seventy years by private owners and dealers too stupid to see what it was under the skin."

The fat man paused to smile and shake his head regretfully. Then he went on: "For seventy years, sir, this marvelous item was, as you might say, a football in the gutters of Paris – until 1911 when a Greek dealer named Charilaos Konstantinides found it in an obscure shop. It didn't take Charilaos long to learn what it was and to acquire it. No thickness of enamel could conceal value from his eyes and nose. Well, sir, Charilaos was the man who traced most of its history and who identified it as what it actually was. I got wind of it and finally forced most of the history out of him, though I've been able to add a few details since.

"Charilaos was in no hurry to convert his find into money at once. He knew that – enormous as its intrinsic value was – a far higher, a terrific, price could be obtained for it once its authenticity was established beyond doubt. Possibly he planned to do business with one of the modern descendants of the old Order – the English Order of St. John of Jerusalem, the Prussian Johanniterorden, or the Italian or German *langues* of the Sovereign Order of Malta – all wealthy orders."

The fat man raised his glass, smiled at its emptiness, and rose to fill it and Spade's. "You begin to believe me a little?" he asked as he worked the siphon.

"I haven't said I didn't."

"No," Gutman chuckled. "But how you looked." He sat down, drank generously, and patted his mouth with a white handkerchief. "Well, sir, to hold it safe while pursuing his researches into its history, Charilaos had re-enameled the bird, apparently just as it is now. One year to the very day after he had acquired it – that was possibly three months after I'd made him confess to me – I picked up the *Times* in London and read that his establishment had been burglarized and him murdered. I was in Paris the next day." He shook his head sadly. "The bird was gone. By Gad, sir, I was wild. I didn't believe anybody else knew what it was. I didn't believe he had told anybody but me. A great quantity of stuff had been stolen. That made me think that the thief had simply taken the bird along with the rest of his plunder, not knowing what it was. Because I assure you that a thief who knew its value would not burden himself with anything else − no, sir − at least not anything less than crown jewels."

He shut his eyes and smiled complacently at an inner thought. He opened his eyes and said: "That was seventeen years ago. Well, sir, it took me seventeen years to locate that bird, but I did it. I wanted it, and I'm not a man that's easily discouraged when he wants something." His smile grew broad. "I wanted it and I found it. I want it and I'm going to have it." He drained his glass, dried his lips again, and returned his handkerchief to his pocket. "I traced it to the home of a Russian general − one Kemidov − in a Constantinople suburb. He didn't know a thing about it. It was nothing but a black enameled figure to him, but his natural contrariness − the natural contrariness of a Russian general − kept him from selling it to me when I made him an offer. Perhaps in my eagerness I was a little unskillful, though not very. I don't know about that. But I did know I wanted it and I was afraid this stupid soldier might begin to investigate his property, might chip off some of the enamel. So I sent some − ah − agents to get it. Well, sir, they got it and I haven't got it." He stood up and carried his empty glass to the table. "But I'm going to get it. Your glass, sir."

"Then the bird doesn't belong to any of you?" Spade asked, "but to a General Kemidov?"

"Belong?" the fat man said jovially. "Well, sir, you might say it belonged to the King of Spain, but I don't see how you can honestly grant anybody else clear title to it − except by right of possession." He clucked. "An article of that value that has passed from hand to hand by such means is clearly the property of whoever can get hold of it."

"Then it's Miss O'Shaughnessy's now?"

"No, sir, except as my agent."

Spade said, "Oh," ironically.

Gutman, looking thoughtfully at the stopper of the whiskey-bottle in his hand, asked: "There's no doubt that she's got it now?"

"Not much."

"Where?"

"I don't know exactly."

The fat man set the bottle on the table with a bang. "But you said you did," he protested.

Spade made a careless gesture with one hand. "I meant to say I know where to get it when the time comes."

The pink bulbs of Gutman's face arranged themselves more happily. "And you do?" he asked.

"Yes."

"Where?"

Spade grinned and said: "Leave that to me. That's my end."

"When?"

"When I'm ready."

The fat man pursed his lips and, smiling with only slight uneasiness, asked: "Mr. Spade, where is Miss O'Shaughnessy now?"

"In my hands, safely tucked away."

Gutman smiled with approval. "Trust you for that, sir," he said. "Well now, sir, before we sit down to talk prices, answer me this: how soon can you – or how soon are you willing to – produce the falcon?"

"A couple of days."

The fat man nodded. "That is satisfactory. We – But I forgot our nourishment." He turned to the table, poured whiskey, squirted charged water into it, set a glass at Spade's elbow and held his own aloft. "Well, sir, here's to a fair bargain and profits large enough for both of us."

They drank. The fat man sat down. Spade asked: "What's your idea of a fair bargain?"

Gutman held his glass up to the light, looked affectionately at it, took another long drink, and said: "I have two proposals to make, sir, and either is fair. Take your choice. I will give you twenty-five thousand dollars when you deliver the falcon to me, and another twenty-five thousand as soon as I get to New York; or I will give you one quarter – twenty-five per cent – of what I realize on the falcon. There you are, sir: an almost immediate fifty thousand dollars or a vastly greater sum within, say, a couple of months."

Spade drank and asked: "How much greater?"

"Vastly," the fat man repeated. "Who knows how much greater? Shall I say a hundred thousand, or a quarter of a million? Will you believe me if I name the sum that seems the probable minimum?"

"Why not?"

The fat man smacked his lips and lowered his voice to a purring murmur. "What would you say, sir, to half a million?"

Spade narrowed his eyes. "Then you think the dingus is worth two million?"

Gutman smiled serenely. "In your own words, why not?" he asked.

Spade emptied his glass and set it on the table. He put his cigar in his mouth, took it out, looked at it, and put it back in. His yellow-gray eyes were faintly muddy. He said: "That's a hell of a lot of dough."

The fat man agreed: "That's a hell of a lot of dough." He leaned forward and patted Spade's knee. "That is the absolute rock-bottom minimum – or Charilaos Konstantinides was a blithering idiot – and he wasn't."

Spade removed the cigar from his mouth again, frowned at it with distaste, and put it on the smoking-stand. He shut his eyes hard, opened them again. Their muddiness had thickened. He said: "The – the minimum, huh? And the maximum?" An unmistakable *sh* followed the x in maximum as he said it.

"The maximum?" Gutman held his empty hand out, palm up. "I refuse to guess. You'd think me crazy. I don't know. There's no telling how high it could go, sir, and that's the one and only truth about it."

Spade pulled his sagging lower lip tight against the upper. He shook his head impatiently. A sharp frightened gleam awoke in his eyes – and was smothered by the deepening muddiness. He stood up, helping himself up with his hands on the arms of his chair. He shook his head again and took an uncertain step forward. He laughed thickly and muttered: "God damn you."

Gutman jumped up and pushed his chair back. His fat globes jiggled. His eyes were dark holes in an oily pink face.

Spade swung his head from side to side until his dull eyes were pointed at – if not focused on – the door. He took another uncertain step.

The fat man called sharply: "Wilmer!"

A door opened and the boy came in.

Spade took a third step. His face was gray now, with jaw-muscles standing out like tumors under his ears. His legs did not straighten again after his fourth step and his muddy eyes were almost covered by their lids. He took his fifth step.

The boy walked over and stood close to Spade, a little in front of him, but not directly between Spade and the door. The boy's right hand was inside his coat over his heart. The corners of his mouth twitched.

Spade essayed his sixth step.

The boy's leg darted out across Spade's leg, in front. Spade tripped over the interfering leg and crashed face-down on the floor. The boy, keeping his right hand under his coat, looked down at Spade. Spade tried to get up. The boy drew his right foot far back and kicked Spade's temple. The kick rolled Spade over on his side. Once more he tried to get up, could not, and went to sleep.

SPADE, COMING AROUND the corner from the elevator at a few minutes past six in the morning, saw yellow light glowing through the frosted glass of his office-door. He halted abruptly, set his lips together, looked up and down the corridor, and advanced to the door with swift quiet strides.

He put his hand on the knob and turned it with care that permitted neither rattle nor click. He turned the knob until it would turn no farther: the door was locked. Holding the knob still, he changed hands, taking it now in his left hand. With his right hand he brought his keys out of his pocket, carefully, so they could not jingle against one another. He separated the office-key from the others and, smothering the others together in his palm, inserted the office-key in the lock. The insertion was soundless. He balanced himself on the balls of his feet, filled his lungs, clicked the door open, and went in.

Effie Perine sat sleeping with her head on her forearms, her forearms on her desk. She wore her coat and had one of Spade's overcoats wrapped cape-fashion around her.

Spade blew his breath out in a muffled laugh, shut the door behind him, and crossed to the inner door. The inner office was empty. He went over to the girl and put a hand on her shoulder.

She stirred, raised her head drowsily, and her eyelids fluttered. Suddenly she sat up straight, opening her eyes wide. She saw Spade, smiled, leaned back in her chair, and rubbed her eyes with her fingers. "So you finally got back?" she said. "What time is it?"

"Six o'clock. What are you doing here?"

She shivered, drew Spade's overcoat closer around her, and yawned. "You told me to stay till you got back or phoned."

"Oh, you're the sister of the boy who stood on the burning deck?"

"I wasn't going to – " She broke off and stood up, letting his coat slide down on the chair behind her. She looked with dark excited eyes at his temple under the brim of his hat and exclaimed: "Oh, your head! What happened?"

His right temple was dark and swollen.

"I don't know whether I fell or was slugged. I don't think it amounts to much, but it hurts like hell." He barely touched it with his fingers, flinched, turned his grimace into a grim smile, and explained: "I went visiting, was fed knockout-drops, and came to twelve hours later all spread out on a man's floor."

She reached up and removed his hat from his head. "It's terrible," she said. "You'll have to get a doctor. You can't walk around with a head like that."

"It's not as bad as it looks, except for the headache, and that might be mostly from the drops." He went to the cabinet in the corner of the office and ran cold water on a handkerchief. "Anything turn up after I left?"

"Did you find Miss O'Shaughnessy, Sam?"

"Not yet. Anything turn up after I left?"

"The District Attorney's office phoned. He wants to see you."

"Himself?"

"Yes, that's the way I understood it. And a boy came in with a message – that Mr. Gutman would be delighted to talk to you before five-thirty."

Spade turned off the water, squeezed the handkerchief, and came away from the cabinet holding the handkerchief to his temple. "I got that," he said. "I met the boy downstairs, and talking to Mr. Gutman got me this."

"Is that the G. who phoned, Sam?"

"Yes."

"And what – ?"

Spade stared through the girl and spoke as if using speech to arrange his thoughts: "He wants something he thinks I can get. I persuaded him I could keep him from getting it if he didn't make the deal with me before five-thirty. Then – uh-huh – sure – it was after I'd told him he'd have to wait a couple of days that he fed me the junk. It's not likely he thought I'd die. He'd know I'd be up and around in ten or twelve hours. So maybe the answer's that he figured he could get it without my help in that time if I was fixed so I couldn't butt in." He scowled. "I hope to Christ he was wrong." His stare became less distant. "You didn't get any word from the O'Shaughnessy?"

The girl shook her head no and asked: "Has this got anything to do with her?"

"Something."

"This thing he wants belongs to her?"

"Or to the King of Spain. Sweetheart, you've got an uncle who teaches history or something over at the University?"

"A cousin. Why?"

"If we brightened his life with an alleged historical secret four centuries old could we trust him to keep it dark awhile?"

"Oh, yes, he's good people."

"Fine. Get your pencil and book."

She got them and sat in her chair. Spade ran more cold water on his handkerchief and, holding it to his temple, stood in front of her and dictated the story of the falcon as he had heard it from Gutman, from Charles V's grant to the Hospitallers up to – but no further than – the enameled bird's arrival in Paris at the time of the Carlist influx. He stumbled over the names of authors and their works that Gutman had mentioned, but managed to achieve some sort of phonetic likeness. The rest of the history he repeated with the accuracy of a trained interviewer.

When he had finished the girl shut her notebook and raised a flushed smiling face to him. "Oh, isn't this thrilling?" she said. "It's –"

"Yes, or ridiculous. Now will you take it over and read it to your cousin and ask him what he thinks of it? Has he ever run across anything that might have some connection with it? Is it probable? Is it possible – even barely possible? Or is it the bunk? If he wants more time to look it up, OK, but get some sort of opinion out of him now. And for God's sake make him keep it under his hat."

"I'll go right now," she said, "and you go see a doctor about that head."

"We'll have breakfast first."

"No, I'll eat over in Berkeley. I can't wait to hear what Ted thinks of this."

"Well," Spade said, "don't start boo-hooing if he laughs at you."

After a leisurely breakfast at the Palace, during which he read both morning papers, Spade went home, shaved, bathed, rubbed ice on his bruised temple, and put on fresh clothes.

He went to Brigid O'Shaughnessy's apartment at the Coronet. Nobody was in the apartment. Nothing had been changed in it since his last visit.

He went to the Alexandria Hotel. Gutman was not in. None of the other occupants of Gutman's suite was in. Spade learned that these other occupants were the fat man's secretary, Wilmer Cook, and his daughter Rhea, a brown-eyed fair-haired smallish girl of seventeen whom the hotel-staff said was beautiful. Spade was told that the Gutman party had arrived at the hotel, from New York, ten days before, and had not checked out.

Spade went to the Belvedere and found the hotel-detective eating in the hotel-café.

"Morning, Sam. Set down and bite an egg." The hotel-detective stared at Spade's temple. "By God, somebody maced you plenty!"

"Thanks, I've had mine," Spade said as he sat down, and then, referring to his temple: "It looks worse than it is. How's my Cairo's conduct?"

"He went out not more than half an hour behind you yesterday and I ain't seen him since. He didn't sleep here again last night."

"He's getting bad habits."

"Well, a fellow like that alone in a big city. Who put the slug to you, Sam?"

"It wasn't Cairo." Spade looked attentively at the small silver dome covering Luke's toast. "How's chances of giving his room a casing while he's out?"

"Can do. You know I'm willing to go all the way with you all the time." Luke pushed his coffee back, put his elbows on the table, and screwed up his eyes at Spade. "But I got a hunch you ain't going all the way with me. What's the honest-to-God on this guy, Sam? You don't have to kick back on me. You know I'm regular."

Spade lifted his eyes from the silver dome. They were clear and candid. "Sure, you are," he said. "I'm not holding out. I gave you it straight. I'm doing a job for him, but he's got some friends that look wrong to me and I'm a little leery of him."

"The kid we chased out yesterday was one of his friends."

"Yes, Luke, he was."

"And it was one of them that shoved Miles across."

Spade shook his head. "Thursby killed Miles."

"And who killed him?"

Spade smiled. "That's supposed to be a secret, but, con-fidentially, I did," he said, "according to the police."

Luke grunted and stood up saying: "You're a tough one to figure out, Sam. Come on, we'll have that look-see."

They stopped at the desk long enough for Luke to "fix it so we'll get a ring if he comes in," and went up to Cairo's room. Cairo's bed was smooth and trim, but paper in the wastebasket, unevenly drawn blinds, and a couple of rumpled towels in the bathroom showed that the chambermaid had not yet been in that morning.

Cairo's luggage consisted of a square trunk, a valise, and a gladstone bag. His bathroom-cabinet was stocked with cosmetics – boxes, cans, jars, and bottles of powders, creams, unguents, perfumes, lotions, and tonics. Two suits and an overcoat hung in the closet over three pairs of carefully treed shoes.

The valise and smaller bag were unlocked. Luke had the trunk unlocked by the time Spade had finished searching elsewhere.

"Blank so far," Spade said as they dug down into the trunk.

They found nothing there to interest them.

"Any particular thing we're supposed to be looking for?" Luke asked as he locked the trunk again.

"No. He's supposed to have come here from Constantinople. I'd like to know if he did. I haven't seen anything that says he didn't."

"What's his racket?"

Spade shook his head. "That's something else I'd like to know." He crossed the room and bent down over the wastebasket. "Well, this is our last shot."

He took a newspaper from the basket. His eyes brightened when he saw it was the previous day's *Call*. It was folded with the classified-advertising page outside. He opened it, examined that page, and nothing there stopped his eyes.

He turned the paper over and looked at the page that had been folded inside, the page that held financial and shipping news, the weather, births, marriages, divorces, and deaths. From the lower left-hand corner, a little more than two inches of the bottom of the second column had been torn out.

Immediately above the tear was a small caption *Arrived Today* followed by:

12:20 A.M. – Capac from Astoria.

5:05 A.M. – Helen P. Drew from Greenwood.

5:06 A.M. – Albarado from Bandon.

The tear passed through the next line, leaving only enough of its letters to make *from Sydney* inferable.

Spade put the *Call* down on the desk and looked into the wastebasket again. He found a small piece of wrapping-paper, a piece of string, two hosiery tags, a haberdasher's sale-ticket for half a dozen pairs of socks, and, in the bottom of the basket, a piece of newspaper rolled in a tiny ball.

He opened the ball carefully, smoothed it out on the desk, and fitted it into the torn part of the *Call*. The fit at the sides was exact, but between the top of the crumpled fragment and the inferable *from Sydney* half an inch was missing, sufficient space to have held announcement of six or seven boats' arrival. He turned the sheet over and saw that the other side of the missing portion could have held only a meaningless corner of a stockbroker's advertisement.

Luke, leaning over his shoulder, asked: "What's this all about?"

"Looks like the gent's interested in a boat."

"Well, there's no law against that, or is there?" Luke said while Spade was folding the torn page and the crumpled fragment together and putting them into his coat-pocket. "You all through here now?"

"Yes. Thanks a lot, Luke. Will you give me a ring as soon as he comes in?"

"Sure."

Spade went to the Business Office of the *Call*, bought a copy of the previous day's issue, opened it to the shipping-news-page, and compared it with the page taken from Cairo's wastebasket. The missing portion had read:

5:17 A.M. – Tahiti from Sydney and Papeete.
6:05 A.M. – Admiral Peoples from Astoria.
8:07 A.M. – Caddopeak from San Pedro.

8:17 A.M. – Silverado from San Pedro.
8:05 A.M. – La Paloma from Hongkong.
9:03 A.M. – Daisy Gray from Seattle.

He read the list slowly and when he had finished he underscored *Hongkong* with a fingernail, cut the list of arrivals from the paper with his pocket-knife, put the rest of the paper and Cairo's sheet into the wastebasket, and returned to his office.

He sat down at his desk, looked up a number in the telephone-book, and used the telephone.

"Kearny one four o one, please.... Where is the *Paloma*, in from Hongkong yesterday morning docked?" He repeated the question. "Thanks."

He held the receiver-hook down with his thumb for a moment, released it, and said: "Davenport two o two o, please.... Detective bureau, please.... Is Sergeant Polhaus there?... Thanks.... Hello, Tom, this is Sam Spade.... Yes, I tried to get you yesterday afternoon.... Sure, suppose you go to lunch with me.... Right."

He kept the receiver to his ear while his thumb worked the hook again.

"Davenport o one seven o, please.... Hello, this is Samuel Spade. My secretary got a message yesterday that Mr. Bryan wanted to see me. Will you ask him what time's the most convenient for him?... Yes, Spade, S-p-a-d-e." A long pause. "Yes.... Two-thirty? All right. Thanks."

He called a fifth number and said: "Hello, darling, let me talk to Sid?... Hello, Sid – Sam. I've got a date with the District Attorney at half-past two this afternoon. Will you give me a ring – here or there – around four, just to see that I'm not in trouble?... Hell with your Saturday afternoon golf: your job's to keep me out of jail.... Right, Sid. 'Bye."

He pushed the telephone away, yawned, and stretched, felt his bruised temple, looked at his watch, and rolled and lighted a cigarette. He smoked sleepily until Effie Perine came in.

Effie Perine came in smiling, bright-eyed and rosy-faced. "Ted says it could be," she reported, "and he hopes it is. He says he's not a specialist in that field, but the names and dates are all right, and at least none of your authorities or their works are out-and-out fakes. He's all excited over it."

"That's swell, as long as he doesn't get too enthusiastic to see through it if it's phoney."

"Oh, he wouldn't – not Ted! He's too good at his stuff for that."

"Uh-huh, the whole damned Perine family's wonderful," Spade said, "including you and the smudge of soot on your nose."

"He's not a Perine, he's a Christy." She bent her head to look at her nose in her vanity-case-mirror. "I must've got that from the fire." She scrubbed the smudge with the corner of a handkerchief.

"The Perine-Christy enthusiasm ignite Berkeley?" he asked.

She made a face at him while patting her nose with a powdered pink disc. "There was a boat on fire when I came back. They were towing it out from the pier and the smoke blew all over our ferry-boat."

Spade put his hands on the arms of his chair. "Were you near enough to see the name of the boat?" he asked.

"Yes. *La Paloma*. Why?"

Spade smiled ruefully. "I'm damned if I know why, sister," he said.

15   EVERY CRACKPOT

SPADE AND DETECTIVE-SERGEANT Polhaus ate pickled pigs' feet at one of big John's tables at the States Hof Brau.

Polhaus, balancing pale bright jelly on a fork half-way between plate and mouth, said: "Hey, listen, Sam! Forget about the other night. He was dead wrong, but you know anybody's liable to lose their head if you ride them thataway."

Spade looked thoughtfully at the police-detective. "Was that what you wanted to see me about?" he asked.

Polhaus nodded, put the forkful of jelly into his mouth, swallowed it, and qualified his nod: "Mostly."

"Dundy send you?"

Polhaus made a disgusted mouth. "You know he didn't. He's as bullheaded as you are."

Spade smiled and shook his head. "No, he's not, Tom," he said. "He just thinks he is."

Tom scowled and chopped at his pig's foot with a knife. "Ain't you ever going to grow up?" he grumbled. "What've you got to beef about? He didn't hurt you. You came out on top. What's the sense of making a grudge of it? You're just making a lot of grief for yourself."

Spade placed his knife and fork carefully together on his plate, and put his hands on the table beside his plate. His smile was faint and devoid of warmth. "With every bull in town working overtime trying to pile up grief for me a little more won't hurt. I won't even know it's there."

Polhaus's ruddiness deepened. He said: "That's a swell thing to say to me."

Spade picked up his knife and fork and began to eat. Polhaus ate.

Presently Spade asked: "See the boat on fire in the bay?"

"I saw the smoke. Be reasonable, Sam. Dundy was wrong and he knows it. Why don't you let it go at that?"

"Think I ought to go around and tell him I hope my chin didn't hurt his fist?"

Polhaus cut savagely into his pig's foot.

Spade said: "Phil Archer been in with any more hot tips?"

"Aw, hell! Dundy didn't think you shot Miles, but what else could he do except run the lead down? You'd've done the same thing in his place, and you know it."

"Yes?" Malice glittered in Spade's eyes. "What made him think I didn't do it? What makes you think I didn't? Or don't you?"

Polhaus's ruddy face flushed again. He said: "Thursby shot Miles."

"You think he did."

"He did. That Webley was his, and the slug in Miles came out of it."

"Sure?" Spade demanded.

"Dead sure," the police-detective replied. "We got hold of a kid – a bellhop at Thursby's hotel – that had seen it in his room just that morning. He noticed it particular because he'd never saw one just like it before. I never saw one. You say they don't make them any more. It ain't likely there'd be another around and – anyway – if that wasn't Thursby's what happened to his? And that's the gun the slug in Miles come out of." He started to put a piece of bread into his mouth, withdrew it, and asked:

"You say you've seen them before: where was that at?" He put the bread into his mouth.

"In England before the war."

"Sure, there you are."

Spade nodded and said: "Then that leaves Thursby the only one I killed."

Polhaus squirmed in his chair and his face was red and shiny. "Christ's sake, ain't you never going to forget that?" he complained earnestly. "That's out. You know it as well as I do. You'd think you wasn't a dick yourself the way you bellyache over things. I suppose you don't never pull the same stuff on anybody that we pulled on you?"

"You mean that you tried to pull on me, Tom – just tried."

Polhaus swore under his breath and attacked the remainder of his pig's foot.

Spade said: "All right. You know it's out and I know it's out. What does Dundy know?"

"He knows it's out."

"What woke him up?"

"Aw, Sam, he never really thought you'd –" Spade's smile checked Polhaus. He left the sentence incomplete and said: "We dug up a record on Thursby."

"Yes? Who was he?"

Polhaus's shrewd small brown eyes studied Spade's face. Spade exclaimed irritably: "I wish to God I knew half as much about this business as you smart guys think I do!"

"I wish we all did," Polhaus grumbled. "Well, he was a St. Louis gunman the first we hear of him. He was picked up a lot of times back there for this and that, but he belonged to the Egan mob, so nothing much was ever done about any of it. I don't know howcome he left that shelter, but they got him once in New York for knocking over a row of stuss-games – his twist turned him up – and he was in a year before Fallon got him sprung. A couple of years later he did a short hitch in Joliet for pistol-whipping another twist that had given him the needle, but after that he took up with Dixie Monahan and didn't have any trouble getting out whenever he happened to get in. That was when Dixie was almost as big a shot as Nick the Greek in Chicago gambling. This Thursby was Dixie's bodyguard and he took the run-out with him when Dixie got in wrong with the rest of the boys over some debts he couldn't or wouldn't pay off. That was a couple of years back – about the time the Newport Beach Boating Club was shut up. I don't know if Dixie had any part in that. Anyways, this is the first time him or Thursby's been seen since."

"Dixie's been seen?" Spade asked.

Polhaus shook his head. "No." His small eyes became sharp, prying. "Not unless you've seen him or know somebody's seen him."

Spade lounged back in his chair and began to make a cigarette. "I haven't," he said mildly. "This is all new stuff to me."

"I guess it is," Polhaus snorted.

Spade grinned at him and asked: "Where'd you pick up all this news about Thursby?"

"Some of it's on the records. The rest – well – we got it here and there."

"From Cairo, for instance?" Now Spade's eyes held the prying gleam.

Polhaus put down his coffee-cup and shook his head. "Not a word of it. You poisoned that guy for us."

Spade laughed. "You mean a couple of high-class sleuths like you and Dundy worked on that lily-of-the-valley all night and couldn't crack him?"

"What do you mean – all night?" Polhaus protested. "We worked on him for less than a couple of hours. We saw we wasn't getting nowhere, and let him go."

Spade laughed again and looked at his watch. He caught John's eye and asked for the check. "I've got a date with the D.A. this afternoon," he told Polhaus while they waited for his change.

"He send for you?"

"Yes."

Polhaus pushed his chair back and stood up, a barrel-bellied tall man, solid and phlegmatic. "You won't be doing me any favor," he said, "by telling him I've talked to you like this."

A lathy youth with salient ears ushered Spade into the District Attorney's office. Spade went in smiling easily, saying easily: "Hello, Bryan!"

District Attorney Bryan stood up and held his hand out across his desk. He was a blond man of medium stature, perhaps forty-five years old, with aggressive blue eyes behind black-ribboned nose-glasses, the over-large mouth of an orator, and a wide dimpled chin. When he said, "How do you do, Spade?" his voice was resonant with latent power.

They shook hands and sat down.

The District Attorney put his finger on one of the pearl buttons in a battery of four on his desk, said to the lathy youth who opened the door again, "Ask Mr. Thomas and Healy to come in," and then, rocking back in his chair, addressed Spade pleasantly: "You and the police haven't been hitting it off so well, have you?"

Spade made a negligent gesture with the fingers of his right hand. "Nothing serious," he said lightly. "Dundy gets too enthusiastic."

The door opened to admit two men. The one to whom Spade said, "Hello, Thomas!" was a sunburned stocky man of thirty in clothing and hair of a kindred unruliness. He clapped Spade on the shoulder with a freckled hand, asked, "How's tricks?" and sat down beside him. The second man was younger and colorless. He took a seat a little apart from the others and balanced a stenographer's notebook on his knee, holding a green pencil over it.

Spade glanced his way, chuckled, and asked Bryan: "Anything I say will be used against me?"

The District Attorney smiled. "That always holds good." He took his glasses off, looked at them, and set them on his nose again. He looked through them at Spade and asked: "Who killed Thursby?"

Spade said: "I don't know."

Bryan rubbed his black eyeglass-ribbon between thumb and fingers and said knowingly: "Perhaps you don't, but you certainly could make an excellent guess."

"Maybe, but I wouldn't."

The District Attorney raised his eyebrows.

"I wouldn't," Spade repeated. He was serene. "My guess might be excellent, or it might be crummy, but Mrs. Spade didn't raise any children dippy enough to make guesses in front of a district attorney, an assistant district attorney, and a stenographer."

"Why shouldn't you, if you've nothing to conceal?"

"Everybody," Spade responded mildly, "has something to conceal."

"And you have – ?"

"My guesses, for one thing."

The District Attorney looked down at his desk and then up at Spade. He settled his glasses more firmly on his nose. He said: "If you'd prefer not having the stenographer here we can dismiss him. It was simply as a matter of convenience that I brought him in."

"I don't mind him a damned bit," Spade replied. "I'm willing to have anything I say put down and I'm willing to sign it."

"We don't intend asking you to sign anything," Bryan assured him. "I wish you wouldn't regard this as a formal inquiry at all. And please don't think I've any belief – much less confidence – in those theories the police seem to have formed."

"No?"

"Not a particle."

Spade sighed and crossed his legs. "I'm glad of that." He felt in his pockets for tobacco and papers. "What's your theory?"

Bryan leaned forward in his chair and his eyes were hard and shiny as the lenses over them. "Tell me who Archer was shadowing Thursby for and I'll tell you who killed Thursby."

Spade's laugh was brief and scornful. "You're as wrong as Dundy," he said.

"Don't misunderstand me, Spade," Bryan said, knocking on the desk with his knuckles. "I don't say your client killed Thursby or had him killed, but I do say that, knowing who your client is, or was, I'll mighty soon know who killed Thursby."

Spade lighted his cigarette, removed it from his lips, emptied his lungs of smoke, and spoke as if puzzled: "I don't exactly get that."

"You don't? Then suppose I put it this way: where is Dixie Monahan?"

Spade's face retained its puzzled look. "Putting it that way doesn't help much," he said. "I still don't get it."

The District Attorney took his glasses off and shook them for emphasis. He said: "We know Thursby was Monahan's bodyguard and went with him when Monahan found it wise to vanish from Chicago. We know Monahan welshed on something like two-hundred-thousand-dollars' worth of bets when he vanished. We don't know – not yet – who his creditors were." He put the glasses on again and smiled grimly. "But we all know what's likely to happen to a gambler who welshes, and to his bodyguard, when his creditors find him. It's happened before."

Spade ran his tongue over his lips and pulled his lips back over his teeth in an ugly grin. His eyes glittered under pulled-down brows. His reddening neck bulged over the rim of his collar. His voice was low and hoarse and passionate. "Well, what do you think? Did I kill him for his creditors? Or just find him and let them do their own killing?"

"No, no!" the District Attorney protested. "You misunder-stand me."

"I hope to Christ I do," Spade said.

"He didn't mean that," Thomas said.

"Then what did he mean?"

Bryan waved a hand. "I only mean that you might have been involved in it without knowing what it was. That could – "

"I see," Spade sneered. "You don't think I'm naughty. You just think I'm dumb."

"Nonsense," Bryan insisted: "Suppose someone came to you and engaged you to find Monahan, telling you they had reasons for thinking he was in the city. The someone might give you a completely false story – any one of a dozen or more would do – or might say he was a debtor who had run away, without giving you any of the details. How could you tell what was behind it? How would you know it wasn't an ordinary piece of detective work? And under those circumstances you certainly couldn't be held responsible for your part in it unless" – his voice sank to a more impressive key and his words came out spaced and distinct – "you made yourself an accomplice by concealing your knowledge of the murderer's identity or information that would lead to his apprehension."

Anger was leaving Spade's face. No anger remained in his voice when he asked: "That's what you meant?"

"Precisely."

"All right. Then there's no hard feelings. But you're wrong."

"Prove it."

Spade shook his head. "I can't prove it to you now. I can tell you."

"Then tell me."

"Nobody ever hired me to do anything about Dixie Monahan."

Bryan and Thomas exchanged glances. Bryan's eyes came back to Spade and he said: "But, by your own admission, somebody did hire you to do something about his bodyguard Thursby."

"Yes, about his ex-bodyguard Thursby."

"Ex?"

"Yes, ex."

"You know that Thursby was no longer associated with Monahan? You know that positively?"

Spade stretched out his hand and dropped the stub of his cigarette into an ashtray on the desk. He spoke carelessly: "I don't know anything positively except that my client wasn't interested in Monahan, had never been interested in Monahan. I heard that Thursby took Monahan out to the Orient and lost him."

Again the District Attorney and his assistant exchanged glances.

Thomas, in a tone whose matter-of-factness did not quite hide excitement, said: "That opens another angle. Monahan's friends could have knocked Thursby off for ditching Monahan."

"Dead gamblers don't have any friends," Spade said.

"It opens up two new lines," Bryan said. He leaned back and stared at the ceiling for several seconds, then sat upright quickly. His orator's face was alight. "It narrows down to three things. Number one: Thursby was killed by the gamblers Monahan had welshed on in Chicago. Not knowing Thursby had sloughed Monahan – or not believing it – they killed him because he had been Monahan's associate, or to get him out of the way so they could get to Monahan, or because he had refused to lead them to Monahan. Number two: he was killed by friends of Monahan. Or number three: he sold Monahan out to his enemies and then fell out with them and they killed him."

"Or number four," Spade suggested with a cheerful smile: "he died of old age. You folks aren't serious, are you?"

The two men stared at Spade, but neither of them spoke. Spade turned his smile from one to the other of them and shook his head in mock pity. "You've got Arnold Rothstein on the brain," he said.

Bryan smacked the back of his left hand down into the palm of his right. "In one of those three catagories lies the solution." The power in his voice was no longer latent. His right hand, a fist except for protruding forefinger, went up and then down to stop with a jerk when the finger was leveled at Spade's chest. "And you can give us the information that will enable us to determine the category."

Spade said, "Yes?" very lazily. His face was somber. He touched his lower lip with a finger, looked at the finger, and then scratched the back of his neck with it. Little irritable lines had appeared in his forehead. He blew his breath out heavily through his nose and his voice was an ill-humored growl. "You wouldn't want the kind of information I could give you, Bryan. You couldn't use it. It'd poop this gambler's-revenge-scenario for you."

Bryan sat up straight and squared his shoulders. His voice was stern without blustering. "You are not the judge of that. Right or wrong, I am nonetheless the District Attorney."

Spade's lifted lip showed his eyetooth. "I thought this was an informal talk."

"I am a sworn officer of the law twenty-four hours a day," Bryan said, "and neither formality nor informality justifies your withholding from me evidence of crime, except of course" – he nodded meaningly – "on certain constitutional grounds."

"You mean if it might incriminate me?" Spade asked. His voice was placid, almost amused, but his face was not. "Well, I've got better grounds than that, or grounds that suit me better. My clients are entitled to a decent amount of secrecy. Maybe I can be made to talk to a Grand Jury or even a Coroner's Jury, but I haven't been called before either yet, and it's a cinch I'm not going to advertise my clients' business until I have to. Then again, you and the police have both accused me of being mixed up in the other night's murders. I've had trouble with both of you before. As far as I can see, my best chance of clearing myself of the trouble you're trying to make for me is by bringing in the murderers – all tied up. And my only chance of ever catching them and tying them up and bringing them in is by keeping away from you and the police, because neither of you show any signs of knowing what in hell it's all about." He rose and turned his head over his shoulder to address the stenographer: "Getting this all right, son? Or am I going too fast for you?"

The stenographer looked at him with startled eyes and replied: "No, sir, I'm getting it all right."

"Good work," Spade said and turned to Bryan again. "Now if you want to go to the Board and tell them I'm obstructing justice and ask them to revoke my license, hop to it. You've tried it before and it didn't get you anything but a good laugh all around." He picked up his hat.

Bryan began: "But look here – "

Spade said: "And I don't want any more of these informal talks. I've got nothing to tell you or the police and I'm God-damned tired of being called things by every crackpot on the city payroll. If you want to see me, pinch me or subpoena me or something and I'll come down with my lawyer." He put his hat on his head, said, "See you at the inquest, maybe," and stalked out.

SPADE WENT INTO the Hotel Sutter and telephoned the Alexandria. Gutman was not in. No member of Gutman's party was in. Spade telephoned the Belvedere. Cairo was not in, had not been in that day.

Spade went to his office.

A swart greasy man in notable clothes was waiting in the outer room. Effie Perine, indicating the swart man, said: "This gentleman wishes to see you, Mr. Spade."

Spade smiled and bowed and opened the inner door. "Come in." Before following the man in Spade asked Effie Perine: "Any news on that other matter?"

"No, sir."

The swart man was the proprietor of a moving-picture-theater in Market Street. He suspected one of his cashiers and a doorman of colluding to defraud him. Spade hurried him through the story, promised to "take care of it," asked for and received fifty dollars, and got rid of him in less than half an hour.

When the corridor-door had closed behind the showman Effie Perine came into the inner office. Her sunburned face was worried and questioning. "You haven't found her yet?" she asked.

He shook his head and went on stroking his bruised temple lightly in circles with his fingertips.

"How is it?" she asked.

"All right, but I've got plenty of headache."

She went around behind him, put his hand down, and stroked his temple with her slender fingers. He leaned back until the back of his head over the chair-top rested against her breast. He said: "You're an angel."

She bent her head forward over his and looked down into his face. "You've got to find her, Sam. It's more than a day and she – "

He stirred and impatiently interrupted her: "I haven't got to do anything, but if you'll let me rest this damned head a minute or two I'll go out and find her."

She murmured, "Poor head," and stroked it in silence awhile. Then she asked: "You know where she is? Have you any idea?"

The telephone-bell rang. Spade picked up the telephone and said: "Hello.... Yes, Sid, it came out all right, thanks. ... No.... Sure. He got snotty, but so did I.... He's nursing a gambler's-war pipe-dream.... Well, we didn't kiss when we parted. I declared my weight and walked out on him.... That's something for you to worry about.... Right. 'Bye." He put the telephone down and leaned back in his chair again.

Effie Perine came from behind him and stood at his side. She demanded: "Do you think you know where she is, Sam?"

"I know where she went," he replied in a grudging tone.

"Where?" She was excited.

"Down to the boat you saw burning."

Her eyes opened until their brown was surrounded by white. "You went down there." It was not a question.

"I did not," Spade said.

"Sam," she cried angrily, "she may be – "

"She went down there," he said in a surly voice. "She wasn't taken. She went down there instead of to your house when she learned the boat was in. Well, what the hell? Am I supposed to run around after my clients begging them to let me help them?"

"But, Sam, when I told you the boat was on fire!"

"That was at noon and I had a date with Polhaus and another with Bryan."

She glared at him between tightened lids. "Sam Spade," she said, "you're the most contemptible man God ever made when you want to be. Because she did something without confiding in you you'd sit here and do nothing when you know she's in danger, when you know she might be – "

Spade's face flushed. He said stubbornly: "She's pretty capable of taking care of herself and she knows where to come for help when she thinks she needs it, and when it suits her."

"That's spite," the girl cried, "and that's all it is! You're sore because she did something on her own hook, without telling you. Why shouldn't she? You're not so damned honest, and you haven't been so much on the level with her, that she should trust you completely."

Spade said: "That's enough of that."

His tone brought a brief uneasy glint into her hot eyes, but she tossed her head and the glint vanished. Her mouth was drawn taut and small. She said: "If you don't go down there this very minute, Sam, I will and I'll take the police down there." Her voice trembled, broke, and was thin and wailing. "Oh, Sam, go!"

He stood up cursing her. Then he said: "Christ! It'll be easier on my head than sitting here listening to you squawk." He looked at his watch. "You might as well lock up and go home."

She said: "I won't. I'm going to wait right here till you come back."

He said, "Do as you damned please," put his hat on, flinched, took it off, and went out carrying it in his hand.

An hour and a half later, at twenty minutes past five, Spade returned. He was cheerful. He came in asking: "What makes you so hard to get along with, sweetheart?"

"Me?"

"Yes, you." He put a finger on the tip of Effie Perine's nose and flattened it. He put his hands under her elbows, lifted her straight up, and kissed her chin. He set her down on the floor again and asked: "Anything doing while I was gone?"

"Luke – what's his name? – at the Belvedere called up to tell you Cairo has returned. That was about half an hour ago."

Spade snapped his mouth shut, turned with a long step, and started for the door.

"Did you find her?" the girl called.

"Tell you about it when I'm back," he replied without pausing and hurried out.

A taxicab brought Spade to the Belvedere within ten minutes of his departure from his office. He found Luke in the lobby. The hotel-detective came grinning and shaking his head to meet Spade. "Fifteen minutes late," he said. "Your bird has fluttered."

Spade cursed his luck.

"Checked out – gone bag and baggage," Luke said. He took a battered memorandum-book from a vest-pocket, licked his thumb, thumbed pages, and held the book out open to Spade. "There's the number of the taxi that hauled him. I got that much for you."

"Thanks." Spade copied the number on the back of an envelope. "Any forwarding address?"

"No. He just come in carrying a big suitcase and went upstairs and packed and come down with his stuff and paid his bill and got a taxi and went without anybody being able to hear what he told the driver."

"How about his trunk?"

Luke's lower lip sagged. "By God," he said, "I forgot that! Come on."

They went up to Cairo's room. The trunk was there. It was closed, but not locked. They raised the lid. The trunk was empty.

Luke said: "What do you know about that!"

Spade did not say anything.

Spade went back to his office. Effie Perine looked up at him, inquisitively.

"Missed him," Spade grumbled and passed into his private room.

She followed him in. He sat in his chair and began to roll a cigarette. She sat on the desk in front of him and put her toes on a corner of his chair-seat.

"What about Miss O'Shaughnessy?" she demanded.

"I missed her too," he replied, "but she had been there."

"On the *La Paloma*?"

"*The La* is a lousy combination," he said.

"Stop it. Be nice, Sam. Tell me."

He set fire to his cigarette, pocketed his lighter, patted her shins, and said: "Yes, *La Paloma*. She got down there at a little after noon yesterday." He pulled his brows down. "That means she went straight there after leaving the cab at the Ferry Building. It's only a few piers away. The Captain wasn't aboard. His name's Jacobi and she asked for him by name. He was uptown on business. That would mean he didn't expect her, or not at that time anyway. She waited there till he came back at four o'clock. They spent the time from then till meal-time in his cabin and she ate with him."

He inhaled and exhaled smoke, turned his head aside to spit a yellow tobacco-flake off his lip, and went on: "After the meal Captain Jacobi had three more visitors. One of them was Gutman and one was Cairo and one was the kid who delivered Gutman's message to you yesterday. Those three came together while Brigid was there and the five of them did a lot of talking in the Captain's cabin. It's hard to get anything out of the crew, but they had a row and somewhere around eleven o'clock that night a gun went off there, in the Captain's cabin. The watchman beat it down there, but the

Captain met him outside and told him everything was all right. There's a fresh bullet-hole in one corner of the cabin, up high enough to make it likely that the bullet didn't go through anybody to get there. As far as I could learn there was only the one shot. But as far as I could learn wasn't very far."

He scowled and inhaled smoke again. "Well, they left around midnight – the Captain and his four visitors all together – and all of them seem to have been walking all right. I got that from the watchman. I haven't been able to get hold of the Custom-Housemen who were on duty there then. That's all of it. The Captain hasn't been back since. He didn't keep a date he had this noon with some shipping-agents, and they haven't found him to tell him about the fire."

"And the fire?" she asked.

Spade shrugged. "I don't know. It was discovered in the hold, aft – in the rear basement – late this morning. The chances are it got started some time yesterday. They got it out all right, though it did damage enough. Nobody liked to talk about it much while the Captain's away. It's the – "

The corridor-door opened. Spade shut his mouth. Effie Perine jumped down from the desk, but a man opened the connecting door before she could reach it.

"Where's Spade?" the man asked.

His voice brought Spade up erect and alert in his chair. It was a voice harsh and rasping with agony and with the strain of keeping two words from being smothered by the liquid bubbling that ran under and behind them.

Effie Perine, frightened, stepped out of the man's way.

He stood in the doorway with his soft hat crushed between his head and the top of the door-frame: he was nearly seven feet tall. A black overcoat cut long and straight and like a sheath, buttoned from throat to knees, exaggerated his leanness. His shoulders stuck out, high, thin, angular. His bony face – weather-coarsened, age-lined – was the color of wet sand and was wet with sweat on cheeks and chin. His eyes were dark and bloodshot and mad above lower lids that hung down to show pink inner membrane. Held tight against the left side of his chest by a black-sleeved arm that ended in a yellowish claw was a brown-paper-wrapped parcel bound with thin rope – an ellipsoid somewhat larger than an American football.

The tall man stood in the doorway and there was nothing to show that he saw Spade. He said, "You know – " and then the liquid bubbling came up in his throat and submerged whatever else he said. He put his other hand over the hand that held the ellipsoid. Holding himself stiffly straight, not putting his hands out to break his fall, he fell forward as a tree falls.

Spade, wooden-faced and nimble, sprang from his chair and caught the falling man. When Spade caught him the man's mouth opened and a little blood spurted out, and the brown-wrapped parcel dropped from the man's hands and rolled across the floor until a foot of the desk stopped it. Then the man's knees bent and he bent at the waist and his thin body became limber inside the sheath-like overcoat, sagging in Spade's arms so that Spade could not hold it up from the floor.

Spade lowered the man carefully until he lay on the floor on his left side. The man's eyes – dark and bloodshot, but not now mad – were wide open and still. His mouth was open as when blood has spurted from it, but no more blood came from it, and all his long body was as still as the floor it lay on.

Spade said: "Lock the door."

While Effie Perine, her teeth chattering, fumbled with the corridor-door's lock Spade knelt beside the thin man, turned him over on his back, and ran a hand down inside his overcoat. When he withdrew the hand presently it came out smeared with blood. The sight of his bloody hand brought not the least nor briefest of changes to Spade's face. Holding that hand up where it would touch nothing, he took his lighter out of his pocket with his other hand. He snapped on the flame and held the flame close to first one and then the other of the thin man's eyes. The eyes – lids, balls, irises, and pupils – remained frozen, immobile.

Spade extinguished the flame and returned the lighter to his pocket. He moved on his knees around to the dead man's side and, using his one clean hand, unbuttoned and opened the tubular overcoat. The inside of the overcoat was wet with blood and the double-breasted blue jacket beneath it was sodden. The jacket's lapels, where they crossed over the man's chest, and both sides of his coat immediately below that point, were pierced by soggy ragged holes.

Spade rose and went to the wash-bowl in the outer office.

Effie Perine, wan and trembling and holding herself upright by means of a hand on the corridor-door's knob and her back against its glass, whispered: "Is – is he – ?"

"Yes. Shot through the chest, maybe half a dozen times." Spade began to wash his hands.

"Oughtn't we – ?" she began, but he cut her short: "It's too late for a doctor now and I've got to think before we do anything." He finished washing his hands and began to rinse the bowl. "He couldn't have come far with those in him. If he – Why in hell couldn't he had stood up long enough to say something?" He frowned at the girl, rinsed his hands again, and picked up a towel. "Pull yourself together. For Christ's sake don't get sick on me now!" He threw the towel down and ran fingers through his hair. "We'll have a look at that bundle."

He went into the inner office again, stepped over the dead man's legs, and picked up the brown-paper-wrapped parcel. When he felt its weight his eyes glowed. He put it on his desk, turning it over so that the knotted part of the rope was uppermost. The knot was hard and tight. He took out his pocket-knife and cut the rope.

The girl had left the door and, edging around the dead man with her face turned away, had come to Spade's side. As she stood there – hands on a corner of the desk – watching him pull the rope loose and push aside brown paper, excitement began to supplant nausea in her face. "Do you think it is?" she whispered.

"We'll soon know," Spade said, his big fingers busy with the inner husk of coarse gray paper, three sheets thick, that the brown paper's removal had revealed. His face was hard and dull. His eyes were shining. When he had put the gray paper out of the way he had an egg-shaped mass of pale excelsior, wadded tight. His fingers tore the wad apart and then he had the foot-high figure of a bird, black as coal and shiny where its polish was not dulled by wood-dust and fragments of excelsior.

Spade laughed. He put a hand down on the bird. His widespread fingers had ownership in their curving. He put his other arm around Effie Perine and crushed her body against his. "We've got the damned thing, angel," he said.

"Ouch!" she said, "you're hurting me."

He took his arm away from her, picked the black bird up in both hands, and shook it to dislodge clinging excelsior. Then he stepped back holding it up in front of him and blew dust off it, regarding it triumphantly.

Effie Perine made a horrified face and screamed, pointing at his feet.

He looked down at his feet. His last backward step had brought his left heel into contact with the dead man's hand, pinching a quarter-inch of flesh at a side of the palm between heel and floor. Spade jerked his foot away from the hand.

The telephone-bell rang.

He nodded at the girl. She turned to the desk and put the receiver to her ear. She said: "Hello.... Yes.... Who?... Oh, yes!" Her eyes became large. "Yes.... Yes.... Hold the line...." Her mouth suddenly stretched wide and fearful. She cried: "Hello! Hello! Hello!" She rattled the prong up and down and cried, "Hello!" twice. Then she sobbed and spun around to face Spade, who was close beside her by now. "It was Miss O'Shaughnessy," she said wildly. "She wants you. She's at the Alexandria – in danger. Her voice was – oh, it was awful, Sam! – and something happened to her before she could finish. Go help her, Sam!"

Spade put the falcon down on the desk and scowled gloomily. "I've got to take care of this fellow first," he said, pointing his thumb at the thin corpse on the floor.

She beat his chest with her fists, crying: "No, no – you've got to go to her. Don't you see, Sam? He had the thing that was hers and he came to you with it. Don't you see? He was helping her and they killed him and now she's – Oh, you've got to go!"

"All right." Spade pushed her away and bent over his desk, putting the back bird back into its nest of excelsior, bending the paper around it, working rapidly, making a larger and clumsy package. "As soon as I've gone phone the police. Tell them how it happened, but don't drag any names in. You don't know. I got the phone-call and I told you I had to go out, but I didn't say where." He cursed the rope for being tangled, yanked it into straightness, and began to bind the package. "Forget this thing. Tell it as it happened, but forget he had a bundle." He chewed his lower lip. "Unless they pin you down. If they seem to know about it you'll have to admit it. But that's not likely. If they do then I took the bundle away with me, unopened." He finished tying the knot and straightened up with the parcel under his left arm. "Get it straight, now. Everything happened the way it did happen, but without this dingus unless they already know about it. Don't deny it – just don't mention it. And I got the phone-call – not you. And you don't know anything about anybody else having any connection with this fellow. You don't know anything about him and you can't talk about my business until you see me. Got it?"

"Yes, Sam. Who – do you know who he is?"

He grinned wolfishly. "Uh-uh," he said, "but I'd guess he was Captain Jacobi, master of *La Paloma*." He picked up his hat and put it on. He looked thoughtfully at the dead man and then around the room.

THE MALTESE FALCON

"Hurry, Sam," the girl begged.

"Sure," he said absent-mindedly, "I'll hurry. Might not hurt to get those few scraps of excelsior off the floor before the police come. And maybe you ought to try to get hold of Sid. No." He rubbed his chin. "We'll leave him out of it awhile. It'll look better. I'd keep the door locked till they come." He took his hand from his chin and rubbed her cheek. "You're a damned good man, sister," he said and went out.

CARRYING THE PARCEL lightly under his arm, walking briskly, with only the ceaseless shifting of his eyes to denote wariness, Spade went, partly by way of an alley and a narrow court, from his office-building to Kearny and Post Streets, where he hailed a passing taxicab.

The taxicab carried him to the Pickwick Stage terminal in Fifth Street. He checked the bird at the Parcel Room there, put the check into a stamped envelope, wrote *M. F. Holland* and a San Francisco Post Office box-number on the envelope, sealed it, and dropped it into a mail-box. From the stage-terminal another taxicab carried him to the Alexandria Hotel.

Spade went up to suite 12-C and knocked on the door. The door was opened, when he had knocked a second time, by a small fair-haired girl in a shimmering yellow dressing-gown – a small girl whose face was white and dim and who clung desperately to the inner doorknob with both hands and gasped: "Mr. Spade?"

Spade said, "Yes," and caught her as she swayed.

Her body arched back over his arm and her head dropped straight back so that her short fair hair hung down her scalp and her slender throat was a firm curve from chin to chest.

Spade slid his supporting arm higher up her back and bent to get his other arm under her knees, but she stirred then, resisting, and between parted lips that barely moved blurred words came: "No! Ma' me wa'!"

Spade made her walk. He kicked the door shut and he walked her up and down the green-carpeted room from wall to wall. One of his arms around her small body, that hand under her armpit, his other hand gripping her other arm, held her erect when she stumbled, checked her swaying, kept urging her forward, but made her tottering legs bear all her weight they could bear. They walked across and across the floor, the girl falteringly, with incoordinate steps, Spade surely on the balls of his feet with balance unaffected by her staggering. Her face was chalk-white and eyeless, his sullen, with eyes hardened to watch everywhere at once.

He talked to her monotonously: "That's the stuff. Left, right, left, right. That's the stuff. One, two, three, four, one, two, three, now we turn." He shook her as they turned from the wall. "Now back again. One, two, three, four. Hold your head up. That's the stuff. Good girl. Left, right, left, right. Now we turn again." He shook her again. "That's the girl. Walk, walk, walk, walk. One, two, three, four. Now we go around." He shook her, more roughly, and increased their pace. "That's the trick. Left, right, left, right. We're in a hurry. One, two, three. . . ."

She shuddered and swallowed audibly. Spade began to chafe her arm and side and he put his mouth nearer her ear. "That's fine. You're doing fine. One, two, three, four. Faster, faster, faster, faster. That's it. Step, step, step, step. Pick them up and lay them down. That's the stuff. Now we turn. Left, right, left, right. What'd they do – dope you? The same stuff they gave me?"

Her eyelids twitched up then for an instant over dulled golden-brown eyes and she managed to say all of "Yes" except the final consonant.

They walked the floor, the girl almost trotting now to keep up with Spade, Spade slapping and kneading her flesh through yellow silk with both hands, talking and talking while his eyes remained hard and aloof and watchful. "Left, right, left, right, left, right, turn. That's the girl. One, two, three, four, one, two, three, four. Keep the chin up. That's the stuff. One, two. . . ."

Her lids lifted again a bare fraction of an inch and under them her eyes moved weakly from side to side.

"That's fine," he said in a crisp voice, dropping his monotone. "Keep them open. Open them wide – wide!" He shook her.

She moaned in protest, but her lids went farther up, though her eyes were without inner light. He raised his hand and slapped her cheek half a dozen times in quick succession. She moaned again and tried to break away from him. His arm held her and swept her along beside him from wall to wall.

"Keep walking," he ordered in a harsh voice, and then: "Who are you?"

Her "Rhea Gutman" was thick but intelligible.

"The daughter?"

"Yes." Now she was no farther from the final consonant than *sh*.

"Where's Brigid?"

She twisted convulsively around in his arms and caught at one of his hands with both of hers. He pulled his hand away quickly and looked at it. Across its back was a thin red scratch an inch and a half or more in length.

"What the hell?" he growled and examined her hands. Her left hand was empty. In her right hand, when he forced it open, lay a three-inch jade-headed steel bouquet-pin. "What the hell?" he growled again and held the pin up in front of her eyes.

When she saw the pin she whimpered and opened her dressing-gown. She pushed aside the cream-colored pajama-coat under it and showed him her body below her left breast – white flesh criss-crossed with thin red lines, dotted with tiny red dots, where the pin had scratched and punctured it. "To stay awake...walk...till you came.... She said you'd come...were so long." She swayed.

Spade tightened his arm around her and said: "Walk."

She fought against his arm, squirming around to face him again. "No...tell you...sleep...save her..."

"Brigid?" he demanded.

"Yes . . . took her . . . Bur–Burlingame . . . twenty-six Ancho . . . hurry . . . too late . . ." Her head fell over on her shoulder.

Spade pushed her head up roughly. "Who took her there? Your father?"

"Yes . . . Wilmer . . . Cairo." She writhed and her eyelids twitched but did not open. ". . . kill her." Her head fell over again, and again he pushed it up.

"Who shot Jacobi?"

She did not seem to hear the question. She tried pitifully to hold her head up, to open her eyes. She mumbled: "Go . . . she . . . "

He shook her brutally. "Stay awake till the doctor comes."

Fear opened her eyes and pushed for a moment the cloudiness from her face. "No, no," she cried thickly, "father . . . kill me . . . swear you won't . . . he'd know . . . I did . . . for her . . . promise . . . won't . . . sleep . . . all right . . . morning . . ."

He shook her again. "You're sure you can sleep the stuff off all right?"

"Ye'." Her head fell down again.

"Where's your bed?"

She tried to raise a hand, but the effort had become too much for her before the hand pointed at anything except the carpet. With the sight of a tired child she let her whole body relax and crumple.

Spade caught her up in his arms – scooped her up as she sank – and, holding her easily against his chest, went to the nearest of the three doors. He turned the knob far enough to release the catch, pushed the door open with his foot, and went into a passageway that ran past an open bathroom-door to a bedroom. He looked into the bathroom, saw it was empty, and carried the girl into the bedroom. Nobody was there. The clothing that was in sight and things on the chiffonier said it was a man's room.

Spade carried the girl back to the green-carpeted room and tried the opposite door. Through it he passed into another passageway, past another empty bathroom, and into a bedroom that was feminine in its accessories. He turned back the bedclothes and laid the girl on the bed, removed her slippers, raised her a little to slide the yellow dressing-gown off, fixed a pillow under her head, and put the covers up over her.

Then he opened the room's two windows and stood with his back to them staring at the sleeping girl. Her breathing was heavy but not troubled. He frowned and looked around, working his lips together. Twilight was dimming the room. He stood there in the weakening light for perhaps five minutes. Finally he shook his thick sloping shoulders impatiently and went out, leaving the suite's outer door unlocked.

Spade went to the Pacific Telephone and Telegraph Company's station in Powell Street and called Davenport 2020. "Emergency Hospital, please. . . . Hello, there's a girl in suite twelve C at the Alexandria Hotel who has been drugged. . . . Yes, you'd better send somebody to take a look at her. . . . This is Mr. Hooper of the Alexandria."

He put the receiver on its prong and laughed. He called another number and said: "Hello, Frank. This is Sam Spade. . . . Can you let me have a car with a driver who'll keep his mouth shut? . . . To go down the peninsula right away. . . . Just a couple of hours. . . . Right. Have him pick me up at John's, Ellis Street, as soon as he can make it."

He called another number – his office's – held the receiver to his ear for a little while without saying anything, and replaced it on its hook.

He went to John's Grill, asked the waiter to hurry his order of chops, baked potato, and sliced tomatoes, ate hurriedly, and was smoking a cigarette with his coffee when a thick-set youngish man with a plaid cap set askew above pale eyes and a tough cheery face came into the Grill and to his table.

"All set, Mr. Spade. She's full of gas and rearing to go."

"Swell." Spade emptied his cup and went out with the thick-set man. "Know where Ancho Avenue, or Road, or Boulevard, is in Burlingame?"

"Nope, but if she's there we can find her."

"Let's do that," Spade said as he sat beside the chauffeur in the dark Cadillac sedan. "Twenty-six is the number we want, and the sooner the better, but we don't want to pull up at the front door."

"Correct."

They rode half a dozen blocks in silence. The chauffeur said: "Your partner got knocked off, didn't he, Mr. Spade?"

"Uh-huh."

The chauffeur clucked. "She's a tough racket. You can have it for mine."

"Well, hack-drivers don't live forever."

"Maybe that's right," the thick-set man conceded, "but, just the same, it'll always be a surprise to me if I don't."

Spade stared ahead at nothing and thereafter, until the chauffeur tired of making conversation, replied with uninterested yeses and noes.

At a drug-store in Burlingame the chauffeur learned how to reach Ancho Avenue. Ten minutes later he stopped the sedan near a dark corner, turned off the lights, and waved his hand at the block ahead. "There she is," he said. "She ought to be on the other side, maybe the third or fourth house."

Spade said, "Right," and got out of the car. "Keep the engine going. We may have to leave in a hurry."

He crossed the street and went up the other side. Far ahead a lone street-light burned. Warmer lights dotted the night on either side where houses were spaced half a dozen to a block. A high thin moon was cold and feeble as the distant street-light. A radio droned through the open windows of a house on the other side of the street.

In front of the second house from the corner Spade halted. On one of the gateposts that were massive out of all proportion to the fence flanking them a 2 and a 6 of pale metal caught what light there was. A square white card was nailed over them. Putting his face close to the card, Spade could see that it was a *For Sale or Rent* sign. There was no gate between the posts. Spade went up the cement walk to the house. He stood still on the walk at the foot of the porch-steps for a long moment. No sound came from the house. The house was dark except for another pale square card nailed on its door.

Spade went up to the door and listened. He could hear nothing. He tried to look through the glass of the door. There was no curtain to keep his gaze out, but inner darkness. He tiptoed to a window and then to another. They, like the door, were uncurtained except by inner darkness. He tried both windows. They were locked. He tried the door. It was locked.

He left the porch and, stepping carefully over dark unfamiliar ground, walked through weeds around the house. The side-windows were too high to be reached from the ground. The back door and the one back window he could reach were locked.

Spade went back to the gatepost and, cupping the flame between his hands, held his lighter up to the *For Sale or Rent* sign. It bore the printed name and address of a San Mateo real-estate-dealer and a line penciled in blue: *Key at 31*.

Spade returned to the sedan and asked the chauffeur: "Got a flashlight?"

"Sure." He gave it to Spade. "Can I give you a hand at anything?"

"Maybe." Spade got into the sedan. "We'll ride up to number thirty-one. You can use your lights."

Number 31 was a square grey house across the street from, but a little farther up than, 26. Lights glowed in its downstairs-windows. Spade went up on the porch and rang the bell. A dark-haired girl of fourteen or fifteen opened the door. Spade, bowing and smiling, said: "I'd like to get the key to number twenty-six."

"I'll call Papa," she said and went back into the house calling: "Papa!"

A plump red-faced man, bald-headed and heavily mustached, appeared, carrying a newspaper.

Spade said: "I'd like to get the key to twenty-six."

The plump man looked more doubtful. He said: "The juice is not on. You couldn't see anything."

Spade patted his pocket. "I've a flashlight."

The plump man looked more doubtful. He cleared his throat uneasily and crumpled the newspaper in his hand.

Spade showed him one of his business-cards, put it back in his pocket, and said in a low voice: "We got a tip that there might be something hidden there."

The plump man's face and voice were eager. "Wait a minute," he said. "I'll go over with you."

A moment later he came back carrying a brass key attached to a black and red tag. Spade beckoned to the chauffeur as they passed the car and the chauffeur joined them.

"Anybody been looking at the house lately?" Spade asked.

"Not that I know of," the plump man replied. "Nobody's been to me for the key in a couple of months."

The plump man marched ahead with the key until they had gone up on the porch. Then he thrust the key into Spade's hand, mumbled, "Here you are," and stepped aside.

Spade unlocked the door and pushed it open. There was silence and darkness. Holding the flashlight – dark – in his left hand, Spade entered. The chauffeur came close behind him and then, at a little distance, the plump man followed them. They searched the house from bottom to top, cautiously at first, then, finding nothing, boldly. The house was empty – unmistakably – and there was nothing to indicate that it had been visited in weeks.

* * *

Saying, "Thanks, that's all," Spade left the sedan in front of the Alexandria. He went into the hotel, to the desk, where a tall young man with a dark grave face said: "Good evening, Mr. Spade."

"Good evening." Spade drew the young man to one end of the desk. "These Gutmans – up in twelve C – are they in?"

The young man replied, "No," darting a quick glance at Spade. Then he looked away, hesitated, looked at Spade again, and murmured: "A funny thing happened in connection with them this evening, Mr. Spade. Somebody called the Emergency Hospital and told them there was a sick girl up there."

"And there wasn't?"

"Oh, no, there was nobody up there. They went out earlier in the evening."

Spade said: "Well, these practical-jokers have to have their fun. Thanks."

He went to a telephone-booth, called a number, and said: "Hello.... Mrs. Perine?... Is Effie there?... Yes, please. ... Thanks.

"Hello, angel! What's the good word?... Fine, fine! Hold it. I'll be out in twenty minutes.... Right."

Half an hour later Spade rang the door-bell of a two-story brick building in Ninth Avenue. Effie Perine opened the door. Her boyish face was tired and smiling. "Hello, boss," she said. "Enter." She said in a low voice: "If Ma says anything to you, Sam, be nice to her. She's all up in the air."

Spade grinned reassuringly and patted her shoulder.

She put her hands on his arm. "Miss O'Shaughnessy?"

"No," he growled. "I ran into a plant. Are you sure it was her voice?"

"Yes."

He made an unpleasant face. "Well, it was hooey."

She took him into a bright living-room, sighed, and slumped down on one end of a Chesterfield, smiling cheerfully up at him through her weariness.

He sat beside her and asked: "Everything went OK? Nothing said about the bundle?"

"Nothing. I told them what you told me to tell them, and they seemed to take it for granted that the phone-call had something to do with it, and that you were out running it down."

"Dundy there?"

"No. Hoff and O'Gar and some others I didn't know. I talked to the Captain too."

"They took you down to the Hall?"

"Oh, yes, and they asked me loads of questions, but it was all – you know – routine."

Spade rubbed his palms together. "Swell," he said and then frowned, "though I guess they'll think up plenty to put to me when we meet. That damned Dundy will, anyway, and Bryan." He moved his shoulders. "Anybody you know, outside of the police, come around?"

"Yes." She sat up straight. "That boy – the one who brought the message from Gutman – was there. He didn't come in, but the police left the corridor-door open while they were there and I saw him standing there."

"You didn't say anything?"

"Oh, no. You had said not to. So I didn't pay any attention to him and the next time I looked he was gone."

Spade grinned at her. "Damned lucky for you, sister, that the coppers got there first."

"Why?"

"He's a bad egg, that lad – poison. Was the dead man Jacobi?"

"Yes."

He pressed her hands and stood up. "I'm going to run along. You'd better hit the hay. You're all in."

She rose. "Sam, what is – ?"

He stopped her words with his hand on her mouth. "Save it till Monday," he said. "I want to sneak out before your mother catches me and gives me hell for dragging her lamb through gutters."

Midnight was a few minutes away when Spade reached his home. He put his key into the street-door's lock. Heels clicked rapidly on the sidewalk behind him. He let go the key and wheeled. Brigid O'Shaughnessy ran up the steps to him. She put her arms around him and hung on him, panting: "Oh, I thought you'd never come!" Her face was haggard, distraught, shaken by the tremors that shook her from head to foot.

With the hand not supporting her he felt for the key again, opened the door, and half lifted her inside. "You've been waiting?" he asked.

"Yes." Panting spaced her words. "In a – doorway – up the – street."

"Can you make it all right?" he asked. "Or shall I carry you?"

She shook her head against his shoulder. "I'll be – all right – when I – get where – I can – sit down."

They rode up to Spade's floor in the elevator and went around to his apartment. She left his arm and stood beside him – panting, both hands to her breast – while he unlocked his door. He switched on the passageway light. They went in. He shut the door and, with his arm around her again, took her back towards the living-room. When they were within a step of the living-room-door the light in the living-room went on.

The girl cried out and clung to Spade.

Just inside the living-room-door fat Gutman stood smiling benevolently at them. The boy Wilmer came out of the kitchen behind them. Black pistols were gigantic in his

176

small hands. Cairo came from the bathroom. He too had a pistol.

Gutman said: "Well, sir, we're all here, as you can see for yourself. Now let's come in and sit down and be comfortable and talk."

SPADE, WITH HIS arms around Brigid O'Shaughnessy, smiled meagerly over her head and said: "Sure, we'll talk."

Gutman's bulbs jounced as he took three waddling backward steps away from the door.

Spade and the girl went in together. The boy and Cairo followed them in. Cairo stopped in the doorway. The boy put away one of his pistols and came up close behind Spade.

Spade turned his head far around to look down over his shoulder at the boy and said: "Get away. You're not going to frisk me."

The boy said: "Stand still. Shut up."

Spade's nostrils went in and out with his breathing. His voice was level. "Get away. Put your paw on me and I'm going to make you use the gun. Ask your boss if he wants me shot up before we talk."

"Never mind, Wilmer," the fat man said. He frowned indulgently at Spade. "You are certainly a most headstrong individual. Well, let's be seated."

Spade said, "I told you I didn't like that punk," and took Brigid O'Shaughnessy to the sofa by the windows. They sat close together, her head against his left shoulder, his left arm around her shoulders. She had stopped trembling, had stopped panting. The appearance of Gutman and his companions seemed to have robbed her of that freedom of personal movement and emotion that is animal, leaving her alive, conscious, but quiescent as a plant.

Gutman lowered himself into the padded rocking chair. Cairo chose the armchair by the table. The boy Wilmer did not sit down. He stood in the doorway where Cairo had stood, letting his one visible pistol hang down at his side, looking under curling lashes at Spade's body. Cairo put his pistol on the table beside him.

Spade took off his hat and tossed it to the other end of the sofa. He grinned at Gutman. The looseness of his lower lip and the droop of his upper eyelids combined with the v's in his face to make his grin lewd as a satyr's. "That daughter of yours has a nice belly," he said, "too nice to be scratched up with pins."

Gutman's smile was affable if a bit oily.

The boy in the doorway took a short step forward, raising his pistol as far as his hip. Everybody in the room looked at him. In the dissimilar eyes with which Brigid O'Shaughnessy and Joel Cairo looked at him there was, oddly, something identically reproving. The boy blushed, drew back his advanced foot, straightened his legs, lowered the pistol and stood as he had stood before, looking under lashes that hid his eyes at Spade's chest. The blush was pale enough and lasted for only an instant, but it was startling on his face that habitually was so cold and composed.

Gutman turned his sleek-eyed fat smile on Spade again. His voice was a suave purring. "Yes, sir, that was a shame, but you must admit that it served its purpose."

Spade's brows twitched together. "Anything would've," he said. "Naturally I wanted to see you as soon as I had the falcon. Cash customers – why not? I went to Burlingame expecting to run into this sort of a meeting. I didn't know you were blundering around, half an hour late, trying to get me out of the way so you could find Jacobi again before he found me."

Gutman chuckled. His chuckle seemed to hold nothing but satisfaction. "Well, sir," he said, "in any case, here we are having our little meeting, if that's what you wanted."

"That's what I wanted. How soon are you ready to make the first payment and take the falcon off my hands?"

Brigid O'Shaughnessy sat up straight and looked at Spade with surprised blue eyes. He patted her shoulder inattentively. His eyes were steady on Gutman's. Gutman's twinkled merrily between sheltering fat-puffs. He said: "Well, sir, as to that," and put a hand inside the breast of his coat.

Cairo, hands on thighs, leaned forward in his chair, breathing between parted soft lips. His dark eyes had the surface-shine of lacquer. They shifted their focus warily from Spade's face to Gutman's, from Gutman's to Spade's.

Gutman repeated, "Well, sir, as to that," and took a white envelope from his pocket. Ten eyes – the boy's now only half obscured by his lashes – looked at the envelope. Turning the envelope over in his swollen hands, Gutman studied for a moment its blank white front and then its back, unsealed, with the flap tucked in. He raised his head, smiled amiably, and scaled the envelope at Spade's lap.

The envelope, though not bulky, was heavy enough to fly true. It struck the lower part of Spade's chest and dropped down on his thighs. He picked it up deliberately and opened it deliberately, using both hands, having taken his left arm from around the girl. The contents of the envelope were thousand-dollar bills, smooth and stiff and new. Spade took them out and counted them. There were ten of them. Spade looked up smiling. He said mildly: "We were talking about more money than this."

"Yes, sir, we were," Gutman agreed, "but we were talking then. This is actual money, genuine coin of the realm, sir. With a dollar of this you can buy more than with ten dollars of talk." Silent laughter shook his bulbs. When their commotion stopped he said more seriously, yet not altogether seriously: "There are more of us to be taken care of now." He moved his twinkling eyes and his fat head to indicate Cairo. "And – well, sir, in short – the situation has changed."

While Gutman talked Spade had tapped the edges of the ten bills into alignment and returned them to their envelope, tucking the flap in over them. Now, with forearms on knees, he sat hunched forward, dangling the envelope from a corner held lightly by finger and thumb down between his legs. His reply to the fat man was careless: "Sure. You're together now, but I've got the falcon."

Joel Cairo spoke. Ugly hands grasping the arms of his chair, he leaned forward and said primly in his high-pitched thin voice: "I shouldn't think it would be necessary to remind you, Mr. Spade, that though you may have the falcon yet we certainly have you."

Spade grinned. "I'm trying to not let that worry me," he said. He sat up straight, put the envelope aside – on the sofa – and addressed Gutman: "We'll come back to the money later. There's another thing that's got to be taken care of first. We've got to have a fall-guy."

The fat man frowned without comprehension, but before he could speak Spade was explaining: "The police have got to have a victim – somebody they can stick for those three murders. We –"

Cairo, speaking in a brittle excited voice, interrupted Spade. "Two – only two – murders, Mr. Spade. Thursby undoubtedly killed your partner."

"All right, two," Spade growled. "What difference does that make? The point is we've got to feed the police some –"

Now Gutman broke in, smiling confidently, talking with good-natured assurance: "Well, sir, from what we've seen and heard of you I don't think we'll have to bother ourselves about that. We can leave the handling of the police to you, all right. You won't need any of our inexpert help."

"If that's what you think," Spade said, "you haven't seen or heard enough."

"Now come, Mr. Spade. You can't expect us to believe at this late date that you are the least bit afraid of the police, or that you are not quite able to handle –"

Spade snorted with throat and nose. He bent forward, resting forearms on knees again, and interrupted Gutman irritably: "I'm not a damned bit afraid of them and I know how to handle them. That's what I'm trying to tell you. The way to handle them is to toss them a victim, somebody they can hang the works on."

"Well, sir, I grant you that's one way of doing it, but – "

" 'But' hell!" Spade said. "It's the only way." His eyes were hot and earnest under a reddening forehead. The bruise on his temple was liver-colored. "I know what I'm talking about. I've been through it all before and expect to go through it again. At one time or another I've had to tell everybody from the Supreme Court down to go to hell, and I've got away with it. I got away with it because I never let myself forget that a day of reckoning was coming. I never forget that when the day of reckoning comes I want to be all set to march into head-quarters pushing a victim in front of me, saying: 'Here, you chumps, is your criminal!' As long as I can do that I can put my thumb to my nose and wriggle my fingers at all the laws in the book. The first time I can't do it my name's Mud. There hasn't been a first time yet. This isn't going to be it. That's flat."

Gutman's eyes flickered and their sleekness became dubious, but he held his other features in their bulbous pink smiling complacent cast and there was nothing of uneasiness in his voice. He said: "That's a system that's got a lot to recommend it, sir – by Gad, it has! And if it was anyway practical this time I'd be the first to say: 'Stick to it by all means, sir.' But this just happens to be a case where it's not possible. That's the way it is with the best of systems. There comes a time when you've got to make exceptions, and a wise man just goes ahead and makes them. Well, sir, that's just the way it is in this case and I don't mind telling you that I think you're being very well paid for making an exception. Now maybe it will be a little more trouble to you than if you had your victim to hand over to the police, but" – he laughed and spread his hands – "you're not the man that's afraid of a little bit of trouble. You know how to do things and you know you'll land on your feet in the end, no matter what happens." He pursed his lips and partly closed one eye. "You'll manage that, sir."

Spade's eyes had lost their warmth. His face was dull and lumpy. "I know what I'm talking about," he said in a low, consciously patient, tone. "This is my city and my game. I could manage to land on my feet – sure – this time, but the next time I tried to put over a fast one they'd stop me so fast I'd swallow my teeth. Hell with that. You birds'll be in New York or Constantinople or some place else. I'm in business here."

"But surely," Gutman began, "you can – "

"I can't," Spade said earnestly. "I won't. I mean it." He sat up straight. A pleasant smile illuminated his face, erasing its dull lumpishness. He spoke rapidly in an agreeable, persuasive tone: "Listen to me, Gutman. I'm telling you what's best for all of us. If we don't give the police a fall-guy it's ten to one they'll sooner or later stumble on information about the falcon. Then you'll have to duck for cover with it – no matter where you are – and that's not going to help you make a fortune off it. Give them a fall-guy and they'll stop right there."

"Well, sir, that's just the point," Gutman replied, and still only in his eyes was uneasiness faintly apparent. "Will they stop right there? Or won't the fall-guy be a fresh clue that as likely as not will lead them to information about the falcon? And, on the other hand, wouldn't you say they were stopped right now, and that the best thing for us to do is leave well enough alone?"

A forked vein began to swell in Spade's forehead. "Jesus! you don't know what it's all about either," he said in a restrained tone. "They're not asleep, Gutman. They're lying low, waiting. Try to get that. I'm in it up to my neck and they know it. That's all right as long as I do something when the time comes. But it won't be all right if I don't." His voice became persuasive again. "Listen, Gutman, we've absolutely got to give them a victim. There's no way out of it. Let's give them the punk." He nodded pleasantly at the boy in the doorway. "He actually did shoot both of them – Thursby and Jacobi – didn't he? Anyway, he's made to order for the part. Let's pin the necessary evidence on him and turn him over to them."

The boy in the doorway tightened the corners of his mouth in what may have been a minute smile. Spade's proposal seemed to have no other effect on him. Joel Cairo's dark face was open-mouthed, open-eyed, yellowish, and amazed. He breathed through his mouth, his round effeminate chest rising and falling, while he gaped at Spade. Brigid O'Shaughnessy had moved away from Spade and had twisted herself around on the sofa to stare at him. There was a suggestion of hysterical laughter behind the startled confusion in her face.

Gutman remained still and expressionless for a long moment. Then he decided to laugh. He laughed heartily and lengthily, not stopping until his sleek eyes had borrowed merriment from his laughter. When he stopped laughing he said: "By Gad, sir, you're a character, that you are!" He took a white handkerchief from his pocket and wiped his eyes. "Yes, sir, there's never any telling what you'll do or say next, except that it's bound to be something astonishing."

"There's nothing funny about it." Spade did not seem offended by the fat man's laughter, nor in any way impressed. He spoke in the manner of one reasoning with a recalcitrant, but not altogether unreasonable, friend. "It's our best bet. With him in their hands, the police will – "

"But, my dear man," Gutman objected, "can't you see? If I even for a moment thought of doing it – But that's ridiculous too. I feel towards Wilmer just exactly as if he were my own son. I really do. But if I even for a moment thought of doing what you propose, what in the world do you think would keep Wilmer from telling the police every last detail about the falcon and all of us?"

Spade grinned with stiff lips. "If we had to," he said softly, "we could have him killed resisting arrest. But we won't have to go that far. Let him talk his head off. I promise you nobody'll do anything about it. That's easy enough to fix."

The pink flesh on Gutman's forehead crawled in a frown. He lowered his head, mashing his chins together over his collar, and asked: "How?" Then, with an abruptness that set all his fat bulbs to quivering and tumbling against one another, he raised his head, squirmed around to look at the boy, and laughed uproariously. "What do you think of this, Wilmer? It's funny, eh?"

The boy's eyes were cold hazel gleams under his lashes. He said in a low distinct voice: "Yes, it's funny – the son of a bitch."

Spade was talking to Brigid O'Shaughnessy: "How do you feel now, angel? Any better?"

"Yes, much better, only" – she reduced her voice until the last words would have been unintelligible two feet away – "I'm frightened."

"Don't be," he said carelessly and put a hand on her gray-stockinged knee. "Nothing very bad's going to happen. Want a drink?"

"Not now, thanks." Her voice sank again. "Be careful, Sam."

Spade grinned and looked at Gutman, who was looking at him. The fat man smiled genially, saying nothing for a moment, and then asked: "How?"

Spade was stupid. "How what?"

The fat man considered more laughter necessary then, and an explanation: "Well, sir, if you're really serious about this – this suggestion of yours, the least we can do in common politeness is to hear you out. Now how are you going about fixing it so that Wilmer" – he paused here to laugh again – "won't be able to do us any harm?"

Spade shook his head. "No," he said, "I wouldn't want to take advantage of anybody's politeness, no matter how common, like that. Forget it."

The fat man puckered up his facial bulbs. "Now come, come," he protested, "you make me decidedly uncomfortable. I shouldn't have laughed, and I apologize most humbly and sincerely. I wouldn't want to seem to ridicule anything you'd suggest, Mr. Spade, regardless of how much I disagreed with you, for you must know that I have the greatest respect and admiration for your astuteness. Now mind you, I don't see how this suggestion of yours can be in any way practical – even leaving out the fact that I couldn't feel any different towards Wilmer if he was my own flesh and blood – but I'll consider it a personal favor as well as a sign that you've accepted my apologies, sir, if you'll go ahead and outline the rest of it."

"Fair enough," Spade said. "Bryan is like most district attorneys. He's more interested in how his record will look on paper than anything else. He'd rather drop a doubtful case than try it and have it go against him. I don't know that he ever deliberately framed anybody he believed innocent, but I can't imagine him letting himself believe them innocent if he could scrape up, or twist into shape, proof of their guilt. To be sure of convicting one man he'll let half a dozen equally guilty accomplices go free – if trying to convict them all might confuse his case.

"That's the choice we'll give him and he'll gobble it up. He wouldn't want to know about the falcon. He'll be tickled pink to persuade himself that anything the punk tells him about it is a lot of chewing-gum, an attempt to muddle things up. Leave that end to me. I can show him that if he starts fooling around trying to gather up everybody he's going to have a tangled case that no jury will be able to make heads or tails of, while if he sticks to the punk he can get a conviction standing on his head."

Gutman wagged his head sidewise in a slow smiling gesture of benign disapproval. "No, sir," he said, "I'm afraid that won't do, won't do at all. I don't see how even this District Attorney of yours can link Thursby and Jacobi and Wilmer together without having to – "

"You don't know district attorneys," Spade told him. "The Thursby angle is easy. He was a gunman and so's your punk. Bryan's already got a theory about that. There'll be no catch there. Well, Christ! they can only hang the punk once. Why try him for Jacobi's murder after he's been convicted of Thursby's? They simply close the record by writing it up against him and let it go at that. If, as is likely enough, he used the same gun on both, the bullets will match up. Everybody will be satisfied."

"Yes, but – " Gutman began, and stopped to look at the boy.

The boy advanced from the doorway, walking stiff-legged, with his legs apart, until he was between Gutman and Cairo, almost in the center of the floor. He halted there, leaning forward slightly from the waist, his shoulders raised towards the front. The pistol in his hand still hung at his side, but his knuckles were white over its grip. His other hand was a small hard fist down at his other side. The indelible youngness of his face gave an indescribably vicious – and inhuman – turn to the white-hot hatred and the cold white malevolence in his face. He said to Spade in a voice cramped by passion: "You bastard, get up on your feet and go for your heater!"

Spade smiled at the boy. His smile was not broad, but the amusement in it seemed genuine and unalloyed.

The boy said: "You bastard, get up and shoot it out if you've got the guts. I've taken all the riding from you I'm going to take."

The amusement in Spade's smile deepened. He looked at Gutman and said: "Young Wild West." His voice matched his smile. "Maybe you ought to tell him that shooting me before you get your hands on the falcon would be bad for business."

187

Gutman's attempt at a smile was not successful, but he kept the resultant grimace on his mottled face. He licked dry lips with a dry tongue. His voice was too hoarse and gritty for the paternally admonishing tone it tried to achieve. "Now, now, Wilmer," he said, "we can't have any of that. You shouldn't let yourself attach so much importance to these things. You – "

The boy, not taking his eyes from Spade, spoke in a choked voice out the side of his mouth: "Make him lay off me then. I'm going to fog him if he keeps it up and there won't be anything that'll stop me from doing it."

"Now, Wilmer," Gutman said and turned to Spade. His face and voice were under control now. "Your plan is, sir, as I said in the first place, not at all practical. Let's not say anything more about it."

Spade looked from one of them to the other. He had stopped smiling. His face held no expression at all. "I say what I please," he told them.

"You certainly do," Gutman said quickly, "and that's one of the things I've always admired in you. But this matter is, as I say, not at all practical, so there's not the least bit of use of discussing it any further, as you can see for yourself."

"I can't see it for myself," Spade said, "and you haven't made me see it, and I don't think you can." He frowned at Gutman. "Let's get this straight. Am I wasting time talking to you? I thought this was your show. Should I do my talking to the punk? I know how to do that."

"No, sir," Gutman replied, "you're quite right in dealing with me."

Spade said: "All right. Now I've got another suggestion. It's not as good as the first, but it's better than nothing. Want to hear it?"

"Most assuredly."

"Give them Cairo."

Cairo hastily picked up his pistol from the table beside him. He held it tight in his lap with both hands. Its muzzle pointed at the floor a little to one side of the sofa. His face had become yellowish again. His black eyes darted their gaze from face to face. The opaqueness of his eyes made them seem flat, two-dimensional.

Gutman, looking as if he could not believe he had heard what he had heard, asked: "Do what?"

"Give the police Cairo."

Gutman seemed about to laugh, but he did not laugh. Finally, he exclaimed: "Well, by Gad, sir!" in an uncertain tone.

"It's not as good as giving them the punk," Spade said. "Cairo's not a gunman and he carries a smaller gun than Thursby and Jacobi were shot with. We'll have to go to more trouble framing him, but that's better than not giving the police anybody."

Cairo cried in a voice shrill with indignation: "Suppose we give them you, Mr. Spade, or Miss O'Shaughnessy? How about that if you're so set on giving them some-body?"

Spade smiled at the Levantine and answered him evenly: "You people want the falcon. I've got it. A fall-guy is part of the price I'm asking. As for Miss O'Shaughnessy" – his dispassionate glance moved to her white perplexed face and then back to Cairo and his shoulders rose and fell a fraction of an inch – "if you think she can be rigged for the part I'm perfectly willing to discuss it with you."

The girl put her hands to her throat, uttered a short strangled cry, and moved farther away from him.

Cairo, his face and body twitching with excitement, exclaimed: "You seem to forget that you are not in a position to insist on anything."

Spade laughed, a harsh derisive snort.

Gutman said, in a voice that tried to make firmness ingratiating: "Come now, gentlemen, let's keep our discussion on a friendly basis; but there certainly is" – he was addressing

Spade – "something in what Mr. Cairo says. You must take into consideration the – "

"Like hell I must." Spade flung his words out with a brutal sort of carelessness that gave them more weight than they could have got from dramatic emphasis or from loudness. "If you kill me, how are you going to get the bird? If I know you can't afford to kill me till you have it, how are you going to scare me into giving it to you?"

Gutman cocked his head to the left and considered these questions. His eyes twinkled between puckered lids. Presently he gave his genial answer: "Well, sir, there are other means of persuasion besides killing and threatening to kill."

"Sure," Spade agreed, "but they're not much good unless the threat of death is behind them to hold the victim down. See what I mean? If you try anything I don't like I won't stand for it. I'll make it a matter of your having to call it off or kill me, knowing you can't afford to kill me."

"I see what you mean." Gutman chuckled. "That is an attitude, sir, that calls for the most delicate judgment on both sides, because, as you know, sir, men are likely to forget in the heat of action where their best interest lies and let their emotions carry them away."

Spade too was all smiling blandness. "That's the trick, from my side," he said, "to make my play strong enough that it ties you up, but yet not make you mad enough to bump me off against your better judgment."

Gutman said fondly: "By Gad, sir, you are a character!"

Joel Cairo jumped up from his chair and went around behind the boy and behind Gutman's chair. He bent over the back of Gutman's chair and, screening his mouth and the fat man's ear with his empty hand, whispered. Gutman listened attentively, shutting his eyes.

Spade grinned at Brigid O'Shaughnessy. Her lips smiled feebly in response, but there was no change in her eyes; they did not lose their numb stare. Spade turned to the boy: "Two to one they're selling you out, son."

The boy did not say anything. A trembling in his knees began to shake the knees of his trousers.

Spade addressed Gutman: "I hope you're not letting yourself be influenced by the guns these pocket-edition desperadoes are waving."

Gutman opened his eyes. Cairo stopped whispering and stood erect behind the fat man's chair.

Spade said: "I've practiced taking them away from both of them, so there'll be no trouble there. The punk is – "

In a voice choked horribly by emotion the boy cried, "All right!" and jerked his pistol up in front of his chest.

Gutman flung a fat hand out at the boy's wrist, caught the wrist, and bore it and the gun down while Gutman's fat body was rising in haste from the rocking chair. Joel Cairo scurried around to the boy's other side and grasped his other arm. They wrestled with the boy, forcing his arms down, holding them down, while he struggled futilely against them. Words came out of the struggling group: fragments of the boy's incoherent speech – "right . . . go . . . bastard . . . smoke" – Gutman's "Now, now, Wilmer!" repeated many times; Cairo's "No, please, don't" and "Don't do that, Wilmer."

Wooden-faced, dreamy-eyed, Spade got up from the sofa and went over to the group. The boy, unable to cope with the weight against him, had stopped struggling. Cairo, still holding the boy's arm, stood partly in front of him, talking to him soothingly. Spade pushed Cairo aside gently and drove his left fist against the boy's chin. The boy's head snapped back as far as it could while his arms were held, and then came forward. Gutman began a desperate "Here, what – ?" Spade drove his right fist against the boy's chin.

Cairo dropped the boy's arm, letting him collapse against Gutman's great round belly. Cairo sprang at Spade, clawing at his face with the curved stiff fingers of both hands. Spade blew his breath out and pushed the Levantine away. Cairo sprang at him again. Tears were in Cairo's eyes and his red lips worked angrily, forming words, but no sound came from between them.

Spade laughed, grunted, "Jesus, you're a pip!" and cuffed the side of Cairo's face with an open hand, knocking him over against the table. Cairo regained his balance and sprang at Spade the third time. Spade stopped him with both palms held out on long rigid arms against his face. Cairo, failing to reach Spade's face with his shorter arms, thumped Spade's arms.

"Stop it," Spade growled. "I'll hurt you."

Cairo cried, "Oh, you big coward!" and backed away from him.

Spade stooped to pick up Cairo's pistol from the floor, and then the boy's. He straightened up holding them in his left hand, dangling them upside-down by their trigger-guards from his forefinger.

Gutman had put the boy in the rocking chair and stood looking at him with troubled eyes in an uncertainly puckered face. Cairo went down on his knees beside the chair and began to chafe one of the boy's limp hands.

Spade felt the boy's chin with his fingers. "Nothing cracked," he said. "We'll spread him on the sofa." He put his right arm under the boy's arm and around his back, put his left forearm under the boy's knees, lifted him without apparent effort, and carried him to the sofa.

Brigid O'Shaughnessy got up quickly and Spade laid the boy there. With his right hand Spade patted the boy's clothes, found his second pistol, added it to the others in his left hand, and turned his back on the sofa. Cairo was already sitting beside the boy's head.

Spade clinked the pistols together in his hand and smiled cheerfully at Gutman. "Well," he said, "there's our fall-guy."

Gutman's face was gray and his eyes were clouded. He did not look at Spade. He looked at the floor and did not say anything.

Spade said: "Don't be a damned fool again. You let Cairo whisper to you and you held the kid while I pasted him. You can't laugh that off and you're likely to get yourself shot trying to."

Gutman moved his feet on the rug and said nothing.

Spade said: "And the other side of it is that you'll either say yes right now or I'll turn the falcon and the whole God-damned lot of you in."

Gutman raised his head and muttered through his teeth: "I don't like that, sir."

"You won't like it," Spade said. "Well?"

The fat man sighed and made a wry face and replied sadly: "You can have him."

Spade said: "That's swell."

THE BOY LAY on his back on the sofa, a small figure that was – except for its breathing – altogether corpse-like to the eye. Joel Cairo sat beside the boy, bending over him, rubbing his cheeks and wrists, smoothing his hair back from his forehead, whispering to him, and peering anxiously down at his white still face.

Brigid O'Shaughnessy stood in an angle made by table and wall. One of her hands was flat on the table, the other to her breast. She pinched her lower lip between her teeth and glanced furtively at Spade whenever he was not looking at her. When he looked at her she looked at Cairo and the boy.

Gutman's face had lost its troubled cast and was becoming rosy again. He had put his hands in his trousers-pockets. He stood facing Spade, watching him without curiosity.

Spade, idly jingling his handful of pistols, nodded at Cairo's rounded back and asked Gutman: "It'll be all right with him?"

"I don't know," the fat man replied placidly. "That part will have to be strictly up to you, sir."

Spade's smile made his v-shaped chin more salient. He said: "Cairo."

The Levantine screwed his dark anxious face around over his shoulder.

Spade said: "Let him rest awhile. We're going to give him to the police. We ought to get the details fixed before he comes to."

Cairo asked bitterly: "Don't you think you've done enough to him without that?"

Spade said: "No."

194

Cairo left the sofa and went close to the fat man. "Please don't do this thing, Mr. Gutman," he begged. "You must realize that – "

Spade interrupted him: "That's settled. The question is, what are you going to do about it? Coming in? Or getting out?"

Though Gutman's smile was a bit sad, even wistful in its way, he nodded his head. "I don't like it either," he told the Levantine, "but we can't help ourselves now. We really can't."

Spade asked: "What are you doing, Cairo? In or out?"

Cairo wet his lips and turned slowly to face Spade. "Suppose," he said, and swallowed. "Have I – ? Can I choose?"

"You can," Spade assured him seriously, "but you ought to know that if the answer is *out* we'll give you to the police with your boy-friend."

"Oh, come, Mr. Spade," Gutman protested, "that is not – "

"Like hell we'll let him walk out on us," Spade said. "He'll either come in or he'll go in. We can't have a lot of loose ends hanging around." He scowled at Gutman and burst out irritably: "Jesus God! is this the first thing you guys ever stole? You're a fine lot of lollipops! What are you going to do next – get down and pray?" He directed his scowl at Cairo. "Well? Which?"

"You give me no choice." Cairo's narrow shoulders moved in a hopeless shrug. "I come in."

"Good," Spade said and looked at Gutman and at Brigid O'Shaughnessy. "Sit down."

The girl sat down gingerly on the end of the sofa by the unconscious boy's feet. Gutman returned to the padded rocking chair, and Cairo to the armchair. Spade put his handful of pistols on the table and sat on the table-corner beside them. He looked at the watch on his wrist and said: "Two o'clock. I can't get the falcon till daylight, or maybe eight o'clock. We've got plenty of time to arrange everything."

Gutman cleared his throat. "Where is it?" he asked and then added in haste: "I don't really care, sir. What I had in mind was that it would be best for all concerned if we did not get out of each other's sight until our business has been transacted." He looked at the sofa and at Spade again, sharply. "You have the envelope?"

Spade shook his head, looking at the sofa and then at the girl. He smiled with his eyes and said: "Miss O'Shaughnessy has it."

"Yes, I have it," she murmured, putting a hand inside her coat. "I picked it up . . . . "

"That's all right," Spade told her. "Hang on to it." He addressed Gutman: "We won't have to lose sight of each other. I can have the falcon brought here."

"That will be excellent," Gutman purred. "Then, sir, in exchange for the ten thousand dollars and Wilmer you will give us the falcon and an hour or two of grace – so we won't be in the city when you surrender him to the authorities."

"You don't have to duck," Spade said. "It'll be air-tight."

"That may be, sir, but nevertheless we'll feel safer well out of the city when Wilmer is being questioned by your District Attorney."

"Suit yourself," Spade replied. "I can hold him here all day if you want." He began to roll a cigarette. "Let's get the details fixed. Why did he shoot Thursby? And why and where and how did he shoot Jacobi?"

Gutman smiled indulgently, shaking his head and purring: "Now come, sir, you can't expect that. We've given you the money and Wilmer. That is our part of the agreement."

"I do expect it," Spade said. He held his lighter to his cigarette. "A fall-guy is what I asked for, and he's not a fall-guy unless he's a cinch to take the fall. Well, to cinch that I've got to know what's what." He pulled his brows together. "What are you belly-aching about? You're not going to be sitting so damned pretty if you leave him with an out."

Gutman leaned forward and wagged a fat finger at the pistols on the table beside Spade's legs. "There's ample evidence of his guilt, sir. Both men were shot with those weapons. It's a very simple matter for the police-department-experts to determine that the bullets that killed the men were fired from those weapons. You know that; you've mentioned it yourself. And that, it seems to me, is ample proof of his guilt."

"Maybe," Spade agreed, "but the thing's more complicated than that and I've got to know what happened so I can be sure the parts that won't fit in are covered up."

Cairo's eyes were round and hot. "Apparently you've forgotten that you assured us it would be a very simple affair," Cairo said. He turned his excited dark face to Gutman. "You see! I advised you not to do this. I don't think –"

"It doesn't make a damned bit of difference what either of you think," Spade said bluntly. "It's too late for that now and you're in too deep. Why did he kill Thursby?"

Gutman interlaced his fingers over his belly and rocked his chair. His voice, like his smile, was frankly rueful. "You are an uncommonly difficult person to get the best of," he said. "I begin to think that we made a mistake in not letting you alone from the very first. By Gad, I do, sir!"

Spade moved his hand carelessly. "You haven't done so bad. You're staying out of jail and you're getting the falcon. What do you want?" He put his cigarette in a corner of his mouth and said around it: "Anyhow you know where you stand now. Why did he kill Thursby?"

Gutman stopped rocking. "Thursby was a notorious killer and Miss O'Shaughnessy's ally. We knew that removing him in just that manner would make her stop and think that perhaps it would be best to patch up her differences with us after all, besides leaving her without so violent a protector. You see, sir, I am being candid with you?"

"Yes. Keep it up. You didn't think he might have the falcon?"

Gutman shook his head so that his round cheeks wobbled. "We didn't think that for a minute," he replied. He smiled benevolently. "We had the advantage of knowing Miss O'Shaughnessy far too well for that and, while we didn't know then that she had given the falcon to Captain Jacobi in Hongkong to be brought over on the *Paloma* while they took a faster boat, still we didn't for a minute think that, if only one of them knew where it was, Thursby was the one."

Spade nodded thoughtfully and asked: "You didn't try to make a deal with him before you gave him the works?"

"Yes, sir, we certainly did. I talked to him myself that night. Wilmer had located him two days before and had been trying to follow him to wherever he was meeting Miss O'Shaughnessy, but Thursby was too crafty for that even if he didn't know he was being watched. So that night Wilmer went to his hotel, learned he wasn't in, and waited outside for him. I suppose Thursby returned immediately after killing your partner. Be that as it may, Wilmer brought him to see me. We could do nothing with him. He was quite determinedly loyal to Miss O'Shaughnessy. Well, sir, Wilmer followed him back to his hotel and did what he did."

Spade thought for a moment. "That sounds all right. Now Jacobi."

Gutman looked at Spade with grave eyes and said: "Captain Jacobi's death was entirely Miss O'Shaughnessy's fault."

The girl gasped, "Oh!" and put a hand to her mouth.

Spade's voice was heavy and even. "Never mind that now. Tell me what happened."

After a shrewd look at Spade, Gutman smiled. "Just as you say, sir," he said. "Well, Cairo, as you know, got in touch with me – I sent for him – after he left police headquarters the night – or morning – he was up here. We recognized the mutual advantage of pooling forces." He directed his smile at the Levantine. "Mr. Cairo is a man of nice judgment. The *Paloma* was his thought. He saw the notice of its arrival in the papers that

198

morning and remembered that he had heard in Hongkong that Jacobi and Miss O'Shaughnessy had been seen together. That was when he had been trying to find her there, and he thought at first that she had left on the *Paloma*, though later he learned that she hadn't. Well, sir, when he saw the notice of arrival in the paper he guessed just what had happened: she had given the bird to Jacobi to bring here for her. Jacobi did not know what it was, of course. Miss O'Shaughnessy is too discreet for that."

He beamed at the girl, rocked his chair twice, and went on: "Mr. Cairo and Wilmer and I went to call on Captain Jacobi and were fortunate enough to arrive while Miss O'Shaughnessy was there. In many ways it was a difficult conference, but finally, by midnight we had persuaded Miss O'Shaughnessy to come to terms, or so we thought. We then left the boat and set out for my hotel, where I was to pay Miss O'Shaughnessy and receive the bird. Well, sir, we mere men should have known better than to suppose ourselves capable of coping with her. *En route*, she and Captain Jacobi and the falcon slipped completely through our fingers." He laughed merrily. "By Gad, sir, it was neatly done."

Spade looked at the girl. Her eyes, large and dark with pleading, met his. He asked Gutman: "You touched off the boat before you left?"

"Not intentionally, no, sir," the fat man replied, "though I dare say we – or Wilmer at least – were responsible for the fire. He had been out trying to find the falcon while the rest of us were talking in the cabin and no doubt was careless with matches."

"That's fine," Spade said. "If any slip-up makes it necessary for us to try him for Jacobi's murder we can also hang an arson-rap on him. All right. Now about the shooting."

"Well, sir, we dashed around town all day trying to find them and we found them late this afternoon. We weren't sure at first that we'd found them. All we were sure of was that we'd found Miss O'Shaughnessy's apartment. But when we listened at the door we heard them moving around inside, so we were pretty confident we had them and rang the bell. When she asked us who we were and we told her – through the door – we heard a window going up.

"We knew what that meant, of course; so Wilmer hurried downstairs as fast as he could and around to the rear of the building to cover the fire-escape. And when he turned into the alley he ran right plumb smack into Captain Jacobi running away with the falcon under his arm. That was a difficult situation to handle, but Wilmer did every bit as well as he could. He shot Jacobi – more than once – but Jacobi was too tough to either fall or drop the falcon, and he was too close for Wilmer to keep out of his way. He knocked Wilmer down and ran on. And this was in broad daylight, you understand, in the afternoon. When Wilmer got up he could see a policeman coming up from the block below. So he had to give it up. He dodged into the open back door of the building next the Coronet, through into the street, and then up to join us – and very fortunate he was, sir, to make it without being seen.

"Well, sir, there we were – stumped again. Miss O'Shaughnessy had opened the door for Mr. Cairo and me after she had shut the window behind Jacobi, and she – " He broke off to smile at a memory. "We persuaded – that is the word, sir – her to tell us that she had told Jacobi to take the falcon to you. It seemed very unlikely that he'd live to go that far, even if the police didn't pick him up, but that was the only chance we had, sir. And so, once more, we persuaded Miss O'Shaughnessy to give us a little assistance. We – well – persuaded her to phone your office in an attempt to draw you away before Jacobi got there, and we sent Wilmer after him. Unfortunately it had taken us too long to decide and to persuade Miss O'Shaughnessy to – "

The boy on the sofa groaned and rolled over on his side. His eyes opened and closed several times. The girl stood up and moved into the angle of table and wall again.

" – cooperate with us," Gutman concluded hurriedly, "and so you had the falcon before we could reach you."

The boy put one foot on the floor, raised himself on an elbow, opened his eyes wide, put the other foot down, sat up, and looked around. When his eyes focused on Spade bewilderment went out of them.

Cairo left his armchair and went over to the boy. He put his arm on the boy's shoulders and started to say something. The boy rose quickly to his feet, shaking Cairo's arm off. He glanced around the room once and then fixed his eyes on Spade again. His face was set hard and he held his body so tense that it seemed drawn in and shrunken.

Spade, sitting on the corner of the table, swinging his legs carelessly, said: "Now listen, kid. If you come over here and start cutting up I'm going to kick you in the face. Sit down and shut up and behave and you'll last longer."

The boy looked at Gutman.

Gutman smiled benignly at him and said: "Well, Wilmer, I'm sorry indeed to lose you, and I want you to know that I couldn't be any fonder of you if you were my own son; but – well, by Gad! – if you lose a son it's possible to get another – and there's only one Maltese falcon."

Spade laughed.

Cairo moved over and whispered in the boy's ear. The boy, keeping his cold hazel eyes on Gutman's face, sat down on the sofa again. The Levantine sat beside him.

Gutman's sigh did not affect the benignity of his smile. He said to Spade: "When you're young you simply don't understand things."

Cairo had an arm around the boy's shoulders again and was whispering to him. Spade grinned at Gutman and addressed Brigid O'Shaughnessy: "I think it'd be swell if you'd see what you can find us to eat in the kitchen, with plenty of coffee. Will you? I don't like to leave my guests."

"Surely," she said and started towards the door.

Gutman stopped rocking. "Just a moment, my dear." He held up a thick hand. "Hadn't you better leave the envelope in here? You don't want to get grease-spots on it."

The girl's eyes questioned Spade. He said in an indifferent tone: "It's still his."

She put her hand inside her coat, took out the envelope, and gave it to Spade. Spade tossed it into Gutman's lap, saying: "Sit on it if you're afraid of losing it."

"You misunderstand me," Gutman replied suavely. "It's not that at all, but business should be transacted in a business-like manner." He opened the flap of the envelope, took out the thousand-dollar bills, counted them, and chuckled so that his belly bounced. "For instance there are only nine bills here now." He spread them out on his fat knees and thighs. "There were ten when I handed it to you, as you very well know." His smile was broad and jovial and triumphant.

Spade looked at Brigid O'Shaughnessy and asked: "Well?"

She shook her head sidewise with emphasis. She did not say anything, though her lips moved slightly, as if she had tried to. Her face was frightened.

Spade held his hand out to Gutman and the fat man put the money into it. Spade counted the money – nine thousand-dollar bills – and returned it to Gutman. Then Spade stood up and his face was dull and placid. He picked up the three pistols on the table. He spoke in a matter-of-fact voice. "I want to know about this. We" – he nodded at the girl, but without looking at her – "are going in the bathroom. The door will be open and I'll be facing it. Unless you want a three-story drop there's no way out of here except past the bathroom door. Don't try to make it."

"Really, sir," Gutman protested, "it's not necessary, and certainly not very courteous of you, to threaten us in this manner. You must know that we've not the least desire to leave."

"I'll know a lot when I'm through." Spade was patient but resolute. "This trick upsets things. I've got to find the answer. It won't take long." He touched the girl's elbow. "Come on."

In the bathroom Brigid O'Shaughnessy found words. She put her hands up flat on Spade's chest and her face up close to his and whispered: "I did not take that bill, Sam."

"I don't think you did," he said, "but I've got to know. Take your clothes off."

"You won't take my word for it?"

"No. Take your clothes off."

"I won't."

"All right. We'll go back to the other room and I'll have them taken off."

She stepped back with a hand to her mouth. Her eyes were round and horrified. "You would?" she asked through her fingers.

"I will," he said. "I've got to know what happened to that bill and I'm not going to be held up by anybody's maidenly modesty."

"Oh, it isn't that." She came close to him and put her hands on his chest again. "I'm not ashamed to be naked before you, but – can't you see? – not like this. Can't you see that if you make me you'll – you'll be killing something?"

He did not raise his voice. "I don't know anything about that. I've got to know what happened to the bill. Take them off."

She looked at his unblinking yellow-gray eyes and her face became pink and then white again. She drew herself up tall and began to undress. He sat on the side of the bathtub watching her and the open door. No sound came from the living-room. She removed her clothes swiftly, without fumbling, letting them fall down on the floor around her feet. When she was naked she stepped back from her clothing and stood looking at him. In her mien was pride without defiance or embarrassment.

He put his pistols on the toilet-seat and, facing the door, went down on one knee in front of her garments. He picked up each piece and examined it with fingers as well as eyes. He did not find the thousand-dollar bill. When he had finished he stood up holding her clothes out in his hands to her. "Thanks," he said. "Now I know."

She took the clothing from him. She did not say anything. He picked up his pistols. He shut the bathroom-door behind him and went into the living-room.

Gutman smiled amiably at him from the rocking chair. "Find it?" he asked.

Cairo, sitting beside the boy on the sofa, looked at Spade with questioning opaque eyes. The boy did not look up. He was leaning forward, head between hands, elbows on knees, staring at the floor between his feet.

Spade told Gutman: "No, I didn't find it. You palmed it."

The fat man chuckled. "I palmed it?"

"Yes," Spade said, jingling the pistols in his hand. "Do you want to say so or do you want to stand for a frisk?"

"Stand for – ?"

"You're going to admit it," Spade said, "or I'm going to search you. There's no third way."

Gutman looked up at Spade's hard face and laughed outright. "By Gad, sir, I believe you would. I really do. You're a character, sir, if you don't mind my saying so."

"You palmed it," Spade said.

"Yes, sir, that I did." The fat man took a crumpled bill from his vest-pocket, smoothed it on a wide thigh, took the envelope holding the nine bills from his coat-pocket, and put the smoothed bill in with the others. "I must have my little joke every now and then and I was curious to know what you'd do in a situation of that sort. I must say that you passed the test with flying colors, sir. It never occurred to me that you'd hit on such a simple and direct way of getting at the truth."

Spade sneered at him without bitterness. "That's the kind of thing I'd expect from somebody the punk's age."

Gutman chuckled.

Brigid O'Shaughnessy, dressed again except for coat and hat, came out of the bathroom, took a step towards the living-room, turned around, went to the kitchen, and turned on the light.

Cairo edged closer to the boy on the sofa and began whispering in his ear again. The boy shrugged irritably.

Spade, looking at the pistols in his hand and then at Gutman, went out into the passageway, to the closet there. He opened the door, put the pistols inside on the top of a trunk, shut the door, locked it, put the key in his trousers-pocket, and went to the kitchen-door.

Brigid O'Shaughnessy was filling an aluminum percolator.

"Find everything?" Spade asked.

"Yes," she replied in a cool voice, not raising her head. Then she set the percolator aside and came to the door. She blushed and her eyes were large and moist and chiding. "You shouldn't have done that to me, Sam," she said softly.

"I had to find out, angel." He bent down, kissed her mouth lightly, and returned to the living-room.

Gutman smiled at Spade and offered him the white envelope, saying: "This will soon be yours; you might as well take it now."

Spade did not take it. He sat in the armchair and said: "There's plenty of time for that. We haven't done enough talking about the money-end. I ought to have more than ten thousand."

Gutman said: "Ten thousand dollars is a lot of money."

Spade said: "You're quoting me, but it's not all the money in the world."

"No, sir, it's not. I grant you that. But it's a lot of money to be picked up in as few days and as easily as you're getting it."

"You think it's been so damned easy?" Spade asked, and shrugged. "Well, maybe, but that's my business."

"It certainly is," the fat man agreed. He screwed up his eyes, moved his head to indicate the kitchen, and lowered his voice. "Are you sharing with her?"

Spade said: "That's my business too."

"It certainly is," the fat man agreed once more, "but" – he hesitated – "I'd like to give you a word of advice."

"Go ahead."

"If you don't – I dare say you'll give her some money in any event, but – if you don't give her as much as she thinks she ought to have, my word of advice is – be careful."

Spade's eyes held a mocking light. He asked: "Bad?"

"Bad," the fat man replied.

Spade grinned and began to roll a cigarette.

Cairo, still muttering in the boy's ear, had put his arm around the boy's shoulders again. Suddenly the boy pushed his arm away and turned on the sofa to face the Levantine. The boy's face held disgust and anger. He made a fist of one small hand and struck Cairo's mouth with it. Cairo cried out as a woman might have cried and drew back to the very end of the sofa. He took a silk handkerchief from his pocket and put it to his mouth. It came away daubed with blood. He put it to his mouth once more and looked reproachfully at the boy. The boy snarled, "Keep away from me," and put his face between his hands again. Cairo's handkerchief released the fragrance of *chypre* in the room.

Cairo's cry had brought Brigid O'Shaughnessy to the door. Spade, grinning, jerked a thumb at the sofa and told her: "The course of true love. How's the food coming along?"

"It's coming," she said and went back to the kitchen.

Spade lighted his cigarette and addressed Gutman: "Let's talk about money."

"Willingly, sir, with all my heart," the fat man replied, "but I might as well tell you frankly right now that ten thousand is every cent I can raise."

Spade exhaled smoke. "I ought to have twenty."

"I wish you could. I'd give it to you gladly if I had it, but ten thousand dollars is every cent I can manage, on my word of honor. Of course, sir, you understand that is simply the first payment. Later – "

Spade laughed. "I know you'll give me millions later," he said, "but let's stick to this first payment now. Fifteen thousand?"

Gutman smiled and frowned and shook his head. "Mr. Spade, I've told you frankly and candidly and on my word of honor as a gentleman that ten thousand dollars is all the money I've got – every penny – and all I can raise."

"But you don't say positively."

Gutman laughed and said: "Positively."

Spade said gloomily: "That's not any too good, but if it's the best you can do – give it to me."

Gutman handed him the envelope. Spade counted the bills and was putting them in his pocket when Brigid O'Shaughnessy came in carrying a tray.

The boy would not eat. Cairo took a cup of coffee. The girl, Gutman, and Spade ate the scrambled eggs, bacon, toast, and marmalade she had prepared, and drank two cups of coffee apiece. Then they settled down to wait the rest of the night through.

Gutman smoked a cigar and read *Celebrated Criminal Cases of America*, now and then chuckling over or commenting on the parts of its contents that amused him. Cairo nursed his mouth and sulked on his end of the sofa. The boy sat with his head in his hands until a little after four o'clock. Then he lay down with his feet towards Cairo, turned his face to the window, and went to sleep. Brigid O'Shaughnessy, in the armchair, dozed, listened to the fat man's comments, and carried on wide-spaced desultory conversations with Spade.

DASHIELL HAMMETT

Spade rolled and smoked cigarettes and moved, without fidgeting or nervousness, around the room. He sat sometimes on an arm of the girl's chair, on the table-corner, on the floor at her feet, on a straight-backed chair. He was wide-awake, cheerful, and full of vigor.

At half-past five he went into the kitchen and made more coffee. Half an hour later the boy stirred, awakened, and sat up yawning. Gutman looked at his watch and questioned Spade: "Can you get it now?"

"Give me another hour."

Gutman nodded and went back to his book.

At seven o'clock Spade went to the telephone and called Effie Perine's number. "Hello, Mrs. Perine?... This is Mr. Spade. Will you let me talk to Effie, please?... Yes, it is.... Thanks." He whistled two lines of *En Cuba*, softly. "Hello, angel. Sorry to get you up.... Yes, very. Here's the plot: in our Holland box at the Post Office you'll find an envelope addressed in my scribble. There's a Pickwick Stage parcel-room-check in it – for the bundle we got yesterday. Will you get the bundle and bring it to me – p. d. q.?... Yes, I'm home.... That's the girl – hustle.... 'Bye."

The street-door-bell rang at ten minutes of eight. Spade went to the telephone-box and pressed the button that released the lock. Gutman put down his book and rose smiling. "You don't mind if I go to the door with you?" he asked.

"OK," Spade told him.

Gutman followed him to the corridor-door. Spade opened it. Presently Effie Perine, carrying the brown-wrapped parcel, came from the elevator. Her boyish face was gay and bright and she came forward quickly, almost trotting. After one glance she did not look at Gutman. She smiled at Spade and gave him the parcel.

He took it saying: "Thanks a lot, lady. I'm sorry to spoil your day of rest, but this – "

"It's not the first one you've spoiled," she replied, laughing, and then, when it was apparent that he was not going to invite her in, asked: "Anything else?"

He shook his head. "No, thanks."

She said, "Bye-bye," and went back to the elevator.

Spade shut the door and carried the parcel into the living-room. Gutman's face was red and his cheeks quivered. Cairo and Brigid O'Shaughnessy came to the table as Spade put the parcel there. They were excited. The boy rose, pale and tense, but he remained by the sofa, staring under curling lashes at the others.

Spade stepped back from the table saying: "There you are."

Gutman's fat fingers made short work of cord and paper and excelsior, and he had the black bird in his hands. "Ah," he said huskily, "now, after seventeen years!" His eyes were moist.

Cairo licked his red lips and worked his hands together. The girl's lower lip was between her teeth. She and Cairo, like Gutman, and like Spade and the boy, were breathing heavily. The air in the room was chilly and stale, and thick with tobacco smoke.

Gutman set the bird down on the table again and fumbled at a pocket. "It's it," he said, "but we'll make sure." Sweat glistened on his round cheeks. His fingers twitched as he took out a gold pocket-knife and opened it.

Cairo and the girl stood close to him, one on either side. Spade stood back a little where he could watch the boy as well as the group at the table.

Gutman turned the bird upside-down and scraped an edge of its base with his knife. Black enamel came off in a tiny curl, exposing blackened metal beneath. Gutman's knife-blade bit into the metal, turning back a thin curved shaving. The inside of the shaving, and the narrow plane its removal had left, had the soft gray sheen of lead.

Gutman's breath hissed between his teeth. His face became turgid with hot blood. He twisted the bird around and hacked at its head. There too the edge of his knife bared lead. He let knife and bird bang down on the table where he wheeled to confront Spade. "It's a fake," he said hoarsely.

Spade's face had become somber. His nod was slow, but there was no slowness in his hand's going out to catch Brigid O'Shaughnessy's wrist. He pulled her to him and grasped her chin with his other hand, raising her face roughly. "All right," he growled into her face. "You've had *your* little joke. Now tell us about it."

She cried: "No, Sam, no! That is the one I got from Kemidov. I swear – "

Joel Cairo thrust himself between Spade and Gutman and began to emit words in a shrill spluttering stream: "That's it! That's it! It was the Russian! I should have known! What a fool we thought him, and what fools he made of us!" Tears ran down the Levantine's cheeks and he danced up and down. "You bungled it!" he screamed at Gutman. "You and your stupid attempt to buy it from him! You fat fool! You let him know it was valuable and he found out how valuable and made a duplicate for us! No wonder we had so little trouble stealing it! No wonder he was so willing to send me off around the world looking for it! You imbecile! You bloated idiot!" He put his hands to his face and blubbered.

Gutman's jaw sagged. He blinked vacant eyes. Then he shook himself and was – by the time his bulbs had stopped jouncing – again a jovial fat man. "Come, sir," he said good-naturedly, "there's no need of going on like that. Everybody errs at times and you may be sure this is every bit as severe a blow to me as to anyone else. Yes, that is the Russian's hand, there's no doubt of it. Well, sir, what do you suggest? Shall we stand here and shed tears and call each other names? Or shall we" – he paused and his smile was a cherub's – "go to Constantinople?"

Cairo took his hands from his face and his eyes bulged. He stammered: "You are – ?" Amazement coming with full comprehension made him speechless.

Gutman patted his fat hands together. His eyes twinkled. His voice was a complacent throaty purring: "For seventeen years I have wanted that little item and have been trying to get it. If I must spend another year on the quest – well, sir – that will be an additional expenditure in time of only" – his lips moved silently as he calculated – "five and fifteen-seventeenths per cent."

The Levantine giggled and cried: "I go with you!"

Spade suddenly released the girl's wrist and looked around the room. The boy was not there. Spade went into the passageway. The corridor-door stood open. Spade made a dissatisfied mouth, shut the door, and returned to the living-room. He leaned against the door-frame and looked at Gutman and Cairo. He looked at Gutman for a long time, sourly. Then he spoke, mimicking the fat man's throaty purr: "Well, sir, I must say you're a swell lot of thieves!"

Gutman chuckled. "We've little enough to boast about, and that's a fact, sir," he said. "But, well, we're none of us dead yet and there's not a bit of use thinking the world's come to an end just because we've run into a little setback." He brought his left hand from behind him and held it out towards Spade, pink smooth hilly palm up. "I'll have to ask you for that envelope, sir."

Spade did not move. His face was wooden. He said: "I held up my end. You got your dingus. It's your hard luck, not mine, that it wasn't what you wanted."

"Now come, sir," Gutman said persuasively, "we've all failed and there's no reason for expecting any one of us to bear the brunt of it, and –" He brought his right hand from behind him. In the hand was a small pistol, an ornately engraved and inlaid affair of silver and gold and mother-of-pearl. "In short, sir, I must ask you to return my ten thousand dollars."

Spade's face did not change. He shrugged and took the envelope from his pocket. He started to hold it out to Gutman, hesitated, opened the envelope, and took out one thousand-dollar bill. He put that bill into his trousers-pocket. He tucked the envelope's flap in over the other bills and held them out to Gutman. "That'll take care of my time and expenses," he said.

Gutman, after a little pause, imitated Spade's shrug and accepted the envelope. He said: "Now, sir, we will say good-bye to you, unless" – the fat puffs around his eyes crinkled – "you care to undertake the Constantinople expedition with us. You don't? Well, sir, frankly I'd like to have you along. You're a man to my liking, a man of many resources and nice judgment. Because we know you're a man of nice judgment we know we can say good-bye with every assurance that you'll hold the details of our little enterprise in confidence. We know we can count on you to appreciate the fact that, as the situation now stands, any legal difficulties that come to us in connection with these last few days would likewise and equally come to you and the charming Miss O'Shaughnessy. You're too shrewd not to recognize that, sir, I'm sure."

"I understand that," Spade replied.

"I was sure you would. I'm also sure that, now there's no alternative, you'll somehow manage the police without a fall-guy."

"I'll make out all right," Spade replied.

"I was sure you would. Well, sir, the shortest farewells are the best. Adieu." He made a portly bow. "And to you, Miss O'Shaughnessy, adieu. I leave you the *rara avis* on the table as a little memento."

FOR ALL OF five minutes after the outer door had closed behind Casper Gutman and Joel Cairo, Spade, motionless, stood staring at the knob of the open living-room-door. His eyes were gloomy under a forehead drawn down. The clefts at the root of his nose were deep and red. His lips protruded loosely, pouting. He drew them in to make a hard v and went to the telephone. He had not looked at Brigid O'Shaughnessy, who stood by the table looking with uneasy eyes at him.

He picked up the telephone, set it on its shelf again, and bent to look into the telephone-directory hanging from a corner of the shelf. He turned the pages rapidly until he found the one he wanted, ran his finger down a column, straightened up, and lifted the telephone from the shelf again. He called a number and said:

"Hello, is Sergeant Polhaus there?.... Will you call him, please? This is Samuel Spade...." He stared into space, waiting. "Hello, Tom, I've got something for you.... Yes, plenty. Here it is: Thursby and Jacobi were shot by a kid named Wilmer Cook." He described the boy minutely. "He's working for a man named Casper Gutman." He described Gutman. "That fellow Cairo you met here is in with them too.... Yes, that's it.... Gutman's staying at the Alexandria, suite twelve C, or was. They've just left here and they're blowing town, so you'll have to move fast, but I don't think they're expecting a pinch.... There's a girl in it too – Gutman's daughter." He described Rhea Gutman. "Watch yourself when you go up against the kid. He's supposed to be pretty good with the gun.... That's right, Tom, and I've got some stuff here for you. I've got the guns he used. . . . That's right. Step on it – and luck to you!"

Spade slowly replaced receiver on prong, telephone on shelf. He wet his lips and looked down at his hands. Their palms were wet. He filled his deep chest with air. His eyes were glittering between straightened lids. He turned and took three long swift steps into the living-room.

Brigid O'Shaughnessy, startled by the suddenness of his approach, let her breath out in a little laughing gasp.

Spade, face to face with her, very close to her, tall, big-boned and thick-muscled, coldly smiling, hard of jaw and eye, said: "They'll talk when they're nailed – about us. We're sitting on dynamite, and we've only got minutes to get set for the police. Give me all of it – fast. Gutman sent you and Cairo to Constantinople?"

She started to speak, hesitated, and bit her lip.

He put a hand on her shoulder. "God damn you, talk!" he said. "I'm in this with you and you're not going to gum it. Talk. He sent you to Constantinople?"

"Y–yes, he sent me. I met Joe there and – and asked him to help me. Then we – "

"Wait. You asked Cairo to help you get it from Kemidov?"

"Yes."

"For Gutman?"

She hesitated again, squirmed under the hard angry glare of his eyes, swallowed, and said: "No, not then. We thought we would get it for ourselves."

"All right. Then?"

"Oh, then I began to be afraid that Joe wouldn't play fair with me, so – so I asked Floyd Thursby to help me."

"And he did. Well?"

"Well, we got it and went to Hongkong."

"With Cairo? Or had you ditched him before that?"

"Yes. We left him in Constantinople, in jail – something about a check."

"Something you fixed up to hold him there?"

She looked shamefacedly at Spade and whispered: "Yes."

"Right. Now you and Thursby are in Hongkong with the bird."

"Yes, and then – I didn't know him very well – I didn't know whether I could trust him. I thought it would be safer – anyway, I met Captain Jacobi and I knew his boat was coming here, so I asked him to bring a package for me – and that was the bird. I wasn't sure I could trust Thursby, or that Joe or – or somebody working for Gutman might not be on the boat we came on – and that seemed the safest plan."

"All right. Then you and Thursby caught one of the fast boats over. Then what?"

"Then – then I was afraid of Gutman. I knew he had people – connections – everywhere, and he'd soon know what we had done. And I was afraid he'd have learned that we had left Hongkong for San Francisco. He was in New York and I knew if he heard that by cable he would have plenty of time to get here by the time we did, or before. He did. I didn't know that then, but I was afraid of it, and I had to wait here until Captain Jacobi's boat arrived. And I was afraid Gutman would find me – or find Floyd and buy him over. That's why I came to you and asked you to watch him for –"

"That's a lie," Spade said. "You had Thursby hooked and you knew it. He was a sucker for women. His record shows that – the only falls he took were over women. And once a chump, always a chump. Maybe you didn't know his record, but you'd know you had him safe."

She blushed and looked timidly at him.

He said: "You wanted to get him out of the way before Jacobi came with the loot. What was your scheme?"

"I – I knew he'd left the States with a gambler after some trouble. I didn't know what it was, but I thought that if it was anything serious and he saw a detective watching him he'd

215

think it was on account of the old trouble, and would be frightened into going away. I didn't think – "

"You told him he was being shadowed," Spade said confidently. "Miles hadn't many brains, but he wasn't clumsy enough to be spotted the first night."

"I told him, yes. When we went out for a walk that night I pretended to discover Mr. Archer following us and pointed him out to Floyd." She sobbed. "But please believe, Sam, that I wouldn't have done it if I had thought Floyd would kill him. I thought he'd be frightened into leaving the city. I didn't for a minute think he'd shoot him like that."

Spade smiled wolfishly with his lips, but not at all with his eyes. He said: "If you thought he wouldn't you were right, angel."

The girl's upraised face held utter astonishment.

Spade said: "Thursby didn't shoot him."

Incredulity joined astonishment in the girl's face.

Spade said: "Miles hadn't many brains, but, Christ! he had too many years' experience as a detective to be caught like that by the man he was shadowing. Up a blind alley with his gun tucked away on his hip and his overcoat buttoned? Not a chance. He was as dumb as any man ought to be, but he wasn't quite that dumb. The only two ways out of the alley could be watched from the edge of Bush Street over the tunnel. You'd told us Thursby was a bad actor. He couldn't have tricked Miles into the alley like that, and he couldn't have driven him in. He was dumb, but not dumb enough for that."

He ran his tongue over the inside of his lips and smiled affectionately at the girl. He said: "But he'd've gone up there with you, angel, if he was sure nobody else was up there. You were his client, so he would have had no reason for not dropping the shadow on your say-so, and if you caught up with him and asked him to go up there he'd've gone. He was just dumb enough for that. He'd've looked you up and down and licked his lips and gone grinning from ear to ear – and then you could've stood as close to him as you liked in the dark and put a hole through him with the gun you had got from Thursby that evening."

Brigid O'Shaughnessy shrank back from him until the edge of the table stopped her. She looked at him with terrified eyes and cried: "Don't – don't talk to me like that, Sam! You know I didn't! You know – "

"Stop it." He looked at the watch on his wrist. "The police will be blowing in any minute now and we're sitting on dynamite. Talk!"

She put the back of a hand on her forehead. "Oh, why do you accuse me of such a terrible – ?"

"Will you stop it?" he demanded in a low impatient voice. "This isn't the spot for the schoolgirl-act. Listen to me. The pair of us are sitting under the gallows." He took hold of her wrists and made her stand up straight in front of him. "Talk!"

"I – I – How did you know he – he licked his lips and looked – ?"

Spade laughed harshly. "I knew Miles. But never mind that. Why did you shoot him?"

She twisted her wrists out of Spade's fingers and put her hands up around the back of his neck, pulling his head down until his mouth all but touched hers. Her body was flat against his from knees to chest. He put his arms around her, holding her tight to him. Her dark-lashed lids were half down over velvet eyes. Her voice was hushed, throbbing: "I didn't mean to, at first. I didn't, really. I meant what I told you, but when I saw Floyd couldn't be frightened I – "

Spade slapped her shoulder. He said: "That's a lie. You asked Miles and me to handle it ourselves. You wanted to be sure the shadower was somebody you knew and who knew you, so they'd go with you. You got the gun from Thursby that day – that night. You had already rented the apartment at the Coronet. You had trunks there and none at the hotel and when I looked the apartment over I found a rent-receipt dated five or six days before the time you told me you rented it."

She swallowed with difficulty and her voice was humble. "Yes, that's a lie, Sam. I did intend to if Floyd – I – I can't look at you and tell you this, Sam." She pulled his head farther down until her cheek was against his cheek, her mouth by his ear, and whispered: "I knew Floyd wouldn't be easily frightened, but I thought that if he knew somebody was shadowing him either he'd – Oh, I can't say it, Sam!" She clung to him, sobbing.

Spade said: "You thought Floyd would tackle him and one or the other of them would go down. If Thursby was the one then you were rid of him. If Miles was, then you could see that Floyd was caught and you'd be rid of him. That it?"

"S-something like that."

"And when you found that Thursby didn't mean to tackle him you borrowed the gun and did it yourself. Right?"

"Yes – though not exactly."

"But exact enough. And you had that plan up your sleeve from the first. You thought Floyd would be nailed for the killing."

"I – I thought they'd hold him at least until after Captain Jacobi had arrived with the falcon and – "

"And you didn't know then that Gutman was here hunting for you. You didn't suspect that or you wouldn't have shaken your gunman. You knew Gutman was here as soon as you heard Thursby had been shot. Then you knew you needed another protector, so you came back to me. Right?"

"Yes, but – oh, sweetheart! – it wasn't only that. I would have come back to you sooner or later. From the first instant I saw you I knew – "

Spade said tenderly: "You angel! Well, if you get a good break you'll be out of San Quentin in twenty years and you can come back to me then."

She took her cheek away from his, drawing her head far back to stare up without comprehension at him.

He was pale. He said tenderly: "I hope to Christ they don't hang you, precious, by that sweet neck." He slid his hands up to caress her throat.

In an instant she was out of his arms, back against the table, crouching, both hands spread over her throat. Her face was wild-eyed, haggard. Her dry mouth opened and closed. She said in a small parched voice: "You're not – " She could get no other words out.

Spade's face was yellow-white now. His mouth smiled and there were smile-wrinkles around his glittering eyes. His voice was soft, gentle. He said: "I'm going to send you over. The chances are you'll get off with life. That means you'll be out again in twenty years. You're an angel. I'll wait for you." He cleared his throat. "If they hang you I'll always remember you."

She dropped her hands and stood erect. Her face became smooth and untroubled except for the faintest of dubious glints in her eyes. She smiled back at him, gently. "Don't, Sam, don't say that even in fun. Oh, you frightened me for a moment! I really thought you – You know you do such wild and unpredictable things that – " She broke off. She thrust her face forward and stared deep into his eyes. Her cheeks and the flesh around her mouth shivered and fear came back into her eyes. "What – ? Sam!" She put her hand to her throat again and lost her erectness.

Spade laughed. His yellow-white face was damp with sweat and though he held his smile he could not hold softness in his voice. He croaked: "Don't be silly. You're taking the fall. One of us has got to take it, after the talking those birds will do. They'd hand me sure. You're likely to get a better break. Well?"

"But – but, Sam, you can't! Not after what we've been to each other. You can't – "

"Like hell I can't."

She took a long trembling breath. "You've been playing with me? Only pretending you cared – to trap me like this? You didn't – care at all? You didn't – don't – l-love me?"

"I think I do," Spade said. "What of it?" The muscles holding his smile in place stood out like wales. "I'm not Thursby. I'm not Jacobi. I won't play the sap for you."

"That is not just," she cried. Tears came to her eyes. "It's unfair. It's contemptible of you. You know it was not that. You can't say that."

"Like hell I can't," Spade said. "You came into my bed to stop me asking questions. You led me out yesterday for Gutman with that phoney call for help. Last night you came here with them and waited outside for me and came in with me. You were in my arms when the trap was sprung – I couldn't have gone for a gun if I'd had one on me and couldn't have made a fight of it if I had wanted to. And if they didn't take you away with them it was only because Gutman's got too much sense to trust you except for short stretches when he has to and because he thought I'd play the sap for you and – not wanting to hurt you – wouldn't be able to hurt him."

Brigid O'Shaughnessy blinked her tears away. She took a step towards him and stood looking him in the eyes, straight and proud. "You called me a liar," she said. "Now you are lying. You're lying if you say you don't know down in your heart that, in spite of anything I've done, I love you."

Spade made a short abrupt bow. His eyes were becoming bloodshot, but there was no other change in his damp and yellowish fixedly smiling face. "Maybe I do," he said. "What of it? I should trust you? You who arranged that nice little trick for – for my predecessor, Thursby? You who knocked off Miles, a man you had nothing against, in cold blood, just like swatting a fly, for the sake of double-crossing Thursby? You who double-crossed Gutman, Cairo, Thursby – one, two, three? You who've never played square with me for half an hour at a stretch since I've known you? I should trust you? No, no, darling. I wouldn't do it even if I could. Why should I?"

Her eyes were steady under his and her hushed voice was steady when she replied: "Why should you? If you've been playing with me, if you do not love me, there is no answer to that. If you did, no answer would be needed."

Blood streaked Spade's eyeballs now and his long-held smile had become a frightful grimace. He cleared his throat huskily and said: "Making speeches is no damned good now." He put a hand on her shoulder. The hand shook and jerked. "I don't care who loves who, I'm not going to play the sap for you. I won't walk in Thursby's and Christ knows who else's footsteps. You killed Miles and you're going over for it. I could have helped you by letting the others go and standing off the police the best way I could. It's too late for that now. I can't help you now. And I wouldn't if I could."

She put a hand on his hand on her shoulder. "Don't help me then," she whispered, "but don't hurt me. Let me go away now."

"No," he said. "I'm sunk if I haven't got you to hand over to the police when they come. That's the only thing that can keep me from going down with the others."

"You won't do that for me?"

"I won't play the sap for you."

"Don't say that, please." She took his hand from her shoulder and held it to her face. "Why must you do this to me, Sam? Surely Mr. Archer wasn't as much to you as – "

"Miles," Spade said hoarsely, "was a son of a bitch. I found that out the first week we were in business together and I meant to kick him out as soon as the year was up. You didn't do me a damned bit of harm by killing him."

"Then what?"

Spade pulled his hand out of hers. He no longer either smiled or grimaced. His wet yellow face was set hard and deeply lined. His eyes burned madly. He said: "Listen. This isn't a damned bit of good. You'll never understand me, but I'll try once more and then we'll give it up. Listen. When a man's partner is killed he's supposed to do something about it. It doesn't make any difference what you thought of him. He was your partner and you're supposed to do something about it. Then it happens we were in the detective business. Well, when one of your organization gets killed it's bad business to let the killer get away with it. It's bad all around – bad for that one organization, bad for every detective everywhere. Third, I'm a detective and expecting me to run criminals down and then let them go free is like asking a dog to catch a rabbit and let it go. It can be done, all right, and sometimes it is done, but it's not the natural thing. The only way I could have let you go was by letting Gutman and Cairo and the kid go. That's – "

"You're not serious," she said. "You don't expect me to think that these things you're saying are sufficient reason for sending me to the – "

"Wait till I'm through and then you can talk. Fourth, no matter what I wanted to do now it would be absolutely impossible for me to let you go without having myself dragged to the gallows with the others. Next, I've no reason in God's world to think I can trust you and if I did this and got away with it you'd have something on me that you could use whenever you happened to want to. That's five of them. The sixth would be that, since I've also got something on you, I couldn't be sure you wouldn't decide to shoot a hole in *me* some day. Seventh, I don't even like the idea of thinking that there might be one chance in a hundred that you'd played me for a sucker. And eighth – but that's enough. All those on one side. Maybe some of them are unimportant. I won't argue about that. But look at the number of them. Now on the other side we've got what? All we've got is the fact that maybe you love me and maybe I love you."

"You know," she whispered, "whether you do or not."

"I don't. It's easy enough to be nuts about you." He looked hungrily from her hair to her feet and up to her eyes again. "But I don't know what that amounts to. Does anybody ever? But suppose I do? What of it? Maybe next month I won't. I've been through it before – when it lasted that long. Then what? Then I'll think I played the sap. And if I did it and got sent over then I'd be sure I was the sap. Well, if I send you over I'll be sorry as hell – I'll have some rotten nights – but that'll pass. Listen." He took her by the shoulders and bent her back, leaning over her. "If that doesn't mean anything to you forget it and we'll make it this: I won't because all of me wants to – wants to say to hell with the consequences and do it – and because – God damn you – you've counted on that with me the same as you counted on that with the others." He took his hands from her shoulders and let them fall to his sides.

She put her hands up to his cheeks and drew his face down again. "Look at me," she said, "and tell me the truth. Would you have done this to me if the falcon had been real and you had been paid your money?"

"What difference does that make now? Don't be too sure I'm as crooked as I'm supposed to be. That kind of reputation might be good business – bringing in high-priced jobs and making it easier to deal with the enemy."

She looked at him, saying nothing.

He moved his shoulders a little and said: "Well, a lot of money would have been at least one more item on the other side of the scales."

She put her face up to his face. Her mouth was slightly open with lips a little thrust out. She whispered: "If you loved me you'd need nothing more on that side."

Spade set the edges of his teeth together and said through them: "I won't play the sap for you."

She put her mouth to his, slowly, her arms around him, and came into his arms. She was in his arms when the door-bell rang.

* * *

Spade, left arm around Brigid O'Shaughnessy, opened the corridor-door. Lieutenant Dundy, Detective-sergeant Tom Polhaus, and two other detectives were there.

Spade said: "Hello, Tom. Get them?"

Polhaus said: "Got them."

"Swell. Come in. Here's another one for you." Spade pressed the girl forward. "She killed Miles. And I've got some exhibits – the boy's guns, one of Cairo's, a black statuette that all the hell was about, and a thousand-dollar bill that I was supposed to be bribed with." He looked at Dundy, drew his brows together, leaned forward to peer into the Lieutenant's face, and burst out laughing. "What in hell's the matter with your little playmate, Tom? He looks heart-broken." He laughed again. "I bet, by God! when he heard Gutman's story he thought he had me at last."

"Cut it out, Sam," Tom grumbled. "We didn't think – "

"Like hell he didn't," Spade said merrily. "He came up here with his mouth watering, though you'd have sense enough to know I'd been stringing Gutman."

"Cut it out," Tom grumbled again, looking uneasily side-wise at his superior. "Anyways we got it from Cairo. Gutman's dead. The kid had just finished shooting him up when we got there."

Spade nodded. "He ought to have expected that," he said.

Effie Perine put down her newspaper and jumped out of Spade's chair when he came into the office at a little after nine o'clock Monday morning.

He said: "Morning, angel."

"Is that – what the papers have – right?" she asked.

"Yes, ma'am." He dropped his hat on the desk and sat down. His face was pasty in color, but its lines were strong and cheerful and his eyes, though still somewhat red-veined, were clear.

The girl's brown eyes were peculiarly enlarged and there was a queer twist to her mouth. She stood beside him, staring down at him.

He raised his head, grinned, and said mockingly: "So much for your woman's intuition."

Her voice was queer as the expression on her face. "You did that, Sam, to her?"

He nodded. "Your Sam's a detective." He looked sharply at her. He put his arm around her waist, his hand on her hip. "She did kill Miles, angel," he said gently, "offhand, like that." He snapped the fingers of his other hand.

She escaped from his arm as if it had hurt her. "Don't, please, don't touch me," she said brokenly. "I know – I know you're right. You're right. But don't touch me now – not now."

Spade's face became pale as his collar.

The corridor-door's knob rattled. Effie Perine turned quickly and went into the outer office, shutting the door behind her. When she came in again she shut it behind her.

She said in a small flat voice: "Iva is here."

Spade, looking down at his desk, nodded almost imperceptibly. "Yes," he said, and shivered. "Well, send her in."

THE THIN MAN

To Lillian

1

I WAS LEANING against the bar in a speakeasy on Fifty-second Street, waiting for Nora to finish her Christmas shopping, when a girl got up from the table where she had been sitting with three other people and came over to me. She was small and blonde, and whether you looked at her face or at her body in powder-blue sports clothes, the result was satisfactory. "Aren't you Nick Charles?" she asked.

I said: "Yes."

She held out her hand. "I'm Dorothy Wynant. You don't remember me, but you ought to remember my father, Clyde Wynant. You – "

"Sure," I said, "and I remember you now, but you were only a kid of eleven or twelve then, weren't you?"

"Yes, that was eight years ago. Listen: remember those stories you told me? Were they true?"

"Probably not. How is your father?"

She laughed. "I was going to ask you. Mamma divorced him, you know, and we never hear from him – except when he gets in the newspapers now and then with some of his carryings on. Don't you ever see him?"

My glass was empty. I asked her what she would have to drink, she said Scotch and soda. I ordered two of them and said: "No, I've been living in San Francisco."

She said slowly: "I'd like to see him. Mamma would raise hell if she found it out, but I'd like to see him."

"Well?"

"He's not where we used to live, on Riverside Drive, and he's not in the phone-book or city directory."

"Try his lawyer," I suggested.

Her face brightened. "Who is he?"

"It used to be a fellow named Mac-something-or-other –
Macaulay, that's it, Herbert Macaulay. He was in the Singer
Building."

"Lend me a nickel," she said, and went out to the telephone. She came back smiling. "I found him. He's just round
the corner on Fifth Avenue."

"Your father?"

"The lawyer. He says my father's out of town. I'm going
round to see him." She raised her glass to me. "Family
reunions. Look, why don't – "

Asta jumped up and punched me in the belly with her front
feet. Nora, at the other end of the leash, said: "She's had a swell
afternoon – knocked over a table of toys at Lord & Taylor's,
scared a fat woman silly by licking her leg in Saks's, and's been
patted by three policemen."

I made introductions. "My wife, Dorothy Wynant. Her
father was once a client of mine, when she was only so high.
A good guy, but screwy."

"I was fascinated by him," Dorothy said, meaning me, "a
real live detective, and used to follow him around making him
tell me about his experiences. He told me awful lies, but
I believed every word."

I said: "You look tired, Nora."

"I am. Let's sit down."

Dorothy Wynant said she had to go back to her table. She
shook hands with Nora; we must drop in for cocktails, they
were living at the Courtland, her mother's name was Jorgensen now. We would be glad to and she must come see us some
time, we were at the Normandie and would be in New York
for another week or two. Dorothy patted the dog's head and
left us.

We found a table. Nora said: "She's pretty."

"If you like them like that."

She grinned at me. "You got types?"

"Only you, darling – lanky brunettes with wicked jaws."

"And how about the red-head you wandered off with at the Quinns' last night?"

"That's silly," I said. "She just wanted to show me some French etchings."

2

THE NEXT DAY Herbert Macaulay telephoned me. "Hello, I didn't know you were back in town till Dorothy Wynant told me. How about lunch?"

"What time is it?"

"Half-past eleven. Did I wake you up?"

"Yes," I said, "but that's all right. Suppose you come up here for lunch: I've got a hangover and don't feel like running around much. . . . OK, say one o'clock." I had a drink with Nora, who was going out to have her hair washed, then another after a shower, and was feeling better by the time the telephone rang again. A female voice asked: "Is Mr. Macaulay there?"

"Not yet."

"Sorry to trouble you, but would you mind asking him to call his office as soon as he gets there? It's important." I promised to do that.

Macaulay arrived about ten minutes later. He was a big curly-haired, rosy-cheeked, rather good-looking chap of about my age – forty-one – though he looked younger. He was supposed to be a pretty good lawyer. I had worked on several jobs for him when I was living in New York and we had always got along nicely. Now we shook hands and patted each other's backs, and he asked me how the world was treating me, and I said, "Fine," and asked him and he said, "Fine," and I told him to call his office.

He came away from the telephone frowning. "Wynant's back in town," he said, "and wants me to meet him."

I turned around with the drinks I had poured. "Well, the lunch can – "

"Let him wait," he said, and took one of the glasses from me.

"Still as screwy as ever?"

"That's no joke," Macaulay said solemnly. "You heard they had him in a sanatorium for nearly a year back in '29?"

"No."

He nodded. He sat down, put his glass on a table beside his chair, and leaned towards me a little. "What's Mimi up to, Charles?"

"Mimi? Oh, the wife – the ex-wife. I don't know. Does she have to be up to something?"

"She usually is," he said dryly, and then very slowly, "and I thought you'd know."

So that was it. I said: "Listen, Mac, I haven't been a detective for six years, since 1927." He stared at me. "On the level," I assured him, "a year after I got married, my wife's father died and left her a lumber mill and a narrow-gauge railroad and some other things and I quit the Agency to look after them. Anyway I wouldn't be working for Mimi Wynant, or Jorgensen, or whatever her name is – she never liked me and I never liked her."

"Oh, I didn't think you – " Macaulay broke off with a vague gesture and picked up his glass. When he took it away from his mouth, he said: "I was just wondering. Here Mimi phones me three days ago – Tuesday – trying to find Wynant; then yesterday Dorothy phones, saying you told her to, and comes around, and – I thought you were still sleuthing, so I was wondering what it was all about."

"Didn't they tell you?"

"Sure – they wanted to see him for old times' sake. That means a lot."

"You lawyers are a suspicious crew," I said. "Maybe they did – that and money. But what's the fuss about? Is he in hiding?"

Macaulay shrugged. "You know as much about it as I do. I haven't seen him since October." He drank again. "How long are you going to be in town?"

"Till after New Year's," I told him and went to the telephone to ask room service for menus.

3

NORA AND I went to the opening of *Honeymoon* at the Little
Theatre that night and then to a party given by some people
named Freeman or Fielding or something. I felt pretty low
when she called me the next morning. She gave me a newspaper and a cup of coffee and said: "Read that."

I patiently read a paragraph or two, then put the paper
down and took a sip of coffee. "Fun's fun," I said, "but right
now I'd swap you all the interviews with Mayor-elect O'Brien
ever printed – and throw in the Indian picture – for a slug of
whis – "

"Not that, stupid." She put a finger on the paper. "That."

INVENTOR'S SECRETARY
MURDERED IN APARTMENT
JULIA WOLF'S BULLET-RIDDLED BODY FOUND;
POLICE SEEK HER EMPLOYER, CLYDE WYNANT

The bullet-riddled body of Julia Wolf, thirty-two-year-
old confidential secretary to Clyde Miller Wynant, well-
known inventor, was discovered late yesterday afternoon
in the dead woman's apartment at 411 East Fifty-fourth
St. by Mrs. Christian Jorgensen, divorced wife of the
inventor, who had gone there in an attempt to learn her
former husband's present address.

Mrs. Jorgensen, who returned Monday after a six-year
stay in Europe, told police that she heard feeble groans
when she rang the murdered woman's door-bell, where-
upon she notified an elevator boy, Mervin Holly,

who called Walter Meany, apartment-house superintendent. Miss Wolf was lying on the bedroom floor with
four .32-caliber bullet-wounds in her chest when they
entered the apartment, and died without having recovered consciousness before police and medical aid arrived.

Herbert Macaulay, Wynant's attorney, told the police
that he had not seen the inventor since October. He
stated that Wynant called him on the telephone yesterday
and made an appointment, but failed to keep it; and
disclaimed any knowledge of his client's whereabouts.
Miss Wolf, Macaulay stated, had been in the inventor's
employ for the past eight years. The attorney said he
knew nothing about the dead woman's family or private
affairs and could throw no light on her murder.

The bullet-wounds could not have been self-inflicted,
according to . . .

The rest of it was the usual police-department handout.

"Do you suppose he killed her?" Nora asked when I put the
paper down again.

"Wynant? I wouldn't be surprised. He's batty as hell."

"Did you know her?"

"Yes. How about a drop of something to cut the phlegm?"

"What was she like?"

"Not bad," I said. "She wasn't bad-looking and she had a
lot of sense and a lot of nerve – and it took both to live with
that guy."

"She lived with him?"

"Yes. I want a drink, please. That is, it was like that when
I knew them."

"Why don't you have some breakfast first? Was she in love
with him or was it just business?"

"I don't know. It's too early for breakfast."

When Nora opened the door to go out, the dog came in
and put her front feet on the bed, her face in my face. I rubbed

her head and tried to remember something Wynant had once said to me, something about women and dogs. It was not the woman-spaniel-walnut-tree line. I could not remember what it was, but there seemed to be some point in trying to remember. Nora returned with two drinks and another question: "What's he like?"

"Tall – over six feet – and one of the thinnest men I've ever seen. He must be about fifty now, and his hair was almost white when I knew him. Usually needs a haircut, ragged brindle mustache, bites his fingernails." I pushed the dog away to reach for my drink.

"Sounds lovely. What were you doing with him?"

"A fellow who'd worked for him accused him of stealing some kind of invention from him. Rosewater was his name. He tried to shake Wynant down by threatening to shoot him, bomb his house, kidnap his children, cut his wife's throat – I don't know what all – if he didn't come across. We never caught him – must've scared him off. Anyway, the threats stopped and nothing happened."

Nora stopped drinking to ask: "Did Wynant really steal it?"

"Tch, tch, tch," I said. "This is Christmas Eve: try to think good of your fellow man."

4

THAT AFTERNOON I took Asta for a walk, explained to two people that she was a Schnauzer and not a cross between a Scottie and an Irish terrier, stopped at Jim's for a couple of drinks, ran into Larry Crowley, and brought him back to the Normandie with me. Nora was pouring cocktails for the Quinns, Margot Innes, a man whose name I did not catch, and Dorothy Wynant. Dorothy said she wanted to talk to me, so we carried our cocktails into the bedroom.

She came to the point right away. "Do you think my father killed her, Nick?"

"No," I said. "Why should I?"

"Well, the police have — Listen, she was his mistress, wasn't she?"

I nodded. "When I knew them."

She stared at her glass while saying, "He's my father. I never liked him. I never liked Mamma." She looked up at me. "I don't like Gilbert." Gilbert was her brother.

"Don't let that worry you. Lots of people don't like their relatives."

"Do you like them?"

"My relatives?"

"Mine." She scowled at me. "And stop talking to me as if I was still twelve."

"It's not that," I explained. "I'm getting tight."

"Well, do you?"

I shook my head. "You were all right, just a spoiled kid. I could get along without the rest of them."

"What's the matter with us?" she asked, not argumentatively, but as if she really wanted to know.

"Different things. Your – "

Harrison Quinn opened the door and said: "Come on over and play some Ping-Pong, Nick."

"In a little while."

"Bring Beautiful along." He leered at Dorothy and went away.

She said: "I don't suppose you know Jorgensen."

"I know a Nels Jorgensen."

"Some people have all the luck. This one's named Christian. He's a honey. That's Mamma – divorces a lunatic and marries a gigolo." Her eyes became wet. She caught her breath in a sob and asked: "What am I going to do, Nick?" Her voice was a frightened child's.

I put an arm around her and made what I hoped were comforting sounds. She cried on my lapel. The telephone beside the bed began to ring. In the next room "Rise and Shine" was coming through the radio. My glass was empty. I said: "Walk out on them."

She sobbed again. "You can't walk out on yourself."

"Maybe I don't know what you're talking about."

"Please don't tease me," she said humbly.

Nora, coming in to answer the telephone, looked questioningly at me. I made a face at her over the girl's head. When Nora said "Hello" into the telephone, the girl stepped quickly back away from me and blushed. "I – I'm sorry," she stammered, "I didn't – "

Nora smiled sympathetically at her. I said: "Don't be a dope." The girl found her handkerchief and dabbed at her eyes with it.

Nora spoke into the telephone. "Yes . . . I'll see if he's in. Who's calling, please?" She put a hand over the mouthpiece and addressed me: "It's a man named Norman. Do you want to talk to him?"

I said I didn't know and took the telephone. "Hello."

A somewhat harsh voice said: "Mr. Charles? ... Mr. Charles, I understand that you were formerly connected with the Trans-American Detective Agency."

"Who is this?" I asked.

"My name is Albert Norman, Mr. Charles, which probably means nothing to you, but I would like to lay a proposition before you. I am sure you will – "

"What kind of a proposition?"

"I can't discuss it over the phone, Mr. Charles, but if you will give me half an hour of your time, I can promise – "

"Sorry," I said. "I'm pretty busy and – "

"But, Mr. Charles, this is – " Then there was a loud noise: it could have been a shot or something falling or anything else that would make a loud noise. I said, "Hello," a couple of times, got no answer, and hung up.

Nora had Dorothy over in front of a looking-glass soothing her with powder and rouge. I said, "A guy selling insurance," and we went into the living-room for a drink. Some more people had come in. I spoke to them. Harrison Quinn left the sofa where he had been sitting with Margot Innes and said: "Now Ping-Pong." Asta jumped up and punched me in the belly with her front feet. I shut off the radio and poured myself a cocktail. The man whose name I had not caught was saying: "Comes the revolution and we'll all be lined up against the wall – first thing." He seemed to think it was a good idea.

Quinn came over to refill his glass. He looked towards the bedroom-door. "Where'd you find the little blonde?"

"Used to bounce it on my knee."

"Which knee?" he asked. "Could I touch it?"

Nora and Dorothy came out of the bedroom. I saw an afternoon paper on the radio and picked it up. Headlines said:

JULIA WOLF ONCE RACKETEER'S GIRL;
ARTHUR NUNHEIM IDENTIFIES BODY;
WYNANT STILL MISSING

Nora, at my elbow, spoke in a low voice: "I asked her to have dinner with us. Be nice to the child" – Nora was twenty-six – "she's all upset."

"Whatever you say." I turned around. Dorothy, across the room, was laughing at something Quinn was telling her. "But if you get mixed up in people's troubles, don't expect me to kiss you where you're hurt."

"I won't. You're a sweet old fool. Don't read that here now." She took the newspaper away from me and stuck it out of sight behind the radio.

5

NORA COULD NOT sleep that night. She read Chaliapin's memoirs until I began to doze and then woke me up by asking: "Are you asleep?" I said I was. She lit a cigarette for me, one for herself. "Don't you ever think you'd like to go back to detecting once in a while just for the fun of it? You know, when something special comes up, like the Lindb –"

"Darling," I said, "my guess is that Wynant killed her, and the police'll catch him without my help. Anyway, it's nothing in my life."

"I didn't mean just that, but –"

"But besides I haven't the time: I'm too busy trying to see that you don't lose any of the money I married you for." I kissed her. "Don't you think maybe a drink would help you to sleep?"

"No, thanks."

"Maybe it would if I took one." When I brought my Scotch and soda back to bed, she was frowning into space. I said: "She's cute, but she's cuckoo. She wouldn't be his daughter if she wasn't. You can't tell how much of what she says is what she thinks and you can't tell how much of what she thinks ever really happened. I like her, but I think you're letting –"

"I'm not sure I like her," Nora said thoughtfully, "she's probably a little bastard, but if a quarter of what she told us is true, she's in a tough spot."

"There's nothing I can do to help her."

"She thinks you can."

"And so do you, which shows that no matter what you think, you can always get somebody else to go along with you."

Nora sighed. "I wish you were sober enough to talk to." She leaned over to take a sip of my drink. "I'll give you your Christmas present now if you'll give me mine."

I shook my head. "At breakfast."

"But it's Christmas now."

"Breakfast."

"Whatever you're giving me," she said, "I hope I don't like it."

"You'll have to keep them anyway, because the man at the Aquarium said he positively wouldn't take them back. He said they'd already bitten the tails off the – "

"It wouldn't hurt you any to find out if you can help her, would it? She's got so much confidence in you, Nicky."

"Everybody trusts Greeks."

"Please."

"You just want to poke your nose into things that – "

"I meant to ask you: did his wife know the Wolf girl was his mistress?"

"I don't know. She didn't like her."

"What's the wife like?"

"I don't know – a woman."

"Good-looking?"

"Used to be very."

"She old?"

"Forty, forty-two. Cut it out, Nora. You don't want any part of it. Let the Charleses stick to the Charleses' troubles and the Wynants stick to the Wynants'."

She pouted. "Maybe that drink would help me."

I got out of bed and mixed her a drink. As I brought it into the bedroom, the telephone began to ring. I looked at my watch on the table. It was nearly five o'clock.

Nora was talking into the telephone: "Hello. . . . Yes, speaking." She looked sidewise at me. I shook my head no.

"Yes. . . . Why, certainly. . . . Yes, certainly." She put the telephone down and grinned at me.

"You're wonderful," I said. "Now what?"

"Dorothy's coming up. I think she's tight."

"That's great." I picked up my bathrobe. "I was afraid I was going to have to go to sleep."

She was bending over looking for her slippers. "Don't be such an old fluff. You can sleep all day." She found her slippers and stood up in them. "Is she really as afraid of her mother as she says?"

"If she's got any sense. Mimi's poison."

Nora screwed up her dark eyes at me and asked slowly: "What are you holding out on me?"

"Oh, dear," I said, "I was hoping I wouldn't have to tell you. Dorothy is really my daughter. I didn't know what I was doing, Nora. It was spring in Venice and I was so young and there was a moon over the – "

"Be funny. Don't you want something to eat?"

"If you do. What do you want?"

"Raw chopped beef sandwich with a lot of onion and some coffee."

Dorothy arrived while I was telephoning an all-night delicatessen. When I went into the living-room, she stood up with some difficulty and said: "I'm awfully sorry, Nick, to keep bothering you and Nora like this, but I can't go home this way tonight. I can't. I'm afraid to. I don't know what'd happen to me, what I'd do. Please don't make me." She was very drunk. Asta sniffed at her ankles.

I said: "Sh-h-h. You're all right here. Sit down. There'll be some coffee in a little while. Where'd you get the snoutful?"

She sat down and shook her head stupidly. "I don't know. I've been everywhere since I left you. I've been everywhere except home because I can't go home this way. Look what I got." She stood up again and took a battered automatic pistol out of her coat-pocket. "Look at that." She waved it at me while Asta, wagging her tail, jumped happily at it.

Nora made a noise with her breathing. The back of my neck was cold. I pushed the dog aside and took the pistol away from Dorothy. "What kind of clowning is this? Sit down." I dropped the pistol into a bathrobe-pocket and pushed Dorothy down in her chair.

"Don't be mad at me, Nick," she whined. "You can keep it. I don't want to make a nuisance of myself."

"Where'd you get it?" I asked.

"In a speakeasy on Tenth Avenue. I gave a man my bracelet – the one with the emeralds and diamonds – for it."

"And then won it back from him in a crap game," I said. "You've still got it on."

She stared at her bracelet. "I thought I did."

I looked at Nora and shook my head. Nora said: "Aw, don't bully her, Nick. She's –"

"He's not bullying me, Nora, he's really not," Dorothy said quickly. "He's – he's the only person I got in the world to turn to."

I remembered Nora had not touched her Scotch and soda, so I went into the bedroom and drank it. When I came back, Nora was sitting on the arm of Dorothy's chair with an arm around the girl. Dorothy was sniffling; Nora was saying: "But Nick's not mad, dear. He likes you." She looked up at me. "You're not mad, are you, Nicky?"

"No, I'm just hurt." I sat on the sofa. "Where'd you get the gun, Dorothy?"

"From a man – I told you."

"What man?"

"I told you – a man in a speakeasy."

"And you gave him a bracelet for it."

"I thought I did, but – look – I've still got my bracelet."

"I noticed that."

Nora patted the girl's shoulder. "Of course you've still got your bracelet."

I said: "When the boy comes with that coffee and stuff, I'm going to bribe him to stick around. I'm not going to stay alone with a couple of – "

Nora scowled at me, told the girl: "Don't mind him. He's been like that all night."

The girl said: "He thinks I'm a silly little drunken fool." Nora patted her shoulder some more.

I asked: "But what'd you want a gun for?"

Dorothy sat up straight and stared at me with wide drunken eyes. "Him," she whispered excitedly, "if he bothered me. I was afraid because I was drunk. That's what it was. And then I was afraid of that, too, so I came here."

"You mean your father?" Nora asked, trying to keep excitement out of her voice.

The girl shook her head. "Clyde Wynant's my father. My stepfather." She leaned against Nora's breast.

Nora said: "Oh," in a tone of very complete understanding. Then she said, "You poor child," and looked significantly at me.

I said: "Let's all have a drink."

"Not me." Nora was scowling at me again. "And I don't think Dorothy wants one."

"Yes, she does. It'll help her sleep." I poured her a terrific dose of Scotch and saw that she drank it. It worked nicely: she was sound asleep by the time our coffee and sandwiches came.

Nora said: "Now you're satisfied."

"Now I'm satisfied. Shall we tuck her in before we eat?"

I carried her into the bedroom and helped Nora undress her. She had a beautiful little body. We went back to our food. I took the pistol out of my pocket and examined it. It had been kicked around a lot. There were two cartridges in it, one in the chamber, one in the magazine.

"What are you going to do with it?" Nora asked.

"Nothing till I find out if it's the one Julia Wolf was killed with. It's a .32."

"But she said – "

"She got it in a speakeasy – from a man – for a bracelet. I heard her."

Nora leaned over her sandwich at me. Her eyes were very shiny and almost black. "Do you suppose she got it from her stepfather?"

"I do," I said, but I said it too earnestly.

Nora said: "You're a Greek louse. But maybe she did; you don't know. And you don't believe her story."

"Listen, darling, tomorrow I'll buy you a whole lot of detective stories, but don't worry your pretty little head over mysteries tonight. All she was trying to tell you was that she was afraid Jorgensen was waiting to try to make her when she got home and she was afraid she was drunk enough to give in."

"But her mother!"

"This family's a family. You can – "

Dorothy Wynant, standing unsteadily in the doorway in a nightgown much too long for her, blinked at the light and said: "Please, can I come in for a little while? I'm afraid in there alone."

"Sure." She came over and curled up beside me on the sofa while Nora went to get something to put around her.

6

THE THREE OF us were at breakfast early that afternoon when the Jorgensens arrived. Nora answered the telephone and came away from it trying to pretend she was not tickled. "It's your mother," she told Dorothy. "She's downstairs. I told her to come up."

Dorothy said: "Damn it. I wish I hadn't phoned her."

I said: "We might just as well be living in the lobby."

Nora said: "He doesn't mean that." She patted Dorothy's shoulder.

The door-bell rang. I went to the door. Eight years had done no damage to Mimi's looks. She was a little riper, showier, that was all. She was larger than her daughter, and her blondness was more vivid. She laughed and held her hands out to me. "Merry Christmas. It's awfully good to see you after all these years. This is my husband. Mr. Charles, Chris."

I said, "I'm glad to see you, Mimi," and shook hands with Jorgensen. He was probably five years younger than his wife, a tall thin erect dark man, carefully dressed and sleek, with smooth hair and a waxed mustache.

He bowed from the waist. "How do you do, Mr. Charles?" His accent was heavy, Teutonic, his hand was lean and muscular. We went inside.

Mimi, when the introductions were over, apologized to Nora for popping in on us. "But I did want to see your husband again, and then I know the only way to get this brat of mine anywhere on time is to carry her off bodily." She turned her smile on Dorothy. "Better get dressed, honey."

Honey grumbled through a mouthful of toast that she didn't see why she had to waste another afternoon at Aunt Alice's even if it was Christmas. "I bet Gilbert's not going."

Mimi said Asta was a lovely dog and asked me if I had *any* idea where that ex-husband of hers might be.

"No." She went on playing with the dog. "He's crazy, absolutely crazy, to disappear at a time like this. No wonder the police at first thought he had something to do with it."

"What do they think now?" I asked.

She looked up at me. "Haven't you seen the papers?"

"No."

"It's a man named Morelli – a gangster. He killed her. He was her lover."

"They caught him?"

"Not yet, but he did it. I wish I could find Clyde. Macaulay won't help me at all. He says he doesn't know where he is, but that's ridiculous. He has powers of attorney from him and everything and I know very well he's in touch with Clyde. Do you think Macaulay's trustworthy?"

"He's Wynant's lawyer," I said. "There's no reason why you should trust him."

"Just what I thought." She moved over a little on the sofa. "Sit down. I've got millions of things to ask you."

"How about a drink first?"

"Anything but egg-nog," she said. "It makes me bilious."

When I came out of the pantry, Nora and Jorgensen were trying their French on each other, Dorothy was still pretending to eat, and Mimi was playing with the dog again. I distributed the drinks and sat down beside Mimi. She said: "Your wife's lovely."

"I like her."

"Tell me the truth, Nick: do you think Clyde's really crazy? I mean crazy enough that something ought to be done about it."

"How do I know?"

DASHIELL HAMMETT

"I'm worried about the children," she said. "I've no claim on him any more – the settlement he made when I divorced him took care of all that – but the children have. We're absolutely penniless now and I'm worried about them. If he is crazy he's just as likely as not to throw away everything and leave them without a cent. What do you think I ought to do?"

"Thinking about putting him in the booby-hatch?"

"No–o," she said slowly, "but I would like to talk to him." She put a hand on my arm. "You could find him."

I shook my head.

"Won't you help me, Nick? We used to be friends." Her big blue eyes were soft and appealing. Dorothy, at the table, was watching us suspiciously.

"For Christ's sake, Mimi," I said, "there's a thousand detectives in New York. Hire one of them. I'm not working at it any more."

"I know, but – Was Dorry very drunk last night?"

"Maybe I was. She seemed all right to me."

"Don't you think she's gotten to be a pretty little thing?"

"I always thought she was."

She thought that over a moment, then said: "She's only a child, Nick."

"What's that got to do with what?" I asked.

She smiled. "How about getting some clothes on, Dorry?"

Dorothy sulkily repeated that she didn't see why she had to waste an afternoon at Aunt Alice's.

Jorgensen turned to address his wife: "Mrs. Charles has the great kindness to suggest that we do not – "

"Yes," Nora said, "why don't you stay awhile? There'll be some people coming in. It won't be very exciting, but – " She waved her glass a little to finish the sentence.

"I'd love to," Mimi replied slowly, "but I'm afraid Alice – "

"Make our apologies to her by telephone," Jorgensen suggested.

"I'll do it," Dorothy said.

252

Mimi nodded. "Be nice to her." Dorothy went into the bedroom. Everybody seemed much brighter. Nora caught my eye and winked merrily and I had to take it and like it because Mimi was looking at me then. Mimi asked me: "You really didn't want us to stay, did you?"

"Of course."

"Chances are you're lying. Weren't you sort of fond of poor Julia?"

" 'Poor Julia' sounds swell from you. I liked her all right."

Mimi put her hand on my arm again. "She broke up my life with Clyde. Naturally I hated her – then – but that's a long time ago. I had no feeling against her when I went to see her Friday. And, Nick, I saw her die. She didn't deserve to die. It was horrible. No matter what I'd felt, there'd be nothing left but pity now. I meant 'poor Julia' when I said it."

"I don't know what you're up to," I said. "I don't know what any of you are up to."

"Any of us," she repeated. "Has Dorry been – "

Dorothy came in from the bedroom. "I squared it." She kissed her mother on the mouth and sat down beside her.

Mimi, looking in her compact-mirror to see her mouth had not been smeared, asked: "She wasn't peevish about it?"

"No, I squared it. What do you have to do to get a drink?"

I said: "You have to walk over to that table where the ice and bottles are and pour it."

Mimi said: "You drink too much."

"I don't drink as much as Nick." She went over to the table.

Mimi shook her head. "These children! I mean you were pretty fond of Julia Wolf, weren't you?"

Dorothy called: "You want one, Nick?"

"Thanks," I said: then to Mimi, "I liked her well enough."

"You're the damnedest evasive man," she complained. "Did you like her as much as you used to like me for instance?"

"You mean those couple of afternoons we killed?"

Her laugh was genuine. "That's certainly an answer." She turned to Dorothy, carrying glasses towards us. "You'll have to get a robe that shade of blue, darling. It's very becoming to you." I took one of the glasses from Dorothy and said I thought I had better get dressed.

WHEN I CAME out of the bathroom, Nora and Dorothy were in the bedroom, Nora combing her hair, Dorothy sitting on the side of the bed dangling a stocking. Nora made a kiss at me in the dressing-table mirror. She looked very happy.

"You like Nick a lot, don't you, Nora?" Dorothy asked.

"He's an old Greek fool, but I'm used to him."

"Charles isn't a Greek name."

"It's Charalambides," I explained. "When the old man came over, the mug that put him through Ellis Island said Charalambides was too long – too much trouble to write – and whittled it down to Charles. It was all right with the old man; they could have called him X so they let him in."

Dorothy stared at me. "I never know when you're lying." She started to put on the stocking, stopped. "What's Mamma trying to do to you?"

"Nothing. Pump me. She'd like to know what you did and said last night."

"I thought so. What'd you tell her?"

"What could I tell her? You don't do or say anything."

She wrinkled her forehead over that, but when she spoke again it was about something else: "I never knew there was anything between you and Mamma. Of course I was only a kid then and wouldn't have known what it was all about even if I'd noticed anything, but I didn't even know you called each other by your first names."

Nora turned from the mirror laughing. "Now we're getting somewhere." She waved the comb at Dorothy. "Go on, dear."

Dorothy said earnestly: "Well, I didn't know."

I was taking laundry pins out of a shirt. "What do you know now?" I asked.

"Nothing," she said slowly, and her face began to grow pink, "but I can guess." She bent over her stocking.

"Can and do," I growled. "You're a dope, but don't look so embarrassed. You can't help it if you've got a dirty mind."

She raised her head and laughed, but when she asked, "Do you think I take after Mamma much?" she was serious.

"I wouldn't be surprised."

"But do you?"

"You want me to say no. No."

"That's what I have to live with," Nora said cheerfully. "You can't do anything with him."

I finished dressing first and went out to the living-room. Mimi was sitting on Jorgensen's knee. She stood up and asked: "What'd you get for Christmas?"

"Nora gave me a watch." I showed it to her.

She said it was lovely, and it was. "What'd you give her?"

"Necklace."

Jorgensen said, "May I?" and rose to mix himself a drink.

The door-bell rang. I let the Quinns and Margot Innes in, introduced them to the Jorgensens. Presently Nora and Dorothy finished dressing and came out of the bedroom, and Quinn attached himself to Dorothy. Larry Crowley arrived with a girl named Denis, and a few minutes later the Edges. I won thirty-two dollars – on the cuff – from Margot at backgammon. The Denis girl had to go into the bedroom and lie down awhile. Alice Quinn, with Margot's help, tore her husband away from Dorothy at a little after six and carried him off to keep a date they had. The Edges left. Mimi put on her coat, got her husband and daughter into their coats.

"It's awful short notice," she said, "but can't you come to dinner tomorrow night?"

Nora said: "Certainly." We shook hands and made polite speeches all around and they went away. Nora shut the door after them and leaned her back against it. "Jesus, he's a handsome guy," she said.

SO FAR I had known just where I stood on the Wolf-Wynant-Jorgensen troubles and what I was doing – the answers were, respectively, nowhere and nothing – but when we stopped at Reuben's for coffee on our way home at four the next morning, Nora opened a newspaper and found a line in one of the gossip columns: "Nick Charles, former Trans-American Detective Agency ace, on from Coast to sift the Julia Wolf murder mystery"; and when I opened my eyes and sat up in bed some six hours later Nora was shaking me and a man with a gun in his hand was standing in the bedroom doorway.

He was a plump dark youngish man of medium height, broad through the jaws, narrow between the eyes. He wore a black derby hat, a black overcoat that fitted him very snugly, a dark suit, and black shoes, all looking as if he had bought them within the past fifteen minutes. The gun, a blunt black .38-caliber automatic, lay comfortably in his hand, not pointing at anything. Nora was saying: "He made me let him in, Nick. He said he had to – "

"I got to talk to you," the man with the gun said. "That's all, but I got to do that." His voice was low, rasping. I had blinked myself awake by then. I looked at Nora. She was excited, but apparently not frightened: she might have been watching a horse she had a bet on coming down the stretch with a nose lead.

I said: "All right, talk, but do you mind putting the gun away? My wife doesn't care, but I'm pregnant and I don't want the child to be born with – "

He smiled with his lower lip. "You don't have to tell me you're tough. I heard about you." He put the pistol in his overcoat-pocket. "I'm Shep Morelli."

"I never heard about you," I said.

He took a step into the room and began to shake his head from side to side. "I didn't knock Julia off."

"Maybe you didn't, but you're bringing the news to the wrong place. I got nothing to do with it."

"I haven't seen her in three months," he said. "We were washed up."

"Tell the police."

"I wouldn't have any reason to hurt her: she was always on the up and up with me."

"That's all swell," I said, "only you're peddling your fish in the wrong market."

"Listen." He took another step towards the bed. "Studsy Burke tells me you used to be OK That's why I'm here. Do the – "

"How is Studsy?" I asked. "I haven't seen him since the time he went up the river in '23 or '24."

"He's all right. He'd like to see you. He's got a joint on West Forty-ninth, the Pigiron Club. But listen, what's the law doing to me? Do they think I did it? Or is it just something else to pin on me?"

I shook my head. "I'd tell you if I knew. Don't let news-papers fool you: I'm not in this. Ask the police."

"That'd be very smart." He smiled with his lower lip again. "That'd be the smartest thing I ever did. Me that a police captain's been in a hospital three weeks on account we had an argument. The boys would like me to come in and ask 'em questions. They'd like it right down to the end of their black-jacks." He turned a hand over, palm up. "I come to you on the level. Studsy says you're on the level. Be on the level."

"I'm being on the level," I assured him. "If I knew anything I'd – "

Knuckles drummed on the corridor-door, three times, sharply. Morelli's gun was in his hand before the noise stopped. His eyes seemed to move in all directions at once. His voice was a metallic snarl deep in his chest: "Well?"

"I don't know." I sat up a little higher in bed and nodded at the gun in his hand. "That makes it your party." The gun pointed very accurately at my chest. I could hear the blood in my ears, and my lips felt swollen. I said: "There's no fire-escape." I put my left hand out towards Nora, who was sitting on the far side of the bed.

The knuckles hit the door again, and a deep voice called: "Open up. Police."

Morelli's lower lip crawled up to lap the upper, and the whites of his eyes began to show under the irises. "You son of a bitch," he said slowly, almost as if he were sorry for me. He moved his feet the least bit, flattening them against the floor.

A key touched the outer lock. I hit Nora with my left hand, knocking her down across the room. The pillow I chucked with my right hand at Morelli's gun seemed to have no weight; it drifted slow as a piece of tissue paper. No noise in the world, before or after, was ever as loud as Morelli's gun going off. Something pushed my left side as I sprawled across the floor. I caught one of his ankles and rolled over with it, bringing him down on me, and he clubbed my back with the gun until I got a hand free and began to hit him as low in the body as I could.

Men came in and dragged us apart. It took us five minutes to bring Nora to. She sat up holding her cheek and looked around the room until she saw Morelli, nippers on one wrist, standing between two detectives. Morelli's face was a mess: the coppers had worked him over a little just for the fun of it. Nora glared at me. "You damned fool," she said, "you didn't have to knock me cold. I knew you'd take him, but I wanted to see it."

One of the coppers laughed. "Jesus," he said admiringly, "there's a woman with hair on her chest."

She smiled at him and stood up. When she looked at me she stopped smiling. "Nick, you're – " I said I didn't think it was much and opened what was left of my pajama-coat. Morelli's bullet had scooped out a gutter perhaps four inches long under my left nipple. A lot of blood was running out of it, but it was not very deep.

Morelli said: "Tough luck. A couple of inches over would make a lot of difference the right way." The copper who had admired Nora – he was a big sandy man of forty-eight or fifty in a gray suit that did not fit him very well – slapped Morelli's mouth.

Keyser, the Normandie's manager, said he would get a doctor and went to the telephone. Nora ran to the bathroom for towels. I put a towel over the wound and lay down on the bed. "I'm all right. Don't let's fuss over it till the doctor comes. How'd you people happen to pop in?"

The copper who had slapped Morelli said: "We happen to hear this is getting to be kind of a meeting-place for Wynant's family and his lawyer and everybody, so we think we'll kind of keep an eye on it in case he happens to show up, and this morning when Mack here, who was the eye we were kind of keeping on it at the time, sees this bird duck in, he gives us a ring and we get hold of Mr. Keyser and come on up, and pretty lucky for you."

"Yes, pretty lucky for me, or maybe I wouldn't've got shot."

He eyed me suspiciously. His eyes were pale gray and watery. "This bird a friend of yours?"

"I never saw him before."

"What'd he want of you?"

"Wanted to tell me he didn't kill the Wolf girl."

"What's that to you?"

"Nothing."

"What'd he think it was to you?"

"Ask him. I don't know."

"I'm asking you."

"Keep on asking."

"I'll ask you another one: you're going to swear to the complaint on him shooting you?"

"That's another one I can't answer right now. Maybe it was an accident."

"Oke. There's plenty of time. I guess we got to ask you a lot more things than we'd figured on." He turned to one of his companions: there were four of them. "We'll frisk the joint."

"Not without a warrant," I told him.

"So you say. Come on, Andy." They began to search the place.

The doctor – a colorless wisp of a man with the snuffles – came in, clucked and sniffed over my side, got the bleeding stopped and a bandage on, and told me I would have nothing to worry about if I lay still for a couple of days. Nobody would tell the doctor anything. The police would not let him touch Morelli. He went away looking even more colorless and vague. The big sandy man had returned from the living-room holding one hand behind him. He waited until the doctor had gone, then asked: "Have you got a pistol permit?"

"No."

"Then what are you doing with this?" He brought from behind him the gun I had taken from Dorothy Wynant. There was nothing I could say.

"You've heard about the Sullivan Act?" he asked.

"Yes."

"Then you know where you stand. This gun yours?"

"No."

"Whose is it?"

"I'll have to try to remember."

He put the pistol in his pocket and sat down on a chair beside the bed. "Listen, Mr. Charles," he said. "I guess we're both of us doing this wrong. I don't want to get tough with you and I don't guess you really want to get tough with me.

That hole in your side can't be making you feel any too good, so I ain't going to bother you any more till you've had a little rest. Then maybe we can get together the way we ought to."

"Thanks," I said and meant it. "We'll buy a drink."

Nora said, "Sure," and got up from the edge of the bed.

The big sandy man watched her go out of the room. He shook his head solemnly. His voice was solemn: "By God, sir, you're a lucky man." He suddenly held out his hand. "My name's Guild, John Guild."

"You know mine." We shook hands.

Nora came back with a siphon, a bottle of Scotch, and some glasses on a tray. She tried to give Morelli a drink, but Guild stopped her. "It's mighty kind of you, Mrs. Charles, but it's against the law to give a prisoner drinks or drugs except on a doctor's say-so." He looked at me. "Ain't that right?" I said it was. The rest of us drank.

Presently Guild set down his empty glass and stood up. "I got to take this gun along with me, but don't you worry about that. We got plenty of time to talk when you're feeling better." He took Nora's hand and made an awkward bow over it. "I hope you didn't mind what I said back there awhile ago, but I meant it in a – "

Nora can smile very nicely. She gave him one of her nicest smiles. "Mind? I liked it." She let the policemen and their prisoner out. Keyser had gone a few minutes before.

"He's sweet," she said when she came back from the door. "Hurt much?"

"No."

"It's pretty much my fault, isn't it?"

"Nonsense. How about another drink?"

She poured me one. "I wouldn't take too many of these today."

"I won't," I promised. "I could do with some kippers for breakfast. And, now our troubles seem to be over for a while, you might have them send up our absentee watchdog. And tell

263

DASHIELL HAMMETT

the operator not to give us any calls; there'll probably be reporters."

"What are you going to tell the police about Dorothy's pistol? You'll have to tell them something, won't you?"

"I don't know yet."

"Tell me the truth, Nick: have I been too silly?"

I shook my head. "Just silly enough."

She laughed, said, "You're a Greek louse," and went around to the telephone.

9

NORA SAID: "YOU'RE just showing off, that's all it is. And what for? I know bullets bounce off you. You don't have to prove it to me."

"It's not going to hurt me to get up."

"And it's not going to hurt you to stay in bed at least one day. The doctor said – "

"If he knew anything he'd cure his own snuffles." I sat up and put my feet on the floor. Asta tickled them with her tongue.

Nora brought me slippers and robe. "All right, hard guy, get up and bleed on the rugs." I stood up cautiously and seemed to be all right as long as I went easy with my left arm and kept out of the way of Asta's front feet.

"Be reasonable," I said. "I didn't want to get mixed up with these people – still don't – but a fat lot of good that's doing me. Well, I can't just blunder out of it. I've got to see."

"Let's go away," she suggested. "Let's go to Bermuda or Havana for a week or two, or back to the Coast."

"I'd still have to tell the police some kind of story about that gun. And suppose it turns out to be the gun she was killed with? If they don't know already they're finding out."

"Do you really think it is?"

"That's guessing. We'll go there for dinner tonight and – "

"We'll do nothing of the kind. Have you gone completely nuts? If you want to see anybody have them come here."

"It's not the same thing." I put my arms around her. "Stop worrying about this scratch. I'm all right."

265

"You're showing off," she said. "You want to let people see you're a hero who can't be stopped by bullets."

"Don't be nasty."

"I will be nasty. I'm not going to have you – "

I shut her mouth with a hand over it. "I want to see the Jorgensens together at home, I want to see Macaulay, and I want to see Studsy Burke. I've been pushed around too much. I've got to see about things."

"You're so damned pig-headed," she complained. "Well, it's only five o'clock. Lie down till it's time to dress."

I made myself comfortable on the living-room sofa. We had the afternoon papers sent up. Morelli, it seemed, had shot me – twice for one of the papers and three times for another – when I tried to arrest him for Julia Wolf's murder, and I was too near death to see anybody or to be moved to a hospital. There were pictures of Morelli and a thirteen-year-old one of me in a pretty funny-looking hat, taken, I remembered, when I was working on the Wall Street explosion. Most of the follow-up stories on the murder of Julia Wolf were rather vague. We were reading them when our little constant visitor, Dorothy Wynant, arrived.

I could hear her at the door when Nora opened it: "They wouldn't send my name up, so I sneaked up. Please don't send me away. I can help you nurse Nick. I'll do anything. Please, Nora."

Nora had a chance then to say: "Come on in."

Dorothy came in. She goggled at me. "B-but the papers said you – "

"Do I look like I'm dying? What's happened to you?" Her lower lip was swollen and cut near one corner, there was a bruise on one cheek-bone and two fingernail scratches down the other cheek, and her eyes were red and swollen.

"Mamma beat me," she said. "Look." She dropped her coat on the floor, tore off a button unbuttoning her dress, took an arm out of its sleeve, and pushed the dress down to show her back. There were dark bruises on her arm, and her back was criss-crossed by long red welts. She was crying now. "See?"

Nora put an arm around her. "You poor kid."

"What'd she beat you for?" I asked.

She turned from Nora and knelt on the floor beside my sofa. Asta came over and nuzzled her. "She thought I came – came to see you about Father and Julia Wolf." Sobs broke up her sentences. "That's why she came over here – to find out – and you made her think I didn't. You – you made her think you didn't care anything about what happened – just like you made me – and she was all right till she saw the papers this afternoon. Then she knew – she knew you'd been lying about not having anything to do with it. She beat me to try to make me tell her what I'd told you."

"What'd you tell her?"

"I couldn't tell her anything. I – I couldn't tell her about Chris. I couldn't tell her anything."

"Was he there?"

"Yes."

"And he let her beat you like this?"

"But he – he never makes her stop."

I said to Nora: "For God's sake, let's have a drink."

Nora said, "Sure," picked up Dorothy's coat, laid it across the back of a chair, and went into the pantry.

Dorothy said: "Please let me stay here, Nick. I won't be any trouble, honestly, and you told me yourself I ought to walk out on them. You know you did, and I've got nowhere else to go. Please."

"Take it easy. This thing needs a little figuring out. I'm as much afraid of Mimi as you are, you know. What did she think you'd told me?"

"She must know something – something about the murder that she thinks I know – but I don't, Nick. Honest to God, I don't."

"That helps a lot," I complained. "But listen, sister: there are things you know and we're going to start with those. You come clean at and from the beginning – or we don't play."

She made a movement as if she were about to cross her heart. "I swear I will," she said.

"That'll be swell. Now let's drink." We took a glass apiece from Nora. "Tell her you were leaving for good?"

"No, I didn't say anything. Maybe she doesn't know yet I'm not in my room."

"That helps some."

"You're not going to make me go back?" she cried.

Nora said over her glass: "The child can't stay and be beaten like that, Nick."

I said: "Sh-h-h. I don't know. I was just thinking that if we're going there for dinner maybe it's better for Mimi not to know – "

Dorothy stared at me with horrified eyes while Nora said: "Don't think you're going to take me there now."

Then Dorothy spoke rapidly: "But Mamma doesn't expect you. I don't even know whether she'll be there. The papers said you were dying. She doesn't think you're coming."

"So much the better," I said. "We'll surprise them."

She put her face, white now, close to mine, spilling some of her drink on my sleeve in her excitement. "Don't go. You can't go there now. Listen to me. Listen to Nora. You can't go." She turned her white face around to look up at Nora. "Can he? Tell him he can't."

Nora, not shifting the focus of her dark eyes from my face, said: "Wait, Dorothy. He ought to know what's best. What is it, Nick?"

I made a face at her. "I'm just fumbling around. If you say Dorothy stays here, she stays. I guess she can sleep with Asta. But you've got to leave me alone on the rest of it. I don't know

268

what I'm going to do because I don't know what's being done to me. I've got to find out. I've got to find out in my own way."

"We won't interfere," Dorothy said. "Will we, Nora?"

Nora continued to look at me, saying nothing.

I asked Dorothy: "Where'd you get that gun? And nothing out of books this time." She moistened her lower lip and her face became pinker. She cleared her throat. "Careful," I said. "If it's another piece of chewing-gum, I'll phone Mimi to come to get you."

"Give her a chance," Nora said.

Dorothy cleared her throat again. "Can – can I tell you something that happened to me when I was a little child?"

"Has it got anything to do with the gun?"

"Not exactly, but it'll help you understand why I – "

"Not now. Some other time. Where'd you get the gun?"

"I wish you'd let me." She hung her head.

"Where'd you get the gun?"

Her voice was barely audible. "From a man in a speakeasy."

I said: "I knew we'd get the truth at last." Nora frowned and shook her head at me. "All right, say you did. What speakeasy?"

Dorothy raised her head. "I don't know. It was on Tenth Avenue, I think. Your friend Mr. Quinn would know. He took me there."

"You met him after you left us that night?"

"Yes."

"By accident, I suppose."

She looked reproachfully at me. "I'm trying to tell you the truth, Nick. I'd promised to meet him at a place called the Palma Club. He wrote the address down for me. So after I said good-night to you and Nora, I met him there and we went to a lot of places, winding up in this place where I got the gun. It was an awful tough place. You can ask him if I'm telling the truth."

"Quinn get the gun for you?"

"No. He'd passed out then. He was sleeping with his head on the table. I left him there. They said they'd get him home all right."

"And the gun?"

"I'm coming to it." She began to blush. "He told me it was a gunmen's hang-out. That's why I'd said let's go there. And after he went to sleep I got to talking to a man there, an awful tough-looking man. I was fascinated. And all the time I didn't want to go home, I wanted to come back here, but I didn't know if you'd let me." Her face was quite red now and in her embarrassment she blurred her words. "So I thought perhaps if I – if you thought I was in a terrible fix – and, besides, that way I wouldn't feel so silly. Anyhow, I asked this awful tough-looking gangster, or whatever he was, if he would sell me a pistol or tell me where I could buy one. He thought I was kidding and laughed at first, but I told him I wasn't, and then he kept on grinning, but he said he'd see, and when he came back he said yes, he could get me one and asked how much I would pay for it. I didn't have much money, but I offered him my bracelet, but I guess he didn't think it was any good, because he said no, he'd have to have cash, so finally I gave him twelve dollars – all I had but a dollar for the taxi – and he gave me the pistol and I came over here and made up that about being afraid to go home because of Chris." She finished so rapidly her words ran together, and she sighed as if very glad to have finished.

"Then Chris hasn't been making passes at you?"

She bit her lip. "Yes, but not – not that bad." She put both hands on my arm, and her face almost touched mine. "You've got to believe me. I couldn't tell you all that, couldn't make myself out such a cheap little lying fool, if it wasn't the truth."

"It makes more sense if I don't believe you," I said. "Twelve bucks isn't enough money. We'll let that rest for a minute, though. Did you know Mimi was going to see Julia Wolf that afternoon?"

"No. I didn't even know she was trying to find my father then. They didn't say where they were going that afternoon."

"They?"

"Yes, Chris left the apartment with her."

"What time was that?"

She wrinkled her forehead. "It must've been pretty close to three o'clock – after two-thirty, anyway – because I remember I was late for a date to go shopping with Elsie Hamilton and was hurrying into my clothes."

"They come back together?"

"I don't know. They were both home before I came."

"What time was that?"

"Some time after six. Nick, you don't think they – Oh, I remember something she said while she was dressing. I don't know what Chris said, but she said: 'When I ask her she'll tell me,' in that Queen-of-France way she talks sometimes. You know. I didn't hear anything else. Does that mean anything?"

"What'd she tell you about the murder when you came home?"

"Oh, just about finding her and how upset she was and about the police and everything."

"She seem very shocked?"

Dorothy shook her head. "No, just excited. You know Mamma." She stared at me for a moment, asked slowly: "You don't think she had anything to do with it?"

"What do you think?"

"I hadn't thought. I just thought about my father." A little later she said gravely: "If he did it, it's because he's crazy, but she'd kill somebody if she wanted to."

"It doesn't have to be either of them," I reminded her. "The police seem to have picked Morelli. What'd she want to find your father for?"

"For money. We're broke: Chris spent it all." She pulled down the corners of her mouth. "I suppose we all helped, but he spent most of it. Mamma's afraid he'll leave her if she hasn't any money."

"How do you know that?"

"I've heard them talk."

"Do you think he will?"

She nodded with certainty. "Unless she has money."

I looked at my watch and said: "The rest of it'll have to wait till we get back. You can stay here tonight, anyhow. Make yourself comfortable and have the restaurant send up your dinner. It's probably better if you don't go out." She stared miserably at me and said nothing.

Nora patted her shoulder. "I don't know what he's doing, Dorothy, but if he says we ought to go there for dinner he probably knows what he's talking about. He wouldn't – "

Dorothy smiled and jumped up from the floor. "I believe you. I won't be silly any more."

I called the desk on the telephone and asked them to send up our mail. There were a couple of letters for Nora, one for me, some belated Christmas cards (including one from Larry Crowley, which was a copy of Haldeman-Julius Little Blue Book Number 1534, with "and a Merry Christmas," followed by Larry's name enclosed in a holly wreath, all printed in red under the book's title, *How to Test Your Urine at Home*), a number of telephone-call memoranda slips, and a telegram from Philadelphia:

NICK CHARLES
THE NORMANDIE NEW YORK NY
WILL YOU COMMUNICATE WITH HERBERT MACAU-
LAY TO DISCUSS TAKING CHARGE OF INVESTIGATION
OF WOLF MURDER STOP AM GIVING HIM FULL INSTRUC-
TIONS STOP BEST REGARDS
CLYDE MILLER WYNANT

I put the telegram in an envelope with a note saying it had just reached me and sent it by messenger to the Police Department Homicide Bureau.

IN THE TAXICAB Nora asked: "You're sure you feel all right?"

"Sure."

"And this isn't going to be too much for you?"

"I'm all right. What'd you think of the girl's story?"

She hesitated. "You don't believe her, do you?"

"God forbid — at least till I've checked it up."

"You know more about this kind of thing than I do," she said, "but I think she was at least trying to tell the truth."

"A lot fancier yarns come from people who are trying to do that. It's not easy once you're out of the habit."

She said: "I bet you know a lot about human nature, Mr. Charles. Now don't you? Some time you must tell me about your experiences as a detective."

I said: "Buying a gun for twelve bucks in a speakeasy. Well, maybe, but . . ."

We rode a couple of blocks in silence. Then Nora asked: "What's really the matter with her?"

"Her old man's crazy: she thinks she is."

"How do you know?"

"You asked me. I'm telling you."

"You mean you're guessing?"

"I mean that's what's wrong with her; I don't know whether Wynant's actually nuts and I don't know whether she inherited any of it if he is, but she thinks both answers are yes, and it's got her doing figure eights."

When we stopped in front of the Courtland she said: "That's horrible, Nick. Somebody ought to — "

I said I didn't know: maybe Dorothy was right. "Likely as not she's making doll clothes for Asta right now."

We sent our name up to the Jorgensens and, after some delay, were told to go up. Mimi met us in the corridor when we stepped out of the elevator, met us with open arms and many words. "Those wretched newspapers. They had me frantic with their nonsense about your being at death's door. I phoned twice, but they wouldn't give me your apartment, wouldn't tell me how you were." She had both of my hands. "I'm so glad, Nick, that it was just a pack of lies, even if you will have to take pot luck with us tonight. Naturally I didn't expect you and – But you're pale. You really have been hurt."

"Not much," I said. "A bullet scraped my side, but it doesn't amount to anything."

"And you came to dinner in spite of that! That is flattering, but I'm afraid it's foolish too." She turned to Nora. "Are you sure it was wise to let him – "

"I'm not sure," Nora said, "but he wanted to come."

"Men are such idiots," Mimi said. She put an arm around me. "They either make mountains out of nothing or utterly neglect things that may – But come in. Here, let me help you."

"It's not that bad," I assured her, but she insisted on leading me to a chair and packing me in with half a dozen cushions.

Jorgensen came in, shook hands with me, and said he was glad to find me more alive than the newspapers had said. He bowed over Nora's hand. "If I may be excused one little minute more I will finish the cocktails." He went out.

Mimi said: "I don't know where Dorry is. Off sulking somewhere, I suppose. You haven't any children, have you?"

Nora said: "No."

"You're missing a lot, though they can be a great trial sometimes." Mimi sighed. "I suppose I'm not strict enough. When I do have to scold Dorry she seems to think I'm a complete monster." Her face brightened. "Here's my other tot. You remember Mr. Charles, Gilbert. And this is

Mrs. Charles." Gilbert Wynant was two years younger than his sister, a gangling pale blond boy of eighteen with not too much chin under a somewhat slack mouth. The size of his remarkably clear blue eyes, and the length of the lashes, gave him a slightly effeminate look. I hoped he had stopped being the whining little nuisance he was as a kid.

Jorgensen brought in his cocktails, and Mimi insisted on being told about the shooting. I told her, making it even more meaningless than it had been. "But why should he have come to you?" she asked.

"God knows. I'd like to know. The police'd like to know."

Gilbert said: "I read somewhere that when habitual criminals are accused of things they didn't do – even little things – they're much more upset by it than other people would be. Do you think that's so, Mr. Charles?"

"It's likely."

"Except," Gilbert added, "when it's something big, you know, something they would like to've done." I said again it was likely.

Mimi said: "Don't be polite to Gil if he starts talking nonsense, Nick. His head's so cluttered up with reading. Get us another cocktail, darling." He went over to get the shaker. Nora and Jorgensen were in a corner sorting phonograph records.

I said: "I had a wire from Wynant today."

Mimi looked warily around the room, then leaned forward, and her voice was almost a whisper: "What did he say?"

"Wanted me to find out who killed her. It was sent from Philadelphia this afternoon."

She was breathing heavily. "Are you going to do it?"

I shrugged. "I turned it over to the police." Gilbert came back with the shaker. Jorgensen and Nora had put Bach's "Little Fugue" on the phonograph. Mimi quickly drank her cocktail and had Gilbert pour her another.

He sat down and said: "I want to ask you: can you tell dope-addicts by looking at them?" He was trembling.

"Very seldom. Why?"

"I was wondering. Even if they're confirmed addicts?"

"The further along they are, the better the chances of noticing that something's wrong, but you can't often be sure it's dope."

"Another thing," he said, "Gross says when you're stabbed you only feel a sort of push at the time and it's not until afterwards that it begins to hurt. Is that so?"

"Yes, if you're stabbed reasonably hard with a reasonably sharp knife. A bullet's the same way: you only feel the blow – and with a small-caliber steel-jacketed bullet not much of that – at first. The rest comes when the air gets to it."

Mimi drank her third cocktail and said: "I think you're both being indecently gruesome, especially after what happened to Nick today. Do try to find Dorry, Gil. You must know some of her friends. Phone them. I suppose she'll be along presently, but I worry about her."

"She's over at our place," I said.

"At your place?" Her surprise may have been genuine.

"She came over this afternoon and asked if she could stay with us awhile."

She smiled tolerantly and shook her head. "These young-sters!" She stopped smiling. "Awhile?" I nodded. Gilbert, apparently waiting to ask me another question, showed no interest in this conversation between his mother and me.

Mimi smiled again and said: "I'm sorry she's bothering you and your wife, but it's a relief to know she's there instead of off the Lord only knows where. She'll have finished her pouting by the time you get back. Send her along home, will you?" She poured me a cocktail. "You've been awfully nice to her." I did not say anything.

Gilbert began: "Mr. Charles, do criminals – I mean profes-sional criminals – usually – "

"Don't interrupt, Gil," Mimi said. "You will send her along home, won't you?" She was pleasant, but she was Dorothy's Queen of France.

"She can stay if she wants. Nora likes her."

She shook a crooked finger at me. "But I won't have you spoiling her like that. I suppose she told you all sorts of nonsense about me."

"She did say something about a beating."

"There you are," Mimi said complacently, as if that proved her point. "No, you'll have to send her home, Nick." I finished my cocktail. "Well?" she asked.

"She can stay with us if she wants, Mimi. We like having her."

"That's ridiculous. Her place is at home. I want her here." Her voice was a little sharp. "She's only a baby. You shouldn't encourage her foolish notions."

"I'm not doing anything. If she wants to stay, she stays."

Anger was a very pretty thing in Mimi's blue eyes. "She's my child and she's a minor. You've been very kind to her, but this isn't being kind to her or to me, and I won't have it. If you won't send her home, I'll take steps to bring her home. I'd rather not be disagreeable about it, but" – she leaned forward and deliberately spaced her words – "she's coming home."

I said: "You don't want to pick a fight with me, Mimi."

She looked at me as if she were going to say I love you, and asked: "Is that a threat?"

"All right," I said, "have me arrested for kidnapping, contributing to the delinquency of a minor and mopery."

She said suddenly in a harsh enraged voice: "And tell your wife to stop pawing my husband." Nora, looking for another phonograph record with Jorgensen, had a hand on his sleeve. They turned to look at Mimi in surprise.

I said: "Nora, Mrs. Jorgensen wants you to keep your hands off Mr. Jorgensen."

"I'm awfully sorry." Nora smiled at Mimi, then looked at me, put a very artificial expression of concern on her face, and in a somewhat singsong voice, as if she were a schoolchild reciting a piece, said: "Oh, Nick, you're pale. I'm sure you have exceeded your strength and will have a relapse. I'm sorry, Mrs. Jorgensen, but I think I should get him home and to bed right away. You will forgive us, won't you?" Mimi said she would. Everybody was the soul of politeness to everybody else. We went downstairs and got a taxicab.

"Well," Nora said, "so you talked yourself out of a dinner. What do you want to do now? Go home and eat with Dorothy?"

I shook my head. "I can do without Wynants for a little while. Let's go to Max's: I'd like some snails."

"Right. Did you find out anything?"

"Nothing."

She said meditatively: "It's a shame that guy's so handsome."

"What's he like?"

"Just a big doll. It's a shame." We had dinner and went back to the Normandie. Dorothy was not there. I felt as if I had expected that. Nora went through the rooms, called up the desk. No note, no message had been left for us. "So what?" she asked.

It was not quite ten o'clock. "Maybe nothing," I said.

"Maybe anything. My guess is she'll show up about three in the morning, tight, with a machine-gun she bought in Childs'."

Nora said: "To hell with her. Get into pajamas and lie down."

MY SIDE FELT a lot better when Nora called me at noon the next day. "My nice policeman wants to see you," she said. "How do you feel?"

"Terrible. I must've gone to bed sober." I pushed Asta out of the way and got up.

Guild rose with a drink in his hand when I entered the living-room, and smiled all across his broad sandy face. "Well, well, Mr. Charles, you look spry enough this morning." I shook hands with him and said yes I felt pretty good, and we sat down. He frowned good-naturedly. "Just the same, you oughtn't've played that trick on me."

"Trick?"

"Sure, running off to see people when I'd put off asking you questions to give you a chance to rest up. I kind of figured that ought to give me first call on you, as you might say."

"I didn't think," I said. "I'm sorry. See that wire I got from Wynant?"

"Uh-huh. We're running it out in Philly."

"Now about that gun," I began, "I —"

He stopped me. "What gun? That ain't a gun any more. The firing pin's busted off, the guts are rusted and jammed. If anybody's fired it in six months — or could — I'm the Pope of Rome. Don't let's waste any time talking about that piece of junk."

I laughed. "That explains a lot. I took it away from a drunk who said he'd bought it in a speakeasy for twelve bucks. I believe him now."

"Somebody'll sell him the City Hall one of these days. Man to man, Mr. Charles, are you working on the Wolf job or ain't you?"

"You saw the wire from Wynant."

"I did. Then you ain't working for him. I'm still asking you."

"I'm not a private detective any more. I'm not any kind of detective."

"I heard that. I'm still asking you."

"All right. No."

He thought for a moment, said: "Then let me put it another way: are you interested in the job?"

"I know the people, naturally I'm interested."

"And that's all?"

"Yes."

"And you don't expect to be working on it?"

The telephone rang and Nora went to answer it.

"To be honest with you, I don't know. If people keep on pushing me into it, I don't know how far they'll carry me."

Guild wagged his head up and down. "I can see that. I don't mind telling you I'd like to have you in on it – on the right side."

"You mean not on Wynant's side. Did he do it?"

"That I couldn't say, Mr. Charles, but I don't have to tell you he ain't helping us any to find out who did it."

Nora appeared in the doorway. "Telephone, Nick."

Herbert Macaulay was on the wire. "Hello, Charles. How's the wounded?"

"I'm all right, thanks."

"Did you hear from Wynant?"

"Yes."

"I got a letter from him saying he had wired you. Are you too sick to – "

"No, I'm up and around. If you'll be in your office late this afternoon I'll drop in."

"Swell," he said. "I'll be here till six."

I returned to the living-room. Nora was inviting Guild to have lunch while we had breakfast. He said it was mighty kind of her. I said I ought to have a drink before breakfast. Nora went to order meals and pour drinks. Guild shook his head and said: "She's a mighty fine woman, Mr. Charles." I nodded solemnly.

He said: "Suppose you should get pushed into this thing, as you say, I'd like it a lot more to feel you were working with us than against us."

"So would I."

"That's a bargain then," he said. He hunched his chair around a little. "I don't guess you remember me, but back when you were working this town I was walking beat on Forty-second Street."

"Of course," I said, lying politely. "I knew there was something familiar about – Being out of uniform makes a difference."

"I guess it does. I'd like to be able to take it as a fact that you're not holding out anything we don't already know."

"I don't mean to. I don't know what you know. I don't know very much. I haven't seen Macaulay since the murder and I haven't even been following it in the newspapers." The telephone was ringing again. Nora gave us our drinks and went to answer it.

"What we know ain't much of a secret," Guild said, "and if you want to take the time to listen I don't mind giving it to you." He tasted his drink and nodded approvingly. "Only there's a thing I'd like to ask first. When you went to Mrs. Jorgensen's last night, did you tell her about getting the telegram from him?"

"Yes, and I told her I'd turned it over to you."

"What'd she say?"

"Nothing. She asked questions. She's trying to find him."

He put his head a little to one side and partly closed one eye. "You don't think there's any chance of them being in

282

cahoots, do you?" He held up a hand. "Understand I don't know why they would be or what it'd be all about if they were, but I'm just asking."

"Anything's possible," I said, "but I'd say it was pretty safe they aren't working together. Why?"

"I guess you're right." Then he added vaguely: "But there's a couple of points." He sighed. "There always is. Well, Mr. Charles, here's just about all we know for certain and if you give us a little something more here and there as we go along I'll be mighty thankful to you." I said something about doing my best.

"Well, along about the 3rd of last October Wynant tells Macaulay he's got to leave town for a while. He don't tell Macaulay where he's going or what for, but Macaulay gets the idea that he's off to work on some invention or other that he wants to keep quiet – and he gets it out of Julia Wolf later that he's right – and he guesses Wynant's gone off to hide somewhere in the Adirondacks, but when he asks her about that later she says she don't know any more about it than he does."

"She know what the invention was?"

Guild shook his head. "Not according to Macaulay, only that it was probably something that he needed room for and machinery or things that cost money, because that's what he was fixing up with Macaulay. He was fixing it so Macaulay could get hold of his stocks and bonds and other things he owned and turn 'em into money when he wanted it and take care of his banking and everything just like Wynant himself."

"Power of attorney covering everything, huh?"

"Exactly. And listen, when he wanted money, he wanted it in cash."

"He was always full of screwy notions," I said.

"That's what everybody says. The idea seems to be he don't want to take any chances on anybody tracing him through checks, or anybody up there knowing he's Wynant. That's why he didn't take the girl along with him – didn't even let her know where he was, if she was telling the truth – and let his whiskers grow." With his left hand he stroked an imaginary beard.

"'Up there,'" I quoted. "So he was in the Adirondacks?"

Guild moved one shoulder. "I just said that because that and Philadelphia are the only ideas anybody's give us. We're trying the mountains, but we don't know. Maybe Australia."

"And how much of this money in cash did Wynant want?"

"I can tell you that exactly." He took a wad of soiled, bent and dog-eared papers out of his pocket, selected an envelope that was a shade dirtier than most of the others, and stuffed the others back in his pocket. "The day after he talked to Macaulay he drew five thousand out of the bank himself, in cash. On the 28th – this is October, you understand – he had Macaulay get another five for him, and twenty-five hundred on the 6th of November, and a thousand on the 15th, and seventy-five hundred on the 30th, and fifteen hundred on the 6th – that would be December – and a thousand on the 18th, and five thousand on the 22nd, which was the day before she was killed."

"Nearly thirty thou," I said. "A nice bank balance he had."

"Twenty-eight thousand five hundred, to be exact." Guild returned the envelope to his pocket. "But you understand it wasn't all in there. After the first call Macaulay would sell something every time to raise the dough." He felt in his pocket again. "I got a list of the stuff he sold, if you want to see it."

I said I didn't. "How'd he turn the money over to Wynant?"

"Wynant would write the girl when he wanted it, and she'd get it from Macaulay. He's got her receipts."

"And how'd she get it to Wynant?"

Guild shook his head. "She told Macaulay she used to meet him places he told her, but he thinks she knew where he was, though she always said she didn't."

"And maybe she still had the last five thousand on her when she was killed, huh?"

"Which might make it robbery, unless" – Guild's watery gray eyes were almost shut – "he killed her when he came there to get it."

"Or unless," I suggested, "somebody else who killed her for some other reason found the money there and thought they might as well take it along."

"Sure," he agreed. "Things like that happen all the time. It even happens sometimes that the first people that find a body like that pick up a little something before they turn in the alarm." He held up a big hand. "Of course, with Mrs. Jorgensen – a lady like that – I hope you don't think I'm – "

"Besides," I said, "she wasn't alone, was she?"

"For a little while. The phone in the apartment was out of whack, and the elevator boy rode the superintendent down to phone from the office. But get me right on this, I'm not saying Mrs. Jorgensen did anything funny. A lady like that wouldn't be likely – "

"What was the matter with the phone?" I asked.

The door-bell rang. "Well," Guild said, "I don't know just what to make of it. The phone had – " He broke off as a waiter came in and began to set a table. "About the phone," Guild said when we were sitting at the table, "I don't know just what to make of it, as I said. It had a bullet right smack through the mouthpiece of it."

"Accidental or – ?"

"I'd just as lief ask you. It was from the same gun as the four that hit her, of course, but whether he missed her with that one or did it on purpose I don't know. It seems like a kind of noisy way to put a phone on the bum."

"That reminds me," I said, "didn't anybody hear all this shooting? A .32's not a shotgun, but somebody ought to've heard it."

"Sure," he said disgustedly. "The place is lousy with people that think they heard things now, but nobody did anything about it then, and God knows they don't get together much on what they think they heard."

"It's always like that," I said sympathetically.

"Don't I know it." He put a forkful of food in his mouth. "Where was I? Oh, yes, about Wynant. He gave up his apartment when he went away, and put his stuff in storage. We been looking through it – the stuff – but ain't found anything yet to show where he went or even what he was working on, which we thought maybe might help. We didn't have any better luck in his shop on First Avenue. It's been locked up too since he went away, except that she used to go down there for an hour or two once or twice a week to take care of his mail and things. There's nothing to tell us anything in the mail that's come since she got knocked off. We didn't find anything in her place to help." He smiled at Nora. "I guess this must be pretty dull to you, Mrs. Charles."

"Dull?" She was surprised. "I'm sitting on the edge of my chair."

"Ladies usually like more color," he said, and coughed, "kind of glamour. Anyways, we got nothing to show where he's been, only he phones Macaulay last Friday and says to meet him at two o'clock in the Plaza lobby. Macaulay wasn't in, so he just left the message."

"Macaulay was here," I said, "for lunch."

"He told me. Well, Macaulay don't get to the Plaza till nearly three and he don't find any Wynant there and Wynant ain't registered there. He tries describing him, with and without a beard, but nobody at the Plaza remembers seeing him. He phones his office, but Wynant ain't called up again. And then he phones Julia Wolf and she tells him she don't even know Wynant's in town, which he figures is a lie, because he had just give her five thousand dollars for Wynant yesterday and figures Wynant's come for it, but he just says all right and hangs up and goes on about his business."

"His business such as what?" I asked.

Guild stopped chewing the piece of roll he had just bitten off. "I guess it wouldn't hurt to know, at that. I'll find out. There didn't seem to be anything pointing at him, so we didn't bother with that, but it don't ever hurt any to know who's got an alibi and who ain't."

I shook my head no at the question he had decided not to ask. "I don't see anything pointing at him, except that he's Wynant's lawyer and probably knows more than he's telling."

"Sure. I understand. Well, that's what people have lawyers for, I guess. Now about the girl: maybe Julia Wolf wasn't her real name at all. We ain't been able to find out for sure yet, but we have found out she wasn't the kind of dame you'd expect him to be trusting to handle all that dough – I mean if he knew about her."

"Had a record?"

He wagged his head up and down. "This is elegant stew. A couple of years before she went to work for him she did six months on a badger-game charge out West, in Cleveland, under the name of Rhoda Stewart."

"You suppose Wynant knew that?"

"Search me. Don't look like he'd turn her loose with that dough if he did, but you can't tell. They tell me he was kind of nuts about her, and you know how guys can go. She was running around off and on with this Shep Morelli and his boys too."

"Have you really got anything on him?" I asked.

"Not on this," he said regretfully, "but we wanted him for a couple of other things." He drew his sandy brows together a little. "I wish I knew what sent him here to see you. Of course these junkies are likely to do anything, but I wish I knew."

"I told you all I knew."

"I'm not doubting that," he assured me. He turned to Nora. "I hope you don't think we were too rough with him, but you see you got to – " Nora smiled and said she understood perfectly and filled his cup with coffee. "Thank you, ma'am."

"What's a junkie?" she asked.

"Hop-head."

She looked at me. "Was Morelli – ?"

"Primed to the ears," I said.

"Why didn't you tell me?" she complained. "I miss everything." She left the table to answer the telephone.

Guild asked: "You going to prosecute him for shooting you?"

"Not unless you need it."

He shook his head. His voice was casual, though there was some curiosity in his eyes. "I guess we got enough on him for a while."

"You were telling me about the girl."

"Yes," he said. "Well, we found out she'd been spending a lot of nights away from her apartment – two or three days at a stretch sometimes. Maybe that's when she was meeting Wynant. I don't know. We ain't been able to knock any holes in Morelli's story of not seeing her for three months. What do you make of that?"

"The same thing you do," I replied. "It's just about three months since Wynant went off. Maybe it means something, maybe not." Nora came in and said Harrison Quinn was on the telephone. He told me he had sold some bonds I was writing off losses on and gave me the prices. "Have you seen Dorothy Wynant?" I asked.

"Not since I left her in your place, but I'm meeting her at the Palma for cocktails this afternoon. Come to think of it, she told me not to tell you. How about that gold, Nick? You're missing something if you don't get in on it. Those wild men from the West are going to give us some kind of inflation as

288

soon as Congress meets, that's certain, and even if they don't, everybody expects them to. As I told you last week, there's already talk of a pool being – "

"All right," I said and gave him an order to buy some Dome Mines at 12½.

He remembered then that he had seen something in the newspapers about my having been shot. He was pretty vague about it and paid very little attention to my assurances that I was all right. "I suppose that means no Ping-Pong for a couple of days," he said with what seemed genuine regret. "Listen: you've got tickets for the opening tonight. If you can't use them I'll be – "

"We're going to use them. Thanks just the same." He laughed and said good-bye.

A waiter was carrying away the table when I returned to the living-room. Guild had made himself comfortable on the sofa. Nora was telling him: " . . . have to go away over the Christmas holidays every year because what's left of my family make a fuss over them and if we're home they come to visit us or we have to visit them, and Nick doesn't like it." Asta was licking her paws in a corner.

Guild looked at his watch. "I'm taking up a lot of you folks' time. I didn't mean to impose – "

I sat down and said: "We were just about up to the murder, weren't we?"

"Just about." He relaxed on the sofa again. "That was on Friday the 23rd at some time before twenty minutes after three in the afternoon, which was the time Mrs. Jorgensen got there and found her. It's kind of hard to say how long she'd been laying there dying before she was found. The only thing we know is that she was all right and answered the phone – and the phone was all right – at about half-past two, when Mrs. Jorgensen called her up and was still all right around three, when Macaulay phoned."

"I didn't know Mrs. Jorgensen phoned."

289

"It's a fact." Guild cleared his throat. "We didn't suspect anything there, you understand, but we checked it up just as a matter of course and found out from the girl at the switch-board at the Courtland that she put the call through for Mrs. J. about two-thirty."

"What did Mrs. J. say?"

"She said she called up to ask where she could find Wynant, but this Julia Wolf said she didn't know, so Mrs. J., thinking she's lying and maybe she can get her to tell the truth if she sees her, asks if she can drop in for a minute, and she says sure." He frowned at my right knee. "Well, she went there and found her. The apartment-house people don't remember seeing any-body going in or out of the Wolf apartment, but that's easy. A dozen people could do it without being seen. The gun wasn't there. There wasn't any signs of anybody busting in, and things in the place hadn't been disturbed any more than I've told you. I mean the place didn't look like it had been frisked. She had on a diamond ring that must've been worth a few hundred and there was thirty-some bucks in her bag. The people there know Wynant and Morelli – both of 'em have been in and out enough – but claim they ain't seen either for some time. The fire-escape window was locked and the fire-escape didn't look like it had been walked on recently." He turned his hands over, palms up. "I guess that's the crop."

"No fingerprints?"

"Hers, some belonging to the people that clean up the place, near as we can figure. Nothing any good to us."

"Nothing out of her friends?"

"She didn't seem to have any – not any close ones."

"How about the – what was his name? – Nunheim who identified her as a friend of Morelli's?"

"He just knew her by sight through seeing her around with Morelli and recognized her picture when he saw it in the paper."

"Who is he?"

"He's all right. We know all about him."

"You wouldn't hold out on me, would you," I asked, "after getting me to promise not to hold out on you?"

Guild said: "Well, if it don't go any further, he's a fellow that does some work for the department now and then."

"Oh."

He stood up. "I hate to say it, but that's just about as far as we've got. You got anything you can help with?"

"No."

He looked at me steadily for a moment. "What do you think of it?"

"That diamond ring, was it an engagement ring?"

"She had it on that finger." After a pause he asked, "Why?"

"It might help to know who bought it for her. I'm going to see Macaulay this afternoon. If anything turns up I'll give you a ring. It looks like Wynant, all right, but – "

He growled good-naturedly, "Uh-huh, but," shook hands with Nora and me, thanked us for our whiskey, our lunch, our hospitality, and our kindness in general, and went away.

I told Nora: "I'm not one to suggest that your charm wouldn't make any man turn himself inside out for you, but don't be too sure that guy isn't kidding us."

"So it's come to that," she said. "You're jealous of policemen."

MACAULAY'S LETTER FROM Clyde Wynant was quite a document. It was very badly typewritten on plain white paper and dated Philadelphia, Pa., December 26, 1932. It read:

Dear Herbert: I am telegraphing Nick Charles who worked for me you will remember some years ago and who is in New York to get in touch with you about the terrible death of poor Julia. I want you to do everything in your power to [a line had been x'd and m'd out here so that it was impossible to make anything at all of it] *persuade him to find her murderer. I don't care what it costs — pay him!*

Here are some facts I want to give him outside of all you know about it yourself. I don't think he should tell these facts to the police, but he will know what is best and I want him to have a completely free hand as I have got the utmost confidence in him. Perhaps you had better just show him this letter, after which I must ask you to carefully destroy it.

Here are the facts. When I met Julia Thursday night to get that $1,000 from her she told me she wanted to quit her job. She said she hadn't been at all well for some time and her doctor had told her she ought to go away and rest and now that her uncle's estate had been settled she could afford to and wanted to do it. She had never said anything about bad health before and I thought she was hiding her real reason and tried to get it out of her, but she stuck to what she had said. I didn't know anything about her uncle dying either. She said it was her Uncle John in Chicago. I suppose that could be looked up if it's important. I couldn't persuade her to change her mind, so she *was to leave the last day of the month. She seemed worried or frightened, but she said she wasn't. I was sorry at first that she was going, but then I wasn't, because I had always been able to trust her and now I wouldn't be if she was lying, as I thought she was.*

The next fact I want Charles to know is that whatever anybody may think or whatever was true some time ago Julia and I ["are now" was x'd out lightly*] were at the time of her murder* and had been for more than a year *not anything more to each other than employee and employer. This relationship was the result of mutual agreement.*

Next, I believe some attempt should be made to learn the present whereabouts of the Victor Rosewater with whom we had trouble some years ago inasmuch as the experiments I am now engaged in are in line with those he claimed I cheated him out of and I consider him quite insane enough to have killed Julia in a rage at her refusal to tell him where I could be found.

Fourth, and most important, *has my divorced wife been in communication with Rosewater? How did she learn I was carrying out the experiments with which he once assisted me?*

Fifth, the police must be convinced at once that I can tell them nothing about the murder so that they will take no steps to find me — steps that might lead to a discovery of and a premature exposure of my experiments, which I would consider very dangerous at this time. This can best be avoided by clearing up the mystery of her murder immediately, and that is what I wish to have done.

I will communicate with you from time to time and if in the meanwhile anything should arise to make communication with me imperative insert the following advertisement in the Times: Abner. Yes. Bunny.

I will thereupon arrange to get in touch with you.

I hope you sufficiently understand the necessity of persuading Charles to act for me, since he is already acquainted with the Rosewater trouble and knows most of the people concerned. Yours truly,

Clyde Miller Wynant

I put the letter down on Macaulay's desk and said: "It makes a lot of sense. Do you remember what his row with Rosewater was about?"

"Something about changes in the structures of crystals. I can look it up." Macaulay picked up the first sheet of the letter and frowned at it. "He says he got a thousand dollars from her that night. I gave her five thousand for him; she told me that's what he wanted."

"Four thousand from Uncle John's estate?" I suggested.

"Looks like it. That's funny: I never thought she'd gyp him. I'll have to find out about the other money I turned over to her."

"Did you know she'd done a jail sentence in Cleveland on a badger-game charge?"

"No. Had she really?"

"According to the police – under the name of Rhoda Stewart. Where'd Wynant find her?"

He shook his head. "I've no idea."

"Know anything about where she came from originally, relatives, things like that?" He shook his head again. "Who was she engaged to?" I asked.

"I didn't know she was engaged."

"She was wearing a diamond ring on her finger."

"That's news to me," he said. He shut his eyes and thought. "No, I can't remember ever noticing an engagement ring." He put his forearms on his desk and grinned over them at me. "Well, what are the chances of getting you to do what he wants?"

"Slim."

"I thought so." He moved a hand to touch the letter. "You know as much about how he feels as I do. What would make you change your mind?"

"I don't – "

"Would it help any if I could persuade him to meet you? Maybe if I told him that was the only way you'd take it – "

294

"I'm willing to talk to him," I said, "but he'd have to talk a lot straighter than he's writing."

Macaulay asked slowly: "You mean you think he may have killed her?"

"I don't know anything about that," I said. "I don't know as much as the police do, and it's a cinch they haven't got enough on him to make the pinch even if they could find him."

Macaulay sighed. "Being a goof's lawyer is not much fun. I'll try to make him listen to reason, but I know he won't."

"I meant to ask, how are his finances these days? Is he as well fixed as he used to be?"

"Almost. The depression's hurt him some, along with the rest of us, and the royalties from his smelting process have gone pretty much to hell now that the metals are dead, but he can still count on fifty or sixty thousand a year from his glassine and soundproofing patents, with a little more coming in from odds and ends like – " He broke off to ask: "You're not worrying about his ability to pay whatever you'd ask?"

"No, I was just wondering." I thought of something else: "Has he any relatives outside of his ex-wife and children?"

"A sister, Alice Wynant, that hasn't been on speaking terms with him for – it must be four or five years now."

I supposed that was the Aunt Alice the Jorgensens had not gone to see Christmas afternoon. "What'd they fall out about?" I asked.

"He gave an interview to one of the papers saying he didn't think the Russian Five Year Plan was necessarily doomed to failure. Actually he didn't make it much stronger than that."

I laughed. "They're a – "

"She's even better than he is. She can't remember things. The time her brother had his appendix out, she and Mimi were in a taxi going to see him the first afternoon and they passed a hearse coming from the direction of the hospital. Miss

Alice turned pale and grabbed Mimi by the arm and said: 'Oh, dear! If that should be what's-his-name!' "

"Where does she live?"

"On Madison Avenue. It's in the phone-book." He hesitated. "I don't think – "

"I'm not going to bother her." Before I could say anything else his telephone began to ring.

He put the receiver to his ear and said: "Hello. . . . Yes, speaking. . . . Who?. . . Oh, yes. . . . " Muscles tightened around his mouth, and his eyes opened a little wider. "Where?" He listened some more. "Yes, surely. Can I make it?" He looked at the watch on his left wrist. "Right. See you on the train." He put the telephone down. "That was Lieutenant Guild," he told me. "Wynant's tried to commit suicide in Allentown, Pennsylvania."

13

DOROTHY AND QUINN were at the bar when I went into the Palma Club. They did not see me until I came up beside Dorothy and said: "Hello, folks." Dorothy had on the same clothes I had last seen her in.

She looked at me and at Quinn and her face flushed. "You had to tell him."

"The girl's in a pet," Quinn said cheerfully. "I got that stock for you. You ought to pick up some more and what are you drinking?"

"Old-fashioned. You're a swell guest – ducking out without leaving a word behind you."

Dorothy looked at me again. The scratches on her face were pale, the bruise barely showed, and her mouth was no longer swollen. "I trusted you," she said. She seemed about to cry.

"What do you mean by that?"

"You know what I mean. Even when you went to dinner at Mamma's I trusted you."

"And why not?"

Quinn said: "She's been in a pet all afternoon. Don't bait her." He put a hand on one of hers. "There, there, darling, don't you – "

"Please shut up." She took her hand away from him. "You know very well what I mean," she told me. "You and Nora both made fun of me to Mamma and – "

I began to see what had happened. "She told you that and you believed it?" I laughed. "After twenty years you're still a sucker for her lies? I suppose she phoned you after we left: we had a row and didn't stay long."

297

DASHIELL HAMMETT

She hung her head and said, "Oh, I'm a fool," in a low miserable voice. Then she grabbed me by both arms and said: "Listen, let's go over and see Nora now. I've got to square myself with her. I'm such an ass. It'd serve me right if she never – "

"Sure. There's plenty of time. Let's have this drink first."

Quinn said: "Brother Charles, I'd like to shake your hand. You've brought sunshine back into the life of our little tot and joy to – " He emptied his glass. "Let's go over and see Nora. The booze there is just as good and costs us less."

"Why don't you stay here?" she asked him.

He laughed and shook his head. "Not me. Maybe you can get Nick to stay here, but I'm going with you. I've put up with your snottiness all afternoon: now I'm going to bask in the sunshine."

Gilbert Wynant was with Nora when we reached the Normandie. He kissed his sister and shook hands with me and, when he had been introduced, Harrison Quinn. Dorothy immediately began to make long and earnest and none too coherent apologies to Nora. Nora said: "Stop it. There's nothing to forgive. If Nick's told you I was sore or hurt or anything of the sort he's just a Greek liar. Let me take your coat."

Quinn turned on the radio. At the stroke of the gong it was five-thirty-one and one quarter, Eastern Standard Time. Nora told Quinn, "Play bar-tender: you know where the stuff is," and followed me into the bathroom. "Where'd you find her?"

"In a speak. What's Gilbert doing here?"

"He came over to see her, so he said. She didn't go home last night and he thought she was still here." She laughed. "He wasn't surprised at not finding her, though. He said she was always wandering off somewhere, she has dromomania, which comes from a mother fixation and is very interesting. He said Stekel claims people who have it usually show kleptomaniac impulses too, and he's left things around to see if she'd steal them, but she never has yet that he knows of."

"He's quite a lad. Did he say anything about his father?"

"No."

"Maybe he hadn't heard. Wynant tried to commit suicide down in Allentown. Guild and Macaulay have gone down to see him. I don't know whether to tell the youngsters or not. I wonder if Mimi had a hand in his coming over here."

"I wouldn't think so, but if you do – "

"I'm just wondering," I said. "Has he been here long?"

"About an hour. He's a funny kid. He's studying Chinese and writing a book on Knowledge and Belief – not in Chinese – and thinks Jack Oakie's very good."

"So do I. Are you tight?"

"Not very."

When we returned to the living-room, Dorothy and Quinn were dancing to "Eadie Was a Lady." Gilbert put down the magazine he was looking at and politely said he hoped I was recovering from my injury. I said I was.

"I've never been hurt, really hurt," he went on, "that I can remember. I've tried hurting myself, of course, but that's not the same thing. It just made me uncomfortable and irritable and sweat a lot."

"That's pretty much the same thing," I said.

"Really? I thought there'd be more – well, more to it." He moved a little closer to me. "It's things like that I don't know. I'm so horribly young I haven't had a chance to – Mr. Charles, if you're too busy or don't want to, I hope you'll say so, but I'd appreciate it very much if you'd let me talk to you some time when there aren't a lot of people around to interrupt us. There are so many things I'd like to ask you, things I don't know anybody else could tell me and – "

"I'm not so sure about that," I said, "but I'll be glad to try any time you want."

"You really don't mind? You're not just being polite?"

"No, I mean it, only I'm not sure you'll get as much help as you expect. It depends on what you want to know."

"Well, things like cannibalism," he said. "I don't mean in places like Africa and New Guinea – in the United States, say. Is there much of it?"

"Not nowadays. Not that I know of."

"Then there was once?"

"I don't know how much, but it happened now and then before the country was completely settled. Wait a minute: I'll give you a sample." I went over to the bookcase and got the copy of Duke's *Celebrated Criminal Cases of America* that Nora had picked up in a second-hand book store, found the place I wanted, and gave it to him. "It's only three or four pages."

ALFRED G. PACKER, THE "MANEATER," WHO
MURDERED HIS FIVE COMPANIONS IN THE MOUNTAINS
OF COLORADO, ATE THEIR BODIES AND
STOLE THEIR MONEY.

In the fall of 1873 a party of twenty daring men left Salt Lake City, Utah, to prospect in the San Juan country. Having heard glowing accounts of the fortunes to be made, they were light-hearted and full of hope as they started on their journey, but as the weeks rolled by and they beheld nothing but barren wastes and snowy mountains, they grew despondent. The further they proceeded, the less inviting appeared the country, and they finally became desperate when it appeared that their only reward would be starvation and death. Just as the prospectors were about to give up in despair, they saw an Indian camp in the distance, and while they had no assurance as to what treatment they would receive at the hands of the "Reds," they decided that any death was preferable to starvation, so they agreed to take a chance.

When they approached the camp they were met by an Indian who appeared to be friendly and escorted them to Chief Ouray. To their great surprise, the Indians treated them with every consideration and insisted upon their remaining in the camp until they had fully recuperated from their hardships. Finally the party decided to make another start, with the Los Pinos Agency as their goal. Ouray attempted to dissuade them from continuing the journey, and did succeed in influencing ten of the party to abandon the trip and return to Salt Lake. The other ten determined to continue, so Ouray supplied them with provisions and admonished them to follow the Gunnison River, which was named after Lieutenant Gunnison, who was murdered in 1852. (See life of Joe Smith, the Mormon.)

Alfred G. Packer, who appeared as the leader of the party which continued the journey, boasted of his knowledge of the topography of the country and expressed confidence in his ability to find his way without difficulty. When his party had traveled a short distance, Packer told them that rich mines had recently been discovered near the headwaters of the Rio Grande River, and he offered to guide the party to the mines. Four of the party insisted that they follow Ouray's instructions, but Packer persuaded five men, named Swan, Miller, Noon, Bell and Humphrey, to accompany him to the mines, while the other four proceeded along the river.

Of the party of four, two died from starvation and exposure, but the other two finally reached the Los Pinos Agency in February, 1874, after enduring indescribable hardships. General Adams was in command of this Agency, and the unfortunate men were treated with every consideration. When they regained their strength they started back to civilization.

In March, 1874, General Adams was called to Denver on business, and one cold, blizzardly morning, while he was still away, the employees of the Agency, who were seated at the breakfast table, were startled by the appearance at the door of a wild-looking man who begged piteously for food and shelter. His face was frightfully bloated but otherwise he appeared to be in fairly good condition, although his stomach would not retain the food given him. He stated that his name was Packer and claimed that his five companions had deserted him while he was ill, but had left a rifle with him which he brought into the Agency.

After partaking of the hospitality of the employees at the Agency for ten days, Packer proceeded to a place called Saquache, claiming that he intended to work his way to Pennsylvania, where he had a brother. At Saquache, Packer drank heavily and appeared to be well supplied with money. While intoxicated, he told many conflicting stories regarding the fate of his companions, and it was suspected that he had disposed of his erstwhile associates by foul means.

At this time General Adams stopped at Saquache on his return from Denver to the Agency, and while at the home of Otto Mears he was advised to arrest Packer and investigate his movements. The General decided to take him back to the Agency, and while en route they stopped at the cabin of Major Downey, where they met the ten men who listened to the Indian chief and abandoned the trip. It was then proven that a great part of Packer's statement was false, so the General decided that the matter required a complete investigation, and Packer was bound and taken to the Agency, where he was held in close confinement.

On April 2, 1874, two wildly excited Indians ran into the Agency, holding strips of flesh in their hands which they called "white man's meat," and which they stated they found just outside the Agency. As it had been lying on the snow and the weather had been extremely cold, it was still in good condition. When Packer caught sight of the exhibits, his face became livid, and with a low moan he sank to the floor. Restoratives were administered and after pleading for mercy, he made a statement substantially as follows:

"When I and five others left Ouray's camp, we estimated that we had sufficient provisions for the long and arduous journey before us, but our food rapidly disappeared and we were soon on the verge of starvation. We dug roots from the ground upon which we subsisted for some days, but as they were not nutritious and as the extreme cold had driven all animals and birds to shelter, the situation became desperate. Strange looks came into the eyes of each of the party and they all became suspicious of each other. One day I went out to gather wood for the fire and when I returned I found that Mr. Swan, the oldest man in the party, had been struck on the head and killed, and the remainder of the party were in the act of cutting up the body preparatory to eating it. His money, amounting to $ 2000.00, was divided among the remainder of the party.

"This food only lasted a few days, and I suggested that Miller be the next victim because of the large amount of flesh he carried. His skull was split open with a hatchet as he was in the act of picking up a piece of wood. Humphrey and Noon were the next victims. Bell and I then entered into a solemn compact that as we were the only ones left we would stand by each other whatever befell, and rather than harm each other we would die of starvation. One day Bell said, 'I can stand it no longer,' and he rushed at me like a famished tiger, at the same time attempting to strike me with his gun. I parried the blow and killed him with a hatchet. I then cut his flesh into strips which I carried with me as I pursued my journey. When I espied the Agency from the top of the hill, I threw away the strips I had left,

303

and I confess I did so reluctantly as I had grown fond of human flesh, especially that portion around the breast."

After relating this gruesome story, Packer agreed to guide a party in charge of H. Lauter to the remains of the murdered men. He led them to some high, inaccessible mountains, and as he claimed to be bewildered, it was decided to abandon the search and start back the next day. That night Packer and Lauter slept side by side, and during the night Packer assaulted him with the intent to commit murder and escape, but he was overpowered, bound, and after the party reached the Agency, he was turned over to the Sheriff.

Early in June of that year, an artist named Reynolds, from Peoria, Ill., while sketching along the shores of Lake Christoval, discovered the remains of the five men lying in a grove of hemlocks. Four of the bodies were lying together in a row, and the fifth, minus the head, was found a short distance away. The bodies of Bell, Swan, Humphrey and Noon had rifle bullet wounds in the back of the head, and when Miller's head was found it was crushed in, evidently by a blow from a rifle which was lying near by, the stock being broken from the barrel.

The appearance of the bodies clearly indicated that Packer had been guilty of cannibalism as well as murder. He probably spoke the truth when he stated his preference for the breast of man, as in each instance the entire breast was cut away to the ribs. A beaten path was found leading from the bodies to a near-by cabin, where blankets and other articles belonging to the murdered men were discovered, and everything indicated that Packer lived in this cabin for many days after the murders, and that he made frequent trips to the bodies for his supply of human meat.

After these discoveries the Sheriff procured warrants charging Packer with five murders, but during his absence the prisoner escaped. Nothing was heard of him again until January 29, 1883, nine years later, when General Adams received a letter from Cheyenne, Wyoming, in which a Salt Lake prospector stated that he had met Packer face to face in that locality. The informant stated that the fugitive was known as John Schwartze, and was suspected of being engaged in operations with a gang of outlaws. Detectives began an investigation, and on March 12, 1883, Sheriff Sharpless of Laramie County arrested Packer, and on the 17th inst. Sheriff Smith of Hinsdale County brought the prisoner back to Lake City, Col.

His trial on the charge of murdering Israel Swan in Hinsdale County on March 1, 1874, was begun on April 3, 1883. It was proven that each member of the party except Packer possessed considerable money. The defendant repeated his former statement, wherein he claimed that he had only killed Bell, and had done so in self-defense. On April 13, the jury found the defendant guilty with the death penalty attached. A stay of execution was granted to Packer, who immediately appealed to the Supreme Court. In the meantime he was transferred to the Gunnison jail to save him from mob violence.

In October, 1885, the Supreme Court granted a new trial and it was then decided to bring him to trial on five charges of manslaughter. He was found guilty on each charge and was sentenced to serve eight years for each offense, making a total of forty years. He was pardoned on January 1, 1901, and died on a ranch near Denver on April 24, 1907.

While Gilbert was reading this, I got myself a drink. Dorothy stopped dancing to join me. "Do you like him?" she asked, jerking her head to indicate Quinn.

"He's all right."

"Maybe, but he can be terribly silly. You didn't ask me where I stayed last night. Don't you care?"

"It's none of my business."

"But I found out something for you."

"What?"

"I stayed at Aunt Alice's. She's not exactly right in the head, but she's awfully sweet. She told me she had a letter from Father today warning her against Mamma."

"Warning her how? Just what did he say?"

"I didn't see it. Aunt Alice had been mad with him for several years and she tore it up. She says he's become a Communist and she's sure the Communists killed Julia Wolf and will kill him in the end. She thinks it's all over some secret they betrayed."

I said: "Oh my God!"

"Well, don't blame me. I'm just telling you what she told me. I told you she wasn't exactly right in the head."

"Did she tell you that junk was in the letter?"

Dorothy shook her head. "No. She only said the warning was. As near as I remember she said he wrote her not to trust anybody connected with her, which I suppose means all of us."

"Try to remember more."

"But there wasn't any more. That's all she told me."

"Where was the letter from?" I asked.

"She didn't know – except that it had come airmail. She said she wasn't interested."

"What did she think of it? I mean, did she take the warning seriously?"

"She said he was a dangerous radical – they're her very words – and she wasn't interested in anything he had to say."

"How seriously do you take it?"

She stared at me for a long moment and she moistened her lips before she spoke. "I think he – "

Gilbert, book in hand, came over to us. He seemed disappointed in the story I had given him. "It's very interesting," he said, "but, if you know what I mean, it's not a pathological case." He put an arm around his sister's waist. "It was more a matter of that or starving."

"Not unless you want to believe him," I said.

Dorothy asked: "What is it?"

"Tell him about the letter your aunt got," I said to Dorothy. She told him.

When she had finished, he grimaced impatiently. "That's silly. Mamma's not really dangerous. She's just a case of arrested development. Most of us have outgrown ethics and morals and so on. Mamma's just not grown up to them yet." He frowned and corrected himself thoughtfully: "She might be dangerous, but it would be like a child playing with matches."

Nora and Quinn were dancing. "And what do you think of your father?" I asked.

Gilbert shrugged. "I haven't seen him since I was a child. I've got a theory about him, but a lot of it's guesswork. I'd like – the chief thing I'd like to know is if he's impotent."

I said: "He tried to kill himself today, down in Allentown."

Dorothy cried, "He didn't," so sharply that Quinn and Nora stopped dancing, and she turned and thrust her face up at her brother's. "Where's Chris?" she demanded.

Gilbert looked from her face to mine and quickly back to hers. "Don't be an ass," he said coldly. "He's off with that girl of his, that Fenton girl."

Dorothy did not look as if she believed him. "She's jealous of him," he explained to me. "It's that mother fixation."

I asked: "Did either of you ever see the Victor Rosewater your father had trouble with back when I first knew you?"

Dorothy shook her head. Gilbert said: "No. Why?"

"Just an idea I had. I never saw him either, but the description they gave me, with some easy changes, could be made to fit your Chris Jorgensen."

14

THAT NIGHT NORA and I went to the opening of the Radio City Music Hall, decided we had had enough of the performance after an hour, and left. "Where to?" Nora asked.

"I don't care. Want to hunt up that Pigiron Club that Morelli told us about? You'll like Studsy Burke. He used to be a safe-burglar. He claims to've cracked the safe in the Hagerstown jail while he was doing thirty days there for disorderly conduct."

"Let's," she said.

We went down to Forty-ninth Street and, after asking two taxi-drivers, two newsboys, and a policeman, found the place. The doorman said he didn't know about any Burkes, but he'd see. Studsy came to the door. "How are you, Nick?" he said. "Come on in."

He was a powerfully built man of medium height, a little fat now, but not soft. He must have been at least fifty, but looked ten years younger than that. He had a broad, pleasantly ugly, pock-marked face under not much hair of no particular color, and even his baldness could not make his forehead seem large. His voice was a deep bass growl. I shook hands with him and introduced him to Nora.

"A wife," he said. "Think of that. By God, you'll drink champagne or you'll fight me." I said we wouldn't fight and we went inside. His place had a comfortably shabby look. It was between hours: there were only three customers in the place. We sat at a table in a corner and Studsy told the waiter exactly which bottle of wine to bring. Then he examined me carefully and nodded. "Marriage done you

308

good." He scratched his chin. "It's a long time I don't see you."

"A long time," I agreed.

"He sent me up the river," he told Nora.

She clucked sympathetically. "Was he a good detective?"

Studsy wrinkled what forehead he had. "Folks say, but I don't know. The once he caught me was a accident: I led with my right."

"How come you sicked this wild man Morelli on me?" I asked.

"You know how foreigners are," he said; "they're hysterical. I don't know he's going to do nothing like that. He's worrying about the coppers trying to hang that Wolf dame's killing on him and we see in the paper you got something to do with it and I say to him, 'Nick might not maybe sell his own mother out and you feel like you got to talk to somebody,' so he says he will. What'd you do, make faces at him?"

"He let himself be spotted sneaking in and then blamed me for it. How'd he find me?"

"He's got friends, and you wasn't hiding, was you?"

"I'd only been in town a week and there was nothing in the paper saying where I was staying."

"Is that so?" Studsy asked with interest. "Where you been?"

"I live in San Francisco now. How'd he find me?"

"That's a swell town. I ain't been there in years, but it's one swell town. I oughtn't tell you, Nick. Ask him. It's his business."

"Except that you sent him to me."

"Well, yes," he said, "except that, of course; but then, see, I was putting in a boost for you." He said it seriously.

I said: "My pal."

"How did I know he was going to blow his top? Anyways, he didn't hurt you much, did he?"

"Maybe not, but it didn't do me any good and I – " I stopped as the waiter arrived with the champagne. We tasted it and said it was swell. It was pretty bad. "Think he killed the girl?" I asked.

Studsy shook his head sidewise with certainty. "No chance."

"He's a fellow you can persuade to shoot," I said.

"I know – these foreigners are hysterical – but he was around here all that afternoon."

"All?"

"All. I'll take my oath to it. Some of the boys and girls were celebrating upstairs and I know for a fact he wasn't off his hip, let alone out of here, all afternoon. No kidding, that's a thing he can prove."

"Then what was he worried about?"

"Do I know? Ain't that what I been asking him myself? But you know how these foreigners are."

I said: "Uh-huh. They're hysterical. He wouldn't've sent a friend around to see her, would he?"

"I think you got the boy wrong," Studsy said. "I knew the dame. She used to come in here with him sometimes. They was just playing. He wasn't nuts enough about her that he'd have any reason for weighting her down like that. On the level."

"Was she on the stuff too?"

"I don't know. I seen her take it sometimes, but maybe she was just being sociable, taking a shot because he did."

"Who else did she play around with?"

"Nobody I know," Studsy replied indifferently. "There was a rat named Nunheim used to come in here that was on the make for her, but he didn't get nowhere that I could see."

"So that's where Morelli got my address."

"Don't be silly. All Morelli'd want of him would be a crack at him. What's it to him telling the police Morelli knew the dame? A friend of yours?"

I thought it over and said: "I don't know him. I hear he does chores for the police now and then."

"M-m-m. Thanks."

"Thanks for what? I haven't said anything."

"Fair enough. Now you tell me something: what's all this fiddlededee about, huh? That guy Wynant killed her, didn't he?"

"A lot of people think so," I said, "but fifty bucks'll get you a hundred he didn't."

He shook his head. "I don't bet with you in your own racket" – his face brightened – "but I tell you what I will do and we can put some dough on it if you want. You know that time you copped me, I did lead with my right like I said, and I always wondered if you could do it again. Some time when you're feeling well I'd like –"

I laughed and said: "No, I'm all out of condition."

"I'm hog-fat myself," he insisted.

"Besides, that was a fluke: you were off balance and I was set."

"You're just trying to let me down easy," he said, and then more thoughtfully, "though I guess you did get the breaks at that. Well, if you won't – Here, let me fill your glasses."

Nora decided that she wanted to go home early and sober, so we left Studsy and his Pigiron Club at a little after eleven o'clock. He escorted us to a taxicab and shook our hands vigorously. "This has been a fine pleasure," he told us. We said equally polite things and rode away.

Nora thought Studsy was marvelous. "Half his sentences I can't understand at all."

"He's all right."

"You didn't tell him you'd quit gum-shoeing."

"He'd've thought I was trying to put something over on him," I explained. "To a mug like him, once a sleuth always a sleuth, and I'd rather lie to him than have him think I'm lying. Have you got a cigarette? He really trusts me, in a way."

"Were you telling the truth when you said Wynant didn't kill her?"

"I don't know. My guess is I was."

At the Normandie there was a telegram for me from Macaulay in Allentown:

MAN HERE IS NOT WYNANT AND DID NOT TRY
TO COMMIT SUICIDE

15

I HAD A stenographer in the next morning and got rid of most of the mail that had been accumulating; had a telephone conversation with our lawyer in San Francisco – we were trying to keep one of the mill's customers from being thrown into bankruptcy; spent an hour going over a plan we had for lowering our state taxes; was altogether the busy business man, and felt pretty virtuous by two o'clock, when I knocked off work for the day and went out to lunch with Nora. She had a date to play bridge after lunch. I went down to see Guild: I had talked with him on the telephone earlier in the day.

"So it was a false alarm?" I said after we had shaken hands and made ourselves comfortable in chairs.

"That's what it was. He wasn't any more Wynant than I am. You know how it is: we told the Philly police he'd sent a wire from there and broadcasted his description, and for the next week anybody that's skinny and maybe got whiskers is Wynant to half of the State of Pennsylvania. This was a fellow named Barlow, a carpenter out of work as near as we can figure out, that got shot by a nigger trying to stick him up. He can't talk much yet."

"He couldn't've been shot by somebody who made the same mistake the Allentown police did?" I asked.

"You mean thought he was Wynant? I guess that could be – if it helps any. Does it?"

I said I didn't know. "Did Macaulay tell you about the letter he got from Wynant?"

"He didn't tell me what was in it." I told him. I told him what I knew about Rosewater. He said: "Now, that's interesting."

313

I told him about the letter Wynant had sent his sister.

He said: "He writes a lot of people, don't he?"

"I thought of that." I told him Victor Rosewater's description with a few easy changes would fit Christian Jorgensen.

He said: "It don't hurt any to listen to a man like you. Don't let me stop you." I told him that was the crop.

He rocked back in his chair and screwed his pale gray eyes up at the ceiling. "There's some work to be done there," he said presently.

"Was this fellow in Allentown shot with a .32?" I asked.

Guild stared curiously at me for a moment, then shook his head. "A .44. You got something on your mind?"

"No. Just chasing the set-up around in my head."

He said, "I know what that is," and leaned back to look at the ceiling some more. When he spoke again it was as if he was thinking of something else. "That alibi of Macaulay's you was asking about is all right. He was late for a date then and we know for a fact he was in a fellow's office named Hermann on Fifty-seventh Street from five minutes after three till twenty after, the time that counts."

"What's the five minutes after three?"

"That's right, you don't know about that. Well, we found a fellow named Caress with a cleaning and dyeing place on First Avenue that called her up at five minutes after three to ask her if she had any work for him, and she said no and told him she was liable to go away. So that narrows the time down to from three-five to three-twenty. You ain't really suspicious of Macaulay?"

"I'm suspicious of everybody," I said. "Where were you between three-five and three-twenty?"

He laughed. "As a matter of fact," he said, "I'm just about the only one of the lot that ain't got an alibi. I was at the moving pictures."

"The rest of them have?"

314

He wagged his head up and down. "Jorgensen left his place with Mrs. Jorgensen – that was about five minutes to three – and sneaked over on West Seventy-third Street to see a girl named Olga Fenton – we promised not to tell his wife – and stayed there till about five. We know what Mrs. Jorgensen did. The daughter was dressing when they left and she took a taxi at a quarter past and went straight to Bergdorf-Goodman's. The son was in the Public Library all afternoon – Jesus, he reads funny books. Morelli was in a joint over in the Forties." He laughed. "And where was you?"

"I'm saving mine till I really need it. None of those look too air-tight, but legitimate alibis seldom do. How about Nun-heim?"

Guild seemed surprised. "What makes you think of him?"

"I hear he had a yen for the girl."

"And where'd you hear it?"

"I heard it."

He scowled. "Would you say it was reliable?"

"Yes."

"Well," he said slowly, "he's one guy we can check up on. But look here, what do you care about these people? Don't you think Wynant done it?"

I gave him the same odds I had given Studsy: "Twenty-five'll get you fifty he didn't."

He scowled at me over that for a long silent moment, then said: "That's an idea, anyways. Who's your candidate?"

"I haven't got that far yet. Understand, I don't know anything. I'm not saying Wynant didn't do it. I'm just saying everything doesn't point at him."

"And saying it two to one. What don't point at him?"

"Call it a hunch, if you want," I said, "but – "

"I don't want to call it anything," he said. "I think you're a smart detective. I want to listen to what you got to say."

"Mostly I've got questions to say. For instance, how long was it from the time the elevator boy let Mrs. Jorgensen off at the Wolf girl's floor until she rang for him and said she heard groans?"

Guild pursed his lips, opened them to ask, "You think she might've –?" and left the rest of the question hanging in the air.

"I think she might've. I'd like to know where Nunheim was. I'd like to know the answers to the questions in Wynant's letter. I'd like to know where the four-thousand-dollar difference between what Macaulay gave the girl and what she seems to have given Wynant went. I'd like to know where her engagement ring came from."

"We're doing the best we can," Guild said. "Me – just now I'd like to know why, if he didn't do it, Wynant don't come in and answer questions for us."

"One reason might be that Mrs. Jorgensen'd like to slam him in the squirrel cage again." I thought of something. "Herbert Macaulay's working for Wynant: you didn't just take Macaulay's word for it that the man in Allentown wasn't him?"

"No. He was a younger man than Wynant, with damned little gray in his hair and no dye, and he didn't look like the pictures we got." He seemed positive. "You got anything to do the next hour or so?"

"No."

"That's fine." He stood up. "I'll get some of the boys working on these things we been discussing and then maybe me and you will pay some visits."

"Swell," I said, and he went out of the office.

There was a copy of the *Times* in his wastebasket. I fished it out and turned to the Public Notices columns. Macaulay's advertisement was there: "*Abner. Yes. Bunny.*"

When Guild returned I asked: "How about Wynant's help, whoever he had working in the shop? Have they been looked up?"

"Uh-huh, but they don't know anything. They was laid off at the end of the week that he went away – there's two of them – and haven't seen him since."

"What were they working on when the shop was closed?"

"Some kind of paint or something – something about a permanent green. I don't know. I'll find out if you want."

"I don't suppose it matters. Is it much of a shop?"

"Looks like a pretty good lay-out, far as I can tell. You think the shop might have something to do with it?"

"Anything might."

"Uh-huh. Well, let's run along."

16

"FIRST THING," GUILD said as we left his office, "we'll go see Mr. Nunheim. He ought to be home: I told him to stick around till I phoned him."

Mr. Nunheim's home was on the fourth floor of a dark, damp, and smelly building made noisy by the Sixth Avenue elevated. Guild knocked on the door. There were sounds of hurried movement inside, then a voice asked: "Who is it?" The voice was a man's, nasal, somewhat irritable.

Guild said: "John."

The door was hastily opened by a small sallow man of thirty-five or -six whose visible clothes were an undershirt, blue pants, and black silk stockings. "I wasn't expecting you, Lieutenant," he whined. "You said you'd phone." He seemed frightened. His dark eyes were small and set close together; his mouth was wide, thin, and loose; and his nose was peculiarly limber, a long, drooping nose, apparently boneless.

Guild touched my elbow with his hand and we went in. Through an open door to the left an unmade bed could be seen. The room we entered was a living-room, shabby and dirty, with clothing, newspapers, and dirty dishes sitting around. In an alcove to the right there was a sink and a stove. A woman stood between them holding a sizzling skillet in her hand. She was a big-boned, full-fleshed, red-haired woman of perhaps twenty-eight, handsome in a rather brutal, sloppy way. She wore a rumpled pink kimono and frayed pink mules with lopsided bows on them. She stared sullenly at us. Guild did not introduce me to Nunheim and he paid no attention to the woman. "Sit down," he said, and pushed some clothing out of the way to make a place for himself on an end of the sofa.

I removed part of a newspaper from a rocking chair and sat down. Since Guild kept his hat on I did the same with mine. Nunheim went over to the table, where there was about two inches of whiskey in a pint bottle and a couple of tumblers, and said: "Have a shot?"

Guild made a face. "Not that vomit. What's the idea of telling me you just knew the Wolf girl by sight?"

"That's all I did, Lieutenant, that's the Christ's truth." Twice his eyes slid sidewise towards me and he jerked them back. "Maybe I said hello to her or how are you or something like that when I saw her, but that's all I knew her. That's the Christ's truth."

The woman in the alcove laughed, once, derisively, and there was no merriment in her face. Nunheim twisted himself around to face her. "All right," he told her, his voice shrill with rage, "put your mouth in and I'll pop a tooth out of it." She swung her arm and let the skillet go at his head. It missed, crashing into the wall. Grease and eggyolks made fresher stains on the wall, floor, and furniture. He started for her. I did not have to rise to put out a foot and trip him. He tumbled down on the floor. The woman had picked up a paring knife.

"Cut it out," Guild growled. He had not stood up either. "We come here to talk to you, not to watch this roughhouse comedy. Get up and behave yourself."

Nunheim got slowly to his feet. "She drives me nuts when she's drinking," he said. "She's been ragging me all day." He moved his right hand back and forth. "I think I sprained my wrist." The woman walked past us without looking at any of us, went into the bedroom, and shut the door.

Guild said: "Maybe if you'd quit sucking around after other women you wouldn't have so much trouble with this one."

"What do you mean, Lieutenant?" Nunheim was surprised and innocent and perhaps pained.

319

"Julia Wolf."

The little sallow man was indignant now. "That's a lie, Lieutenant. Anybody that say I ever – "

Guild interrupted him by addressing me: "If you want to take a poke at him, I wouldn't stop on account of his bum wrist: he couldn't ever hit hard anyhow."

Nunheim turned to me with both hands out. "I didn't mean you were a liar. I meant maybe somebody made a mistake if they – "

Guild interrupted him again: "You wouldn't've taken her if you could've gotten her?"

Nunheim moistened his lower lip and looked warily at the bedroom-door. "Well," he said slowly in a cautiously low voice, "of course she was a classy number. I guess I wouldn't've turned it down."

"But you never tried to make her?"

Nunheim hesitated, then moved his shoulders and said: "You know how it is. A fellow knocking around tries most everything he runs into."

Guild looked sourly at him. "You'd've done better to tell me that in the beginning. Where were you the afternoon she was knocked off?"

The little man jumped as if he had been stuck with a pin. "For Christ's sake, Lieutenant, you don't think I had anything to do with that. What would I want to hurt her for?"

"Where were you?"

Nunheim's loose lips twitched nervously. "What day was she – " He broke off as the bedroom-door opened. The big woman came out carrying a suitcase. She had put on street clothes.

"Miriam," Nunheim said.

She stared at him dully and said: "I don't like crooks, and even if I did, I wouldn't like crooks that are stool-pigeons, and if I liked crooks that are stool-pigeons, I still wouldn't like you." She turned to the outer door.

Guild, catching Nunheim's arm to keep him from following the woman, repeated: "Where were you?"

Nunheim called: "Miriam. Don't go. I'll behave, I'll do anything. Don't go, Miriam." She went out and shut the door.

"Let me go," he begged Guild. "Let me bring her back. I can't get along without her. I'll bring her right back and tell you anything you want to know. Let me go. I've got to have her."

Guild said: "Nuts. Sit down." He pushed the little man down in a chair. "We didn't come here to watch you and that broad dance around a maypole. Where were you the afternoon the girl was killed?"

Nunheim put his hands over his face and began to cry. "Keep on stalling," Guild said, "and I'm going to slap you silly." I poured some whiskey in a tumbler and gave it to Nunheim.

"Thank you, sir, thank you." He drank it, coughed, and brought out a dirty handkerchief to wipe his face with. "I can't remember offhand, Lieutenant," he whined. "Maybe I was over at Charlie's shooting pool, maybe I was here. Miriam would remember if you'll let me go bring her back."

Guild said: "The hell with Miriam. How'd you like to be thrown in the can on account of not remembering?"

"Just give me a minute. I'll remember. I'm not stalling, Lieutenant. You know I always come clean with you. I'm just upset now. Look at my wrist." He held up his right wrist to let us see it was swelling. "Just one minute." He put his hands over his face again. Guild winked at me and we waited for the little man's memory to work.

Suddenly he took his hands down from his face and laughed. "Holy hell! It would serve me right if you had pinched me. That's the afternoon I was – Wait, I'll show you." He went into the bedroom.

After a few minutes Guild called: "Hey, we haven't got all night. Shake it up." There was no answer. The bedroom was empty when we went into it and when we opened the

DASHIELL HAMMETT

bathroom-door the bathroom was empty. There was an open window and a fire-escape.

I said nothing, tried to look nothing. Guild pushed his hat back a little from his forehead and said: "I wish he hadn't done that." He went to the telephone in the living-room. While he was telephoning, I poked around in drawers and closets, but found nothing. My search was not very thorough and I gave it up as soon as he had finished putting the police machinery in action.

"I guess we'll find him, all right," he said. "I got some news. We've identified Jorgensen as Rosewater."

"Who made the identification?"

"I sent a man over to talk to the girl that gave him his alibi, this Olga Fenton, and he finally got it out of her. He says he couldn't shake her on the alibi, though. I'm going over and have a try at her. Want to come along?"

I looked at my watch and said: "I'd like to, but it's too late. Picked him up yet?"

"The order's out." He looked thoughtfully at me. "And will that baby have to do some talking!"

I grinned at him. "Now who do you think killed her?"

"I'm not worrying," he said. "Just let me have things to squeeze enough people with and I'll turn up the right one before the whistle blows." In the street he promised to let me know what happened, and we shook hands and separated. He ran after me a couple of seconds later to send his very best regards to Nora.

322

17

HOME, I DELIVERED Guild's message to Nora and told her the day's news.

"I've got a message for you, too," she said. "Gilbert Wynant dropped in and was quite disappointed at missing you. He asked me to tell you he has something of the 'utmost import-ance' to tell you."

"He's probably discovered that Jorgensen has a mother fixation."

"Do you think Jorgensen killed her?" she asked.

"I thought I knew who did it," I said, "but it's too mixed up right now for anything but guesses."

"And what's your guess?"

"Mimi Jorgensen, Wynant, Nunheim, Gilbert, Dorothy, Aunt Alice, Morelli, you, me, or Guild. Maybe Studsy did it. How about shaking up a drink?"

She mixed some cocktails. I was on my second or third when she came back from answering the telephone and said: "Your friend Mimi wants to talk to you."

I went to the telephone. "Hello, Mimi."

"I'm awfully sorry I was so rude the other night, Nick, but I was so upset and I just simply lost my temper and made a show of myself. Please forgive me." She ran through this very rapidly, as if anxious to get it over with.

"That's all right," I said.

She hardly let me get my three words out before she was speaking again, but slower and more earnestly now: "Can I see you, Nick? Something horrible has happened, something – I don't know what to do, which way to turn."

"What is it?"

"I can't tell you over the phone, but you've got to tell me what to do. I've got to have somebody's advice. Can't you come over?"

"You mean now?"

"Yes. Please."

I said, "All right," and went back to the living-room. "I'm going to run over and see Mimi. She says she's in a jam and needs help."

Nora laughed. "Keep your legs crossed. She apologize to you? She did to me."

"Yes, all in one breath. Is Dorothy home or still at Aunt Alice's?"

"Still at Auntie's, according to Gilbert. How long will you be?"

"No longer than I have to. The chances are they've copped Jorgensen and she wants to know if it can be fixed."

"Can they do anything to him? I mean if he didn't kill the Wolf girl."

"I suppose the old charges against him – threats by mail, attempted extortion – could be raked up." I stopped drinking to ask Nora and myself a question: "I wonder if he and Nunheim know each other." I thought that over, but could make nothing more than a possibility of it. "Well, I'm on my way."

MIMI RECEIVED ME with both hands. "It's awfully, awfully nice of you to forgive me, Nick, but then you've always been awfully nice. I don't know what got into me Monday night."

I said: "Forget it." Her face was somewhat pinker than usual and the firmness of its muscles made it seem younger. Her blue eyes were very bright. Her hands had been cold on mine. She was tense with excitement, but I could not figure out what kind of excitement it was.

She said: "It was awfully sweet of your wife, too, to – "

"Forget it."

"Nick, what can they do to you for concealing evidence that somebody's guilty of a murder?"

"Make you an accomplice – accomplice after the fact is the technical term – if they want."

"Even if you voluntarily change your mind and give them the evidence?"

"They can. Usually they don't."

She looked around the room as if to make sure there was nobody else there and said: "Clyde killed Julia. I found the proof and hid it. What'll they do to me?"

"Probably nothing except give you hell – if you turn it in. He was once your husband: you and he are close enough together that no jury'd be likely to blame you for trying to cover him up – unless, of course, they had reason to think you had some other motive."

She asked coolly, deliberately: "Do you?"

"I don't know," I said. "My guess would be that you had intended to use this proof of his guilt to shake him down for some dough as soon as you could get in touch with him, and that now something else has come up to make you change your mind." She made a claw of her right hand and struck at my face with her pointed nails. Her teeth were together, her lips drawn far back over them.

I caught her wrist. "Women are getting tough," I said, trying to sound wistful. "I just left one that heaved a skillet at a guy."

She laughed, though her eyes did not change. "You're such a bastard. You always think the worst of me, don't you?" I took my hand away from her wrist and she rubbed the marks my fingers had left on it.

"Who was the woman who threw the skillet?" she asked. "Anyone I know?"

"It wasn't Nora, if that's what you mean. Have they arrested Victor-Christian Rosewater-Jorgensen yet?"

"What?"

I believed in her bewilderment, though both it and my belief in it surprised me. "Jorgensen is Rosewater," I said. "You remember him. I thought you knew."

"You mean that horrible man who – "

"Yes."

"I won't believe it." She stood up working her fingers together. "I won't. I won't." Her face was sick with fear, her voice strained, unreal as a ventriloquist's. "I won't believe it."

"That'll help a lot," I said. She was not listening to me. She turned her back to me and went to a window, where she stood with her back to me.

I said: "There's a couple of men in a car out front who look like they might be coppers waiting to pick him up when he – "

She turned around and asked sharply: "Are you sure he's Rosewater?" Most of the fear had already gone out of her face and her voice was at least human again.

"The police are." We stared at each other, both of us busy thinking. I was thinking she had not been afraid that Jorgensen killed Julia Wolf, or even that he might be arrested: she was afraid his only reason for marrying her had been as a move in some plot against Wynant.

When I laughed – not because the idea was funny, but because it had come to me so suddenly – she started and smiled uncertainly. "I won't believe it," she said, and her voice was very soft now, "until he tells me himself."

"And when he does – then what?"

She moved her shoulders a little, and her lower lip quivered. "He is my husband."

That should have been funny, but it annoyed me. I said: "Mimi, this is Nick. You remember me, N-i-c-k."

"I know you never think any good of me," she said gravely. "You think I'm – "

"All right. All right. Let it pass. Let's get back to the dope on Wynant you found."

"Yes, that," she said, and turned away from me. When she turned back her lip was quivering again. "That was a lie, Nick. I didn't find anything." She came close to me. "Clyde had no right to send those letters to Alice and Macaulay trying to make everybody suspicious of me and I thought it would serve him right if I made up something against him, because I really did think – I mean, I do think – he killed her and it was only – "

"What'd you make up?" I asked.

"I – I hadn't made it up yet. I wanted to find out about what they could do – you know, the things I asked you – first. I might've pretended she came to a little when I was alone with her, while the others were phoning, and told me he did it."

"You didn't say you heard something and kept quiet, you said you found something and hid it."

"But I hadn't really made up my mind what I – "

"When'd you hear about Wynant's letter to Macaulay?"

"This afternoon," she said, "there was a man here from the police."

"Didn't he ask you anything about Rosewater?"

"He asked me if I knew him or had ever known him, and I thought I was telling the truth when I said no."

"Maybe you did," I said, "and for the first time I now believe you were telling the truth when you said you found some sort of evidence against Wynant."

She opened her eyes wider. "I don't understand."

"Neither do I, but it could be like this: you could've found something and decided to hold it out, probably with the idea of selling it to Wynant; then when his letters started people looking you over, you decided to give up the money idea and both pay him back and protect yourself by turning it over to the police; and, finally, when you learn that Jorgensen is Rosewater, you make another about-face and hold it out, not for money this time, but to leave Jorgensen in as bad a spot as possible as punishment for having married you as a trick in his game against Wynant and not for love."

She smiled calmly and asked: "You really think me capable of anything, don't you?"

"That doesn't matter," I said. "What ought to matter to you is that you'll probably wind up your life in prison somewhere."

Her scream was not loud, but it was horrible, and the fear that had been in her face before was as nothing to that there now. She caught my lapels and clung to them, babbling: "Don't say that, please don't. Say you don't think it." She was trembling so I put an arm around her to keep her from falling.

We did not hear Gilbert until he coughed and asked: "Aren't you well, Mamma?"

She slowly took her hands down from my lapels and moved back a step and said: "Your mother's a silly woman." She was still trembling, but she smiled at me and she made her voice playful: "You're a brute to frighten me like that."

I said I was sorry. Gilbert put his coat and hat on a chair and looked from one to the other of us with polite interest. When it became obvious that neither of us was going to tell him anything he coughed again, said, "I'm awfully glad to see you," and came over to shake hands with me. I said I was glad to see him.

Mimi said: "Your eyes look tired. I bet you've been reading all afternoon without your glasses again." She shook her head and told me: "He's as unreasonable as his father."

"Is there any news of Father?" he asked.

"Not since that false alarm about his suicide," I said. "I suppose you heard it was a false alarm."

"Yes." He hesitated. "I'd like to see you for a few minutes before you go."

"Sure."

"But you're seeing him now, darling," Mimi said. "Are there secrets between you that I'm not supposed to know about?" Her tone was light enough. She had stopped trembling.

"It would bore you." He picked up his hat and coat, nodded at me, and left the room.

Mimi shook her head again and said: "I don't understand that child at all. I wonder what he made of our tableau." She did not seem especially worried. Then, more seriously: "What made you say that, Nick?"

"About you winding up in – ?"

"No, never mind." She shuddered. "I don't want to hear it. Can't you stay for dinner? I'll probably be all alone."

"I'm sorry I can't. Now how about this evidence you found?"

"I didn't really find anything. That was a lie." She frowned earnestly. "Don't look at me like that. It really was a lie."

"So you sent for me just to lie to me?" I asked. "Then why'd you change your mind?"

She chuckled. "You must really like me, Nick, or you wouldn't always be so disagreeable."

I could not follow that line of reasoning. I said: "Well, I'll see what Gilbert wants and run along."

"I wish you could stay."

"I'm sorry I can't," I said again. "Where'll I find him?"

"The second door to the – Will they really arrest Chris?"

"That depends," I told her, "on what kind of answers he gives them. He'll have to talk pretty straight to stay out."

"Oh, he'll – " She broke off, looked sharply at me, asked, "You're not playing a trick on me? He's really that Rose-water?"

"The police are sure enough of it."

"But the man who was here this afternoon didn't ask a single question about Chris," she objected. "He only asked me if I knew – "

"They weren't sure then," I explained. "It was just a half-idea."

"But they're sure now?" I nodded.

"How'd they find out?"

"From a girl he knows," I said.

"Who?" Her eyes darkened a little, but her voice was under control.

"I can't remember her name." Then I went back to the truth: "The one that gave him his alibi for the afternoon of the murder."

"Alibi?" she asked indignantly. "Do you mean to tell me the police would take the word of a girl like that?"

"Like what?"

"You know what I mean."

"I don't. Do you know the girl?"

"No," she said as if I had insulted her. She narrowed her eyes and lowered her voice until it was not much more than a whisper: "Nick, do you suppose he killed Julia?"

"What would he do that for?"

"Suppose he married me to get revenge on Clyde," she said, "and – You know he did urge me to come over here and try to get some money from Clyde. Maybe I suggested it – I don't know – but he did urge me. And then suppose he happened to run into Julia. She knew him, of course, because they worked for Clyde at the same time. And he knew I was going over to see her that afternoon and was afraid if I made her mad she might expose him to me and so – Couldn't that be?"

"That doesn't make any sense at all. Besides, you and he left here together that afternoon. He wouldn't've had time to – "

"But my taxicab was awfully slow," she said, "and then I may have stopped somewhere on – I think I did. I think I stopped at a drug-store to get some aspirin." She nodded energetically. "I remember I did."

"And he knew you were going to stop, because you had told him," I suggested. "You can't go on like this, Mimi. Murder's serious. It's nothing to frame people for just because they played tricks on you."

"Tricks?" she asked, glaring at me. "Why, that..." She called Jorgensen all the usual profane, obscene, and otherwise insulting names, her voice gradually rising until towards the end she was screaming into my face.

When she stopped for breath I said: "That's pretty cursing, but it – "

"He even had the nerve to hint that I might've killed her," she told me. "He didn't have nerve enough to ask me, but he kept leading up to it until I told him positively that – well, that I didn't do it."

"That's not what you started to say. You told him positively what?"

She stamped her foot. "Stop heckling me."

"All right and to hell with you," I said. "Coming here wasn't my idea." I started towards my hat and coat.

She ran after me, caught my arm. "Please, Nick, I'm sorry. It's this rotten temper of mine. I don't know what I – "

Gilbert came in and said: "I'll go along part of the way with you."

Mimi scowled at him. "You were listening."

"How could I help it, the way you screamed?" he asked. "Can I have some money?"

"And we haven't finished talking," she said.

I looked at my watch. "I've got to run, Mimi. It's late."

"Will you come back after you get through with your date?"

"If it's not too late. Don't wait for me."

"I'll be here," she said. "It doesn't matter how late it is." I said I would try to make it. She gave Gilbert his money. He and I went downstairs.

"I WAS LISTENING," Gilbert told me as we left the building. "I think it's silly not to listen whenever you get a chance if you're interested in studying people, because they're never exactly the same as when you're with them. People don't like it when they know about it, of course, but" – he smiled – "I don't suppose birds and animals like having naturalists spying on them either."

"Hear much of it?" I asked.

"Oh, enough to know I didn't miss any of the important part."

"And what'd you think of it?"

He pursed his lips, wrinkled his forehead, said judicially: "It's hard to say exactly. Mamma's good at hiding things sometimes, but she's never much good at making them up. It's a funny thing – I suppose you've noticed it – the people who lie the most are nearly always the clumsiest at it, and they're easier to fool with lies than most people, too. You'd think they'd be on the look-out for lies, but they seem to be the very ones that will believe almost anything at all. I suppose you've noticed that, haven't you?"

"Yes."

He said: "What I wanted to tell you: Chris didn't come home last night. That's why Mamma's more upset than usual, and when I got the mail this morning there was a letter for him that I thought might have something in it, so I steamed it open." He took a letter from his pocket and held it out to me. "You'd better read it and then I'll seal it again and put it with tomorrow's mail in case he comes back, though I don't think he will."

"Why don't you?" I asked as I took the letter.

"Well, he's really Rosewater. . . . "

"You say anything to him about it?"

"I didn't have a chance. I haven't seen him since you told me."

I looked at the letter in my hand. The envelope was post-marked Boston, Massachusetts, December 27, 1932, and addressed in a slightly childish feminine hand to Mr. Christian Jorgensen, Courtland Apts., New York, N. Y. "How'd you happen to open it?" I asked, taking the letter out of the envelope.

"I don't believe in intuition," he said, "but there are probably odors, sounds, maybe something about the handwriting, that you can't analyze, maybe aren't even conscious of, that influence you sometimes. I don't know what it was: I just felt there might be something important in it."

"You often feel that way about the family's mail?"

He glanced quickly at me as if to see whether I was spoofing, then said: "Not often, but I have opened their mail before. I told you I was interested in studying people."

I read the letter:

Dear Vic – Olga wrote me about you being back in the U.S. married to another woman and using the name of Christian Jorgensen. That is not right Vic as you very well know the same as leaving me without word of any kind all these years. And no money. I know that you had to go away on account of that trouble you had with Mr. Wynant but am sure he has long since forgot all about that and I do think you might have written to me as you know very well I have always been your friend and am willing to do anything within my power for you at any time. I do not want to scold you Vic but I have to see you. I will be off from the store Sunday and Monday on account of New Years and will come down to N. Y. Saturday night and must have a talk with you. Write me where you will meet me and what time as I do not

*want to make any trouble for you. Be sure and write me right
away so I will get it in time.*

Your true wife,
Georgia

There was a street address. I said, "Well, well, well," and
put the letter back in its envelope. "And you resisted the
temptation to tell your mother about this?"

"Oh, I know what her reaction would be. You saw how
she carried on with just what you told her. What do you think
I ought to do about it?"

"You ought to let me tell the police."

He nodded immediately. "If you think that's the best thing.
You can show it to them if you want."

I said, "Thanks," and put the letter in my pocket.

He said: "Now there's another thing: I had some morphine
I was experimenting with and somebody stole it, about twenty
grains."

"Experimenting how?"

"Taking it. I wanted to study the effects."

"And how'd you like them?" I asked.

"Oh, I didn't expect to like it. I just wanted to know about
it. I don't like things that dull my mind. That's why I don't
very often drink, or even smoke. I want to try cocaine,
though, because that's supposed to sharpen the brain, isn't it?"

"It's supposed to. Who do you think copped the stuff?"

"I suspect Dorothy, because I have a theory about her.
That's why I'm going over to Aunt Alice's for dinner: Dorry's
still there and I want to find out. I can make her tell me
anything."

"Well, if she's been over there," I asked, "how could she – "

"She was home for a little while last night," he said, "and,
besides, I don't know exactly when it was taken. Today
was the first time I opened the box it was in for three or four
days."

335

"Did she know you had it?"

"Yes. That's one of the reasons I suspect her. I don't think anybody else did. I experimented on her too."

"How'd she like it?"

"Oh, she liked it all right, but she'd have taken it anyhow. But what I want to ask you is could she have become an addict in a little time like that?"

"Like what?"

"A week – no – ten days."

"Hardly, unless she thought herself into it. Did you give her much?"

"No."

"Let me know if you find out," I said. "I'm going to grab a taxi here. Be seeing you."

"You're coming over later tonight, aren't you?"

"If I can make it. Maybe I'll see you then."

"Yes," he said, "and thanks awfully."

At the first drug-store I stopped to telephone Guild, not expecting to catch him in his office, but hoping to learn how to reach him at his home. He was still there, though. "Working late," I said.

His "That's what" sounded very cheerful.

I read Georgia's letter to him, gave him her address.

"Good pickings," he said.

I told him Jorgensen had not been home since the day before. "Think we'll find him in Boston?" he asked.

"Either there," I guessed, "or as far south as he could manage to get by this time."

"We'll try 'em both," he said, still cheerful. "Now I got a bit of news for you. Our friend Nunheim was filled full of .32s just about an hour after he copped the sneak on us – deader'n hell. The pills look like they come from the same gun that cut down the Wolf dame. The experts are matching 'em up now. I guess he wishes he'd stayed and talked to us."

NORA WAS EATING a piece of cold duck with one hand and working on a jig-saw puzzle with the other when I got home.

"I thought you'd gone to live with her," she said. "You used to be a detective: find me a brownish piece shaped something like a snail with a long neck."

"Piece of duck or puzzle? Don't let's go to the Edges' tonight: they're dull folk."

"All right, but they'll be sore."

"We wouldn't be that lucky," I complained. "They'd get sore at the Quinns and – "

"Harrison called you up. He told me to tell you now's the time to buy some McIntyre Porcupine – I think that's right – to go with your Dome stock. He said it closed at twenty and a quarter." She put a finger on her puzzle. "The piece I want goes in there." I found the piece she wanted and told her, almost word for word, what had been done and said at Mimi's.

"I don't believe it," she said. "You made it up. There aren't any people like that. What's the matter with them? Are they the first of a new race of monsters?"

"I just tell you what happens; I don't explain it."

"How would you explain it? There doesn't seem to be a single one in the family – now that Mimi's turned against her Chris – who has even the slightest reasonably friendly feeling for any of the others, and yet there's something very alike in all of them."

"Maybe that explains it," I suggested.

"I'd like to see Aunt Alice," she said. "Are you going to turn that letter over to the police?"

"I've already phoned Guild," I replied, and told her about Nunheim.

"What does that mean?" she asked.

"For one thing, if Jorgensen's out of town, as I think he is, and the bullets are from the same gun that was used on Julia Wolf, and they probably are, then the police'll have to find his accomplice if they want to hang anything on him."

"I'm sure if you were a good detective you'd be able to make it much clearer to me than it is." She went to work on her puzzle again. "Are you going back to see Mimi?"

"I doubt it. How about letting that dido rest while we get some dinner?"

The telephone rang and I said I would get it. It was Dorothy Wynant. "Hello. Nick?"

"The same. How are you, Dorothy?"

"Gil just got here and asked me about that you-know, and I wanted to tell you I did take it, but I only took it to try to keep him from becoming a dope-fiend."

"What'd you do with it?" I asked.

"He made me give it back to him and he doesn't believe me, but, honestly, that's the only reason I took it."

"I believe you."

"Will you tell Gil, then? If you believe me, he will, because he thinks you know all about things like that."

"I'll tell him as soon as I see him," I promised.

There was a pause, then she asked: "How's Nora?"

"Looks all right to me. Want to talk to her?"

"Well, yes, but there's something I want to ask you. Did – did Mamma say anything about me when you were over there today?"

"Not that I remember. Why?"

"And did Gil?"

"Only about the morphine."

"Are you sure?"

"Pretty sure," I said. "Why?"

338

"It's nothing, really — if you're sure. It's just silly."

"Right. I'll call Nora." I went into the living-room. "Dorothy wants to talk to you. Don't ask her to eat with us."

When Nora returned from the telephone she had a look in her eye. "Now what's up?" I asked.

"Nothing. Just 'how are you' and all that."

I said: "If you're lying to the old man, God'll punish you."

We went over to a Japanese place on Fifty-eighth Street for dinner and then I let Nora talk me into going to the Edges' after all. Halsey Edge was a tall scrawny man of fifty-something with a pinched yellow face and no hair at all. He called himself "a ghoul by profession and inclination" — his only joke, if that is what it was — by which he meant he was an archaeologist, and he was very proud of his collection of battle-axes. He was not so bad once you had resigned yourself to the fact that you were in for occasional cataloguings of his armory — stone axes, copper axes, bronze axes, double-bladed axes, faceted axes, polygonal axes, scalloped axes, hammer axes, adze axes, Meso-potamian axes, Hungarian axes, Nordic axes, and all of them looking pretty moth-eaten. It was his wife we objected to. Her name was Leda, but he called her Tip. She was very small and her hair, eyes, and skin, though naturally of different shades, were all muddy. She seldom sat — she perched on things — and liked to cock her head a little to one side. Nora had a theory that once when Edge opened an antique grave, Tip ran out of it, and Margot Innes always spoke of her as the gnome, pronouncing all the letters. She once told me that she did not think any literature of twenty years ago would live, because it had no psychiatry in it. They lived in a pleasant old three-story house on the edge of Greenwich Village and their liquor was excellent.

A dozen or more people were there when we arrived. Tip introduced us to the ones we did not know and then backed me into a corner. "Why didn't you tell me that those people I met at your place Christmas were mixed up in a murder mystery?" she asked, tilting her head to the left until her ear was practically resting on her shoulder.

"I don't know that they are. Besides, what's one murder mystery nowadays?"

She tilted her head to the right. "You didn't even tell me you had taken the case."

"I had done what? Oh, I see what you mean. Well, I hadn't and haven't. My getting shot ought to prove I was an innocent bystander."

"Does it hurt much?"

"It itches. I forgot to have the dressing changed this afternoon."

"Wasn't Nora utterly terrified?"

"So was I and so was the guy that shot me. There's Halsey. I haven't spoken to him yet."

As I slid around her to escape she said: "Harrison's promised to bring the daughter tonight."

I talked to Edge for a few minutes – chiefly about a place in Pennsylvania he was buying – then found myself a drink and listened to Larry Crowley and Phil Thames swap dirty stories until some woman came over and asked Phil – he taught at Columbia – one of the questions about technocracy that people were asking that week. Larry and I moved away. We went over to where Nora was sitting. "Watch yourself," she told me. "The gnome's hell-bent on getting the inside story of Julia Wolf's murder out of you."

"Let her get it out of Dorothy," I said. "She's coming with Quinn."

"I know."

Larry said: "He's nuts over that girl, isn't he? He told me he was going to divorce Alice and marry her."

Nora said, "Poor Alice," sympathetically. She did not like Alice.

Larry said: "That's according to how you look at it." He liked Alice. "I saw that fellow who's married to the girl's mother yesterday. You know, the tall fellow I met at your house."

"Jorgensen?"

"That's it. He was coming out of a pawnshop on Sixth Avenue near Forty-sixth."

"Talk to him?"

"I was in a taxi. It's probably polite to pretend you don't see people coming out of pawnshops, anyhow."

Tip said, "Sh-h-h," in all directions, and Levi Oscant began to play the piano. Quinn and Dorothy arrived while he was playing. Quinn was drunk as a lord and Dorothy seemed to have something better than a glow.

She came over to me and whispered: "I want to leave when you and Nora do."

I said: "You won't be here for breakfast."

Tip said, "Sh-h-h," in my direction. We listened to some more music.

Dorothy fidgeted beside me for a minute and whispered again: "Gil says you're going over to see Mamma later. Are you?"

"I doubt it."

Quinn came unsteadily around to us. "How're you, boy? How're you, Nora? Give him my message?" (Tip said, "Sh-h-h," at him. He paid no attention to her. Other people looked relieved and began to talk.) "Listen, boy, you bank at the Golden Gate Trust in San Francisco, don't you?"

"Got a little money there."

"Get it out, boy. I heard tonight they're plenty shaky."

"All right. I haven't got much there, though."

"No? What do you do with all your money?"

"Me and the French hoard gold."

He shook his head solemnly. "It's fellows like you that put the country on the bum."

"And it's fellows like me that don't go on the bum with it," I said. "Where'd you get the skinful?"

"It's Alice. She's been sulking for a week. If I didn't drink I'd go crazy."

"What's she sulking about?"

"About my drinking. She thinks – " He leaned forward and lowered his voice confidentially. "Listen. You're all my friends and I'm going to tell you what I'm going to do. I'm going to get a divorce and marry – "

He had tried to put an arm around Dorothy. She pushed it away and said: "You're silly and you're tiresome. I wish you'd leave me alone."

"She thinks I'm silly and tiresome," he told me. "You know why she don't want to marry me? I bet you don't. It's because she's in – "

"Shut up! Shut up, you drunken fool!" Dorothy began to beat his face with both hands. Her face was red, her voice shrill. "If you say that again I'll kill you!"

I pulled Dorothy away from Quinn; Larry caught him, kept him from falling. He whimpered: "She hit me, Nick." Tears ran down his cheeks. Dorothy had her face against my coat and seemed to be crying.

We had what audience there was. Tip came running, her face bright with curiosity. "What is it, Nick?"

I said: "Just a couple of playful drunks. They're all right. I'll see that they get home all right."

Tip was not for that: she wanted them to stay at least until she had a chance to discover what had happened. She urged Dorothy to lie down awhile, offered to get something – whatever she meant by that – for Quinn, who was having trouble standing up now.

Nora and I took them out. Larry offered to go along, but we decided that was not necessary. Quinn slept in a corner of the taxicab during the ride to his apartment, and Dorothy sat stiff and silent in the other corner, with Nora between them. I clung to a folding seat and thought that anyway we had not stayed long at the Edges'. Nora and

Dorothy remained in the taxicab while I took Quinn upstairs. He was pretty limp.

Alice opened the door when I rang. She had on green pajamas and held a hairbrush in one hand. She looked wearily at Quinn and spoke wearily: "Bring it in."

I took it in and spread it on a bed. It mumbled something I could not make out and moved one hand feebly back and forth, but its eyes stayed shut. "I'll tuck him in," I said and loosened his tie.

Alice leaned on the foot of the bed. "If you want to. I've given up doing it." I took off his coat, vest, and shirt.

"Where'd he pass out this time?" she asked with not much interest. She was still standing at the foot of the bed, brushing her hair now.

"The Edges'." I unbuttoned his pants.

"With that little Wynant bitch?" The question was casual.

"There were a lot of people there."

"Yes," she said. "He wouldn't pick a secluded spot." She brushed her hair a couple of times. "So you don't think it's clubby to tell me anything."

Her husband stirred a little and mumbled: "Dorry." I took off his shoes.

Alice sighed. "I can remember when he had muscles." She stared at her husband until I took off the last of his clothes and rolled him under the covers. Then she sighed again and said: "I'll get you a drink."

"You'll have to make it short: Nora's waiting in the cab."

She opened her mouth as if to speak, shut it, opened it again to say: "Righto." I went into the kitchen with her.

Presently she said: "It's none of my business, Nick, but what do people think of me?"

"You're like everybody else: some people like you, some people don't, and some have no feeling about it one way or the other."

343

She frowned. "That's not exactly what I meant. What do people think about my staying with Harrison with him chasing everything that's hot and hollow?"

"I don't know, Alice."

"What do you think?"

"I think you probably know what you're doing and whatever you do is your own business."

She looked at me with dissatisfaction. "You'll never talk yourself into any trouble, will you?" She smiled bitterly. "You know I'm only staying with him for his money, don't you? It may not be a lot to you, but it is to me – the way I was raised."

"There's always divorce and alimony. You ought to have – "

"Drink your drink and get to hell out of here," she said wearily.

NORA MADE A place for me between her and Dorothy in the taxicab. "I want some coffee," she said. "Reuben's?"

I said, "All right," and gave the driver the address.

Dorothy asked timidly: "Did his wife say anything?"

"She sent her love to you."

Nora said: "Stop being nasty."

Dorothy said: "I don't really like him, Nick. I won't ever see him again – honestly." She seemed pretty sober now. "It was – well, I was lonesome and he was somebody to run around with." I started to say something, but stopped when Nora poked me in the side.

Nora said: "Don't worry about it. Harrison's always been a simpleton."

"I don't want to stir things up," I said, "but I think he's really in love with the girl." Nora poked me in the side again.

Dorothy peered at my face in the dim light. "You're – you're not – You're not making fun of me, Nick?"

"I ought to be."

"I heard a new story about the gnome tonight," Nora said in the manner of one who did not mean to be interrupted, and explained to Dorothy, "That's Mrs. Edge. Levi says..." The story was funny enough if you knew Tip. Nora went on talking about her until we got out of the taxicab at Reuben's.

Herbert Macaulay was in the restaurant, sitting at a table with a plump dark-haired girl in red. I waved at him and, after we had ordered some food, went over to speak to him. "Nick Charles, Louise Jacobs," he said. "Sit down. What's news?"

"Jorgensen's Rosewater," I told him.

"The hell he is!"

I nodded. "And he seems to have a wife in Boston."

"I'd like to see him," he said slowly. "I knew Rosewater. I'd like to make sure."

"The police seem sure enough. I don't know whether they've found him yet. Think he killed Julia?"

Macaulay shook his head with emphasis. "I can't see Rosewater killing anybody – not as I knew him – in spite of those threats he made. You remember I didn't take them very seriously at the time. What else has happened?" When I hesitated, he said: "Louise is all right. You can talk."

"It's not that. I've got to go back to my folks and food. I came over to ask you if you'd got an answer to your ad in this morning's *Times*."

"Not yet. Sit down, Nick, there's a lot I want to ask you. You told the police about Wynant's letter, didn't – "

"Come up to lunch tomorrow and we'll bat it around. I've got to get back to my folks."

"Who is the little blonde girl?" Louise Jacobs asked. "I've seen her places with Harrison Quinn."

"Dorothy Wynant."

"You know Quinn?" Macaulay asked me.

"Ten minutes ago I was putting him to bed."

Macaulay grinned. "I hope you keep his acquaintance like that – social."

"Meaning what?"

Macaulay's grin became rueful. "He used to be my broker, and his advice led me right up to the poorhouse steps."

"That's sweet," I said. "He's my broker now and I'm following his advice." Macaulay and the girl laughed. I pretended I was laughing and returned to my table.

Dorothy said: "It's not midnight yet and Mamma said she'd be expecting you. Why don't we all go to see her?"

Nora was very carefully pouring coffee into her cup. "What for?" I asked. "What are you two up to now?" It would have been hard to find two more innocent faces than theirs.

"Nothing, Nick," Dorothy said. "We thought it would be nice. It's early and – "

"And we all love Mimi."

"No–o, but – "

"It's too early to go home," Nora said.

"There are speakeasies," I suggested, "and nightclubs and Harlem."

Nora made a face. "All your ideas are alike."

"Want to go over to Barry's and try our luck at faro?" Dorothy started to say yes, but stopped when Nora made another face.

"That's the way I feel about seeing Mimi again," I said. "I've had enough of her for one day."

Nora sighed to show she was being patient. "Well, if we're going to wind up in a speakeasy as usual, I'd rather go to your friend Studsy's, if you won't let him give us any more of that awful champagne. He's cute."

"I'll do my best," I promised and asked Dorothy, "Did Gilbert tell you he caught Mimi and me in a compromising position?"

She tried to exchange glances with Nora, but Nora's glance was occupied with a cheese blintz on her plate. "He – he didn't exactly say that."

"Did he tell you about the letter?"

"From Chris's wife? Yes." Her blue eyes glittered. "Won't Mamma be furious!"

"You like it, though."

"Suppose I do? What of it? What did she ever do to make me – "

Nora said: "Nick, stop bullying the child." I stopped.

22

BUSINESS WAS GOOD at the Pigiron Club. The place was full of people, noise, and smoke. Studsy came from behind the cash register to greet us. "I was hoping you'd come in." He shook my hand and Nora's and grinned broadly at Dorothy.

"Anything special?" I asked.

He made a bow. "Everything's special with ladies like these." I introduced him to Dorothy.

He bowed to her and said something elaborate about any friend of Nick's and stopped a waiter. "Pete, put a table up here for Mr. Charles."

"Pack them in like this every night?" I asked.

"I got no kick," he said. "They come once, they come back again. Maybe I ain't got no black marble cuspidors, but you don't have to spit out what you buy here. Want to lean against the bar whilst they're putting up that table?" We said we did and ordered drinks.

"Hear about Nunheim?" I asked.

He looked at me for a moment before making up his mind to say: "Uh-huh, I heard. His girl's down there" – he moved his head to indicate the other end of the room – "celebrating, I guess."

I looked past Studsy down the room and presently picked out big red-haired Miriam sitting at a table with half a dozen men and women. "Hear who did it?" I asked.

"She says the police done it – he knew too much."

"That's a laugh," I said.

"That's a laugh," he agreed. "There's your table. Set right down. I'll be back in a minute."

348

We carried our glasses over to a table that had been squeezed in between two tables which had occupied a space large enough for one and made ourselves as nearly comfortable as we could.

Nora tasted her drink and shuddered. "Do you suppose this could be the 'bitter vetch' they used to put in crossword puzzles?"

Dorothy said: "Oh, look."

We looked and saw Shep Morelli coming towards us. His face had attracted Dorothy's attention. Where it was not dented it was swollen and its coloring ranged from deep purple around one eye to the pale pink of a piece of court-plaster on his chin. He came to our table and leaned over a little to put both fists on it. "Listen," he said, "Studsy says I ought to apologize."

Nora murmured, "Old Emily Post Studsy," while I asked, "Well?"

Morelli shook his battered head. "I don't apologize for what I do – people've got to take it or leave it – but I don't mind telling you I'm sorry I lost my noodle and cracked down on you and I hope it ain't bothering you much and if there's anything I can do to square it I – "

"Forget it. Sit down and have a drink. This is Mr. Morelli, Miss Wynant." Dorothy's eyes became wide and interested.

Morelli found a chair and sat down. "I hope you won't hold it against me, neither," he told Nora.

She said: "It was fun." He looked at her suspiciously.

"Out on bail?" I asked.

"Uh-huh, this afternoon." He felt his face gingerly with one hand. "That's where the new ones come from. They had me resisting some more arrest just for good measure before they turned me loose."

Nora said indignantly: "That's horrible. You mean they really – " I patted her hand.

Morelli said: "You got to expect it." His swollen lower lip moved in what was meant for a scornful smile. "It's all right as long as it takes two or three of 'em to do it."

Nora turned to me. "Did you do things like that?"

"Who? Me?"

Studsy came over to us carrying a chair. "They lifted his face, huh?" he said, nodding at Morelli. We made room for him and he sat down. He grinned complacently at Nora's drink and at Nora. "I guess you don't get no better than that in your fancy Park Avenue joints – and you pay four bits a slug for it here." Nora's smile was weak, but it was a smile. She put her foot on mine under the table

I asked Morelli: "Did you know Julia Wolf in Cleveland?"

He looked sidewise at Studsy, who was leaning back in his chair, gazing around the room, watching his profits mount.

"When she was Rhoda Stewart," I added.

He looked at Dorothy. I said: "You don't have to be cagey. She's Clyde Wynant's daughter."

Studsy stopped gazing around the room and beamed on Dorothy. "So you are? And how is your pappy?"

"But I haven't seen him since I was a little girl," she said.

Morelli wet the end of a cigarette and put it between his swollen lips. "I come from Cleveland." He struck a match. His eyes were dull – he was trying to keep them dull. "She wasn't Rhoda Stewart except once – Nancy Kane." He looked at Dorothy again. "Your father knows it."

"Do you know my father?"

"We had some words once."

"What about?" I asked.

"Her." The match in his hand had burned down to his fingers. He dropped it, struck another, and lit his cigarette. He raised his eyebrows at me, wrinkling his forehead. "Is this OK?"

"Sure. There's nobody here you can't talk in front of."

"OK. He was jealous as hell. I wanted to take a poke at him, but she wouldn't let me. That was all right: he was her bank-roll."

"How long ago was this?"

"Six months, eight months."

"Have you seen him since she got knocked off?"

He shook his head. "I never seen him but a couple of times, and this time I'm telling you about is the last."

"Was she gypping him?"

"She don't say she is. I figure she is."

"Why?"

"She's a wise head – plenty smart. She was getting dough somewheres. Once I wanted five grand." He snapped his fingers. "Cash."

I decided against asking if he had paid her back. "Maybe he gave it to her."

"Sure – maybe."

"Did you tell any of this to the police?" I asked.

He laughed once, contemptuously. "They thought they could smack it out of me. Ask 'em what they think now. You're a right guy. I don't – " He broke off, took the cigarette from between his lips. "The earysipelas kid," he said and put out a hand to touch the ear of a man who, sitting at one of the tables we had been squeezed in between, had been leaning further and further back towards us. The man jumped and turned a startled pale pinched face around over his shoulder at Morelli.

Morelli said: "Pull in that lug – it's getting in our drinks."

The man stammered, "I d-didn't mean nothing, Shep," and rammed his belly into his table trying to get as far as possible from us, which still did not take him out of earshot.

Morelli said, "You won't ever mean nothing, but that don't keep you from trying," and returned his attention to me. "I'm willing to go all the way with you – the kid's dead, it's not going to hurt her any – but Mulrooney ain't got a wrecking crew that can get it out of me."

"Swell," I said. "Tell me about her, where you first ran into her, what she did before she tied up with Wynant, where he found her."

"I ought to have a drink." He twisted himself around in his chair and called: "Hey, garsong – you with the boy on your back!"

The somewhat hunchbacked waiter Studsy had called Pete pushed through people to our table and grinned affectionately down at Morelli. "What'll it be?" He sucked a tooth noisily. We gave our orders and the waiter went away.

Morelli said: "Me and Nancy lived in the same block. Old man Kane had a candy-store on the corner. She used to pinch cigarettes for me." He laughed. "Her old man kicked hell out of me once for showing her how to get nickels out of the telephone with a piece of wire. You know, the old-style ones. Jesus, we couldn't've been more than in the third grade." He laughed again, low in his throat. "I wanted to glaum some fixtures from a row of houses they were building around the corner and plant 'em in his cellar and tell Schultz, the cop on the beat, to pay him back, but she wouldn't let me."

Nora said: "You must've been a little darling."

"I was that," he said fondly. "Listen. Once when I was no more'n five or – "

A feminine voice said: "I thought that was you."

I looked up and saw it was red-haired Miriam speaking to me. I said: "Hello."

She put her hands on her hips and stared somberly at me. "So he knew too much for you."

"Maybe, but he took it on the lam down the fire-escape with his shoes in his hand before he told us any of it."

"Balls!"

"All right. What do you think he knew that was too much for us?"

"Where Wynant is," she said.

"So? Where is he?"

"I don't know. Art knew."

"I wish he'd told us. We – "

"Balls!" she said again. "You know and the police know. Who do you think you're kidding?"

"I'm not kidding. I don't know where Wynant is."

"You're working for him and the police are working with you. Don't kid me. Art thought knowing was going to get him a lot of money, poor sap. He didn't know what it was going to get him."

"Did he tell you he knew?" I asked.

"I'm not as dumb as you think. He told me he knew something that was going to get him big dough and I've seen how it worked out. I guess I can put two and two together."

"Sometimes the answer's four," I said, "and sometimes it's twenty-two. I'm not working for Wynant. Now don't say, 'Balls,' again. Do you want to help – "

"No. He was a rat and he held out on the people he was ratting for. He asked for what he got, only don't expect me to forget that I left him with you and Guild, and the next time anybody saw him he was dead."

"I don't want you to forget anything. I'd like you to remember whether – "

"I've got to go to the can," she said and walked away. Her carriage was remarkably graceful.

"I don't know as I'd want to be mixed up with that dame," Studsy said thoughtfully. "She's mean medicine." Morelli winked at me.

Dorothy touched my arm.

"I don't understand, Nick."

I told her that was all right and addressed Morelli: "You were telling us about Julia Wolf."

"Uh-huh. Well, old man Kane booted her out when she was fifteen or sixteen and got in some kind of a jam with a high-school teacher and she took up with a guy called Face Peppler, a smart kid if he didn't talk too much. I remember once me and Face were – " He broke off and cleared his throat. "Anyways, Face and her stuck together – it must be five, six years,

353

throwing out the time he was in the army and she was living with some guy that I can't remember his name – a cousin of Dick O'Brien's, a skinny dark-headed guy that liked his liquor. But she went back to Face when he come out of the army, and they stuck together till they got nailed trying to shake down some bird from Toronto. Face took it and got her off with six months – they gave him the business. Last I heard he was still in. I saw her when she came out – she touched me for a couple hundred to blow town. I hear from her once, when she sends it back to me and tells me Julia Wolf's her name now and she likes the big city fine, but I know Face is hearing from her right along. So when I move here in '28, I look her up. She's – "

Miriam came back and stood with her hands on her hips as before. "I've been thinking over what you said. You must think I'm pretty dumb."

"No," I said, not very truthfully.

"It's a cinch I'm not dumb enough to fall for that song and dance you tried to give me. I can see things when they're right in front of me."

"All right."

"It's not all right. You killed Art and – "

"Not so loud, girlie." Studsy rose and took her arm. His voice was soothing. "Come along. I want to talk to you." He led her towards the bar.

Morelli winked again. "He likes that. Well, I was saying I looked her up when I moved here, and she told me she had this job with Wynant and he was nuts about her and she was sitting pretty. It seems they learned her shorthand in Ohio when she was doing her six months and she figures maybe it'll be an in to something – you know, maybe she can get a job somewheres where they'll go out and leave the safe open. A agency had sent her over to do a couple days' work for Wynant and she figured maybe he'd be worth more for a long pull than for a quick tap and a get-away, so she give him the business and wound up with a steady connection. She was smart enough to tell him she had a record and was trying to go straight now and all that, so's not to have the racket spoiled if he found out anyhow, because she said his lawyer was a little leery of her and might have her looked up. I don't know just what she was doing, you understand, because it's her game and she don't need my help, and even if we are pals in a way, there's no sense in telling me anything I might want to go to her boss with. Understand, she wasn't my girl or anything – we was just a couple old friends, been kids playing together. Well, I used to see her every once in a while – we used to come here a lot – till he kicked up too much of a fuss and then she said she was going to cut it out, she wasn't going to lose a soft bed over a few drinks with me. So that was that. That was October, I guess, and she stuck to it. I haven't seen her since."

"Who else did she run around with?" I asked.

Morelli shook his head. "I don't know. She don't do much talking about people."

"She was wearing a diamond engagement ring. Know anything about it?"

"Nothing except she didn't get it from me. She wasn't wearing it when I seen her."

"Do you think she meant to throw in with Peppler again when he got out?"

"Maybe. She didn't seem to worry much about him being in, but she liked to work with him all right and I guess they'd've teamed up again."

"And how about the cousin of Dick O'Brien, the skinny dark-headed lush? What became of him?"

Morelli looked at me in surprise. "Search me."

Studsy returned alone. "Maybe I'm wrong," he said as he sat down, "but I think somebody could do something with that cluck if they took hold of her right."

Morelli said: "By the throat."

Studsy grinned good-naturedly. "No. She's trying to get somewhere. She works hard at her singing lessons and – "

Morelli looked at his empty glass and said: "This tiger milk of yours must be doing her pipes a lot of good." He turned his head to yell at Pete: "Hey, you with the knapsack, some more of the same. We got to sing in the choir tomorrow."

Pete said: "Coming up, Sheppy." His lined gray face lost its dull apathy when Morelli spoke to him.

An immensely fat blond man – so blond he was nearly albino – who had been sitting at Miriam's table came over and said to me in a thin, tremulous, effeminate voice: "So you're the party who put it to little Art Nunhei – "

Morelli hit the fat man in his fat belly, as hard as he could without getting up. Studsy, suddenly on his feet, leaned over Morelli and smashed a big fist into the fat man's face. I noticed, foolishly, that he still led with his right. Hunchbacked Pete came up behind the fat man and banged his empty tray down with full force on the fat man's head. The fat man fell back, upsetting three people and a table. Both bar-tenders were with us by then. One of them hit the fat man with a blackjack as he tried to get up, knocking him forward on hands and knees, the other put a hand down inside the fat man's collar in back, twisting the collar to choke him. With Morelli's help they got the fat man to his feet and hustled him out.

Pete looked after them and sucked a tooth. "That god-damned Sparrow," he explained to me, "you can't take no chances on him when he's drinking."

Studsy was at the next table, the one that had been upset, helping people pick up themselves and their possessions. "That's bad," he was saying, "bad for business, but where you going to draw the line? I ain't running a dive, but I ain't trying to run a young ladies' seminary neither."

Dorothy was pale, frightened; Nora wide-eyed and amazed. "It's a madhouse," she said. "What'd they do that for?"

"You know as much about it as I do," I told her.

Morelli and the bar-tenders came in again, looking pretty pleased with themselves. Morelli and Studsy returned to their seats at our table. "You boys are impulsive," I said.

Studsy repeated, "Impulsive," and laughed, "Ha-ha-ha."

Morelli was serious. "Any time that guy starts anything, you got to start it first. It's too late when he gets going. We seen him like that before, ain't we, Studsy?"

"Like what?" I asked. "He hadn't done anything."

"He hadn't, all right," Morelli said slowly, "but it's a kind of feeling you get about him sometimes. Ain't that right, Studsy?"

Studsy said: "Uh-huh, he's hysterical."

IT WAS ABOUT two o'clock when we said goodnight to Studsy and Morelli and left the Pigiron Club. Dorothy slumped down in her corner of the taxicab and said: "I'm going to be sick. I know I am." She sounded as if she was telling the truth.

Nora said: "That booze." She put her head on my shoulder. "Your wife is drunk, Nicky. Listen, you've got to tell me what happened—everything. Not now, tomorrow. I don't understand a thing that was said or a thing that was done. They're marvelous."

Dorothy said: "Listen, I can't go to Aunt Alice's like this. She'd have a fit."

Nora said: "They oughtn't've hit that fat man like that, though it must've been funny in a cruel way."

Dorothy said: "I suppose I'd better go to Mamma's."

Nora said: "Erysipelas hasn't got anything to do with ears. What's a lug, Nicky?"

"An ear."

Dorothy said: "Aunt Alice would have to see me because I forgot the key and I'd have to wake her up."

Nora said: "I love you, Nicky, because you smell nice and know such fascinating people."

Dorothy said: "It's not much out of your way to drop me at Mamma's, is it?"

I said, "No," and gave the driver Mimi's address.

Nora said: "Come home with us."

Dorothy said: "No—o, I'd better not."

Nora asked, "Why not?" and Dorothy said, "Well, I don't think I ought to," and that kind of thing went on until the taxicab stopped at the Courtland.

I got out and helped Dorothy out. She leaned heavily on my arm. "Please come up, just for a minute."

Nora said, "Just for a minute," and got out of the taxicab.

I told the driver to wait. We went upstairs. Dorothy rang the bell. Gilbert, in pajamas and bathrobe, opened the door. He raised one hand in a warning gesture and said in a low voice: "The police are here."

Mimi's voice came from the living-room: "Who is it, Gil?"

"Mr. and Mrs. Charles and Dorothy."

Mimi came to meet us as we went in. "I never was so glad to see anybody. I just didn't know which way to turn." She had on a pinkish satin robe over a pinkish silk nightgown, and her face was pink, and by no means unhappy. She ignored Dorothy, squeezed one of Nora's hands, one of mine. "Now I'm going to stop worrying and leave it all up to you, Nick. You'll have to tell the foolish little woman what to do."

Dorothy, behind me, said, "Balls!" under her breath, but with a lot of feeling.

Mimi did not show that she had heard her daughter. Still holding our hands, she drew us back towards the living-room, chattering: "You know Lieutenant Guild. He's been very nice, but I'm sure I must have tried his patience. I've been so – well – I mean I've been so bewildered. But now you're here and – " We went into the living-room.

Guild said, "Hello," to me and, "Good evening, ma'am," to Nora. The man with him, the one he had called Andy and who had helped him search our rooms the morning of Morelli's visit, nodded and grunted at us.

"What's up?" I asked.

Guild looked at Mimi out of the corners of his eyes, then at me, and said: "The Boston police found Jorgensen or Rosewater or whatever you want to call him at his first wife's place and asked him some questions for us. The chief answer seems to be he don't have anything to do with Julia Wolf getting killed or not getting killed and Mrs. Jorgensen can prove it because she's been holding out what amounts to the goods on Wynant." His eyes slid sidewise in their sockets to focus on Mimi again. "The lady kind of don't want to say yes and kind of don't want to say no. To tell you the truth, Mr. Charles, I don't know what to make of her in a lot of ways."

I could understand that. I said, "She's probably frightened," and Mimi tried to look frightened. "Has he been divorced from the first wife?"

"Not according to the first wife."

Mimi said: "She's lying, I bet."

I said: "Sh-h-h. Is he coming back to New York?"

"It looks like he's going to make us extradite him if we want him. Boston says he's squawking his head off for a lawyer."

"Do you want him that bad?"

Guild moved his big shoulders. "If bringing him back'll help us on this murder. I don't care much about any of the old charges or the bigamy. I never believe in hounding a man over things that are none of my business."

I asked Mimi: "Well?"

"Can I talk to you alone?"

I looked at Guild, who said: "Anything that'll help."

Dorothy touched my arm. "Nick, listen to me first. I – " She broke off. Everybody was staring at her.

"What?" I asked.

"I – I wanted to talk to you first."

"Go ahead."

"I mean alone," she said.

I patted her hand. "Afterwards."

Mimi led me into her bedroom and carefully shut the door. I sat on the bed and lit a cigarette. Mimi leaned back against the door and smiled at me very gently and trustingly. Half a minute passed that way.

Then she said, "You do like me, Nick," and when I said nothing she asked, "Don't you?"

"No."

She laughed and came away from the door. "You mean you don't approve of me." She sat on the bed beside me. "But you do like me well enough to help me?"

"That depends."

"Depends on wha – "

The door opened and Dorothy came in: "Nick, I've got to – "

Mimi jumped up and confronted her daughter. "Get out of here," she said through her teeth.

Dorothy flinched, but she said: "I won't. You're not going to make a – "

Mimi slashed Dorothy across the mouth with the back of her right hand. "Get out of here."

Dorothy screamed and put a hand to her mouth. Holding it there, holding her wide frightened eyes on Mimi's face, she backed out of the room. Mimi shut the door again.

I said: "You must come over to our place some time and bring your little white whips."

She did not seem to hear me. Her eyes were heavy, brooding, and her lips were thrust out a little in a half-smile, and when she spoke, her voice seemed heavier, throatier, than usual. "My daughter's in love with you."

"Nonsense."

"She is and she's jealous of me. She has absolute spasms whenever I get within ten feet of you." She spoke as if thinking of something else.

"Nonsense. Maybe she's got a little hangover from that crush she had on me when she was twelve, but that's all it is."

Mimi shook her head. "You're wrong, but never mind." She sat down on the bed beside me again. "You've got to help me out of this. I – "

"Sure," I said. "You're a delicate *fleur* that needs a great big man's protection."

"Oh, that?" She waved a hand at the door through which Dorothy had gone. "You're surely not getting – Why, it's

361

nothing you haven't heard about before – and seen and done, for that matter. It's nothing to worry you." She smiled as before with heavy, brooding eyes, and lips thrust out a little. "If you want Dorry, take her, but don't get sentimental about it. But never mind that. Of course I'm not a delicate *fleur*. You never thought I was."

"No," I agreed.

"Well, then," she said with an air of finality.

"Well then what?"

"Stop being so damned coquettish," she said. "You know what I mean. You understand me as well as I understand you."

"Just about, but you've been doing the coquetting ever since – "

"I know. That was a game. I'm not playing now. That son of a bitch made a fool of me, Nick, an out and out fool, and now he's in trouble and expects me to help him. I'll help him." She put a hand on my knee and her pointed nails dug into my flesh. "The police, they don't believe me. How can I make them believe that he's lying, that I know nothing more than I've told them about the murder?"

"You probably can't," I said slowly, "especially since Jorgensen's only repeating what you told me a few hours ago."

She caught her breath, and her nails dug into me again. "Did you tell them that?"

"Not yet." I took her hand off my knee.

She sighed with relief. "And of course you won't tell them now, will you?"

"Why not?"

"Because it's a lie. He lied and I lied. I didn't find anything, anything at all."

I said: "We're back where we were earlier, and I believe you just as much now as I did then. What happened to those new terms we were on? You understanding me, me under-standing you, no coquetting, no games, no playing."

She slapped my hand lightly. "All right. I did find something – not much, but something – and I'm not going to give it up to help that son of a bitch. You can understand how I feel about it, Nick. You'd feel the same – "

"Maybe," I said, "but the way it stands, I've got no reason for putting in with you. Your Chris is no enemy of mine. I've got nothing to gain by helping you frame him."

She sighed. "I've been thinking about that a lot. I don't suppose what money I could give you would mean much to you now" – she smiled crookedly – "nor my beautiful white body. But aren't you interested in saving Clyde?"

"Not necessarily."

She laughed at that. "I don't know what that means."

"It might mean I don't think he needs saving. The police haven't got much on him. He's screwy, he was in town the day Julia was killed, and she had been gypping him. That's not enough to arrest him on."

She laughed again. "But with my contribution?"

"I don't know. What is it?" I asked, and went on without waiting for the answer I did not expect. "Whatever it is, you're being a sap, Mimi. You've got Chris cold on bigamy. Sock that to him. There's no – "

She smiled sweetly and said: "But I am holding that in reserve to use after this if he – "

"If he gets past the murder charge, huh? Well, it won't work out that way, lady. You can get him about three days in jail. By that time the District Attorney will have questioned him and checked up on him enough to know that he didn't kill Julia and that you've been making a chump of the D. A., and when you spring your little bigamy charge the D. A. will tell you to go jump in the lake, and he'll refuse to prosecute."

"But he can't do that, Nick."

"Can and will," I assured her, "and if he can dig up proof that you're holding out something he'll make it as tough for you as he can."

She chewed her lower lip, asked: "You're being honest with me?"

"I'm telling you exactly what'll happen, unless district attorneys have changed a lot since my day."

She chewed her lip some more. "I don't want him to get off," she said presently, "and I don't want to get into any trouble myself." She looked up at me. "If you're lying to me, Nick . . . "

"There's nothing you can do about it except believe me or disbelieve me."

She smiled and put a hand on my cheek and kissed me on the mouth and stood up. "You're such a bastard. Well, I'm going to believe you." She walked down to the other end of the room and back again. Her eyes were shiny, her face pleasantly excited.

"I'll call Guild," I said.

"No, wait. I'd rather – I'd rather see what you think of it first."

"All right, but no clowning."

"You're certainly afraid of your shadow," she said, "but don't worry, I'm not going to play any tricks on you."

I said that would be swell and how about showing me whatever she had to show me. "The others will be getting restless."

She went around the bed to a closet, opened the door, pushed some clothes aside, and put a hand among other clothes behind them. "That's funny," she said.

"Funny?" I stood up. "It's a panic. It'll have Guild rolling on the floor." I started towards the door.

"Don't be so bad-tempered," she said. "I've got it." She turned to me holding a wadded handkerchief in her hand. As I approached, she opened the handkerchief to show me a three-inch length of watch-chain, broken at one end, attached at the other to a small gold knife. The handkerchief was a woman's and there were brown stains on it.

"Well?" I asked.

"It was in her hand and I saw it when they left me with her and I knew it was Clyde's, so I took it."

"You're sure it's his?"

"Yes," she said impatiently. "See, they're gold, silver, and copper links. He had it made out of the first batches of metal that came through that smelting process he invented. Anybody who knows him at all well can identify it – there can't be another like it." She turned the knife over to let me see the *C M W* engraved in it. "They're his initials. I never saw the knife before, but I'd know the chain anywhere. Clyde's worn it for years."

"Did you remember it well enough that you could've described it without seeing it again?"

"Of course."

"Is that your handkerchief?"

"Yes."

"And the stain on it's blood?"

"Yes. The chain was in her hand – I told you – and there was some blood on them." She frowned at me. "Don't you – You act as if you don't believe me."

"Not exactly," I said, "but I think you ought to be sure you're telling your story straight this time."

She stamped her foot. "You're – " She laughed and anger went out of her face. "You can be the most annoying man. I'm telling the truth now, Nick. I've told you everything that happened exactly as it happened."

"I hope so. It's about time. You're sure Julia didn't come to enough to say anything while you were alone with her?"

"You're trying to make me mad again. Of course I'm sure."

"All right," I said. "Wait here. I'll get Guild, but if you tell him the chain was in Julia's hand and she wasn't dead yet he's going to wonder whether you didn't have to rough her up a little to get it away from her."

She opened her eyes wide. "What should I tell him?"

I went out and shut the door.

NORA, LOOKING A little sleepy, was entertaining Guild and Andy in the living-room. The Wynant offspring were not in sight. "Go ahead," I told Guild. "First door to the left. I think she's readied up for you."

"Crack her?" he asked. I nodded.

"What'd you get?"

"See what you get and we'll put them together and see how they add up," I suggested.

"OK. Come on, Andy." They went out.

"Where's Dorothy?" I asked.

Nora yawned. "I thought she was with you and her mother. Gilbert's around somewhere. He was here till a few minutes ago. Do we have to hang around long?"

"Not long." I went back down the passageway past Mimi's door to another bedroom-door, which was open, and looked in. Nobody was there. A door facing it was shut. I knocked on it.

Dorothy's voice said: "What is it?"

"Nick," I said and went in. She was lying on her side on a bed, dressed except for her slippers. Gilbert was sitting on the bed beside her. Her mouth seemed a little puffy, but it may have been from crying: her eyes were red. She raised her head to stare sullenly at me.

"Still want to talk to me?" I asked.

Gilbert got up from the bed. "Where's Mamma?"

"Talking to the police." He said something I did not catch and left the room.

Dorothy shuddered. "He gives me the creeps," she cried, and then remembered to stare sullenly at me again.

"Still want to talk to me?"

"What made you turn against me like that?"

"You're being silly." I sat down where Gilbert had been sitting. "Do you know anything about this knife and chain your mother's supposed to have found?"

"No. Where?"

"What'd you want to tell me?"

"Nothing – now," she said disagreeably, "except you might at least wipe her lipstick off your mouth." I wiped it off. She snatched the handkerchief from my hand and rolled over to pick up a package of matches from the table on that side of the bed. She struck a match.

"That's going to stink like hell," I said.

She said, "I don't care," but she blew out the match. I took the handkerchief, went to a window, opened it, dropped the handkerchief out, shut the window, and went back to my seat on the bed. "If that makes you feel any better."

"What did Mamma say – about me?"

"She said you're in love with me."

She sat up abruptly. "What did you say?"

"I said you just liked me from when you were a kid."

Her lower lip twitched. "Do – do you think that's what it is?"

"What else could it be?"

"I don't know." She began to cry. "Everybody's made so much fun about it – Mamma and Gilbert and Harrison – I – "

I put my arms around her. "To hell with them."

After a while she asked: "Is Mamma in love with you?"

"Good God, no! She hates men more than any woman I've ever known who wasn't a Lesbian."

"But she's always having some sort of – "

"That's the body. Don't let it fool you. Mimi hates men – all of us – bitterly."

She had stopped crying. She wrinkled her forehead and said: "I don't understand. Do you hate her?"

"Not as a rule."

"Now?"

"I don't think so. She's being stupid and she's sure she's being very clever, and that's a nuisance, but I don't think I hate her."

"I do," Dorothy said.

"So you told me last week. Something I meant to ask you: did you know or did you ever see the Arthur Nunheim we were talking about in the speakeasy tonight?"

She looked sharply at me. "You're just trying to change the subject."

"I want to know. Did you?"

"No."

"He was mentioned in the newspapers," I reminded her. "He was the one who told the police about Morelli knowing Julia Wolf."

"I didn't remember his name," she said. "I don't remember ever having heard it until tonight."

I described him. "Ever see him?"

"No."

"He may have been known as Albert Norman sometimes. Does that sound familiar?"

"No."

"Know any of the people we saw at Studsy's tonight? Or anything about them?"

"No. Honestly, Nick, I'd tell you if I knew anything at all that might help you."

"No matter who it hurt?"

"Yes," she said immediately, then, "What do you mean?"

"You know damned well what I mean."

She put her hands over her face, and her words were barely audible: "I'm afraid, Nick. I – " She jerked her hands down as someone knocked on the door.

"All right," I called.

Andy opened the door far enough to stick his head in. He tried to keep curiosity from showing in his face while saying: "The Lieutenant wants to see you."

"Be right out," I promised.

He opened the door wider. "He's waiting." He gave me what was probably meant to be a significant wink, but a corner of his mouth moved more than his eye did and the result was a fairly startling face.

"I'll be back," I told Dorothy, and followed him out.

He shut the door behind me and put his mouth close to my ear. "The kid was at the keyhole," he muttered.

"Gilbert?"

"Yep. He had time to get away from it when he heard me coming, but he was there, right enough."

"That's mild for him," I said. "How'd you all make out with Mrs. J.?"

He puckered his thick lips up in an o and blew breath out noisily. "What a dame!"

WE WENT INTO Mimi's bedroom. She was sitting in a deep chair by a window looking very pleased with herself. She smiled gayly at me and said: "My soul is spotless now. I've confessed everything."

Guild stood by a table wiping his face with a handkerchief. There were still some drops of sweat on his temples, and his face seemed old and tired. The knife and chain, and the handkerchief they had been wrapped in, were on the table. "Finished?" I asked.

"I don't know, and that's a fact," he said. He turned his head to address Mimi: "Would you say we were finished?"

Mimi laughed. "I can't imagine what more there would be."

"Well," Guild said slowly, somewhat reluctantly, "in that case I guess I'd like to talk to Mr. Charles, if you'll excuse us for a couple of minutes." He folded his handkerchief carefully and put it in his pocket.

"You can talk here." She got up from the chair. "I'll go out and talk to Mrs. Charles till you're through." She tapped my cheek playfully with the tip of a forefinger as she passed me. "Don't let them say too horrid things about me, Nick." Andy opened the door for her, shut it behind her, and made the o and the blowing noise again.

I lay down on the bed. "Well," I asked, "what's what?"

Guild cleared his throat. "She told us about finding this here chain and knife on the floor where the Wolf dame had most likely broke it off fighting with Wynant, and she told us the reasons why she'd hid it till now. Between me and you, that

370

don't make any too much sense, looking at it reasonably, but maybe that ain't the way to look at it in this case. To tell you the plain truth, I don't know what to make of her in a lot of ways, I don't for a fact."

"The chief thing," I advised them, "is not to let her tire you out. When you catch her in a lie, she admits it and gives you another lie to take its place and, when you catch her in that one, admits it and gives you still another, and so on. Most people – even women – get discouraged after you've caught them in the third or fourth straight lie and fall back on either the truth or silence, but not Mimi. She keeps trying and you've got to be careful or you'll find yourself believing her, not because she seems to be telling the truth, but simply because you're tired of disbelieving her."

Guild said: "Hm-m-m. Maybe." He put a finger inside his collar. He seemed very uncomfortable. "Look here, do you think she killed that dame?"

I discovered that Andy was staring at me so intently that his eyes bulged. I sat up and put my feet on the floor. "I wish I knew. That chain business looks like a plant, all right, but . . . We can find out whether he had a chain like that, maybe whether he still has it. If she remembered the chain as well as she said she did, there's no reason why she couldn't have told a jeweler how to make one, and anybody can buy a knife and have any initials they want engraved on it. There's plenty to be said against the probability of her having gone that far. If she did plant it, it's more likely she had the original chain – maybe she's had it for years – but all that's something for you folks to check up."

"We're doing the best we can," Guild said patiently. "So you do think she did it?"

"The murder?" I shook my head. "I haven't got that far yet. How about Nunheim? Did the bullets match up?"

"They did – from the same gun as was used on the dame – all five of them."

"He was shot five times?"

"He was, and close enough to burn his clothes."

"I saw his girl, the big red-head, tonight in a speak," I told him. "She's saying you and I killed him because he knew too much."

He said: "Hm-m-m. What speak was that? I might want to talk to her."

"Studsy Burke's Pigiron Club," I said, and gave him the address. "Morelli hangs out there too. He tells me Julia Wolf's real name is Nancy Kane and she has a boy-friend doing time in Ohio – Face Peppler."

From the tone of Guild's "Yes?" I imagined he had already found out about Peppler and about Julia's past. "And what else did you pick up in your travels?"

"A friend of mine – Larry Crowley, a press agent – saw Jorgensen coming out of a hock-shop on Sixth near Forty-sixth yesterday afternoon."

"Yes?"

"You don't seem to get excited about my news. I'm – "

Mimi opened the door and came in with glasses, whiskey, and mineral water on a tray. "I thought you'd like a drink," she said cheerfully. We thanked her.

She put the tray on the table, said, "I don't mean to inter-rupt," smiled at us with that air of amused tolerance which women like to affect towards male gatherings, and went out.

"You were saying something," Guild reminded me.

"Just that if you people think I'm not coming clean with you, you ought to say so. We've been playing along together so far and I wouldn't want – "

"No, no," Guild said hastily, "it's nothing like that, Mr. Charles." His face had reddened a little. "I been – The fact is the Commissioner's been riding us for action and I guess I been kind of passing it on. This second murder's made things tough." He turned to the tray on the table. "How'll you have yours?"

"Straight, thanks. No leads on it?"

"Well, the same gun and a lot of bullets, same as with her, but that's about all. It was a rooming-house hallway in between a couple stores. Nobody there claims they know Nunheim or Wynant or anybody else we can connect. The door's left unlocked, anybody could walk in, but that don't make too much sense when you come to think of it."

"Nobody saw or heard anything?"

"Sure, they heard the shooting, but they didn't see anybody doing it." He gave me a glass of whiskey.

"Find any empty shells?" I asked.

He shook his head. "Neither time. Probably a revolver."

"And he emptied it both times – counting the shot that hit her telephone – if, like a lot of people, he carried an empty chamber under the hammer."

Guild lowered the glass he was raising towards his mouth. "You're not trying to find a Chinese angle on it, are you," he complained, "just because they shoot like that?"

"No, but any kind of angle would help some. Find out where Nunheim was the afternoon the girl was killed?"

"Uh-huh. Hanging around the girl's building – part of the time anyhow. He was seen in front and he was seen in back, if you're going to believe people that didn't think much of it at the time and haven't got any reason for lying about it. And the day before the killing he had been up to her apartment, according to an elevator boy. The boy says he came down right away and he don't know whether he got in or not."

I said: "So. Maybe Miriam's right, maybe he did know too much. Find out anything about the four-thousand difference between what Macaulay gave her and what Clyde Wynant says he got from her?"

"No."

"Morelli says she always had plenty of money. He says she once lent him five thousand in cash."

Guild raised his eyebrows. "Yes?"

"Yes. He also says Wynant knew about her record."

"Seems to me," Guild said slowly, "Morelli did a lot of talking to you."

"He likes to talk. Find out anything more about what Wynant was working on when he left, or what he was going away to work on?"

"No. You're kind of interested in that shop of his."

"Why not? He's an inventor, the shop's his place. I'd like to have a look at it some time."

"Help yourself. Tell me some more about Morelli, and how you go about getting him to open up."

"He likes to talk. Do you know a fellow called Sparrow? A big fat pale fellow with a pansy voice?"

Guild frowned. "No. Why?"

"He was there – with Miriam – and wanted to take a crack at me, but they wouldn't let him."

"And what'd he want to do that for?"

"I don't know. Maybe because she told him I helped knock Nunheim off – helped you."

Guild said: "Oh." He scratched his chin with a thumbnail, looked at his watch. "It's getting kind of late. Suppose you drop in and see me some time tomorrow – today."

I said, "Sure," instead of the things I was thinking, nodded at him and Andy, and went out to the living-room.

Nora was sleeping on the sofa. Mimi put down the book she was reading and asked: "Is the secret session over?"

"Yes." I moved towards the sofa.

Mimi said: "Let her sleep awhile, Nick. You're going to stay till after your police friends have gone, aren't you?"

"All right. I want to see Dorothy again."

"But she's asleep."

"That's all right. I'll wake her up."

"But –" Guild and Andy came in, said their good-nights, Guild looked regretfully at the sleeping Nora, and they left.

Mimi sighed. "I'm tired of policemen," she said. "You remember that story?"

"Yes."

Gilbert came in. "Do they really think Chris did it?"

"No," I said.

"Who do they think?"

"I could've told you yesterday. I can't today."

"That's ridiculous," Mimi protested. "They know very well and you know very well that Clyde did it." When I said nothing she repeated, more sharply: "You know very well that Clyde did it."

"He didn't," I said.

An expression of triumph brightened Mimi's face. "You *are* working for him, now aren't you?" My "No" bounced off her with no effect whatever.

Gilbert asked, not argumentatively, but as if he wanted to know: "Why couldn't he?"

"He could've, but he didn't. Would he have written those letters throwing suspicion on Mimi, the one person who's helping him by hiding the chief evidence against him?"

"But maybe he didn't know that. Maybe he thought the police were simply not telling all they knew. They often do that, don't they? Or maybe he thought he could discredit her, so they wouldn't believe her if – "

"That's it," Mimi said. "That's exactly what he did, Nick."

I said to Gilbert: "You don't think he killed her."

"No, I don't think he did, but I'd like to know why you don't think so – you know – your method."

"And I'd like to know yours."

His face flushed a little and there was some embarrassment in his smile. "Oh, but I – it's different."

"He *knows* who killed her," Dorothy said from the doorway. She was still dressed. She stared at me fixedly, as if afraid to look at anybody else. Her face was pale and she held her small body stiffly erect.

Nora opened her eyes, pushed herself up on an elbow, and asked, "What?" sleepily. Nobody answered her.

Mimi said: "Now, Dorry, don't let's have one of those idiotic dramatic performances."

Dorothy said: "You can beat me after they've gone. You will." She said it without taking her eyes off mine. Mimi tried to look as if she did not know what her daughter was talking about.

"Who does he know killed her?" I asked.

Gilbert said: "You're making an ass of yourself, Dorry, you're — "

I interrupted him: "Let her. Let her say what she's got to say. Who killed her, Dorothy?"

She looked at her brother and lowered her eyes and no longer held herself erect. Looking at the floor, she said indistinctly: "I don't know. He knows." She raised her eyes to mine and began to tremble. "Can't you see I'm afraid?" she cried. "I'm afraid of them. Take me away and I'll tell you, but I'm afraid of them."

Mimi laughed at me. "You asked for it. It serves you right."

Gilbert was blushing. "It's so silly," he mumbled.

I said: "Sure, I'll take you away, but I'd like to have it out now while we're all together."

Dorothy shook her head. "I'm afraid."

Mimi said: "I wish you wouldn't baby her so, Nick. It only makes her worse. She — "

I asked Nora: "What do you say?"

She stood up and stretched without lifting her arms. Her face was pink and lovely as it always is when she has been sleeping. She smiled drowsily at me and said: "Let's go home. I don't like these people. Come on, get your hat and coat, Dorothy."

Mimi said to Dorothy: "Go to bed."

Dorothy put the tips of the fingers of her left hand to her mouth and whimpered through them: "Don't let her beat me, Nick." I was watching Mimi, whose face wore a placid half-smile, but her nostrils moved with her breathing and I could hear her breathing.

Nora went around to Dorothy. "Come on, we'll wash your face and –" Mimi made an animal noise in her throat, muscles thickened on the back of her neck, and she put her weight on the balls of her feet.

Nora stepped between Mimi and Dorothy. I caught Mimi by a shoulder as she started forward, put my other arm around her waist from behind, and lifted her off her feet. She screamed and hit back at me with her fists and her hard sharp high-heels made dents in my shins.

Nora pushed Dorothy out of the room and stood in the doorway watching us. Her face was very live. I saw it clearly, sharply: everything else was blurred. When clumsy, ineffectual blows on my back and shoulder brought me around to find Gilbert pommeling me, I could see him but dimly and I hardly felt the contact when I shoved him aside. "Cut it out. I don't want to hurt you, Gilbert." I carried Mimi over to the sofa and dumped her on her back on it, sat on her knees, got a wrist in each hand.

Gilbert was at me again. I tried to pop his kneecap, but kicked him too low, kicked his leg from under him. He went down on the floor in a tangle. I kicked at him again, missed, and said: "We can fight afterwards. Get some water."

Mimi's face was becoming purple. Her eyes protruded, glassy, senseless, enormous. Saliva bubbled and hissed between clenched teeth with her breathing, and her red throat – her whole body – was a squirming mass of veins and muscles swollen until it seemed they must burst. Her wrists were hot in my hands and sweat made them hard to hold. Nora beside me with a glass of water was a welcome sight. "Chuck it in her face," I said.

Nora chucked it. Mimi separated her teeth to gasp and she shut her eyes. She moved her head violently from side to side, but there was less violence in the squirming of her body. "Do it again," I said. The second glass of water brought a spluttering protest from Mimi and the fight went out of her body. She lay still, limp, panting.

I took my hands away from her wrists and stood up. Gilbert, standing on one foot, was leaning against a table nursing the leg I kicked. Dorothy, big-eyed and pale, was in the doorway, undecided whether to come in or run off and hide. Nora, beside me, holding the empty glass in her hand, asked: "Think she's all right?"

"Sure."

Presently Mimi opened her eyes, tried to blink the water out of them. I put a handkerchief in her hand. She wiped her face, gave a long shivering sigh, and sat up on the sofa. She looked around the room, still blinking a little. When she saw me she smiled feebly. There was guilt in her smile, but nothing you could call remorse. She touched her hair with an unsteady hand and said: "I've certainly been drowned."

I said: "Some day you're going into one of those things and not come out of it."

She looked past me at her son. "Gil. What's happened to you?" she asked.

He hastily took his hand off his leg and put his foot down on the floor. "I – uh – nothing," he stammered. "I'm perfectly all right." He smoothed his hair, straightened his necktie.

She began to laugh. "Oh, Gil, did you really try to protect me? And from Nick?" Her laughter increased. "It was awfully sweet of you, but awfully silly. Why, he's a monster, Gil. Nobody could – " She put my handkerchief over her mouth and rocked back and forth.

I looked sidewise at Nora. Her mouth was set and her eyes were almost black with anger. I touched her arm. "Let's blow. Give your mother a drink, Gilbert. She'll be all right in a minute or two."

Dorothy, hat and coat in her hands, tiptoed to the outer door. Nora and I found our hats and coats and followed her out, leaving Mimi laughing into my handkerchief on the sofa. None of the three of us had much to say in the taxicab that carried us over to the Normandie. Nora was brooding, Dorothy seemed still pretty frightened, and I was tired – it had been a full day.

It was nearly five o'clock when we got home. Asta greeted us boisterously. I lay down on the floor to play with her while Nora went into the pantry to make coffee. Dorothy wanted to tell me something that happened to her when she was a little child. I said: "No. You tried that Monday. What is it? a gag? It's late. What was it you were afraid to tell me over there?"

"But you'd understand better if you'd let me – "

"You said *that* Monday. I'm not a psychoanalyst. I don't know anything about early influences. I don't give a damn about them. And I'm tired – I been ironing all day."

She pouted at me. "You seem to be trying to make it as hard for me as you can."

"Listen, Dorothy," I said, "you either know something you were afraid to say in front of Mimi and Gilbert or you don't. If you do, spit it out. I'll ask you about any of it I find myself not understanding."

She twisted a fold of her skirt and looked sulkily at it, but when she raised her eyes they became bright and excited. She spoke in a whisper loud enough for anybody in the room to hear: "Gil's been seeing my father and he saw him today and my father told him who killed Miss Wolf."

"Who?"

She shook her head. "He wouldn't tell me. He'd just tell me that."

"And that's what you were afraid to say in front of Gil and Mimi?"

"Yes. You'd understand that if you'd let me tell you – "

"Something that happened when you were a little child. Well, I won't. Stop it. What else did he tell you?"

"Nothing."

"Nothing about Nunheim?"

"No, nothing."

"Where is your father?"

"Gil didn't tell me."

"When did he meet him?"

"He didn't tell me. Please don't be mad, Nick. I've told you everything he told me."

"And a fat lot it is," I growled. "When'd he tell you this?"

"Tonight. He was telling me when you came in my room, and, honest, that's all he told me."

I said: "It'd be swell if just once one of you people would make a clear and complete statement about something – it wouldn't matter what."

Nora came in with the coffee. "What's worrying you now, son?" she asked.

"Things," I said, "riddles, lies, and I'm too old and too tired for them to be any fun. Let's go back to San Francisco."

"Before New Year's?"

"Tomorrow, today."

"I'm willing." She gave me a cup. "We can fly back, if you want, and be there for New Year's Eve."

Dorothy said tremulously: "I didn't lie to you, Nick. I told you everything I – Please, please don't be mad with me. I'm so –" She stopped talking to sob. I rubbed Asta's head and groaned.

Nora said: "We're all worn out and jumpy. Let's send the pup downstairs for the night and turn in and do our talking after we've had some rest. Come on, Dorothy, I'll bring your coffee into the bedroom and give you some night-clothes."

Dorothy got up, said, "Good-night," to me, "I'm sorry I'm so silly," and followed Nora out.

When Nora returned she sat down on the floor beside me. "Our Dorry does her share of weeping and whining," she said. "Admitting life's not too pleasant for her just now, still . . ." She yawned. "What was her fearsome secret?"

I told her what Dorothy had told me. "It sounds like a lot of hooey."

"Why?"

"Why not? Everything else we've got from them has been hooey."

Nora yawned again. "That may be good enough for a detective, but it's not convincing enough for me. Listen, why don't we make a list of all the suspects and all the motives and clues, and check them off against – "

"You do it. I'm going to bed. What's a clue, Mamma?"

"It's like when Gilbert tiptoed over to the phone tonight when I was alone in the living-room, and he thought I was asleep, and told the operator not to put through any incoming calls until morning."

"Well, well."

"And," she said, "it's like Dorothy discovering that she had Aunt Alice's key all the time."

"Well, well."

"And it's like Studsy nudging Morelli under the table when he started to tell you about the drunken cousin of – what was it? – Dick O'Brien's that Julia Wolf knew."

I got up and put our cups on a table. "I don't see how any detective can hope to get along without being married to you, but, just the same, you're overdoing it. Studsy nudging Morelli is my idea of something to spend a lot of time not worrying about. I'd rather worry about whether they pushed Sparrow around to keep me from being hurt or to keep me from being told something. I'm sleepy."

"So am I. Tell me something, Nick. Tell me the truth: when you were wrestling with Mimi, didn't you get excited?"

"Oh, a little."

She laughed and got up from the floor. "If you aren't a disgusting old lecher," she said. "Look, it's daylight."

NORA SHOOK ME awake at quarter-past ten. "The telephone," she said. "It's Herbert Macaulay and he says it's important."

I went into the bedroom – I had slept in the living-room – to the telephone. Dorothy was sleeping soundly. I mumbled, "Hello," into the telephone.

Macaulay said: "It's too early for that lunch, but I've got to see you right away. Can I come up now?"

"Sure. Come up for breakfast."

"I've had it. Get yours and I'll be up in fifteen minutes."

"Right."

Dorothy opened her eyes less than half-way, said, "It must be late," sleepily, turned over, and returned to unconsciousness.

I put cold water on my face and hands, brushed my teeth and hair, and went back to the living-room. "He's coming up," I told Nora. "He's had breakfast, but you'd better order some coffee for him. I want chicken livers."

"Am I invited to your party or do I –"

"Sure. You've never met Macaulay, have you? He's a pretty good guy. I was attached to his outfit for a few days once, up around Vaux, and we looked each other up after the war. He threw a couple of jobs my way, including the Wynant one. How about a drop of something to cut the phlegm?"

"Why don't you stay sober today?"

"We didn't come to New York to stay sober. Want to see a hockey game tonight?"

"I'd like to." She poured me a drink and went to order breakfast.

I looked through the morning papers. They had the news of Jorgensen's being picked up by the Boston police and of Nunheim's murder, but further developments of what the tabloids called "The Hell's Kitchen Gang War," the arrest of "Prince Mike" Gerguson, and an interview with the "Jafsie" of the Lindbergh kidnapping negotiations got more space. Macaulay and the bellboy who brought Asta up arrived together. Asta liked Macaulay because when he patted her he gave her something to set her weight against: she was never very fond of gentleness.

He had lines around his mouth this morning and some of the rosiness was gone from his cheeks. "Where'd the police get this new line?" he asked. "Do you think – " He broke off as Nora came in. She had dressed.

"Nora, this is Herbert Macaulay," I said. "My wife."

They shook hands and Nora said: "Nick would only let me order some coffee for you. Can't I – "

"No, thanks, I've just finished breakfast."

I said: "Now what's this about the police?" He hesitated.

"Nora knows practically everything I know," I assured him, "so unless it's something you'd rather not – "

"No, no, nothing like that," he said. "It's – well – for Mrs. Charles's sake. I don't want to cause her anxiety."

"Then out with it. She only worries about things she doesn't know. What's the new police line?"

"Lieutenant Guild came to see me this morning," he said. "First he showed me a piece of watch-chain with a knife attached to it and asked me if I'd ever seen them before. I had: they were Wynant's. I told him I thought I had: I thought they looked like Wynant's. Then he asked me if I knew of any way in which they could have come into anybody else's possession and, after some beating about the bush, I discovered that by anybody else he meant you or Mimi. I told him certainly – Wynant could have given them to either of you, you could have stolen them or found them on the street or have been given them by somebody who stole them or found them on the street, or you could have got them from somebody Wynant gave them to. There were other ways, too, for you to have got them, I told him, but he knew I was kidding him, so he wouldn't let me tell him about them."

There were spots of color in Nora's cheeks and her eyes were dark. "The idiot!"

"Now, now," I said. "Maybe I should have warned you – he was heading in that direction last night. I think it's likely my old pal Mimi gave him a prod or two. What else did he turn the searchlight on?"

"He wanted to know about – what he asked was: 'Do you figure Charles and the Wolf dame was still playing around together? Or was that all washed up?'"

"That's the Mimi touch, all right," I said. "What'd you tell him?"

"I told him I didn't know whether you were 'still' playing around together because I didn't know that you had ever played around together, and reminded him that you hadn't been living in New York for a long time anyway."

Nora asked me: "Did you?"

I said: "Don't try to make a liar out of Mac. What'd he say to that?"

"Nothing. He asked me if I thought Jorgensen knew about you and Mimi and, when I asked him what about you and Mimi, he accused me of acting the innocent – they were his words – so we didn't get very far. He was interested in the times I had seen you, also, where and when to the exact inch and second."

"That's nice," I said. "I've got lousy alibis."

A waiter came in with our breakfast. We talked about this and that until he had set the table and gone away. Then Macaulay said: "You've nothing to be afraid of. I'm going to turn Wynant over to the police." His voice was unsteady and a little choked.

"Are you sure he did it?" I asked. "I'm not."

He said simply: "I know." He cleared his throat. "Even if there was a chance in a thousand of my being wrong – and there isn't – he's a madman, Charles. He shouldn't be loose."

"That's probably right enough," I began, "and if you know–"

"I know," he repeated. "I saw him the afternoon he killed her; it couldn't've been half an hour after he'd killed her, though I didn't know that, didn't even know she'd been killed. I – well – I know it now."

"You met him in Hermann's office?"

"What?"

"You were supposed to have been in the office of a man named Hermann, on Fifty-seventh Street, from around three o'clock till around four that afternoon. At least, that's what the police told me."

"That's right," he said. "I mean that's the story they got. What really happened: after I failed to find Wynant or any news of him at the Plaza and phoned my office and Julia with no better results, I gave him up and started walking down to Hermann's. He's a mining engineer, a client of mine; I had just finished drawing up some articles of incorporation for him, and there were some minor changes to be made in them. When I got to Fifty-seventh Street I suddenly got a feeling that I was being followed – you know the feeling. I couldn't think of any reason for anybody shadowing me, but, still, I'm a lawyer and there might be. Anyhow, I wanted to find out, so I turned east on Fifty-seventh and walked over to Madison and still wasn't sure. There was a small sallow man I thought I'd seen around the Plaza, but – The quickest way to find out seemed to be by taking a taxi, so I did that and told the driver to drive east. There was too much traffic there for me to see whether this small man or anybody else took a taxi after me, so I had my driver turn south at Third, east again on Fifty-sixth, and south again on Second Avenue, and by that time I was pretty sure a yellow taxi was following me. I couldn't see whether my small man was in it, of course; it wasn't close enough for that. And at the next corner, when a red light stopped us, I saw Wynant. He was in a taxicab going west on Fifty-fifth Street. Naturally, that didn't surprise me very much: we were only two blocks from Julia's and I took it for granted she hadn't wanted me to know he was there when I phoned and that he was now on his way over to meet me at the Plaza. He was never very punctual. So I told my driver to turn west, but at Lexington Avenue – we were half a block behind him – Wynant's taxicab turned south. That wasn't the way to the Plaza and wasn't even the way to my office, so I said to hell with him and turned my attention back to the taxi following me – and it wasn't there any more. I kept a look-out behind all the way over to Hermann's and saw no sign at all of anybody following me."

"What time was it when you saw Wynant?" I asked.

"It must've been fifteen or twenty minutes past three. It was twenty minutes to four when I got to Hermann's and I imagine that was twenty or twenty-five minutes later. Well, Hermann's secretary – Louise Jacobs, the girl I was with when I saw you last night – told me he had been locked up in a conference all afternoon, but would probably be through in a few minutes, and he was, and I got through with him in ten or fifteen minutes and went back to my office."

"I take it you weren't close enough to Wynant to see whether he looked excited, was wearing his watch-chain, smelled of gunpowder – things like that."

"That's right. All I saw was his profile going past, but don't think I'm not sure it was Wynant."

"I won't. Go ahead," I said.

"He didn't phone again. I'd been back about an hour when the police phoned – Julia was dead. Now you must understand that I didn't think Wynant had killed her – not for a minute. You can understand that – you still don't think he did. So when I went over there and the police began to ask me questions about him and I could see they suspected him, I did what ninety-nine out of a hundred lawyers would've done for their clients – I said nothing about having seen him in that neighborhood at about the time that the murder must have been committed. I told them what I told you – about having the date with him and him not showing up – and let them understand that I had gone over to Hermann's straight from the Plaza."

"That's understandable enough," I agreed. "There was no sense in your saying anything until you had heard his side of the story."

"Exactly and, well, the catch is I never heard his side of the story. I'd expected him to show up, phone me, something, but he didn't – until Tuesday, when I got that letter from him from Philadelphia, and there was not a word in it about his failure to meet me Friday, nothing about – but you saw the letter. What'd you think of it?"

"You mean did it sound guilty?"

"Yes."

"Not particularly," I said. "It's about what could be expected from him if he didn't kill her – no great alarm over the police suspecting him except as it might interfere with his work, a desire to have it all cleaned up with no inconvenience to him – not too bright a letter to have come from anybody else, but in line with his particular form of goofiness. I can see him sending it off without the faintest notion that the best thing he could do would be to account for his own actions on the day of the murder. How sure are you he was coming from Julia's when you saw him?"

"I'm sure now. I thought it likely at first. Then I thought he may have been to his shop. It's on First Avenue, just a few blocks from where I saw him, and, though it's been closed since he went away, we renewed the lease last month and everything's there waiting for him to come back to it, and he could have been there that afternoon. The police couldn't find anything there to show whether he had or hadn't."

"I meant to ask you: there was some talk about his having grown whiskers. Was he – "

"No – the same long bony face with the same ragged near-white mustache."

"Another thing: there was a fellow named Nunheim killed yesterday, a small – "

"I'm coming to that," he said.

"I was thinking about the little fellow you thought might be shadowing you."

Macaulay stared at me. "You mean that might've been Nunheim?"

"I don't know. I was wondering."

"And I don't know," he said. "I never saw Nunheim, far as I – "

"He was a little fellow, not more than five feet three, and would weigh maybe a hundred and twenty. I'd say he was thirty-five or -six. Sallow, dark hair and eyes, with the eyes set pretty close together, big mouth, long limp nose, bat-wing ears – shifty-looking."

"That could easily be him," he said, "though I didn't get too close a view of my man. I suppose the police would let me see him" – he shrugged – "not that it matters now. Where was I? Oh, yes, about not being able to get in touch with Wynant. That put me in an uncomfortable position, since the police clearly thought I was in touch with him and lying about it. So did you, didn't you?"

"Yes," I admitted.

"And you also, like the police, probably suspected that I *had* met him, either at the Plaza or later, on the day of the murder."

"It seemed possible."

"Yes. And of course you were partly right. I had at least seen him, and seen him at a place and time that would've spelled Guilty with a capital G to the police, so, having lied instinctively and by inference, I now lied directly and deliberately. Hermann had been tied up in a conference all that afternoon and didn't know how long I had been waiting to see him. Louise Jacobs is a good friend of mine. Without going into details, I told her she could help me help a client by saying I had arrived there at a minute or two after three o'clock and she agreed readily enough. To protect her in case of trouble, I told her that if anything went wrong she could always say that she hadn't remembered what time I arrived, but that I, the next day, had casually mentioned my arrival at that time and she had no reason for doubting me – throwing the whole thing on me." Macaulay took a deep breath. "None of that's important now. What's important is that I heard from Wynant this morning."

"Another one of those screwy letters?" I asked.

"No, he phoned. I made a date with him for tonight – for you and me. I told him you wouldn't do anything for him unless you could see him, so he promised to meet us tonight. I'm going to take the police, of course. I can't go on justifying my shielding him like this. I can get him an acquittal on grounds of insanity and have him put away. That's all I can do, all I want to do."

"Have you told the police yet?"

"No. He didn't phone till just after they'd left. Anyway, I wanted to see you first. I wanted to tell you I hadn't forgotten what I owed you and – "

"Nonsense," I said.

"It's not." He turned to Nora. "I don't suppose he ever told you he saved my life once in a shell-hole in – "

"He's nuts," I told her. "He fired at a fellow and missed and I fired at him and didn't and that's all there was to it." I addressed him again: "Why don't you let the police wait awhile? Suppose you and I keep this date tonight and hear what he's got to say. We can sit on him and blow whistles when the meeting's about to break up if we're convinced he's the murderer."

Macaulay smiled wearily. "You're still doubtful, aren't you? Well, I'm willing to do it that way if you want, though it seems like a – But perhaps you'll change your mind when I tell you about our telephone conversation."

Dorothy, wearing a nightgown and a robe of Nora's, both much too long for her, came in yawning. "Oh!" she exclaimed when she saw Macaulay, and then, when she had recognized him, "Oh, hello, Mr. Macaulay. I didn't know you were here. Is there any news of my father?"

He looked at me. I shook my head. He told her: "Not yet, but perhaps we'll have some today."

I said: "Dorothy's had some, indirectly. Tell Macaulay about Gilbert."

"You mean about – about my father?" she asked hesitantly, staring at the floor.

"Oh, dear me, no," I said.

Her face flushed and she glanced reproachfully at me; then, hastily, she told Macaulay: "Gil saw my father yesterday and he told Gil who killed Miss Wolf."

"What?" She nodded four or five times, earnestly. Macaulay looked at me with puzzled eyes.

"This doesn't have to've happened," I reminded him. "It's what Gil says happened."

"I see. Then you think he might be – ?"

"You haven't done much talking to that family since hell broke loose, have you?" I asked.

"No."

"It's an experience. They're all sex-crazy, I think, and it backs up into their heads. They start off – "

Dorothy said angrily: "I think you're horrid. I've done my best to – "

"What are you kicking about?" I demanded. "I'm giving you the break this time: I'm willing to believe Gil did tell you that. Don't expect too much of me."

Macaulay asked: "And who killed her?"

"I don't know. Gil wouldn't tell me."

"Had your brother seen him often?"

"I don't know how often. He said he had been seeing him."

"And was anything said – well – about the man Nunheim?"

"No. Nick asked me that. He didn't tell me anything else at all."

I caught Nora's eye and made signals. She stood up saying: "Let's go in the other room, Dorothy, and give these lads a chance to do whatever it is they think they're doing." Dorothy went reluctantly, but she went out with Nora.

Macaulay said: "She's grown up to be something to look at." He cleared his throat. "I hope your wife won't – "

"Forget it. Nora's all right. You started to tell me about your conversation with Wynant."

"He phoned right after the police left and said he'd seen the ad in the *Times* and wanted to know what I wanted. I told him you weren't anxious to get yourself mixed up in his troubles and had said you wouldn't touch it at all without talking it over with him first, and we made the date for tonight. Then he asked if I'd seen Mimi and I told him I'd seen her once or twice since her return from Europe and had also seen his daughter. And then he said this: 'If my wife should ask for money, give her any sum in reason.'"

"I'll be damned," I said.

Macaulay nodded. "That's the way I felt about it. I asked him why and he said what he'd read in the morning papers had convinced him that she was Rosewater's dupe, not his confederate, and he had reason to believe she was 'kindly disposed' towards him, Wynant. I began to see what he was up to, then, and I told him she had already turned the knife and chain over to the police. And try to guess what he said to that."

"I give up."

"He hemmed and hawed a bit – not much, mind you – and then as smooth as you like asked: 'You mean the chain and knife on the watch I left with Julia to be repaired?'"

I laughed. "What'd you say?"

"That stumped me. Before I could think up an answer he was saying: 'However, we can discuss that more fully when we meet tonight.' I asked him where and when we'd meet him and he said he'd have to phone me, he didn't know where he'd be. He's to phone me at my house at ten o'clock. He was in a hurry now, though he had seemed leisurely enough before, and hadn't time to answer any of the things I wanted to ask, so he hung up and I phoned you. What do you think of his innocence now?"

"Not as much as I did," I replied slowly. "How sure are you of hearing from him at ten tonight?"

Macaulay shrugged. "You know as much about that as I do."

"Then if I were you I wouldn't bother the police till we've grabbed our wild man and can turn him over to them. This story of yours isn't going to make them exactly love you and, even if they don't throw you in the can right away, they'll make things pretty disagreeable for you if Wynant gives us a run-around tonight."

"I know, but I'd like to get the load off my shoulders."

"A few hours more oughtn't to matter much," I said. "Did either of you say anything about his not keeping the date at the Plaza?"

"No. I didn't get a chance to ask him. Well, if you say wait, I'll wait, but – "

"Let's wait till tonight, anyhow, till he phones you – if he does – and then we can make up our minds whether to take the police along."

"You don't think he'll phone?"

"I'm not too sure," I said. "He didn't keep his last date with you, and he seems to have gone pretty vague on you as soon as he learned that Mimi had turned in the watch-chain and knife. I wouldn't be too optimistic about it. We'll see though. I'd better get out to your house at about nine o'clock, hadn't I?"

"Come for dinner."

"I can't, but I'll make it as early as I can, in case he's ahead of time. We'll want to move fast. Where do you live?"

Macaulay gave me his address, in Scarsdale, and stood up. "Will you say good-bye to Mrs. Charles for me and thank – Oh, by the way, I hope you didn't misunderstand me about Harrison Quinn last night. I meant only just what I said, that I'd had bad luck taking his advice on the market. I didn't mean to insinuate that there was anything – you know – or that he might not've made money for his other customers."

"I understand," I said, and called Nora. She and Macaulay shook hands and made polite speeches to each other and he pushed Asta around a little and said, "Make it as early as you can," to me and went away.

"There goes the hockey game," I said, "unless you find somebody else to go with."

"Did I miss anything?" Nora asked.

"Not much." I told her what Macaulay had told me. "And don't ask me what I think of it. I don't know. I know Wynant's crazy, but he's not acting like a murderer. He's acting like a man playing some kind of game. God only knows what the game is."

"I think," she said, "that he's shielding somebody else."

"Why don't you think he did it?"

She looked surprised. "Because you don't."

I said that was a swell reason. "Who is the somebody else?"

"I don't know yet. Now don't make fun of me: I've thought about it a lot. It wouldn't be Macaulay, because he's using him to help shield whoever it is and – "

"And it wouldn't be me," I suggested, "because he wants to use me."

"That's right," she said, "and you're going to feel very silly if you make fun of me and then I guess who it is before you do. And it wouldn't be either Mimi or Jorgensen, because he tried to throw suspicion on them. And it wouldn't be Nunheim, because he was most likely killed by the same person and, furthermore, wouldn't have to be shielded now. And it wouldn't be Morelli, because Wynant was jealous of him and they'd had a row." She frowned at me. "I wish you'd found out more about that big fat man they called Sparrow and that big red-haired woman."

"But how about Dorothy and Gilbert?"

"I wanted to ask you about them. Do you think he's got any very strong paternal feeling for them?"

"No."

"You're probably just trying to discourage me," she said. "Well, knowing them, it's hard to think either of them might've been guilty, but I tried to throw out my personal feelings and stick to logic. Before I went to sleep last night I made a list of all the – "

"There's nothing like a little logic-sticking to ward off insomnia. It's like – "

"Don't be so damned patronizing. Your performance so far has been a little less than dazzling."

"I didn't mean no harm," I said and kissed her. "That a new dress?"

"Ah! Changing the subject, you coward."

I WENT TO see Guild early in the afternoon and went to work on him as soon as we had shaken hands. "I didn't bring my lawyer along. I thought it looked better if I came by myself."

He wrinkled his forehead and shook his head as if I had hurt him. "Now it was nothing like that," he said patiently.

"It was too much like that."

He sighed. "I wouldn't've thought you'd make the mistake that a lot of people make thinking just because we – You know we got to look at every angle, Mr. Charles."

"That sounds familiar. Well, what do you want to know?"

"All I want to know is who killed her – and him."

"Try asking Gilbert," I suggested.

Guild pursed his lips. "Why him exactly?"

"He told his sister he knew who did it, told her he got it from Wynant."

"You mean he's been seeing the old man?"

"So she says he said. I haven't had a chance to ask him about it."

He squinted his watery eyes at me. "Just what is that lay-out over there, Mr. Charles?"

"The Jorgensen family? You probably know as much about it as I do."

"I don't," he said, "and that's a fact. I just can't size them up at all. This Mrs. Jorgensen, now, what is she?"

"A blonde."

He nodded gloomily. "Uh-huh, and that's all I know. But look, you've known them a long time and from what she says you and her – "

DASHIELL HAMMETT

"And me and her daughter," I said, "and me and Julia Wolf and me and Mrs. Astor. I'm hell with the women."

He held up a hand. "I'm not saying I believe everything she says, and there's nothing to get sore about. You're taking the wrong attitude, if you don't mind me saying it. You're acting like you thought we were out to get you, and that's all wrong, absolutely all wrong."

"Maybe, but you've been talking double to me ever since last – "

He looked at me with steady pale eyes and said calmly: "I'm a copper and I got my work to do."

"That's reasonable enough. You told me to come in today. What do you want?"

"I didn't tell you to come in, I asked you."

"All right. What do you want?"

"I don't want this," he said. "I don't want anything like this. We've been talking man to man up to this time and I'd kind of like to go on thataway."

"You made the change."

"I don't think that's a fact. Look here, Mr. Charles, would you take your oath, or even just tell me straight out, that you've been emptying your pockets to me right along?"

There was no use saying yes – he would not have believed me. I said: "Practically."

"Practically, yes," he grumbled. "Everybody's been telling me practically the whole truth. What I want's some impractical son of a gun that'll shoot the works."

I could sympathize with him: I knew how he felt. I said: "Maybe nobody you've found knows the whole truth."

He made an unpleasant face. "That's very likely, ain't it? Listen, Mr. Charles, I've talked to everybody I could find. If you can find any more for me, I'll talk to them too. You mean Wynant? Don't you suppose we got every facility the department's got working night and day trying to turn him up?"

"There's his son," I suggested.

"There's his son," he agreed. He called in Andy and a swarthy bow-legged man named Kline. "Get me that Wynant kid – the punk – I want to talk to him." They went out. He said: "See, I want people to talk to."

I said: "Your nerves are in pretty bad shape this afternoon, aren't they? Are you bringing Jorgensen down from Boston?"

He shrugged his big shoulders. "His story listens all right to me. I don't know. Want to tell me what you think of it?"

"Sure."

"I'm kind of jumpy this afternoon, for a fact," he said. "I didn't get a single solitary wink of sleep last night. It's a hell of a life. I don't know why I stick at it. A fellow can get a piece of land and some wire fencing and a few head of silver fox and – Well, anyways, when you people scared Jorgensen off back in '25, he says he lit out for Germany, leaving his wife in the lurch – though he don't say much about that – and changing his name to give you more trouble finding him, and on the same account he's afraid to work at his regular job – he calls himself some kind of a technician or something – so pickings are kind of slim. He says he worked at one thing and another, whatever he could get, but near as I can figure out he was mostly gigoloing, if you know what I mean, and not finding too many heavy-money dames. Well, along about '27 or '28 he's in Milan – that's a city in Italy – and he sees in the Paris *Herald* where this Mimi, recently divorced wife of Clyde Miller Wynant, has arrived in Paris. He don't know her personally and she don't know him, but he knows she's a dizzy blonde that likes men and fun and hasn't got much sense. He figures a bunch of Wynant's dough must've come to her with the divorce and, the way he looks at it, any of it he could take away from her wouldn't be any more than what Wynant had gypped him out of – he'd only be getting some of what belonged to him. So he scrapes up the fare to Paris and goes up there. All right so far?"

"Sounds all right."

"That's what I thought. Well, he don't have any trouble getting to know her in Paris – either picking her up or getting somebody to introduce him or whatever happened – and the rest of it's just as easy. She goes for him in a big way – bing, according to him – right off the bat, and the first thing you know she's one jump ahead of him, she's thinking about marrying him. Naturally he don't try to talk her out of that. She'd gotten a lump sum – two hundred thousand berries, by God! – out of Wynant instead of alimony, so her marrying again wasn't stopping any payments, and it'll put him right in the middle of the cash-drawer. So they do it. According to him, it was a trick marriage up in some mountains he says are between Spain and France and was done by a Spanish priest on what was really French soil, which don't make it legal, but I figure he's just trying to discourage a bigamy rap. Personally, I don't care one way or the other. The point is he got his hands on the dough and kept them on it till there wasn't any more dough. And all this time, understand, he says she didn't know he was anybody but Christian Jorgensen, a fellow she met in Paris, and still didn't know it up to the time we grabbed him in Boston. Still sound all right?"

"Still sounds all right," I said, "except, as you say, about the marriage, and even that could be all right."

"Uh-huh, and what difference does it make anyways? So comes the winter and the bank-roll's getting skinny and he's getting ready to take a run-out on her with the last of it, and then she says maybe they could come back to America and tap Wynant for some more. He thinks that's fair enough if it can be done, and she thinks it can be done, so they get on a boat and – "

"That story cracks a little there," I said.

"What makes you think so? He's not figuring on going to Boston, where he knows his first wife is, and he's figuring on keeping out of the way of the few people that know him, including especially Wynant, and somebody's told him there's a statute of limitation making everything just lovely after seven years. He don't figure he's running much risk. They ain't even going to stay here long."

"I still don't like that part of his story," I insisted, "but go ahead."

"Well, the second day he's here – while they're still trying to find Wynant – he gets a bad break. He runs into a friend of his first wife's – this Olga Fenton – on the street and she recognizes him. He tries to talk her out of tipping off the first wife and does manage to stall her along a couple days with a moving-picture story he makes up – what an imagination that guy's got! – but he don't fool her long, and she goes to her parson and tells him about it and asks him what she ought to do and he says she ought to tell the first wife, and so she does, and the next time she sees Jorgensen she tells him what she'd done, and he lights out for Boston to try to keep his wife from kicking up trouble and we pick him up there."

"How about his visit to the hock-shop?" I asked.

"That was part of it. He says there was a train for Boston leaving in a few minutes and he didn't have any dough with him and didn't have time to go home for some – besides not being anxious to face the second wife till he had the first one quieted down – and the banks were closed, so he soaked his watch. It checks up."

"Did you see the watch?"

"I can. Why?"

"I was wondering. You don't think it was once on the other end of that piece of chain Mimi turned over to you?"

He sat up straight. "By God!" Then he squinted at me suspiciously and asked: "Do you know anything about it or are you –"

"No. I was just wondering. What does he say about the murders now? Who does he think did them?"

"Wynant. He admits for a while he thought Mimi might've, but he says she convinced him different. He claims she wouldn't tell him what she had on Wynant. He might be just trying to cover himself up on that. I don't guess there's any doubt about them meaning to use it to shake him down for that money they wanted."

"Then you don't think she planted the knife and chain?"

Guild pulled down the ends of his mouth. "She could've planted them to shake him down with. What's wrong with that?"

"It's a little complicated for a fellow like me," I said. "Find out if Face Peppler's still in the Ohio pen?"

"Uh-huh. He gets out next week. That accounts for the diamond ring. He had a pal of his on the outside send it to her for him. Seems they were planning to get married and go straight together after he got out, or some such. Anyways, the warden says he saw letters passing between them reading like that. This Peppler won't tell the warden that he knows anything that'll help us, and the warden don't call to mind anything that was in their letters that's any good to us. Of course, even this much helps some, with the motive. Say Wynant's jealous and she's wearing this other guy's ring and getting ready to go away with him. That'll – " He broke off to answer his telephone. "Yes," he said into it. "Yes. . . . What? . . . Sure. . . . Sure, but leave somebody there. . . . That's right." He pushed the telephone aside. "Another bum steer on that West Twenty-ninth Street killing yesterday."

"Oh," I said, "I thought I heard Wynant's name. You know how some telephone voices carry."

He blushed, cleared his throat. "Maybe something sounded like it – why not, I guess. Uh-huh, that could sound like it – why not. I almost forgot: we looked up that fellow Sparrow for you."

"What'd you find out?"

"It looks like there's nothing there for us. His name's Jim Brophy. It figures out that he was making a play for that girl of Nunheim's and she was sore at you and he was just drunk enough to think he could put himself in solid with her by taking a poke at you."

"A nice idea," I said. "I hope you didn't make any trouble for Studsy."

"A friend of yours? He's an ex-con, you know, with a record as long as your arm."

"Sure. I sent him over once." I started to gather up my hat and overcoat. "You're busy. I'll run along and – "

"No, no," he said. "Stick around if you got the time. I got a couple things coming in that'll maybe interest you, and you can give me a hand with that Wynant kid, too, maybe." I sat down again.

"Maybe you'd like a drink," he suggested, opening a drawer of his desk, but I had never had much luck with policemen's liquor, so I said: "No, thanks."

His telephone rang again and he said into it: "Yes. . . . Yes. . . . That's all right. Come on in." This time no words leaked out to me.

He rocked back in his chair and put his feet on his desk. "Listen, I'm on the level about that silver fox farming and I want to ask you what you think of California for a place."

I was trying to decide whether to tell him about the lion and ostrich farms in the lower part of the state when the door opened and a fat red-haired man brought Gilbert Wynant in. One of Gilbert's eyes was completely shut by swollen flesh around it and his left knee showed through a tear in his pants-leg.

I SAID TO Guild: "When you say bring 'em in, they bring 'em in, don't they?"

"Wait," he told me. "This is more'n you think." He addressed the fat red-haired man: "Go ahead, Flint, let's have it."

Flint wiped his mouth with the back of a hand. "He's a wildcat for fair, the young fellow. He don't look tough, but, man, he didn't want to come along. I can tell you that. And can he run!"

Guild growled: "You're a hero and I'll see the Commissioner about your medal right away, but never mind that now. Talk turkey."

"I wasn't saying I did anything great," Flint protested. "I was just – "

"I don't give a damn what you did," Guild said. "I want to know what he did."

"Yes, sir, I was getting to that. I relieved Morgan at eight o'clock this morning and everything went along smooth and quiet as per usual, with not a creature was stirring, as the fellow says, till along about ten minutes after two, and then what do I hear but a key in the lock." He sucked in his lips and gave us a chance to express our amazement.

"The Wolf dame's apartment," Guild explained to me. "I had a hunch."

"And what a hunch!" Flint exclaimed, practically top-heavy with admiration. "Man, what a hunch!" Guild glared at him and he went on hastily: "Yes, sir, a key, and then the door opens and this young fellow comes in." He grinned proudly, affectionately, at Gilbert. "Scared stiff, he looked, and when I went for him he was out and away like a streak and it wasn't till the first floor that I caught him, and then, by golly, he put up a tussle and I had to bat him in the eye to tone him down. He don't look tough, but – "

"What'd he do in the apartment?" Guild asked.

"He didn't have a chance to do nothing. I – "

"You mean you jumped him without waiting to see what he was up to?" Guild's neck bulged over the edge of his collar, and his face was as red as Flint's hair.

"I thought it was best not to take no chances."

Guild stared at me with angry incredulous eyes. I did my best to keep my face blank. He said in a choking voice: "That'll do, Flint. Wait outside."

The red-haired man seemed puzzled. He said, "Yes, sir," slowly. "Here's his key." He put the key on Guild's desk and went to the door. There he twisted his head over a shoulder to say: "He claims he's Clyde Wynant's son." He laughed merrily.

Guild, still having trouble with his voice, said: "Oh, he does, does he?"

"Yeah. I seen him somewhere before. I got an idea he used to belong to Big Shorty Dolan's mob. Seems to me I used to see him around – "

"Get out!" Guild snarled, and Flint got out. Guild groaned from deep down in his big body. "That mug gets me. Big Shorty Dolan's mob. Christ." He shook his head hopelessly and addressed Gilbert: "Well, son?"

Gilbert said: "I know I shouldn't've done it."

"That's a fair start," Guild said genially. His face was becoming normal again. "We all make mistakes. Pull yourself up a chair and let's see what we can do about getting you out of the soup. Want anything for that eye?"

"No, thank you, it's quite all right." Gilbert moved a chair two or three inches towards Guild and sat down.

"Did that bum smack you just to be doing something?"

"No, no, it was my fault. I – I did resist."

"Oh, well," Guild said, "nobody likes to be arrested, I guess. Now what's the trouble?" Gilbert looked at me with his one good eye.

"You're in as bad a hole as Lieutenant Guild wants to put you," I told him. "You'll make it easy for yourself by making it easy for him."

Guild nodded earnestly. "And that's a fact." He settled himself comfortably in his chair and asked, in a friendly tone: "Where'd you get the key?"

"My father sent it to me in his letter." He took a white envelope from his pocket and gave it to Guild.

I went around behind Guild and looked at the envelope over his shoulder. The address was typewritten, *Mr. Gilbert Wynant, The Courtland*, and there was no postage stamp stuck on it. "When'd you get it?" I asked.

"It was at the desk when I got in last night, around ten o'clock. I didn't ask the clerk how long it had been there, but I don't suppose it was there when I went out with you, or they'd have given it to me."

Inside the envelope were two sheets of paper covered with the familiar unskillful typewriting. Guild and I read together:

Dear Gilbert:

If all these years have gone by without my having communicated with you, it is only because your mother wished it so and if now I break this silence with a request for your assistance it is because only great need could make me go against your mother's wishes. Also you are a man now and I feel that you yourself are the one to decide whether or not we should act in accordance with our ties of blood. That I am in an embarrassing situation now in connection with Julia Wolf's so-called murder I think you know and I trust that you still have remaining enough affection for me to at least hope that I am in all ways guiltless of any complicity therein, which is indeed the case. I turn to you now for help in demonstrating my innocence once and for all to the police and to the world with every confidence that even could I not count on your affection for me I nevertheless could count on your natural desire to do anything within your power to keep unblemished the name that is yours and your sister's as well as your Father's. I turn to you also because while I have a lawyer who is able and who believes in my innocence and who is leaving no stone unturned to prove it and have hopes of engaging Mr. Nick Charles to assist him I cannot ask either of them to undertake what is after all a patently illegal act nor do I know anybody else except you that I dare confide in. What I wish you to do is this, tomorrow go to Julia Wolf's apartment at 411 East 54th St. to which the enclosed key will admit you and between the pages of a book called The Grand Manner *you will find a certain paper or statement which you are to read and destroy immediately. You are to be sure you destroy it completely leaving not so much as an ash and when you have read it you will know why this must be done and will understand why I have entrusted this task to you. In the event that something should develop to make a change in our plans advisable I will call you on the telephone late tonight. If you do not hear from me I will telephone you tomorrow evening to learn if you have carried out my instructions and to make arrangements for a meeting. I have every confidence that you will realize the tremendous responsibility I am placing on your shoulders and that my confidence is not misplaced.*

Affectionately,
Your Father

Wynant's sprawling signature was written in ink beneath "Your Father."

Guild waited for me to say something. I waited for him. After a little of that he asked Gilbert: "And did he phone?"

"No, sir."

"How do you know?" I asked. "Didn't you tell the operator not to put any calls through?"

"I – yes, I did. I was afraid you'd find out who it was if he called up while you were there, but he'd've left some kind of message with the operator, I think, and he didn't."

"Then you haven't been seeing him?"

"No."

"And he didn't tell you who killed Julia Wolf?"

"No."

"You were lying to Dorothy?"

He lowered his head and nodded at the floor. "I was – it was – I suppose it was jealousy really." He looked up at me now and his face was pink. "You see, Dorry used to look up to me and think I knew more than anybody else about almost everything and – you know – she'd come to me if there was anything she wanted to know and she always did what I told her, and then, when she got to seeing you, it was different. She looked up to you and respected you more – She naturally would, I mean, she'd've been silly if she hadn't, because there's no comparison, of course, but I – I suppose I was jealous and resented – well, not exactly resented it, because I looked up to you too – but I wanted to do something to impress her again – show off, I guess you'd call it – and when I got that letter I pretended I'd been seeing my father and he'd told me who committed those murders, so she'd think I knew things even you didn't." He stopped, out of breath, and wiped his face with a handkerchief.

I outwaited Guild again until presently he said: "Well, I guess there ain't been a great deal of harm done, sonny, if you're sure you ain't doing harm by holding back some other things we ought to know."

The boy shook his head. "No, sir, I'm not holding back anything."

"You don't know anything about that knife and chain your mother give us?"

"No, sir, and I didn't know a thing about it till after she had given it to you."

"How is she?" I asked.

"Oh, she's all right, I think, though she said she was going to stay in bed today."

Guild narrowed his eyes. "What's the matter with her?"

"Hysteria," I told him. "She and the daughter had a row last night and she blew up."

"A row about what?"

"God knows – one of those feminine brain-storms."

Guild said, "Hm-m-m," and scratched his chin.

"Was Flint right in saying you didn't get a chance to hunt for your paper?" I asked the boy.

"Yes. I hadn't even had time to shut the door when he ran at me."

"They're grand detectives I got working for me," Guild growled. "Didn't he yell, 'Boo!' when he jumped out at you? Never mind. Well, son, I can do one of two things, and the which depends on you. I can hold you for a while or I can let you go in exchange for a promise that you'll let me know as soon as your father gets in touch with you and let me know what he tells you and where he wants you to meet him, if any."

I spoke before Gilbert could speak: "You can't ask that of him, Guild. It's his own father."

"I can't, huh?" He scowled at me. "Ain't it for his father's good if he's innocent?" I said nothing.

Guild's face cleared slowly. "All right, then, son, suppose I put you on a kind of parole. If your father or anybody else asks you to do anything, will you promise to tell them you can't because you give me your word of honor you wouldn't?" The boy looked at me.

I said: "That sounds reasonable."

Gilbert said: "Yes, sir, I'll give you my word."

Guild made a large gesture with one hand. "Oke. Run along."

The boy stood up saying: "Thank you very much, sir." He turned to me. "Are you going to be – "

407

"Wait for me outside," I told him, "if you're not in a hurry."

"I will. Good-bye, Lieutenant Guild, and thank you." He went out.

Guild grabbed his telephone and ordered *The Grand Manner* and its contents found and brought to him. That done, he clasped his hands behind his head and rocked back in his chair. "So what?"

"It's anybody's guess," I said.

"Look here, you don't still think Wynant didn't do it?"

"What difference does it make what I think? You've got plenty on him now with what Mimi gave you."

"It makes a lot of difference," he assured me. "I'd like a lot to know what you think and why."

"My wife thinks he's trying to cover up somebody else."

"Is that so? Hm-m-m. I was never one to belittle women's intuition and, if you don't mind me saying so, Mrs. Charles is a mighty smart woman. Who does she think it is?"

"She hadn't decided, the last I heard."

He sighed, "Well, maybe the paper he sent the kid for will tell us something." But the paper told us nothing that afternoon: Guild's men could not find it, could not find a copy of *The Grand Manner* in the dead woman's rooms.

GUILD HAD RED-HAIRED Flint in again and put the thumb-screws on him. The red-haired man sweat away ten pounds, but he stuck to it that Gilbert had had no opportunity to disturb anything in the apartment and throughout Flint's guardianship nobody hadn't touched nothing. He did not remember having seen a book called *The Grand Manner*, but he was not a man you would expect to memorize book titles. He tried to be helpful and made idiotic suggestions until Guild chased him out.

"The kid's probably waiting for me outside," I said, "if you think talking to him again will do any good."

"Do you?"

"No."

"Well, then. But, by God, somebody took that book and I'm going to – "

"Why?" I asked.

"Why what?"

"Why'd it have to be there for somebody to take?"

Guild scratched his chin. "Just what do you mean by that?"

"He didn't meet Macaulay at the Plaza the day of the murder, he didn't commit suicide in Allentown, he says he only got a thousand from Julia Wolf when he thought he was getting five thousand, he says they were just friends when we think they were lovers, he disappoints us too much for me to have much confidence in what he says."

"It's a fact," Guild said, "that I'd understand it better if he'd either come in or run away. Him hanging around like this, just messing things up, don't fit in anywheres that I can see."

"Are you watching his shop?"

"We're kind of keeping an eye on it. Why?"

"I don't know," I said truthfully, "except that he's pointed his finger at a lot of things that got us nowhere. Maybe we ought to pay some attention to the things he hasn't pointed at, and the shop's one of them."

Guild said: "Hm-m-m."

I said, "I'll leave you with that bright thought," and put on my hat and coat. "Suppose I wanted to get hold of you late at night, how would I reach you?" He gave me his telephone-number, we shook hands, and I left.

Gilbert Wynant was waiting for me in the corridor. Neither of us said anything until we were in a taxicab. Then he asked: "He thinks I was telling the truth, doesn't he?"

"Sure. Weren't you?"

"Oh, yes, but people don't always believe you. You won't say anything to Mamma about this, will you?"

"Not if you don't want me to."

"Thank you," he said. "In your opinion, is there more opportunity for a young man out West than here in the East?"

I thought of him working on Guild's fox farm while I replied: "Not now. Thinking of going west?"

"I don't know. I want to do something." He fidgeted with his necktie. "You'll think it's a funny question: is there much incest?"

"There's some," I told him; "that's why they've got a name for it." His face flushed.

I said: "I'm not making fun of you. It's one of the things nobody knows. There's no way of finding out."

We had a couple of blocks of silence after that. Then he said: "There's another funny question I'd like to ask you: what do you think of me?" He was more self-conscious about it than Alice Quinn had been.

"You're all right," I told him, "and you're all wrong."

He looked away, out the window. "I'm so awfully young."
We had some more silence. Then he coughed and a little
blood trickled from one corner of his mouth.

"That guy did hurt you," I said.

He nodded shamefacedly and put his handkerchief to his
mouth. "I'm not very strong."

At the Courtland he would not let me help him out of the
taxicab and he insisted he could manage alone, but I went
upstairs with him, suspecting that otherwise he would say
nothing to anybody about his condition. I rang the apartment
bell before he could get his key out, and Mimi opened the
door. She goggled at his black eye.

I said: "He's hurt. Get him to bed and get him a doctor."

"What happened?"

"Wynant sent him into something."

"Into what?"

"Never mind that until we get him fixed up."

"But Clyde was here," she said. "That's why I phoned
you."

"What?"

"He was." She nodded vigorously. "And he asked where
Gil was. He was here for an hour or more. He hasn't been
gone ten minutes."

"All right, let's get him to bed." Gilbert stubbornly insisted
that he needed no help, so I left him in the bedroom with his
mother and went out to the telephone.

"Any calls?" I asked Nora when I had her on the line.

"Yes, sir. Messrs. Macaulay and Guild want you to phone
them, and Mesdames Jorgensen and Quinn want you to
phone them. No children so far."

"When did Guild call?"

"About five minutes ago. Mind eating alone? Larry
asked me to go see the new Osgood Perkins show with
him."

"Go ahead. See you later." I called up Herbert Macaulay.

"The date's off," he told me. "I heard from our friend and he's up to God knows what. Listen, Charles, I'm going to the police. I've had enough of it."

"I guess there's nothing else to do now," I said. "I was thinking about telephoning some policemen myself. I'm at Mimi's. He was here a few minutes ago. I just missed him."

"What was he doing there?"

"I'm going to try to find out now."

"Were you serious about phoning the police?"

"Sure."

"Then suppose you do that and I'll come on over."

"Right. Be seeing you."

I called up Guild. "A little news came in right after you left," he said. "Are you where I can give it to you?"

"I'm at Mrs. Jorgensen's. I had to bring the kid home. That red-head lad of yours had got him bleeding somewhere inside."

"I'll kill that mug," he snarled. "Then I better not talk."

"I've got some news, too. Wynant was here for about an hour this afternoon, according to Mrs. Jorgensen, and left only a few minutes before I got here."

There was a moment of silence, then he said: "Hold everything. I'll be right up."

Mimi came into the living-room while I was looking up the Quinns' telephone-number. "Do you think he's seriously hurt?" she asked.

"I don't know, but you ought to get your doctor right away." I pushed the telephone towards her. When she was through with it, I said: "I told the police Wynant had been here."

She nodded. "That's what I phoned you for, to ask if I ought to tell them."

"I phoned Macaulay, too. He's coming over."

"He can't do anything," she said indignantly. "Clyde gave them to me of his own free will – they're mine."

"What's yours?"

"Those bonds, the money."

"What bonds? what money?"

She went to the table and pulled the drawer out. "See?"

Inside were three packages of bonds held together by thick rubber bands. Across the top of them lay a pink check on the Park Avenue Trust Company to the order of Mimi Jorgensen for ten thousand dollars, signed Clyde Miller Wynant, and dated January 3, 1933.

"Dated five days ahead," I said. "What kind of nonsense is that?"

"He said he hadn't that much in his account and might not be able to make a deposit for a couple of days."

"There's going to be hell about this," I warned her. "I hope you're ready for it."

"I don't see why," she protested. "I don't see why my husband – my former husband – can't provide for me and his children if he wants to."

"Cut it out. What'd you sell him?"

"Sell him?"

"Uh-huh. What'd you promise to do in the next few days or he fixes it so the check's no good?"

She made an impatient face. "Really, Nick, I think you're a half-wit sometimes with your silly suspicions."

"I'm studying to be one. Three more lessons and I get my diploma. But remember I warned you yesterday that you'll probably wind up in – "

"Stop it," she cried. She put a hand over my mouth. "Do you have to keep saying that? You know it terrifies me and – " Her voice became soft and wheedling. "You must know what I'm going through these days, Nick. Can't you be a little kinder?"

"Don't worry about me," I said. "Worry about the police." I went back to the telephone and called up Alice Quinn. "This is Nick. Nora said you – "

"Yes. Have you seen Harrison?"

"Not since I left him with you."

"Well, if you do, you won't say anything about what I said last night, will you? I didn't mean it, really I didn't mean a word of it."

"I didn't think you did," I assured her, "and I wouldn't say anything about it anyway. How's he feeling today?"

"He's gone," she said.

"What?"

"He's gone. He's left me."

"He's done that before. He'll be back."

"I know, but I'm afraid this time. He didn't go to his office. I hope he's just drunk somewhere and – but this time I'm afraid. Nick, do you think he's really in love with that girl?"

"He seems to think he is."

"Did he tell you he was?"

"That wouldn't mean anything."

"Do you think it would do any good to have a talk with her?"

"No."

"Why don't you? Do you think she's in love with him?"

"No."

"What's the matter with you?" she asked irritably.

"No, I'm not home."

"What? Oh, you mean you're some place where you can't talk?"

"That's it."

"Are you – are you at her house?"

"Yes."

"Is she there?"

"No."

"Do you think she's with him?"

"I don't know. I don't think so."

"Will you call me when you can talk, or, better still, will you come up to see me?"

"Sure," I promised, and we hung up.

Mimi was looking at me with amusement in her blue eyes. "Somebody's taking my brat's affairs seriously?"

When I did not answer her, she laughed and asked: "Is Dorry still being the maiden in distress?"

"I suppose so."

"She will be, too, as long as she can get anybody to believe in it. And you, of all people, to be fooled, you who are afraid to believe that – well – that I, for instance, am ever telling the truth."

"That's a thought," I said. The door-bell rang before I could go on. Mimi let the doctor in – he was a roly-poly elderly man with a stoop and a waddle – and took him in to Gilbert.

I opened the table-drawer again and looked at the bonds, Postal Telegraph & Cable 5s, Sao Paulo City 6½s, American Type Founders 6s, Certain-teed Products 5½s, Upper Austria 6½s, United Drugs 5s, Philippine Railway 4s, Tokio Electric Lighting 6s, about sixty thousand dollars at face value, I judged, and – guessing – between a quarter and a third of that at the market.

When the door-bell rang I shut the drawer and let Macaulay in. He looked tired. He sat down without taking off his overcoat and said: "Well, tell me the worst. What was he up to here?"

"I don't know yet, except that he gave Mimi some bonds and a check."

"I know that." He fumbled in his pocket and gave me a letter:

Dear Herbert:

I am today giving Mrs. Mimi Jorgensen the securities listed below and a ten thousand dollar check on the Park Ave. Trust dated Jan. 3. Please arrange to have sufficient money there on that date to cover it. I would suggest that you sell some more of the public utility bonds, but use your own judgment. I find that

I cannot spend any more time in New York at present and probably will not be able to get back here for several months, but will communicate with you from time to time. I am sorry I will not be able to wait over to see you and Charles tonight.

Yours truly,
Clyde Miller Wynant

Under the sprawling signature was a list of the bonds.

"How'd it come to you?" I asked.

"By messenger. What do you suppose he was paying her for?"

I shook my head. "I tried to find out. She said he was 'providing for her and his children.'"

"That's likely, as likely as that she'd tell the truth."

"About these bonds?" I asked. "I thought you had all his property in your hands."

"I thought so too, but I didn't have these, didn't know he had them." He put his elbows on his knees, his head in his hands. "If all the things I don't know were laid end to end. . . ."

MIMI CAME IN with the doctor, said, "Oh, how do you do," a little stiffly to Macaulay, and shook hands with him. "This is Doctor Grant, Mr. Macaulay, Mr. Charles."

"How's the patient?" I asked.

Doctor Grant cleared his throat and said he didn't think there was anything seriously the matter with Gilbert, effects of a beating, slight hemorrhage of course, should rest, though. He cleared his throat again and said he was happy to have met us, and Mimi showed him out.

"What happened to the boy?" Macaulay asked me.

"Wynant sent him on a wild-goose chase over to Julia's apartment and he ran into a tough copper."

Mimi returned from the door. "Has Mr. Charles told you about the bonds and the check?" she asked.

"I had a note from Mr. Wynant saying he was giving them to you," Macaulay said.

"Then there will be no – "

"Difficulty? Not that I know of."

She relaxed a little and her eyes lost some of their coldness. "I didn't see why there should be but he" – pointing at me – "likes to frighten me."

Macaulay smiled politely. "May I ask whether Mr. Wynant said anything about his plans?"

"He said something about going away, but I don't suppose I was listening very attentively. I don't remember whether he told me when he was going or where."

I grunted to show skepticism; Macaulay pretended he believed her. "Did he say anything that you could repeat to me about Julia Wolf, or about his difficulties, or about any-thing connected with the murder and all?" he asked.

She shook her head emphatically. "Not a word I could either repeat or couldn't, not a word at all. I asked him about it, but you know how unsatisfactory he can be when he wants. I couldn't get as much as a grunt out of him about it."

I asked the question Macaulay seemed too polite to ask: "What did he talk about?"

"Nothing, really, except ourselves and the children, particu-larly Gil. He was very anxious to see him and waited nearly an hour, hoping he'd come home. He asked about Dorry, but he didn't seem very interested."

"Did he say anything about having written Gilbert?"

"Not a word. I can repeat our whole conversation, if you want me to. I didn't know he was coming, he didn't even phone from downstairs. The door-bell just rang and when I went to the door there he was, looking a lot older than when I'd seen him last and even thinner, and I said, 'Why, Clyde!' or something like that, and he said: 'Are you alone?' I told him I was and he came in. Then he – '" The door-bell rang and she went to answer it.

"What do you think of it?" Macaulay asked in a low voice.

"When I start believing Mimi," I said, "I hope I have sense enough not to admit it."

She returned from the door with Guild and Andy. Guild nodded to me and shook hands with Macaulay, then turned to Mimi and said: "Well, ma'am, I'll have to ask you to tell – "

Macaulay interrupted him: "Suppose you let me tell what I have to tell first, Lieutenant. It belongs ahead of Mrs. Jor-gensen's story and – "

Guild waved a big hand at the lawyer "Go ahead." He sat down on an end of the sofa. Macaulay told him what he had told me that morning. When he mentioned having told it to me that morning Guild glanced bitterly at me, once, and thereafter ignored me completely. Guild did not interrupt Macaulay, who

418

told his story clearly and concisely. Twice Mimi started to say something, but each time broke off to listen. When Macaulay had finished, he handed Guild the note about the bonds and check. "That came by messenger this afternoon."

Guild read the note very carefully and addressed Mimi: "Now then, Mrs. Jorgensen."

She told him what she had told us about Wynant's visit, elaborating the details as he patiently questioned her, but sticking to her story that he had refused to say a word about anything connected with Julia Wolf or her murder, that in giving her the bonds and check he had simply said that he wished to provide for her and the children, and that though he had said he was going away she did not know where or when. She seemed not at all disturbed by everybody's obvious disbelief. She wound up smiling, saying: "He's a sweet man in a lot of ways, but quite mad."

"You mean he's really insane, do you," Guild asked, "not just nutty?"

"Yes."

"What makes you think that?"

"Oh, you'd have to live with him to really know how mad he is," she replied airily.

Guild seemed dissatisfied. "What kind of clothes was he wearing?"

"A brown suit and brown overcoat and hat and I think brown shoes and a white shirt and a grayish necktie with either red or reddish brown figures in it."

Guild jerked his head at Andy. "Tell 'em." Andy went out.

Guild scratched his jaw and frowned thoughtfully. The rest of us watched. When he stopped scratching, he looked at Mimi and Macaulay, but not at me, and asked: "Any of you know anybody that's got the initials of D. W. Q.?"

Macaulay shook his head from side to side slowly.

Mimi said: "No. Why?"

Guild looked at me now. "Well?"

"I don't know them."

419

"Why?" Mimi repeated.

Guild said: "Try to remember back. He'd most likely've had dealings with Wynant."

"How far back?" Macaulay asked.

"That's hard to say right now. Maybe a few months, maybe a few years. He'd be a pretty large man, big bones, big belly, and maybe lame."

Macaulay shook his head again. "I don't remember anybody like that."

"Neither do I," Mimi said, "but I'm bursting with curiosity. I wish you'd tell us what it's all about."

"Sure, I'll tell you." Guild took a cigar from his vest-pocket, looked at it, and returned it to the pocket. "A dead man like that's buried under the floor of Wynant's shop."

I said: "Ah." Mimi put both hands to her mouth and said nothing. Her eyes were round and glassy.

Macaulay, frowning, asked: "Are you sure?"

Guild sighed. "Now you know that ain't something anybody would guess at," he said wearily.

Macaulay's face flushed and he smiled sheepishly. "That was a silly question. How did you happen to find him – it?"

"Well, Mr. Charles here kept hinting that we ought to pay more attention to that shop, so, figuring that Mr. Charles here is a man that's liable to know a lot more things than he tells anybody right out, I sent some men around this morning to see what they could find. We'd give it the once-over before and hadn't turned up nothing, but this time I told 'em to take the dump apart, because Mr. Charles here had said we ought to pay more attention to it. And Mr. Charles here was right." He looked at me with cool unfriendliness. "By and by they found a corner of the cement floor looking a little newer maybe than the rest and they cracked it and there was the mortal remains of Mr. D. W. Q. What do you think of that?"

Macaulay said: "I think it was a damned good guess of Charles's." He turned to me. "How did you – "

420

Guild interrupted him. "I don't think you ought to say that. When you call it just a guess, you ain't giving Mr. Charles here the proper credit for being as smart as he is."

Macaulay was puzzled by Guild's tone. He looked questioningly at me. "I'm being stood in the corner for not telling Lieutenant Guild about our conversation this morning," I explained.

"There's that," Guild agreed calmly, "among other things." Mimi laughed, and smiled apologetically at Guild when he stared at her.

"How was Mr. D. W. Q. killed?" I asked.

Guild hesitated, as if making up his mind whether to reply, then moved his big shoulders slightly and said: "I don't know yet, or how long ago. I haven't seen the remains yet, what there is of them, and the Medical Examiner wasn't through the last I heard."

"What there is of them?" Macaulay repeated.

"Uh-huh. He'd been sawed up in pieces and buried in lime or something so there wasn't much flesh left on him, according to the report I got, but his clothes had been stuck in with him rolled up in a bundle, and enough was left of the inside ones to tell us something. There was part of a cane, too, with a rubber tip. That's why we thought he might be lame, and we –" He broke off as Andy came in. "Well?"

Andy shook his head gloomily. "Nobody sees him come, nobody sees him go. What was that joke about a guy being so thin he had to stand in the same place twice to throw a shadow?"

I laughed – not at the joke – and said: "Wynant's not that thin, but he's thin enough, say as thin as the paper in that check and in those letters people have been getting."

"What's that?" Guild demanded, his face reddening, his eyes angry and suspicious.

"He's dead. He's been dead a long time except on paper. I'll give you even money they're his bones in the grave with the fat lame man's clothes."

Macaulay leaned towards me. "Are you sure of that, Charles?"

Guild snarled at me: "What are you trying to pull?"

"There's the bet if you want it. Who'd go to all that trouble with a corpse and then leave the easiest thing of all to get rid of – the clothes – untouched unless they – "

"But they weren't untouched. They – "

"Of course not. That wouldn't look right. They'd have to be partly destroyed, only enough left to tell you what they were supposed to tell. I bet the initials were plenty conspicuous."

"I don't know," Guild said with less heart. "They were on a belt buckle." I laughed.

Mimi said angrily: "That's ridiculous, Nick. How could that be Clyde? You know he was here this afternoon. You know he – "

"Sh-h-h. It's very silly of you to play along with him," I told her. "Wynant's dead, your children are probably his heirs, that's more money than you've got over there in the drawer. What do you want to take part of the loot for when you can get it all?"

"I don't know what you mean," she said. She was very pale.

Macaulay said: "Charles thinks Wynant wasn't here this afternoon and that you were given those securities and the check by somebody else, or perhaps stole them yourself. Is that it?" he asked me.

"Practically."

"But that's ridiculous," she insisted.

"Be sensible, Mimi," I said. "Suppose Wynant was killed three months ago and his corpse disguised as somebody else. He's supposed to have gone away leaving powers of attorney with Macaulay. All right, then, the estate's completely in Macaulay's hands forever and ever, or at least until he finishes plundering it, because you can't even – "

Macaulay stood up saying: "I know what you're getting at, Charles, but I'm – "

"Take it easy," Guild told him. "Let him have his say out."

"He killed Wynant and he killed Julia and he killed Nunheim," I assured Mimi. "What do you want to do? Be next on the list? You ought to know damned well that once you've come to his aid by saying you've seen Wynant alive – because that's his weak spot, being the only person up to now who claims to have seen Wynant since October – he's not going to take any chances on having you change your mind – not when it's only a matter of knocking you off with the same gun and putting the blame on Wynant. And what are you doing it for? For those few crummy bonds in the drawer, a fraction of what you get your hands on through your children if we prove Wynant's dead."

Mimi turned to Macaulay and said: "You son of a bitch." Guild gaped at her, more surprised by that than by anything else that had been said.

Macaulay started to move. I did not wait to see what he meant to do, but slammed his chin with my left fist. The punch was all right, it landed solidly and dropped him, but I felt a burning sensation on my left side and knew I had torn the bullet-wound open. "What do you want me to do?" I growled at Guild. "Put him in cellophane for you?"

IT WAS NEARLY three in the morning when I let myself into our apartment at the Normandie. Nora, Dorothy, and Larry Crowley were in the living-room, Nora and Larry playing backgammon, Dorothy reading a newspaper.

"Did Macaulay really kill them?" Nora asked immediately.

"Yes. Did the morning papers have anything about Wynant?"

Dorothy said: "No, just about Macaulay being arrested. Why?"

"Macaulay killed him too."

Nora said, "Really?" Larry said, "I'll be damned." Dorothy began to cry. Nora looked at Dorothy in surprise.

Dorothy sobbed: "I want to go home to Mamma."

Larry said not very eagerly: "I'll be glad to take you home if . . ."

Dorothy said she wanted to go. Nora fussed over her, but did not try to talk her out of going. Larry, trying not to look too unwilling, found his hat and coat. He and Dorothy left. Nora shut the door behind them and leaned against it. "Explain that to me, Mr. Charalambides," she said. I shook my head.

She sat on the sofa beside me. "Now out with it. If you skip a single word, I'll – "

"I'd have to have a drink before I could do any talking."

She cursed me and brought me a drink. "Has he confessed?"

"Why should he? You can't plead guilty of murder in the first degree. There were too many murders – and at least two

424

of them were too obviously done in cold blood – for the District Attorney to let him plead guilty of second-degree murder. There's nothing for him to do but fight it out."

"But he did commit them?"

"Sure."

She pushed my glass down from my mouth. "Stop stalling and tell me about it."

"Well, it figures out that he and Julia had been gypping Wynant for some time. He'd dropped a lot of money in the market and he'd found out about her past – as Morelli hinted – and the pair of them teamed up on the old man. We're sicking accountants on Macaulay's books and Wynant's and shouldn't have much trouble tracing some of the loot from one to the other."

"Then you don't know positively that he was robbing Wynant?"

"Sure we know. It doesn't click any other way. The chances are Wynant was going away on a trip the 3rd of October, because he did draw five thousand dollars out of the bank in cash, but he didn't close up his shop and give up his apartment. That was done by Macaulay a few days later. Wynant was killed at Macaulay's in Scarsdale on the night of the 3rd. We know that because on the morning of the 4th, when Macaulay's cook, who slept at home, came to work, Macaulay met her at the door with some kind of trumped-up complaint and two weeks' wages and fired her on the spot, not letting her in the house to find any corpses or blood-stains."

"How did you find that out? Don't skip details."

"Ordinary routine. Naturally after we grabbed him we went to his office and house to see what we could find out – you know, where-were-you-on-the-night-of-June-6,-1894-stuff – and the present cook said she'd only been working for him since the 8th of October, and that led to that. We also found a table with a very faint trace of what we hope is human blood not quite scrubbed out. The scientific boys are making

425

shavings of it now to see if they can soak out any results for us."
(It turned out to be beef blood.)

"Then you're not sure he —"

"Stop saying that. Of course we're sure. That's the only way
it clicks. Wynant had found out that Julia and Macaulay were
gypping him and also thought, rightly or wrongly, that Julia
and Macaulay were cheating on him — and we know he was
jealous — so he went up there to confront him with whatever
proof he had, and Macaulay, with prison looking him in the
face, killed the old man. Now don't say we're not sure. It
doesn't make any sense otherwise. Well, there he is with a
corpse, one of the harder things to get rid of. Can I stop to take
a swallow of whiskey?"

"Just one," Nora said. "But this is just a theory, isn't it?"

"Call it any name you like. It's good enough for me."

"But I thought everybody was supposed to be considered
innocent until they were proved guilty and if there was any
reasonable doubt, they —"

"That's for juries, not detectives. You find the guy you
think did the murder and you slam him in the can and let
everybody know you think he's guilty and put his picture all
over newspapers, and the District Attorney builds up the best
theory he can on what information you've got and meanwhile
you pick up additional details here and there, and people who
recognize his picture in the paper — as well as people who'd
think he was innocent if you hadn't arrested him — come in
and tell you things about him and presently you've got him
sitting on the electric chair." (Two days later a woman in
Brooklyn identified Macaulay as a George Foley who for the
past three months had been renting an apartment from her.)

"But that seems so loose."

"When the murders are committed by mathematicians,"
I said, "you can solve them by mathematics. Most of them
aren't and this one wasn't. I don't want to go against your
idea of what's right and wrong, but when I say he probably

dissected the body so he could carry it into town in bags I'm only saying what seems most probable. That would be on the 6th of October or later, because it wasn't until then that he laid off the two mechanics Wynant had working in the shop – Prentice and McNaughton – and shut it up. So he buried Wynant under the floor, buried him with a fat man's clothes and a lame man's stick and a belt marked D. W. Q., all arranged so they wouldn't get too much of the lime – or whatever he used to eat off the dead man's features and flesh – on them, and he re-cemented the floor over the grave. Between police routine and publicity we've got more than a fair chance of finding out where he bought or otherwise got the clothes and stick and the cement." (We traced the cement to him later – he had bought it from a coal and wood dealer uptown – but had no luck with the other things.)

"I hope so," she said, not too hopefully.

"So now that's taken care of. By renewing the lease on the shop and keeping it vacant – supposedly waiting for Wynant to return – he can make sure – reasonably sure – that nobody will discover the grave, and if it is accidentally discovered, then fat Mr. D. W. Q. – by that time Wynant's bones would be pretty bare and you can't tell whether a man was thin or fat by his skeleton – was murdered by Wynant, which explains why Wynant has made himself scarce. That taken care of, Macaulay forges the power of attorney and, with Julia's help, settles down to the business of gradually transferring the late Clyde's money to themselves. Now I'm going theoretical again. Julia doesn't like murder, and she's frightened, and he's not too sure she won't weaken on him. That's why he makes her break with Morelli – giving Wynant's jealousy as an excuse. He's afraid she might confide to Morelli in a weak moment and, as the time draws near for her still closer friend, Face Peppler, to get out of prison, he gets more and more worried. He's been safe there as long as Face stayed in, because she's not likely to put anything dangerous in a letter that has to pass through the warden's hands, but now ... Well, he starts to plan, and then all hell breaks loose. Mimi and her children arrive and start hunting for Wynant and I come to town and am in touch with them and he thinks I'm helping them. He decides to play safe on Julia by putting her out of the way. Like it so far?"

"Yes, but ..."

"It gets worse as it goes along," I assured her. "On his way here for lunch that day he stops and phones his office, pretending he's Wynant, and making that appointment at the Plaza, the idea being to establish Wynant's presence in town. When he leaves here he goes to the Plaza and asks people if they've seen Wynant, to make that plausible, and for the same reason phones his office to ask if any further word has come in from Wynant, and phones Julia. She tells him she's expecting Mimi and she tells him Mimi thought she was lying when she said she didn't know where Wynant was, and Julia probably sounds pretty frightened. So he decides he's got to beat Mimi to the interview and he does. He beats it over there and kills her. He's a terrible shot. I saw him shoot during the war. It's likely he missed her with the first shot, the one that hit the telephone, and didn't succeed in killing her right away with the other four, but he probably thought she was dead, and, anyhow, he had to get out before Mimi arrived, so he dropped the piece of Wynant's chain that he had brought along as a clincher – and his having saved that for three months makes it look as if he'd intended killing her from the beginning – and scoots over to the engineer Hermann's office, where he takes advantage of the breaks and fixes himself up with an alibi. The two things he doesn't expect – couldn't very well have foreseen – are that Nunheim, hanging around trying to get at the girl, had seen him leave her apartment – may even have heard the shots – and that Mimi, with blackmail in her heart, was going to conceal the chain for use in shaking down her ex-husband. That's why he had to go down to Philadelphia and send me that wire and the letter to himself and one to Aunt

Alice later – if Mimi thinks Wynant's throwing suspicion on her she'll get mad enough to give the police the evidence she's got against him. Her desire to hurt Jorgensen nearly gummed that up, though. Macaulay, by the way, knew Jorgensen was Rosewater. Right after he killed Wynant he had detectives look Mimi and her family up in Europe – their interest in the estate made them potentially dangerous – and the detectives found out who Jorgensen was. We found the reports in Macaulay's files. He pretended he was getting the information for Wynant, of course. Then he started worrying about me, about my not thinking Wynant guilty and – "

"And why didn't you?"

"Why should he write letters antagonizing Mimi, the one who was helping him by holding back incriminating evidence? That's why I thought the chain had been planted when she did turn it in, only I was a little bit too willing to believe she had done the planting. Morelli worried Macaulay, too, because he didn't want suspicion thrown on anybody who might, in clearing themselves, throw it in the wrong direction. Mimi was all right, because she'd throw it back on Wynant, but everybody else was out. Suspicion thrown on Wynant was the one thing that was guaranteed to keep anybody from suspecting that Wynant was dead, and if Macaulay hadn't killed Wynant, then there was no reason for his having killed either of the others. The most obvious thing in the whole lay-out and the key to the whole lay-out was that Wynant had to be dead."

"You mean you thought that from the beginning?" Nora demanded, fixing me with a stern eye.

"No, darling, though I ought to be ashamed of myself for not seeing it, but once I heard there was a corpse under the floor, I wouldn't have cared if doctors swore it was a woman's, I'd have insisted it was Wynant's. It had to be. It was the right thing."

"I guess you're awfully tired. That must be what makes you talk like this."

"Then he had Nunheim to worry about too. After pointing the finger at Morelli, just to show the police he was being useful, he went to see Macaulay. I'm guessing again, sweetheart. I had a phone-call from a man who called himself Albert Norman, and the conversation ended with a noise on his end of the wire. My guess is that Nunheim went to see Macaulay and demanded some dough to keep quiet and, when Macaulay tried to bluff him, Nunheim said he'd show him and called me up to make a date with me to see if I'd buy his information – and Macaulay grabbed the phone and gave Nunheim something, if only a promise, but when Guild and I had our little talk with Nunheim, and he ran out on us, then he phoned Macaulay and demanded real action, probably a lump sum, with a promise to beat it out of town, away from us meddling sleuths. We do know he called up that afternoon – Macaulay's telephone-operator remembers a Mr. Albert Norman calling up, and she remembers that Macaulay went out right after talking to him, so don't get snooty about this – uh – reconstruction of mine. Macaulay wasn't silly enough to think Nunheim was to be trusted even if he paid him, so he lured him down to this spot he had probably picked out ahead of time and let him have it – and that took care of that."

"Probably," Nora said.

"It's a word you've got to use a lot in this business. The letter to Gilbert was only for the purpose of showing that Wynant had a key to the girl's apartment, and sending Gilbert there was only a way of making sure that he'd fall into the hands of the police, who'd squeeze him and not let him keep the information about the letter and the key to himself. Then Mimi finally comes through with the watch-chain, but meanwhile another worry comes up. She's persuaded Guild to suspect me a little. I've an idea that when Macaulay came to me this morning with that hooey he intended to get me up to Scarsdale and knock me off, making me number three on the list of Wynant's victims. Maybe he just changed his mind, maybe he thought I was suspicious, too willing to go up there without policemen. Anyhow, Gilbert's lie about having seen Wynant gave him another idea. If he could get somebody to say they had seen Wynant and stick to it . . . Now this part we know definitely."

"Thank God."

"He went to see Mimi this afternoon – riding up two floors above hers and walking down so the elevator boys wouldn't remember having carried him to her floor – and made her a proposition. He told her there was no question about Wynant's guilt, but that it was doubtful if the police would ever catch him. Meanwhile he, Macaulay, had the whole estate in his hands. He couldn't take a chance on appropriating any of it, but he'd fix it so she could – if she would split with him. He'd give her these bonds he had in his pocket and this check, but she'd have to say that Wynant had given them to her and she'd have to send this note, which he also had, over to Macaulay as if from Wynant. He assured her that Wynant, a fugitive, could not show up to deny his gift, and, except for herself and her children, there was no one else who had any interest in the estate, any reason for questioning the deal. Mimi's not very sensible where she sees a chance to make a profit, so it was all OK with her, and he had what he wanted – somebody who'd seen Wynant alive. He warned her that everybody would think Wynant was paying her for some service, but if she simply denied it there would be nothing anybody could prove."

"Then what he told you this morning about Wynant instructing him to give her any amount she asked for was simply in preparation?"

"Maybe, maybe it was an earlier fumbling towards that idea. Now are you satisfied with what we've got on him?"

"Yes, in a way. There seems to be enough of it, but it's not very neat."

"It's neat enough to send him to the chair," I said, "and that's all that counts. It takes care of all the angles and I can't think of any other theory that would. Naturally it wouldn't hurt to find the pistol, and the typewriter he used for the Wynant letters, and they must be somewhere around where he can get at them when he needs them. (We found them in the Brooklyn apartment he had rented as George Foley.)

"Have it your own way," she said, "but I always thought detectives waited until they had every little detail fixed in – "

"And then wonder why the suspect's had time to get to the farthest country that has no extradition treaty."

She laughed. "All right, all right. Still want to leave for San Francisco tomorrow?"

"Not unless you're in a hurry. Let's stick around awhile. This excitement has put us behind in our drinking."

"It's all right by me. What do you think will happen to Mimi and Dorothy and Gilbert now?"

"Nothing new. They'll go on being Mimi and Dorothy and Gilbert just as you and I will go on being us and the Quinns will go on being the Quinns. Murder doesn't round out anybody's life except the murdered's and sometimes the murderer's."

"That may be," Nora said, "but it's all pretty unsatisfactory."

RED HARVEST

To Joseph Thompson Shaw

1 A WOMAN IN GREEN AND A MAN IN GRAY

I FIRST HEARD Personville called Poisonville by a red-haired mucker named Hickey Dewey in the Big Ship in Butte. He also called his shirt a shoit. I didn't think anything of what he had done to the city's name. Later I heard men who could manage their r's give it the same pronunciation. I still didn't see anything in it but the meaningless sort of humor that used to make richardsnary the thieves' word for dictionary. A few years later I went to Personville and learned better.

Using one of the phones in the station, I called the *Herald*, asked for Donald Willsson, and told him I had arrived.

"Will you come out to my house at ten this evening?" He had a pleasantly crisp voice. "It's 2101 Mountain Boulevard. Take a Broadway car, get off at Laurel Avenue, and walk two blocks west."

I promised to do that. Then I rode up to the Great Western Hotel, dumped my bags, and went out to look at the city.

The city wasn't pretty. Most of its builders had gone in for gaudiness. Maybe they had been successful at first. Since then the smelters whose brick stacks stuck up tall against a gloomy mountain to the south had yellow-smoked everything into uniform dinginess. The result was an ugly city of forty thousand people, set in an ugly notch between two ugly mountains that had been all dirtied up by mining. Spread over this was a grimy sky that looked as if it had come out of the smelters' stacks.

The first policeman I saw needed a shave. The second had a couple of buttons off his shabby uniform. The third stood in the center of the city's main intersection – Broadway and

Union Street – directing traffic, with a cigar in one corner of his mouth. After that I stopped checking them up.

At nine-thirty I caught a Broadway car and followed the directions Donald Willsson had given me. They brought me to a house set in a hedged grassplot on a corner.

The maid who opened the door told me Mr. Willsson was not home. While I was explaining that I had an appointment with him a slender blonde woman of something less than thirty in green crêpe came to the door. When she smiled her blue eyes didn't lose their stoniness. I repeated my explanation to her.

"My husband isn't in now." A barely noticeable accent slurred her s's. "But if he's expecting you he'll probably be home shortly."

She took me upstairs to a room on the Laurel Avenue side of the house, a brown and red room with a lot of books in it. We sat in leather chairs, half facing each other, half facing a burning coal grate, and she set about learning my business with her husband.

"Do you live in Personville?" she asked first.

"No. San Francisco."

"But this isn't your first visit?"

"Yes."

"Really? How do you like our city?"

"I haven't seen enough of it to know." That was a lie. I had. "I got in only this afternoon."

Her shiny eyes stopped prying while she said:

"You'll find it a dreary place." She returned to her digging with: "I suppose all mining towns are like this. Are you engaged in mining?"

"Not just now."

She looked at the clock on the mantel and said:

"It's inconsiderate of Donald to bring you out here and then keep you waiting, at this time of night, long after business hours."

I said that was all right.

"Though perhaps it isn't a business matter," she suggested.

I didn't say anything.

She laughed – a short laugh with something sharp in it.

"I'm really not ordinarily so much of a busybody as you probably think," she said gaily. "But you're so excessively secretive that I can't help being curious. You aren't a boot-legger, are you? Donald changes them so often."

I let her get whatever she could out of a grin.

A telephone-bell rang downstairs. Mrs. Willsson stretched her green-slippered feet out towards the burning coal and pretended she hadn't heard the bell. I didn't know why she thought that necessary.

She began: "I'm afraid I'll ha –" and stopped to look at the maid in the doorway.

The maid said Mrs. Willsson was wanted at the phone. She excused herself and followed the maid out. She didn't go downstairs, but spoke over an extension within earshot.

I heard: "Mrs. Willsson speaking.... Yes.... I beg your pardon?... Who?... Can't you speak a little louder?... *What?*... Yes.... Yes.... Who is this?... Hello! Hello!"

The telephone-hook rattled. Her steps sounded down the hallway – rapid steps.

I set fire to a cigarette and stared at it until I heard her going down the steps. Then I went to a window, lifted an edge of the blind, and looked out at Laurel Avenue, and at the square white garage that stood in the rear of the house on that side.

Presently a slender woman in dark coat and hat came into sight hurrying from house to garage. It was Mrs. Willsson. She drove away in a Buick coupé. I went back to my chair and waited.

Three-quarters of an hour went by. At five minutes after eleven, automobile brakes screeched outside. Two minutes later Mrs. Willsson came into the room. She had taken off hat and coat. Her face was white, her eyes almost black.

"I'm awfully sorry," she said, her tight-lipped mouth moving jerkily, "but you've had all this waiting for nothing. My husband won't be home tonight."

I said I would get in touch with him at the *Herald* in the morning.

I went away wondering why the green toe of her left slipper was dark and damp with something that could have been blood.

I walked over to Broadway and caught a street-car. Three blocks north of my hotel I got off to see what the crowd was doing around a side-entrance of the City Hall.

Thirty or forty men and a sprinkling of women stood on the sidewalk looking at a door marked *Police Department*. There were men from mines and smelters still in their working clothes, gaudy boys from pool rooms and dance halls, sleek men with slick pale faces, men with the dull look of respectable husbands, a few just as respectable and dull women, and some ladies of the night.

On the edge of this congregation I stopped beside a square-set man in rumpled gray clothes. His face was grayish too, even the thick lips, though he wasn't much older than thirty. His face was broad, thick-featured and intelligent. For color he depended on a red windsor tie that blossomed over his gray flannel shirt.

"What's the rumpus?" I asked him.

He looked at me carefully before he replied, as if he wanted to be sure that the information was going into safe hands. His eyes were gray as his clothes, but not so soft.

"Don Willsson's gone to sit on the right hand of God, if God don't mind looking at bullet-holes."

"Who shot him?" I asked.

The gray man scratched the back of his neck and said:

440

"Somebody with a gun."

I wanted information, not wit. I would have tried my luck with some other member of the crowd if the red tie hadn't interested me. I said:

"I'm a stranger in town. Hang the Punch and Judy on me. That's what strangers are for."

"Donald Willsson, Esquire, publisher of the *Morning* and *Evening Herald*s, was found in Hurricane Street a little while ago, shot very dead by parties unknown," he recited in a rapid sing-song. "Does that keep your feelings from being hurt?"

"Thanks." I put out a finger and touched a loose end of his tie. "Mean anything? Or just wearing it?"

"I'm Bill Quint."

"The hell you are!" I exclaimed, trying to place the name. "By God, I'm glad to meet you!"

I dug out my card case and ran through the collection of credentials I had picked up here and there by one means or another. The red card was the one I wanted. It identified me as Henry F. Neill, A. B. seaman, member in good standing of the Industrial Workers of the World. There wasn't a word of truth in it.

I passed this card to Bill Quint. He read it carefully, front and back, returned it to my hand, and looked me over from hat to shoes, not trustfully.

"He's not going to die any more," he said. "Which way you going?"

"Any."

We walked down the street together, turned a corner, aimlessly as far as I knew.

"What brought you in here, if you're a sailor?" he asked casually.

"Where'd you get that idea?"

"There's the card."

"I got another that proves I'm a timber beast," I said. "If you want me to be a miner I'll get one for that tomorrow."

441

"You won't. I run 'em here."

"Suppose you got a wire from Chi?" I asked.

"Hell with Chi! I run 'em here." He nodded at a restaurant-door and asked: "Drink?"

"Only when I can get it."

We went through the restaurant, up a flight of steps, and into a narrow second-story room with a long bar and a row of tables. Bill Quint nodded and said, "Hullo!" to some of the boys and girls at tables and bar, and steered me into one of the green-curtained booths that lined the wall opposite the bar.

We spent the next two hours drinking whiskey and talking.

The gray man didn't think I had any right to the card I had showed him, nor to the other one I had mentioned. He didn't think I was a good wobbly. As chief muckademuck of the I. W. W. in Personville, he considered it his duty to get the low-down on me, and to not let himself be pumped about radical affairs while he was doing it.

That was all right with me. I was interested in Personville affairs. He didn't mind discussing them between casual pokings into my business with the red cards.

What I got out of him amounted to this:

For forty years old Elihu Willsson – father of the man who had been killed this night – had owned Personville, heart, soul, skin and guts. He was president and majority stockholder of the Personville Mining Corporation, ditto of the First National Bank, owner of the *Morning Herald*, and *Evening Herald*, the city's only newspapers, and at least part owner of nearly every other enterprise of any importance. Along with these pieces of property he owned a United States senator, a couple of representatives, the governor, the mayor, and most of the state legislature. Elihu Willsson was Personville, and he was almost the whole state.

Back in the war days the I. W. W. – in full bloom then throughout the West – had lined up the Personville Mining Corporation's help. The help hadn't been exactly pampered.

They used their new strength to demand the things they wanted. Old Elihu gave them what he had to give them, and bided his time.

In 1921 it came. Business was rotten. Old Elihu didn't care whether he shut down for a while or not. He tore up the agreements he had made with his men and began kicking them back into their pre-war circumstances.

Of course the help yelled for help. Bill Quint was sent out from I. W. W. headquarters in Chicago to give them some action. He was against a strike, an open walk-out. He advised the old sabotage racket, staying on the job and gumming things up from the inside. But that wasn't active enough for the Personville crew. They wanted to put themselves on the map, make labor history.

They struck.

The strike lasted eight months. Both sides bled plenty. The wobblies had to do their own bleeding. Old Elihu hired gun-men, strike-breakers, national guardsmen and even parts of the regular army, to do his. When the last skull had been cracked, the last rib kicked in, organized labor in Personville was a used firecracker.

But, said Bill Quint, old Elihu didn't know his Italian history. He won the strike, but he lost his hold on the city and the state. To beat the miners he had to let his hired thugs run wild. When the fight was over he couldn't get rid of them. He had given his city to them and he wasn't strong enough to take it away from them. Personville looked good to them and they took it over. They had won his strike for him and they took the city for their spoils. He couldn't openly break with them. They had too much on him. He was responsible for all they had done during the strike.

Bill Quint and I were both fairly mellow by the time we had got this far. He emptied his glass again, pushed his hair out of his eyes and brought his history up to date:

"The strongest of 'em now is probably Pete the Finn. This stuff we're drinking's his. Then there's Lew Yard. He's got a loan shop down on Parker Street, does a lot of bail bond business, handles most of the burg's hot stuff, so they tell me, and is pretty thick with Noonan, the chief of police. This kid Max Thaler – Whisper – had got a lot of friends too. A little slick dark guy with something wrong with his throat. Can't talk. Gambler. Those three, with Noonan, just about help Elihu run his city – help him more than he wants. But he's got to play with 'em or else –"

"This fellow who was knocked off tonight – Elihu's son – where did he stand?" I asked.

"Where papa put him, and he's where papa put him now."

"You mean the old man had him –?"

"Maybe, but that's not my guess. This Don just came home and began running the papers for the old man. It wasn't like the old devil, even if he was getting close to the grave, to let anybody cop anything from him without hitting back. But he had to be cagey with these guys. He brought the boy and his French wife home from Paris and used him for his monkey – a damned nice fatherly trick. Don starts a reform campaign in the papers. Clear the burg of vice and corruption – which means clear it of Pete and Lew and Whisper, if it goes far enough. Get it? The old man's using the boy to shake 'em loose. I guess they got tired of being shook."

"There seems to be a few things wrong with that guess," I said.

"There's more than a few things wrong with everything in this lousy burg. Had enough of this paint?"

I said I had. We went down to the street. Bill Quint told me he was living in the Miners' Hotel in Forest Street. His way home ran past my hotel, so we walked down together. In front of my hotel a beefy fellow with the look of a plain-clothes man stood on the curb and talked to the occupant of a Stutz touring car.

"That's Whisper in the car," Bill Quint told me.

I looked past the beefy man and saw Thaler's profile. It was young, dark and small, with pretty features as regular as if they had been cut by a die.

"He's cute," I said.

"Uh-huh," the gray man agreed, "and so's dynamite."

THE *MORNING HERALD* gave two pages to Donald Willsson and his death. His picture showed a pleasant intelligent face with curly hair, smiling eyes and mouth, a cleft chin and a striped necktie.

The story of his death was simple. At ten-forty the previous night he had been shot four times in stomach, chest and back, dying immediately. The shooting had taken place in the eleven-hundred block of Hurricane Street. Residents of that block who looked out after hearing the shots saw the dead man lying on the sidewalk. A man and a woman were bending over him. The street was too dark for anyone to see anybody or anything clearly. The man and woman had disappeared before anybody else reached the street. Nobody knew what they looked like. Nobody had seen them go away.

Six shots had been fired at Willsson from a .32 caliber pistol. Two of them had missed him, going into the front wall of a house. Tracing the course of these two bullets, the police had learned that the shooting had been done from a narrow alley across the street. That was all anybody knew.

Editorially the *Morning Herald* gave a summary of the dead man's short career as a civic reformer and expressed a belief that he had been killed by some of the people who didn't want Personville cleaned up. The *Herald* said the chief of police could best show his own lack of complicity by speedily catching and convicting the murderer or murderers. The editorial was blunt and bitter.

I finished it with my second cup of coffee, jumped a Broadway car, dropped off at Laurel Avenue, and turned down towards the dead man's house.

I was half a block from it when something changed my mind and my destination.

A smallish young man in three shades of brown crossed the street ahead of me. His dark profile was pretty. He was Max Thaler, alias Whisper. I reached the corner of Mountain Boulevard in time to catch the flash of his brown-covered rear leg vanishing into the late Donald Willsson's doorway.

I went back to Broadway, found a drug-store with a phone-booth in it, searched the directory for Elihu Willsson's residence number, called it, told somebody who claimed to be the old man's secretary that I had been brought from San Francisco by Donald Willsson, that I knew something about his death, and that I wanted to see his father.

When I made it emphatic enough I got an invitation to call.

The czar of Poisonville was propped up in bed when his secretary – a noiseless slim sharp-eyed man of forty – brought me into the bedroom.

The old man's head was small and almost perfectly round under its close-cut crop of white hair. His ears were too small and plastered too flat to the sides of his head to spoil the spherical effect. His nose also was small, carrying down the curve of his bony forehead. Mouth and chin were straight lines chopping the sphere off. Below them a short thick neck ran down into white pajamas between square meaty shoulders. One of his arms was outside the covers, a short compact arm that ended in a thick-fingered blunt hand. His eyes were round, blue, small and watery. They looked as if they were hiding behind the watery film and under the bushy white brows only until the time came to jump out and grab something. He wasn't the sort of man whose pocket you'd try to pick unless you had a lot of confidence in your fingers.

447

He ordered me into a bedside chair with a two-inch jerk of his round head, chased the secretary away with another, and asked:

"What's this about my son?"

His voice was harsh. His chest had too much and his mouth too little to do with his words for them to be very clear.

"I'm a Continental Detective Agency operative, San Francisco branch," I told him. "A couple of days ago we got a check from your son and a letter asking that a man be sent here to do some work for him. I'm the man. He told me to come out to his house last night. I did, but he didn't show up. When I got downtown I learned he had been killed."

Elihu Willsson peered suspiciously at me and asked:

"Well, what of it?"

"While I was waiting your daughter-in-law got a phone-message, went out, came back with what looked like blood on her shoe, and told me her husband wouldn't be home. He was shot at ten-forty. She went out at ten-twenty, came back at eleven-five."

The old man sat straight up in bed and called young Mrs. Willsson a flock of things. When he ran out of words of that sort he still had some breath left. He used it to shout at me:

"Is she in jail?"

I said I didn't think so.

He didn't like her not being in jail. He was nasty about it. He bawled a lot of things I didn't like, winding up with:

"What the hell are you waiting for?"

He was too old and too sick to be smacked. I laughed and said:

"For evidence."

"Evidence? What do you need? You've –"

"Don't be a chump," I interrupted his bawling. "Why should she kill him?"

"Because she's a French hussy! Because she –"

The secretary's frightened face appeared at the door.

448

"Get out of here!" the old man roared at it, and the face went.

"She jealous?" I asked before he could go on with his shouting. "And if you don't yell maybe I'll be able to hear you anyway. My deafness is a lot better since I've been eating yeast."

He put a fist on top of each hump his thighs made in the covers and pushed his square chin at me.

"Old as I am and sick as I am," he said very deliberately, "I've a great mind to get up and kick your behind."

I paid no attention to that, repeating:

"Was she jealous?"

"She was," he said, not yelling now, "and domineering, and spoiled, and suspicious, and greedy, and mean, and unscrupulous, and deceitful, and selfish, and damned bad – altogether damned bad!"

"Any reason for her jealousy?"

"I hope so," he said bitterly. "I'd hate to think a son of mine would be faithful to her. Though likely enough he was. He'd do things like that."

"But you don't know any reason why she should have killed him?"

"Don't know any reason?" He was bellowing again. "Haven't I been telling you that –"

"Yeah. But none of that means anything. It's kind of childish."

The old man flung the covers back from his legs and started to get out of bed. Then he thought better of it, raised his red face and roared:

"Stanley!"

The door opened to let the secretary glide in.

"Throw this bastard out!" his master ordered, waving a fist at me.

The secretary turned to me. I shook my head and suggested:

"Better get help."

He frowned. We were about the same age. He was weedy, nearly a head taller than I, but fifty pounds lighter. Some of my hundred and ninety pounds were fat, but not all of them. The secretary fidgeted, smiled apologetically, and went away.

"What I was about to say," I told the old man: "I intended talking to your son's wife this morning. But I saw Max Thaler go into the house, so I postponed my visit."

Elihu Willsson carefully pulled the covers up over his legs again, leaned his head back on the pillows, screwed his eyes up at the ceiling, and said:

"Hm-m-m, so that's the way it is, is it?"

"Mean anything?"

"She killed him," he said certainly. "That's what it means."

Feet made noises in the hall, huskier feet than the secretary's. When they were just outside the door I began a sentence:

"You were using your son to run a —"

"Get out of here!" the old man yelled at those in the doorway. "And keep that door closed." He glowered at me and demanded: "What was I using my son for?"

"To put the knife in Thaler, Yard and the Finn."

"You're a liar."

"I didn't invent the story. It's all over Personville."

"It's a lie. I gave him the papers. He did what he wanted with them."

"You ought to explain that to your playmates. They'd believe you."

"What they believe be damned! What I'm telling you is so."

"What of it? Your son won't come back to life just because he was killed by mistake — if he was."

"That woman killed him."

"Maybe."

"Damn you and your maybes! She did."

"Maybe. But the other angle has got to be looked into too — the political end. You can tell me —"

"I can tell you that that French hussy killed him, and I can tell you that any other damned numbskull notions you've got are way off the lode."

"But they've got to be looked into," I insisted. "And you know the inside of Personville politics better than anyone else I'm likely to find. He was your son. The least you can do is —"

"The least I can do," he bellowed, "is tell you to get to hell back to Frisco, you and your numbskull —"

I got up and said unpleasantly:

"I'm at the Great Western Hotel. Don't bother me unless you want to talk sense for a change."

I went out of the bedroom and down the stairs. The secretary hovered around the bottom step, smiling apologetically.

"A fine old rowdy," I growled.

"A remarkably vital personality," he murmured.

At the office of the *Herald*, I hunted up the murdered man's secretary. She was a small girl of nineteen or twenty with wide chestnut eyes, light brown hair and a pale pretty face. Her name was Lewis.

She said she hadn't known anything about my being called to Personville by her employer.

"But then," she explained, "Mr. Willsson always liked to keep everything to himself as long as he could. It was — I don't think he trusted anybody here, completely."

"Not you?"

She flushed and said:

"No. But of course he had been here such a short while and didn't know any of us very well."

"There must have been more to it than that."

"Well," she bit her lip and made a row of forefinger prints down the polished edge of the dead man's desk, "his father wasn't — wasn't in sympathy with what he was doing. Since his father really owned the papers, I suppose it was natural for

Mr. Donald to think some of the employees might be more loyal to Mr. Elihu than to him."

"The old man wasn't in favor of the reform campaign? Why did he stand for it, if the papers were his?"

She bent her head to study the fingerprints she had made. Her voice was low.

"It's not easy to understand unless you know – The last time Mr. Elihu was taken sick he sent for Donald – Mr. Donald. Mr. Donald had lived in Europe most of his life, you know. Dr. Pride told Mr. Elihu that he'd have to give up the management of his affairs, so he cabled his son to come home. But when Mr. Donald got here Mr. Elihu couldn't make up his mind to let go of everything. But he wanted Mr. Donald to stay here, so he gave him the newspapers – that is, made him publisher. Mr. Donald liked that. He had been interested in journalism in Paris. When he found out how terrible everything was here – in civic affairs and so on – he started that reform campaign. He didn't know – he had been away since he was a boy – he didn't know –"

"He didn't know his father was in it as deep as anybody else," I helped her along.

She squirmed a little over her examination of the fingerprints, didn't contradict me, and went on:

"Mr. Elihu and he had a quarrel. Mr. Elihu told him to stop stirring things up, but he wouldn't stop. Maybe he would have stopped if he had known – all there was to know. But I don't suppose it would have occurred to him that his father was really seriously implicated. And his father wouldn't tell him. I suppose it would be hard for a father to tell a son a thing like that. He threatened to take the papers away from Mr. Donald. I don't know whether he intended to or not. But he was taken sick again, and everything went along as it did."

"Donald Willsson didn't confide in you?" I asked.

"No." It was almost a whisper.

"Then, you learned all this where?"

"I'm trying – trying to help you learn who murdered him," she said earnestly. "You've no right to –"

"You'll help me most just now by telling me where you learned all this," I insisted.

She stared at the desk, chewing her lower lip. I waited. Presently she said:

"My father is Mr. Willsson's secretary."

"Thanks."

"But you mustn't think that we –"

"It's nothing to me," I assured her. "What was Willsson doing in Hurricane Street last night when he had a date with me at his house?"

She said she didn't know. I asked her if she had heard him tell me, over the phone, to come to his house at ten o'clock. She said she had.

"What did he do after that? Try to remember every least thing that was said and done from then until you left at the end of the day."

She leaned back in her chair, shut her eyes and wrinkled her forehead.

"You called up – if it was you he told to come to his house – at about two o'clock. After that Mr. Donald dictated some letters, one to a paper mill, one to Senator Keefer about some changes in post office regulations, and – Oh, yes! He went out for about twenty minutes, a little before three. And before he went he wrote out a check."

"Who for?"

"I don't know, but I saw him writing it."

"Where's his check book? Carry it with him?"

"It's here." She jumped up, went around to the front of his desk, and tried the top drawer. "Locked."

I joined her, straightened out a wire clip, and with that and a blade of my knife fiddled the drawer open.

453

The girl took out a thin, flat First National Bank check book. The last used stub was marked $5,000. Nothing else. No name. No explanation.

"He went out with this check," I said, "and was gone twenty minutes? Long enough to get to the bank and back?"

"It wouldn't have taken him more than five minutes to get there."

"Didn't anything else happen before he wrote out the check? Think. Any messages? Letters? Phone-calls?"

"Let's see." She shut her eyes again. "He was dictating some mail and – Oh, how stupid of me! He did have a phone-call. He said: 'Yes, I can be there at ten, but I shall have to hurry away.' Then again he said: 'Very well, at ten.' That was all he said except, 'Yes, yes,' several times."

"Talking to a man or a woman?"

"I didn't know."

"Think. There'd be a difference in his voice."

She thought and said:

"Then it was a woman."

"Which of you – you or he – left first in the evening?"

"I did. He – I told you my father is Mr. Elihu's secretary. He and Mr. Donald had an engagement for the early part of the evening – something about the paper's finances. Father came in a little after five. They were going to dinner together, I think."

That was all the Lewis girl could give me. She knew nothing that would explain Willsson's presence in the eleven-hundred block of Hurricane Street, she said. She admitted knowing nothing about Mrs. Willsson.

We frisked the dead man's desk, and dug up nothing in any way informative. I went up against the girls at the switchboard, and learned nothing. I put in an hour's work on messengers, city editors, and the like, and my pumping brought up nothing. The dead man, as his secretary said, had been a good hand at keeping his affairs to himself.

3   DINAH BRAND

AT THE FIRST National Bank I got hold of an assistant cashier named Albury, a nice-looking blond youngster of twenty-five or so.

"I certified the check for Willsson," he said after I had explained what I was up to. "It was drawn to the order of Dinah Brand – $5,000."

"Know who she is?"

"Oh, yes! I know her."

"Mind telling me what you know about her?"

"Not at all. I'd be glad to, but I'm already eight minutes overdue at a meeting with –"

"Can you have dinner with me this evening and give it to me then?"

"That'll be fine," he said.

"Seven o'clock at the Great Western?"

"Righto."

"I'll run along and let you get to your meeting, but tell me, has she an account here?"

"Yes, and she deposited the check this morning. The police have it."

"Yeah? And where does she live?"

"1232 Hurricane Street."

I said: "Well, well!" and, "See you tonight," and went away.

My next stop was in the office of the chief of police, in the City Hall.

Noonan, the chief, was a fat man with twinkling greenish eyes set in a round jovial face. When I told him what I was

455

doing in his city he seemed glad of it. He gave me a hand-shake, a cigar and a chair.

"Now," he said when we were settled, "tell me who turned the trick."

"The secret's safe with me."

"You and me both," he said cheerfully through smoke. "But what do you guess?"

"I'm not good at guessing, especially when I haven't got the facts."

"'Twon't take long to give you all the facts there is," he said. "Willsson got a five-grand check in Dinah Brand's name certi-fied yesterday just before bank closing. Last night he was killed by slugs from a .32 less than a block from her house. People that heard the shooting saw a man and a woman bending over the remains. Bright and early this morning the said Dinah Brand deposits the said check in the said bank. Well?"

"Who is this Dinah Brand?"

The chief dumped the ash off his cigar in the center of his desk, flourished the cigar in his fat hand, and said:

"A soiled dove, as the fellow says, a de luxe hustler, a big-league gold-digger."

"Gone up against her yet?"

"No. There's a couple of slants to be taken care of first. We're keeping an eye on her and waiting. This I've told you is under the hat."

"Yeah. Now listen to this," and I told him what I had seen and heard while waiting in Donald Willsson's house the pre-vious night.

When I had finished the chief bunched his fat mouth, whistled softly, and exclaimed:

"Man, that's an interesting thing you've been telling me! So it was blood on her slipper? And she said her husband wouldn't be home?"

"That's what I took it for," I said to the first question, and, "Yeah," to the second.

"Have you done any talking to her since then?" he asked.

"No. I was up that way this morning, but a young fellow named Thaler went into the house ahead of me, so I put off my visit."

"Grease us twice!" His greenish eyes glittered happily. "Are you telling me the Whisper was there?"

"Yeah."

He threw his cigar on the floor, stood up, planted his fat hands on the desk-top, and leaned over them towards me, oozing delight from every pore.

"Man, you've done something," he purred. "Dinah Brand is this Whisper's woman. Let's me and you just go out and kind of talk to the widow."

We climbed out of the chief's car in front of Mrs. Willsson's residence. The chief stopped for a second with one foot on the bottom step to look at the black crêpe hanging over the bell. Then he said, "Well, what's got to be done has got to be done," and we went up the steps.

Mrs. Willsson wasn't anxious to see us, but people usually see the chief of police if he insists. This one did. We were taken upstairs to where Donald Willsson's widow sat in the library. She was in black. Her blue eyes had frost in them.

Noonan and I took turns mumbling condolences and then he began:

"We just wanted to ask you a couple of questions. For instance, like where'd you go last night?"

She looked disagreeably at me, then back to the chief, frowned, and spoke haughtily:

"May I ask why I am being questioned in this manner?"

I wondered how many times I had heard that question, word for word and tone for tone, while the chief, disregarding it, went on amiably:

457

"And then there was something about one of your shoes being stained. The right one, or maybe the left. Anyways it was one or the other."

A muscle began twitching in her upper lip.

"Was that all?" the chief asked me. Before I could answer he made a clucking noise with his tongue and turned his genial face to the woman again. "I almost forgot. There was a matter of how you knew your husband wouldn't be home."

She got up, unsteadily, holding the back of her chair with one white hand.

"I'm sure you'll excuse –"

"'S all right." The chief made a big-hearted gesture with one beefy paw. "We don't want to bother you. Just where you went, and about the shoe, and how you knew he wasn't coming back. And, come to think of it, there's another – What Thaler wanted here this morning."

Mrs. Willsson sat down again, very rigidly. The chief looked at her. A smile that tried to be tender made funny lines and humps in his fat face. After a little while her shoulders began to relax, her chin went lower, a curve came in her back.

I put a chair facing her and sat on it.

"You'll have to tell us, Mrs. Willsson," I said, making it as sympathetic as I could. "These things have got to be explained."

"Do you think I have anything to hide?" she asked defiantly, sitting up straight and stiff again, turning each word out very precisely, except that the s's were a bit slurred. "I did go out. The stain was blood. I knew my husband was dead. Thaler came to see me about my husband's death. Are your questions answered now?"

"We knew all that," I said. "We're asking you to explain them."

She stood up again, said angrily:

"I dislike your manner. I refuse to submit to –"

Noonan said:

"That's perfectly all right, Mrs. Willsson, only we'll have to ask you to go down to the Hall with us."

She turned her back to him, took a deep breath and threw words at me:

"While we were waiting here for Donald I had a telephone-call. It was a man who wouldn't give his name. He said Donald had gone to the home of a woman named Dinah Brand with a check for five thousand dollars. He gave me her address. Then I drove out there and waited down the street in the car until Donald came out.

"While I was waiting there I saw Max Thaler, whom I knew by sight. He went to the woman's house, but didn't go in. He went away. Then Donald came out and walked down the street. He didn't see me. I didn't want him to. I intended to drive home – get here before he came. I had just started the engine when I heard the shots, and I saw Donald fall. I got out of the car and ran over to him. He was dead. I was frantic. Then Thaler came. He said if I were found there they would say I had killed him. He made me run back to the car and drive home."

Tears were in her eyes. Through the water her eyes studied my face, apparently trying to learn how I took the story. I didn't say anything. She asked:

"Is that what you wanted?"

"Practically," Noonan said. He had walked around to one side. "What did Thaler say this afternoon?"

"He urged me to keep quiet." Her voice had become small and flat. "He said either or both of us would be suspected if anyone learned we were there, because Donald had been killed coming from the woman's house after giving her money."

"Where did the shots come from?" the chief asked.

"I don't know. I didn't see anything – except – when I looked up – Donald falling."

"Did Thaler fire them?"

DASHIELL HAMMETT

"No," she said quickly. Then her mouth and eyes spread.
She put a hand to her breast. "I don't know. I didn't think so,
and he said he didn't. I don't know where he was. I don't
know why I never thought he might have."

"What do you think now?" Noonan asked.

"He – he may have."

The chief winked at me, an athletic wink in which all his
facial muscles took part, and cast a little farther back:

"And you don't know who called you up?"

"He wouldn't tell me his name."

"Didn't recognize his voice?"

"No."

"What kind of voice was it?"

"He talked in an undertone, as if afraid of being overheard.
I had difficulty understanding him."

"He whispered?" The chief's mouth hung open as the last
sound left it. His greenish eyes sparkled greedily between their
pads of fat.

"Yes, a hoarse whisper."

The chief shut his mouth with a click, opened it again to say
persuasively:

"You've heard Thaler talk. . . ."

The woman started and stared big-eyed from the chief
to me.

"It was he," she cried. "It was he."

Robert Albury, the young assistant cashier of the First National
Bank, was sitting in the lobby when I returned to the Great
Western Hotel. We went up to my room, had some ice-water
brought, used its ice to put chill in Scotch, lemon juice, and
grenadine, and then went down to the dining-room.

"Now tell me about the lady," I said when we were working on the soup.

"Have you seen her yet?" he asked.

"Not yet."

"But you've heard something about her?"

"Only that she's an expert in her line."

"She is," he agreed. "I suppose you'll see her. You'll be disappointed at first. Then, without being able to say how or when it happened, you'll find you've forgotten your disappointment, and the first thing you know you'll be telling her your life's history, and all your troubles and hopes." He laughed with boyish shyness. "And then you're caught, absolutely caught."

"Thanks for the warning. How'd you come by the information?"

He grinned shamefacedly across his suspended soup spoon and confessed:

"I bought it."

"Then I suppose it cost you plenty. I hear she likes *dinero*."

"She's money-mad, all right, but somehow you don't mind it. She's so thoroughly mercenary, so frankly greedy, that there's nothing disagreeable about it. You'll understand what I mean when you know her."

"Maybe. Mind telling me how you happened to part with her?"

"No, I don't mind. I spent it all, that's how."

"Cold-blooded like that?"

His face flushed a little. He nodded.

"You seem to have taken it well," I said.

"There was nothing else to do." The flush in his pleasant young face deepened and he spoke hesitantly. "It happens I owe her something for it. She – I'm going to tell you this. I want you to see this side of her. I had a little money. After that was gone – You must remember I was young and head over heels. After my money was gone there was the bank's. I had – You don't care whether I had actually done anything or was simply thinking about it. Anyway, she found it out. I never could hide anything from her. And that was the end."

"She broke off with you?"

461

"Yes, thank God! If it hadn't been for her you might be looking for me now – for embezzlement. I owe her that!" He wrinkled his forehead earnestly. "You won't say anything about this – you know what I mean. But I wanted you to know she has her good side too. You'll hear enough about the other."

"Maybe she has. Or maybe it was just that she didn't think she'd get enough to pay for the risk of being caught in a jam."

He turned this over in his mind and then shook his head.

"That may have had something to do with it, but not all."

"I gathered she was strictly pay-as-you-enter."

"How about Dan Rolff?" he asked.

"Who's he?"

"He's supposed to be her brother, or half-brother, or something of the sort. He isn't. He's a down-and-outer – t. b. He lives with her. She keeps him. She's not in love with him or anything. She simply found him somewhere and took him in."

"Any more?"

"There was that radical chap she used to run around with. It's not likely she got much money out of him."

"What radical chap?"

"He came here during the strike – Quint is his name."

"So he was on her list?"

"That's supposed to be the reason he stayed here after the strike was over."

"So he's still on her list?"

"No. She told me she was afraid of him. He had threatened to kill her."

"She seems to have had everybody on her string at one time or another," I said.

"Everybody she wanted," he said, and he said it seriously.

"Donald Willsson was the latest?" I asked.

"I don't know," he said. "I had never heard anything about them, had never seen anything. The chief of police had us try to find any checks he may have issued to her before yesterday, but we found nothing. Nobody could remember ever having seen any."

"Who was her last customer, so far as you know?"

"Lately I've seen her around town quite often with a chap named Thaler – he runs a couple of gambling houses here. They call him Whisper. You've probably heard of him."

At eight-thirty I left young Albury and set out for the Miners' Hotel in Forest Street. Half a block from the hotel I met Bill Quint.

"Hello!" I hailed him. "I was on my way down to see you."

He stopped in front of me, looked me up and down, growled:

"So you're a gum-shoe."

"That's the bunk," I complained. "I come all the way down here to rope you, and you're smarted up."

"What do you want to know now?" he asked.

"About Donald Willsson. You knew him, didn't you?"

"I knew him."

"Very well?"

"No."

"What did you think of him?"

He pursed his gray lips, by forcing breath between them made a noise like a rag tearing, and said:

"A lousy liberal."

"You know Dinah Brand?" I asked.

"I know her." His neck was shorter and thicker than it had been.

"Think she killed Willsson?"

"Sure. It's a kick in the pants."

"Then you didn't?"

"Hell, yes," he said, "the pair of us together. Got any more questions?"

"Yeah, but I'll save my breath. You'd only lie to me."

I walked back to Broadway, found a taxi, and told the driver to take me to 1232 Hurricane Street.

4   HURRICANE STREET

MY DESTINATION WAS a gray frame cottage. When I rang the bell the door was opened by a thin man with a tired face that had no color in it except a red spot the size of a half-dollar high on each cheek. This, I thought, is the lunger Dan Rolff.

"I'd like to see Miss Brand," I told him.

"What name shall I tell her?" His voice was a sick man's and an educated man's.

"It wouldn't mean anything to her. I want to see her about Willsson's death."

He looked at me with level tired dark eyes and said: "Yes?"

"I'm from the San Francisco office of the Continental Detective Agency. We're interested in the murder."

"That's nice of you," he said ironically. "Come in."

I went in, into a ground-floor room where a young woman sat at a table that had a lot of papers on it. Some of the papers were financial service bulletins, stock and bond market forecasts. One was a racing chart.

The room was disorderly, cluttered up. There were too many pieces of furniture in it, and none of them seemed to be in its proper place.

"Dinah," the lunger introduced me, "this gentleman has come from San Francisco on behalf of the Continental Detective Agency to inquire into Mr. Donald Willsson's demise."

The young woman got up, kicked a couple of newspapers out of her way, and came to me with one hand out.

She was an inch or two taller than I, which made her about five feet eight. She had a broad-shouldered, full-breasted,

465

round-hipped body and big muscular legs. The hand she gave me was soft, warm, strong. Her face was the face of a girl of twenty-five already showing signs of wear. Little lines crossed the corners of her big ripe mouth. Fainter lines were beginning to make nets around her thick-lashed eyes. They were large eyes, blue and a bit blood-shot.

Her coarse hair – brown – needed trimming and was parted crookedly. One side of her upper lip had been rouged higher than the other. Her dress was of a particularly unbecoming wine color, and it gaped here and there down one side, where she had neglected to snap the fasteners or they had popped open. There was a run down the front of her left stocking.

This was the Dinah Brand who took her pick of Poisonville's men, according to what I had been told.

"His father sent for you, of course," she said while she moved a pair of lizard-skin slippers and a cup and saucer off a chair to make room for me.

Her voice was soft, lazy.

I told her the truth:

"Donald Willsson sent for me. I was waiting to see him while he was being killed."

"Don't go away, Dan," she called to Rolff.

He came back into the room. She returned to her place at the table. He sat on the opposite side, leaning his thin face on a thin hand, looking at me without interest.

She drew her brows together, making two creases between them, and asked:

"You mean he knew someone meant to kill him?"

"I don't know. He didn't say what he wanted. Maybe just help in the reform campaign."

"But do you –"

I made a complaint:

"It's no fun being a sleuth when somebody steals your stuff, does all the questioning."

"I like to find out what's going on," she said, a little laugh gurgling down in her throat.

"I'm that way too. For instance, I'd like to know why you made him have the check certified."

Very casually, Dan Rolff shifted in his chair, leaning back, lowering his thin hands out of sight below the table's edge.

"So you found out about that?" Dinah Brand asked. She crossed left leg over right and looked down. Her eyes focused on the run in her stocking. "Honest to God, I'm going to stop wearing them!" she complained. "I'm going bare-footed. I paid five bucks for these socks yesterday. Now look at the damned things. Every day – runs, runs, runs!"

"It's no secret," I said. "I mean the check, not the runs. Noonan's got it."

She looked at Rolff, who stopped watching me long enough to nod once.

"If you talked my language," she drawled, looking narrow-eyed at me, "I might be able to give you some help."

"Maybe if I knew what it was."

"Money," she explained, "the more the better. I like it."

I became proverbial:

"Money saved is money earned. I can save you money and grief."

"That doesn't mean anything to me," she said, "though it sounds like it's meant to."

"The police haven't asked you anything about the check?"

She shook her head, no.

I said:

"Noonan's figuring on hanging the rap on you as well as on Whisper."

"Don't scare me," she lisped. "I'm only a child."

"Noonan knows that Thaler knew about the check. He knows that Thaler came here while Willsson was here, but didn't get in. He knows that Thaler was hanging around the neighborhood when Willsson was shot. He knows that Thaler and a woman were seen bending over the dead man."

The girl picked up a pencil from the table and thoughtfully scratched her cheek with it. The pencil made little curly black lines over the rouge.

Rolff's eyes had lost their weariness. They were bright, feverish, fixed on mine. He leaned forward, but kept his hands out of sight below the table.

"Those things," he said, "concern Thaler, not Miss Brand."

"Thaler and Miss Brand aren't strangers," I said. "Willsson brought a five-thousand-dollar check here, and was killed leaving. That way, Miss Brand might have had trouble cashing it – if Willsson hadn't been thoughtful enough to get it certified."

"My God!" the girl protested, "if I'd been going to kill him I'd have done it in here where nobody could have seen it, or waited until he got out of sight of the house. What kind of a dumb onion do you take me for?"

"I'm not sure you killed him," I said. "I'm just sure that the fat chief means to hang it on you."

"What are you trying to do?" she asked.

"Learn who killed him. Not who could have or might have, but who did."

"I could give you some help," she said, "but there'd have to be something in it for me."

"Safety," I reminded her, but she shook her head.

"I mean it would have to get me something in a financial way. It'd be worth something to you, and you ought to pay something, even if not a fortune."

"Can't be done." I grinned at her. "Forget the bank-roll and go in for charity. Pretend I'm Bill Quint."

Dan Rolff started up from his chair, lips white as the rest of his face. He sat down again when the girl laughed – a lazy, good-natured laugh.

"He thinks I didn't make any profit out of Bill, Dan." She leaned over and put a hand on my knee. "Suppose you knew far enough ahead that a company's employees were going to strike, and when, and then far enough ahead when they were going to call the strike off. Could you take that info and some capital to the stock market and do yourself some good playing with the company's stock? You bet you could!" she wound up triumphantly. "So don't go around thinking that Bill didn't pay his way."

"You've been spoiled," I said.

"What in the name of God's the use of being so tight?" she demanded. "It's not like it had to come out of your pocket. You've got an expense account, haven't you?"

I didn't say anything. She frowned at me, at the run in her stocking, and at Rolff. Then she said to him:

"Maybe he'd loosen up if he had a drink."

The thin man got up and went out of the room.

She pouted at me, prodded my shin with her toe, and said:

"It's not so much the money. It's the principle of the thing. If a girl's got something that's worth something to somebody, she's a boob if she doesn't collect."

I grinned.

"Why don't you be a good guy?" she begged.

Dan Rolff came in with a siphon, a bottle of gin, some lemons, and a bowl of cracked ice. We had a drink apiece. The lunger went away. The girl and I wrangled over the money question while we had more drinks. I kept trying to keep the conversation on Thaler and Willsson. She kept switching it to the money she deserved. It went on that way until the gin bottle was empty. My watch said one-fifteen.

She chewed a piece of lemon peel and said for the thirtieth or fortieth time:

"It won't come out of your pocket. What do you care?"

"It's not the money," I said, "it's the principle of the thing."

469

She made a face at me and put her glass where she thought the table was. She was eight inches wrong. I don't remember if the glass broke when it hit the floor, or what happened to it. I do remember that I was encouraged by her missing the table.

"Another thing," I opened up a new argumentative line, "I'm not sure I really need whatever you can tell me. If I have to get along without it, I think I can."

"It'll be nice if you can, but don't forget I'm the last person who saw him alive, except whoever killed him."

"Wrong," I said. "His wife saw him come out, walk away, and fall."

"His wife!"

"Yeah. She was sitting in a coupé down the street."

"How did she know he was here?"

"She says Thaler phoned her that her husband had come here with the check."

"You're trying to kid me," the girl said. "Max couldn't have known it."

"I'm telling you what Mrs. Willsson told Noonan and me."

The girl spit what was left of the lemon peel out on the floor, further disarranged her hair by running her fingers through it, wiped her mouth with the back of her hand, and slapped the table.

"All right, Mr. Knowitall," she said, "I'm going to play with you. You can think it's not going to cost you anything, but I'll get mine before we're through. You think I won't?" she challenged me, peering at me as if I were a block away.

This was no time to revive the money argument, so I said: "I hope you do." I think I said it three or four times, quite earnestly.

"I will. Now listen to me. You're drunk, and I'm drunk, and I'm just exactly drunk enough to tell you anything you want to know. That's the kind of girl I am. If I like a person I'll tell them anything they want to know. Just ask me. Go ahead, ask me."

470

I did:

"What did Willsson give you five thousand dollars for?"

"For fun." She leaned back to laugh. Then: "Listen. He was hunting for scandal. I had some of it, some affidavits and things that I thought might be good for a piece of change some day. I'm a girl that likes to pick up a little jack when she can. So I had put these things away. When Donald began going after scalps I let him know that I had these things, and that they were for sale. I gave him enough of a peep at them to let him know they were good. And they were good. Then we talked about how much. He wasn't as tight as you – nobody ever was – but he was a little bit close. So the bargain hung fire, till yesterday.

"Then I gave him the rush, phoned him and told him I had another customer for the stuff and that if he wanted it he'd have to show up that night with either five thousand smacks in cash or a certified check. That was hooey, but he hadn't been around much, so he fell for it."

"Why ten o'clock?" I asked.

"Why not? That's as good a time as any other. The main thing on a deal like that is to give them a definite time. Now you want to know why it had to be cash or a certified check? All right, I'll tell you. I'll tell you anything you want to know. That's the kind of girl I am. Always was."

She went on that way for five minutes, telling me in detail just which and what sort of a girl she was, and always had been, and why. I yes-yes'd her until I got a chance to cut in with:

"All right, now why did it have to be a certified check?"

She shut one eye, waggled a forefinger at me, and said:

"So he couldn't stop payment. Because he couldn't have used the stuff I sold him. It was good, all right. It was too good. It would have put his old man in jail with the rest of them. It would have nailed Papa Elihu tighter than anyone else."

I laughed with her while I tried to keep my head above the gin I had guzzled.

"Who else would it nail?" I asked.

"The whole damned lot of them." She waved a hand. "Max, Lew Yard, Pete, Noonan, and Elihu Willsson – the whole damned lot of them."

"Did Max Thaler know what you were doing?"

"Of course not – nobody but Donald Willsson."

"Sure of that?"

"Sure I'm sure. You don't think I was going around bragging about it ahead of time, do you?"

"Who do you think knows about it now?"

"I don't care," she said. "It was only a joke on him. He couldn't have used the stuff."

"Do you think the birds whose secrets you sold will see anything funny in it? Noonan's trying to hang the killing on you and Thaler. That means he found the stuff in Donald Willsson's pocket. They all thought old Elihu was using his son to break them, didn't they?"

"Yes, sir," she said, "and I'm one who thinks the same thing."

"You're probably wrong, but that doesn't matter. If Noonan found the things you sold Donald Willsson in his pocket, and learned you had sold them to him, why shouldn't he add that up to mean that you and your friend Thaler had gone over to old Elihu's side?"

"He can see that old Elihu would be hurt as much as anybody else."

"What was this junk you sold him?"

"They built a new City Hall three years ago," she said, "and none of them lost any money on it. If Noonan got the papers he'll pretty soon find out that they tied as much on old Elihu, or more, than on anybody else."

"That doesn't make any difference. He'll take it for granted that the old man had found an out for himself. Take my word for it, sister, Noonan and his friends think you and Thaler and Elihu are double-crossing them."

"I don't give a damn what they think," she said obstinately. "It was only a joke. That's all I meant it for. That's all it was."

"That's good," I growled. "You can go to the gallows with a clear conscience. Have you seen Thaler since the murder?"

"No, but Max didn't kill him, if that's what you think, even if he was around."

"Why?"

"Lots of reasons. First place, Max wouldn't have done it himself. He'd have had somebody else do it, and he'd have been way off with an alibi nobody could shake. Second place, Max carries a .38, and anybody he sent to do the job would have had that much gun or more. What kind of a gunman would use a .32?"

"Then who did it?"

"I've told you all I know," she said. "I've told you too much."

I stood up and said:

"No, you've told me just exactly enough."

"You mean you think you know who killed him?"

"Yeah, though there's a couple of things I'll have to cover before I make the pinch."

"Who? Who?" She stood up, suddenly almost sober, tugging at my lapels. "Tell me who did it."

"Not now."

"Be a good guy."

"Not now."

She let go my lapels, put her hands behind her, and laughed in my face.

"All right. Keep it to yourself – and try to figure out which part of what I told you is the truth."

I said:

"Thanks for the part that is, anyhow, and for the gin. And if Max Thaler means anything to you, you ought to pass him the word that Noonan's trying to rib him."

5   OLD ELIHU TALKS SENSE

IT WAS CLOSE to two-thirty in the morning when I reached the hotel. With my key the night clerk gave me a memorandum that asked me to call Poplar 605. I knew the number. It was Elihu Willsson's.

"When did this come?" I asked the clerk.

"A little after one."

That sounded urgent. I went back to a booth and put in the call. The old man's secretary answered, asking me to come out at once. I promised to hurry, asked the clerk to get me a taxi, and went up to my room for a shot of Scotch.

I would rather have been cold sober, but I wasn't. If the night held more work for me I didn't want to go it with alcohol dying in me. The snifter revived me a lot. I poured more of the King George into a flask, pocketed it, and went down to the taxi.

Elihu Willsson's house was lighted from top to bottom. The secretary opened the front door before I could get my finger on the button. His thin body was shivering in pale blue pajamas and dark blue bathrobe. His thin face was full of excitement.

"Hurry!" he said. "Mr. Willsson is waiting. And, please, will you try to persuade him to let us have the body removed?"

I promised and followed him up to the old man's bedroom.

Old Elihu was in bed as before, but now a black automatic pistol lay on the covers close to one of his pink hands.

As soon as I appeared he took his head off the pillows, sat upright and barked at me:

"Have you got as much guts as you've got gall?"

His face was an unhealthy dark red. The film was gone from his eyes. They were hard and hot.

I let his question wait while I looked at the corpse on the floor between door and bed.

A short thick-set man in brown lay on his back with dead eyes staring at the ceiling from under the visor of a gray cap. A piece of his jaw had been knocked off. His chin was tilted to show where another bullet had gone through tie and collar to make a hole in his neck. One arm was bent under him. The other hand held a blackjack as big as a milk bottle. There was a lot of blood.

I looked up from this mess to the old man. His grin was vicious and idiotic.

"You're a great talker," he said. "I know that. A two-fisted, you-be-damned man with your words. But have you got anything else? Have you got the guts to match your gall? Or is it just the language you've got?"

There was no use in trying to get along with the old boy. I scowled and reminded him:

"Didn't I tell you not to bother me unless you wanted to talk sense for a change?"

"You did, my lad." There was a foolish sort of triumph in his voice. "And I'll talk you your sense. I want a man to clean this pig-sty of a Poisonville for me, to smoke out the rats, little and big. It's a man's job. Are you a man?"

"What's the use of getting poetic about it?" I growled. "If you've got a fairly honest piece of work to be done in my line, and you want to pay a decent price, maybe I'll take it on. But a lot of foolishness about smoking rats and pig-pens doesn't mean anything to me."

"All right. I want Personville emptied of its crooks and grafters. Is that plain enough language for you?"

"You didn't want it this morning," I said. "Why do you want it now?"

The explanation was profane and lengthy and given to me in a loud and blustering voice. The substance of it was that he had built Personville brick by brick with his own hands and he was going to keep it or wipe it off the side of the hill. Nobody could threaten him in his own city, no matter who they were. He had let them alone, but when they started telling him, Elihu Willsson, what he had to do and what he couldn't do, he would show them who was who. He brought the speech to an end by pointing at the corpse and boasting:

"That'll show them there's still a sting in the old man."

I wished I were sober. His clowning puzzled me. I couldn't put my finger on the something behind it.

"Your playmates sent him?" I asked, nodding at the dead man.

"I only talked to him with this," he said, patting the automatic on the bed, "but I reckon they did."

"How did it happen?"

"It happened simple enough. I heard the door opening, and I switched on the light, and there he was, and I shot him, and there he is."

"What time?"

"It was about one o'clock."

"And you've let him lie there all this time?"

"That I have." The old man laughed savagely and began blustering again: "Does the sight of a dead man turn your stomach? Or is it his spirit you're afraid of?"

I laughed at him. Now I had it. The old boy was scared stiff. Fright was the something behind his clowning. That was why he blustered, and why he wouldn't let them take the body away. He wanted it there to look at, to keep panic away, visible proof of his ability to defend himself. I knew where I stood.

"You really want the town cleaned up?" I asked.

"I said I did and I do."

"I'd have to have a free hand – no favors to anybody – run the job as I pleased. And I'd have to have a ten-thousand-dollar retainer."

"Ten thousand dollars! Why in hell should I give that much to a man I don't know from Adam? A man who's done nothing I know of but talk?"

"Be serious. When I say *me*, I mean the Continental. You know them."

"I do. And they know me. And they ought to know I'm good for –"

"That's not the idea. These people you want taken to the cleaners were friends of yours yesterday. Maybe they will be friends again next week. I don't care about that. But I'm not playing politics for you. I'm not hiring out to help you kick them back in line – with the job being called off then. If you want the job done you'll plank down enough money to pay for a complete job. Any that's left over will be returned to you. But you're going to get a complete job or nothing. That's the way it'll have to be. Take it or leave it."

"I'll damned well leave it," he bawled.

He let me get half-way down the stairs before he called me back.

"I'm an old man," he grumbled. "If I was ten years younger –" He glared at me and worked his lips together. "I'll give you your damned check."

"And authority to go through with it in my own way?"

"Yes."

"We'll get it done now. Where's your secretary?"

Willsson pushed a button on his bedside-table and the silent secretary appeared from wherever he had been hiding. I told him:

"Mr. Willsson wants to issue a ten-thousand-dollar check to the Continental Detective Agency, and he wants to write the Agency – San Francisco branch – a letter authorizing the Agency to use the ten thousand dollars investigating crime and political corruption in Personville. The letter is to state clearly that the Agency is to conduct the investigation as it sees fit."

The secretary looked questioningly at the old man, who frowned and ducked his round white head.

"But first," I told the secretary as he glided towards the door, "you'd better phone the police that we've got a dead burglar here. Then call Mr. Willsson's doctor."

The old man declared he didn't want any damned doctors.

"You're going to have a nice shot in the arm so you can sleep," I promised him, stepping over the corpse to take the black gun from the bed. "I'm going to stay here tonight and we'll spend most of tomorrow sifting Poisonville affairs."

The old man was tired. His voice, when he profanely and somewhat long-windedly told me what he thought of my impudence in deciding what was best for him, barely shook the windows.

I took off the dead man's cap for a better look at his face. It didn't mean anything to me. I put the cap back in place.

When I straightened up the old man asked, moderately:

"Are you getting anywhere in your hunt for Donald's murderer?"

"I think so. Another day ought to see it finished."

"Who?" he asked.

The secretary came in with the letter and the check. I gave them to the old man instead of an answer to his question. He put a shaky signature on each, and I had them folded in my pocket when the police arrived.

The first copper into the room was the chief himself, fat Noonan. He nodded amiably at Willsson, shook hands with me, and looked with twinkling greenish eyes at the dead man.

"Well, well," he said. "It's a good job he did, whoever did it. Yakima Shorty. And will you look at the sap he's toting?" He kicked the blackjack out of the dead man's hand. "Big enough to sink a battleship. You drop him?" he asked me.

"Mr. Willsson."

"Well, that certainly is fine," he congratulated the old man. "You saved a lot of people a lot of troubles, including me. Pack him out, boys," he said to the four men behind him.

The two in uniform picked Yakima Shorty up by legs and arm-pits and went away with him, while one of the others gathered up the blackjack and a flashlight that had been under the body.

"If everybody did that to their prowlers, it would certainly be fine," the chief babbled on. He brought three cigars out of a pocket, threw one over on the bed, stuck one at me, and put the other in his mouth. "I was just wondering where I could get hold of you," he told me as we lighted up. "I got a little job ahead that I thought you'd like to be in on. That's how I happened to be on tap when the rumble came." He put his mouth close to my ear and whispered: "Going to pick up Whisper. Want to go along?"

"Yeah."

"I thought you would. Hello, Doc!"

He shook hands with a man who had just come in, a little plump man with a tired oval face and gray eyes that still had sleep in them.

The doctor went to the bed, where one of Noonan's men was asking Willsson about the shooting. I followed the sec-retary into the hall and asked him:

"Any men in the house besides you?"

"Yes, the chauffeur, the Chinese cook."

"Let the chauffeur stay in the old man's room tonight. I'm going out with Noonan. I'll get back as soon as I can. I don't think there'll be any more excitement here, but no matter what happens don't leave the old man alone. And don't leave him alone with Noonan or any of Noonan's crew."

The secretary's mouth and eyes popped wide.

"What time did you leave Donald Willsson last night?" I asked.

"You mean night before last, the night he was killed?"

"Yeah."

479

"At precisely half-past nine."

"You were with him from five o'clock till then?"

"From a quarter after five. We went over some statements and that sort of thing in his office until nearly eight o'clock. Then we went to Bayard's and finished our business over our dinners. He left at half-past nine, saying he had an engagement."

"What else did he say about this engagement?"

"Nothing else."

"Didn't give you any hint of where he was going, who he was going to meet?"

"He merely said he had an engagement."

"And you didn't know anything about it?"

"No. Why? Did you think I did?"

"I thought he might have said something." I switched back to tonight's doings: "What visitors did Willsson have today, not counting the one he shot?"

"You'll have to pardon me," the secretary said, smiling apologetically, "I can't tell you that without Mr. Willsson's permission. I'm sorry."

"Weren't some of the local powers here? Say Lew Yard, or – "

The secretary shook his head, repeating:

"I'm sorry."

"We won't fight over it," I said, giving it up and starting back towards the bedroom-door.

The doctor came out, buttoning his overcoat.

"He will sleep now," he said hurriedly. "Someone should stay with him. I shall be in in the morning." He ran downstairs.

I went into the bedroom. The chief and the man who had questioned Willsson were standing by the bed. The chief grinned as if he were glad to see me. The other man scowled. Willsson was lying on his back, staring at the ceiling.

"That's about all there is here," Noonan said. "What say we mosey along?"

I agreed and said, "Good-night," to the old man. He said, "Good-night," without looking at me. The secretary came in with the chauffeur, a tall sunburned young husky.

The chief, the other sleuth – a police lieutenant named McGraw – and I went downstairs and got into the chief's car. McGraw sat beside the driver. The chief and I sat in back.

"We'll make the pinch along about daylight," Noonan explained as we rode. "Whisper's got a joint over on King Street. He generally leaves there along about daylight. We could crash the place, but that'd mean gun-play, and it's just as well to take it easy. We'll pick him up when he leaves."

I wondered if he meant pick him up or pick him off. I asked:

"Got enough on him to make the rap stick?"

"Enough?" He laughed good-naturedly. "If what the Willsson dame give us ain't enough to stretch him I'm a pickpocket."

I thought of a couple of wisecrack answers to that. I kept them to myself.

6 WHISPER'S JOINT

OUR RIDE ENDED under a line of trees in a dark street not far from the center of town. We got out of the car and walked down to the corner.

A burly man in a gray overcoat, with a gray hat pulled down over his eyes, came to meet us.

"Whisper's hep," the burly man told the chief. "He phoned Donohoe that he's going to stay in his joint. If you think you can pull him out, try it, he says."

Noonan chuckled, scratched an ear, and asked pleasantly:

"How many would you say was in there with him?"

"Fifty, anyhow."

"Aw, now! There wouldn't be that many, not at this time of morning."

"The hell there wouldn't," the burly man snarled. "They been drifting in since midnight."

"Is that so? A leak somewheres. Maybe you oughtn't to have let them in."

"Maybe I oughtn't." The burly man was angry. "But I did what you told me. You said let anybody go in or out that wanted to, but when Whisper showed to –"

"To pinch him," the chief said.

"Well, yes," the burly man agreed, looking savagely at me.

More men joined us and we held a talk-fest. Everybody was in a bad humor except the chief. He seemed to enjoy it all. I didn't know why.

Whisper's joint was a three-story brick building in the middle of the block, between two two-story buildings. The ground floor of his joint was occupied by a cigar-store that served as entrance and cover for the gambling establishment upstairs. Inside, if the burly man's information was to be depended on, Whisper had collected half a hundred friends, loaded for a fight. Outside, Noonan's force was spread around the building, in the street in front, in the alley in back, and on the adjoining roofs.

"Well, boys," the chief said amiably after everybody had had his say, "I don't reckon Whisper wants trouble any more than we do, or he'd have tried to shoot his way out before this, if he's got that many with him, though I don't mind saying I don't think he has — not that many."

The burly man said: "The hell he ain't."

"So if he don't want trouble," Noonan went on, "maybe talking might do some good. You run over, Nick, and see if you can't argue him into being peaceable."

The burly man said: "The hell I will."

"Phone him, then," the chief suggested.

The burly man growled: "That's more like it," and went away. When he came back he looked completely satisfied.

"He says," he reported, " 'Go to hell.' "

"Get the rest of the boys down here," Noonan said cheerfully. "We'll knock it over as soon as it gets light."

The burly Nick and I went around with the chief while he made sure his men were properly placed. I didn't think much of them — a shabby, shifty-eyed crew without enthusiasm for the job ahead of them.

The sky became a faded gray. The chief, Nick, and I stopped in a plumber's doorway diagonally across the street from our target.

Whisper's joint was dark, the upper windows blank, blinds down over cigar-store windows and door.

"I hate to start this without giving Whisper a chance," Noonan said. "He's not a bad kid. But there's no use me trying to talk to him. He never did like me much."

483

He looked at me. I said nothing.

"You wouldn't want to make a stab at it?" he asked.

"Yeah, I'll try it."

"That's fine of you. I'll certainly appreciate it if you will. You just see if you can talk him into coming along without any fuss. You know what to say – for his own good and all that, like it is."

"Yeah," I said and walked across to the cigar-store, taking pains to let my hands be seen swinging empty at my sides.

Day was still a little way off. The street was the color of smoke. My feet made a lot of noise on the pavement.

I stopped in front of the door and knocked the glass with a knuckle, not heavily. The green blind down inside the door made a mirror of the glass. In it I saw two men moving up the other side of the street.

No sound came from inside. I knocked harder, then slid my hand down to rattle the knob.

Advice came from indoors:

"Get away from there while you're able."

It was a muffled voice, but not a whisper, so probably not Whisper's.

"I want to talk to Thaler," I said.

"Go talk to the lard-can that sent you."

"I'm not talking for Noonan. Is Thaler where he can hear me?"

A pause. Then the muffled voice said: "Yes."

"I'm the Continental op who tipped Dinah Brand off that Noonan was framing you," I said. "I want five minutes' talk with you. I've got nothing to do with Noonan except to queer his racket. I'm alone. I'll drop my rod in the street if you say so. Let me in."

I waited. It depended on whether the girl had got to him with the story of my interview with her. I waited what seemed a long time.

The muffled voice said:

"When we open, come in quick. And no stunts."

"All set."

The latch clicked. I plunged in with the door.

Across the street a dozen guns emptied themselves. Glass shot from door and windows tinkled around us.

Somebody tripped me. Fear gave me three brains and half a dozen eyes. I was in a tough spot. Noonan had slipped me a pretty dose. These birds couldn't help thinking I was playing his game.

I tumbled down, twisting around to face the door. My gun was in my hand by the time I hit the floor.

Across the street, burly Nick had stepped out of a doorway to pump slugs at us with both hands.

I steadied my gun-arm on the floor. Nick's body showed over the front sight. I squeezed the gun. Nick stopped shooting. He crossed his guns on his chest and went down in a pile on the sidewalk.

Hands on my ankles dragged me back. The floor scraped pieces off my chin. The door slammed shut. Some comedian said:

"Uh-huh, people don't like you."

I sat up and shouted through the racket:

"I wasn't in on this."

The shooting dwindled, stopped. Door and window blinds were dotted with gray holes. A husky whisper said in the darkness:

"Tod, you and Slats keep an eye on things down here. The rest of us might as well go upstairs."

We went through a room behind the store, into a passageway, up a flight of carpeted steps, and into a second-story room that held a green table banked for crap-shooting. It was a small room, had no windows, and the lights were on.

There were five of us. Thaler sat down and lit a cigarette, a small dark young man with a face that was pretty in a chorus-man way until you took another look at the thin hard mouth.

An angular blond kid of no more than twenty in tweeds sprawled on his back on a couch and blew cigarette-smoke at the ceiling. Another boy, as blond and as young, but not so angular, was busy straightening his scarlet tie, smoothing his yellow hair. A thin-faced man of thirty with little or no chin under a wide loose mouth wandered up and down the room looking bored and humming *Rosy Cheeks*.

I sat in a chair two or three feet from Thaler's.

"How long is Noonan going to keep this up?" he asked. There was no emotion in his hoarse whispering voice, only a shade of annoyance.

"He's after you this trip," I said. "I think he's going through with it."

The gambler smiled a thin, contemptuous smile.

"He ought to know what a swell chance he's got of hanging a one-legged rap like that on me."

"He's not figuring on proving anything in court," I said.

"No?"

"You're to be knocked off resisting arrest, or trying to make a get-away. He won't need much of a case after that."

"He's getting tough in his old age." The thin lips curved in another smile. He didn't seem to think much of the fat chief's deadliness. "Any time he rubs me out I deserve rubbing. What's he got against you?"

"He's guessed I'm going to make a nuisance of myself."

"Too bad. Dinah told me you were a pretty good guy, except kind of Scotch with the roll."

"I had a nice visit. Will you tell me what you know about Donald Willsson's killing?"

"His wife plugged him."

"You saw her?"

"I saw her the next second – with the gat in her hand."

"That's no good to either of us," I said. "I don't know how far you've got it cooked. Rigged right, you could make it stick in court, maybe, but you'll not get a chance to make your play there. If Noonan takes you at all he'll take you stiff. Give me the straight of it. I only need that to pop the job."

He dropped his cigarette on the floor, mashed it under his foot, and asked:

"You that hot?"

"Give me your slant on it and I'm ready to make the pinch – if I can get out of here."

He lit another cigarette and asked:

"Mrs. Willsson said it was me that phoned her?"

"Yeah – after Noonan had persuaded her. She believes it now – maybe."

"You dropped Big Nick," he said. "I'll take a chance on you. A man phoned me that night. I don't know him, don't know who he was. He said Willsson had gone to Dinah's with a check for five grand. What the hell did I care? But, see, it was funny somebody I didn't know cracked it to me. So I went around. Dan stalled me away from the door. That was all right. But still it was funny as hell that guy phoned me.

"I went up the street and took a plant in a vestibule. I saw Mrs. Willsson's heap standing in the street, but I didn't know then that it was hers or that she was in it. He came out pretty soon and walked down the street. I didn't see the shots. I heard them. Then this woman jumps out of the heap and runs over to him. I knew she hadn't done the shooting. I ought to have beat it. But it was all funny as hell, so when I saw the woman was Willsson's wife I went over to them, trying to find out what it was all about. That was a break, see? So I had to make an out for myself, in case something slipped. I strung the woman. That's the whole damned works – on the level."

"Thanks," I said. "That's what I came for. Now the trick is to get out of here without being mowed down."

"No trick at all," Thaler assured me. "We go any time we want to."

"I want to now. If I were you, I'd go too. You've got Noonan pegged as a false-alarm, but why take a chance? Make the sneak and keep under cover till noon, and his frame-up will be a wash-out."

Thaler put his hand in his pants-pocket and brought out a fat roll of paper money. He counted off a hundred or two, some fifties, twenties, tens, and held them out to the chinless man, saying:

"Buy us a get-away, Jerry, and you don't have to give anybody any more dough than he's used to."

Jerry took the money, picked up a hat from the table, and strolled out. Half an hour later he returned and gave some of the bills back to Thaler, saying casually:

"We wait in the kitchen till we get the office."

We went down to the kitchen. It was dark there. More men joined us.

Jerry opened the door and we went down three steps into the back yard. It was almost full daylight. There were ten of us in the party.

"This all?" I asked Thaler.

He nodded.

"Nick said there were fifty of you."

"Fifty of us to stand off that crummy force!" he sneered.

A uniformed copper held the back gate open, muttering nervously:

"Hurry it up, boys, please."

I was willing to hurry, but nobody else paid any attention to him.

We crossed an alley, were beckoned through another gate by a big man in brown, passed through a house, out into the next street, and climbed into a black automobile that stood at the curb.

One of the blond boys drove. He knew what speed was.

I said I wanted to be dropped off somewhere in the neighborhood of the Great Western Hotel. The driver looked at

Whisper, who nodded. Five minutes later I got out in front of my hotel.

"See you later," the gambler whispered, and the car slid away.

The last I saw of it was its police department license plate vanishing around a corner.

IT WAS HALF-PAST five. I walked around a few blocks until I came to an unlighted electric sign that said *Hotel Crawford*, climbed a flight of steps to the second-floor office, registered, left a call for ten o'clock, was shown into a shabby room, moved some of the Scotch from my flask to my stomach, and took old Elihu's ten-thousand-dollar check and my gun to bed with me.

At ten I dressed, went up to the First National Bank, found young Albury, and asked him to certify Willsson's check for me. He kept me waiting a while. I suppose he phoned the old man's residence to find out if the check was on the up-and-up. Finally he brought it back to me, properly scribbled on.

I sponged an envelope, put the old man's letter and check in it, addressed it to the Agency in San Francisco, stuck a stamp on it, and went out and dropped it in the mail-box on the corner.

Then I returned to the bank and said to the boy:

"Now tell me why you killed him."

He smiled and asked:

"Cock Robin or President Lincoln?"

"You're not going to admit off-hand that you killed Donald Willsson?"

"I don't want to be disagreeable," he said, still smiling, "but I'd rather not."

"That's going to make it bad," I complained. "We can't stand here and argue very long without being interrupted. Who's the stout party with cheaters coming this way?"

The boy's face pinkened. He said:

490

"Mr. Dritton, the cashier."

"Introduce me."

The boy looked uncomfortable, but he called the cashier's name. Dritton – a large man with a smooth pink face, a fringe of white hair around an otherwise bald pink head, and rimless nose glasses – came over to us.

The assistant cashier mumbled the introductions. I shook Dritton's hand without losing sight of the boy.

"I was just saying," I addressed Dritton, "that we ought to have a more private place to talk in. He probably won't confess till I've worked on him a while, and I don't want everybody in the bank to hear me yelling at him."

"Confess?" The cashier's tongue showed between his lips.

"Sure." I kept my face, voice and manner bland, mimicking Noonan. "Didn't you know that Albury is the fellow who killed Donald Willsson?"

A polite smile at what he thought an asinine joke started behind the cashier's glasses, and changed to puzzlement when he looked at his assistant. The boy was rouge-red and the grin he was forcing his mouth to wear was a terrible thing.

Dritton cleared his throat and said heartily:

"It's a splendid morning. We've been having splendid weather."

"But isn't there a private room where we can talk?" I insisted.

Dritton jumped nervously and questioned the boy:

"What – what is this?"

Young Albury said something nobody could have understood.

I said: "If there isn't I'll have to take him down to the City Hall."

Dritton caught his glasses as they slid down his nose, jammed them back in place and said:

"Come back here."

We followed him down the length of the lobby, through a gate, and into an office whose door was labeled *President* – old Elihu's office. Nobody was in it.

I motioned Albury into one chair and picked another for myself. The cashier fidgeted with his back against the desk, facing both of us.

"Now, sir, will you explain this," he said.

"We'll get around to that," I told him and turned to the boy. "You're an ex-boy-friend of Dinah's who was given the air. You're the only one who knew her intimately who could have known about the certified check in time to phone Mrs. Willsson and Thaler. Willsson was shot with a .32. Banks like that caliber. Maybe the gun you used wasn't a bank gun, but I think it was. Maybe you didn't put it back. Then there'll be one missing. Anyway, I'm going to have a gun expert put his microscopes and micrometers on the bullets that killed Willsson and bullets fired from all the bank guns."

The boy looked calmly at me and said nothing. He had himself under control again. That wouldn't do. I had to be nasty. I said:

"You were cuckoo over the girl. You confessed to me that it was only because she wouldn't stand for it that you didn't –"

"Don't – please don't," he gasped. His face was red again.

I made myself sneer at him until his eyes went down. Then I said:

"You talked too much, son. You were too damned anxious to make your life an open book for me. That's a way you amateur criminals have. You've always got to overdo the frank and open business."

He was watching his hands. I let him have the other barrel:

"You know you killed him. You know if you used a bank gun, and if you put it back. If you did you're nailed now, without an out. The gun-sharks will take care of that. If you didn't, I'm going to nail you anyhow. All right. I don't have to tell you whether you've got a chance or not. You know.

"Noonan is framing Whisper Thaler for the job. He can't convict him, but the frame-up is tight enough that if Thaler's killed resisting arrest, the chief will be in the clear. That's what he means to do – kill Thaler. Thaler stood off the police all night in his King Street joint. He's still standing them off – unless they've got to him. The first copper that gets to him – exit Thaler.

"If you figure you've got a chance to beat your rap, and you want to let another man be killed on your account, that's your business. But if you know you haven't got a chance – and you haven't if the gun can be found – for God's sake give Thaler one by clearing him."

"I'd like." Albury's voice was an old man's. He looked up from his hands, saw Dritton, said, "I'd like," again and stopped.

"Where is the gun?" I asked.

"In Harper's cage," the boy said.

I scowled at the cashier and asked him:

"Will you get it?"

He went out as if he were glad to go.

"I didn't mean to kill him," the youngster said. "I don't think I meant to."

I nodded encouragingly, trying to look solemnly sympathetic.

"I don't think I meant to kill him," he repeated, "though I took the gun with me. You were right about my being cuckoo over Dinah – then. It was worse some days than others. The day Willsson brought the check in was one of the bad ones. All I could think about was that I had lost her because I had no more money, and he was taking five thousand dollars to her. It was the check. Can you understand that? I had known that she and Thaler were – you know. If I had learned that Willsson and she were too, without seeing the check, I wouldn't have done anything. I'm sure of it. It was seeing the check – and knowing I'd lost her because my money was gone.

493

"I watched her house that night and saw him go in. I was afraid of what I might do, because it was one of the bad days, and I had the gun in my pocket. Honestly I didn't want to do anything. I was afraid. I couldn't think of anything but the check, and why I had lost her. I knew Willsson's wife was jealous. Everybody knew that. I thought if I called her up and told her – I don't know exactly what I thought, but I went to a store around the corner and phoned her. Then I phoned Thaler. I wanted them there. If I could have thought of anyone else who had anything to do with either Dinah or Willsson I'd have called them too.

"Then I went back and watched Dinah's house again. Mrs. Willsson came, and then Thaler, and both of them stayed there, watching the house. I was glad of that. With them there I wasn't so afraid of what I might do. After a while Willsson came out and walked down the street. I looked up at Mrs. Willsson's car and at the doorway where I knew Thaler was. Neither of them did anything, and Willsson was walking away. I knew then why I had wanted them there. I had hoped they would do something – and I wouldn't have to. But they didn't, and he was walking away. If one of them had gone over and said something to him, or even followed him, I wouldn't have done anything.

"But they didn't. I remember taking the gun out of my pocket. Everything was blurred in front of my eyes, like I was crying. Maybe I was. I don't remember shooting – I mean I don't remember deliberately aiming and pulling the trigger – but I can remember the sound the shots made, and that I knew the noise was coming from the gun in my hand. I don't remember how Willsson looked, if he fell before I turned and ran up the alley, or not. When I got home I cleaned and reloaded the pistol, and put it back in the paying teller's cage the next morning."

* * *

494

On the way down to the City Hall with the boy and the gun I apologized for the village cut-up stuff I had put in the early part of the shake-down, explaining:

"I had to get under your skin, and that was the best way I knew. The way you'd talked about the girl showed me you were too good an actor to be broken down by straight hammering."

He winced, and said slowly:

"That wasn't acting, altogether. When I was in danger, facing the gallows, she didn't – didn't seem so important to me. I couldn't – I can't now – quite understand – fully – why I did what I did. Do you know what I mean? That somehow makes the whole thing – and me – cheap. I mean, the whole thing from the beginning."

I couldn't find anything to say except something meaningless, like:

"Things happen that way."

In the chief's office we found one of the men who had been on the storming party the night before – a red-faced official named Biddle. He goggled at me with curious gray eyes, but asked no questions about the King Street doings.

Biddle called in a young lawyer named Dart from the prosecuting attorney's office. Albury was repeating his story to Biddle, Dart and a stenographer, when the chief of police, looking as if he had just crawled out of bed, arrived.

"Well, it certainly is fine to see you," Noonan said, pumping my hand up and down while patting my back. "By God! You had a narrow one last night – the rats! I was dead sure they'd got you till we kicked in the doors and found the joint empty. Tell me how those son-of-a-guns got out of there."

"A couple of your men let them out the back door, took them through the house in back, and sent them away in a department car. They took me along so I couldn't tip you off."

"A couple of my men did that?" he asked, with no appearance of surprise. "Well, well! What kind of looking men were they?"

I described them.

"Shore and Riordan," he said. "I might of known it. Now what's all this?" nodding his fat face at Albury.

I told him briefly while the boy went on dictating his statement.

The chief chuckled and said:

"Well, well, I did Whisper an injustice. I'll have to hunt him up and square myself. So you landed the boy? That certainly is fine. Congratulations and thanks." He shook my hand again. "You'll not be leaving our city now, will you?"

"Not just yet."

"That's fine," he assured me.

I went out for breakfast-and-lunch. Then I treated myself to a shave and haircut, sent a telegram to the Agency asking to have Dick Foley and Mickey Linehan shipped to Personville, stopped in my room for a change of clothes, and set out for my client's house.

Old Elihu was wrapped in blankets in an armchair at a sunny window. He gave me a stubby hand and thanked me for catching his son's murderer.

I made some more or less appropriate reply. I didn't ask him how he had got the news.

"The check I gave you last night," he said, "is only fair pay for the work you have done."

"Your son's check more than covered that."

"Then call mine a bonus."

"The Continental's got rules against taking bonuses or rewards," I said.

His face began to redden.

"Well, damn it —"

"You haven't forgotten that your check was to cover the cost of investigating crime and corruption in Personville, have you?" I asked.

"That was nonsense," he snorted. "We were excited last night. That's called off."

"Not with me."

He threw a lot of profanity around. Then:

"It's my money and I won't have it wasted on a lot of damn-foolery. If you won't take it for what you've done, give it back to me."

"Stop yelling at me," I said. "I'll give you nothing except a good job of city-cleaning. That's what you bargained for, and that's what you're going to get. You know now that your son was killed by young Albury, and not by your playmates. They know now that Thaler wasn't helping you double-cross them. With your son dead, you've been able to promise them that the newspapers won't dig up any more dirt. All's lovely and peaceful again.

"I told you I expected something like that. That's why I sewed you up. And you are sewed up. The check has been certified, so you can't stop payment. The letter of authority may not be as good as a contract, but you'll have to go into court to prove that it isn't. If you want that much of that kind of publicity, go ahead. I'll see that you get plenty.

"Your fat chief of police tried to assassinate me last night. I don't like that. I'm just mean enough to want to ruin him for it. Now I'm going to have my fun. I've got ten thousand dollars of your money to play with. I'm going to use it opening Poisonville up from Adam's apple to ankles. I'll see that you get my reports as regularly as possible. I hope you enjoy them."

And I went out of the house with his curses sizzling around my head.

8   A TIP ON KID COOPER

I SPENT MOST of the afternoon writing my three days' reports on the Donald Willsson operation. Then I sat around, burned Fatimas, and thought about the Elihu Willsson operation until dinner time.

I went down to the hotel dining-room and had just decided in favor of pounded rump steak with mushrooms when I heard myself being paged.

The boy took me to one of the lobby booths. Dinah Brand's lazy voice came out of the receiver:

"Max wants to see you. Can you drop in tonight?"

"Your place?"

"Yes."

I promised to drop in and returned to the dining-room and my meal. When I had finished eating I went up to my room, fifth floor front. I unlocked the door and went in, snapping on the light.

A bullet kissed a hole in the door-frame close to my noodle.

More bullets made more holes in door, door-frame and wall, but by that time I had carried my noodle into a safe corner, one out of line with the window.

Across the street, I knew, was a four-story office-building with a roof a little above the level of my window. The roof would be dark. My light was on. There was no percentage in trying to peep out under those conditions.

I looked around for something to chuck at the light globe, found a Gideon Bible, and chucked it. The bulb popped apart, giving me darkness.

The shooting had stopped.

I crept to the window, kneeling with an eye to one of its lower corners. The roof across the street was dark and too high for me to see beyond its rim. Ten minutes of this one-eyed spying got me nothing except a kink in my neck.

I went to the phone and asked the girl to send the house-copper up.

He was a portly, white-mustached man with the round undeveloped forehead of a child. He wore a too-small hat on the back of his head to show the forehead. His name was Keever. He got too excited over the shooting.

The hotel-manager came in, a plump man with carefully controlled face, voice and manner. He didn't get excited at all. He took the this-is-unheard-of-but-not-really-serious-of-course attitude of a street fakir whose mechanical dingus flops during a demonstration.

We risked light, getting a new globe, and added up the bullet-holes. There were ten of them.

Policemen came, went, and returned to report no luck in picking up whatever trail there might have been. Noonan called up. He talked to the sergeant in charge of the police detail, and then to me.

"I just this minute heard about the shooting," he said. "Now who do you reckon would be after you like that?"

"I couldn't guess," I lied.

"None of them touched you?"

"No."

"Well, that certainly is fine," he said heartily. "And we'll nail that baby, whoever he was, you can bet your life on that. Would you like me to leave a couple of the boys with you, just to see nothing else happens?"

"No, thanks."

"You can have them if you want them," he insisted.

"No, thanks."

He made me promise to call on him the first chance I got, told me the Personville police department was at my disposal, gave me to understand that if anything happened to me his whole life would be ruined, and I finally got rid of him.

The police went away. I had my stuff moved into another room, one into which bullets couldn't be so easily funneled. Then I changed my clothes and set out for Hurricane Street, to keep my date with the whispering gambler.

Dinah Brand opened the door for me. Her big ripe mouth was rouged evenly this evening, but her brown hair still needed trimming, was parted haphazardly, and there were spots down the front of her orange silk dress.

"So you're still alive," she said. "I suppose nothing can be done about it. Come on in."

We went into her cluttered-up living-room. Dan Rolff and Max Thaler were playing pinochle there. Rolff nodded to me. Thaler got up to shake hands.

His hoarse whispering voice said:

"I hear you've declared war on Poisonville."

"Don't blame me. I've got a client who wants the place ventilated."

"Wanted, not wants," he corrected me as we sat down. "Why don't you chuck it?"

I made a speech:

"No. I don't like the way Poisonville has treated me. I've got my chance now, and I'm going to even up. I take it you're back in the club again, all brothers together, let bygones be bygones. You want to be let alone. There was a time when I wanted to be let alone. If I had been, maybe now I'd be riding back to San Francisco. But I wasn't. Especially I wasn't let alone by that fat Noonan. He's had two tries at my scalp in two days. That's plenty. Now it's my turn to run him ragged, and that's exactly what I'm going to do. Poisonville is ripe for the harvest. It's a job I like, and I'm going to do it."

"While you last," the gambler said.

"Yeah," I agreed. "I was reading in the paper this morning about a fellow choking to death eating a chocolate eclair in bed."

"That may be good," said Dinah Brand, her big body sprawled in an armchair, "but it wasn't in this morning's paper."

She lit a cigarette and threw the match out of sight under the chesterfield. The lunger had gathered up the cards and was shuffling them over and over, purposelessly.

Thaler frowned at me and said:

"Willsson's willing for you to keep the ten grand. Let it go at that."

"I've got a mean disposition. Attempted assassinations make me mad."

"That won't get you anything but a box. I'm for you. You kept Noonan from framing me. That's why I'm telling you, forget it and go back to Frisco."

"I'm for you," I said. "That's why I'm telling you, split with them. They crossed you up once. It'll happen again. Anyway, they're slated for the chutes. Get out while the getting's good."

"I'm sitting too pretty," he said. "And I'm able to take care of myself."

"Maybe. But you know the racket's too good to last. You've had the cream of the pickings. Now it's get-away day."

He shook his little dark head and told me:

"I think you're pretty good, but I'm damned if I think you're good enough to crack this camp. It's too tight. If I thought you could swing it, I'd be with you. You know how I stand with Noonan. But you'll never make it. Chuck it."

"No. I'm in it to the last nickel of Elihu's ten thousand."

"I told you he was too damned pig-headed to listen to reason," Dinah Brand said, yawning. "Isn't there anything to drink in the dump, Dan?"

The lunger got up from the table and went out of the room.

Thaler shrugged, said:

"Have it your way. You're supposed to know what you're doing. Going to the fights tomorrow night?"

I said I thought I would. Dan Rolff came in with gin and trimmings. We had a couple of drinks apiece. We talked about the fights. Nothing more was said about me versus Poisonville. The gambler apparently had washed his hands of me, but he didn't seem to hold my stubbornness against me. He even gave me what seemed to be a straight tip on the fights – telling me any bet on the main event would be good if its maker remembered that Kid Cooper would probably knock Ike Bush out in the sixth round. He seemed to know what he was talking about, and it didn't seem to be news to the others.

I left a little after eleven, returning to the hotel without anything happening.

I WOKE NEXT morning with an idea in my skull. Personville had only some forty thousand inhabitants. It shouldn't be hard to spread news. Ten o'clock found me out spreading it.

I did my spreading in pool rooms, cigar-stores, speakeasies, soft-drink joints, and on street-corners – wherever I found a man or two loafing. My spreading technique was something like this:

"Got a match? . . . Thanks. . . . Going to the fights tonight? . . . I hear Ike Bush takes a dive in the sixth. . . . It ought to be straight: I got it from Whisper. . . . Yeah, they all are."

People like inside stuff, and anything that had Thaler's name to it was very inside in Personville. The news spread nicely. Half the men I gave it to worked almost as hard as I did spreading it, just to show they knew what was what.

When I started out, seven to four was being offered that Ike Bush would win, and two to three that he would win by a knockout. By two o'clock none of the joints taking bets were offering anything better than even money, and by half-past three Kid Cooper was a two-to-one favorite.

I made my last stop a lunch counter, where I tossed the news out to a waiter and a couple of customers while eating a hot beef sandwich.

When I went out I found a man waiting by the door for me. He had bowed legs and a long sharp jaw, like a hog's. He nodded and walked down the street beside me, chewing a toothpick and squinting sidewise into my face. At the corner he said:

"I know for a fact that ain't so."

"What?" I asked.

"About Ike Bush flopping. I know for a fact that ain't so."

"Then it oughtn't bother you any. But the wise money's going two to one on Cooper, and he's not that good unless Bush lets him be."

The hog jaw spit out the mangled toothpick and snapped yellow teeth at me.

"He told me his own self that Cooper was a set-up for him, last night, and he wouldn't do nothing like that – not to me."

"Friend of yours?"

"Not exactly, but he knows I – Hey, listen! Did Whisper give you that, on the level?"

"On the level."

He cursed bitterly. "And I put my last thirty-five bucks in the world on that rat on his say-so. Me, that could send him over for –" He broke off and looked down the street.

"Could send him over for what?" I asked.

"Plenty," he said. "Nothing."

I had a suggestion:

"If you've got something on him, maybe we ought to talk it over. I wouldn't mind seeing Bush win, myself. If what you've got is any good, what's the matter with putting it up to him?"

He looked at me, at the sidewalk, fumbled in his vest-pocket for another toothpick, put it in his mouth, and mumbled:

"Who are you?"

I gave him a name, something like Hunter or Hunt or Huntington, and asked him his. He said his name was MacSwain, Bob MacSwain, and I could ask anybody in town if it wasn't right.

I said I believed him and asked:

"What do you say? Will we put the squeeze to Bush?"

Little hard lights came into his eyes and died.

"No," he gulped. "I ain't that kind of fellow. I never –"

"You never did anything but let people gyp you. You don't have to go up against him, MacSwain. Give me the dope, and I'll make the play – if it's any good."

He thought that over, licking his lips, letting the toothpick fall down to stick on his coat front.

"You wouldn't let on about me having any part in it?" he asked. "I belong here, and I wouldn't stand a chance if it got out. And you won't turn him up? You'll just use it to make him fight?"

"Right."

He took my hand excitedly and demanded:

"Honest to God?"

"Honest to God."

"His real moniker is Al Kennedy. He was in on the Keystone Trust knock-over in Philly two years ago, when Scissors Haggerty's mob croaked two messengers. Al didn't do the killing, but he was in on the caper. He used to scrap around Philly. The rest of them got copped, but he made the sneak. That's why he's sticking out here in the bushes. That's why he won't never let them put his mug in the papers or on any cards. That's why he's a pork-and-beaner when he's as good as the best. See? This Ike Bush is Al Kennedy that the Philly bulls want for the Keystone trick. See? He was in on the —"

"I see. I see," I stopped the merry-go-round. "The next thing is to get to see him. How do we do that?"

"He flops at the Maxwell, on Union Street. I guess maybe he'd be there now, resting up for the mill."

"Resting for what? He doesn't know he's going to fight. We'll give it a try, though."

"We! We! Where do you get that *we* at? You said — you swore you'd keep me covered."

"Yeah," I said, "I remember that now. What does he look like?"

"A black-headed kid, kind of slim, with one tin ear and eyebrows that run straight across. I don't know if you can make him like it."

"Leave that to me. Where'll I find you afterwards?"

"I'll be hanging around Murry's. Mind you don't tip my mitt. You promised."

The Maxwell was one of a dozen hotels along Union Street with narrow front doors between stores, and shabby stairs leading up to second-story offices. The Maxwell's office was simply a wide place in the hall, with a key- and mail-rack behind a wooden counter that needed paint just as badly. A brass bell and a dirty day-book register were on the counter. Nobody was there.

I had to run back eight pages before I found *Ike Bush, Salt Lake City, 214*, written in the book. The pigeon-hole that had that number was empty. I climbed more steps and knocked on a door that had it. Nothing came of that. I tried it two or three times more and then turned back to the stairs.

Somebody was coming up. I stood at the top, waiting for a look at him. There was just light enough to see by.

He was a slim muscular lad in army shirt, blue suit, gray cap. Black eyebrows made a straight line above his eyes.

I said: "Hello."

He nodded without stopping or saying anything.

"Win tonight?" I asked.

"Hope so," he said shortly, passing me.

I let him take four steps towards his room before I told him:

"So do I. I'd hate to have to ship you back to Philly, Al."

He took another step, turned around very slowly, rested a shoulder against the wall, let his eyes get sleepy, and grunted:

"Huh?"

"If you were smacked down in the sixth or any other round by a palooka like Kid Cooper, it'd make me peevish," I said. "Don't do it, Al. You don't want to go back to Philly."

The youngster put his chin down in his neck and came back to me. When he was within arm's reach, he stopped, letting his

506

left side turn a bit to the front. His hands were hanging loose. Mine were in my overcoat-pockets.

He said, "Huh?" again.

I said:

"Try to remember that – if Ike Bush doesn't turn in a win tonight, Al Kennedy will be riding east in the morning."

He lifted his left shoulder an inch. I moved the gun around in my pocket, enough. He grumbled:

"Where do you get that stuff about me not winning?"

"Just something I heard. I didn't think there was anything in it, except maybe a ducat back to Philly."

"I oughta bust your jaw, you fat crook."

"Now's the time to do it," I advised him. "If you win tonight you're not likely to see me again. If you lose, you'll see me, but your hands won't be loose."

I found MacSwain in Murry's, a Broadway pool room.

"Did you get to him?" he asked.

"Yeah. It's all fixed – if he doesn't blow town, or say something to his backers, or just pay no attention to me, or –"

MacSwain developed a lot of nervousness.

"You better damn sight be careful," he warned me. "They might try to put you out of the way. He – I got to see a fellow down the street," and he deserted me.

Poisonville's prize fighting was done in a big wooden ex-casino in what had once been an amusement park on the edge of town. When I got there at eight-thirty, most of the population seemed to be on hand, packed tight in close rows of folding chairs on the main floor, packed tighter on benches in two dinky balconies.

Smoke. Stink. Heat. Noise.

My seat was in the third row, ringside. Moving down to it, I discovered Dan Rolff in an aisle seat not far away, with Dinah Brand beside him. She had her hair trimmed at last, and marcelled, and looked like a lot of money in a big gray fur coat.

"Get down on Cooper?" she asked after we had swapped hellos.

"No. You playing him heavy?"

"Not as heavy as I'd like. We held off, thinking the odds would get better, but they went to hell."

"Everybody in town seems to know Bush is going to dive," I said. "I saw a hundred put on Cooper at four to one a few minutes ago." I leaned past Rolff and put my mouth close to where the gray fur collar hid the girl's ear, whispering: "The dive is off. Better copper your bets while there's time."

Her big bloodshot eyes went wide and dark with anxiety, greed, curiosity, suspicion.

"You mean it?" she asked huskily.

"Yeah."

She chewed her reddened lips, frowned, asked:

"Where'd you get it?"

I wouldn't say. She chewed her mouth some more and asked:

"Is Max on?"

"I haven't seen him. Is he here?"

"I suppose so," she said absent-mindedly, a distant look in her eyes. Her lips moved as if she were counting to herself.

I said: "Take it or leave it, but it's a gut."

She leaned forward to look sharply into my eyes, clicked her teeth together, opened her bag, and dragged out a roll of bills the size of a coffee can. Part of the roll she pushed at Rolff.

"Here, Dan, get it down on Bush. You've got an hour anyway to look over the odds."

Rolff took the money and went off on his errand. I took his seat. She put a hand on my forearm and said:

"Christ help you if you've made me drop that dough."

I pretended the idea was ridiculous.

The preliminary bouts got going, four-round affairs between assorted hams. I kept looking for Thaler, but couldn't see him. The girl squirmed beside me, paying little attention to the fighting, dividing her time between asking me where I had got my information and threatening me with hell-fire and damnation if it turned out to be a bust.

The semi-final was on when Rolff came back and gave the girl a handful of tickets. She was straining her eyes over them when I left for my own seat. Without looking up she called to me:

"Wait outside for us when it's over."

Kid Cooper climbed into the ring while I was squeezing through to my seat. He was a ruddy straw-haired solid-built boy with a dented face and too much meat around the top of his lavender trunks. Ike Bush, alias Al Kennedy, came through the ropes in the opposite corner. His body looked better – slim, nicely ridged, snaky – but his face was pale, worried.

They were introduced, went to the center of the ring for the usual instructions, returned to their corners, shed bath-robes, stretched on the ropes, the gong rang, and the scrap was on.

Cooper was a clumsy bum. He had a pair of wide swings that might have hurt when they landed, but anybody with two feet could have kept away from them. Bush had class – nimble legs, a smooth fast left hand, and a right that got away quick. It would have been murder to put Cooper in the ring with the slim boy if he had been trying. But he wasn't. That is, he wasn't trying to win. He was trying not to, and had his hands full doing it.

Cooper waddled flat-footed around the ring, throwing his wide swings at everything from the lights to the corner posts. His system was simply to turn them loose and let them take their chances. Bush moved in and out, putting a glove on the ruddy boy whenever he wanted to, but not putting anything in the glove.

The customers were booing before the first round was over. The second round was just as sour. I didn't feel so good. Bush didn't seem to have been much influenced by our little conversation. Out of the corner of my eye I could see Dinah Brand trying to catch my attention. She looked hot. I took care not to have my attention caught.

The room-mate act in the ring was continued in the third round to the tune of yelled Throw-em-outs, Why-don't-you-kiss-hims and Make-em-fights from the seats. The pugs' waltz brought them around to the corner nearest me just as the booing broke off for a moment.

I made a megaphone of my hands and bawled:

"Back to Philly, Al."

Bush's back was to me. He wrestled Cooper around, shoving him into the ropes, so he – Bush – faced my way.

From somewhere far back in another part of the house another yelling voice came:

"Back to Philly, Al."

MacSwain, I supposed.

A drunk off to one side lifted his puffy face and bawled the same thing, laughing as if it were a swell joke. Others took up the cry for no reason at all except that it seemed to disturb Bush.

His eyes jerked from side to side under the black bar of his eyebrows.

One of Cooper's wild mitts clouted the slim boy on the side of the jaw.

Ike Bush piled down at the referee's feet.

The referee counted five in two seconds, but the gong cut him off.

I looked over at Dinah Brand and laughed. There wasn't anything else to do. She looked at me and didn't laugh. Her face was sick as Dan Rolff's, but angrier.

Bush's handlers dragged him into his corner and rubbed him up, not working very hard at it. He opened his eyes and watched his feet. The gong was tapped.

Kid Cooper paddled out hitching up his trunks. Bush waited until the bum was in the center of the ring, and then came to him, fast.

Bush's left glove went down, out – practically out of sight in Cooper's belly. Cooper said, "Ugh," and backed away, folding up.

Bush straightened him with a right-hand poke in the mouth, and sank the left again. Cooper said, "Ugh," again and had trouble with his knees.

Bush cuffed him once on each side of the head, cocked his right, carefully pushed Cooper's face into position with a long left, and threw his right hand straight from under his jaw to Cooper's.

Everybody in the house felt the punch.

Cooper hit the floor, bounced, and settled there. It took the referee half a minute to count ten seconds. It would have been just the same if he had taken half an hour. Kid Cooper was out.

When the referee had finally stalled through the count, he raised Bush's hand. Neither of them looked happy.

A high twinkle of light caught my eye. A short silvery streak slanted down from one of the small balconies.

A woman screamed.

The silvery streak ended its flashing slant in the ring, with a sound that was partly a thud, partly a snap.

Ike Bush took his arm out of the referee's hand and pitched down on top of Kid Cooper. A black knife-handle stuck out of the nape of Bush's neck.

HALF AN HOUR later, when I left the building, Dinah Brand was sitting at the wheel of a pale blue little Marmon, talking to Max Thaler, who stood in the road.

The girl's square chin was tilted up. Her big red mouth was brutal around the words it shaped, and the lines crossing its ends were deep, hard.

The gambler looked as unpleasant as she. His pretty face was yellow and tough as oak. When he talked his lips were paper-thin.

It seemed to be a nice family party. I wouldn't have joined it if the girl hadn't seen me and called:

"My God, I thought you were never coming."

I went over to the car. Thaler looked across the hood at me with no friendliness at all.

"Last night I advised you to go back to Frisco." His whisper was harsher than anybody's shout could have been. "Now I'm telling you."

"Thanks just the same," I said as I got in beside the girl.

While she was stirring the engine up he said to her:

"This isn't the first time you've sold me out. It's the last."

She put the car in motion, turned her head back over her shoulder, and sang to him:

"To hell, my love, with you!"

We rode into town rapidly.

"Is Bush dead?" she asked as she twisted the car into Broadway.

"Decidedly. When they turned him over the point of the knife was sticking out in front."

"He ought to have known better than to double-cross them. Let's get something to eat. I'm almost eleven hundred ahead on the night's doings, so if the boy-friend doesn't like it, it's just too bad. How'd you come out?"

"Didn't bet. So your Max doesn't like it?"

"Didn't bet?" she cried. "What kind of an ass are you? Whoever heard of anybody not betting when they had a thing like that sewed up?"

"I wasn't sure it was sewed up. So Max didn't like the way things turned out?"

"You guessed it. He dropped plenty. And then he gets sore with me because I had sense enough to switch over and get in on the win." She stopped the car violently in front of a Chinese restaurant. "The hell with him, the little tin-horn runt!"

Her eyes were shiny because they were wet. She jabbed a handkerchief into them as we got out of the car.

"My God, I'm hungry," she said, dragging me across the sidewalk. "Will you buy me a ton of *chow mein*?"

She didn't eat a ton of it, but she did pretty well, putting away a piled-up dish of her own and half of mine. Then we got back into the Marmon and rode out to her house.

Dan Rolff was in the dining-room. A water-glass and a brown bottle with no label stood on the table in front of him. He sat straight up in his chair, staring at the bottle. The room smelled of laudanum.

Dinah Brand slid her fur coat off, letting it fall half on a chair and half on the floor, and snapped her fingers at the lunger, saying impatiently:

"Did you collect?"

Without looking up from the bottle, he took a pad of paper money out of his inside pocket and dropped it on the table. The girl grabbed it, counted the bills twice, smacked her lips, and stuffed the money in her bag.

She went out to the kitchen and began chopping ice. I sat down and lit a cigarette. Rolff stared at his bottle. He and

I never seemed to have much to say to one another. Presently the girl brought in some gin, lemon juice, seltzer and ice.

We drank and she told Rolff:

"Max is sore as hell. He heard you'd been running around putting last-minute money on Bush, and the little monkey thinks I double-crossed him. What did I have to do with it? All I did was what any sensible person would have done – get in on the win. I didn't have any more to do with it than a baby, did I?" she asked me.

"No."

"Of course not. What's the matter with Max is he's afraid the others will think he was in on it too, that Dan was putting his dough down as well as mine. Well, that's his hard luck. He can go climb trees for all I care, the lousy little runt. Another drink would go good."

She poured another for herself and for me. Rolff hadn't touched his first one. He said, still staring at the brown bottle:

"You can hardly expect him to be hilarious about it."

The girl scowled and said disagreeably:

"I can expect anything I want. And he's got no right to talk to me that way. He doesn't own me. Maybe he thinks he does, but I'll show him different." She emptied her glass, banged it on the table, and twisted around in her chair to face me. "Is that on the level about your having ten thousand dollars of Elihu Willsson's money to use cleaning up the city?"

"Yeah."

Her blood-shot eyes glistened hungrily.

"And if I help you will I get some of the ten – ?"

"You can't do that, Dinah." Rolff's voice was thick, but gently firm, as if he were talking to a child. "That would be utterly filthy."

The girl turned her face slowly towards him. Her mouth took on the look it had worn while talking to Thaler.

"I am going to do it," she said. "That makes me utterly filthy, does it?"

He didn't say anything, didn't look up from the bottle. Her face got red, hard, cruel. Her voice was soft, cooing:

"It's just too bad that a gentleman of your purity, even if he is a bit consumptive, has to associate with a filthy bum like me."

"That can be remedied," he said slowly, getting up. He was laudanumed to the scalp.

Dinah Brand jumped out of her chair and ran around the table to him. He looked at her with blank dopey eyes. She put her face close to his and demanded:

"So I'm too utterly filthy for you now, am I?"

He said evenly:

"I said to betray your friends to this chap would be utterly filthy, and it would."

She caught one of his thin wrists and twisted it until he was on his knees. Her other hand, open, beat his hollow-cheeked face, half a dozen times on each side, rocking his head from side to side. He could have put his free arm up to protect his face, but didn't.

She let go his wrist, turned her back to him, and reached for gin and seltzer. She was smiling. I didn't like the smile.

He got up, blinking. His wrist was red where she had held it, his face bruised. He steadied himself upright and looked at me with dull eyes.

With no change in the blankness of his face and eyes, he put a hand under his coat, brought out a black automatic pistol, and fired at me.

But he was too shaky for either speed or accuracy. I had time to toss a glass at him. The glass hit his shoulder. His bullet went somewhere overhead.

I jumped before he got the next one out – jumped at him – was close enough to knock the gun down. The second slug went into the floor.

I socked his jaw. He fell away from me and lay where he fell.

I turned around.

515

Dinah Brand was getting ready to bat me over the head with the seltzer-bottle, a heavy glass siphon that would have made pulp of my skull.

"Don't," I yelped.

"You didn't have to bust him like that," she snarled.

"Well, it's done. You'd better get him straightened out."

She put down the siphon and I helped her carry him up to his bedroom. When he began moving his eyes, I left her to finish the work and went down to the dining-room again. She joined me there fifteen minutes later.

"He's all right," she said. "But you could have handled him without that."

"Yeah, but I did that for him. Know why he took the shot at me?"

"So I'd have nobody to sell Max out to?"

"No. Because I'd seen you maul him around."

"That doesn't make sense to me," she said. "I was the one who did it."

"He's in love with you, and this isn't the first time you've done it. He acted like he had learned there was no use matching muscle with you. But you can't expect him to enjoy having another man see you slap his face."

"I used to think I knew men," she complained, "but, by God! I don't. They're lunatics, all of them."

"So I poked him to give him back some of his self-respect. You know, treated him as I would a man instead of a down-and-outer who could be slapped around by girls."

"Anything you say," she sighed. "I give up. We ought to have a drink."

We had the drink, and I said:

"You were saying you'd work with me if there was a cut of the Willsson money in it for you. There is."

"How much?"

"Whatever you earn. Whatever what you do is worth."

"That's uncertain."

"So's your help, so far as I know."

"Is it? I can give you the stuff, brother, loads of it, and don't think I can't. I'm a girl who knows her Poisonville." She looked down at her gray-stockinged knees, waved one leg at me, and exclaimed indignantly: "Look at that. Another run. Did you ever see anything to beat it? Honest to God! I'm going bare-foot."

"Your legs are too big," I told her. "They put too much strain on the material."

"That'll do out of you. What's your idea of how to go about purifying our village?"

"If I haven't been lied to, Thaler, Pete the Finn, Lew Yard and Noonan are the men who've made Poisonville the sweet-smelling mess it is. Old Elihu comes in for his share of the blame, too, but it's not all his fault, maybe. Besides, he's my client, even if he doesn't want to be, so I'd like to go easy on him.

"The closest I've got to an idea is to dig up any and all the dirty work I can that might implicate the others, and run it out. Maybe I'll advertise – *Crime Wanted – Male or Female*. If they're as crooked as I think they are I shouldn't have a lot of trouble finding a job or two that I can hang on them."

"Is that what you were up to when you uncooked the fight?"

"That was only an experiment – just to see what would happen."

"So that's the way you scientific detectives work. My God! for a fat, middle-aged, hard-boiled, pig-headed guy, you've got the vaguest way of doing things I ever heard of."

"Plans are all right sometimes," I said. "And sometimes just stirring things up is all right – if you're tough enough to survive, and keep your eyes open so you'll see what you want when it comes to the top."

"That ought to be good for another drink," she said.

11 THE SWELL SPOON

WE HAD ANOTHER drink.

She put her glass down, licked her lips, and said:

"If stirring things up is your system, I've got a swell spoon for you. Did you ever hear of Noonan's brother Tim, the one who committed suicide out at Mock Lake a couple of years ago?"

"No."

"You wouldn't have heard much good. Anyway, he didn't commit suicide. Max killed him."

"Yeah?"

"For God's sake wake up. This I'm giving you is real. Noonan was like a father to Tim. Take the proof to him and he'll be after Max like nobody's business. That's what you want, isn't it?"

"We've got proof?"

"Two people got to Tim before he died, and he told them Max had done it. They're both still in town, though one won't live a lot longer. How's that?"

She looked as if she were telling the truth, though with women, especially blue-eyed women, that doesn't always mean anything.

"Let's listen to the rest of it," I said. "I like details and things."

"You'll get them. You ever been out to Mock Lake? Well, it's our summer resort, thirty miles up the canyon road. It's a dump, but it's cool in summer, so it gets a good play. This was summer a year ago, the last week-end in August. I was out there with a fellow named Holly. He's back in England now, but you don't care anything about that, because he's got nothing to do with it. He was a funny sort of old woman – used to wear white silk socks turned inside out so the loose threads wouldn't hurt his feet. I got a letter from him last week. It's around here somewhere, but that doesn't make any difference.

"We were up there, and Max was up there with a girl he used to play around with – Myrtle Jennison. She's in the hospital now – City – dying of Bright's disease or something. She was a classy-looking kid then, a slender blonde. I always liked her, except that a few drinks made her too noisy. Tim Noonan was crazy about her, but she couldn't see anybody but Max that summer.

"Tim wouldn't let her alone. He was a big good-looking Irishman, but a sap and a cheap crook who only got by because his brother was chief of police. Wherever Myrtle went, he'd pop up sooner or later. She didn't like to say anything to Max about it, not wanting Max to do anything to put him in wrong with Tim's brother, the chief.

"So of course Tim showed up at Mock Lake this Saturday. Myrtle and Max were just by themselves. Holly and I were with a bunch, but I saw Myrtle to talk to and she told me she had got a note from Tim, asking her to meet him for a few minutes that night, in one of the little arbor things on the hotel grounds. He said if she didn't he would kill himself. That was a laugh for us – the big false alarm. I tried to talk Myrtle out of going, but she had just enough booze in her to feel gay and she said she was going to give him an earful.

"We were all dancing in the hotel that night. Max was there for a while, and then I didn't see him any more. Myrtle was dancing with a fellow named Rutgers, a lawyer here in town. After a while she left him and went out one of the side-doors. She winked at me when she passed, so I knew she was going down to see Tim. She had just got out when I heard the shot. Nobody else paid any attention to it. I suppose

I wouldn't have noticed it either if I hadn't known about Myrtle and Tim.

"I told Holly I wanted to see Myrtle, and went out after her, by myself. I must have been about five minutes behind her in getting out. When I got outside I saw lights down by one of the summer houses, and people. I went down there, and – This talking is thirsty work."

I poured out a couple of hookers of gin. She went into the kitchen for another siphon and more ice. We mixed them up, drank, and she settled down to her tale again:

"There was Tim Noonan, dead, with a hole in his temple and his gun lying beside him. Perhaps a dozen people were standing around, hotel people, visitors, one of Noonan's men, a dick named MacSwain. As soon as Myrtle saw me she took me away from the crowd, back in the shade of some trees.

"'Max killed him,' she said. 'What'll I do?'

"I asked her about it. She told me she had seen the flash of the gun and at first she thought Tim had killed himself after all. She was too far away and it was too dark for her to see anything else. When she ran down to him, he was rolling around, moaning, 'He didn't have to kill me over her. I'd have – ' She couldn't make out the rest of it. He was rolling around, bleeding from the hole in his temple.

"Myrtle was afraid Max had done it, but she had to be sure, so she knelt down and tried to pick up Tim's head, asking: 'Who did it, Tim?'

"He was almost gone, but before he passed out he got enough strength to tell her, 'Max!'

"She kept asking me, 'What'll I do?' I asked her if anybody else had heard Tim, and she said the dick had. He came running up while she was trying to lift Tim's head. She didn't think anybody else had been near enough to hear, but the dick had.

"I didn't want Max to get in a jam over killing a mutt like Tim Noonan. Max didn't mean anything to me then, except that I liked him, and I didn't like any of the Noonans. I knew the dick – MacSwain. I used to know his wife. He had been a pretty good guy, straight as ace-deuce-trey-four-five, till he got on the force. Then he went the way of the rest of them. His wife stood as much of it as she could and then left him.

"Knowing this dick, I told Myrtle I thought we could fix things. A little jack would ruin MacSwain's memory, or, if he didn't like that, Max could have him knocked off. She had Tim's note threatening suicide. If the dick would play along, the hole in Tim's head from his own gun and the note would smooth everything over pretty.

"I left Myrtle under the trees and went out to hunt for Max. He wasn't around. There weren't many people there, and I could hear the hotel orchestra still playing dance music. I couldn't find Max, so I went back to Myrtle. She was all worked up over another idea. She didn't want Max to know that she had found out that he had killed Tim. She was afraid of him.

"See what I mean? She was afraid that if she and Max ever broke off he'd put her out of the way if he knew she had enough on him to swing him. I know how she felt. I got the same notion later, and kept just as quiet as she did. So we figured that if it could be fixed up without his knowing about it, so much the better. I didn't want to show in it either.

"Myrtle went back alone to the group around Tim and got hold of MacSwain. She took him off a little way and made the deal with him. She had some dough on her. She gave him two hundred and a diamond ring that had cost a fellow named Boyle a thousand. I thought he'd be back for more later, but he wasn't. He shot square with her. With the help of the letter he put over the suicide story.

"Noonan knew there was something fishy about the lay-out, but he could never peg it. I think he suspected Max of having something to do with it. But Max had an air-tight alibi – trust him for that – and I think even Noonan finally counted him out.

But Noonan never believed it happened the way it was made to look. He broke MacSwain – kicked him off the force.

"Max and Myrtle slid apart a little while after that. No row or anything – they just slid apart. I don't think she ever felt easy around him again, though so far as I know he never suspected her of knowing anything. She's sick now, as I told you, and hasn't got long to live. I think she'd not so much mind telling the truth if she were asked. MacSwain's still hanging around town. He'd talk if there was something in it for him. Those two have got the stuff on Max – and wouldn't Noonan eat it up! Is that good enough to give your stirring-up a start?"

"Couldn't it have been suicide?" I asked. "With Tim Noonan getting a last-minute bright idea to stick it on Max?"

"That four-flusher shoot himself? Not a chance."

"Could Myrtle have shot him?"

"Noonan didn't overlook that one. But she couldn't have been a third of the distance down the slope when the shot was fired. Tim had powder-marks on his head, and hadn't been shot and rolled down the slope. Myrtle's out."

"But Max had an alibi?"

"Yes, indeed. He always has. He was in the hotel bar, on the other side of the building, all the time. Four men said so. As I remember it, they said it openly and often, long before anybody asked them. There were other men in the bar who didn't remember whether Max had been there or not, but those four remembered. They'd remember anything Max wanted remembered."

Her eyes got large and then narrowed to black-fringed slits. She leaned towards me, upsetting her glass with an elbow.

"Peak Murry was one of the four. He and Max are on the outs now. Peak might tell it straight now. He's got a pool room on Broadway."

"This MacSwain, does he happen to be named Bob?" I asked. "A bow-legged man with a long jaw like a hog's?"

"Yes. You know him?"

"By sight. What does he do now?"

"A small-time grifter. What do you think of the stack-up?"

"Not bad. Maybe I can use it."

"Then let's talk scratch."

I grinned at the greed in her eyes and said:

"Not just yet, sister. We'll have to see how it works out before we start scattering pennies around."

She called me a damned nickel-nurser and reached for the gin.

"No more for me, thanks," I told her, looking at my watch. "It's getting along towards five a.m. and I've got a busy day ahead."

She decided she was hungry again. That reminded me that I was. It took a half an hour or more to get waffles, ham and coffee off the stove. It took some more time to get them into our stomachs and to smoke some cigarettes over extra cups of coffee. It was quite a bit after six when I got ready to leave.

I went back to my hotel and got into a tub of cold water. It braced me a lot, and I needed bracing. At forty I could get along on gin as a substitute for sleep, but not comfortably.

When I had dressed I sat down and composed a document:

Just before he died, Tim Noonan told me he had been shot by Max Thaler. Detective Bob MacSwain heard him tell me. I gave Detective MacSwain $200 and a diamond ring worth $1,000 to keep quiet and make it look like suicide.

With this document in my pocket I went downstairs, had another breakfast that was mostly coffee, and went up to the City Hospital.

Visiting hours were in the afternoon, but by flourishing my Continental Detective Agency credentials and giving everybody to understand that an hour's delay might cause thousands of deaths, or words to that effect, I got to see Myrtle Jennison.

She was in a ward on the third floor, alone. The other four beds were empty. She could have been a girl of twenty-five or a woman of fifty-five. Her face was a bloated spotty mask. Lifeless yellow hair in two stringy braids lay on the pillow beside her.

I waited until the nurse who had brought me up left. Then I held my document out to the invalid and said:

"Will you sign this, please, Miss Jennison?"

She looked at me with ugly eyes that were shaded into no particular dark color by the pads of flesh around them, then at the document, and finally brought a shapeless fat hand from under the covers to take it.

She pretended it took her nearly five minutes to read the forty-two words I had written. She let the document fall down on the covers and asked:

"Where'd you get that?" Her voice was tinny, irritable.

"Dinah Brand sent me to you."

She asked eagerly:

"Has she broken off with Max?"

"Not that I know of," I lied. "I imagine she just wants to have this on hand in case it should come in handy."

"And get her fool throat slit. Give me a pencil."

I gave her my fountain-pen and held my notebook under the document, to stiffen it while she scribbled her signature at the bottom, and to have it in my hands as soon as she had finished. While I fanned the paper dry she said:

"If that's what she wants it's all right with me. What do I care what anybody does now? I'm done. Hell with them all!" She sniggered and suddenly threw the bedclothes down to her knees, showing me a horrible swollen body in a coarse white nightgown. "How do you like me? See, I'm done."

I pulled the covers up over her again and said:

"Thanks for this, Miss Jennison."

"That's all right. It's nothing to me any more. Only" – her puffy chin quivered – "it's hell to die ugly as this."

I WENT OUT to hunt for MacSwain. Neither city directory nor telephone-book told me anything. I did the pool rooms, cigar-stores, speakeasies, looking around first, then asking cautious questions. That got me nothing. I walked the streets, looking for bowed legs. That got me nothing. I decided to go back to my hotel, grab a nap, and resume the hunting at night.

In a far corner of the lobby a man stopped hiding behind a newspaper and came out to meet me. He had bowed legs, a hog jaw, and was MacSwain.

I nodded carelessly at him and walked on towards the elevators. He followed me, mumbling:

"Hey, you got a minute?"

"Yeah, just about." I stopped, pretending indifference.

"Let's get out of sight," he said nervously.

I took him up to my room. He straddled a chair and put a match in his mouth. I sat on the side of the bed and waited for him to say something. He chewed his match a while and began:

"I'm going to come clean with you, brother. I'm —"

"You mean you're going to tell me you knew me when you braced me yesterday?" I asked. "And you're going to tell me Bush hadn't told you to bet on him? And you didn't until afterwards? And you knew about his record because you used to be a bull? And you thought if you could get me to put it to him you could clean up a little dough playing him?"

"I'll be damned if I was going to come through with that much," he said, "but since it's been said I'll put a yes to it."

"Did you clean up?"

526

"I win myself six hundred iron men." He pushed his hat back and scratched his forehead with the chewed end of his match. "And then I lose myself that and my own two hundred and some in a crap game. What do you think of that? I pick up six hundred berries like shooting fish, and have to bum four bits for breakfast."

I said it was a tough break but that was the kind of a world we lived in.

He said, "Uh-huh," put the match back in his mouth, ground it some more, and added: "That's why I thought I'd come to see you. I used to be in the racket myself and –"

"What did Noonan put the skids under you for?"

"Skids? What skids? I quit. I come into a piece of change when the wife got killed in an automobile accident – insurance – and I quit."

"I heard he kicked you out the time his brother shot himself."

"Well, then you heard wrong. It was just after that, but you can ask him if I didn't quit."

"It's not that much to me. Go on telling me why you came to see me."

"I'm busted, flat. I know you're a Continental op, and I got a pretty good hunch what you're up to here. I'm close to a lot that's going on on both sides of things in this burg. There's things I could do for you, being an ex-dick, knowing the ropes both ways."

"You want to stool-pigeon for me?"

He looked me straight in the eye and said evenly:

"There's no sense in a man picking out the worst name he can find for everything."

"I'll give you something to do, MacSwain." I took out Myrtle Jennison's document and passed it to him. "Tell me about that."

He read it through carefully, his lips framing the words, the match wavering up and down in his mouth. He got up, put the paper on the bed beside me, and scowled down at it.

"There's something I'll have to find out about first," he said, very solemnly. "I'll be back in a little while and give you the whole story."

I laughed and told him:

"Don't be silly. You know I'm not going to let you walk out on me."

"I don't know that." He shook his head, still solemn. "Neither do you. All you know is whether you're going to try to stop me."

"The answer's yeah," I said while I considered that he was fairly hard and strong, six or seven years younger than I, and twenty or thirty pounds lighter.

He stood at the foot of the bed and looked at me with solemn eyes. I sat on the side of the bed and looked at him with whatever kind of eyes I had at the time. We did this for nearly three minutes.

I used part of the time measuring the distance between us, figuring out how, by throwing my body back on the bed and turning on my hip, I could get my heels in his face if he jumped me. He was too close for me to pull the gun. I had just finished this mental map-making when he spoke:

"That lousy ring wasn't worth no grand. I did swell to get two centuries for it."

He shook his head again and said:

"First I want to know what you're meaning to do about it."

"Cop Whisper."

"I don't mean that. I mean with me."

"You'll have to go over to the Hall with me."

"I won't."

"Why not? You're only a witness."

"I'm only a witness that Noonan can hang a bribe-taking, or an accomplice after the act rap on, or both. And he'd be tickled simple to have the chance."

This jaw-wagging didn't seem to be leading anywhere. I said:

"That's too bad. But you're going to see him."

"Try and take me."

I sat up straighter and slid my right hand back to my hip.

He grabbed for me. I threw my body back on the bed, did the hip-spin, swung my feet at him. It was a good trick, only it didn't work. In his hurry to get at me he bumped the bed aside just enough to spill me off on the floor.

I landed all sprawled out on my back. I kept dragging at my gun while I tried to roll under the bed.

Missing me, his lunge carried him over the low footboard, over the side of the bed. He came down beside me, on the back of his neck, his body somersaulting over.

I put the muzzle of my gun in his left eye and said:

"You're making a fine pair of clowns of us. Be still while I get up or I'll make an opening in your head for brains to leak in."

I got up, found and pocketed my document, and let him get up.

"Knock the dents out of your hat and put your necktie in front, so you won't disgrace me going through the streets," I ordered after I had run a hand over his clothes and found nothing that felt like a weapon. "You can suit yourself about remembering that this gat is going to be in my overcoat-pocket, with a hand on it."

He straightened his hat and tie and said:

"Hey, listen: I'm in this, I guess, and cutting up won't get me nothing. Suppose I be good. Could you forget about the tussle? See – maybe it'd be smoother for me if they thought I come along without being dragged."

"OK."

"Thanks, brother."

Noonan was out eating. We had to wait half an hour in his outer office. When he came in he greeted me with the usual

How are you? . . . That certainly is fine. . . . and the rest of it. He didn't say anything to MacSwain – simply eyed him sourly.

We went into the chief's private office. He pulled a chair over to his desk for me and then sat in his own, ignoring the ex-dick.

I gave Noonan the sick girl's document.

He gave it one glance, bounced out of his chair, and smashed a fist the size of a cantaloup into MacSwain's face.

The punch carried MacSwain across the room until a wall stopped him. The wall creaked under the strain, and a framed photograph of Noonan and other city dignitaries welcoming somebody in spats dropped down to the floor with the hit man.

The fat chief waddled over, picked up the picture and beat it to splinters on MacSwain's head and shoulders. Noonan came back to his desk, puffing, smiling, saying cheerfully to me:

"That fellow's a rat if there ever was one."

MacSwain sat up and looked around, bleeding from nose, mouth and head.

Noonan roared at him:

"Come here, you."

MacSwain said, "Yes, chief," scrambled up and ran over to the desk.

Noonan said: "Come through or I'll kill you."

MacSwain said:

"Yes, chief. It was like she said, only that rock wasn't worth no grand. But she give me it and the two hundred to keep my mouth shut, because I got there just when she asks him, 'Who did it, Tim?' and he says, 'Max!' He says it kind of loud and sharp, like he wanted to get it out before he died, because he died right then, almost before he'd got it out. That's the way it was, chief, but the rock wasn't worth no –"

"Damn the rock," Noonan barked. "And stop bleeding on my rug."

MacSwain hunted in his pocket for a dirty handkerchief, mopped his nose and mouth with it, and jabbered on:

"That's the way it was, chief. Everything else was like I said at the time, only I didn't say anything about hearing him say Max done it. I know I hadn't ought to –"

"Shut up," Noonan said, and pressed one of the buttons on his desk.

A uniformed copper came in. The chief jerked a thumb at MacSwain and said:

"Take this baby down cellar and let the wrecking crew work on him before you lock him up."

MacSwain started a desperate plea, "Aw, chief!" but the copper took him away before he could get any farther.

Noonan stuck a cigar at me, tapped the document with another and asked:

"Where's this broad?"

"In the City Hospital, dying. You'll have the 'cuter get a stiff out of her? That one's not so good legally – I framed it for effect. Another thing – I hear that Peak Murry and Whisper aren't playmates any more. Wasn't Murry one of his alibis?"

The chief said, "He was," picked up one of his phones, said, "McGraw," and then: "Get hold of Peak Murry and ask him to drop in. And have Tony Agosti picked up for that knife-throwing."

He put the phone down, stood up, made a lot of cigar-smoke, and said through it:

"I haven't always been on the up-and-up with you."

I thought that was putting it mildly, but I didn't say anything while he went on:

"You know your way around. You know what these jobs are. There's this one and that one that's got to be listened to. Just because a man's chief of police doesn't mean he's chief. Maybe you're a lot of trouble to somebody that can be a lot of trouble to me. Don't make any difference if I think you're a right guy. I got to play with them that play with me. See what I mean?"

I wagged my head to show I did.

"That's the way it was," he said. "But no more. This is something else, a new deal. When the old woman kicked off Tim was just a lad. She said to me, 'Take care of him, John,' and I promised I would. And then Whisper murders him on account of that tramp." He reached down and took my hand. "See what I'm getting at? That's a year and a half ago, and you give me my first chance to hang it on him. I'm telling you there's no man in Personville that's got a voice big enough to talk you down. Not after today."

That pleased me and I said so. We purred at each other until a lanky man with any extremely up-turned nose in the middle of a round and freckled face was ushered in. It was Peak Murry.

"We were just wondering about the time when Tim died," the chief said when Murry had been given a chair and a cigar, "where Whisper was. You were out to the Lake that night, weren't you?"

"Yep," Murry said and the end of his nose got sharper.

"With Whisper?"

"I wasn't with him all the time."

"Were you with him at the time of the shooting?"

"Nope."

The chief's greenish eyes got smaller and brighter. He asked softly:

"You know where he was?"

"Nope."

The chief sighed in a thoroughly satisfied way and leaned back in his chair.

"Damn it, Peak," he said, "you told us before that you were with him at the bar."

"Yep, I did," the lanky man admitted. "But that don't mean nothing except that he asked me to and I didn't mind helping out a friend."

"Meaning you don't mind standing a perjury rap?"

"Don't kid me." Murry spit vigorously at the cuspidor. "I didn't say nothing in no court rooms."

"How about Jerry and George Kelly and O'Brien?" the chief asked. "Did they say they were with him just because he asked them to?"

"O'Brien did. I don't know nothing about the others. I was going out of the bar when I run into Whisper, Jerry and Kelly, and went back to have a shot with them. Kelly told me Tim had been knocked off. Then Whisper says, 'It never hurts anybody to have an alibi. We were here all the time, weren't we?' and he looks at O'Brien, who's behind the bar. O'Brien says, 'Sure you was,' and when Whisper looks at me I say the same thing. But I don't know no reasons why I've got to cover him up nowadays."

"And Kelly said Tim had been knocked off? Didn't say he had been found dead?"

"'Knocked off' was the words he used."

The chief said:

"Thanks, Peak. You oughtn't to have done like you did, but what's done is done. How are the kids?"

Murry said they were doing fine, only the baby wasn't as fat as he'd like to have him. Noonan phoned the prosecuting attorney's office and had Dart and a stenographer take Peak's story before he left.

Noonan, Dart and the stenographer set out for the City Hospital to get a complete statement from Myrtle Jennison. I didn't go along. I decided I needed sleep, told the chief I would see him later, and returned to the hotel.

I HAD MY vest unbuttoned when the telephone-bell rang.

It was Dinah Brand, complaining that she had been trying to get me since ten o'clock.

"Have you done anything on what I told you?" she asked.

"I've been looking it over. It seems pretty good. I think maybe I'll crack it this afternoon."

"Don't. Hold it till I see you. Can you come up now?"

I looked at the vacant white bed and said, "Yes," without much enthusiasm.

Another tub of cold water did me so little good that I almost fell asleep in it.

Dan Rolff let me in when I rang the girl's bell. He looked and acted as if nothing out of the ordinary had happened the night before. Dinah Brand came into the hall to help me off with my overcoat. She had on a tan woolen dress with a two-inch rip in one shoulder seam.

She took me into the living-room. She sat on the chesterfield beside me and said:

"I'm going to ask you to do something for me. You like me enough, don't you?"

I admitted that. She counted the knuckles of my left hand with a warm forefinger and explained:

"I want you to not do anything more about what I told you last night. Now wait a minute. Wait till I get through. Dan was right. I oughtn't sell Max out like that. It would be utterly filthy. Besides, it's Noonan you chiefly want, isn't it? Well, if you'll be a nice darling and lay off Max this time, I'll give you enough on Noonan to nail him forever. You'd like that better, wouldn't you? And you like me too much to want to take advantage of me by using information I gave you when I was mad at what Max had said, don't you?"

"What is the dirt on Noonan?" I asked.

She kneaded my biceps and murmured: "You promise?"

"Not yet."

She pouted at me and said:

"I'm off Max for life, on the level. You've got no right to make me turn rat."

"What about Noonan?"

"Promise first."

"No."

She dug fingers into my arm and asked sharply:

"You've already gone to Noonan?"

"Yeah."

She let go my arm, frowned, shrugged, and said gloomily:

"Well, how can I help it?"

I stood up and a voice said:

"Sit down."

It was a hoarse whispering voice – Thaler's.

I turned to see him standing in the dining-room doorway, a big gun in one of his little hands. A red-faced man with a scarred cheek stood behind him.

The other doorway – opening to the hall – filled as I sat down. The loose-mouthed chinless man I had heard Whisper call Jerry came a step through it. He had a couple of guns. The more angular one of the blond kids who had been in the King Street joint looked over his shoulder.

Dinah Brand got up from the chesterfield, put her back to Thaler, and addressed me. Her voice was husky with rage.

"This is none of my doing. He came here by himself, said he was sorry for what he had said, and showed me how we could make a lot of coin by turning Noonan up for you. The whole thing was a plant, but I fell for it. Honest to Christ! He was to wait upstairs while I put it to you. I didn't know anything about the others. I didn't —"

Jerry's casual voice drawled:

"If I shoot a pin from under her, she'll sure sit down, and maybe shut up. OK?"

I couldn't see Whisper. The girl was between us. He said:

"Not now. Where's Dan?"

The angular blond youngster said:

"Up on the bathroom-floor. I had to sap him."

Dinah Brand turned around to face Thaler. Stocking seams made s's up the ample backs of her legs. She said:

"Max Thaler, you're a lousy little —"

He whispered, very deliberately:

"Shut up and get out of the way."

She surprised me by doing both, and she kept quiet while he spoke to me:

"So you and Noonan are trying to paste his brother's death on me?"

"It doesn't need pasting. It's a natural."

He curved his thin lips at me and said:

"You're as crooked as he is."

I said:

"You know better. I played your side when he tried to frame you. This time he's got you copped to rights."

Dinah Brand flared up again, waving her arms in the center of the room, storming:

"Get out of here, the whole lot of you. Why should I give a goddamn about your troubles? Get out."

The blond kid who had sapped Rolff squeezed past Jerry and came grinning into the room. He caught one of the girl's flourished arms and bent it behind her.

She twisted towards him, socked him in the belly with her other fist. It was a very respectable wallop — man-size. It broke his grip on her arm, sent him back a couple of steps.

536

The kid gulped a wide mouthful of air, whisked a blackjack from his hip, and stepped in again. His grin was gone.

Jerry laughed what little chin he had out of sight.

Thaler whispered harshly: "Lay off!"

The kid didn't hear him. He was snarling at the girl.

She watched him with a face hard as a silver dollar. She was standing with most of her weight on her left foot. I guessed blondy was going to stop a kick when he closed in.

The kid feinted a grab with his empty left hand, started the blackjack at her face.

Thaler whispered, "Lay off," again, and fired.

The bullet smacked blondy under the right eye, spun him around, and dropped him backwards into Dinah Brand's arms.

This looked like the time, if there was to be any.

In the excitement I had got my hand to my hip. Now I yanked the gun out and snapped a cap at Thaler, trying for his shoulder.

That was wrong. If I had tried for a bull's-eye I would have winged him. Chinless Jerry hadn't laughed himself blind. He beat me to the shot. His shot burnt my wrist, throwing me off the target. But, missing Thaler, my slug crumpled the red-faced man behind him.

Not knowing how badly my wrist was nicked, I switched the gun to my left hand.

Jerry had another try at me. The girl spoiled it by heaving the corpse at him. The dead yellow head banged into his knees. I jumped for him while he was off-balance.

The jump took me out of the path of Thaler's bullet. It also tumbled me and Jerry out into the hall, all tangled up together.

Jerry wasn't tough to handle, but I had to work quick. There was Thaler behind me. I socked Jerry twice, kicked him, butted him at least once, and was hunting for a place to bite when he went limp under me. I poked him again where his chin should have been – just to make sure he wasn't faking

– and went away on hands and knees, down the hall a bit, out of line with the door.

I sat on my heels against the wall, held my gun level at Thaler's part of the premises, and waited. I couldn't hear anything for the moment except blood singing in my head.

Dinah Brand stepped out of the door I had tumbled through, looked at Jerry, then at me. She smiled with her tongue between her teeth, beckoned with a jerk of her head, and returned to the living-room. I followed her cautiously.

Whisper stood in the center of the floor. His hands were empty and so was his face. Except for his vicious little mouth he looked like something displaying suits in a clothing-store window.

Dan Rolff stood behind him, with a gun-muzzle tilted to the little gambler's left kidney. Rolff's face was mostly blood. The blond kid – now dead on the floor between Rolff and me – had sapped him plenty.

I grinned at Thaler and said, "Well, this is nice," before I saw that Rolff had another gun, centered on my chubby middle. That wasn't so nice. But my gun was reasonably level in my hand. I didn't have much worse than an even break.

Rolff said:

"Put down your pistol."

I looked at Dinah, looked puzzled, I suppose. She shrugged and told me:

"It seems to be Dan's party."

"Yeah? Somebody ought to tell him I don't like to play this way."

Rolff repeated: "Put down your pistol."

I said disagreeably:

"I'm damned if I will. I've shed twenty pounds trying to nab this bird, and I can spare twenty more for the same purpose."

Rolff said:

"I'm not interested in what is between you two, and I have no intention of giving either of you —"

Dinah Brand had wandered across the room. When she was behind Rolff, I interrupted his speech by telling her:

"If you upset him now you're sure of making two friends — Noonan and me. You can't trust Thaler any more, so there's no use helping him."

She laughed and said:

"Talk money, darling."

"Dinah!" Rolff protested. He was caught. She was behind him and she was strong enough to handle him. It wasn't likely that he would shoot her, and it wasn't likely that anything else would keep her from doing whatever she decided to do.

"A hundred dollars," I bid.

"My God!" she exclaimed, "I've actually got a cash offer out of you. But not enough."

"Two hundred."

"You're getting reckless. But I still can't hear you."

"Try," I said. "It's worth that to me not to have to shoot Rolff's gun out of his hand, but no more than that."

"You got a good start. Don't weaken. One more bid, anyway."

"Two hundred dollars and ten cents and that's all."

"You big bum," she said, "I won't do it."

"Suit yourself." I made a face at Thaler and cautioned him: "When what happens happens be damned sure you keep still."

Dinah cried:

"Wait! Are you really going to start something?"

"I'm going to take Thaler out with me, regardless."

"Two hundred and a dime?"

"Yeah."

"Dinah," Rolff called without turning his face from me, "you won't —"

539

But she laughed, came close to his back, and wound her strong arms around him, pulling his arms down, pinning them to his sides.

I shoved Thaler out of the way with my right arm, and kept my gun on him while I yanked Rolff's weapons out of his hands. Dinah turned the lunger loose.

He took two steps towards the dining-room-door, said wearily, "There is no —" and collapsed on the floor.

Dinah ran to him. I pushed Thaler through the hall-door, past the still sleeping Jerry, and to the alcove beneath the front stairs, where I had seen a phone.

I called Noonan, told him I had Thaler, and where.

"Mother of God!" he said. "Don't kill him till I get there."

THE NEWS OF Whisper's capture spread quickly. When Noonan, the coppers he had brought along, and I took the gambler and the now conscious Jerry into the City Hall there were at least a hundred people standing around watching us.

All of them didn't look pleased. Noonan's coppers – a shabby lot at best – moved around with whitish strained faces. But Noonan was the most triumphant guy west of the Mississippi. Even the bad luck he had trying to third-degree Whisper couldn't spoil his happiness.

Whisper stood up under all they could give him. He would talk to his lawyer, he said, and to nobody else, and he stuck to it. And, as much as Noonan hated the gambler, here was a prisoner he didn't give the works, didn't turn over to the wrecking crew. Whisper had killed the chief's brother, and the chief hated his guts, but Whisper was still too much somebody in Poisonville to be roughed around.

Noonan finally got tired of playing with his prisoner, and sent him up – the prison was on the City Hall's top floor – to be stowed away. I lit another of the chief's cigars and read the detailed statement he had got from the woman in the hospital. There was nothing in it that I hadn't learned from Dinah and MacSwain.

The chief wanted me to come out to his house for dinner, but I lied out of it, pretending that my wrist – now in a bandage – was bothering me. It was really little more than a burn.

While we were talking about it, a pair of plain-clothes men brought in the red-faced bird who had stopped the slug I had missed Whisper with. It had broken a rib for him, and he had

taken a back-door sneak while the rest of us were busy.
Noonan's men had picked him up in a doctor's office. The
chief failed to get any information out of him, and sent him off
to the hospital.

I got up and prepared to leave, saying:

"The Brand girl gave me the tip-off on this. That's why
I asked you to keep her and Rolff out of it."

The chief took hold of my left hand for the fifth or sixth
time in the past couple of hours.

"If you want her taken care of, that's enough for me," he
assured me. "But if she had a hand in turning that bastard up,
you can tell her for me that any time she wants anything, all
she's got to do is name it."

I said I'd tell her that, and went over to my hotel, thinking
about that neat white bed. But it was nearly eight o'clock, and
my stomach needed attention. I went into the hotel dining-
room and had that fixed up.

Then a leather chair tempted me into stopping in the lobby
while I burnt a cigar. That led to conversation with a traveling
railroad auditor from Denver, who knew a man I knew in St.
Louis. Then there was a lot of shooting in the street.

We went to the door and decided that the shooting was in
the vicinity of the City Hall. I shook the auditor and moved up
that way.

I had done two-thirds of the distance when an automobile
came down the street towards me, moving fast, leaking gun-
fire from the rear.

I backed into an alley entrance and slid my gun loose. The
car came abreast. An arc-light brightened two faces in the front
of the car. The driver's meant nothing to me. The upper part
of the other's was hidden by a pulled-down hat. The lower
part was Whisper's.

Across the street was the entrance to another block of my
alley, lighted at the far end. Between the light and me, somebody moved just as Whisper's car roared past. The somebody

had dodged from behind one shadow that might have been an ash-can to another.

What made me forget Whisper was that the somebody's legs had a bowed look.

A load of coppers buzzed past, throwing lead at the first car.

I skipped across the street, into the section of alley that held a man who might have bowed legs.

If he was my man, it was a fair bet he wasn't armed. I played it that way, moving straight up the slimy middle of the alley, looking into shadows with eyes, ears and nose.

Three-quarters of a block of this, and a shadow broke away from another shadow – a man going pell-mell away from me.

"Stop!" I bawled, pounding my feet after him. "Stop, or I'll plug you, MacSwain."

He ran half a dozen strides farther and stopped, turning.

"Oh, it's you," he said, as if it made any difference who took him back to the hoosegow.

"Yeah," I confessed. "What are all you people doing wandering around loose?"

"I don't know nothing about it. Somebody dynamited the floor out of the can. I dropped through the hole with the rest of them. There was some mugs standing off the bulls. I made the back-trotters with one bunch. Then we split, and I was figuring on cutting over and making the hills. I didn't have nothing to do with it. I just went along when she blew open."

"Whisper was pinched this evening," I told him.

"Hell! Then that's it. Noonan had ought to know he'd never keep that guy screwed up – not in this burg."

We were standing still in the alley where MacSwain had stopped running.

"You know what he was pinched for?" I asked.

"Uh-huh, for killing Tim."

"You know who killed Tim?"

"Huh? Sure, he did."

"You did."

"Huh? What's the matter? You simple?"

"There's a gun in my left hand," I warned him.

"But look here – didn't he tell the broad that Whisper done it? What's the matter with you?"

"He didn't say *Whisper*. I've heard women call Thaler *Max*, but I've never heard a man here call him anything but *Whisper*. Tim didn't say *Max*. He said *MacS* – the first part of *MacSwain* – and died before he could finish it. Don't forget about the gun."

"What would I have killed him for? He was after Whisper's –"

"I haven't got around to that yet," I admitted, "but let's see: You and your wife had busted up. Tim was a ladies' man, wasn't he? Maybe there's something there. I'll have to look it up. What started me thinking about you was that you never tried to get any more money out of the girl."

"Cut it out," he begged. "You know there ain't any sense to it. What would I have hung around afterwards for? I'd have been out getting an alibi, like Whisper."

"Why? You were a dick then. Close by was the spot for you – to see that everything went right – handle it yourself."

"You know damned well it don't hang together, don't make sense. Cut it out, for God's sake."

"I don't mind how goofy it is," I said. "It's something to put to Noonan when we get back. He's likely all broken up over Whisper's crush-out. This will take his mind off it."

MacSwain got down on his knees in the muddy alley and cried:

"Oh, Christ, no! He'd croak me with his hands."

"Get up and stop yelling," I growled. "Now will you give it to me straight?"

He whined: "He'd croak me with his hands."

"Suit yourself. If you won't talk, I will, to Noonan. If you'll come through to me, I'll do what I can for you."

"What can you do?" he asked hopelessly, and started sniveling again. "How do I know you'll try to do anything?"

I risked a little truth on him:

"You said you had a hunch what I'm up to here in Poisonville. Then you ought to know that it's my play to keep Noonan and Whisper split. Letting Noonan think Whisper killed Tim will keep them split. But if you don't want to play with me, come on, we'll play with Noonan."

"You mean you won't tell him?" he asked eagerly. "You promise?"

"I promise you nothing," I said. "Why should I? I've got you with your pants down. Talk to me or Noonan. And make up your mind quick. I'm not going to stand here all night."

He made up his mind to talk to me.

"I don't know how much you know, but it was like you said, my wife fell for Tim. That's what put me on the tramp. You can ask anybody if I wasn't a good guy before that. I was this way: what she wanted I wanted her to have. Mostly what she wanted was tough on me. But I couldn't be any other way. We'd have been a damned sight better off if I could. So I let her move out and put in divorce papers, so she could marry him, thinking he meant to.

"Pretty soon I begin to hear he's chasing this Myrtle Jennison. I couldn't go that. I'd given him his chance with Helen, fair and square. Now he was giving her the air for this Myrtle. I wasn't going to stand for that. Helen wasn't no hanky-panky. It was accidental, though, running into him at the Lake that night. When I saw him go down to them summer houses I went after him. That looked like a good quiet place to have it out.

"I guess we'd both had a little something to drink. Anyway, we had it hot and heavy. When it got too hot for him, he pulled the gun. He was yellow. I grabbed it, and in the tussle it went off. I swear to God I didn't shoot him except like that. It went off while the both of us had our hands on it. I beat it back in some bushes. But when I got in the bushes I could hear him moaning and talking. There was people coming – a girl running down from the hotel, that Myrtle Jennison.

"I wanted to go back and hear what Tim was saying, so I'd know where I stood, but I was leery of being the first one there. So I had to wait till the girl got to him, listening all the time to his squawking, but too far away to make it out. When she got to him, I ran over and got there just as he died trying to say my name.

"I didn't think about that being Whisper's name till she propositioned me with the suicide letter, the two hundred, and the rock. I'd just been stalling around, pretending to get the job lined up – being on the force then – and trying to find out where I stood. Then she makes the play and I know I'm sitting pretty. And that's the way it went till you started digging it up again."

He slopped his feet up and down in the mud and added:

"Next week my wife got killed – an accident. Uh-huh, an accident. She drove the Ford square in front of No. 6 where it comes down the long grade from Tanner and stopped it there."

"Is Mock Lake in this county?" I asked.

"No, Boulder County."

"That's out of Noonan's territory. Suppose I take you over there and hand you to the sheriff?"

"No. He's Senator Keefer's son-in-law – Tom Cook. I might as well be here. Noonan could get to me through Keefer."

"If it happened the way you say, you've got at least an even chance of beating the rap in court."

"They won't give me a chance. I'd have stood it if there'd been a chance in the world of getting an even break – but not with them."

"We're going back to the Hall," I said. "Keep your mouth shut."

Noonan was waddling up and down the floor, cursing the half a dozen bulls who stood around wishing they were some-where else.

"Here's something I found roaming around," I said, pushing MacSwain forward.

Noonan knocked the ex-detective down, kicked him, and told one of the coppers to take him away.

Somebody called Noonan on the phone. I slipped out without saying, "Good-night," and walked back to the hotel.

Off to the north some guns popped.

A group of three men passed me, shifty-eyed, walking pigeon-toed.

A little farther along, another man moved all the way over to the curb to give me plenty of room to pass. I didn't know him and didn't suppose he knew me.

A lone shot sounded not far away.

As I reached the hotel, a battered black touring car went down the street, hitting fifty at least, crammed to the curtains with men.

I grinned after it. Poisonville was beginning to boil out under the lid, and I felt so much like a native that even the memory of my very un-nice part in the boiling didn't keep me from getting twelve solid end-to-end hours of sleep.

15　CEDAR HILL INN

MICKEY LINEHAN USED the telephone to wake me a little after noon.

"We're here," he told me. "Where's the reception committee?"

"Probably stopped to get a rope. Check your bags and come up to the hotel. Room 537. Don't advertise your visit."

I was dressed when they arrived.

Mickey Linehan was a big slob with sagging shoulders and a shapeless body that seemed to be coming apart at all its joints. His ears stood out like red wings, and his round red face usually wore the meaningless smirk of a half-wit. He looked like a comedian and was.

Dick Foley was a boy-sized Canadian with a sharp irritable face. He wore high heels to increase his height, perfumed his handkerchiefs and saved all the words he could.

They were both good operatives.

"What did the Old Man tell you about the job?" I asked when we had settled into seats. The Old Man was the manager of the Continental's San Francisco branch. He was also known as Pontius Pilate, because he smiled pleasantly when he sent us out to be crucified on suicidal jobs. He was a gentle, polite, elderly person with no more warmth in him than a hangman's rope. The Agency wits said he could spit icicles in July.

"He didn't seem to know much what it was all about," Mickey said, "except that you had wired for help. He said he hadn't got any reports from you for a couple of days."

"The chances are he'll wait a couple more. Know anything about this Personville?"

548

Dick shook his head. Mickey said:

"Only that I've heard parties call it Poisonville like they meant it."

I told them what I knew and what I had done. The telephone-bell interrupted my tale in the last quarter.

Dinah Brand's lazy voice:

"Hello! How's the wrist?"

"Only a burn. What do you think of the crush-out?"

"It's not my fault," she said. "I did my part. If Noonan couldn't hold him, that's just too bad. I'm coming downtown to buy a hat this afternoon. I thought I'd drop in and see you for a couple of minutes if you're going to be there."

"What time?"

"Oh, around three."

"Right, I'll expect you, and I'll have that two hundred and a dime I owe you."

"Do," she said. "That's what I'm coming in for. Ta-ta."

I went back to my seat and my story.

When I had finished, Mickey Linehan whistled and said:

"No wonder you're scared to send in any reports. The Old Man wouldn't do much if he knew what you've been up to, would he?"

"If it works out the way I want it to, I won't have to report all the distressing details," I said. "It's right enough for the Agency to have rules and regulations, but when you're out on a job you've got to do it the best way you can. And anybody that brings any ethics to Poisonville is going to get them all rusty. A report is no place for the dirty details, anyway, and I don't want you birds to send any writing back to San Francisco without letting me see it first."

"What kind of crimes have you got for us to pull?" Mickey asked.

"I want you to take Pete the Finn. Dick will take Lew Yard. You'll have to play it the way I've been playing – do what you can when you can. I've an idea that the pair of them will try to make Noonan let Whisper alone. I don't know what he'll do. He's shifty as hell and he does want to even up his brother's killing."

"After I take this Finnish gent," Mickey said, "what do I do with him? I don't want to brag about how dumb I am, but this job is plain as astronomy to me. I understand everything about it except what you have done and why, and what you're trying to do and how."

"You can start off by shadowing him. I've got to have a wedge that can be put between Pete and Yard, Yard and Noonan, Pete and Noonan, Pete and Thaler, or Yard and Thaler. If we can smash things up enough – break the combination – they'll have their knives in each other's backs, doing our work for us. The break between Thaler and Noonan is a starter. But it'll sag on us if we don't help it along.

"I could buy more dope on the whole lot from Dinah Brand. But there's no use taking anybody into court, no matter what you've got on them. They own the courts, and, besides, the courts are too slow for us now. I've got myself tangled up in something and as soon as the Old Man smells it – and San Francisco isn't far enough away to fool his nose – he's going to be sitting on the wire, asking for explanations. I've got to have results to hide the details under. So evidence won't do. What we've got to have is dynamite."

"What about our respected client, Mr. Elihu Willsson?" Mickey asked. "What are you planning to do with or to him?"

"Maybe ruin him, maybe club him into backing us up. I don't care which. You'd better stay at the Hotel Person, Mickey, and Dick can go to the National. Keep apart, and, if you want to keep me from being fired, burn the job up before the Old Man tumbles. Better write these down."

I gave them names, descriptions, and addresses when I had them, of Elihu Willsson; Stanley Lewis, his secretary; Dinah Brand; Dan Rolff; Noonan; Max Thaler, alias Whisper; his right-hand man, the chinless Jerry; Mrs. Donald Willsson;

Lewis's daughter, who had been Donald Willsson's secretary; and Bill Quint, Dinah's radical ex-boy-friend.

"Now hop to it," I said. "And don't kid yourselves that there's any law in Poisonville except what you make for yourself."

Mickey said I'd be surprised how many laws he could get along without. Dick said: "So long," and they departed.

After breakfast I went over to the City Hall.

Noonan's greenish eyes were bleary, as if they hadn't been sleeping, and his face had lost some of its color. He pumped my hand up and down as enthusiastically as ever, and the customary amount of cordiality was in his voice and manner.

"Any line on Whisper?" I asked when we had finished the glad-handing.

"I think I've got something." He looked at the clock on the wall and then at his phone. "I'm expecting word any minute. Sit down."

"Who else got away?"

"Jerry Hooper and Tony Agosti are the only other ones still out. We picked up the rest. Jerry is Whisper's man-Friday, and the wop's one of his mob. He's the bozo that put the knife in Ike Bush the night of the fight."

"Any more of Whisper's mob in?"

"No. We just had the three of them, except Buck Wallace, the fellow you potted. He's in the hospital."

The chief looked at the wall clock again, and at his watch. It was exactly two o'clock. He turned to the phone. It rang. He grabbed it, said:

"Noonan talking.... Yes.... Yes.... Yes.... Right."

He pushed the phone aside and played a tune on the row of pearl buttons on his desk. The office filled up with coppers.

"Cedar Hill Inn," he said. "You follow me out with your detail, Bates. Terry, shoot out Broadway and hit the dump from behind. Pick up the boys on traffic duty as you go along.

551

It's likely we'll need everybody we can get. Duffy, take yours out Union Street and around by the old mine road. McGraw will hold headquarters down. Get hold of everybody you can and send them after us. Jump!"

He grabbed his hat and went after them, calling over his thick shoulder to me:

"Come on, man, this is the kill."

I followed him down to the department garage, where the engines of half a dozen cars were roaring. The chief sat beside his driver. I sat in back with four detectives.

Men scrambled into the other cars. Machine-guns were unwrapped. Arm-loads of rifles and riot-guns were distributed, and packages of ammunition.

The chief's car got away first, off with a jump that hammered our teeth together. We missed the garage-door by half an inch, chased a couple of pedestrians diagonally across the sidewalk, bounced off the curb into the roadway, missed a truck as narrowly as we had missed the door, and dashed out King Street with our siren wide open.

Panicky automobiles darted right and left, regardless of traffic rules, to let us through. It was a lot of fun.

I looked back, saw another police car following us, a third turning into Broadway. Noonan chewed a cold cigar and told the driver:

"Give her a bit more, Pat."

Pat twisted us around a frightened woman's coupé, put us through a slot between street-car and laundry wagon – a narrow slot that we couldn't have slipped through if our car hadn't been so smoothly enameled – and said:

"All right, but the brakes ain't no good."

"That's nice," the gray-mustached sleuth on my left said. He didn't sound sincere.

Out of the center of the city there wasn't much traffic to bother us, but the paving was rougher. It was a nice half-hour's ride, with everybody getting a chance to sit in everybody else's lap. The last ten minutes of it was over an uneven road that had hills enough to keep us from forgetting what Pat had said about the brakes.

We wound up at a gate topped by a shabby electric sign that had said *Cedar Hill Inn* before it lost its globes. The roadhouse, twenty feet behind the gate, was a squat wooden building painted a moldy green and chiefly surrounded by rubbish. Front door and windows were closed, blank.

We followed Noonan out of the car. The machine that had been trailing us came into sight around a bend in the road, slid to rest beside ours, and unloaded its cargo of men and weapons.

Noonan ordered this and that.

A trio of coppers went around each side of the building. Three others, including a machine-gunner, remained by the gate. The rest of us walked through tin cans, bottles, and ancient newspaper to the front of the house.

The gray-mustached detective who had sat beside me in the car carried a red ax. We stepped up on the porch.

Noise and fire came out under a window sill.

The gray-mustached detective fell down, hiding the ax under his corpse.

The rest of us ran away.

I ran with Noonan. We hid in the ditch on the Inn side of the road. It was deep enough, and banked high enough, to let us stand almost erect without being targets.

The chief was excited.

"What luck!" he said happily. "He's here, by God, he's here!"

"That shot came from under the sill," I said. "Not a bad trick."

"We'll spoil it, though," he said cheerfully. "We'll sieve the dump. Duffy ought to be pulling up on the other road by now, and Terry Shane won't be many minutes behind him. Hey, Donner!" he called to a man who was peeping around a boulder. "Swing around back and tell Duffy and Shane to start closing in as soon as they come, letting fly with all they got. Where's Kimble?"

The peeper jerked a thumb towards a tree beyond him. We could see only the upper part of it from our ditch.

"Tell him to set up his mill and start grinding," Noonan ordered. "Low, across the front, ought to do it like cutting cheese."

The peeper disappeared.

Noonan went up and down the ditch, risking his noodle over the top now and then for a look around, once in a while calling or gesturing to his men.

He came back, sat on his heels beside me, gave me a cigar, and lit one for himself.

"It'll do," he said complacently. "Whisper won't have a chance. He's done."

The machine-gun by the tree fired, haltingly, experiment-ally, eight or ten shots. Noonan grinned and let a smoke ring float out of his mouth. The machine-gun settled down to business, grinding out metal like the busy little death factory it was. Noonan blew another smoke ring and said:

"That's exactly what'll do it."

I agreed that it ought to. We leaned against the clay bank and smoked while, farther away, another machine-gun got going, and then a third. Irregularly, rifles, pistols, shot-guns joined in. Noonan nodded approvingly and said:

"Five minutes of that will let him know there's a hell."

When the five minutes were up I suggested a look at the remains. I gave him a boost up the bank and scrambled up after him.

The roadhouse was as bleak and empty-looking as before, but more battered. No shots came from it. Plenty were going into it.

"What do you think?" Noonan asked.

"If there's a cellar there might be a mouse alive in it."

"Well, we could finish him afterwards."

He took a whistle out of his pocket and made a lot of noise. He waved his fat arms, and the gun-fire began dwindling. We had to wait for the word to go all the way around.

Then we crashed the door.

The first floor was ankle-deep with booze that was still gurgling from bullet-holes in the stacked-up cases and barrels that filled most of the house.

Dizzy with the fumes of spilled hooch, we waded around until we had found four dead bodies and no live ones. The four were swarthy foreign-looking men in laborers' clothes. Two of them were practically shot to pieces.

Noonan said:

"Leave them here and get out."

His voice was cheerful, but in a flashlight's glow his eyes showed white-ringed with fear.

We went out gladly, though I did hesitate long enough to pocket an unbroken bottle labeled *Dewar*.

A khaki-dressed copper was tumbling off a motorcycle at the gate. He yelled at us:

"The First National's been stuck up."

Noonan cursed savagely, bawled:

"He's foxed us, damn him! Back to town, everybody."

Everybody except us who had ridden with the chief beat it for the machines. Two of them took the dead detective with them.

Noonan looked at me out of his eye-corners and said:

"This is a tough one, no fooling."

I said, "Well," shrugged, and sauntered over to his car, where the driver was sitting at the wheel. I stood with my back to the house, talking to Pat. I don't remember what we talked about. Presently Noonan and the other sleuths joined us.

Only a little flame showed through the open roadhouse door before we passed out of sight around the bend in the road.

16 EXIT JERRY

THERE WAS A mob around the First National Bank. We pushed through it to the door, where we found sour-faced McGraw.

"Was six of them, masked," he reported to the chief as we went inside. "They hit it about two-thirty. Five of them got away clean with the jack. The watchman here dropped one of them, Jerry Hooper. He's over on the bench, cold. We got the roads blocked, and I wired around, if it ain't too late. Last seen of them was when they made the turn into King Street, in a black Lincoln."

We went over to look at the dead Jerry, lying on one of the lobby benches with a brown robe over him. The bullet had gone under his left shoulder blade.

The bank watchman, a harmless-looking old duffer, pushed up his chest and told us about it:

"There wasn't no chance to do nothing at first. They were in 'fore anybody knew anything. And maybe they didn't work fast. Right down the line, scooping it up. No chance to do anything then. But I says to myself. 'All righty, young fellows, you've got it all your own way now, but wait till you try to leave.'

"And I was as good as my word, you bet you. I runs right to the door after them and cut loose with the old firearm. I got that fellow just as he was stepping into the car. I bet you I'd of got more of them if I'd of had more cartridges, because it's kind of hard shooting down like that, standing in the —"

Noonan stopped the monologue by patting the old duffer's

back till his lungs were empty, telling him, "That certainly is fine. That certainly is fine."

McGraw pulled the robe up over the dead man again and growled:

"Nobody can identify anybody. But with Jerry on it, it's a cinch it was Whisper's caper."

The chief nodded happily and said:

"I'll leave it in your hands, Mac. Going to poke around here, or going back to the Hall with me?" he asked me.

"Neither. I've got a date, and I want to get into dry shoes."

Dinah Brand's little Marmon was standing in front of the hotel. I didn't see her. I went up to my room, leaving the door unlocked. I had got my hat and coat off when she came in without knocking.

"My God, you keep a boozy smelling room," she said.

"It's my shoes. Noonan took me wading in rum."

She crossed to the window, opened it, sat on the sill, and asked:

"What was that for?"

"He thought he was going to find your Max out in a dump called Cedar Hill Inn. So we went out there, shot the joint silly, murdered some dagoes, spilled gallons of liquor, and left the place burning."

"Cedar Hill Inn? I though it had been closed up for a year or more."

"It looked it, but it was somebody's warehouse."

"But you didn't find Max there?" she asked.

"While we were there he seems to have been knocking over Elihu's First National Bank."

"I saw that," she said. "I had just come out of Bengren's, the store two doors away. I had just got in my car when I saw a big boy backing out of the bank, carrying a sack and a gun, with a black handkerchief over his face."

"Was Max with them?"

"No, he wouldn't be. He'd send Jerry and the boys. That's what he has them for. Jerry was there. I knew him as soon as he got out of the car, in spite of the black handkerchief. They all had black ones. Four of them came out of the bank, running down to the car at the curb. Jerry and another fellow were in the car. When the four came across the sidewalk, Jerry jumped out and went to meet them. That's when the shooting started and Jerry dropped. The others jumped in the bus and lit out. How about that dough you owe me?"

I counted out ten twenty-dollar bills and a dime. She left the window to come for them.

"That's for pulling Dan off, so you could cop Max," she said when she had stowed the money away in her bag. "Now how about what I was to get for showing you where you could turn up the dope on his killing Tim Noonan?"

"You'll have to wait till he's indicted. How do I know the dope's any good?"

She frowned and asked:

"What do you do with all the money you don't spend?" Her face brightened. "You know where Max is now?"

"No."

"What's it worth to know?"

"Nothing."

"I'll tell you for a hundred bucks."

"I wouldn't want to take advantage of you that way."

"I'll tell you for fifty bucks."

I shook my head.

"Twenty-five."

"I don't want him," I said. "I don't care where he is. Why don't you peddle the news to Noonan?"

"Yes, and try to collect. Do you only perfume yourself with booze, or is there any for drinking purposes?"

"Here's a bottle of so-called Dewar that I picked up at Cedar Hill this afternoon. There's a bottle of King George in my bag. What's your choice?"

She voted for King George. We had a drink apiece, straight, and I said:

"Sit down and play with it while I change clothes."

When I came out of the bathroom twenty-five minutes later she was sitting at the secretary, smoking a cigarette and studying a memoranda book that had been in a side-pocket of my gladstone bag.

"I guess these are the expenses you've charged up on other cases," she said without looking up. "I'm damned if I can see why you can't be more liberal with me. Look, here's a six-hundred-dollar item marked *Inf*. That's information you bought from somebody, isn't it? And here's a hundred and fifty below it – *Top* – whatever that is. And here's another day when you spent nearly a thousand dollars."

"They must be telephone numbers," I said, taking the book from her. "Where were you raised? Fanning my baggage!"

"I was raised in a convent," she told me. "I won the good behavior prize every year I was there. I thought little girls who put extra spoons of sugar in their chocolate went to hell for gluttony. I didn't even know there was such a thing as profanity until I was eighteen. The first time I heard any I damned near fainted." She spit on the rug in front of her, tilted her chair back, put her crossed feet on my bed, and asked: "What do you think of that?"

I pushed her feet off the bed and said:

"I was raised in a water-front saloon. Keep your saliva off my floor or I'll toss you out on your neck."

"Let's have another drink first. Listen, what'll you give me for the inside story of how the boys didn't lose anything building the City Hall – the story that was in the papers I sold Donald Willsson?"

"That doesn't click with me. Try another."

"How about why the first Mrs. Lew Yard was sent to the insane asylum?"

"No."

"King, our sheriff, eight thousand dollars in debt four years ago, now the owner of as nice a collection of downtown business blocks as you'd want to see. I can't give you all of it, but I can show you where to get it."

"Keep trying," I encouraged her.

"No. You don't want to buy anything. You're just hoping you'll pick up something for nothing. This isn't bad Scotch. Where'd you get it?"

"Brought it from San Francisco with me."

"What's the idea of not wanting any of this information I'm offering? Think you can get it cheaper?"

"Information of that kind's not much good to me now. I've got to move quick. I need dynamite—something to blow them apart."

She laughed and jumped up, her big eyes sparkling.

"I've got one of Lew Yard's cards. Suppose we sent the bottle of Dewar you copped to Pete with the card. Wouldn't he take it as a declaration of war? If Cedar Hill was a liquor cache, it was Pete's. Wouldn't the bottle and Lew's card make him think Noonan had knocked the place over under orders?"

I considered it and said:

"Too crude. It wouldn't fool him. Besides, I'd just as lief have Pete and Lew both against the chief at this stage."

She pouted and said:

"You think you know everything. You're just hard to get along with. Take me out tonight? I've got a new outfit that'll knock them cockeyed."

"Yeah."

"Come up for me around eight."

She patted my cheek with a warm hand, said "Ta-ta," and went out as the telephone-bell began jingling.

* * *

"My chinch and Dick's are together at your client's joint," Mickey Linehan reported over the wire. "Mine's been generally busier than a hustler with two bunks, though I don't know what the score is yet. Anything new?"

I said there wasn't and went into conference with myself across the bed, trying to guess what would come of Noonan's attack on Cedar Hill Inn and Whisper's on the First National Bank. I would have given something for the ability to hear what was being said up at old Elihu's house by him, Pete the Finn, and Lew Yard. But I hadn't that ability, and I was never much good at guessing, so after half an hour I stopped tormenting my brain and took a nap.

It was nearly seven o'clock when I came out of the nap. I washed, dressed, loaded my pockets with a gun and a pint flask of Scotch, and went up to Dinah's.

17 RENO

SHE TOOK ME into her living-room, backed away from me, revolved, and asked me how I liked the new dress. I said I liked it. She explained that the color was rose beige and that the dinguses on the side were something or other, winding up:

"And you really think I look good in it?"

"You always look good," I said. "Lew Yard and Pete the Finn went calling on old Elihu this afternoon."

She made a face at me and said:

"You don't give a damn about my dress. What did they do there?"

"A pow-wow, I suppose."

She looked at me through her lashes and asked:

"Don't you really know where Max is?"

Then I did. There was no use admitting I hadn't known all along. I said:

"At Willsson's, probably, but I haven't been interested enough to make sure."

"That's goofy of you. He's got reasons for not liking you and me. Take mama's advice and nail him quick, if you like living and like having mama live too."

I laughed and said:

"You don't know the worst of it. Max didn't kill Noonan's brother. Tim didn't say *Max*. He tried to say *MacSwain*, and died before he could finish."

She grabbed my shoulders and tried to shake my hundred and ninety pounds. She was almost strong enough to do it.

"God damn you!" Her breath was hot in my face. Her face was white as her teeth. Rouge stood out sharply like red labels

562

pasted on her mouth and cheeks. "If you've framed him and made me frame him, you've got to kill him – now."

I don't like being manhandled, even by young women who look like something out of mythology when they're steamed up. I took her hands off my shoulders, and said:

"Stop belly-aching. You're still alive."

"Yes, still. But I know Max better than you do. I know how much chance anybody that frames him has got of staying alive long. It would be bad enough if we had got him right, but –"

"Don't make so much fuss over it. I've framed my millions and nothing's happened to me. Get your hat and coat and we'll feed. You'll feel better then."

"You're crazy if you think I'm going out. Not with that –"

"Stop it, sister. If he's that dangerous he's just as likely to get you here as anywhere. So what difference does it make?"

"It makes a – You know what you're going to do? You're going to stay here until Max is put out of the way. It's your fault and you've got to look out for me. I haven't even got Dan. He's in the hospital."

"I can't," I said. "I've got work to do. You're all burnt up over nothing. Max has probably forgotten all about you by now. Get your hat and coat. I'm starving."

She put her face close to mine again, and her eyes looked as if they had found something horrible in mine.

"Oh, you're rotten!" she said. "You don't give a damn what happens to me. You're using me as you use the others – that dynamite you wanted. I trusted you."

"You're dynamite, all right, but the rest of it's kind of foolish. You look a lot better when you're happy. Your features are heavy. Anger makes them downright brutal. I'm starving, sister."

"You'll eat here," she said. "You're not going to get me out after dark."

She meant it. She swapped the rose beige dress for an apron, and took inventory of the ice box. There were potatoes, lettuce, canned soup and half a fruit cake. I went out and got a couple of steaks, rolls, asparagus, and tomatoes.

When I came back she was mixing gin, vermouth and orange bitters in a quart shaker, not leaving a lot a space for them to move around in.

"Did you see anything?" she asked.

I sneered at her in a friendly way. We carried the cocktails into the dining-room and played bottoms-up while the meal cooked. The drinks cheered her a lot. By the time we sat down to the food she had almost forgotten her fright. She wasn't a very good cook, but we ate as if she were.

We put a couple of gin-gingerales in on top the dinner.

She decided she wanted to go places and do things. No lousy little runt could keep her cooped up, because she had been as square with him as anybody could be until he got nasty over nothing, and if he didn't like what she did he could go climb trees or jump in lakes, and we'd go out to the Silver Arrow where she had meant to take me, because she had promised Reno she'd show up at his party, and by God she would, and anybody who thought she wouldn't was crazy as a pet cuckoo, and what did I think of that?

"Who's Reno?" I asked while she tied herself tighter in the apron by pulling the strings the wrong way.

"Reno Starkey. You'll like him. He's a right guy. I promised him I'd show at his celebration and that's just what I'll do."

"What's he celebrating?"

"What the hell's the matter with this lousy apron? He was sprung this afternoon."

"Turn around and I'll unwind you. What was he in for? Stand still."

"Blowing a safe six or seven months ago – Turlock's, the jeweler. Reno, Put Collings, Blackie Whalen, Hank O'Marra, and a little lame guy called Step-and-a-Half. They had plenty of cover – Lew Yard – but the jewelers' association dicks tied the job to them last week. So Noonan had to go through the motions. It doesn't mean anything. They got out on bail at five o'clock this afternoon, and that's the last anybody will ever hear about it. Reno's used to it. He was already out on bail for three other capers. Suppose you mix another little drink while I'm inserting myself in the dress."

The Silver Arrow was half-way between Personville and Mock Lake.

"It's not a bad dump," Dinah told me as her little Marmon carried us towards it. "Polly De Voto is a good scout and anything she sells you is good, except maybe the bourbon. That always tastes a little bit like it had been drained off a corpse. You'll like her. You can get away with anything out here so long as you don't get noisy. She won't stand for noise. There it is. See the red and blue lights through the trees?"

We rode out of the woods into full view of the roadhouse, a very electric-lighted imitation castle set close to the road.

"What do you mean she won't stand for noise?" I asked, listening to the chorus of pistols singing *Bang-bang-bang*.

"Something up," the girl muttered, stopping the car.

Two men dragging a woman between them ran out of the roadhouse's front-door, ran away into the darkness. A man sprinted out a side-door, away. The guns sang on. I didn't see any flashes.

Another man broke out and vanished around the back.

A man leaned far out a front second-story window, a black gun in his hand.

Dinah blew her breath out sharply.

From a hedge by the road, a flash of orange pointed briefly up at the man in the window. His gun flashed downward. He leaned farther out. No second flash came from the hedge.

The man in the window put a leg over the sill, bent, hung by his hands, dropped.

Our car jerked forward. Dinah's lower lip was between her teeth.

The man who had dropped from the window was gathering himself up on hands and knees.

Dinah put her face in front of mine and screamed:

"Reno!"

The man jumped up, his face to us. He made the road in three leaps, as we got to him.

Dinah had the little Marmon wide open before Reno's feet were on the running-board beside me. I wrapped my arms around him, and damned near dislocated them holding him on. He made it as tough as he could for me by leaning out to try for a shot at the guns that were tossing lead all around us.

Then it was all over. We were out of range, sight and sound of the Silver Arrow, speeding away from Personville.

Reno turned around and did his own holding on. I took my arms in and found that all the joints still worked. Dinah was busy with the car.

Reno said:

"Thanks, kid. I needed pulling out."

"That's all right," she told him. "So that's the kind of parties you throw?"

"We had guests that wasn't invited. You know the Tanner Road?"

"Yes."

"Take it. It'll put us over to Mountain Boulevard, and we can get back to town that-a-way."

The girl nodded, slowed up a little, and asked:

"Who were the uninvited guests?"

"Some plugs that don't know enough to leave me alone."

"Do I know them?" she asked, too casually, as she turned the car into a narrower and rougher road.

"Let it alone, kid," Reno said. "Better get as much out of the heap as it's got."

She prodded another fifteen miles an hour out of the Marmon. She had plenty to do now holding the car to the road, and Reno had plenty holding himself to the car. Neither of them made any more conversation until the road brought us into one that had more and better paving.

Then he asked:

"So you paid Whisper off?"

"Um-hmm."

"They're saying you turned rat on him."

"They would. What do you think?"

"Ditching him was all right. But throwing in with a dick and cracking the works to him is kind of sour. Damned sour, if you ask me."

He looked at me while he said it. He was a man of thirty-four or -five, fairly tall, broad and heavy without fat. His eyes were large, brown, dull, and set far apart in a long, slightly sallow horse face. It was a humorless face, stolid, but somehow not unpleasant. I looked at him and said nothing.

The girl said: "If that's the way you feel about it, you can —"

"Look out," Reno grunted.

We had swung around a curve. A long black car was straight across the road ahead of us — a barricade.

Bullets flew around us. Reno and I threw bullets around while the girl made a polo pony of the little Marmon.

She shoved it over to the left of the road, let the left wheels ride the bank high, crossed the road again with Reno's and my weight on the inside, got the right bank under the left wheels just as our side of the car began to lift in spite of our weight, slid us down in the road with our backs to the enemy, and took us out of the neighborhood by the time we had emptied our guns.

A lot of people had done a lot of shooting, but so far as we could tell nobody's bullets had hurt anybody.

Reno, holding to the door with his elbows while he pushed another clip into his automatic, said:

"Nice work, kid. You handle the bus like you meant it."

Dinah asked: "Where now?"

"Far away first. Just follow the road. We'll have to figure it out. Looks like they got the burg closed up on us. Keep your dog on it."

We put ten or twelve more miles between Personville and us. We passed a few cars, saw nothing to show we were being chased. A short bridge rumbled under us. Reno said:

"Take the right turn at the top of the hill."

We took it, into a dirt road that wound between trees down the side of a rock-ridged hill. Ten miles an hour was fast going here. After five minutes of creeping along Reno ordered a halt. We heard nothing, saw nothing, during the half-hour we sat in darkness. Then Reno said:

"There's an empty shack a mile down the way. We'll camp there, huh? There's no sense trying to crash the city line again tonight."

Dinah said she would prefer anything to being shot at again. I said it was all right with me, though I would rather have tried to find some path back to the city.

We followed the dirt track cautiously until our headlights settled on a small clapboard building that badly need the paint it had never got.

"Is this it?" Dinah asked Reno.

"Uh-huh. Stay here till I look it over."

He left us, appearing soon in the beam of our lights at the shack door. He fumbled with keys at the padlock, got it off, opened the door, and went in. Presently he came to the door and called:

"All right. Come in and make yourselves at home."

Dinah cut off the engine and got out of the car.

"Is there a flashlight in the car?" I asked.

She said, "Yes," gave it to me, yawned, "My God, I'm tired. I hope there's something to drink in the hole."

I told her I had a flask of Scotch. The news cheered her up.

The shack was a one-room affair that held an army cot covered with brown blankets, a deal table with a deck of cards and some gummy poker chips on it, a brown iron stove, four chairs, an oil lamp, dishes, pots, pans and buckets, three shelves with canned food on them, a pile of firewood and a wheelbarrow.

Reno was lighting the lamp when we came in. He said:

"Not so tough. I'll hide the heap and then we'll be all set till daylight."

Dinah went over to the cot, turned back the covers, and reported:

"Maybe there's things in it, but anyway it's not alive with them. Now let's have that drink."

I unscrewed the flask and passed it to her while Reno went out to hide the car. When she had finished, I took a shot.

The purr of the Marmon's engine got fainter. I opened the door and looked out. Downhill, through trees and bushes, I could see broken chunks of white light going away. When I lost them for good I returned indoors and asked the girl:

"Have you ever had to walk home before?"

"What?"

"Reno's gone with the car."

"The lousy tramp! Thank God he left us where there's a bed, anyway."

"That'll get you nothing."

"No?"

"No. Reno had a key to this dump. Ten to one the birds after him know about it. That's why he ditched us here. We're supposed to argue with them, hold them off his trail a while."

She got up wearily from the cot, cursed Reno, me, all men from Adam on, and said disagreeably:

"You know everything. What do we do next?"

"We find a comfortable spot in the great open spaces, not too far away, and wait to see what happens."

"I'm going to take the blankets."

"Maybe one won't be missed, but you'll tip our mitts if you take more than that."

"Damn your mitts," she grumbled, but she took only one blanket.

I blew out the lamp, padlocked the door behind us, and with the help of the flashlight picked a way through the undergrowth.

On the hillside above we found a little hollow from which road and shack could be not too dimly seen through foliage thick enough to hide us unless we showed a light.

I spread that blanket there and we settled down.

The girl leaned against me and complained that the ground was damp, that she was cold in spite of her fur coat, that she had a cramp in her leg, and that she wanted a cigarette.

I gave her another drink from the flask. That bought me ten minutes of peace.

Then she said:

"I'm catching cold. By the time anybody comes, if they ever do, I'll be sneezing and coughing loud enough to be heard in the city."

"Just once," I told her. "Then you'll be all strangled."

"There's a mouse or something crawling under the blanket."

"Probably only a snake."

"Are you married?"

"Don't start that."

"Then you are?"

"No."

"I'll bet your wife's glad of it."

I was trying to find a suitable come-back to that wise-crack when a distant light gleamed up the road. It disappeared as I sh-sh'd the girl.

"What is it?" she asked.

"A light. It's gone now. Our visitors have left their car and are finishing the trip afoot."

A lot of time went by. The girl shivered with her cheek warm against mine. We heard footsteps, saw dark figures

570

moving on the road and around the shack, without being sure whether we did or didn't.

A flashlight ended our doubt by putting a bright circle on the shack's door. A heavy voice said:

"We'll let the broad come out."

There was a half-minute of silence while they waited for a reply from indoors. Then the same heavy voice asked: "Coming?" Then more silence.

Gun-fire, a familiar sound tonight, broke the silence. Something hammered boards.

"Come on," I whispered to the girl. "We'll have a try at their car while they're making a racket."

"Let them alone," she said, pulling my arm down as I started up. "I've had enough of it for one night. We're all right here."

"Come on," I insisted.

She said, "I won't," and she wouldn't, and presently, while we argued, it was too late. The boys below had kicked in the door, found the hut empty, and were bellowing for their car.

It came, took eight men aboard, and followed Reno's track downhill.

"We might as well move in again," I said. "It's not likely they'll be back this way tonight."

"I hope to God there's some Scotch left in that flask," she said as I helped her stand up.

THE SHACK'S SUPPLY of canned goods didn't include anything that tempted us for breakfast. We made the meal of coffee cooked in very stale water from a galvanized pail.

A mile of walking brought us to a farmhouse where there was a boy who didn't mind earning a few dollars by driving us to town in the family Ford. He had a lot of questions, to which we gave him phoney answers or none. He set us down in front of a little restaurant in upper King Street, where we ate quantities of buckwheat cakes and bacon.

A taxi put us at Dinah's door a little before nine o'clock. I searched the place for her, from roof to cellar, and found no signs of visitors.

"When will you be back?" she asked as she followed me to the door.

"I'll try to pop in between now and midnight, if only for a few minutes. Where does Lew Yard live?"

"1622 Painter Street. Painter's three blocks over. 1622's four blocks up. What are you going to do there?" Before I could answer, she put her hands on my arm and begged: "Get Max, will you? I'm afraid of him."

"Maybe I'll sic Noonan on him a little later. It depends on how things work out."

She called me a damned double-crossing something or other who didn't care what happened to her as long as his dirty work got done.

I went over to Painter Street. 1622 was a red brick house with a garage under the front porch.

A block up the street I found Dick Foley in a hired drive-yourself Buick. I got in beside him, asking:

"What's doing?"

"Spot two. Out three-thirty, office to Willsson's. Mickey. Five. Home. Busy. Kept plant. Off three, seven. Nothing yet."

That was supposed to inform me that he had picked up Lew Yard at two the previous afternoon; had shadowed him to Willsson's at three-thirty, where Mickey had tailed Pete; had followed Yard away at five, to his residence; had seen people going in and out of the house, but had not shadowed any of them; had watched the house until three this morning, and had returned to the job at seven; and since then had seen nobody go in or out.

"You'll have to drop this and take a plant on Willsson's," I said. "I hear Whisper Thaler's holing-up there, and I'd like an eye kept on him till I make up my mind whether to turn him up for Noonan or not."

Dick nodded and started the engine grinding. I got out and returned to the hotel.

There was a telegram from the Old Man:

SEND BY FIRST MAIL FULL EXPLANATION OF PRESENT OPERATION AND CIRCUMSTANCES UNDER WHICH YOU ACCEPTED IT WITH DAILY REPORTS TO DATE

I put the telegram in my pocket and hoped things would keep on breaking fast. To have sent him the dope he wanted at that time would have been the same as sending in my resignation.

I bent a fresh collar around my neck and trotted over to the City Hall.

"Hello," Noonan greeted me. "I was hoping you'd show up. Tried to get you at your hotel but they told me you hadn't been in."

He wasn't looking well this morning, but under his glad-handing he seemed, for a change, genuinely glad to see me.

573

As I sat down one of his phones rang. He put the receiver to his ear, said "Yes?" listened for a moment, said, "You better go out there yourself, Mac," and had to make two attempts to get the receiver back on its prong before he succeeded. His face had gone a little doughy, but his voice was almost normal as he told me:

"Lew Yard's been knocked off – shot coming down his front steps just now."

"Any details?" I asked while I cursed myself for having pulled Dick Foley away from Painter Street an hour too soon. That was a tough break.

Noonan shook his head, staring at his lap.

"Shall we go out and look at the remains?" I suggested, getting up.

He neither got up nor looked up.

"No," he said wearily to his lap. "To tell the truth, I don't want to. I don't know as I could stand it just now. I'm getting sick of this killing. It's getting to me – on my nerves, I mean."

I sat down again, considered his low spirits, and asked:

"Who do you guess killed him?"

"God knows," he mumbled. "Everybody's killing everybody. Where's it going to end?"

"Think Reno did it?"

Noonan winced, started to look up at me, changed his mind, and repeated:

"God knows."

I went at him from another angle:

"Anybody knocked off in the battle at the Silver Arrow last night?"

"Only three."

"Who were they?"

"A pair of Johnson-brothers named Blackie Whalen and Put Collings that only got out on bail around five yesterday, and Dutch Jake Wahl, a guerrilla."

"What was it all about?"

"Just a roughhouse, I guess. It seems that Put and Blackie and the others that got out with them were celebrating with a lot of friends, and it wound up in smoke."

"All of them Lew Yard's men?"

"I don't know anything about that," he said.

I got up, said, "Oh, all right," and started for the door.

"Wait," he called. "Don't run off like that. I guess they were."

I came back to my chair. Noonan watched the top of his desk. His face was gray, flabby, damp, like fresh putty.

"Whisper's staying at Willsson's," I told him.

He jerked his head up. His eyes darkened. Then his mouth twitched, and he let his head sag again. His eyes faded.

"I can't go through with it," he mumbled. "I'm sick of this butchering. I can't stand any more of it."

"Sick enough to give up the idea of evening the score for Tim's killing, if it'll make peace?" I asked.

"I am."

"That's what started it," I reminded him. "If you're willing to call it off, it ought to be possible to stop it."

He raised his face and looked at me with eyes that were like a dog's looking at a bone.

"The others ought to be as sick of it as you are," I went on. "Tell them how you feel about it. Have a get-together and make peace."

"They'd think I was up to some kind of a trick," he objected miserably.

"Have the meeting at Willsson's. Whisper's camping there. You'd be the one risking tricks going there. Are you afraid of that?"

He frowned and asked:

"Will you go with me?"

"If you want me."

"Thanks," he said. "I – I'll try it."

19   THE PEACE CONFERENCE

ALL THE OTHER delegates to the peace conference were on hand when Noonan and I arrived at Willsson's home at the appointed time, nine o'clock that night. Everybody nodded to us, but the greetings didn't go any further than that.

Pete the Finn was the only one I hadn't met before. The bootlegger was a big-boned man of fifty with a completely bald head. His forehead was small, his jaws enormous – wide, heavy, bulging with muscle.

We sat around Willsson's library table.

Old Elihu sat at the head. The short-clipped hair on his round pink skull was like silver in the light. His round blue eyes were hard, domineering, under their bushy white brows. His mouth and chin were horizontal lines.

On his right Pete the Finn sat watching everybody with tiny black eyes that never moved. Reno Starkey sat next to the bootlegger. Reno's sallow horse face was as stolidly dull as his eyes.

Max Thaler was tilted back in a chair on Willsson's left. The little gambler's carefully pressed pants legs were carelessly crossed. A cigarette hung from one corner of his tight-lipped mouth.

I sat next to Thaler. Noonan sat on my other side.

Elihu Willsson opened the meeting.

He said things couldn't go on the way they were going. We were all sensible men, reasonable men, grown men who had seen enough of the world to know that a man couldn't have everything his own way, no matter who he was. Compromises were things everybody had to make sometimes. To get what he wanted, a man had to give other people what they wanted. He said he was sure that what we all most wanted now was to stop this insane killing. He said he was sure that everything could be frankly discussed and settled in an hour without turning Personville into a slaughterhouse.

It wasn't a bad oration.

When it was over there was a moment of silence. Thaler looked past me, at Noonan, as if he expected something of him. The rest of us followed his example, looking at the chief of police.

Noonan's face turned red and he spoke huskily:

"Whisper, I'll forget you killed Tim." He stood up and held out a beefy paw. "Here's my hand on it."

Thaler's thin mouth curved into a vicious smile.

"Your bastard of a brother needed killing, but I didn't kill him," he whispered coldly.

Red became purple in the chief's face.

I said loudly:

"Wait, Noonan. We're going at this wrong. We won't get anywhere unless everybody comes clean. Otherwise we'll all be worse off than before. MacSwain killed Tim, and you know it."

He stared at me with dumbfounded eyes. He gaped. He couldn't understand what I had done to him.

I looked at the others, tried to look virtuous as hell, asked:

"That's settled, isn't it? Let's get the rest of the kicks squared." I addressed Pete the Finn: "How do you feel about yesterday's accident to your warehouse and the four men?"

"One hell of an accident," he rumbled.

I explained:

"Noonan didn't know you were using the joint. He went there thinking it empty, just to clear the way for a job in town. Your men shot first, and then he really thought he had stumbled into Thaler's hideout. When he found he'd been stepping in your puddle he lost his head and touched the place off."

Thaler was watching me with a hard small smile in eyes and mouth. Reno was all dull stolidity. Elihu Willsson was leaning towards me, his old eyes sharp and wary. I don't know what Noonan was doing. I couldn't afford to look at him. I was in a good spot if I played my hand right, and in a terrible one if I didn't.

"The men, they get paid for taking chances," Pete the Finn said. "For the other, twenty-five grand will make it right."

Noonan spoke quickly, eagerly:

"All right, Pete, all right, I'll give it to you."

I pushed my lips together to keep from laughing at the panic in his voice.

I could look at him safely now. He was licked, broken, willing to do anything to save his fat neck, or to try to. I looked at him.

He wouldn't look at me. He sat down and looked at nobody. He was busy trying to look as if he didn't expect to be carved apart before he got away from these wolves to whom I had handed him.

I went on with the work, turning to Elihu Willsson:

"Do you want to squawk about your bank being knocked over, or do you like it?"

Max Thaler touched my arm and suggested:

"We could tell better maybe who's entitled to beef if you'd give us what you've got first."

I was glad to.

"Noonan wanted to nail you," I told him, "but he either got word, or expected to get word, from Yard and Willsson here to let you alone. So he thought if he had the bank looted and framed you for it, your backers would ditch you, and let him go after you right. Yard, I understand, was supposed to put his OK on all the capers in town. You'd be cutting into his territory, and gypping Willsson. That's how it would look.

578

RED HARVEST

And that was supposed to make them hot enough that they'd help Noonan cop you. He didn't know you were here.

"Reno and his mob were in the can. Reno was Yard's pup, but he didn't mind crossing up his headman. He already had the idea that he was about ready to take the burg away from Lew." I turned to Reno and asked: "Isn't that it?"

He looked at me woodenly and said:

"You're telling it."

I continued telling it:

"Noonan fakes a tip that you're at Cedar Hill, and takes all the coppers he can't trust out there with him, even cleaning the traffic detail out of Broadway, so Reno would have a clear road. McGraw and the bulls that are in on the play let Reno and his mob sneak out of the hoosegow, pull the job, and duck back in. Nice thing in alibis. Then they got sprung on bail a couple of hours later.

"It looks as if Lew Yard tumbled. He sent Dutch Jake Wahl and some other boys out to the Silver Arrow last night to teach Reno and his pals not to take things in their own hands like that. But Reno got away, and got back to the city. It was either him or Lew then. He made sure which it would be by being in front of Lew's house with a gun when Lew came out this morning. Reno seems to have had the right dope, because I notice that right now he's holding down a chair that would have been Lew Yard's if Lew hadn't been put on ice."

Everybody was sitting very still, as if to call attention to how still they were sitting. Nobody could count on having any friends among those present. It was no time for careless motions on anybody's part.

If what I had said meant anything one way or the other to Reno he didn't show it.

Thaler whispered softly:

"Didn't you skip some of it?"

"You mean the part about Jerry?" I kept on being the life of the party. "I was coming back to that. I don't know whether

579

he got away from the can when you crushed out, and was caught later, or whether he didn't get away, or why. And I don't know how willingly he went along on the bank caper. But he did go along, and he was dropped and left in front of the bank because he was your right bower, and his being killed there would pin the trick to you. He was kept in the car till the get-away was on. Then he was pushed out, and was shot in the back. He was facing the bank, with his back to the car, when he got his."

Thaler looked at Reno and whispered:

"Well?"

Reno looked with dull eyes at Thaler and asked calmly:

"What of it?"

Thaler stood up, said, "Deal me out," and walked to the door.

Pete the Finn stood up, leaning on the table with big bony hands, speaking from deep in his chest:

"Whisper." And when Thaler had stopped and turned to face him: "I'm telling you this. You, Whisper, and all of you. That damn gun-work is out. All of you understand it. You've got no brains to know what is best for yourselves. So I'll tell you. This busting the town open is no good for business. I won't have it any more. You be nice boys or I'll make you.

"I got one army of young fellows that know what to do on any end of a gun. I got to have them in my racket. If I got to use them on you I'll use them on you. You want to play with gunpowder and dynamite? I'll show you what playing is. You like to fight? I'll give you fighting. Mind what I tell you. That's all."

Pete the Finn sat down.

Thaler looked thoughtful for a moment, and went away without saying or showing what he had thought.

His going made the others impatient. None wanted to remain until anybody else had time to accumulate a few guns in the neighborhood.

In a very few minutes Elihu Willsson and I had the library to ourselves.

We sat and looked at one another.

Presently he said:

"How would you like to be chief of police?"

"No. I'm a rotten errand boy."

"I don't mean with this bunch. After we've got rid of them."

"And got another just like them."

"Damn you," he said, "it wouldn't hurt to take a nicer tone to a man old enough to be your father."

"Who curses me and hides behind his age."

Anger brought a vein out blue in his forehead. Then he laughed.

"You're a nasty talking lad," he said, "but I can't say you haven't done what I paid you to do."

"A swell lot of help I've got from you."

"Did you need wet-nursing? I gave you the money and a free hand. That's what you asked for. What more did you want?"

"You old pirate," I said, "I blackmailed you into it, and you played against me all the way till now, when even you can see that they're hell-bent on gobbling each other up. Now you talk about what you did for me."

"Old pirate," he repeated. "Son, if I hadn't been a pirate I'd still be working for the Anaconda for wages, and there'd be no Personville Mining Corporation. You're a damned little woolly lamb yourself, I suppose. I was had, son, where the hair was short. There were things I didn't like – worse things that I didn't know about until tonight – but I was caught and had to bide my time. Why since that Whisper Thaler has been here I've been a prisoner in my own home, a damned hostage!"

"Tough. Where do you stand now?" I demanded. "Are you behind me?"

"If you win."

I got up and said:

"I hope to Christ you get caught with them."

He said:

"I reckon you do, but I won't." He squinted his eyes merrily at me. "I'm financing you. That shows I mean well, don't it? Don't be too hard on me, son, I'm kind of –"

I said, "Go to hell," and walked out.

DICK FOLEY IN his hired car was at the next corner. I had him drive me over to within a block of Dinah Brand's house, and walked the rest of the way.

"You look tired," she said when I had followed her into the living-room. "Been working?"

"Attending a peace conference out of which at least a dozen killings ought to grow."

The telephone rang. She answered it and called me.

Reno Starkey's voice:

"I thought maybe you'd like to hear about Noonan being shot to hell and gone when he got out of his heap in front of his house. You never saw anybody that was deader. Must have had thirty pills pumped in him."

"Thanks."

Dinah's big blue eyes asked questions.

"First fruits of the peace conference, plucked by Whisper Thaler," I told her. "Where's the gin?"

"Reno talking, wasn't it?"

"Yeah. He thought I'd like to hear about Poisonville being all out of police chiefs."

"You mean – ?"

"Noonan went down tonight, according to Reno. Haven't you got any gin? Or do you like making me ask for it?"

"You know where it is. Been up to some of your cute tricks?"

I went back into the kitchen, opened the top of the refrigerator, and attacked the ice with an ice pick that had a six-inch awl-sharp blade set in a round blue and white handle.

The girl stood in the doorway and asked questions. I didn't answer them while I put ice, gin, lemon juice and seltzer together in two glasses.

"What have you been doing?" she demanded as we carried our drinks into the dining-room. "You look ghastly."

I put my glass on the table, sat down facing it, and complained:

"This damned burg's getting me. If I don't get away soon I'll be going blood-simple like the natives. There's been what? A dozen and a half murders since I've been here. Donald Willsson; Ike Bush; the four wops and the dick at Cedar Hill; Jerry; Lew Yard; Dutch Jake, Blackie Whalen and Put Collings at the Silver Arrow; Big Nick, the copper I potted; the blond kid Whisper dropped here; Yakima Shorty, old Elihu's prowler; and now Noonan. That's sixteen of them in less than a week, and more coming up."

She frowned at me and said sharply:

"Don't look like that."

I laughed and went on:

"I've arranged a killing or two in my time, when they were necessary. But this is the first time I've ever got the fever. It's this damned burg. You can't go straight here. I got myself tangled at the beginning. When old Elihu ran out on me there was nothing I could do but try to set the boys against each other. I had to swing the job the best way I could. How could I help it if the best way was bound to lead to a lot of killing? The job couldn't be handled any other way without Elihu's backing."

"Well, if you couldn't help it, what's the use of making a lot of fuss over it? Drink your drink."

I drank half of it and felt the urge to talk some more.

"Play with murder enough and it gets you one of two ways. It makes you sick, or you get to like it. It got Noonan the first way. He was green around the gills after Yard was knocked off, all the stomach gone out of him, willing to do anything to make peace. I took him in, suggested that he and the other survivors get together and patch up their differences.

"We had the meeting at Willsson's tonight. It was a nice party. Pretending I was trying to clear away everybody's misunderstandings by coming clean all around, I stripped Noonan naked and threw him to them – him and Reno. That broke up the meeting. Whisper declared himself out. Pete told everybody where they stood. He said battling was bad for his bootlegging racket, and anybody who started anything from then on could expect to have his booze guards turned loose on them. Whisper didn't look impressed. Neither did Reno."

"They wouldn't be," the girl said. "What did you do to Noonan? I mean how did you strip him and Reno?"

"I told the others that he had known all along that Mac-Swain killed Tim. That was the only lie I told them. Then I told them about the bank stick-up being turned by Reno and the chief, with Jerry taken along and dropped on the premises to tie the job to Whisper. I knew that's the way it was if what you told me was right, about Jerry getting out of the car, starting towards the bank and being shot. The hole was in his back. Fitting in with that, McGraw said the last seen of the stick-up car was when it turned into King Street. The boys would be returning to the City Hall, to their jail alibi."

"But didn't the bank watchman say he shot Jerry? That's the way it was in the papers."

"He said so, but he'd say anything and believe it. He probably emptied his gun with his eyes shut, and anything that fell was his. Didn't you see Jerry drop?"

"Yes, I did, and he was facing the bank, but it was all too confused for me to see who shot him. There were a lot of men shooting, and –"

"Yeah. They'd see to that. I also advertised the fact – at least, it looks like a fact to me – that Reno plugged Lew Yard. This Reno is a tough egg, isn't he? Noonan went watery, but all they got out of Reno was a 'What of it?' It was all nice and gentlemanly. They were evenly divided – Pete and Whisper against Noonan and Reno. But none of them could count on his partner backing him up if he made a play, and by the time the meeting was over the pairs had been split. Noonan was out of the count, and Reno and Whisper, against each other, had Pete against them. So everybody sat around and behaved and watched everybody else while I juggled death and destruction.

"Whisper was the first to leave, and he seems to have had time to collect some rods in front of Noonan's house by the time the chief reached home. The chief was shot down. If Pete the Finn meant what he said – and he has the look of a man who would – he'll be out after Whisper. Reno was as much to blame for Jerry's death as Noonan, so Whisper ought to be gunning for him. Knowing it, Reno will be out to get Whisper first, and that will set Pete on his trail. Besides that, Reno will likely have his hands full standing off those of the late Lew Yard's underlings who don't fancy Reno as boss. All in all it's one swell dish."

Dinah Brand reached across the table and patted my hand. Her eyes were uneasy. She said:

"It's not your fault, darling. You said yourself that there was nothing else you could do. Finish your drink and we'll have another."

"There was plenty else I could do," I contradicted her. "Old Elihu ran out on me at first simply because these birds had too much on him for him to risk a break unless he was sure they could be wiped out. He couldn't see how I could do it, so he played with them. He's not exactly their brand of cut-throat, and, besides, he thinks the city is his personal property, and he doesn't like the way they've taken it away from him.

"I could have gone to him this afternoon and showed him that I had them ruined. He'd have listened to reason. He'd have come over to my side, have given me the support I needed to swing the play legally. I could have done that. But it's easier to have them killed off, easier and surer, and, now that I'm feeling this way, more satisfying. I don't know how I'm going to come out with the Agency. The Old Man will boil me in oil if he ever finds out what I've been doing. It's this damned town. Poisonville is right. It's poisoned me.

"Look. I sat at Willsson's table tonight and played them like you'd play trout, and got just as much fun out of it. I looked at Noonan and knew he hadn't a chance in a thousand of living another day because of what I had done to him, and I laughed, and felt warm and happy inside. That's not me. I've got hard skin all over what's left of my soul, and after twenty years of messing around with crime I can look at any sort of a murder without seeing anything in it but my bread and butter, the day's work. But this getting a rear out of planning deaths is not natural to me. It's what this place has done to me."

She smiled too softly and spoke too indulgently:

"You exaggerate so, honey. They deserve all they get. I wish you wouldn't look like that. You make me feel creepy."

I grinned, picked up the glasses, and went out to the kitchen for more gin. When I came back she frowned at me over anxious dark eyes and asked:

"Now what did you bring the ice pick in for?"

"To show you how my mind's running. A couple of days ago, if I thought about it at all, it was as a good tool to pry off chunks of ice." I ran a finger down its half-foot of round steel blade to the needle point. "Not a bad thing to pin a man to his clothes with. That's the way I'm begging, on the level. I can't even see a mechanical cigar lighter without thinking of filling one with nitroglycerine for somebody you don't like. There's a piece of copper wire lying in the gutter in front of your house – thin, soft, and just long enough to go around a neck with two ends to hold on. I had one hell of a time to keep from picking it up and stuffing it in my pocket, just in case –"

"You're crazy."

"I know it. That's what I've been telling you. I'm going blood-simple."

"Well, I don't like it. Put that thing back in the kitchen and sit down and be sensible."

I obeyed two-thirds of the order.

"The trouble with you is," she scolded me, "your nerves are shot. You've been through too much excitement in the last few days. Keep it up and you're going to have the heebie-jeebies for fair, a nervous breakdown."

I held up a hand with spread fingers. It was steady enough. She looked at it and said:

"That doesn't mean anything. It's inside you. Why don't you sneak off for a couple of days' rest? You've got things here so they'll run themselves. Let's go down to Salt Lake. It'll do you good."

"Can't, sister. Somebody's got to stay here to count the dead. Besides, the whole program is based on the present combination of people and events. Our going out of town would change that, and the chances are the whole thing would have to be gone over again."

"Nobody would have to know you were gone, and I've got nothing to do with it."

"Since when?"

She leaned forward, made her eyes small, and asked:

"Now what are you getting at?"

"Nothing. Just wondering how you got to be a disinterested bystander all of a sudden. Forgotten that Donald Willsson was killed because of you, starting the whole thing? Forgotten that it was the dope you gave me on Whisper that kept the job from petering out in the middle?"

"You know just as well as I do that none of that was my fault," she said indignantly. "And it's all past, anyway. You're just bringing it up because you're in a rotten humor and want to argue."

"It wasn't past last night, when you were scared stiff Whisper was going to kill you."

"Will you stop talking about killing!"

"Young Albury once told me Bill Quint had threatened to kill you," I said.

"Stop it."

"You seem to have a gift for stirring up murderous notions in your boy-friends. There's Albury waiting trial for killing Willsson. There's Whisper who's got you shivering in corners. Even I haven't escaped your influence. Look at the way I've turned. And I've always had a private notion that Dan Rolff's going to have a try at you some day."

"Dan! You're crazy. Why, I –"

"Yeah. He was a lunger and down and out, and you took him in. You gave him a home and all the laudanum he wants. You use him for errand boy, you slap his face in front of me, and slap him around in front of others. He's in love with you. One of these mornings you're going to wake up and find he's whittled your neck away."

She shivered, got up and laughed.

"I'm glad one of us knows what you're talking about, if you do," she said as she carried our empty glasses through the kitchen-door.

I lit a cigarette and wondered why I felt the way I did, wondered if I were getting psychic, wondered whether there was anything in this presentiment business or whether my nerves were just ragged.

"The next best thing for you to do if you won't go away," the girl advised me when she returned with full glasses, "is to get plastered and forget everything for a few hours. I put a double slug of gin in yours. You need it."

"It's not me," I said, wondering why I was saying it, but somehow enjoying it. "It's you. Every time I mention killing, you jump on me. You're a woman. You think if nothing's said about it, maybe none of the God only knows how many people in town who might want to will kill you. That's silly. Nothing we say or don't say is going to make Whisper, for instance –"

589

"Please, please stop! I am silly. I am afraid of the words. I'm afraid of him. I – Oh, why didn't you put him out of the way when I asked you?"

"Sorry," I said, meaning it.

"Do you think he –?"

"I don't know," I told her, "and I reckon you're right. There's no use talking about it. The thing to do is drink, though there doesn't seem to be much body to this gin."

"That's you, not the gin. Do you want an honest to God rear?"

"I'd drink nitroglycerine tonight."

"That's just about what you're going to get," she promised me.

She rattled bottles in the kitchen and brought me in a glass of what looked like the stuff we had been drinking. I sniffed at it and said:

"Some of Dan's laudanum, huh? He still in the hospital?"

"Yes. I think his skull is fractured. There's your kick, mister, if that's what you want."

I put the doped gin down my throat. Presently I felt more comfortable. Time went by as we drank and talked in a world that was rosy, cheerful, and full of fellowship and peace on earth.

Dinah stuck to gin. I tried that for a while too, and then had another gin and laudanum.

For a while after that I played a game, trying to hold my eyes open as if I were awake, even though I couldn't see anything out of them. When the trick wouldn't fool her any more I gave it up.

The last thing I remembered was her helping me onto the living-room chesterfield.

I DREAMED I was sitting on a bench, in Baltimore, facing the tumbling fountain in Harlem Park, beside a woman who wore a veil. I had come there with her. She was somebody I knew well. But I had suddenly forgotten who she was. I couldn't see her face because of the long black veil.

I thought that if I said something to her I would recognize her voice when she answered. But I was very embarrassed and was a long time finding anything to say. Finally I asked her if she knew a man named Carroll T. Harris.

She answered me, but the roar and swish of the tumbling fountain smothered her voice, and I could hear nothing.

Fire engines went out Edmondson Avenue. She left me to run after them. As she ran she cried, "Fire! Fire!" I recognized her voice then and knew who she was, and knew she was someone important to me. I ran after her, but it was too late. She and the fire engines were gone.

I walked streets hunting for her, half the streets in the United States, Gay Street and Mount Royal Avenue in Baltimore, Colfax Avenue in Denver, Aetna Road and St. Clair Avenue in Cleveland, McKinney Avenue in Dallas, Lemartine and Cornell and Amory Streets in Boston, Berry Boulevard in Louisville, Lexington Avenue in New York, until I came to Victoria Street in Jacksonville, where I heard her voice again, though I still could not see her.

I walked more streets, listening to her voice. She was calling a name, not mine, one strange to me, but no matter how fast I walked or in what direction, I could get no nearer her voice. It was the same distance from me in the street that runs past the

Federal Building in El Paso as in Detroit's Grand Circus Park. Then the voice stopped.

Tired and discouraged, I went into the lobby of the hotel that faces the railroad station in Rocky Mount, North Carolina, to rest. While I sat there a train came in. She got off it and came into the lobby, over to me, and began kissing me. I was very uncomfortable because everybody stood around looking at us and laughing.

That dream ended there.

I dreamed I was in a strange city hunting for a man I hated. I had an open knife in my pocket and meant to kill him with it when I found him. It was Sunday morning. Church bells were ringing, crowds of people were in the streets, going to and from church. I walked almost as far as in the first dream, but always in this same strange city.

Then the man I was after yelled at me, and I saw him. He was a small brown man who wore an immense sombrero. He was standing on the steps of a tall building on the far side of a wide plaza, laughing at me. Between us, the plaza was crowded with people, packed shoulder to shoulder.

Keeping one hand on the open knife in my pocket, I ran towards the little brown man, running on the heads and shoulders of the people in the plaza. The heads and shoulders were of unequal heights and not evenly spaced. I slipped and floundered over them.

The little brown man stood on the steps and laughed until I had almost reached him. Then he ran into the tall building. I chased him up miles of spiral stairway, always just an inch more than a hand's reach behind him. We came to the roof. He ran straight across to the edge and jumped just as one of my hands touched him.

His shoulder slid out of my fingers. My hand knocked his sombrero off, and closed on his head. It was a smooth hard round head no larger than a large egg. My fingers went all the way around it. Squeezing his head in one hand, I tried to bring the knife out of my pocket with the other – and realized that I had gone off the edge of the roof with him. We dropped giddily down towards the millions of upturned faces in the plaza, miles down.

I opened my eyes in the dull light of morning sun filtered through drawn blinds.

I was lying face down on the dining-room floor, my head resting on my left forearm. My right arm was stretched straight out. My right hand held the round blue and white handle of Dinah Brand's ice pick. The pick's six-inch needle-sharp blade was buried in Dinah Brand's left breast.

She was lying on her back, dead. Her long muscular legs were stretched out towards the kitchen-door. There was a run down the front of her right stocking.

Slowly, gently, as if afraid of awakening her, I let go the ice pick, drew in my arm, and got up.

My eyes burned. My throat and mouth were hot, woolly. I went into the kitchen, found a bottle of gin, tilted it to my mouth, and kept it there until I had to breathe. The kitchen clock said seven-forty-one.

With the gin in me I returned to the dining-room, switched on the lights, and looked at the dead girl.

Not much blood was in sight: a spot the size of a silver dollar around the hole the ice pick made in her blue silk dress. There was a bruise on her right cheek, just under the cheek-bone. Another bruise, finger-made, was on her right wrist. Her hands were empty. I moved her enough to see that nothing was under her.

I examined the room. So far as I could tell, nothing had been changed in it. I went back to the kitchen and found no recognizable changes there.

The spring lock on the back door was fastened, and had no marks to show it had been monkeyed with. I went to the front door and failed to find any marks on it. I went through the house from top to bottom, and learned nothing. The windows were all right. The girl's jewelry, on her dressing-table (except the two diamond rings on her hands), and four hundred odd dollars in her handbag, on a bedroom chair, were undisturbed.

In the dining-room again, I knelt beside the dead girl and used my handkerchief to wipe the ice pick handle clean of any prints my fingers had left on it. I did the same to glasses, bottles, doors, light buttons, and the pieces of furniture I had touched, or was likely to have touched.

Then I washed my hands, examined my clothes for blood, made sure I was leaving none of my property behind, and went to the front door. I opened it, wiped the inner knob, closed it behind me, wiped the outer knob, and went away.

From a drug-store in upper Broadway I telephoned Dick Foley and asked him to come over to my hotel. He arrived a few minutes after I got there.

"Dinah Brand was killed in her house last night or early this morning," I told him. "Stabbed with an ice pick. The police don't know it yet. I've told you enough about her for you to know that there are any number of people who might have had reason for killing her. There are three I want looked up first – Whisper, Dan Rolff and Bill Quint, the radical fellow. You've got their descriptions. Rolff is in the hospital with a dented skull. I don't know which hospital. Try the City first. Get hold of Mickey Linehan – he's still camped on Pete the Finn's trail – and have him let Pete rest while he gives you a hand on this. Find out where those three birds were last night. And time means something."

The little Canadian op had been watching me curiously while I talked. Now he started to say something, changed his mind, grunted, "Righto," and departed.

I went out to look for Reno Starkey. After an hour of searching I located him, by telephone, in a Ronney Street rooming-house.

"By yourself?" he asked when I had said I wanted to see him.

"Yeah."

He said I could come out, and told me how to get there. I took a taxi. It was a dingy two-story house near the edge of town.

A couple of men loitered in front of a grocer's on the corner above. Another pair sat on the low wooden steps of the house down at the next corner. None of the four was conspicuously refined in appearance.

When I rang the bell two men opened the door. They weren't so mild-looking either.

I was taken upstairs to a front room where Reno, collarless and in shirt-sleeves and vest, sat tilted back in a chair with his feet on the window sill.

He nodded his sallow horse face and said:

"Pull a chair over."

The men who had brought me up went away, closing the door. I sat down and said:

"I want an alibi. Dinah Brand was killed last night after I left her. There's no chance of my being copped for it, but with Noonan dead I don't know how I'm hitched up with the department. I don't want to give them any openings to even try to hang anything on me. If I've got to I can prove where I was last night, but you can save me a lot of trouble if you will."

Reno looked at me with dull eyes and asked:

"Why pick on me?"

"You phoned me there last night. You're the only person who knows I was there the first part of the night. I'd have to fix it with you even if I got the alibi somewhere else, wouldn't I?"

He asked:

"You didn't croak her, did you?"

I said, "No," casually.

He stared out the window a little while before he spoke. He asked:

"What made you think I'd give you the lift? Do I owe you anything for what you done to me at Willsson's last night?"

I said:

"I didn't hurt you any. The news was half-out anyhow. Whisper knew enough to guess the rest. I only gave you a show-down. What do you care? You can take care of yourself."

"I aim to try," he agreed. "All right. You was at the Tanner House in Tanner. That's a little burg twenty–thirty miles up the hill. You went up there after you left Willsson's and stayed till morning. A guy named Ricker that hangs around Murry's with a hire heap drove you up and back. You ought to know what you was doing up there. Give me your sig and I'll have it put on the register."

"Thanks," I said as I unscrewed my fountain-pen.

"Don't say them. I'm doing this because I need all the friends I can get. When the time comes that you sit in with me and Whisper and Pete, I don't expect the sour end of it."

"You won't get it," I promised. "Who's going to be chief of police?"

"McGraw's acting chief. He'll likely cinch it."

"How'll he play?"

"With the Finn. Rough stuff will hurt his shop just like it does Pete's. It'll have to be hurt some. I'd be a swell mutt to sit still while a guy like Whisper is on the loose. It's me or him. Think he croaked the broad?"

"He had reason enough," I said as I gave him the slip of paper on which I had written my name. "She double-crossed him, sold him out, plenty."

"You and her was kind of thick, wasn't you?" he asked.

I let the question alone, lighting a cigarette. Reno waited a while and then said:

"You better hunt up Ricker and let him get a look at you so's he'll know how to describe you if he's asked."

A long-legged youngster of twenty-two or so with a thin freckled face around reckless eyes opened the door and came into the room. Reno introduced him to me as Hank O'Marra. I stood up to shake his hand, and then asked Reno:

"Can I reach you here if I need to?"

"Know Peak Murry?"

"I've met him, and I know his joint."

"Anything you give him will get to me," he said. "We're getting out of here. It's not so good. That Tanner lay is all set."

"Right. Thanks." I went out of the house.

DOWNTOWN, I WENT first to police headquarters. McGraw was holding down the chief's desk. His blond-lashed eyes looked suspiciously at me, and the lines in his leathery face were even deeper and sourer than usual.

"When'd you see Dinah Brand last?" he asked without any preliminaries, not even a nod. His voice rasped disagreeably through his bony nose.

"Ten-forty last night, or thereabout," I said. "Why?"

"Where?"

"Her house."

"How long were you there?"

"Ten minutes, maybe fifteen."

"Why?"

"Why what?"

"Why didn't you stay any longer than that?"

"What," I asked, sitting down in the chair he hadn't offered me, "makes it any of your business?"

He glared at me while he filled his lungs so he could yell, "Murder!" in my face.

I laughed and said:

"You don't think she had anything to do with Noonan's killing?"

I wanted a cigarette, but cigarettes were too well known as first aids to the nervous for me to take a chance on one just then.

McGraw was trying to look through my eyes. I let him look, having all sorts of confidence in my belief that, like a lot of people, I looked most honest when I was lying. Presently he gave up the eye-study and asked:

"Why not?"

That was weak enough. I said, "All right, why not?" indifferently, offered him a cigarette, and took one myself. Then I added: "My guess is that Whisper did it."

"Was he there?" For once McGraw cheated his nose, snapping the words off his teeth.

"Was he where?"

"At Brand's?"

"No," I said, wrinkling my forehead. "Why should he be – if he was off killing Noonan?"

"Damn Noonan!" the acting chief exclaimed irritably. "What do you keep dragging him in for?"

I tried to look at him as if I thought him crazy.

He said:

"Dinah Brand was murdered last night."

I said: "Yeah?"

"Now will you answer my questions?"

"Of course. I was at Willsson's with Noonan and the others. After I left there, around ten-thirty, I dropped in at her house to tell her I had to go up to Tanner. I had a halfway date with her. I stayed there about ten minutes, long enough to have a drink. There was nobody else there, unless they were hiding. When was she killed? And how?"

McGraw told me he had sent a pair of his dicks – Shepp and Vanaman – to see the girl that morning, to see how much help she could and would give the department in copping Whisper for Noonan's murder. The dicks got to her house at nine-thirty. The front door was ajar. Nobody answered their ringing. They went in and found the girl lying on her back in the dining-room, dead, with a stab wound in her left breast.

The doctor who examined the body said she had been killed with a slender, round, pointed blade about six inches in length, at about three o'clock in the morning. Bureaus, closets, trunks, and so on, had apparently been skillfully and thoroughly ransacked. There was no money in the girl's handbag, or elsewhere in the house. The jewel case on her dressing-table was empty. Two diamond rings were on her fingers.

The police hadn't found the weapon with which she had been stabbed. The fingerprint experts hadn't turned up anything they could use. Neither doors nor windows seemed to have been forced. The kitchen showed that the girl had been drinking with a guest or guests.

"Six inches, round, slim, pointed," I repeated the weapon's description. "That sounds like her ice pick."

McGraw reached for the phone and told somebody to send Shepp and Vanaman in. Shepp was a stoop-shouldered tall man whose wide mouth had a grimly honest look that probably came from bad teeth. The other detective was short, stocky, with purplish veins in his nose and hardly any neck.

McGraw introduced us and asked them about the ice pick. They had not see it, were positive it hadn't been there. They wouldn't have overlooked an article of its sort.

"Was it there last night?" McGraw asked me.

"I stood beside her while she chipped off pieces of ice with it."

I described it. McGraw told the dicks to search her house again, and then to try to find the pick in the vicinity of the house.

"You knew her," he said when Shepp and Vanaman had gone. "What's your slant on it?"

"Too new for me to have one," I dodged the question. "Give me an hour or two to think it over. What do you think?"

He fell back into sourness, growling, "How the hell do I know?"

But the fact that he let me go away without asking me any more questions told me he had already made up his mind that Whisper had killed the girl.

I wondered if the little gambler had done it, or if this was another of the wrong raps that Poisonville police chiefs liked to hang on him. It didn't seem to make much difference now. It was a cinch he had – personally or by deputy – put Noonan out, and they could only hang him once.

There were a lot of men in the corridor when I left McGraw. Some of these men were quite young – just kids – quite a few were foreigners, and most of them were every bit as tough-looking as any men should be.

Near the street door I met Donner, one of the coppers who had been on the Cedar Hill expedition.

"Hello," I greeted him. "What's the mob? Emptying the can to make room for more?"

"Them's our new specials," he told me, speaking as if he didn't think much of them. "We're going to have a augmented force."

"Congratulations," I said and went on out.

In his pool room I found Peak Murry sitting at a desk behind the cigar counter talking to three men. I sat down on the other side of the room and watched two kids knock balls around. In a few minutes the lanky proprietor came over to me.

"If you see Reno some time," I told him, "you might let him know that Pete the Finn's having his mob sworn in as special coppers."

"I might," Murry agreed.

Mickey Linehan was sitting in the lobby when I got back to my hotel. He followed me up to my room, and reported:

"Your Dan Rolff pulled a sneak from the hospital some-where after midnight last night. The croakers are kind of steamed up about it. Seems they were figuring on pulling a lot of little pieces of bone out of his brain this morning. But him and his duds were gone. We haven't got a line on Whisper yet. Dick's out now trying to place Bill Quint. What's what on this girl's carving? Dick tells me you got it before the coppers."

"It —"

The telephone-bell rang.

A man's voice, carefully oratorical, spoke my name with a question mark after it.

I said: "Yeah."

The voice said:

"This is Mr. Charles Proctor Dawn speaking. I think you will find it well worth your while to appear at my offices at your earliest convenience."

"Will I? Who are you?"

"Mr. Charles Proctor Dawn, attorney-at-law. My suite is in the Rutledge Block, 310 Green Street. I think you will find it well —"

"Mind telling me part of what it's about?" I asked.

"There are affairs best not discussed over the telephone. I think you will find —"

"All right," I interrupted him again. "I'll be around to see you this afternoon if I get a chance."

"You will find it very, very advisable," he assured me.

I hung up on that.

Mickey said:

"You were going to give me the what's what on the Brand slaughter."

I said:

"I wasn't. I started to say it oughtn't to be hard to trace Rolff — running around with a fractured skull and probably a lot of bandages. Suppose you try it. Give Hurricane Street a play first."

Mickey grinned all the way across his comedian's red face, said, "Don't tell me anything that's going on — I'm only working with you," picked up his hat, and left me.

I spread myself on the bed, smoked cigarettes end to end, and thought about last night — my frame of mind, my passing out, my dreams, and the situation into which I woke. The thinking was unpleasant enough to make me glad when it was interrupted.

Fingernails scratched the outside of my door. I opened the door.

The man who stood there was a stranger to me. He was young, thin, and gaudily dressed. He had heavy eyebrows and a small mustache that were coal-black against a very pale, nervous, but not timid, face.

"I'm Ted Wright," he said, holding out a hand as if I were glad to meet him. "I guess you've heard Whisper talk about me."

I gave him my hand, let him in, closed the door, and asked: "You're a friend of Whisper's?"

"You bet." He held up two thin fingers pressed tightly together. "Just like that, me and him."

I didn't say anything. He looked around the room, smiled nervously, crossed to the open bathroom-door, peeped in, came back to me, rubbed his lips with his tongue, and made his proposition:

"I'll knock him off for you for a half a grand."

"Whisper?"

"Yep, and it's dirt cheap."

"Why do I want him killed?" I asked.

"He un-womaned you, didn't he?"

"Yeah?"

"You ain't that dumb."

A notion stirred in my noodle. To give it time to crawl around I said: "Sit down. This needs talking over."

"It don't need nothing," he said, looking at me sharply, not moving towards either chair. "You either want him knocked off or you don't."

"Then I don't."

He said something I didn't catch, down in his throat, and turned to the door. I got between him and it. He stopped, his eyes fidgeting.

I said:

"So Whisper's dead?"

He stepped back and put a hand behind him. I poked his jaw, leaning my hundred and ninety pounds on the poke.

He got his legs crossed and went down.

I pulled him up by the wrists, yanked his face close to mine, and growled:

"Come through. What's the racket?"

"I ain't done nothing to you."

"Let me catch you. Who got Whisper?"

"I don't know nothing a –"

I let go of one of his wrists, slapped his face with my open hand, caught his wrist again, and tried my luck at crunching both of them while I repeated:

"Who got Whisper?"

"Dan Rolff," he whined. "He walked up to him and stuck him with the same skewer Whisper had used on the twist. That's right."

"How do you know it was the one Whisper killed the girl with?"

"Dan said so."

"What did Whisper say?"

"Nothing. He looked funny as hell, standing there with the butt of the sticker sticking out his side. Then he flashes the rod and puts two pills in Dan just like one, and the both of them go down together, cracking heads, Dan's all bloody through the bandages."

"And then what?"

"Then nothing. I roll them over, and they're a pair of stiffs. Every word I'm telling you is gospel."

"Who else was there?"

"Nobody else. Whisper was hiding out, with only me to go between him and the mob. He killed Noonan hisself, and he didn't want to have to trust nobody for a couple of days, till he could see what was what, excepting me."

"So you, being a smart boy, thought you could run around to his enemies and pick up a little dough for killing him after he was dead?"

"I was clean, and this won't be no place for Whisper's pals when the word gets out that he's croaked," Wright whined. "I had to raise a get-away stake."

"How'd you make out so far?"

"I got a century from Pete and a century and a half from Peak Murry – for Reno – with more promised from both when I turn the trick." The whine changed into boasting as he talked. "I bet you I could get McGraw to come across too, and I thought you'd kick in with something."

"They must be high in the air to toss dough at a woozy racket like that."

"I don't know," he said superiorly. "It ain't such a lousy one at that." He became humble again. "Give me a chance, chief. Don't gum it on me. I'll give you fifty bucks now and a split of whatever I get from McGraw if you'll keep your clam shut till I can put it over and grab a rattler."

"Nobody but you knows where Whisper is?"

"Nobody else, except Dan, that's as dead as he is."

"Where are they?"

"The old Redman warehouse down on Porter Street. In the back, upstairs, Whisper had a room fixed up with a bed, stove, and some grub. Give me a chance. Fifty bucks now and a cut on the rest."

I let go of his arm and said:

"I don't want the dough, but go ahead. I'll lay off for a couple of hours. That ought to be long enough."

"Thanks, chief. Thanks, thanks," and he hurried away from me.

I put on my coat and hat, went out, found Green Street and the Rutledge Block. It was a wooden building a long while past any prime it might ever have had. Mr. Charles Proctor

Dawn's establishment was on the second floor. There was no elevator. I climbed a worn and rickety flight of wooden steps.

The lawyer had two rooms, both dingy, smelly, and poorly lighted. I waited in the outer one while a clerk who went well with the rooms carried my name in to the lawyer. Half a minute later the clerk opened the door and beckoned me in.

Mr. Charles Proctor Dawn was a little fat man of fifty-something. He had prying triangular eyes of a very light color, a short fleshy nose, and a fleshier mouth whose greediness was only partly hidden between a ragged gray mustache and a ragged gray Vandyke beard. His clothes were dark and unclean-looking without actually being dirty.

He didn't get up from his desk, and throughout my visit he kept his right hand on the edge of a desk-drawer that was some six inches open.

He said:

"Ah, my dear sir, I am extremely gratified to find that you had the good judgment to recognize the value of my counsel."

His voice was even more oratorical than it had been over the wire.

I didn't say anything.

Nodding his whiskers as if my not saying anything was another exhibition of good judgment, he continued:

"I may say, in all justice, that you will find it the invariable part of sound judgment to follow the dictates of my counsel in all cases. I may say this, my dear sir, without false modesty, appreciating with both fitting humility and a deep sense of true and lasting values, my responsibilities as well as my prerogatives as a – and why should I stoop to conceal the fact that there are those who feel justified in preferring to substitute the definite article for the indefinite? – recognized and accepted leader of the bar in this thriving state."

He knew a lot of sentences like those, and he didn't mind using them on me. Finally he got along to:

"Thus, that conduct which in a minor practitioner might seem irregular, becomes, when he who exercises it occupies such indisputable prominence in his community – and, I might say, not merely the immediate community – as serves to place him above fear of reproach, simply that greater ethic which scorns the pettier conventionalities when confronted with an opportunity to serve mankind through one of its individual representatives. Therefore, my dear sir, I have not hesitated to brush aside scornfully all trivial considerations of accepted precedent, to summon you, to say to you frankly and candidly, my dear sir, that your interests will best be served by and through retaining me as your legal representative."

I asked:

"What'll it cost?"

"That," he said loftily, "is of but secondary importance. However, it is a detail which has its deserved place in our relationship, and must be not overlooked or neglected. We shall say, a thousand dollars now. Later, no doubt –"

He ruffled his whiskers and didn't finish the sentence.

I said I hadn't, of course, that much money on me.

"Naturally, my dear sir. Naturally. But that is of not the least importance in any degree. None whatever. Any time will do for that, any time up to ten o'clock tomorrow morning."

"At ten tomorrow," I agreed. "Now I'd like to know why I'm supposed to need legal representatives."

He made an indignant face.

"My dear sir, this is no matter for jesting, of that I assure you."

I explained that I hadn't been joking, that I really was puzzled.

He cleared his throat, frowned more or less importantly, said:

"It may well be, my dear sir, that you do not fully comprehend the peril that surrounds you, but it is indubitably preposterous that you should expect me to suppose that you are

607

without any inkling of the difficulties – the legal difficulties, my dear sir – with which you are about to be confronted, growing, as they do, out of occurrences that took place at no more remote time than last night, my dear sir, last night. However, there is no time to go into that now. I have a pressing appointment with Judge Leffner. On the morrow I shall be glad to go more thoroughly into each least ramification of the situation – and I assure you they are many – with you. I shall expect you at ten tomorrow morning."

I promised to be there, and went out. I spent the evening in my room, drinking unpleasant whiskey, thinking unpleasant thoughts, and waiting for reports that didn't come from Mickey and Dick. I went to sleep at midnight.

I WAS HALF dressed the next morning when Dick Foley came in. He reported, in his word-saving manner, that Bill Quint had checked out of the Miners' Hotel at noon the previous day, leaving no forwarding address.

A train left Personville for Ogden at twelve-thirty-five. Dick had wired the Continental's Salt Lake branch to send a man up to Ogden to try to trace Quint.

"We can't pass up any leads," I said, "but I don't think Quint's the man we want. She gave him the air long ago. If he had meant to do anything about it he would have done it before this. My guess is that when he heard she had been killed he decided to duck, being a discarded lover who had threatened her."

Dick nodded and said:

"Gun-play out the road last night. Hijacking. Four trucks of hooch nailed, burned."

That sounded like Reno Starkey's answer to the news that the big bootlegger's mob had been sworn in as special coppers.

Mickey Linehan arrived by the time I had finished dressing.

"Dan Rolff was at the house, all right," he reported. "The Greek grocer on the corner saw him come out around nine yesterday morning. He went down the street wobbling and talking to himself. The Greek thought he was drunk."

"Howcome the Greek didn't tell the police? Or did he?"

"Wasn't asked. A swell department this burg's got. What do we do: find him for them and turn him in with the job all tacked up?"

609

"McGraw has decided Whisper killed her," I said, "and he's not bothering himself with any leads that don't lead that way. Unless he came back later for the ice pick, Rolff didn't turn the trick. She was killed at three in the morning. Rolff wasn't there at eight-thirty, and the pick was still sticking in her. It was –"

Dick Foley came over to stand in front of me and ask:

"How do you know?"

I didn't like the way he looked or the way he spoke. I said:

"You know because I'm telling you."

Dick didn't say anything. Mickey grinned his half-wit's grin and asked:

"Where do we go from here? Let's get this thing polished off."

"I've got a date for ten," I told them. "Hang around the hotel till I get back. Whisper and Rolff are probably dead – so we won't have to hunt for them." I scowled at Dick and said: "I was told that. I didn't kill either of them."

The little Canadian nodded without lowering his eyes from mine.

I ate breakfast alone, and then set out for the lawyer's office.

Turning off King Street, I saw Hank O'Marra's freckled face in an automobile that was going up Green Street. He was sitting beside a man I didn't know. The long-legged youngster waved an arm at me and stopped the car. I went over to him.

He said:

"Reno wants to see you."

"Where will I find him?"

"Jump in."

"I can't go now," I said. "Probably not till afternoon."

"See Peak when you're ready."

I said I would. O'Marra and his companion drove on up Green Street. I walked half a block south to the Rutledge Block.

With a foot on the first of the rickety steps that led up to the lawyer's floor, I stopped to look at something.

It was barely visible back in a dim corner of the first floor. It was a shoe. It was lying in a position that empty shoes don't lie in.

I took my foot off the step and went towards the shoe. Now I could see an ankle and the cuff of a black pants-leg above the shoe-top.

That prepared me for what I found.

I found Mr. Charles Proctor Dawn huddled among two brooms, a mop and a bucket, in a little alcove formed by the back of the stairs and a corner of the wall. His Vandyke beard was red with blood from a cut that ran diagonally across his forehead. His head was twisted sidewise and backward at an angle that could only be managed with a broken neck.

I quoted Noonan's "What's got to be done has got to be done" to myself, and, gingerly pulling one side of the dead man's coat out of the way, emptied his inside coat-pocket, transferring a black book and a sheaf of papers to my own pocket. In two of his other pockets I found nothing I wanted. The rest of his pockets couldn't be got at without moving him, and I didn't care to do that.

Five minutes later I was back in the hotel, going in through a side-door, to avoid Dick and Mickey in the lobby, and walking up to the mezzanine to take an elevator.

In my room I sat down and examined my loot.

I took the book first, a small imitation-leather memoranda book of the sort that sells for not much money in any stationery store. It held some fragmentary notes that meant nothing to me, and thirty-some names and addresses that meant as little, with one exception:

Helen Albury
1229A Hurricane St.

That was interesting because, first, a young man named Robert Albury was in prison, having confessed that he shot and killed Donald Willsson in a fit of jealousy aroused by Willsson's supposed success with Dinah Brand; and, second, Dinah Brand had lived, and had been murdered, at 1232 Hurricane Street, across the street from 1229A.

I did not find my name in the book.

I put the book aside and began unfolding and reading the papers I had taken with it. Here too I had to wade through a lot that didn't mean anything to find something that did.

This find was a group of four letters held together by a rubber band.

The letters were in slitted envelopes that had postmarks dated a week apart, on the average. The latest was a little more than six months old. The letters were addressed to Dinah Brand. The first – that is, the earliest – wasn't so bad, for a love letter. The second was a bit goofier. The third and fourth were swell examples of how silly an ardent and unsuccessful wooer can be, especially if he's getting on in years. The four letters were signed by Elihu Willsson.

I had not found anything to tell me definitely why Mr. Charles Proctor Dawn had thought he could blackmail me out of a thousand dollars, but I had found plenty to think about. I encouraged my brain with two Fatimas, and then went downstairs.

"Go out and see what you can raise on a lawyer named Charles Proctor Dawn," I told Mickey. "He's got offices in Green Street. Stay away from them. Don't put in a lot of time on him. I just want a rough line quick."

I told Dick to give me a five-minute start and then follow me out to the neighborhood of 1229A Hurricane Street.

1229A was the upper flat in a two-story building almost directly opposite Dinah's house. 1229 was divided into two flats, with a private entrance for each. I rang the bell at the one I wanted.

The door was opened by a thin girl of eighteen or nineteen with dark eyes set close together in a shiny yellowish face under short-cut brown hair that looked damp.

She opened the door, made a choked, frightened sound in her throat, and backed away from me, holding both hands to her mouth.

"Miss Helen Albury?" I asked.

She shook her head violently from side to side. There was no truthfulness in it. Her eyes were crazy.

I said:

"I'd like to come in and talk to you a few minutes," going in as I spoke, closing the door behind me.

She didn't say anything. She went up the steps in front of me, her head twisted around so she could watch me with her scary eyes.

We went into a scantily furnished living-room. Dinah's house could be seen from its windows.

The girl stood in the center of the floor, her hands still to her mouth.

I wasted time and words trying to convince her that I was harmless. It was no good. Everything I said seemed to increase her panic. It was a damned nuisance. I quit trying, and got down to business.

"You are Robert Albury's sister?" I asked.

No reply, nothing but the senseless look of utter fear.

I said:

"After he was arrested for killing Donald Willsson you took this flat so you could watch her. What for?"

Not a word from her. I had to supply my own answer:

"Revenge. You blamed Dinah Brand for your brother's trouble. You watched for your chance. It came the night before last. You sneaked into her house, found her drunk, stabbed her with the ice pick you found there."

She didn't say anything. I hadn't succeeded in jolting the blankness out of her frightened face. I said:

"Dawn helped you, engineered it for you. He wanted Elihu Willsson's letters. Who was the man he sent to get them, the man who did the actual killing? Who was he?"

That got me nothing. No change in her expression, or lack of expression. No word. I thought I would like to spank her. I said:

"I've given you your chance to talk. I'm willing to listen to your side of the story. But suit yourself."

She suited herself by keeping quiet, I gave it up. I was afraid of her, afraid she would do something even crazier than her silence if I pressed her further. I went out of the flat not sure that she had understood a single word I had said.

At the corner I told Dick Foley:

"There's a girl in there, Helen Albury, eighteen, five six, skinny, not more than a hundred, if that, eyes close together, brown, yellow skin, brown short hair, straight, got on a gray suit now. Tail her. If she cuts up on you throw her in the can. Be careful – she's crazy as a bedbug."

I set out for Peak Murry's dump, to locate Reno and see what he wanted. Half a block from my destination I stepped into an office building doorway to look the situation over.

A police patrol wagon stood in front of Murry's. Men were being led, dragged, carried, from pool room to wagon. The leaders, draggers, and carriers, did not look like regular coppers. They were, I supposed, Pete the Finn's crew, now special officers. Pete, with McGraw's help, apparently was making good his threat to give Whisper and Reno all the war they wanted.

While I watched, an ambulance arrived, was loaded, and drove away. I was too far away to recognize anybody or any bodies. When the height of the excitement seemed past I circled a couple of blocks and returned to my hotel.

Mickey Linehan was there with information about Mr. Charles Proctor Dawn.

"He's the guy that the joke was wrote about: 'Is he a criminal lawyer?' 'Yes, very.' This fellow Albury that you nailed, some of his family hired this bird Dawn to defend him. Albury wouldn't have anything to do with him when Dawn came to see him. This three-named shyster nearly went over himself last year, on a blackmail rap, something to do with a person named Hill, but squirmed out of it. Got some property out on Libert Street, wherever that is. Want me to keep digging?"

"That'll do. We'll stick around till we hear from Dick."

Mickey yawned and said that was all right with him, never being one that had to run around a lot to keep his blood circulating, and asked if I knew we were getting nationally famous.

I asked him what he meant by that.

"I just ran into Tommy Robins," he said. "The Consolidated Press sent him here to cover the doings. He tells me some of the other press associations and a big-city paper or two are sending in special correspondents, beginning to play our troubles up."

I was making one of my favorite complaints – that newspapers were good for nothing except to hash things up so nobody could unhash them – when I heard a boy chanting my name. For a dime he told me I was wanted on the phone.

Dick Foley:

"She showed right away. To 310 Green Street. Full of coppers. Mouthpiece named Dawn killed. Police took her to the Hall."

"She still there?"

"Yes, in the chief's office."

"Stick, and get anything you pick up to me quick."

I went back to Mickey Linehan and gave him my room key and instructions:

"Camp in my room. Take anything that comes for me and pass it on. I'll be at the Shannon around the corner, registered as J. W. Clark. Tell Dick and nobody."

Mickey asked, "What the hell?" got no answer, and moved his loose-jointed bulk towards the elevators.

24 WANTED

I WENT AROUND to the Shannon Hotel, registered my alias, paid my day's rent, and was taken to room 321.

An hour passed before the phone rang.

Dick Foley said he was coming up to see me.

He arrived within five minutes. His thin worried face was not friendly. Neither was his voice. He said:

"Warrants out for you. Murder. Two counts — Brand and Dawn. I phoned. Mickey said he'd stick. Told me you were here. Police got him. Grilling him now."

"Yeah, I expected that."

"So did I," he said sharply.

I said, making myself drawl the words:

"You think I killed them, don't you, Dick?"

"If you didn't, it's a good time to say so."

"Going to put the finger on me?" I asked.

He pulled his lips back over his teeth. His face changed from tan to buff.

I said:

"Go back to San Francisco, Dick. I've got enough to do without having to watch you."

He put his hat on very carefully and very carefully closed the door behind him when he went out.

At four o'clock, I had some lunch, cigarettes, and an *Evening Herald* sent up to me.

Dinah Brand's murder, and the newer murder of Charles Proctor Dawn, divided the front page of the *Herald*, with Helen Albury connecting them.

Helen Albury was, I read, Robert Albury's sister, and she

was, in spite of his confession, thoroughly convinced that her brother was not guilty of murder, but the victim of a plot. She had retained Charles Proctor Dawn to defend him. (I could guess that the late Charles Proctor had hunted her up, and not she him.) The brother refused to have Dawn or any other lawyer, but the girl (properly encouraged by Dawn, no doubt) had not given up the fight.

Finding a vacant flat across the street of Dinah Brand's house, Helen Albury had rented it, and had installed herself therein with a pair of field glasses and one idea – to prove that Dinah and her associates were guilty of Donald Willsson's murder.

I, it seems, was one of the "associates." The *Herald* called me "a man supposed to be a private detective from San Francisco, who has been in the city for several days, apparently on intimate terms with Max ('Whisper') Thaler, Daniel Rolff, Oliver ('Reno') Starkey, and Dinah Brand." We were the plotters who had framed Robert Albury.

The night that Dinah had been killed, Helen Albury, peeping through her window, had seen things that were, according to the *Herald*, extremely significant when considered in connection with the subsequent finding of Dinah's dead body. As soon as the girl heard of the murder, she took her important knowledge to Charles Proctor Dawn. He, the police learned from his clerks, immediately sent for me, and had been closeted with me that afternoon. He had later told his clerks that I was to return the next – this – morning at ten. This morning I had not appeared to keep my appointment. At twenty-five minutes past ten, the janitor of the Rutledge Block had found Charles Proctor Dawn's body in a corner behind the staircase, murdered. It was believed that valuable papers had been taken from the dead man's pockets.

At the very moment that the janitor was finding the dead lawyer, I, it seems, was in Helen Albury's flat, having forced an entrance, and was threatening her. After she succeeded in throwing me out, she hurried to Dawn's offices, arriving while the police were there, telling them her story. Police sent to my hotel had not found me there, but in my room they had found one Michael Linehan, who also represented himself to be a San Francisco private detective. Michael Linehan was still being questioned by the police. Whisper, Reno, Rolff and I were being hunted by the police, charged with murder. Important developments were expected.

Page two held an interesting half-column. Detectives Shepp and Vanaman, the discoverers of Dinah Brand's body, had mysteriously vanished. Foul play on the part of us "associates" was feared.

There was nothing in the paper about last night's hijacking, nothing about the raid on Peak Murry's joint.

I went out after dark. I wanted to get in touch with Reno.

From a drug-store I phoned Peak Murry's pool room.

"Is Peak there?" I asked.

"This is Peak," said a voice that didn't sound anything at all like his. "Who's talking?"

I said disgustedly, "This is Lillian Gish," hung up the receiver, and removed myself from the neighborhood.

I gave up the idea of finding Reno and decided to go calling on my client, old Elihu, and try to blackjack him into good behavior with the love letters he had written Dinah Brand, and which I had stolen from Dawn's remains.

I walked, keeping to the darker side of the darkest streets. It was a fairly long walk for a man who sneers at exercise. By the time I reached Willsson's block I was in bad enough humor to be in good shape for the sort of interviews he and I usually had. But I wasn't to see him for a little while yet.

I was two pavements from my destination when somebody S-s-s-s-s'd at me.

I probably didn't jump twenty feet.

"'S all right," a voice whispered.

It was dark there. Peeping out under my bush – I was on my hands and knees in somebody's front yard – I could make out the form of a man crouching close to a hedge, on my side of it.

My gun was in my hand now. There was no special reason why I shouldn't take his word for it that it was all right.

I got up off my knees and went to him. When I got close enough I recognized him as one of the men who had let me into the Ronney Street house the day before.

I sat on my heels beside him and asked:

"Where'll I find Reno? Hank O'Marra said he wanted to see me."

"He does that. Know where Kid McLeod's place is at?"

"No."

"It's on Martin Street above King, corner the alley. Ask for the Kid. Go back that-away three blocks, and then down. You can't miss it."

I said I'd try not to, and left him crouching behind his hedge, watching my client's place, waiting, I guessed, for a shot at Pete the Finn, Whisper, or any of Reno's other unfriends who might happen to call on old Elihu.

Following directions, I came to a soft drink and rummy establishment with red and yellow paint all over it. Inside I asked for Kid McLeod. I was taken into a back room, where a fat man with a dirty collar, a lot of gold teeth, and only one ear, admitted he was McLeod.

"Reno sent for me," I said. "Where'll I find him?"

"And who does that make you?" he asked.

I told him who I was. He went out without saying anything. I waited ten minutes. He brought a boy back with him, a kid of fifteen or so with a vacant expression on a pimply red face.

"Go with Sonny," Kid McLeod told me.

I followed the boy out a side-door, down two blocks of back street, across a sandy lot, through a ragged gate, and up to the back door of a frame house.

The boy knocked on the door and was asked who he was.

"Sonny, with a guy the Kid sent," he replied.

The door was opened by long-legged O'Marra. Sonny went away. I went into a kitchen where Reno Starkey and four other men sat around a table that had a lot of beer on it. I noticed that two automatic pistols hung on nails over the top of the door through which I had come. They would be handy if any of the house's occupants opened the door, found an enemy with a gun there, and were told to put up their hands.

Reno poured me a glass of beer and led me through the dining-room into a front room. A man lay on his belly there, with one eye to the crack between the drawn blind and the bottom of the window, watching the street.

"Go back and get yourself some beer," Reno told him.

He got up and went away. We made ourselves comfortable in adjoining chairs.

"When I fixed up that Tanner alibi for you," Reno said, "I told you I was doing it because I needed all the friends I could get."

"You got one."

"Crack the alibi yet?" he asked.

"Not yet."

"It'll hold," he assured me, "unless they got too damned much on you. Think they have?"

I did think so. I said:

"No. McGraw's just feeling playful. That'll take care of itself. How's your end holding up?"

He emptied his glass, wiped his mouth on the back of a hand, and said.

"I'll make out. But that's what I wanted to see you about. Here's how she stacks up. Pete's throwed in with McGraw. That lines coppers and beer mob up against me and Whisper. But hell! Me and Whisper are busier trying to put the chive in each other than bucking the combine. That's a sour racket. While we're tangling, them bums will eat us up."

I said I had been thinking the same thing. He went on:

"Whisper'll listen to you. Find him, will you? Put it to him. Here's the proposish: he means to get me for knocking off Jerry Hooper, and I mean to get him first. Let's forget that for a couple of days. Nobody won't have to trust nobody else. Whisper don't ever show in any of his jobs anyways. He just sends the boys. I'll do the same this time. We'll just put the mobs together to swing the caper. We run them together, rub out the damned Finn, and then we'll have plenty of time to go gunning among ourselves.

"Put it to him cold. I don't want him to get any ideas that I'm dodging a rumpus with him or any other guy. Tell him I say if we put Pete out of the way we'll have more room to do our own scrapping in. Pete's holed-up down in Whiskeytown. I ain't got enough men to go down there and pull him out. Neither has Whisper. The two of us together has. Put it to him."

"Whisper," I said, "is dead."

Reno said, "Is that so?" as if he thought it wasn't.

"Dan Rolff killed him yesterday morning, down in the old Redman warehouse, stuck him with the ice pick Whisper had used on the girl."

Reno asked:

"You know this? You're not just running off at the head?"

"I know it."

"Damned funny none of his mob act like he was gone," he said, but he was beginning to believe me.

"They don't know it. He was hiding out, with Ted Wright the only one in on the where. Ted knew it. He cashed in on it. He told me he got a hundred or a hundred and fifty from you, through Peak Murry."

"I'd have given the big umpchay twice that for the straight dope," Reno grumbled. He rubbed his chin and said: "Well, that settles the Whisper end."

I said: "No."

"What do you mean, no?"

"If his mob don't know where he is," I suggested, "let's tell them. They blasted him out of the can when Noonan copped him. Think they'd try it again if the news got around that McGraw had picked him up on the quiet?"

"Keep talking," Reno said.

"If his friends try to crack the hoosegow again, thinking he's in it, that'll give the department, including Pete's specials, something to do. While they're doing it, you could try your luck in Whiskeytown."

"Maybe," he said slowly, "maybe we'll try just that thing."

"It ought to work," I encouraged him, standing up. "I'll see you – "

"Stick around. This is as good a spot as any while there's a reader out for you. And we'll need a good guy like you on the party."

I didn't like that so much. I knew enough not to say so. I sat down again.

Reno got busy arranging the rumor. The telephone was worked overtime. The kitchen-door was worked as hard, letting men in and out. More came in than went out. The house filled with men, smoke, tension.

AT HALF-PAST ONE Reno turned from answering a phone-call to say:

"Let's take a ride."

He went upstairs. When he came down he carried a black valise. Most of the men had gone out the kitchen-door by then.

Reno gave me the black valise, saying:

"Don't wrastle it around too much."

It was heavy.

The seven of us left in the house went out the front door and got into a curtained touring car that O'Marra had just driven up to the curb. Reno sat beside O'Marra. I was squeezed in between men in the back seat, with the valise squeezed between my legs.

Another car came out of the first cross street to run ahead of us. A third followed us. Our speed hung around forty, fast enough to get us somewhere, not fast enough to get us a lot of attention.

We had nearly finished the trip before we were bothered.

The action started in a block of one-story houses of the shack type, down in the southern end of the city.

A man put his head out of a door, put his fingers in his mouth, and whistled shrilly.

Somebody in the car behind us shot him down.

At the next corner we ran through a volley of pistol bullets.

Reno turned around to tell me:

"If they pop the bag, we'll all of us hit the moon. Get it open. We got to work fast when we get there."

I had the fasteners unsnapped by the time we came to rest at the curb in front of a dark three-story brick building.

Men crawled all over me, opening the valise, helping themselves to the contents, bombs made of short sections of two-inch pipe, packed in sawdust in the bag. Bullets bit chunks out of the car's curtains.

Reno reached back for one of the bombs, hopped out to the sidewalk, paid no attention to a streak of blood that suddenly appeared in the middle of his left cheek, and heaved his piece of stuffed pipe at the brick building's door.

A sheet of flame was followed by deafening noise. Hunks of things pelted us while we tried to keep from being knocked over by the concussion. Then there was no door to keep anybody out of the red brick building.

A man ran forward, swung his arm, let a pipeful of hell go through the doorway. The shutters came off the downstairs windows, fire and glass flying behind them.

The car that had followed us was stationary up the street, trading shots with the neighborhood. The car that had gone ahead of us had turned into a side-street. Pistol shots from behind the red brick building, between the explosions of our cargo, told us that our advance car was covering the back door.

O'Marra, out in the middle of the street, bent far over, tossed a bomb to the brick building's roof. It didn't explode. O'Marra put one foot high in the air, clawed at his throat, and fell solidly backward.

Another of our party went down under the slugs that were cutting at us from a wooden building next to the brick one.

Reno cursed stolidly and said:

"Burn them out, Fat."

Fat spit on a bomb, ran around the back of our car, and swung his arm.

We picked ourselves up off the sidewalk, dodged flying things, and saw that the frame house was all out of whack, with flames climbing its torn edges.

"Any left?" Reno asked as we looked around, enjoying the novelty of not being shot at.

"Here's the last one," Fat said, holding out a bomb.

Fire was dancing inside the upper windows of the brick house. Reno looked at it, took the bomb from Fat, and said:

"Back off. They'll be coming out."

We moved away from the front of the house.

A voice indoors yelled:

"Reno!"

Reno slipped into the shadow of our car before he called back:

"Well?"

"We're done," a heavy voice shouted. "We're coming out. Don't shoot."

Reno asked, "Who's we're?"

"Well?"

"This is Pete," the heavy voice said. "There's four left of us."

"You come first," Reno ordered, "with your mitts on the top of your head. The others come out one at a time, same way, after you. And half a minute apart is close enough. Come on."

We waited a moment, and then Pete the Finn appeared in the dynamited doorway, his hands holding the top of his bald head. In the glare from the burning next-door house we could see that his face was cut, his clothes almost all torn off.

Stepping over wreckage, the bootlegger came slowly down the steps to the sidewalk.

Reno called him a lousy fish-eater and shot him four times in face and body.

Pete went down. A man behind me laughed.

Reno hurled the remaining bomb through the doorway.

We scrambled into our car. Reno took the wheel. The engine was dead. Bullets had got to it.

Reno worked the horn while the rest of us piled out.

The machine that had stopped at the corner came for us. Waiting for it, I looked up and down the street that was bright with the glow of two burning buildings. There were a few faces at windows, but whoever besides us was in the street had taken to cover. Not far away, firebells sounded.

The other machine slowed up for us to climb aboard. It was already full. We packed it in layers, with the overflow hanging on the running-boards.

We bumped over dead Hank O'Marra's legs and headed for home. We covered one block of the distance with safety if not comfort. After that we had neither.

A limousine turned into the street ahead of us, came half a block towards us, put its side to us, and stopped. Out of the side, gun-fire.

Another car came around the limousine and charged us. Out of it, gun-fire.

We did our best, but we were too damned amalgamated for good fighting. You can't shoot straight holding a man in your lap, another hanging on your shoulder, while a third does his shooting from an inch behind your ear.

Our other car – the one that had been around at the building's rear – came up and gave us a hand. But by then two more had joined the opposition. Apparently Thaler's mob's attack on the jail was over, one way or the other, and Pete's army, sent to help there, had returned in time to spoil our get-away. It was a sweet mess.

I leaned over a burning gun and yelled in Reno's ear:

"This is the bunk. Let's us extras get out and do our wrangling from the street."

He thought that a good idea, and gave orders:

"Pile out some of you hombres, and take them from the pavements."

I was the first man out, with my eye on a dark alley entrance.

Fat followed me to it. In my shelter, I turned on him and growled:

"Don't pile up on me. Pick your own hole. There's a cellar-way that looks good."

He agreeably trotted off towards it, and was shot down at his third step.

I explored my alley. It was only twenty feet long, and ended against a high board fence with a locked gate.

A garbage can helped me over the gate into a brick-paved yard. The side-fence of that yard let me into another, and from that I got into another, where a fox terrier raised hell at me.

I kicked the pooch out of the way, made the opposite fence, untangled myself from a clothes line, crossed two more yards, got yelled at from a window, had a bottle thrown at me, and dropped into a cobblestoned back street.

The shooting was behind me, but not far enough. I did all I could to remedy that. I must have walked as many streets as I did in my dreams the night Dinah was killed.

My watch said it was three-thirty a.m. when I looked at it on Elihu Willsson's front steps.

I HAD TO push my client's door-bell a lot before I got any play on it.

Finally the door was opened by the tall sunburned chauffeur. He was dressed in undershirt and pants, and had a billiard cue in one fist.

"What do you want?" he demanded, and then, when he got another look at me: "It's you, is it? Well, what do you want?"

"I want to see Mr. Willsson."

"At four in the morning? Go on with you," and he started to close the door.

I put a foot against it. He looked from my foot to my face, hefted the billiard cue, and asked:

"You after getting your kneecap cracked?"

"I'm not playing," I insisted. "I've got to see the old man. Tell him."

"I don't have to tell him. He told me no later than this afternoon that if you come around he didn't want to see you."

"Yeah?" I took the four love letters out of my pocket, picked out the first and least idiotic of them, held it out to the chauffeur, and said: "Give him that and tell him I'm sitting on the steps with the rest of them. Tell him I'll sit here five minutes and then carry the rest of them to Tommy Robins of the Consolidated Press."

The chauffeur scowled at the letter, said, "To hell with Tommy Robins and his blind aunt!" took the letter, and closed the door.

Four minutes later he opened the door again and said:

"Inside, you."

I followed him upstairs to old Elihu's bedroom.

My client sat up in bed with his love letter crushed in one round pink fist, its envelope in the other.

His short white hair bristled. His round eyes were as much red as blue. The parallel lines of his mouth and chin almost touched. He was in a lovely humor.

As soon as he saw me he shouted:

"So after all your brave talking you had to come back to the old pirate to have your neck saved, did you?"

I said I didn't anything of the sort. I said if he was going to talk like a sap he ought to lower his voice so that people in Los Angeles wouldn't learn what a sap he was.

The old boy let his voice out another notch, bellowing:

"Because you've stolen a letter or two that don't belong to you, you needn't think you –"

I put fingers in my ears. They didn't shut out the noise, but they insulted him into cutting the bellowing short.

I took the fingers out and said:

"Send the flunkey away so we can talk. You won't need him. I'm not going to hurt you."

He said, "Get out," to the chauffeur.

The chauffeur, looking at me without fondness, left us, closing the door.

Old Elihu gave me the rush act, demanding that I surrender the rest of the letters immediately, wanting to know loudly and profanely where I had got them, what I was doing with them, threatening me with this, that, and the other, but mostly just cursing me.

I didn't surrender the letters. I said:

"I took them from the man you hired to recover them. A tough break for you that he had to kill the girl."

Enough red went out of the old man's face to leave it normally pink. He worked his lips over his teeth, screwed up his eyes at me, and said:

630

"Is that the way you're going to play it?"

His voice came comparatively quiet from his chest. He had settled down to fight.

I pulled a chair over beside the bed, sat down, put as much amusement as I could in a grin, and said:

"That's one way."

He watched me, working his lips, saying nothing. I said:

"You're the damnedest client I ever had. What do you do? You hire me to clean town, change your mind, run out on me, work against me until I begin to look like a winner, then get on the fence, and now when you think I'm licked again, you don't even want to let me in the house. Lucky for me I happened to run across those letters."

He said: "Blackmail."

I laughed and said:

"Listen who's naming it. All right, call it that." I tapped the edge of the bed with a forefinger. "I'm not licked, old top. I've won. You came crying to me that some naughty men had taken your little city away from you. Pete the Finn, Lew Yard, Whisper Thaler, and Noonan. Where are they now?

"Yard died Tuesday morning, Noonan the same night, Whisper Wednesday morning, and the Finn a little while ago. I'm giving your city back to you whether you want it or not. If that's blackmail, OK. Now here's what you're going to do. You're going to get hold of your mayor, I suppose the lousy village has got one, and you and he are going to phone the governor – Keep still until I get through.

"You're going to tell the governor that your city police have got out of hand, what with bootleggers sworn in as officers, and so on. You're going to ask him for help – the national guard would be best. I don't know how various ruckuses around town have come out, but I do know the big boys – the ones you were afraid of – are dead. The ones that had too much on you for you to stand up to them. There are plenty of busy young men working like hell right now, trying to get into the dead men's shoes. The more, the better. They'll make it easier for the white-collar soldiers to take hold while everything is disorganized. And none of the substitutes are likely to have enough on you to do much damage.

"You're going to have the mayor, or the governor, whichever it comes under, suspend the whole Personville police department, and let the mail-order troops handle things till you can organize another. I'm told that the mayor and the governor are both pieces of your property. They'll do what you tell them. And that's what you're going to tell them. It can be done, and it's got to be done.

"Then you'll have your city back, all nice and clean and ready to go to the dogs again. If you don't do it, I'm going to turn these love letters of yours over to the newspaper buzzards, and I don't mean your *Herald* crew – the press associations. I got the letters from Dawn. You'll have a lot of fun proving that you didn't hire him to recover them, and that he didn't kill the girl doing it. But the fun you'll have is nothing to the fun people will have reading these letters. They're hot. I haven't laughed so much over anything since the hogs ate my kid brother."

I stopped talking.

The old man was shaking, but there was no fear in his shaking. His face was purple again. He opened his mouth and roared:

"Publish them and be damned!"

I took them out of my pocket, dropped them on his bed, got up from my chair, put on my hat, and said:

"I'd give my right leg to be able to believe that the girl was killed by somebody you sent to get the letters. By God, I'd like to top off the job by sending you to the gallows!"

He didn't touch the letters. He said:

"You told me the truth about Thaler and Pete?"

"Yeah. But what difference does it make? You'll only be pushed around by somebody else."

He threw the bedclothes aside and swung his stocky pajamaed legs and pink feet over the edge of the bed.

"Have you got the guts," he barked, "to take the job I offered you once before – chief of police?"

"No. I lost my guts out fighting your fights while you were hiding in bed and thinking up new ways of disowning me. Find another wet-nurse."

He glared at me. Then shrewd wrinkles came around his eyes.

He nodded his old head and said:

"You're afraid to take the job. So you did kill the girl?"

I left him as I had left him the last time, saying, "Go to hell!" and walking out.

The chauffeur, still toting his billiard cue, still regarding me without fondness, met me on the ground floor and took me to the door, looking as if he hoped I would start something. I didn't. He slammed the door after me.

The street was gray with the beginning of daylight.

Up the street a black coupé stood under some trees. I couldn't see if anyone was in it. I played safe by walking in the opposite direction. The coupé moved after me.

There is nothing in running down streets with automobiles in pursuit. I stopped, facing this one. It came on. I took my hand away from my side when I saw Mickey Linehan's red face through the windshield.

He swung the door open for me to get in.

"I thought you might come up here," he said as I sat beside him, "but I was a second or two too late. I saw you go in, but was too far away to catch you."

"How'd you make out with the police?" I asked. "Better keep driving while we talk."

"I didn't know anything, couldn't guess anything, didn't have any idea of what you were working on, just happened to hit town and meet you. Old friends – that line. They were still trying when the riot broke. They had me in one of the little offices across from the assembly room. When the circus cut loose I back-windowed them."

"How'd the circus wind up?" I asked.

"The coppers shot hell out of them. They got the tip-off half an hour ahead of time, and had the whole neighborhood packed with specials. Seems it was a juicy row while it lasted – no duck soup for the coppers at that. Whisper's mob, I hear."

"Yeah. Reno and Pete the Finn tangled tonight. Hear anything about it?"

"Only that they'd had it."

"Reno killed Pete and ran into an ambush on the get-away. I don't know what happened after that. Seen Dick?"

"I went up to his hotel and was told he'd checked out to catch the evening train."

"I sent him back home," I explained. "He seemed to think I'd killed Dinah Brand. He was getting on my nerves with it."

"Well?"

"You mean, did I kill her? I don't know, Mickey. I'm trying to find out. Want to keep riding with me, or want to follow Dick back to the Coast?"

Mickey said:

"Don't get so cocky over one lousy murder that maybe didn't happen. But what the hell? You know you didn't lift her dough and pretties."

"Neither did the killer. They were still there after eight that morning, when I left. Dan Rolff was in and out between then and nine. He wouldn't have taken them. The – I've got it! The coppers that found the body – Shepp and Vanaman – got there at nine-thirty. Besides the jewelry and money, some letters old Willsson had written the girl were – must have been – taken. I found them later in Dawn's pocket. The two dicks disappeared just about then. See it?

"When Shepp and Vanaman found the girl dead they looted the joint before they turned in the alarm. Old Willsson being a millionaire, his letters looked good to them, so they took them along with the other valuables, and turned them – the letters – over to the shyster to peddle back to Elihu. But Dawn was killed before he could do anything on that end. I took the letters. Shepp and Vanaman, whether they did or didn't know that the letters were not found in the dead man's possession, got cold feet. They were afraid the letters would be traced to them. They had the money and jewelry. They lit out."

"Sounds fair enough," Mickey agreed, "but it don't seem to put any fingers on any murderers."

"It clears the way some. We'll try to clear it some more. See if you can find Porter Street and an old warehouse called Redman. The way I got it, Rolff killed Whisper there, walked up to him and stabbed him with the ice pick he had found in the girl. If he did it that way, then Whisper hadn't killed her. Or he would have been expecting something of the sort, and wouldn't have let the lunger get that close to him. I'd like to look at their remains and check up."

"Porter's over beyond King," Mickey said. "We'll try the south end first. It's nearer and more likely to have warehouses. Where do you set this Rolff guy?"

"Out. If he killed Whisper for killing the girl, that marks him off. Besides, she had bruises on her wrist and cheek, and he wasn't strong enough to rough her. My notion is that he left the hospital, spent the night God knows where, showed up at the girl's house after I left that morning, let himself in with his key, found her, decided Whisper had done the trick, took the sticker out of her, and went hunting Whisper."

"So?" Mickey said. "Now where do you get the idea that you might be the boy who put it over."

"Stop it," I said grouchily as we turned into Porter Street. "Let's find our warehouse."

WE RODE DOWN the street, jerking our eyes around, hunting for buildings that looked like deserted warehouses. It was light enough by now to see well.

Presently I spotted a big square rusty-red building set in the center of a weedy lot. Disuse stuck out all over lot and building. It had the look of a likely candidate.

"Pull up at the next corner," I said. "That looks like the dump. You stick with the heap while I scout it."

I walked two unnecessary blocks so I could come into the lot behind the building. I crossed the lot carefully, not sneaking, but not making any noise I could avoid.

I tried the back door cautiously. It was locked, of course. I moved over to a window, tried to look in, couldn't because of gloom and dirt, tried the window, and couldn't budge it.

I went to the next window with the same luck. I rounded the corner of the building and began working my way along the north side. The first window had me beaten. The second went up slowly with my push, and didn't make much noise doing it.

Across the inside of the window frame, from top to bottom, boards were nailed. They looked solid and strong from where I stood.

I cursed them, and remembered hopefully that the window hadn't made much noise when I raised it. I climbed up on the sill, put a hand against the boards, and tried them gently.

They gave.

I put more weight behind my hand. The boards went away from the left side of the frame, showing me a row of shiny nail points.

I pushed them back farther, looked past them, saw nothing but darkness, heard nothing.

With my gun in my right fist, I stepped over the sill, down into the building. Another step to the left put me out of the window's gray light.

I switched my gun to my left hand and used my right to push the boards back over the window.

A full minute of breathless listening got me nothing. Holding my gun-arm tight to my side, I began exploring the joint. Nothing but the floor came under my feet as I inch-by-inched them forward. My groping left hand felt nothing until it touched a rough wall. I seemed to have crossed a room that was empty.

I moved along the wall, hunting for a door. Half a dozen of my undersized steps brought me to one. I leaned an ear against it, and heard no sound.

I found the knob, turned it softly, eased the door back.

Something swished.

I did four things all together: let go the knob, jumped, pulled trigger, and had my left arm walloped with something hard and heavy as a tombstone.

The flare of my gun showed me nothing. It never does, though it's easy to think you've seen things. Not knowing what else to do, I fired again, and once more.

An old man's voice pleaded:

"Don't do that, partner. You don't have to do that."

I said: "Make a light."

A match spluttered on the floor, kindled, and put flickering yellow light on a battered face. It was an old face of the useless, characterless sort that goes well with park benches. He was sitting on the floor, his stringy legs sprawled far apart. He didn't seem hurt anywhere. A table leg lay beside him.

"Get up and make a light," I ordered, "and keep matches burning until you've done it."

He struck another match, sheltered it carefully with his hands as he got up, crossed the room, and lit a candle on a three-legged table.

I followed him, keeping close. My left arm was numb or I would have taken hold of him for safety.

"What are you doing here?" I asked when the candle was burning.

I didn't need his answer. One end of the room was filled with wooden cases piled six high, branded *Perfection Maple Syrup*.

While the old man explained that as God was his keeper he didn't know nothing about it, that all he knew was that a man named Yates had two days ago hired him as night watchman, and if anything was wrong he was as innocent as innocent, I pulled part of the top off one case.

The bottles inside had Canadian Club labels that looked as if they had been printed with a rubber stamp.

I left the cases and, driving the old man in front of me with the candle, searched the building. As I expected, I found nothing to indicate that this was the warehouse Whisper had occupied.

By the time we got back to the room that held the liquor my left arm was strong enough to lift a bottle. I put it in my pocket and gave the old man some advice:

"Better clear out. You were hired to take the place of some of the men Pete the Finn turned into special coppers. But Pete's dead now and his racket has gone blooey."

When I climbed out the window the old man was standing in front of the cases, looking at them with greedy eyes while he counted on his fingers.

"Well?" Mickey asked when I returned to him and his coupé.

I took out the bottle of anything but Canadian Club, pulled the cork, passed it to him, and then put a shot into my own system.

He asked, "Well?" again.

I said: "Let's try to find the old Redman warehouse."

He said: "You're going to ruin yourself some time telling people too much," and started the car moving.

Three blocks farther up the street we saw a faded sign, *Redman & Company*. The building under the sign was long, low, and narrow, with corrugated-iron roof and few windows.

"We'll leave the boat around the corner," I said. "And you'll go with me this time. I didn't have a whole lot of fun by myself last trip."

When we climbed out of the coupé, an alley ahead promised a path to the warehouse's rear. We took it.

A few people were wandering through the streets, but it was still too early for the factories that filled most of this part of town to come to life.

At the rear of our building we found something interesting. The back door was closed. Its edge, and the edge of the frame, close to the lock, were scarred. Somebody had worked there with a jimmy.

Mickey tried the door. It was unlocked. Six inches at a time, with pauses between, he pushed it far enough back to let us squeeze in.

When we squeezed in we could hear a voice. We couldn't make out what the voice was saying. All we could hear was the faint rumble of a distant man's voice, with a suggestion of quarrelsomeness in it.

Mickey pointed a thumb at the door's scar and whispered. "Not coppers."

I took two steps inside, keeping my weight on my rubber heels. Mickey followed, breathing down the back of my neck.

Ted Wright had told me Whisper's hiding place was in the back, upstairs. The distant rumbling voice could have been coming from there.

I twisted my face around to Mickey and said:
"Flashlight?"

He put it in my left hand. I had my gun in my right. We crept forward.

The door, still a foot open, let in enough light to show us the way across this room to a doorless doorway. The other side of the doorway was black.

I flicked the light across the blackness, found a door, shut off the light, and went forward. The next squirt of light showed us steps leading up.

We went up the steps as if we were afraid they would break under our feet.

The rumbling voice had stopped. There was something else in the air. I didn't know what. Maybe a voice not quite loud enough to be heard, if that meant anything.

I had counted nine steps when a voice spoke clearly above us. It said:

"Sure, I killed the bitch."

A gun said something, the same thing four times, roaring like a 16-inch rifle under the iron roof.

The first voice said: "All right."

By that time Mickey and I had put the rest of the steps behind us, had shoved a door out of the way, and were trying to pull Reno Starkey's hands away from Whisper's throat.

It was a tough job and a useless one. Whisper was dead.

Reno recognized me and let his hands go limp.

His eyes were as dull, his horse face as wooden, as ever.

Mickey carried the dead gambler to the cot that stood in one end of the room, spreading him on it.

The room, apparently once an office, had two windows. In their light I could see a body stowed under the cot – Dan Rolff. A Colt's service automatic lay in the middle of the floor.

Reno bent his shoulders, swaying.

"Hurt?" I asked.

"He put all four in me," he said, calmly, bending to press both forearms against his lower body.

"Get a doc," I told Mickey.

"No good," Reno said. "I got no more belly left than Peter Collins."

I pulled a folding chair over and sat him down on it, so he could lean forward and hold himself together.

Mickey ran out and down the stairs.

"Did you know he wasn't croaked?" Reno asked.

"No. I gave it to you the way I got it from Ted Wright."

"Ted left too soon," he said. "I was leary of something like that, and came to make sure. He trapped me pretty, playing dead till I was under the gun." He stared dully at Whisper's corpse. "Game at that, damn him. Dead, but wouldn't lay down, bandaging hisself, laying here waiting by hisself." He smiled, the only smile I had ever seen him use. "But he's just meat and not much of it now."

His voice was thickening. A little red puddle formed under the edge of his chair. I was afraid to touch him. Only the pressure of his arms, and his bent-forward position, were keeping him from falling apart.

He stared at the puddle and asked:

"How the hell did you figure you didn't croak her?"

"I had to take it out in hoping I hadn't, till just now," I said. "I had you pegged for it, but couldn't be sure. I was all hopped up that night, and had a lot of dreams, with bells ringing and voices calling, and a lot of stuff like that. I got an idea maybe it wasn't straight dreaming so much as hop-head nightmares stirred up by things that were happening around me.

"When I woke up, the lights were out. I didn't think I killed her, turned off the light, and went back to take hold of the ice pick. But it could have happened other ways. You knew I was there that night. You gave me my alibi without stalling. That got me thinking. Dawn tried blackmailing me after he heard Helen Albury's story. The police, after hearing her story, tied you, Whisper, Rolff and me together. I found Dawn dead after seeing O'Marra half a block away. It looked like the shyster had tried blackmailing you. That and the police tying us together

641

started me thinking the police had as much on the rest of you as on me. What they had on me was that Helen Albury had seen me go in or out or both that night. It was a good guess they had the same on the rest of you. There were reasons for counting Whisper and Rolff out. That left you – and me. But why you killed her's got me puzzled."

"I bet you," he said, watching the red puddle grow on the floor. "It was her own damned fault. She calls me up, tells me Whisper's coming to see her, and says if I get there first I can bushwhack him. I'd like that. I go over there, stick around, but he don't show."

He stopped, pretending interest in the shape the red puddle was taking. I knew pain had stopped him, but I knew he would go on talking as soon as he got himself in hand. He meant to die as he had lived, inside the same tough shell. Talking could be torture, but he wouldn't stop on that account, not while anybody was there to see him. He was Reno Starkey who could take anything the world had without batting an eye, and he would play it out that way to the end.

"I got tired of waiting," he went on after a moment. "I hit her door and asked howcome. She takes me in, telling me there's nobody there. I'm doubtful, but she swears she's alone, and we go back in the kitchen. Knowing her, I'm beginning to think maybe it's me and not Whisper that's being trapped."

Mickey came in, telling us he had phoned for an ambulance.

Reno used the interruption to rest his voice, and then continued with his story:

"Later, I find that Whisper did phone her he was coming, and got there before me. You were coked. She was afraid to let him in, so he beat it. She don't tell me that, scared I'll go and leave her. You're hopped and she wants protection against Whisper coming back. I don't know none of that then. I'm leery that I've walked into something, knowing her. I think I'll take hold of her and slap the truth out of her. I try it, and she grabs the pick and screams. When she squawks, I hear a man's feet hitting the floor. The trap's sprung, I think."

He spoke slower, taking more time and pains to turn each word out calmly and deliberately, as talking became harder. His voice had become blurred, but if he knew it he pretended he didn't.

"I don't mean to be the only one that's hurt. I twist the pick out of her hand and stick it in her. You gallop out, coked to the edges, charging at the whole world with both eyes shut. She tumbles into you. You go down, roll around till your hand hits the butt of the pick. Holding on to that, you go to sleep, peaceful as she is. I see it then, what I've done. But hell! she's croaked. There's nothing to do about it. I turn off the lights and go home. When you –"

A tired-looking ambulance crew – Poisonville gave them plenty of work – brought a litter into the room, ending Reno's tale. I was glad of it. I had all the information I wanted, and sitting there listening to and watching him talk himself to death wasn't pleasant.

I took Mickey over to a corner of the room and muttered in his ear:

"The job's yours from now on. I'm going to duck. I ought to be in the clear, but I know my Poisonville too well to take any chances. I'll drive your car to some way station where I can catch a train for Ogden. I'll be at the Roosevelt Hotel there, registered as P. F. King. Stay with the job, and let me know when it's wise to either take my own name again or a trip to Honduras."

I spent most of my week in Ogden trying to fix up my reports so they would not read as if I had broken as many Agency rules, state laws and human bones as I had.

Mickey arrived on the sixth night.

He told me that Reno was dead, that I was no longer officially a criminal, that most of the First National Bank stick-up loot had been recovered, that MacSwain had confessed

643

killing Tim Noonan, and that Personville, under martial law, was developing into a sweet-smelling thornless bed of roses.

Mickey and I went back to San Francisco.

I might just as well have saved the labor and sweat I had put into trying to make my reports harmless. They didn't fool the Old Man. He gave me merry hell.